PRAISE FOR THOMAS LIGOTTI

"If there were a literary genre called 'philosophical horror,' Thomas Ligotti's [*Grimscribe*] would easily fit within it . . . interesting and original ideas . . . provocative images and a style that is both entertaining and lyrical."
New York Times Book Review

"Restrained, lyrical prose and subtly disturbing images that Poe himself might have admired."
USA Today

"Thomas Ligotti is the best kept secret in contemporary horror fiction . . . a canon of short stories [*Grimscribe*] so idiosyncratic as to defy almost any description save demented . . . the best new American writer of weird fiction to appear in years."
The Washington Post

"*Grimscribe* confirms [Ligotti] as an accomplished conjuror of nightmares in the tradition of H.P. Lovecraft . . . the dreamlike mood – of gloomy, deserted streets, and banal objects invested with cabbalistic significance – lingers long after the book has been put down."
The Times

"[*Noctuary* is] another colorful collection of horror stories . . . which spring on the unsuspecting reader the combination of supernatural characters, natural props and 'weird' circumstances."
Library Journal

"The most disturbing terror comes from within, springs unexpectedly from bland or half-formed memories of the past. This is the terror that Ligotti cultivates in the richly evocative tales of *Noctuary* . . . For those willing to immerse themselves in Ligotti's world, the rewards are great."
Booklist

THE
NIGHTMARE
FACTORY

THOMAS LIGOTTI

Carroll & Graf Publishers, Inc.
NEW YORK

Carroll & Graf Publishers, Inc.
260 Fifth Avenue
New York
NY 10001

First published in the UK by Robinson Publishing 1996

First Carroll & Graf edition 1996

ISBN 0–7867–0302–4

Printed and bound in the United Kingdom

10 9 8 7 6 5 4 3 2 1

CONTENTS

FOREWORD

Poppy Z. Brite

Are you out there, Thomas Ligotti? You have a lot to answer for, but I've never been able to discover anything of substance about you. That's the way you seem to want it. Even in the single interview I managed to glean from the wasteland of the small press, you spoke exclusively about the craft of writing. Don't mistake my meaning; there is no one I'd rather read upon the craft. But not a scrap of personal information escaped those lines of print. As someone who gives numerous, messy, highly personal interviews that I suspect I may yet live to regret, I wonder how you are able to do it.

I was twenty, on my first trip to San Francisco, when a friend first handed me your work *Songs of a Dead Dreamer*, the Silver Scarab limited edition with Harry O. Morris illustrations that approached the fabulousness of the stories. My interest was aroused at least partly by the fact that Ramsey Campbell, then and now one of my favourite writers, had seen fit to pen an introduction; so being asked to write this introduction has a certain poignancy.

Riding stoned in the back seat of a car across the Bay Bridge, I opened the book at random and read a sentence that will haunt me all my days, a sentence I'd give a thumb to have written:

> We leave this behind in your capable hands, for in the black-foaming gutters and back alleys of paradise, in the dank windowless gloom of some galactic cellar, in the hollow pearly whorls found in sewerlike seas, in starless cities of insanity, and in their slums . . . my awe-struck little deer and I have gone frolicking.
>
> *from 'The Frolic'*

The glittering panorama of San Francisco, a city I already suspected of harbouring deep mystery from Fritz Leiber's *Our Lady of Darkness*, became inextricably linked in my mind with this prose jewel. For me, those black-foaming gutters and back alleys (not to mention the Street of Wavering Peaks) will always be just across the bay from Berkeley.

Will you hate me if I confess that I photocopied the entire book? I'd promised to send it back to my friend, and I am no book thief. But I could not bear to part with your words, and I could not find another copy anywhere; those few precious copies had been snapped up and hoarded.

Songs of a Dead Dreamer has since been released by major publishers on at least two continents. I have three editions myself. But, until it was destroyed in a flood last year, I still had the looseleaf binder with that pathetic photocopy in it too.

I have followed your career since then – nearly a decade – and I still know nothing more of you than your fiction reveals. Though I know that fictional self-revelation can be considerable, I also know that it is frequently misinterpreted by the reader. If you were to call up and invite me over for coffee, I would expect to meet a slightly dissipated aesthete, sarcastic and decadent and wry, given to odd word-associations, with a taste not just for the macabre but for the truly, nakedly gruesome. (Let the critics blather on about subtle half-hidden horrors; you make *me* see it all.) But perhaps I would encounter someone else entirely. I suspect I'll never know.

You have a lot to answer for, Thomas Ligotti. For every score of horrorheads who don't 'get' your work, there will always be the one who is profoundly impressed and appalled by it, for it seems as though you have reached into his dreaming brain and pulled out the stuff of intensely private nightmares. I am one of those readers. Upon reading your stories, I often experience two distinct sensations: a faint *déjà vu*, not as if I've read the words before, but as if the images have already appeared somewhere in the murk of my subconscious; and a sense of Lovecraftian awe shading into existential nausea. More than any other author I can think of, you write decidedly *weird* fiction. And I can only marvel. Are you out there, Thomas Ligotti?

I believe I've just answered my own question.

INTRODUCTION: THE CONSOLATIONS OF HORROR

Darkness, we welcome and embrace you

Horror, at least in its artistic presentations, can be a comfort. And, like any agent of enlightenment, it may even confer – if briefly – a sense of power, wisdom, and transcendence, especially if the conferee is a willing one with a true feeling for ancient mysteries and a true fear of the skulduggery which a willing heart usually senses in the unknown.

Clearly we (just the willing conferees, remember) want to know the worst, both about ourselves and the world. The oldest, possibly the only theme is that of forbidden knowledge. And no forbidden knowledge ever consoled its possessor. (Which is probably why it's forbidden.) At best it is one of the more sardonic gifts bestowed upon the individual (for knowledge of the forbidden is first and foremost an individual ordeal). It is particularly forbidden because the mere possibility of such knowledge introduces a monstrous and perverse temptation to trade the quiet pleasures of mundane existence for the bright lights of alienage, doom, and, in some rare cases, eternal damnation.

So we not only wish to *know* the worst, but to experience it as well.

Hence that arena of artificial experience, supposedly of the worst kind – the horror story – where gruesome conspiracies may be trumped up to our soul's satisfaction, where the deck is stacked with shivers, shocks, and dismembered hands for every player; and, most importantly, where one, at a safe distance, can come to grips (after a fashion) with death, pain, and loss in the, quote, real world, unquote.

But does it ever work the way we would like it to?

A test case

I am watching *Night of the Living Dead*. I see the ranks of the deceased reanimated by a double-edged marvel of the modern age (atomic radiation, I think. Or is it some wonder chemical which found its way into the water supply? And does this detail even matter?). I see a group of average, almost documentary types holed up in a house, fighting off wave after wave of hungry ghouls. I see the group hopelessly losing their ground and succumb each one of them to the same disease as their sleepwalking attackers: A husband tries to eat his wife (or is it mother tries to eat child?), a daughter stabs her father with a gardener's trowel (or perhaps brother stabs sister with a bricklayer's trowel). In any case, they all die, and horribly. This is the important thing.

When the movie is over, I am invigorated by the sense of having rung the ear-shattering changes of harrowing horror; I've got another bad one under my belt that will serve to bolster my nerves for whatever shocking days and nights are to come; I have, in a phrase, *an expanded capacity for fear*. I can really take it!

At the movies, that is.

The fearful truth is that all of the above brutalities can be "taken" only too well. And then, at some point, one starts to adopt unnatural strategies to ward off not the bogey but the sand man. Talking to the characters in a horror film, for instance: Hi, Mr. Decomposing Corpse lapping up a lump of sticky entrails, Hi! But even this tactic loses its charm after a while, especially if you're watching some "shocker" by yourself and lack an accomplice to share your latest stage of jadedness and immunity to primitive fright. (At the movies, I mean. Otherwise you're the same old vulnerable self.)

So after a devoted horror fan is stuffed to the gills, thoroughly sated and consequently bored – what does he (the he's traditionally out-number the she's here) do next? Haunt the emergency rooms of hospitals or the local morgues? Keep an eye out for bloody mishaps on the freeway? Become a war correspondent? But now the issue has been blatantly shifted to a completely different plane – from movies to life – and clearly it doesn't belong there.

The one remedy for the horror addict's problem seems this: that if the old measure of medicine is just not strong enough – increase the dosage! (This pharmaceutical parallel is ancient but apt.) And thus we have the well-known and very crude basis for the horror film's history of ever-escalating scare tactics. Have you already seen such old classics as *Werewolf of London* too many times? Sample one of its gore-enriched, yet infinitely inferior versions of the early 1980s. Of course the relief is only temporary; one's tolerance to the drug tends to increase. And looking down that long open road there appears to be no ultimate drugstore in sight, no final pharmacy where the horror hunger can be glutted on a sufficiently enormous dose, where the once insatiable addict may, at last, be laden with all the demonic dope there is, collapse with sated obesity into the shadows, and quietly gasp: "enough."

The empty pit of boredom is ever renewing itself, while horror films become less tantalizing to the marginally sadistic movie-goer.

And what is the common rationale for justifying what would otherwise be considered a just barely frustrated case of sadomasochism? Now we remember: to present us with horrors inside the theater (or the books, let's not forget those) and thereby help us to assimilate the horrors on the outside, and also to ready us for the Big One. This does sound reasonable, it sounds right and rational. But none of this has anything to do with these three R's. We are in the great forest of fear, where you can't fight real experiences of the worst with fake ones (no matter how well synchronized a symbolic correspondence they may have). When is the last time you heard of someone screaming himself awake from a nightmare, only to shrug it off with: "Yeah, but I've seen worse at the movies" (or read worse in the books; we'll get to them)? Nothing is worse than that which happens personally to a person. And though a bad dream may momentarily register quite high on the fright meter, it is, realistically speaking, one of the less enduring, smaller time terrors a person is up against. Try drawing solace from your half-dozen viewings of the *Texas Chain-Saw Massacre* when they're prepping you for brain surgery.

In all truth, frequenters of horror films are a jumpier, more casually hysterical class of person than most. We need the most reassurance that we can take it as well as anyone, and we tend to be the most complacent in thinking that seventeen straight nights of supernatural-psycho films is good for the nerves and will give us a special power which non-horror-fanatics don't have. After all, this is supposed to be a major psychological selling point of the horror racket, the first among its consolations.

It is undoubtedly the first consolation, but it's also a false one.

Interlude: so long, consolations of mayhem

Perhaps it was a mistake selecting *Night of the Living Dead* to illustrate the consolations of horror. As a delegate from Horrorland this film is admirably incorruptible, oozing integrity. It hasn't sold out to the kindergarten moral codes of most "modern horror" movies and it has no particular message to deliver: its only news is nightmare. For pure brain-chomping, nerve-chewing, sight-cursing insanity, this is a very effective work, at least the first couple of times or so. It neither tries nor pretends to be anything beyond that. (And as we have already found, nothing exists beyond that anyway, except more and more of *that*.) But the big trouble is that sometimes we forget how much more can be done in horror movies (books too!) than that. We sometimes forget that supernatural stories – and this is a very good time to boot nonsupernatural ones right off the train: psycho, suspense, and the like – are capable of all the functions and feelings of *real* stories. For the supernatural can serve as a trusty vehicle for careening into realms where the Strange and the Familiar charge each other with the opposing poles of their passion.

The Haunting, for example. Besides being the greatest haunted house film ever made, it is also a great haunted human one. In it the ancient spirit of mortal tragedy passes easily through walls dividing the mysteries of the mundane world from those of the extra-mundane. And this supertragic specter never comes to rest in either one of these worlds; it never lingers long enough to give us forbidden knowledge of either the stars or ourselves, or anything else for that matter. To what extent may the "derangement of Hill House" (Dr. Markway's diagnosis) be blamed on the derangement of the people who were, are, and probably will be in it? And vice versa of course. Is there something wrong with that spiral staircase in the library or just with the clumsy persons who try to climb it? The only safe bet is that something is wrong, wherever the wrongness lies . . . and lies and lies. Our poor quartet of spook-chasers – Dr. Markway, Theo, Luke, and Eleanor – are not only helpless to untie themselves from entangling puppet strings; they can't even find the knots!

The ghosts at Hill House always remain unseen, except in their effects: savagely pummeling enormous oak doors, bending them like cardboard; writing assonant messages on walls ("Help Eleanor come home") with an unspecified substance ("Chalk," says Luke. "Or something *like* chalk," corrects Markway); and in general giving the place a very bad feeling. We're not even sure who the ghosts are, or rather were. The pious and demented Hugh Crane, who built Hill House? His spinster daughter Abigail, who wasted away in Hill House? Her neglectful companion, who hung herself in Hill House? None of them emerges as a discrete, clearly definable haunter of the old mansion. Instead we have an undefined presence which seems a sort of melting pot of deranged forces from the past, an anti-America where the very poorest in spirit settle and stagnate and lose themselves in a massive and insane spectral body.

Easier to identify are the personal specters of the living, at least for the viewer. But the characters in the film are too busy with outside things to look inside one another's houses, or even their own. Dr. Markway doesn't acknowledge Eleanor's spooks. (She loves him, hopelessly.) Eleanor can't see Theo's spooks (she's lesbian) and Theo avoids dwelling on her own. ("And what are you afraid of, Theo?" asks Eleanor. "Of knowing what I really want," she replies, somewhat uncandidly.) Best of all, though, is Luke, who doesn't think there even are any spooks, until near the end of the film when this affable fun-seeker gains an excruciating sense of the alienation, perversity, and strangeness of the world around him. "It should be burned to the ground," he says of the high-priced house he is to inherit, "and the earth sown with salt." This quasi-biblical quote indicates that more than a few doors have been kicked down in Luke's private passageways. He *knows* now! Poor Eleanor, of course, has been claimed by the house as one of its lonely, faceless citizens of eternity. It is her voice that gets to deliver the reverberant last lines of the film: "Hill House has stood for eighty years and will probably stand for eighty more . . . and we who walk there, walk alone." With these words the viewer glimpses a realm of unimaginable pain and horror, an unfathomable region of aching Gothic turmoil, a weird nevermoresville.

The experience is extremely disconsoling but nonetheless exhilarating.

But for a movie to convey such intense feeling for the supernatural is rare. (This one of course is a scrupulously faithful adaptation of Shirley Jackson's unarguably excellent novel.) The thing that is quite common, especially with fiction, is the phenomenon that produced the single-sentence paragraph above; in other words – the horror story's paradox of entertainment. The thumping heart of the question, though, is what really entertains us? In opposition, that is, to what we only imagine entertains us. Entertainment, whatever we imagine its real source, is rightly regarded as its own justification, and this seems to be one of the unassailable consolations of horror.

But is it? (This won't take long.)

Another test case

We are reading – in a quiet, cozy room, it goes without saying – one of M.R. James' powerful ghost stories. It is "Count Magnus," in which a curious scholar gains knowledge he didn't even know was forbidden and suffers the resultant doom at the hands of the count and his betentacled companion. The story actually ends before we have a chance to witness its fabulous coup de grace, but we know that a sucked-off face is in store for our scholar. Meanwhile we sit on the sidelines (sipping a warm drink, probably) as the doomed academic meets a fate worse than any we'll ever know. At least we think it's worse, we hope it is . . . deep, deep in the subcellars of our minds we pray: "Please don't let anything even *like* that happen to me! Not to *me*. Let it always be the other guy and I'll read about him, even tremble for him a little. Besides, I'm having so much fun, it can't be all that terrible. For him, that is. For me it would be unbearable. See how shaky and excitable I get just *reading* about it. So please let it always be the other guy."

But it can't always be the other guy, for in the long run we're all, each of us, the other guy.

Of course in the short run it's one of life's minor ecstasies – an undoubted entertainment – to read about a world in which the very worst doom takes place in a restricted area we would never ever wander into and befalls somebody else. And this is the run in which all stories are read, as well as written. (If something with eyes like two runny eggs were after your carcass, would you sit down and write a story about it?) It's another world, the short run; it's a world where horror really is a true consolation. But it's no compliment to Dr. James or to ourselves as readers to put too much stock in ghost stories as a consolation for our mortality, our vulnerability to real-life terrors. As consolations go, this happens to be a pretty low-grade one – demented complacency posing as beatitude.

So our second consolation lives on borrowed time at best. And in the long-run – where no mere tale can do you much good – is delusory.

(Perhaps the stories of H.P. Lovecraft offer a more threatening and admirable role to those of us devoted to doom. In Lovecraft's work doom is not restricted to eccentric characters in eccentric situations. It begins there but ultimately expands to violate the safety zone of the reader (and the non-reader for that matter, though the latter remains innocent of Lovecraft's forbidden knowledge). M.R. James' are cautionary tales, lessons in how to stay out of spectral trouble and how nice and safe it feels to do so. But within the cosmic boundaries of Lovecraft's universe, which many would call the universe itself, we are already in trouble, and feeling safe is out of the question for anyone with some brains and chance access to the manuscripts of Albert Wilmarth, Nathaniel Wingate Peaslee, or Prof. Angell's nephew. These isolated narrators take us with them into their doom, which is the world's. (No one ever gives a hoot what happens to Lovecraft's characters as individuals.) If we knew what they know about the world and about our alarmingly tentative place in it, our brains would indeed reel with revelation. And if we found out what Arthur Jermyn found out about ourselves and our humble origins in a mere madness of biology, we would do as he did with a few gallons of gasoline and a merciful match. Of course Lovecraft insists on telling us things it does no good to know: things that can't help us or protect us or even prepare us for the awful and inevitable apocalypse to come. The only comfort is to accept it, live in it, and sigh yourself into the balm of living oblivion. If you can only maintain this constant sense of doom, you may be spared the pain of foolish hopes and their impending demolishment.

But we can't maintain it; only a saint of doom could. Hope leaks into our lives by way of spreading cracks we always meant to repair but never did. (Oddly enough, when the cracks yawn their widest, and the promised deluge comes at last, it is not hope at all that finally breaks through and drowns us.)

Interlude: see you later, consolations of doom

So when a fictional state of absolute doom no longer offers us possibilities of comfort – what's left? Well, another stock role casts one not as the victim of a horror story but as its villain. That is, we get to be the monster for a change. To a certain extent this is supposed to happen when we walk onto those resounding floor-boards behind the Gothic footlights. It's traditional to identify with and feel sorry for the vampire or the werewolf in their ultimate moment of weakness, a time when they're most human. Sometimes, though, it seems as if there's more fun to be had playing a vampire or werewolf at the height of their monstrous, people-maiming power. To play them in our hearts, I mean. After all, it would be kind of great to wake up at dusk every day and cruise around in the shadows and fly on batwings through the night, stare strangers in the eye and have them under your power. Not bad for someone who's supposed to be dead. Or rather, for someone who can't die and whose soul is not his own; for someone who – no matter how seemingly suave – is doomed to ride eternity with a single and highly embarrassing obsession, the most debased junkie immortalized.

But maybe you could make it as a werewolf. For most of a given month you're just like anybody else. Then for a few days you can take a vacation from your puny human self and spill the blood of puny human others. And once you return to your original clothes size, no one is any the wiser . . . until next month rolls around and you've got to do the whole thing again, month after month, over and over. Still, the werewolf's lifestyle might not be so bad, as long as you don't get caught ripping out someone's throat. Of course, there might be some guilt involved and, yes, bad dreams.

Vampirism and lycanthropy do have their drawbacks, anyone would admit that. But there would also be some memorable moments too, moments humans rarely, if ever, have: feeling your primal self at one with the inhuman forces around you, fearless in the face of night and nature and solitude and all those things from which mere people have much to fear. There you are under the moon – a raging storm in human form. And you'll always be like that, forever if you're careful. Being a human being is a dead end anyway. It would seem that supernatural sociopaths have more possibilities open to them. So wouldn't it be great to be one? What I mean, of course, is: is it a consolation of horror fiction to let us be one for a little while? Yes, it really is; the attractions of this life are sometimes irresistible. But are we missing some point if we only see the glamour and ignore the drudgery in the existence of these free-spirited nyctophiles? Well, are we?

The last test

Test cancelled. The consolation is patently a trick one, done with invisible writing, mirrors, and camera magic.

Substitute consolation: "The Fall of the House of Usher, or Doom Revisited"

Did you ever wonder how a Gothic story like Poe's masterpiece can be so great without enlisting the reader's care for its characters' doom? Plenty of horrible events and concepts are woven together; the narrator and his friend Roderick experience a fair amount of FEAR. But unlike a horror story whose effect depends on reader sympathy with its fictional victims, this one doesn't want us to get involved with the characters in that way. Our fear does not derive from theirs. Though Roderick, his sister, and the visiting narrator are fascinating companions, they do not burden us with their individual catastrophes. Are we sad for Roderick and his sister's terrible fate? No. Are we happy the narrator makes a safe flight from the sinking house? Not particularly. Then why get upset about this calamity which takes place in the backwoods, miles from the nearest town and everyday human concerns?

In this story individuals are not the issue. Everywhere in Poe's literary universe (Lovecraft's too) the individual is horribly and comfortably irrelevant. During the reading of "The Fall of the House of Usher" we don't look over any character's shoulder but have our attention distributed god-wise into every corner of a foul factory which manufactures only one product: total and inescapable doom. Whether a given proper noun escapes this doom or is caught by it is beside the point. Poe's is a world created with built-in obsolescence, and to appreciate fully this downrunning cosmos one must take the perspective of its creator, which is all perspectives without getting sidetracked into a single one. Therefore we as readers *are* the House of Usher (both family and structure), we are the fungi clustering across its walls and the violent storm over its ancient head; we sink with the Ushers and get away with the narrator. In brief, we play all the roles. And the consolation in this is that we are supremely removed from the maddeningly tragic viewpoint of the human.

Of course, when the story is over we must fall from our god's perch and sink back into humanness, which is perhaps what the Ushers and their house are doing. This is always a problem for would-be gods! We can't maintain for very long a godlike point of view. Wouldn't it be great if we could; if life could be lived outside the agony of the individual? But we are always doomed and redoomed to become involved with our own lives, which is the only life there is, and godlikeness has nothing at all to do with it.

But still, wouldn't it be great . . .

Darkness, you've done a lot for us

At this point it may seem that the consolations of horror are not what we thought they were, that all this time we've been keeping company with illusions. Well, we have. And we'll continue to do so, continue to seek the appalling scene which short-circuits our brain, continue to sit in our numb coziness with a book of terror on our laps like a cataleptic predator, and continue to draw smug solace, if only for the space of a story, from a world made snug and simple by absolute hopelessness and doom. These consolations are still effective, even if they don't work as well as we would prefer them to. But they are only effective, like most things of value in art or life, *as illusions*. And there's no point attributing to them powers of therapy or salvation they don't and can't have. There are enough disappointments in the world without adding that one.

Perhaps, though, our illusion of consolation could be enhanced by acquiring a better sense of what we are being consoled by. What, in fact, is a horror story? And what does it do? First the latter.

The horror story does the work of a certain kind of dream we all know. Sometimes it does this so well that even the most irrational and unlikely subject matter can infect the reader with a sense of realism beyond the realistic, a trick usually not seen outside the vaudeville of sleep. When is the last time you failed to be fooled by a nightmare, didn't suspend disbelief because its incidents weren't sufficiently true-to-life? The horror story is only true to dreams, especially those which involve us in mysterious ordeals, the passing of secrets, the passages of forbidden knowledge, and, in more ways than one, the spilling of guts.

What distinguishes horror from other kinds of stories is the exclusive devotion of their practitioners, their true practitioners, to self-consciously imagining and isolating the most demonic aspects and episodes of human existence, undiminished by any consolation whatever. For here no consolation on earth is sufficient to the horrors it will struggle in vain to make bearable.

Are horror stories truer than other stories? They may be, but not necessarily. They are limited to depicting conditions of extraordinary suffering, and while this is not the only game in town, such depictions can be as close to truth as any others. Nevertheless, what simple fictional horror – no matter how grossly magnified – can ever hold a candle to the complex mesh of misery and disenchantment which is merely the human routine? Of course, the fundamental horror of existence is not always apparent to us, its constantly menaced but unwary existers. But in true horror stories we can see it even in the dark. All eternal hopes, optimistic outs, and ultimate redemptions are cleared away, and for a little while we can pretend to stare the very worst right in its rotting face.

Why, though? Why?

Just to do it, that's all. Just to see how much unmitigated weirdness, sorrow, desolation, and cosmic anxiety the human heart can take and still have enough heart left over to translate these agonies into artistic forms: James' stained glass monstrosities, Lovecraft's narrow-passaged blasphemies, Poe's symphonic paranoia. As in any satisfying relationship, the creator of horror and its consumer approach oneness with each other. In other words, you get the horrors you deserve, those you can understand. For contrary to conventional wisdom, you *cannot* be frightened by what you don't understand.

This, then, is the ultimate, that is only, consolation: simply that someone shares some of your own feelings and has made of these a work of art which you have the insight, sensitivity, and – like it or not – peculiar set of experiences to appreciate. Amazing thing to say, the consolation of horror in art is that it actually intensifies our panic, loudens it on the sounding-board of our horror-hollowed hearts, turns terror up full blast, all the while reaching for that perfect and deafening amplitude at which we may dance to the bizarre music of our own misery.

*To the memory of my aunt
and godmother, Virginia Cianciolo*

PART 1
from *Songs of a Dead Dreamer*

THE FROLIC

In a beautiful home in a beautiful part of town – the town of Nolgate, site of the state prison – Dr. Munck examined the evening newspaper while his young wife lounged on a sofa nearby, lazily flipping through the colorful parade of a fashion magazine. Their daughter Norleen was upstairs asleep, or perhaps she was illicitly enjoying an after-hours session with the new color television she'd received on her birthday the week before. If so, her violation of the bedtime rule went undetected due to the affluent expanse between bedroom and living room, where her parents heard no sounds of disobedience. The house was quiet. The neighborhood and the rest of the town were also quiet in various ways, all of them slightly distracting to the doctor's wife. But so far Leslie had only dared complain of the town's social lethargy in the most joking fashion ("Another exciting evening at the Munck's monastic hideaway"). She knew her husband was quite dedicated to this new position of his in this new place. Perhaps tonight, though, he would exhibit some encouraging symptoms of disenchantment with his work.

"How did it go today, David?" she asked, her radiant eyes peeking over the magazine cover, where another pair of eyes radiated a glossy gaze. "You were pretty quiet at dinner."

"It went about the same," said David, without lowering the small-town newspaper to look at his wife.

"Does that mean you don't want to talk about it?"

He folded the newspaper backwards and his upper body appeared. "That's how it sounded, didn't it?"

"Yes, it certainly did. Are you okay today?" she asked, laying aside the magazine on the coffee table and offering her complete attention.

"Severely doubting, that's how I am." He said this with a kind of far-off reflectiveness.

"Anything particularly doubtful, Dr. Munck?"

"Only everything," he answered.

"Shall I make us drinks?"

"That would be much appreciated."

Leslie walked to another part of the living room and from a large cabinet pulled out some bottles and some glasses. From the kitchen she brought out a supply of ice cubes in a brown plastic bucket. The sounds of drink-making were unusually audible in the living room's plush quiet. The drapes were drawn on all windows except the one in the corner where an Aphrodite sculpture posed. Beyond that window was a deserted streetlighted street and a piece of moon above the opulent leafage of spring trees.

"There you go, doctor," she said, handing him a glass that was very thick at its base and tapered almost undetectably toward its rim.

"Thanks, I really need one of these."

"Why? Aren't things going well with your work?"

"You mean my work at the prison?"

"Yes, of course."

"You could say *at the prison* once in a while. Not always talk in the abstract. Overtly recognize my chosen professional environment, my—"

"All right, all right. How's things at the wonderful prison, dear? Is that better?" She paused and took a deep gulp from her glass, then calmed a little. "I'm sorry about the snideness, David."

"No, I deserved it. I'm blaming you for long realizing something I can't bring myself to admit."

"Which is?" she prompted.

"Which is that maybe it was not the wisest decision to move here and take this saintly mission upon my psychologist's shoulders."

This remark was an indication of even deeper disenchantment than Leslie had hoped for. But somehow these words did not cheer her the way she thought they would. She could distantly hear the moving vans pulling up to the house, but the sound was no longer as pleasing as it once was.

"You said you wanted to do something more than treat urban neuroses. Something more meaningful, more challenging."

"What I wanted, masochistically, was a thankless job, an impossible one. And I got it."

"Is it really that bad?" Leslie inquired, not quite believing she asked the question with such encouraging skepticism about the actual severity of the situation. She congratulated herself for placing David's self-esteem above her own desire for a change of venue, important as she felt this was.

"I'm afraid it is that bad. When I first visited the prison's psychiatric section and met the other doctors, I swore I wouldn't become as hopeless and cruelly cynical as they were. Things would be different with me. I overestimated myself by a wide margin, though. Today one of the orderlies was beaten up again by two of the prisoners, excuse me, 'patients'. Last week it was Dr. Valdman, that's why I was so moody on Norleen's birthday. So far I've been lucky. All they do is spit at me. Well, they can all rot in that hellhole as far as I'm concerned."

David felt his own words lingering atmospherically in the room, tainting the serenity of the house. Until then their home had been an insular haven beyond the contamination of the prison, an imposing structure outside the town limits. Now its psychic imposition transcended the limits of physical distance. Inner distance constricted, and David sensed the massive prison walls shadowing the cozy neighborhood outside.

"Do you know why I was late tonight?" he asked his wife.

"No, why?"

"Because I had an overlong chat with a fellow who hasn't got a name yet."

"The one you told me about who won't tell anyone where he's from or what his real name is?"

"That's him. He's just an example of the pernicious monstrosity of the place. Worse than a beast, a rabid animal. Demented blind aggression . . . and clever. Because of this cute name game of his, he was classified as unsuitable for the regular prison population and thus we in the psychiatric section ended up with him. According to him, though, he has plenty of names, no less than a thousand, none of which he's condescended to speak in anyone's presence. From my point of view, he doesn't really have use for any human name. But we're stuck with him, no name and all."

"Do you call him that, 'no name'?"

"Maybe we should, but no, we don't."

"So what do you call him, then?"

"Well, he was convicted as John Doe, and since then everyone refers to him by that name. They've yet to uncover any official documentation on him. Neither his fingerprints nor photograph corresponds to any record of previous convictions. I understand he was picked up in a stolen car parked in front of an elementary school. An observant neighbor reported him as a suspicious character frequently seen in the area. Everyone was on the alert, I guess, after the first few disappearances from the school, and the police were watching him just as he was walking a new victim to his car. That's when they made the arrest. But his version of the story is a little different. He says he was fully aware of his pursuers and expected, even wanted, to be caught, convicted, and exiled to the penitentiary."

"Why?"

"Why? Why ask why? Why ask a psychotic to explain his own motivation, it only becomes more confusing. And John Doe is even less scrutable than most."

"What do you mean?" asked Leslie.

"I can tell you by narrating a little scene from the interview I had with him today. I asked him if he knew why he was in prison.

" 'For frolicking,' he said.

" 'What does that mean?' I asked.

"His reply was: 'Mean, mean, mean. You're a meany.'

"That childish ranting somehow sounded to me as if he were mimicking his victims. I'd really had enough right then but foolishly continued the interview.

" 'Do you know why you can't leave here'? I calmly asked with a poor variant of my original inquiry.

" 'Who says I can't? I'll just go when I want to. But I don't want to yet.'

" 'Why not?' I naturally questioned.

" 'I just got here,' he said. 'Thought I'd take a rest after frolicking so hard. But I want to be in with all the others. Unquestionably stimulating atmosphere. When can I go with them, when can I?'

"Can you believe that? It would be cruel, though, to put him in with the regular prison population, not to say he doesn't deserve this cruelty. The average inmate despises Doe's kind of crime, and there's really no predicting what would happen if we put him in there and the others found out what he was convicted for."

"So he has to stay in the psychiatric section for the rest of his term?" asked Leslie.

"He doesn't think so. He thinks he can leave whenever he wants."

"And can he?" questioned Leslie with a firm absence of facetiousness in her voice. This had always been one of her weightiest fears about living in this prison town, that every moment of the day and night there were horrible fiends plotting to escape through what she envisioned as rather papery walls. To raise a child in such surroundings was another of her objections to her husband's work.

"I told you before, Leslie, there have been a very few successful escapes from that prison. If an inmate does get beyond the walls, his first impulse is usually one of practical self-preservation, and he tries to get as far away as possible from this town, which is probably the safest place to be in the event of an escape. Anyway, most escapees are apprehended within hours after they've gotten out."

"What about a prisoner like John Doe? Does he have this sense of 'practical self-preservation,' or would he rather just hang around and do damage to someone?"

"Prisoners like that don't escape in the normal course of things. They just bounce off the walls but not over them. You know what I mean?"

Leslie said she understood, but this did not in the least lessen the potency of her fears, which found their source in an imaginary prison in an imaginary town, one where anything could happen as long as it approached the hideous. Morbidity had never been among her strong points, and she loathed its intrusion on her character. And for all his ready reassurance about the able security of the prison, David also seemed to be profoundly uneasy. He was sitting very still now, holding his drink between his knees and appearing to listen for something.

"What's wrong, David?" asked Leslie.

"I thought I heard . . . a sound."

"A sound like what?"

"Can't describe it exactly. A faraway noise."

He stood up and looked around, as if to see whether the sound had left some tell-tale clue in the surrounding stillness of the house, perhaps a smeary sonic print somewhere.

"I'm going to check on Norleen," he said, setting his glass down rather abruptly on the table beside his chair and splashing the drink around. He walked across the living room, down the front hallway, up the three segments of the stairway, and then down the upstairs hall. Peeking into his daughter's room he saw her tiny figure resting comfortably, a sleepy embrace wrapped about the form of a stuffed Bambi. She still occasionally slept with an inanimate companion, even though she was getting a little old for this. But her psychologist father was careful not to question her right to this childish comfort. Before leaving the room Dr. Munck lowered the window which was partially open on that warm spring evening.

When he returned to the living room he delivered the wonderfully routine message that Norleen was peacefully asleep. In a gesture containing faint overnotes of celebratory relief, Leslie made them two fresh drinks, after which she said:

"David, you said you had an 'overlong chat' with that John

Doe. Not that I'm morbidly curious or anything, but did you ever get him to reveal very much about himself?"

"Sure," Dr. Munck replied, rolling an ice cube around in his mouth. His voice was now more relaxed.

"He told me everything about himself, and on the surface all of it was nonsense. I asked him in a casually interested sort of way where he was from.

" 'No place,' he replied like a psychotic simpleton.

" 'No place?' I probed.

" 'Yes, precisely there, Herr Doktor.'

" 'Where were you born?' I asked in another brilliant alternate form of the question.

" 'Which time do you mean, you meany?' he said back to me, and so forth. I could go on with this dialogue—"

"You do a pretty good John Doe imitation, I must say."

"Thank you, but I couldn't keep it up for very long. It wouldn't be easy to imitate all his different voices and levels of articulateness. He may be something akin to a multiple personality, I'm not sure. I'd have to go over the tape of the interview to see if any patterns of coherency turn up, possibly something the detectives could use to establish the man's identity, if he has one left. The tragic part is that this is all, of course, totally useless information as far as the victims of Doe's crimes are concerned . . . and as far as I'm concerned it really is too. I'm no aesthete of pathology. It's never been my ambition to study disease merely for its own sake, without effecting some kind of improvement, trying to help someone who would just as soon see me dead, or worse. I used to believe in rehabilitation, maybe with too much naiveté and idealism. But those people, those *things* at the prison are only an ugly stain on existence. The hell with them," he concluded, draining his glass until the ice cubes rattled.

"Want another?" Leslie asked with a smooth therapeutic tone to her voice.

David smiled now, the previous outburst having purged him somewhat. "Let's get drunk, shall we?"

Leslie collected his glass for a refill. Now there was reason to celebrate, she thought. Her husband was not giving up his work from a sense of ineffectual failure but from anger. The anger would turn to resignation, the resignation to indifference, and then everything would be as it had been before; they could leave the prison town and move back home. In fact, they could move anywhere they liked, maybe take a long vacation first, treat Norleen to some sunny place. Leslie thought of all this as she made the drinks in the quiet of that beautiful room. This quiet was no longer an indication of soundless stagnancy but a delicious lulling prelude to the promising days to come. The indistinct happiness of the future glowed inside her along with the alcohol; she was gravid with pleasant prophecies. Perhaps the time was now right to have another child, a little brother for Norleen. But that could wait just a while longer . . . a lifetime of possibilities lay ahead, awaiting their wishes like a distinguished and fatherly genie.

Before returning with the drinks, Leslie went into the kitchen. She had something she wanted to give her husband, and this was the perfect time to do it. A little token to show David that although his job had proved a sad waste of his worthy efforts, she had nevertheless supported his work in her own way. With a drink in each hand, she held under her left elbow the small box she had got from the kitchen.

"What's that?" asked David, taking his drink.

"Something for you, art lover. I bought it at that little shop where they sell things the inmates at the penitentiary make – belts, jewelry, ashtrays, you know."

"I know," David said with an unusual lack of enthusiasm. "I didn't think anyone actually bought that stuff."

"I, for one, did. I thought it would help to support those prisoners who are doing something *creative*, instead of . . . well, instead of destructive things."

"Creativity isn't always an index of niceness, Leslie," David admonished.

"Wait'll you see it before passing judgement," she said, opening the flap of the box. "There – isn't that nice work?" She set the piece on the coffee table.

Dr. Munck now plunged into that depth of sobriety which can only be reached by falling from a prior alcoholic height. He looked at the object. Of course he had seen it before, watched it being tenderly molded and caressed by creative hands, until he sickened and could watch no more. It was the head of a young boy, discovered in gray formless clay and glossily glazed in blue. The work radiated an extraordinary and intense beauty, the subject's face expressing a kind of ecstatic serenity, the labyrinthine simplicity of a visionary's gaze.

"Well, what do you think of it?" asked Leslie.

David looked at his wife and said solemnly: "Please put it back in the box. And then get rid of it."

"Get rid of it? Why?"

"Why? Because I know which of the inmates did this work. He was very proud of it, and I even forced a grudging compliment for the craftsmanship of the thing. It's obviously remarkable. But then he told me who the boy was. That expression of sky-blue peacefulness wasn't on the boy's face when they found him lying in a field about six months ago."

"No, David," said Leslie as a premature denial of what she was expecting her husband to reveal.

"This was his last – and according to him most memorable – 'frolic'."

"Oh my God," Leslie murmured softly, placing her right hand to her cheek. Then with both hands she gently placed the boy of blue back in his box. "I'll return it to the shop," she said quietly.

"Do it soon, Leslie. I don't know how much longer we'll be residing at this address."

In the moody silence that followed, Leslie briefly contemplated the now openly expressed, and definite reality of their departure from the town of Nolgate, their escape. Then she said: "David, did he actually talk about the things he did. I mean about—"

"I know what you mean. Yes, he did," answered Dr. Munck with a professional seriousness.

"Poor David," Leslie sympathized.

"Actually it wasn't that much of an ordeal. The conversation we had could even be called stimulating in a clinical sort of way. He described his 'frolicking' in a kind of unreal and highly imaginative manner that wasn't always hideous to listen to. The strange beauty of this thing in the box here – disturbing as it is – somewhat parallels the language he used when talking about those poor kids. At times I couldn't help being fascinated, though maybe I was shielding my feelings with a psychologist's detachment. Sometimes you just have to distance yourself, even if it means becoming a little less human.

"Anyway, nothing that he said was sickeningly graphic in the way you might imagine. When he told me about his last and 'most memorable frolic,' it was with a powerful sense of wonder and nostalgia, shocking as that sounds to me now. It seemed to be a kind of homesickness, though his 'home' is a ramshackle ruin of his decaying mind. His psychosis had bred this blasphemous fairyland which exists in a powerful way for him, and despite the demented grandeur of his thousand names, he actually sees himself as only a minor figure in this world – a mediocre courtier in a broken-down kingdom of horror. This is really interesting when you consider the egoistical magnificence that a lot of psychopaths would attribute to themselves given a limitless imaginary realm in which they could play any imaginary role. But not John Doe. He's a comparatively lazy demi-demon from a place, a No Place, where dizzy chaos is the norm, a state of affairs on which he gluttonously thrives. Which is as good a description as any of the metaphysical economy of a psychotic's universe.

"There's actually quite a poetic geography to his interior dreamland as he describes it. He talked about a place that sounded like the back alleys of some cosmic slum, an innerdimensional dead end. Which might be an indication of a ghetto upbringing in Doe's past. And if so, his insanity has transformed these ghetto memories into a realm that cross-breeds a banal streetcorner reality with a psychopath's paradise. This is where he does his 'frolicking' with what he calls his 'awe-struck company,' the place possibly being an abandoned building, or even an accomodating sewer. I say this based on his repeated mentioning of 'the jolly river of refuse' and 'the jagged heaps in shadows,' which are certainly mad transmutations of a literal wasteland. Less fathomable are his memories of a moonlit corridor where mirrors scream and laugh, dark peaks of some kind that won't remain still, a stairway that's 'broken' in a very strange way, though this last one fits in with the background of a dilapidated slum.

"But despite all these dreamy back-drops in Doe's imagination, the mundane evidence of his frolics still points to a crime of very familiar, down-to-earth horrors. A run-of-the-mill atrocity. Consistently enough, Doe says he made the evidence look that way as a deliberate afterthought, that what he really means by 'frolicking' is a type of activity quite different from, even opposed to, the crime for which he was convicted. This term probably has some private associations rooted in his past."

Dr. Munck paused and rattled around the ice cubes in his empty glass. Leslie seemed to have drifted into herself while he was speaking. She had lit a cigarette and was now leaning on the arm of the sofa with her legs up on its cushions, so that her knees pointed at her husband.

"You should really quit smoking someday," he said.

Leslie lowered her eyes like a child mildly chastised. "I promise that as soon as we move – I'll quit. Is that a deal?"

"Deal," said David. "And I have another proposal for you. First let me tell you that I've definitely decided to hand in my resignation no later than tomorrow morning."

"Isn't that a little soon?" asked Leslie, hoping it wasn't.

"Believe me, no one will be surprised. I don't think anyone will even care. Anyway, my proposal is that tomorrow we take Norleen and rent a place up north for a few days or so. We could go horseback riding. Remember how she loved it last summer? What do you say?"

"That sounds nice," Leslie agreed with a deep glow of enthusiasm. "Very nice, in fact."

"And on the way back we can drop off Norleen at your parents'. She can stay there while we take care of the business of moving out of this house, maybe find an apartment temporarily. I don't think they'll mind having her for a week or so, do you?"

"No, of course not, they'll love it. But what's the great rush? Norleen's still in school, you know. Maybe we should wait till she gets out. It's just a month away."

David sat in silence for a moment, apparently ordering his thoughts.

"What's wrong?" asked Leslie with just a slight quiver of anxiety in her voice.

"Nothing is actually wrong, nothing at all. But—"

"But what?"

"Well, it has to do with the prison. I know I sounded very smug in telling you how safe we are from prison escapes, and I still maintain that we are. But the one prisoner I've told you about is very strange, as I'm sure you've gathered. He is positively criminally psychotic . . . and then again he's something else."

Leslie quizzed her husband with her eyes. "I thought you said he just bounces off the walls, not—"

"Yes, much of the time he's like that. But sometimes, well . . ."

"What are you trying to say, David?" asked an uneasy Leslie.

"It's something that Doe said when I was talking with him today. Nothing really definite. But I'd feel infinitely more comfortable about the whole thing if Norleen stayed with your parents until we can organize ourselves."

Leslie lit another cigarette. "Tell me what he said that bothers you so much," she said firmly. "I should know too."

"When I tell you, you'll probably just think I'm a little crazy myself. You didn't talk to him, though, and I did. The tone, or rather the many different tones of his voice; the shifting expressions on that lean face. Much of the time I talked to him I had the feeling he was beyond me in some way, I don't know exactly how. I'm sure it was just the customary behavior of the psychopath – trying to shock the doctor. It gives them a sense of power."

"Tell me what he said," Leslie insisted.

"All right, I'll tell you. As I said, it's probably nothing. But toward the end of the interview today, when we were talking about those kids, and actually kids in general, he said something I didn't like at all. He said it with an affected accent, Scottish this time with a little German flavor thrown in. He said: 'You wouldn't be havin' a misbehavin' laddie nor a little colleen of your own, now would you, Professor von Munck?' Then he grinned at me silently.

"Now I'm sure he was deliberately trying to upset me without, however, having any purpose in mind other than that."

"But what he said, David: 'nor a little colleen.' "

"Grammatically, of course, it should have been 'or' not 'nor', but I'm sure it wasn't anything except a case of bad grammar."

"You didn't mention anything about Norleen, did you?"

"Of course I didn't. That's not exactly the kind of thing I would talk about with these . . . people."

"Then why did he say it like that?"

"I have no idea. He possesses a very weird sort of cleverness, speaking much of the time with vague suggestions, even subtle jokes. He could have heard things about me from someone on the staff, I suppose. Then again, it might be just an innocent coincidence." He looked to his wife for comment.

"You're probably right," Leslie agreed with an ambivalent eagerness to believe in this conclusion. "All the same, I think I understand why you want Norleen to stay with my parents. Not that anything might happen—"

"Not at all. There's no reason to think anything would happen. Maybe this is a case of the doctor being out-psyched by his patient, but I don't really care anymore. Any reasonable person would be a little spooked after spending day after day in the chaos and physical danger of that place . . . the murderers, the rapists, the dregs of the dregs. It's impossible to lead a normal family life while working under those conditions. You saw how I was on Norleen's birthday."

"I know. Not the best surroundings in which to bring up a child."

David nodded slowly. "When I think of how she looked when I went to check on her a little while ago, hugging one of those stuffed security blankets of hers." He took a sip of his drink. "It was a new one, I noticed. Did you buy it when you were out shopping today?"

Leslie gazed blankly. "The only thing I bought was that," she said, pointing at the box on the coffee table. "What 'new one' do you mean?"

"The stuffed Bambi. Maybe she had it before and I just never noticed it," he said, partially dismissing the issue.

"Well, if she had it before, it didn't come from me," Leslie said quite resolutely.

"Nor me."

"I don't remember her having it when I put her to bed," said Leslie.

"Well, she had it when I looked in on her after hearing . . ."

David paused with a look on his face of intense thought, an indication of some frantic, rummaging search within.

"What's the matter, David?" Leslie asked, her voice weakening.

"I'm not sure exactly. It's as if I know something and don't know it at the same time."

But Dr. Munck was beginning to know. With his left hand he covered the back of his neck, warming it. Was there a draft coming from somewhere, another part of the house? This was not the kind of house to be drafty, not a broken-down place where the wind gets in through ancient attic boards and warped window-frames. There actually was quite a wind blowing now; he could hear it hunting around outside and could see the restless trees through the window behind the Aphrodite sculpture. The goddess posed languidly with her flawless head leaning back, her blind eyes contemplating the ceiling and beyond. But beyond the ceiling? Beyond the hollow snoozing of the wind, cold and dead? And the draft?

What?

"David, do you feel a draft?" asked his wife.

"Yes," he replied very loudly and with unusual force.

"Yes," he repeated, rising out of the chair, walking across the room, his steps quickening toward the stairs, up the three segments, then running down the second-floor hallway. "Norleen, Norleen," he chanted before reaching the half-closed door of her room. He could feel the breeze coming from there.

He knew and did not know.

He groped for the light switch. It was low, the height of a child. He turned on the light. The child was gone. Across the room the window was wide open, the white translucent curtains flapping upwards on the invading wind. Alone on the bed was the stuffed animal, torn, its soft entrails littering the mattress. Now stuffed inside, blooming out like a flower, was a piece of paper, and Dr. Munck could discern within its folds a fragment of the prison's letterhead. But the note was not a typed message of official business: the handwriting varied from a neat italic script to a child's scrawl. He desperately stared at the words for what seemed an infinite interval without comprehending their message. Then, finally, the meaning sank heavily in.

Dr. Monk, read the note from inside the animal, *We leave this behind in your capable hands, for in the black-foaming gutters and back alleys of paradise, in the dank windowless gloom of some galactic cellar, in the hollow pearly whorls found in sewerlike seas, in starless cities of insanity, and in their slums . . . my awe-struck little deer and I have gone frolicking. See you anon. Jonathan Doe.*

"David?" he heard his wife's voice inquire from the bottom of the stairs. "Is everything all right?"

Then the beautiful house was no longer quiet, for there rang a bright freezing scream of laughter, the perfect sound to accompany a passing anecdote of some obscure hell.

LES FLEURS

April 17th. Flowers sent out today in the early a.m.

May 1st. Today – and I thought it would never happen again – I have met someone about whom, I think, I can be hopeful. Her name is Daisy. She works in a florist shop! *The* florist shop, I might add, where I quietly paid a visit to gather some sorrowful flowers for Clare, who to the rest of the world is still a missing person. At first, of course, Daisy was politely reserved when I asked about some lilting blossoms for a loved one's memorial. I soon cured her, however, of this unnecessarily detached manner. In my deeply shy and friendly tone of voice I asked about some of the other flowers in the shop, ones having nothing to do with loss, if not everything to do with gain. She was quite glad to take me on a trumped-up tour of hyacinths and hibiscuses. I confessed to knowing next to nothing about commercial plants and things, and remarked on her enthusiasm for this field of study, hoping all the while that at least part of her animation was inspired by me. "Oh, I love working with flowers," she said. "I think they're real interesting." Then she asked if I was aware that there were plants having flowers which opened only at night, and that certain types of violets bloomed only in darkness underground. My inner flow of thoughts and sensations suddenly quickened. Though I had already sensed she was a girl of special imagination, this was the first hint I received of just how special it was. I judged my efforts to know her better would not be wasted, as they have been with others. "That *is* real interesting about those flowers," I said, smiling a hothouse warm smile. There was a pause which I filled in with my name. She then told me hers. "Now what kind of flowers would you like?" she asked. I sedately requested an arrangement suitable for the grave of a departed grandmother. Before leaving the shop I told Daisy I might need to stop by again to satisfy some future floral needs. She seemed to have no objection to this. With the vegetation nestled in my arm I songfully walked out of the store. I then proceeded directly to Chapel Gardens cemetery. For a while I sincerely made the effort to find a headstone that might by coincidence display my lost one's name. And any dates would just have to do. I thought she deserved this much at least. As events transpired, however, the recipient of my floral memorial had to be someone named Clarence.

May 16th. Daisy visited my apartment for the first time and fell in love with its quaint refurbishments. "I adore well-preserved old places," she said. It seemed to me she really did. I thought she would. She remarked what decorative wonders a few plants – of varying species – would do for the ancient rooms. She was obviously sensitive to the absence of natural adornments in my bachelor quarters. "Night-blooming cereuses?" I asked, trying not to mean too much by this and give myself away. A mild grin appeared on her face, but it was not an issue I thought I could press at the time, and even now I only delicately press it within these scrapbook pages. She wandered about the apartment at great length. I watched her, seeing the place with new eyes. Then suddenly I realized I had regrettably overlooked something. She looked it over. The object was positioned on a low table before a high window and between its voluminous curtains. It seemed so vulgarly prominent to me then, especially since I hadn't intended to let her see anything of this sort so early in our friendship. "What is this?" she asked, her voice expressing a kind of outraged curiosity bordering on plain outrage. "It's just a sculpture. I told you I do things like that. It's not very good. Kind of dumb." She examined the piece more closely. "Watch that," I warned. She let out a tiny, unserious "Ow." "Is it supposed to be some type of cactus?" she inquired. For a moment she seemed to take a genuine interest in that obscure objet d'art. "It has little teeth," she observed, "on these big tongue things." They do look like tongues; I'd never thought of that. Rather ingenious comparison, considering. I hoped her imagination had found fertile ground in which to grow, but instead she revealed a moribund disgust. "You might have better luck passing it off as an animal than a plant, or a sculpture of a plant, or whatever. It's got a velvety kind of fur and looks like it might crawl away." I felt like crawling away myself at that point. I asked her, as a quasi-botanist, if there were not plants resembling birds and other animal life. This was my feeble attempt to exculpate my creation from any charges of unnaturalness. It's strange how you're sometimes forced to assume an unsympathetic view of yourself through borrowed eyes. Finally I mixed some drinks and we went on to other things. I put on some music.

Soon afterward, however, the bland harmony of the music was undermined by an unfortunate dissonance. That detective (Briceberg, I think) arrived for an unexpected encore of his interrogation re: the Clare affair. Fortunately I was able to keep him and his questions out in the hallway the entire time. We reviewed the previous dialogue we'd had. I reiterated to him that Clare was just someone I worked with and with whom I was professionally friendly. It appears that some of my co-workers, unidentified, suspect that Clare and I were romantically involved. "Office gossip," I countered, knowing she was one girl who knew how to keep certain secrets, even if she could not be trusted with others. No, I said, I definitely had no idea where she could have disappeared to. I did manage to subversively hint, however, that I would not be surprised if in a sudden flight of neurotic despair she had impulsively relocated in some land of her heart's desire. I myself had despaired to find that within Clare's dark and promisingly moody borders lay a disappointing dreamland of white picket fences and flower-printed curtains. No, I didn't tell that to the detective. Besides, I further argued, it was well known in the office that Clare had begun dating someone approximately seven to ten days (my personal estimation of the term of her disloyalty) before her disappearance. So why bother me? This, I found out, was the reason: he had also been informed, he informed me, of my belonging to a certain offbeat organization. I replied there was nothing offbeat in serious philosophical study; furthermore, I was an artist, as he well knew, and, as anybody knows, artistic personalities have a perfectly natural tendency toward such things. I thought he would understand if I put it that way. He did. The man appeared satisfied with my every statement. Indeed, he seemed overly eager to dismiss me as a suspect in the case, no doubt trying to create a false sense of security on my part and lead me to make an unwitting admission to the foulest kind of play. "Was that about the girl in your office?" Daisy asked me afterward. "Mm-hm," I noised. I was brooding and silent for a while, hoping she would attribute this to my inward lament for that strange girl at the office and not to the lamentably imperfect evening we'd had. "Maybe I'd better go," she said, and very soon did. There was not much of our date left to salvage anyway. After she abandoned me I got very drunk on a liqueur tasting of flowers from open fields, or so it seemed. I also took this opportunity to reread a story about some men who visit the white waste regions of a polar wonderland. I don't expect to dream tonight, having already sated myself with this frigid fantasy. Brotherhood of Paradise offbeat indeed!

September 21st. Day came up to the cool, clean offices of G.R. Glacy, the advertising house of whores and horrors, to meet me for lunch. I introduced her around the department to the few people I get along with, and definitely not to those vicious copy-slingers who spread rumors about me. I also showed her my little corner of commercial artistry, including my latest project. "Oh, that's lovely," she said when I pointed out the drawing of a nymph with flowers in her freshly shampooed hair. "That's really nice." That "nice" remark almost spoiled my day. I asked her to look closely at the flowers mingling freshly in the fresh locks of this mythical being. It was barely noticeable that one of the flower stems was growing out of, or perhaps into, the creature's head. Day didn't seem to appreciate the craftiness of my craft very much. And I thought we were making such progress along "offbeat" paths. (Damn that Briceberg!) Perhaps I should wait until we return from our trip before showing her any of my paintings. I want her to be prepared. Everything is all prepared for our vacation, at least; Day finally found someone to take care of the cat who shares her flat.

October 10th. Good-bye diary. See you when I get back.

November 1st. With ecstasy and exasperation, I here record a particular episode from Day's and my tropical sojourn. I'm not sure whether the following adventure represents an impasse or a turning point in the course of our relationship. Perhaps there is some point that I have failed to entirely get. As yet I am, not surprisingly, in the dark. Here, nevertheless, is a fragment from our escapist interlude.

An Hawaiian paradise at midnight. Actually we were just gazing upon the beachside luxuriance from our hotel veranda. Day was bemused by several exotic drinks that wore flowers on their foamy heads. I was in a condition similar to hers. A few moments of heady silence passed, punctuated by an occasional sigh from Day. We heard the flapping of invisible wings whipping the warm air in darkness. We listened closely to the sounds of black orchids growing, even if there were none. "Mmmm," hummed Day. We were ripe for a whim. I had one, not knowing yet if I could pull it thoroughly off. "Can you smell the mysterious cereus?" I asked, placing one hand on her far shoulder and dramatically passing the other in a horizontal arc before the jungle beyond. "Can you?" I hypnotically repeated. "I can," said a game Day. "But can we find them, Day, and watch them open in the moonlight?" "We can, we can," she chanted giddily. We could. Suddenly the smooth-skinned leaves of the night garden were brushing against our smooth-skinned selves. Day paused to touch a flower that was orange or red but smelled of a deep violet. I encouraged us to press on across the flower-bedded earth. We plunged deeper into the dream garden. Faster, faster, faster the sounds and smells rushed by us. It was easier than I thought. At some point, with almost no effort at all, I successfully managed our full departure from known geography. "Day, Day," I shouted in the initial confusion and excitement. "We're here. I've never shown this to anyone. It's been such a torturous secret, Day. I've wanted to tell you for so long, and show you. No, don't speak. Look, look." Oh, the thrill of seeing this dark paradise with new eyes. With doubled intensity would I now see my world. My world. She was somewhere near me in the darkness. I waited, seeing her a thousand ways in my mind before actually gazing at the real Day. I looked. "What's wrong with the stars, the sky?" was all she said. She was trembling.

At breakfast the next morning I subtly probed her for impressions and judgements of the night before. But she was badly hung over and had only a chaotic recall of the previous night. Oh, well.

Since our return I have been working on a painting entitled "Sanctum Obscurum." Though I have done this kind of work many times before, I am including in this one elements that I hope will stir Day's memory and precipitate a conscious recollection of not only a certain night in the islands but of all the subtle and not so subtle messages I have tried to communicate to her. I only pray she will understand.

November 14th. Stars of disaster! Earthly, and not unearthly asters are all that fill Day's heart with gladness. She is too much a lover of natural flora to be anything else. I know this now. I showed her the painting, and even imagined she anticipated seeing it with some excitement. But I think she was just anxiously waiting to see what kind of fool I would make of myself. She sat on the sofa, scraping her lower lip with a nervous forefinger. Opposite her I let a little cloth drop. She looked up as if there had been a startling noise. I was not wholly satisfied with the painting myself, but this exhibition was designed to serve an extra-aesthetic purpose. I searched her eyes for a reflection of understanding, a ripple of empathetic insight. "Well?" I asked, the necessity of the word tolling doom. Her gaze told me all I needed to know, and the fatal clarity of the message was reminiscent of another girl I once knew. She gave me a second chance, looking at the picture with a theatrical scrutiny. The picture itself? An inner refuge, cozily crowding about the periphery of a central window of leaded glass. The interior beams with a honeyed haze, as of light glowing evenly through a patterned tapestry. Beyond the window, too, is a sanctuary of sorts, but not of man or terrestrial nature. Outside is an opulent kingdom of glittering colors and velvety jungle-shapes, a realm of contorted rainbows and twisted auroras. Hyperradiant hues are calmed by the glass, so that their strange intensity does not threaten the chromatic integrity of the world within. Some stars, coloured from the most spectral part of the spectrum, blossom in the high darkness. The outer world glistens in stellar light and also gleams with a labyrinthine glare inside each twisted form. And upon the window's surface is the watery reflection of a lone figure gazing out at this unearthly paradise.

"Of course, it's very good," she observed. "Very realistic."

Not at all, Daisy Day. Not realistic in the least.

Some uncomfortable moments later I found out she had to be leaving. It seemed she had made girl plans with a girlfriend of hers to do some things girls do when they get together with others of their kind. I said I understood, and I did. There was no doubt in my mind of the gender of Day's companion this evening. But it was for a different reason that I was distressed to see her go. Tonight marks the first time, and this I could read in her every move and expression, that she has truly possessed a sure knowledge of my secrets. Of course, she already knew about the meetings I attend and all such things. I've even paraphrased and abridged for her the discussion which goes on at these gatherings, always obscuring their real nature in progressively more transparent guises, hoping one day to show her the naked truth. And now, I think, the secret has been stripped bare. Whether she believes them or not, which doesn't make any difference, she has as clear a notion as Clare ever did of the fabulous truth about me and the others. She has positively gotten the picture now.

November 16th. Tonight we held an emergency meeting, our assembly in crisis. The others feel there's a problem, and of course I know they're right. Ever since I met that girl I could sense their growing uneasiness, which was their prerogative. Now, however, all has changed; my romantic misjudgement has seen to that. They expressed absolute horror that an outsider should know so much. I feel it myself. Day is a stranger now, and I wonder what her loquacious self might disclose about her former friend, not to mention his present ones. A marvelous arcana is threatened with exposure. The secretness we need for our lives could be lost, and with it would go the keys to a strange kingdom.

We've confronted these situations before, and I'm not the only one to have jeopardized our secrecy. We, of course, have no secrets from each other. They know everything about me, and I about them. They knew every step of the way my relationship with Daisy. Some of them even predicted the outcome. And though I thought I was right in taking the extravagant chance that they were wrong, I must now defer to their prophecy. Those lonely souls, *mes frères!* "Do you want us to see it through?" they asked in so many words. I consented, finally, in a score of ambiguous, half-hesitant ways. Then they sent me back to my unflowered sanctum. I'll never do this again, I thought, even though I've made this resolution before. I stared at the razory dentes of my furry sculpture for a perilously long while. What that poor girl saw as tongue-like floral appendages were silent: the preservation of such silence, of course, is their whole purpose. I remember that Daisy once jokingly asked me on what I modeled my art . . .

November 17th.

> *To Eden with me you will not leave*
> *To live in a cottage of crazy crooked*
> *eaves.*
> *In your own happy home you take care*
> *these nights;*
> *When you let your little cat in, turn*
> *on the lights!*
> *Something scurries behind and finds*
> *a cozy place to stare,*
> *Something sent to you from paradise,*
> *paradisically so rare:*
> *Tongues flowering; they leap out*
> *laughing, lapping. Disappear!*

I do this to pass the hours. Only to pass the hours.

November 17th. 12.00 a.m. Flowers.

ALICE'S LAST
ADVENTURE

Preston, stop laughing. They ate the whole backyard. They ate your
mother's favorite flowers! It's not funny, Preston."
"Aaaaa ha-ha-ha-ha-ha. Aaaaa ha-ha-ha-ha-ha."
— *Preston and the Starving Shadows*

A long time ago, Preston Penn made up his mind to ignore the
passing years and join the ranks of those who remain forever
in a kind of half-world between childhood and adolescence. He
would not give up the bold satisfaction of eating insects (cripsy flies
and crunchy beetles are his favorites), nor that peculiar drunkenness of a child's brain, induplicable once grown-up sobriety has set
perniciously in. The result was that Preston successfully negotiated
several decades without ever coming within hailing distance of
puberty; he lived unchanged throughout many a perverse adventure in the forties and fifties and even into the sixties. He lived long
after I ceased writing about him.

Did he have a prototype? I should say so. One doesn't just *invent*
a character like Preston using only the pitiful powers of imagination. He was very much a concoction of reality, later adapted for
my popular series of children's books. Preston's status in both
reality and imagination has always had a great fascination for me.
In the past year, however, this issue has especially demanded my
attention, not without some personal annoyance and even anxiety.
Then again, perhaps I'm just getting senile.

My age is no secret, since it can be looked up in a number of
literary reference sources (see *Children's Authors of Today*) whose
information is only a few years off — I won't tell you in which
direction. Over two decades ago, when the last Preston book
appeared *(Preston and the Upside-Down Face)*, one reviewer rather

snootily referred to me as the " 'Grande Damned' of a particular sort of children's literature." What *sort* you can imagine if you don't otherwise know, if you didn't grow up – or not grow up, as it were – reading Preston's adventures with the Dead Mask, the Starving Shadows, or the Lonely Mirror.

Even as a little girl, I knew I wanted to be an author; and I also knew just the kinds of things I would write. Let someone else give the preadolescents their literary introductions to life and love, guiding them through those volatile years when *anything* might go wrong, and landing them safely on the shores of incipient maturity. That was never my destiny. I would write about my adventures with Preston – my real-life childhood playmate, as everybody knew. Preston would then initiate others into the mysteries of an upside-down, inside-out, sinistral, always faintly askew (if not entirely reversed) universe. A true avatar of topsy-turveydom, Preston gave himself body and soul to the search – in common places such as pools of rainwater, tarnished ornaments, November afternoons – for zones of fractured numinosity, usually with the purpose of fracturing in turn the bizarre icons of his foul and bloated twin, the adult world. He became a conjurer of stylish nightmares, and what he could do with mirrors gave the grown-ups fits and sleepless nights. No dilettante of the extraordinary, but its embodiment. Such is the spiritual biography of Preston Penn.

But I suppose it was my father, as much as Preston's original, who inspired the stories I've written. To put it briefly, Father had the blood of a child coursing through his big adult body, nourishing the over-sophisticated brain of Foxborough College's associate professor of philosophy. Typical of his character was a love for the books of Lewis Carroll, and thus the genesis of my name, if not my subsequent career. (My mother told me that while she was pregnant, Father *willed* me into a little Alice.) Father thought of Carroll not merely as a clever storyteller but more as an inhumanly jaded aesthete of the imagination, no doubt projecting some of his own private values onto poor Mr. Dodgson. To him the author of the Alice books was, I think, a personal symbol of power, the strange ideal of an unstrictured mind manipulating reality to its whim and gaining a kind of objective force through the minds of others.

It was very important that I share these books, and many other things, in the same spirit. "See, honey," he would say while rereading *Through the Looking Glass* to me, "see how smart little Alice right away notices that the room on the other side of the mirror is not as 'tidy' as the one she just came from. Not as *tidy*," he repeated with professorial emphasis but chuckling like a child, a strange little laugh that I inherited from him. "Not tidy. We know what *that* means, don't we?" I would look up at him and nod with all the solemnity that my six, seven, eight years could muster.

And I did know what *that* meant. I felt intimations of a thousand discrete and misshapen marvels: of things going wrong in curious ways, of the edge of the world where an endless ribbon of road continued into space by itself, of a universe handed over to new gods. Father would gaze at my round little face, squinting his eyes as if I were giving off light. "Moon face," he called me. When I got older, my features became more angular, an involuntary betrayal of my father's conception of his little Alice, among all the other betrayals once I'd broken the barrier of maturity. I suppose it was a blessing that he did not live to see me grow up and change, saved from disappointment by a sudden explosion in his brain while he was giving a lecture at the college.

But perhaps he would have perceived, as I did not for many years, that my "change" was illusory, that I merely picked up the conventional gestures of an aging soul (nervous breakdown, divorce, remarriage, alcoholism, widowhood, stoic tolerance of a second-rate reality) without destroying the Alice he loved. She was always kept very much alive, though relegated to the role of an author for children. *Obviously* she endured, because it was she who wrote all those books about her soul mate Preston, even if she has not written one for many years now. Not too many, I hope. Oh, those years, those years.

So much for the past.

At present I would like to deal with just a single year, the one ending today – about an hour from now, judging by the clock that five minutes ago chimed eleven p.m. from the shadows on the other side of this study. During the past three hundred and sixty-five days I have noticed, sometimes just barely, an accumulation of peculiar episodes in my life. A lack of *tidiness*, you might say. (As a result, I've been drinking heavily again; and loneliness is getting to me in ways it never did in the past. Ah, the past.)

Some of these episodes are so elusive and insubstantial that it would be impossible to talk about them sensibly, except perhaps in the moods they leave behind like fingerprints, and which I've learned to read like divinatory signs. My task will be much easier if I confine myself to recounting but a few of the incidents, thereby giving them a certain form and structure I so badly need just now. A tidying up, so to speak.

I should start by identifying tonight as that sacred eve which

Preston always devotedly observed, celebrating it most intensely in *Preston and the Ghost of the Gourd*. (At least there should be a few minutes remaining of this immovable feast, according to the clock ticking at my back; though from the look of things, the hands seem stuck on the time I reported a couple of paragraphs ago. Perhaps I misjudged it before.)

For the past several years I've made an appearance at the local suburban library on this night to give a reading from one of my books as the main event of an annual Hallowe'en fest. Tonight I managed to show up once again for the reading, even if I hesitate to say everything went *as usual*. Last year, however, I did not make it at all to the costume party. This brings me to what I *think* is the first in a year-long series of disruptions unknown to a biography previously marked by nothing more than episodes of conventional chaos. My apologies for taking two steps backward before one step forward. As an old hand at storytelling, I realize this is always a risky approach when bidding for a reader's attention. But here goes.

Around this time last year I attended the funeral of someone from my past, long past. This was none other than that sprite of special genius whose exploits served as the *prima materia* for my Preston Penn books. The gesture was one of pure nostalgia, for I hadn't actually seen this person since my twelfth birthday party. It was soon afterward that my father died, and my mother and I moved out of our house in North Sable, Mass. (see *Childhood Homes of Children's Authors* for a photo of the old two-story frame job), heading for the big city and away from sad reminders. A local teacher who knew of my work, and its beginnings in North S, sent me a newspaper clipping from the *Sable Sentinel*, that reported the demise of my former playmate and even mentioned his second-hand literary fame.

I arrived in town very quietly and was immediately over-whelmed by the lack of change in the place, as if it had existed all those years in a state of suspended animation and had been only recently reanimated for my benefit. It almost seemed that I might run into my old neighbors, schoolmates, and even Mr. So and So who ran the ice-cream shop, which I was surprised to see still in operation. On the other side of the window, a big man with a walrus mustache was digging ice cream from large cardboard cylinders, while two chubby kids pressed their bellies against the counter. The man hadn't changed in the least over the years. He looked up and saw me staring into the shop, and there really seemed to be a twinkle of recognition in his puffy eyes. But that was impossible. He could have never perceived behind my ancient mask the child's face he once knew, even if he had been Mr. So and So and not his look-alike (son? grandson?). Two complete strangers gawking at each other through a window smeared with the sticky handprints of sloppy patrons. The scene depressed me more than I can say.

Unfortunately, an even more depressing reunion waited a few steps down the street. G. V. Ness and Sons, Funeral Directors. For all the years I'd lived in North Sable, this was only my second visit ("Good-bye, Daddy") to that cold colonial building. But such placcs always seem familiar, having that perfectly vacant, neutral atmosphere common to all funeral homes, the same in my home-town as in the suburb outside New York ("Good riddance, Hubby") where I'm now secluded.

I strolled into the proper room unnoticed, another anonymous mourner who was a bit shy about approaching the casket. Although I drew a couple of small-town stares, the elderly, elegant author from New York did not stand out as much as she thought she would. But with or without distinction, it remained my intention to introduce myself to thc widow as a childhood friend of her deceased husband. This intention, how-ever, was shot all to hell by two oxlike men who rose from their seats on either side of the grieving lady and lumbered my way. For some reason I panicked.

"You must be Dad's Cousin Winnie from Boston. The family's heard so much about you over the years," they said.

I smiled widely and gulped deeply, which must have looked like a nod of affirmation to them. In any case, they led me over to "Mom" and introduced me under my inadvertent pseudonym to the red-eyed, half-delirious old woman. (Why, I wonder, did I allow this goof to go on?)

"Nice to finally meet you, and thank you for the lovely card you sent," she said, sniffing loudly and working on her eyes with a grotesquely soiled handkerchief. "I'm Elsie."

Elsie Chester, I thought immediately, though I wasn't entirely sure that this was the same person who was rumored to have sold kisses and other things to the boys at North Sable Elementary. So he had married *her*, whaddaya know? Possibly they *had* to get married, I speculated cattily. At least one of her sons looked old enough to have been the consequence of teenage impatience. Oh, well. So much for Preston's vow to wed no one less than the Queen of Nightmares.

But even greater disappointments awaited my notice. After

chatting emptily with the widow for a few more moments, I excused myself to pay my respects at the coffinside of the deceased. Until then I'd deliberately averted my gaze from that flower-crazed area at the front of the room, where a shiny, pearl-grey casket held its occupant in much the same position as the "Traveling Tomb" racer he'd once constructed. This part of the mortuary ritual never fails to put me in mind of those corpse-viewing sessions to which children in the nineteenth century were subjected in order to acquaint them with their own mortality. At my age this was unnecessary, so allow me to skip quickly over this scene with a few tragic and inevitable words . . .

Bald and blemished, that was unconsciously expected. *Totally* unfamiliar, that wasn't. The mosquito-faced child I once knew had had his features smushed and spread by the years – bloated, not with death but with having overfed himself at the turgid banquet of life, lethargically pushing away from the table just prior to explosion. A portrait of lazy indulgence. Defunct. Used up. The eternal adult. (But perhaps in death, I consoled myself, a truer self was even now ripping off the false face of the thing before me. This must be so, for the idea of an afterworld populated with a preponderance of old, withered souls is too hideous to contemplate.)

After paying homage to the remains of a memory, I slipped out of that room with a stealth my Preston would have been proud of. I'd left behind an envelope with a modest contribution to the widow's fund. I had half a mind to send a batch of gaping black orchids to the funeral home with a note signed by Laetitia Simpson, Preston's dwarfish girlfriend. But this was something that the other Alice would have done – the one who wrote those strange books.

As for me, I got into my car and drove out of town to a nice big Holiday Inn near the interstate, where I found a nice suite – spoils of a successful literary career – and a bar. And as it turned out, this overnight layover must take us down another side road (or back road, if you like) of my narrative. Please stand by.

A late-afternoon crowd had settled into the hotel's bar-room, relieving me of the necessity of drinking in total solitude, which at the time I was quite prepared to do. After a couple of Scotches on the rocks, I noticed a young man looking my way from the other side of that greenish room. At least he appeared young, extremely so, from a distance. But as I walked over to sit at his table, with a boldness I've never attributed to alcohol, he seemed to gain a few years with every step I took. He was now only relatively young –

from an old dowager's point of view, that is. His name was Hank De Vere, and he worked for a distributor of gardening tools and other such products, in Maine. But let's not pretend to care about the details. Later we had dinner together, after which I invited him to my suite.

It was the next morning, by the way, that inaugurated that year-long succession of experiences which I'm methodically trying to sort out with a few select examples. Half step forward coming up: pawn to king three.

I awoke in the darkness peculiar to hotel bedrooms, abnormally heavy curtains masking the morning light. Immediately it became apparent that I was alone. My new acquaintance seemed to have a more developed sense of tact and timing than I had given him credit for. At least I thought so at first. But then I looked through the open doorway into the other room, where I could see a convex mirror in an artificial wood frame on the wall. -

The bulging eye of the mirror reflected almost the entire next room in convexed perspective, and I noticed someone moving around in there. In the mirror, that is. A tiny, misshapen figure seemed to be gyring about, leaping almost, in a way that should have been audible to me. But it wasn't.

I called out a name I barely remembered from the night before. There came no answer from the next room, but the movement in the mirror stopped, and the tiny figure (whatever it was) disappeared. Very cautiously I got up from the bed, robed myself, and peeked around the corner of the doorway like a curious child on Christmas morning. A strange combination of relief and confusion arose in me when I saw that there was no one else in the suite.

I approached the mirror, perhaps to search its surface for the little *something* that might have caused the illusion. My memory is vague on this point, since at the time I was a bit hung over. But I can recall with spectacular vividness what I finally saw after gazing into the mirror for a few moments. Suddenly the sphered glass before me became clouded with a mysterious fog, from the depths of which appeared the waxy face of a corpse. It was the visage of that old cadaver I'd seen at the funeral home, now with eyes open and staring reproachfully into mine . . .

Of course I really saw nothing of the kind. I did not even imagine it, except just now. But somehow this imaginary manifestation seems more fitting and conclusive than what I actually found in the mirror, which was only my old and haggard face . . . a corpselike countenance if ever there was one.

But there was another conclusion, let's say *encore*, to this episode with the mirror. A short while later I was checking out, and as the desk clerk was fiddling with my bill, I happened to look out of a nearby window, beyond which two children were romping on the lawn in front of the hotel: an arm-swinging, leaping mime show. After a few seconds the kids caught me watching them. They stopped and stared back at me, standing perfectly still, side by side . . . then suddenly they were running away. The room took a little spin that only I seemed to notice, while others went calmly about their business. Possibly this experience can be attributed to my failure to employ the usual post-debauch remedies that morning. The old nerves were somewhat shot, and my stomach was giving me no peace. Still, I've remained in pretty fair health over the years, all things considered, and I drove back home without further incident.

That was a year ago. (Get ready for one giant step forward: the old queen is now in play.)

In the succeeding months I noted a number of similar happenings, though they occurred with varying degrees of clarity. Most of them approached the fleeting nature of déjà vu phenomena. A few could be pegged as self-manufactured, while others lacked a definite source. I might see a phrase or the fragment of an image that would make my heart flip over (not a healthy thing at my age), while my mind searched for some correspondence that triggered this powerful sense of repetition and familiarity: the sound of a delayed echo with oblique origins. I delved into dreams, half-conscious perceptions, and the distortions of memory, but all that remained was a chain of occurrences with links as weak as smoke rings.

And today, one year later, this tenuous haunting has regained the clarity of the first incident at the hotel. Specifically I refer to a pair of episodes that have caused me to become a little insecure about my psychic balance and to attempt to confirm my lucidity by writing it all out. Organization is what's needed. Thus:

Episode One. Place: The Bathroom. Time: A Little After Eight a.m., the Last Day of October.

The water was running for my morning bath, cascading into the tub a bit noisily for my sensitive ears. The night before, I suffered from an advanced case of insomnia, which even extra doses of my beloved Guardsman's Reserve Stock did not help. I was very glad to see a sunny autumn morning come and rescue me. My bathroom mirror, however, would not let me forget the sleepless night I'd spent, and I combed and creamed myself without noticeable improvement. Sandal was with me, lying atop the toilet tank and scrutinizing the waters of the bowl below. She was actually staring very hard and deliberately at something. I'd never seen a cat stare at its own reflection and have always been under the impression that they cannot see reflected images of themselves. (Lucky them!) But this one saw something. "What is it, Sandal?" I asked with the patronizing voice of a pet owner. Her tail had a life of its own; she stood up and hissed, then yowled in that horribly demonic falsetto of threatened felines. Finally she dashed out of the bathroom, relinquishing her ground for the first time in all my memory of her.

I had been loitering at the other side of the room, a groggy bystander to an unexpected scene. With a large plastic hairbrush gripped in my left hand, I investigated. I gazed down into the same waters, and though at first they seemed clear enough, something soon appeared from within that porcelain burrow . . . It had dozens of legs and looked all backward and inside out, but what was most disgusting about the thing was that it had a tiny human head, one like a baby's except all blue and shriveled.

This latter part, of course, is an exaggeration; or rather, it's an alarm without a fire. It helps if I can tack a neat storybook finish onto these episodes, because what seem to be their real conclusions just leave me hanging. You can't have stories end that way and still expect to hold your reader's esteem. Some genius once said that literature was invented the first time a certain boy cried "Wolf!" and there was none. I suppose this is what I'm doing now. Crying wolf. Not that it's my intention to make a fiction out of what is real. (Much too real, judging by my recent overdrinking and resultant late-night vomiting sessions.) But stories, even very nasty ones, are traditionally considered more satisfying than reality – which, as we all know, is a grossly overrated affair. So don't worry about my cries of wolf. Even if it turns out that I'm making *everything* up, at least what you have left can be enjoyed as a story – no small value to my mind. It's just a different story, that's all: one about *another* old-lady author of children's yarns, which, incidentally, has nothing to do with the "truth" one way or the other.

So: Yes, I was in the bathroom, staring into the toilet bowl. The truth is that there was nothing in there, except nice, disinfected water of a bluish tint. The water was still, like a miniature lake, and cruelly reflected a miniature face. That's all I really saw, my hysterical kitty notwithstanding. I gazed at my wrinkled self in the magic pool for a few moments longer and then cocked the handle to flush it away. (You were right, Father, it doesn't pay to get old and ugly.)

I spent the rest of the morning lying around the baggy old

suburban home my second husband left me when he died some years ago. An old war movie on television helped me pass the time. (And vain lady that I am, what I remember most about the war is the shortage of silk and other luxury items, like the quicksilver needed to make a mirror of superior reflective powers.)

In the afternoon I began preparing myself for the reading I was to give at the library, the preparation being mostly alcoholic. I've never looked forward to this annual ordeal and only put up with it out of a sense of duty, vanity, and other less comprehensible motives. Maybe this is why I welcomed the excuse to skip it last year. And I wanted to skip it this year, too, if only I could have come up with a reason satisfactory to the others involved – and, more importantly, to myself. Wouldn't want to disappoint the children, would I? Of course not, though heaven only knows why. Children have made me nervous ever since I stopped being one of them. Perhaps this is why I never had any of my own – adopted any, that is – for the doctors told me long ago that I'm about as fertile as the seas of the moon.

The other Alice is the one who's really comfortable with kids and kiddish things. How else could she have written *Preston and the Laughing This* or *Preston and the Twitching That?* So when it comes time to do this reading every year, I try to put *her* onstage as much as possible, something that's becoming more difficult with the passing years. Oddly enough, it's my grown-up's weakness for booze that allows me to do this most effectively. Each drink I had this afternoon peeled away a few more winters, and soon I was ready to confront the most brattish child without fear. Which leads me to introduce:

Episode Two. Place: The Car in the Driveway. Time: A Radiant Twilight.

With a selection of Preston stories on the seat beside me (I was still undecided on which to read, hoping for inspiration), I was off to do my duty at the library. A routine adjustment of the rearview mirror straightened the slack-mouthed angle it had somehow assumed since I'd last driven the car. The image I saw in the mirror was also routine. Across the street and staring into my car by way of the rear window was the odious and infinitely old Mr. Thompson. (Worse than E. Nesbit's U. W. Ugli, let me assure you.)

He seemed to appear out of nowhere, for I hadn't seen him when I was getting into the car. But there he was now, ogling the back of my head. This was quite normal for the lecherous old boy, and I didn't think anything of it. While I was adjusting the mirror, however, a strange little trick took place. I must have hit the switch that changes the position of the mirror for night driving, flipping it back and forth very quickly like the snap of a camera. So what I saw for an instant was a nighttime, negative version of Mr. Thompson as he stood there with his hands deep in his trouser pockets. What a horrendous idea. The unappealingly lubricious Thompson on this side of reality is bad enough without *anti*-Thompsons running around and harassing me for dates. (Thank goodness there's only one of everybody, I thought.) I didn't pull out of the driveway until I saw Thompson move on down the sidewalk, which he did after a few moments, leaving me to stare at my own shriveled eye sockets in the rearview mirror.

The sun was going down in a pumpkin-colored blaze when I arrived at the little one-story library. Some costumed kids were hanging around outside: a werewolf, a black cat with a long curling tail, and what looked like an Elvis Presley, or at least some teen idol of a bygone age. And coming up the walk were two identical Tinkerbells, who I later found out were Tracy and Trina Martin. I had forgotten about twins. So much for the comforting notion that there's only one of everybody.

I was actually feeling quite confident, even as I entered the library and suddenly found myself confronted with a huddling mass of youngsters. But then the spell was broken maliciously when some anonymous smart aleck called out from the crowd, saying: "Hey, lookit the mask *she's* wearing." After that I propelled myself down several glossy linoleum hallways in search of a friendly adult face. (Someone should give that wisecracker a copy of *Struwwelpeter*; let him see what happens to his kind of kid.)

Finally I passed the open door of a tidy little room where a group of ladies and the head librarian, Mr. Grosz, were sipping coffee. Mr. Grosz said how nice it was to see me again and introduced me to the moms who were helping out with the party.

"My William's read all your books," said a Mrs. Harley, as if she were relating a fact to which she was completely indifferent. "I can't keep him away from them."

I didn't know whether or not to thank her for this comment, and ended up replying with a dignified and slightly liquorish smile. Mr. Grosz offered me some coffee and I declined: bad for the stomach. Then he wickedly suggested that, as it was starting to get dark outside, the time seemed right for the festivities to begin. My reading was to inaugurate the evening's fun, a good spooky story "to get everyone in the mood." First, though, I needed to get myself in the mood, and discreetly retired to a nearby ladies' room where I could refortify my fluttering nerves. Mr. Grosz, in one of the strangest and most embarrassing social gestures I've ever witnessed, offered to wait right outside the lavatory until I finished.

"I'm quite ready now, Mr. Grosz," I said, glaring down at the little man from atop an uneldernly pair of high heels. He cleared his throat, and I almost thought he was going to extend a crooked arm for me to take. But instead, he merely stretched it out, indicating the way to an old woman who might not see as well as she once did.

He led me back down the hallway toward the children's section of the library, where I assumed my reading would take place as it always had in the past. However, we walked right by this area, which was dark and ominously empty, and proceeded down a flight of stairs leading to the library's basement. "Our *new* facility," bragged Mr. Grosz. "Converted one of the storage rooms into a small auditorium of sorts." Down at the end of the hallway, two large green doors faced each other on opposite walls. "Which one will it be tonight?" asked Mr. Grosz while staring at my left hand. "*Preston and the Starving Shadows*," I answered, showing him the book I was holding. He smiled and confided that it was one of his favorites. Then he opened the door to the library's *new* facility.

Over fifty kids were sitting (quietly!) in their seats. At the front of the long, narrow room, a big witch was outlining the party activities for the night; and when she saw Mr. Grosz and me enter, she began telling the children about a "special treat for us all," meaning that the half-crocked lady author was about to give her half-cocked oration. Walking a very straight line to the front, I took the platform and thanked everyone for that nice applause – most of it, in fact, coming from the sweaty hands of Mr. Grosz. On the platform was a lamp-bearing podium decorated with wizened cornstalks. I fixed my book in place before me, disguising my apprehension with a little stage patter about the story everyone was going to hear. When I invoked the name of Preston Penn, a few kids actually cheered, or at least one did. Just as I was ready to begin reading, however, the lights went out, which was rather unexpected. And for the first time I noticed that facing each other on opposite sides of the room were two rows of jack-o'-lanterns shining bright orange and yellow in the darkness. They all had identical faces – triangular eyes and noses, wailing *O's* for mouths – and could have been mirror reflections of themselves. (As a child, I was convinced that pumpkins naturally grew this way, complete with facial features and phosphorescent insides.) Furthermore, they seemed to be suspended in space, darkness concealing their means of support. Since that darkness also prevented my seeing the faces of the children, these jack-o'-lanterns became my audience.

But as I read, the real audience asserted itself with giggles, whispers, and some rather ingenious noises made with the folding wooden chairs they were sitting in. At one point, toward the end of the reading, there came a low moan from somewhere in the back, and it sounded as if someone had fallen out of his seat. "It's all right," I heard an adult voice call out. The door at the back opened, allowing a moment of brightness to break the spooky spell, and some shadows exited. When the lights came on at the end of the story, one of the seats toward the back was missing its occupant.

"Okay, kids," said the big witch after some minor applause for Preston, "everyone move their chairs back to the walls and make room for the games and stuff."

The games and stuff had the room in a low-grade uproar. Masked and costumed children ruled the night, indulging their appetite for movement, sweet things to eat and drink, and noise. I stood at the periphery of the commotion and chatted with Mr. Grosz.

"What exactly was the disturbance all about?" I asked him.

He took a sip from a plastic cup of cider and smacked his lips offensively. "Oh, nothing, really. You see that child there with the black-cat outfit? She seemed to have fainted. Not entirely, of course. Once we got her outside, she was all right. She was wearing her kitty mask all through your reading, and I think the poor thing hyperventilated or something like that. Complained that she saw something horrible in her mask and was very frightened for a while. At any rate, you can see she's fine now, and she's even wearing her mask again. Amazing how children can put things right out of their minds and recover so quickly."

I agreed that it was amazing, and then asked precisely what it was the child thought she saw in her mask. I couldn't help being reminded of another cat earlier in the day who also saw something that gave her a fright.

"She couldn't really explain it," replied Mr. Grosz. "You know how it is with children. Yes, I daresay you *do* know how it is with them, considering you've spent your life exploring the subject."

I took credit for knowing how it is with children, knowing instead that Mr. Grosz was really talking about someone else, about *her*. Not to overdo this quaint notion of a split between my professional and my private personas, but at the time I was already quite self-conscious about the matter. While I was reading the Preston book to the kids, I had suffered the uncanny experience of having almost no recognition of my own words. Of course, this is rather a cliché with writers, and it has happened to me many times throughout my long career. But never so completely. They were the words of a mind (I stop just short of writing *soul*) entirely alien to me. This much I would like to note in passing, never to be mentioned again.

"I do hope," I said to Mr. Grosz, "that it wasn't the story that scared the child. I have enough angry parents on my hands as it is."

"Oh, I'm sure it wasn't. Not that it wasn't a good scary children's story. I didn't mean to imply that, of course. But you know, it's that time of year. Imaginary things are supposed to seem more real. Like your Preston. He was always a big one for Hallowe'en, am I right?"

I said he was quite right and hoped he would not pursue the subject. The reality of fictional characters was not at all what I wanted to talk about just then. I tried to laugh it away. And you know, Father, for a moment it was exactly like your own laugh, and not my usual hereditary impersonation of it.

Much to everyone's regret, I did not stay very long at the party. The reading had largely sobered me up, and my tolerance level was running quite low. Yes, Mr. Grosz, I promise to do it again next year, anything you say; just let me get back to my car and my bar.

The drive home through the suburban streets was something of an ordeal, made hazardous by pedestrian trick-or-treaters. The costumes did me no good. (The same ghost was everywhere.) The masks did me no good. And those Prestonian shadows fluttering against two-story facades (why did I have to choose *that* book?) certainly did me no good at all. This was not my place anymore. Not my style. Dr. Guardsman, administer your medicine in tall glasses . . . but please not looking-ones.

And now I'm safe at home with one of the tallest of those glasses resting full and faithful on my desk as I write. A lamp with a shade of Tiffany glass (circa 1922) casts its amiable glow on the many pages I've filled over the past few hours. (Although the hands of the clock seem locked in the same V position as when I started writing.) The lamplight shines upon the window directly in front of my desk, allowing me to see a relatively flattering reflection of myself in the black mirror of the glass. The house is soundless, and I'm a rich, retired authoress-widow.

Is there still a problem? I'm really not sure.

I remind you that I've been drinking steadily since early this afternoon. I remind you that I'm old and no stranger to the mysteries of geriatric neuroticism. I remind you that some part of me has written a series of children's books whose hero is a disciple of the bizarre. I remind you of what night this is and to what zone the imagination can fly on this particular eve. (But we can discount this last one, owing to my status as an elderly cynic and disbeliever.) I need not, however, remind you that this world is stranger than we know, or at least mine seems to be, especially this past year. And I now notice that it's *very* strange – and, once again, untidy.

Exhibit One. Outside my window is an autumn moon hanging in the blackness. Now, I have to confess that I'm not up on lunar phases ("loony faces," as Preston might say), but there seems to have been a switch since I last peeked out the window – the thing looks reversed. Where it used to be concaving to the right, it's now con*vex*ing in that direction, last quarter changed to first quarter, or something of that nature. But I doubt Nature has anything to do with it; more likely the explanation lies with Memory. And there's really not much troubling me about the moon, which, even if reversed, would still look as neat as a storybook illustration. The trouble is with everything else below, or at least what I can see of the suburbanscape in the darkness. Like writing that can only be read in a mirror, the shapes outside my window – trees, houses, but thank goodness no people – now look awkward and wrong.

Exhibit Two. To the earlier list of reasons for my diminished competence, I would like to add an upcoming alcohol withdrawal. The last sip I took out of that glass on my desk tasted indescribably strange, to the point where I doubt I'll be having any more. I almost wrote, and now will, that the booze tasted inside out. Of course, there are certain diseases with the power to turn the flavor of one's favorite drink into that of a hellbroth. So perhaps I've fallen victim to such a malady. But I remind you that although my mind may be terminally soused, it has always resided *in corpore sano*.

Exhibit Three (the last). My reflection in the window before me. Perhaps something unusual in the melt of the glass. My face. The surrounding shadows seem to be overlapping it a little at a time, like bugs attracted to something sweet. But the only thing sweet about Alice is her blood, highly sugared over the years from her drinking habit. So what is it, then? Shadows of senility? Or those starving things I read about earlier this evening come back for a repeat performance, another in a year-long series of echoes? But whenever that happens, it's always the reflection, the warped or imaginary image first . . . and then the real-life echo. Since when does reading a story constitute an incantation calling up its imagery before the body's eyes and not the mind's?

Something's backward here. Backward into a corner: *checkmate*.

Now, perhaps this seems like merely another cry of wolf, the most elaborate one so far. I can't actually say that it isn't. I can't say that what I'm hearing right now isn't some Hallowe'en trick of my besotted brain.

The laughing out in the hallway, I mean. That childish chuckling. Even when I concentrate, I'm still not able to tell if the sound is inside or outside my head. It's like looking at one of those toy pictures that yield two distinct scenes when tilted this way or that, but, at a certain angle, form only a merging blur of them both. Nonetheless, the laughing is there, somewhere. And the voice is extremely familiar. Of course, it is. No, it isn't. Yes, it is, it is!

Aaaaa ha-ha-ha-ha-ha.

Ex. 4 (the shadows again). They're all over my face in the window. Stripping away, as in the story. But there's nothing under that old mask; no child's face there, Preston. It *is* you, isn't it? I've never heard your laughter, except in my imagination, but that's exactly how I imagined it sounds. Or has my imagination given you, too, a hand-me-down, inherited laugh?

My only fear is that it isn't you but some impostor. The moon, the clock, the drink, the window. This is all very much your style, only it's not being done in fun, is it? It's *not funny*. Too horrible for me, Preston, or whoever you are. And who is it? Who could be doing this to a harmless old lady? Too horrible. The shadows in the window. No, not my face.

I can't   see anymore   I can't see
Help me
Father

DREAM OF A MANNIKIN

O nce upon a Wednesday afternoon, promptly at two o'clock, a girl stepped into my office. It was her first session, and she introduced herself as Amy Locher. (And didn't you once tell me that long ago you had a doll with this same first name?) Under the present circumstances I don't think it too gross a violation of professional ethics to use the subject's real name in describing her case to you. Certainly there's something more than simple ethics between us, *ma chère amie*. Besides, I understood from Miss Locher that you recommended me to her. This didn't seem necessarily ominous at first; perhaps, I speculated, your relationship with the girl was such that made it awkward for you to take her on as one of your own patients. Actually it's still not clear to me, my love, just how deeply you can be implicated in the overall experience I had with the petite Miss L. So you'll have to forgive any stupidities of mine which may crudely crop up in the body of this correspondence.

My first impression of Miss Locher, as she positioned herself almost sidesaddle in a leather chair before me, was that of a tense and disturbed but basically efficient and self-seeking young woman. She was dressed and accessoried, I noticed, in much the classic style which you normally favor. I won't go into our first visit preliminaries here (though we can discuss these and other matters at dinner this Saturday if only you are willing). After a brief chat we zeroed in on the girl's immediate impetus for consulting me. This involved, as you may or may not know, a distressing dream she had recently suffered. What will follow, as I have composed them from my tape of the September 10th session, are the events of that dream.

In the dream our subject has entered into a new life, at least to the extent that she holds down a different job from her waking one. She had already informed me that for some five years she has worked as a secretary for a tool and die firm. (And could this possibly be *your* delicate touch? Tooling into oblivion.) However, her working day in the dream finds her as a long-time employee of

a fashionable clothes shop. Like those state witnesses the government wishes to protect with new identities, she has been out-fitted
by the dream with what seems to be a mostly tacit but somehow
complete biography; a marvelous trick of the mind, this. It appears
that the duties of her new job require her to change the clothes of
the mannikins in the front window, this according to some
mysterious schedule. She in fact feels as if her entire existence is
slavishly given over to dressing and undressing these dummies. She
is profoundly dissatisfied with her lot, and the mannikins become
the focal point of her animus.

Such is the general background pre-supposed by the dream,
which now begins in proper. On a particularly gloomy day in her
era of thralldom, our dummy dresser approaches her work. She is
resentful and frightened, the latter emotion an irrational "given"
at this point in the dream. An awesome load of new clothes is
waiting to attire a windowful of naked mannikins. Their unwarm,
uncold bodies repel her touch. (Note this rare awareness of
temperature in a dream, albeit neutral.) She bitterly surveys the
ranks of these putty-faced creatures and then says: "Time to stop
dancing and get dressed, sleeping beauties." These words are
spoken without spontaneity, as if ritually uttered to inaugurate
each dressing session. But the dream changes before the dresser is
able to put one stitch on the dummies, who stare at nothing with
"anticipating" eyes.

The working day is now finished. She has returned to her small
apartment, where she retires to bed . . . and has a dream. (This
dream is that of the mannikin dresser and not hers, she empha-
tically pointed out!)

The mannikin dresser dreams she is in her bedroom. But what
she now thinks of as her "bedroom" is to all appearances actually
an archaically furnished hall with the dimensions of a small
theater. The room is dimly lit by some jeweled lamps along the
walls, the lights shining "with a strange glaziness" upon an
intricately patterned carpet and upon the massive pieces of
antique furniture around the room. She perceives the objects of
the scene more as pure ideas than material phenomena, for details
are blurry and there are many shadows. There is something,
however, which she visualizes quite clearly: one of the walls of
this lofty room is missing, and beyond this great gap is a view of
star-clustered blackness which, irrationally, may in truth represent
the depths of a colossal mirror. In any case, this maze of stars and
blackness appears as an enormous mural and suggests an uncertain
location for a room formerly thought to be nestled at the cozy

crossroads of well-known coordinates. Now it is truly just a lost point within the unfathomable universe of sleep.

The dreamer is positioned on the other side of the room from the brink of the starry abyss. Sitting on the edge of an armless, backless couch of complex brocade, she stares and waits "without breath or heartbeat," these functions being quite unnecessary to her dream self. Everything is in silence. This silence, however, is somehow charged with strange currents of force which she can't really explain, an insane physics electrifying the atmosphere with demonic powers lurking just beyond the threshold of sensory perception. All is perceived with elusive dream senses.

Then a new feeling enters the dream, one slightly more tangible. There seems to be an iciness drifting in from that dazzling starscape across the room. Suddenly our dreamer experiences a premonitory dread of something unknown. Without moving from her place on that uncomfortable couch, she visually searches the room for clues to the source of her terror. Many areas are inaccessible to her sight – like a picture that has been scribbled out in places – but she sees nothing particularly frightening and is relieved for a moment. Then her anxiety begins anew when she realizes for the first time that she hasn't looked behind her, and indeed she seems physically unable to do so.

Something is back there. She feels this to be a horrible truth. She *almost* knows what the thing is, but, afflicted with some kind of oneiric aphasia, she cannot find the word for the thing she fears. She can only wait, hoping that sudden shock will soon bring her out of the dream, for she is now aware that "she is dreaming," thinking of herself in the third person.

The words "she is dreaming" somehow form a ubiquitous motif for the present situation: as a legend written somewhere at the bottom of the dream, as echoing voices bouncing here and there around the room, as a motto printed upon fortune cookie-like strips of paper and hidden in bureau drawers, and as a broken record repeating itself on an ancient victrola inside the dreamer's head. Then all the words of this monotonous slogan gather from their divers places and like an alighting flock of birds settle in the area behind the dreamer's back. There they twitter for a moment, as upon the frozen shoulders of a statue in a park. This is actually the way it seems to the dreamer, including the statue comparison. Something of a statuesque nature is back there, approaching her. Something that is radiating a searing field of tension, coming closer, its great shadow falling across and enlarging her own upon the floor. Still she cannot turn around, cannot move her body, which is stiff-jointed and rigid. Perhaps she can scream, she thinks, and makes an attempt to do so. But this fails, because by then there is already a firm and tepid hand that has covered her mouth from behind. The fingers on her lips feel like thick, naked crayons. Then she sees a long slim arm extending itself over her left shoulder, and a hand that is holding some filthy rags before her eyes and shaking them, "making them dance." And at that moment a dry sibilant voice whispers into her ear: "It's time to get dressed, little dolling."

She tries to look away, her eyes being the only things she can move. Now, for the first time, she notices that all around the room – in the shadowed places – are people dressed as dolls. Their forms are collapsed, their mouths opened wide. They do not look as if they are still alive. Some of them have actually become dolls, their flesh no longer supple and their eyes having lost the appearance of teary moistness. Others are at various intermediate stages between humanness and dollhood. With horror, the dreamer now becomes aware that her own mouth is opened wide and will not close.

But at last, through the power of her fear, she is able to turn around and face the menacing agent. The dream now reaches a shattering crescendo and she awakes. She does not, however, awake in the bed of the mannikin dresser in her dream within a dream, but instead finds herself directly transported into the tangled, though real, bedcovers of her secretary self. Not exactly sure where or who she is for a moment, her first impulse on awaking is to complete the movement she began in the dream; that is, turning around to look behind her. (The hypnopompic hallucination that followed served as a "strong motivating factor" in her decision to seek the powers of a psychiatrist.) What she saw, upon pivoting about, was more than just a simple headboard with a blank wall above. For projecting out of that moon-whitened wall was the face of a female mannikin. And what particularly disturbed her about this illusion (and here we go deeper into already dubious realms) was that the face didn't melt away into the background of the wall the way post-dream projections usually do. It seems, rather, that this protruding visage, in one smooth movement, *withdrew* back into the wall. Her screams summoned more than a few concerned persons from neighboring apartments.

End of dream and related experiences.

Now, my darling, you can probably imagine my reaction to the above psychic yarn. Every loose skein I followed led me back to you. The character of Miss Locher's dream is strongly reminiscent, in both mood and scenario, of matters you have been exploring for some years now. I'm referring, of course, to the all-around astral ambiance of Miss Locher's dream and how eerily it relates to certain notions (very well, *theories*) that in my opinion have become altogether too central to your *oeuvre* as well as to your *vie*. Above all, I refer to those "otherworlds" you say you've detected through a combination of occult studies and depth analysis.

Let me digress for a brief lecture apropos of the preceding.

It's not that I object to your delving into speculative models of reality, sweetheart, but why this particular one? Why posit these "little zones," as I've heard you call them, having such hideous attributes, or should I say *anti*-attributes (to keep up with your theoretical lingo)? To whimsically joke about such bizarrerie with phrases like "pockets of interference" and "cosmic static," belies your talents as a thoughtful member of our profession. And the rest of it: the hyper-uncanniness, the warped relationships that are supposed to obtain in these places, the "games with reality," and all the other transcendent nonsense. I realize that psychology has charted some awfully weird areas in its maps of the mind, but you've gone so far into the ultra-mental hinterlands of metaphysics that I fear you will not return (at least not with your reputation intact).

To speak of your ideas with regard to Miss Locher's dream, you can see the connections, especially in the tortuous plot of her narrative. But I'll tell you when these connections really struck me with a hammerblow. It was just after she had related her dream to me. She was now riding the saddle of her chair in the normal position, and she made a few remarks obviously intended to convey the full extent of her distress. I'm sure she thought it de rigueur to tell me that after her dream episode she began entertaining doubts concerning who she really was. Secretary? Attirer of mannikins? Other? Other other? She knew, of course, the identity of her genuine, factual self; it was just some "new sense of unreality" that undermined complete assurance in this matter.

Surely you can see how the above identity tricks fit in with those "harassments of the self" that you say are one of the characteristic happenings in these zones of yours. And just what are the boundaries of the self? Is there a secret communion of seemingly separate things? How do animate and inanimate relate? Very boring, m'dear . . . zzzzz.

It all reminds me of that trite little fable of the Chinese (Chuang Tzu?) who dreamed he was a butterfly but upon waking affected not to know whether he was a man who'd dreamed he was a butterfly or a butterfly now dreaming . . . you get the idea. The question is: "Do things like butterflies dream?" (Ans.:no. Recall the lab studies in this field, if you will for once.) The issue is ended right there. However – as I'm sure you would contest – suppose the dreamer is not a man or butterfly, but both . . . or neither, something else altogether. Or suppose . . . really we could go on and on like this, and we have. Possibly the most repellent concept you've developed is that which you call "divine masochism," or the doctrine of a Bigger Self terrorizing its little splinter selves, precisely that Something Else Altogether scarifying the man-butterfly with uncanny suspicions that there's a game going on over its collective head.

The trouble with all this, my beloved, is the way you're so adamant about its objective reality, and how you sometimes manage to infect others with your peculiar convictions. Me, for instance. After hearing Miss Locher tell her dream story, I found myself unconsciously analyzing it much as you might have. Her multiplication of roles (including the role reversal with the mannikin) really did put me in mind of some divine being that was splintering and scarring itself to relieve its cosmic ennui, as indeed a few of the well-reputed gods of world religion supposedly do. I also thought of your "divinity of the dream," that thing which is all-powerful in its own realm. Contemplating the realm of Miss Locher's dream, I came to deeply feel that old truism of a solipsistic dream deity commanding all it sees, all of which is only itself. And a corollary to solipsism even occurred to me: if, in any dream of a universe, one has to *always* allow that there is another, waking universe, then the problem becomes, as with our Chinese sleepyhead, knowing when one is actually dreaming and what form the waking self may have; and this one can *never* know. The fact that the overwhelming majority of thinkers rejects any doctrine of solipsism suggests the basic horror and disgusting unreality of its implications. And after all, the horrific feeling of unreality is much more prevalent (to certain people) in what we call human "reality" than in human dreams, where everything is absolutely real.

See what you've done to me! For reasons that you well know, I always try to argue your case, my love. I can't help myself. But I don't think it's right to be exerting your influence upon innocents like Miss Locher. I should tell you that I hypnotized the girl. Her unconscious testimony seems very much to incriminate you. She almost demanded the hypnosis, feeling this to be an easy way of unveiling the source of her problems. And because of her frantic demands, I obliged her. A serendipitous discovery ensued.

She was an excellent subject. In hypnosis we restricted ourselves to penetrating the mysteries of her dream. I had her recount the events of this nightmare with the more accurate memory of her hypnotized state. Her earlier version was amazingly factual, with the exception of one important datum which I'll get to in a moment. I asked her to elaborate on her feelings in the dream and any sense of meaning she experienced. Her responses to these questions were sometimes given in the incoherent language of delirium and dream. She said some quite horrible things about life and lies and "this dream of flesh." I don't think I need expand on the chilling nonsense she uttered, for I've heard you say much the same in one of your "states." (Really, it's appalling the way you dwell both on and in your zones of the metaphysically flayed self.)

That little thing which Miss Locher mentioned only under hypnosis, and which I temporarily omitted above, was a very telling piece of info. It told on you. For when my patient first described the scenes of her dream drama to me, she had forgotten – or just neglected to mention – the presence of another character hidden in the background. This character was the proprietor of the nameless clothing store, a domineering boss who was played by a certain lady psychoanalyst. Not that you were ever on stage, even in a cameo appearance. But the hypnotized Miss Locher did remark in passing on the identity of the employer of that oneiric working girl, this being one of the many underlying suppositions of the dream. So you, my dear, were present in Miss Locher's hypnotic statement in more than just spirit.

I found this revelation immensely helpful in coordinating the separate items of evidence against you. The nature of the evidence, however, was such that I could not rule out the possibility of a conspiracy between you and Miss Locher. So I refrained from asking my new patient anything about her relationship with you, and I didn't inform her of what she disclosed under hypnosis. My assumption was that she was guilty until proven otherwise.

Alternatives did occur to me, though, especially when I realized Miss Locher's extraordinary susceptibility to hypnosis. Isn't it just possible, sweet love, that Miss Locher's incredible dream was induced by one of those post-hypnotic suggestions at which you're so well practised? I know that lab experiments in this area are sometimes eerily successful; and eeriness is, without argument, your specialty. Still another possibility involves the study of dream telepathy, in which you have no small interest. So what were you doing the night Miss Locher underwent her dream ordeal? (You weren't with me, I know that!) And how many of those eidola on my poor patient's mental screen were images projected from an outside source? These are just some of the bizarre questions which lately seem so necessary to ask.

But the answers to such questions would still only establish your means in this crime. What about your motive? On this point I need not exert my psychic resources. It seems there is nothing you won't do to impose your ideas upon common humanity – deplorably on your patients, obnoxiously on your colleagues, and affectionately (I hope) on me. I know it must be hard for a lonely visionary like yourself to remain mute and ignored, but you've chosen such an eccentric path to follow that I fear there are few spirits brave enough to accompany you into those zones of deception and pain, at least not voluntarily.

Which brings us back to Miss Locher. By the end of our first, and only, session I still wasn't sure whether she was a willing or unwilling agent of yours; hence, I kept mum, very mum, about anything concerning you. Nor did she happen to speak of you in any significant way, except of course unconsciously in hypnosis. At any rate, she certainly appeared to be a genuinely disturbed young lady, and she asked me to prescribe for her. As Dr. Bovary tried to assuage the oppressive dreams of his wife with a prescription of valerian and camphor baths, I supplied Miss Locher with a program for serenity that included valium and companionship (the latter of which I also recommend for us, dolling). Then we made a date for the following Wednesday at the same time. Miss Locher seemed most grateful, though not enough, according to my secretary, to pay up what she owed. And wait till you find out where she wanted us to send the bill.

The following week Miss Locher did not appear for her appointment. This did not really alarm me, for as you know many patients – armed with a script for tranquilizers and a single experience of therapy – decide they don't need any more help. But by then I had developed such a personal interest in Miss Locher's case that I was seriously disappointed at the prospect of not being able to pursue it further.

After fifteen patientless minutes had elapsed, I had my secretary call Miss Locher at the number she gave us. (With my former secretary – poor thing! – this would have been done automatically; so the new girl is not as good as you said she was, doctor. I shouldn't have let you insinuate her into my employ . . . but that's my fault, isn't it?) Maggie came into my office a few minutes later, presumably after she'd tried to reach Miss Locher. With rather cryptic impudence she suggested I dial the number myself, giving me the form containing all the information on our new patient. Then she left the room without saying another word. The nerve of that soon-to-be-unemployed girl.

I called the number – which incidentally plays the song about Mary's lamb on the push-button phone in my office – and it rang twice before someone answered. This someone had the voice of a young woman but was not our Miss Locher. In any case, the way this person answered the phone told me I had a wrong number (the right wrong number). Nevertheless, I asked if a Miss Locher could be reached at that number or any of its possible extensions; but the answering voice expressed total ignorance regarding the existence of any person by that name. I thanked her and hung up.

You will have to forgive me, my lovely, if by this time I began to feel like the victim of a hoax, your hoax to be exact. "Maggie," I intercommed, "how many more appointments for this afternoon?" "Just one," she immediately answered, and then without being asked, said: "But I can cancel it if you'd like." I said I would like, that I would be gone for the rest of the afternoon.

My intention was to call on Miss Locher at the, probably also phony, address on her new patient form. I had the suspicion that the address would lead to the same geographical spot as had the electronic nexus of the false phone number. Of course I could have easily verified this without leaving my office; but knowing you, sweet one, I thought that a personal visit was warranted. And I was right.

The address was an hour's drive away. It was in a fashionable suburb on the other side of town from that fashionable suburb in which I have my office. (And I wish you would remove your own place of business from its present location, unless for some reason you need to be near a skid-row source that broadcasts on frequencies of chaos and squalor, which you'd probably claim.) I parked my big black car down the block from the street number I was seeking, which turned out to be located in the middle of the suburb's shopping district.

This was last Wednesday, and if you'll recall it was quite an unusual day (an accomplishment I *do not* list among all your orchestrated connivings of my adventure). It was dim and moody most of the morning, and so prematurely dark by late afternoon that there were stars seemingly visible in the sky. A storm was imminent and the air was appropriately galvanized with a pre-deluge feeling of suspense. Display windows were softly glowing, and one jewelry store I passed twinkled with electric glory in the corner of my eye. In the stillness I strolled beside a row of trees, each of their slender trunks planted in a complex mosaic along the sidewalk, all of their tiny leaves fluttering.

Of course, there's no further need to describe the atmosphere of a place you've visited many times, dear love. But I just wanted to show how sensitive I was to a certain kind of portentous mood, and how ripe I'd become for the staged antics to follow. Very good, doctor!

Distancewise, I only had to walk a few gloomy steps before arriving at the place purported to be the home of our Miss L. By then it was quite clear what I would find. There were no surprises so far. When I looked up at the neon-inscribed name of the shop, I heard a young woman's telephone voice whispering the words into my ear: Mademoiselle Fashions. A fake French accent here, S.V.P. And this is the store – no? – where it seems you acquire so many of your own lovely ensembles. But I'm jumping ahead with my expectations.

What I did not expect were the sheer *lengths* to which you would go in order to arouse my sense of strange revelation. Was this, I pray, done to bring us closer in the divine bonds of unreality? Anyway, I saw what you wanted me to see, or what I thought you wanted me to see, in the window of Mlle Fashions. The thing was even dressed in the same plaid-skirted outfit that I recall Miss Locher was wearing on her only visit to my office. And I have to admit that I was a bit shocked – perhaps attributable in part to the unstable climatic conditions of the day – when I focused on the frozen face of the mannikin. Then again, perhaps I was subliminally looking for a resemblance between Miss Locher (your fellow conspirator, whether she knows it or not) and the figure in the window. You can probably guess what I noticed, or thought I noticed, about its eyes – what you would have me perceive as a certain *moistness* in their fixed gaze. Oh, woe is this Wednesday's child!

Unfortunately, I was unable to linger long enough to positively confirm the above perception, for a medium-intensity shower began to descend at that point. The rain sent me running to a nearby phone booth, where I had some business to conduct anyway. Retrieving the number of the clothes store from my memory, I phoned them for the second time that afternoon. That was easy. What was not quite as easy was imitating your voice, my high-pitched love, and asking if the store's accounting department had mailed out a bill that month for my, I mean your, charge account. My impersonation of you must have been adequate, for the voice on the phone reminded me that I'd already taken care of all my recent expenditures. You thanked the salesgirl for this information, apologizing for your forgetfulness, and then said goodbye. Perhaps I should have asked the girl if she was the one who helped rig up that mannikin to look like Miss Locher, if indeed the situation was not the other way around, with Miss Locher following the fashion of display-window dummies. In any case, I did establish a definite link between you and the clothes store. It seemed you might have accomplices anywhere, and to tell you the truth I was beginning to feel a bit paranoid standing in that little phone booth.

The rain was coming down even harder as I made a mad dash back to my black sedan. A bit soaked, I sat in the car for a few moments wiping off my rain-spotted glasses with a handkerchief. I said that I felt a slight case of paranoia coming on, and what follows proves it. While sitting there with my glasses off, I thought I saw something move in the rearview mirror. My visual vulnerability, combined with the claustrophobic sensation of being in a car with rain-blinded windows, together added up to a momentary but very definite panic on my part. Of course I quickly put on my glasses and found that there was nothing whatever in the back seat. But the point is that I was forced to physically verify this fact in order to relieve my spasm of anxiety. You succeeded, my love, in getting me to experience a moment of self-terror, and in that moment I, too, became your accomplice against myself. Brava!

You have indeed succeeded – assuming all my inferences thus far are for the most part true – perhaps more than you know or ever intended. Having confessed this much, I can now get to the *real* focus and "motivating factor" of my appeal to you. This has far less to do with A. Locher than it does with us, dearest. Please try to be sympathetic and, above all, patient.

I have not been well lately, and you know the reason why. This business with Miss Locher, far from bringing us to a more intimate understanding of each other, has only made the situation worse. Horrible nightmares have been plaguing me every night. Me, of all people! And they are directly due to the well-intentioned (I think) influence of you and Miss L. Let me describe one of these nightmares for you, and thereby describe them all. This will be the last dream story, I promise.

In the dream I am in my bedroom, sitting upon my unmade bed and wearing my pajamas (Oh, will you never see them?). The room is partially illuminated by beams from a streetlight shining through the window. And it also seems to me that a whole galaxy of constellations, although not actually witnessed firsthand, are contributing their light to the scene, a ghastly glowing which unnaturally blanches the entire upstairs of the house. I have to use the bathroom and walk sleepily out to the hallway . . . where I get the shock of my life.

In the whitened hallway – I cannot say *brightened*, because it is almost as if a very fine and luminous powder coats everything – are these things lying up and down the floor, at the top of the stairway, and even upon the stairs themselves as they disappear into the darker regions below. These things are people dressed as dolls, or else dolls made up to look like people. I remember being confused about which it was.

Their heads are turned in all directions as I emerge from the bedroom, and their eyes shine in the white darkness. Paralyzed – yes! – with terror, I merely return a fixed gaze, wondering if my eyes are shining the same as theirs. Then one of the doll people, slouching against the wall on my left, turns its head haltingly upon a stiff little neck and looks into my eyes. Worse, it talks. And its voice is an horrific cackling parody of speech. Even more horrible are its words, as it says: "Become as we are, sweetie. Die *into* us." Suddenly I begin to feel very weak, as if my life were being drained out of me. Summoning all my powers of movement, I manage to rush back to my bed to end the dream.

After I awake, screaming, my heart pounds like a mad prisoner inside me and doesn't let up until morning. This is very disturbing, for there's truth in those studies relating nightmares to cardiac arrest. For some poor souls, that imaginary incubus squatting upon their sleeping forms can do real medical harm. And I do not want to become one of these cases.

You can help me, sweetheart. I know you didn't intend things to turn out this way, but that elaborate joke you perpetrated with the help of Miss Locher has really gotten to me. Consciously, of course, I still uphold the criticism I've already expressed about the basic absurdity of your work. Unconsciously, however, you seem to have awakened me to a stratum (*zone*, I know you would say) of uncanny terror in my mind-soul. I will at least admit that your ideas form a powerful psychic metaphor, though no more than that. Which is quite enough, isn't it? It's certainly quite enough to inspire the writing of this letter, in which I plead for your attention, since I've failed to attract it in any other way. I can't go on like this! You have strange powers over me, as if you didn't already know it. Please release me from your spell, and let's begin a normal romance. Who really gives a damn about the metaphysics of invisible realms anyway? It's only emotions, not abstractions, that count. Love and terror are the true realities, whatever the unknowable mechanics are that turn their wheels, and our own.

In Miss Locher I believe you sent me the embodiment of your deepest convictions. But suppose I start admitting weird things about Miss L? Suppose I admit that she was somehow just a dream. (Then she must have been my secretary's dream too, for she saw her.) Suppose I even admit that Miss Locher was not a girl but actually a multi-selved *thing* – part Man, part mannikin – and with your assistance dreamed itself for a time into existence, reproduced itself in human form just as we reproduce ourselves as an infinite variety of images and shapes, all those impersonations of our flesh? You would like to have me think of things like this. You would like to have me think of all the mysterious connections among the things of this world, and of other worlds. So what if there are? I don't care anymore.

Forget other selves. Forget the third (fourth, nth) person view of life; only first and second persons are important (I and thou). And by all means forget dreams. I, for one, know I'm not a dream. I am real, Dr.— (There, how do you like being anonymized?) So please be so kind as to acknowledge my existence.

It is now after midnight, and I dread going to sleep and having another of those nightmares. You can save me from this fate, if only you can find it in your heart to do so. But you must hurry. Time is running out for us, my love, just as these last few waking moments are now running out for me. Tell me it is still not too late for our love. Please don't destroy everything for us. You will only hurt yourself. And despite your high-flown theory of masochism, there is really nothing divine about it. So no more of your strange psychic deceptions. Be simple, be nice. Oh, I am so tired. I must say good night, then, but not good

Bye, my foolish love. Hear me now. Sleep your singular sleep and dream of the many, the others. They are also part of you, part of us. Die into them and leave me in peace. I will come for you later, and then you can always be with me in a special corner all your own, just as my little Amy once was. This is what you've wanted, and this you shall have. Die into them. Yes, die into them, you simple soul, you silly dolling. Die with a nice bright gleam in your eyes.

THE CHYMIST

Hello, miss. Why, yes, as a matter of fact I *am* looking for some company this evening. My name is Simon, and you are . . . Rosemary. Funny, I was just daydreaming in the key of Rosicrucianism. Never mind. Please sit, and watch out for splinters on your chair, so you don't catch your dress. It appears that everything around here has come to the point of frays and splinters. But what this old place lacks in freshness of decor it amply makes up in atmosphere, don't you think? Yes, as you say, I suppose it does serve its purpose. It's a little lax as far as table service, though. I'm afraid that in the way of drinks one must procure for one's self. Thank you, I'm glad you think I have a nice way of talkin'. Now, can I get you something from the bar? All right, a beer you shall have. And do me a favor please: before I come back, you will already have taken that wad of gum out of your mouth. Thank you, and I'll return shortly with our drinks.

Here you are, Rosie, one beer from the bar. Just don't belch and we'll get along fine. I'm pleased to see you've gotten rid of your gum, though I hope you didn't swallow it. The human stomach should probably remain ignorant of what it's like to accomodate beer and bubble gum in the same digestive episode. I know it's *your* stomach, but I'm concerned about what gets mixed up inside any human vessel. No, I said *vessel*, not that anatomical cavity to which you smuttily refer: Man's hole is not his vessel. We're talking about things in which other things may be contained.

That's right, like that dirty little glass in your immaculate hand, now you're getting it. My glass? Yes, you do see a lot of red in there. I like red drinks. Created this one myself. A Red Rum Ginny, I call it. White rum, gin, pale ginger ale, and, ideally, cranberry juice, though the bartender here had to substitute some undistilled maraschino solution, which has neither the rich red color nor a fraction of the tartness of your smile. Would you like a sip? Go ahead, take a good belt. If you don't like it, say so. Yes, different is the word for it, the wellspring of its interest, as you've observed. I wonder, though, in whose mouth it tastes more different – mine or yours? We'll never know. Even adhering to the same mixological formula there's always some difference in taste, if only you have the *sensitivity* to notice it. In general, I think, there are always those varying factors that make every moment of our lives unique and strange to every other moment.

I have a high tolerance for *diversity* myself. You're smiling at my emphasis. You think you know something about me, and perhaps you do. Sharp girl! Of course, the imp of perversity in *your* thoughts is only one of the many offspring of the imp of the *diverse*. And diversity is the soul of life, or at least of life's amusement.

Pardon me? Yes, I have created other drinks. There's another red one I've pioneered that's actually just a variation on a standard number, but I like it. The Sweet and Sour Bloody Mary, made with high-test vodka, sugar, a lemon slice, and ketchup. It does sound like a meal in itself at that. Very fortifying. No, sorry to spoil your joke, my fondness for red drinks does not extend to the vampire's neck-drawn nectar. Besides, I'm quite able to work during daylight hours.

Where? Well, I suppose I can tell you, *sub rosa*, that I'm employed by a pharmaceutical company not far from here, near that run-down warehouse district. I'm a chemist there. Yes, really. Well, it's nice the way you could see right off that I wasn't no average guy just comin' round after work lookin' for some fun. Perceptive girl! However, I did in fact come directly here after working a little overtime. I noticed while I was at the bar that you were eyeing and toeing the briefcase I brought in with me and set so discreetly under the table. Yes, there are papers in there relating to my work, among other things, never mind just now about that. But you're right that it would be foolish to leave anything important outside in one's car in this neighborhood.

Well, I wouldn't say that this part of town is simply a *pit*. It is, of course, that; but the word doesn't begin to describe the various dimensions of decrepitude in the local geography. *Decrepitude*, Ro. It has your *pit* in it and a lot more besides. I speak from experience, more than you would believe. This whole city is a pitiful corpse, and the neighborhood outside the walls of this bar has the distinction of being the withering heart of the deceased. Yes, I've gotten to know it over the years. I've gone out of my way to note its outlandish points of interest.

For instance, have you ever been to that place not far from here called Speakeasy? Well, then you have some acquaintance with the beautiful corruption of nostalgia, the putrescence of things past. Yes, up a flight of stairs from a crooked little street facade is a high echoey hall with a leftover Deco decor of silvery mirrors and sequined globes. And there the giant painted silhouettes of bony flappers and gaunt Gatsbys sport about the curving ballroom walls, towering over the dance floor, their funereal elegance mocking the awkward gyrations of the living. An old dream with a shiny new veneer. It's fascinating, you know, how an obsolete madness is sometimes adopted and stylized in an attempt to ghoulishly preserve it. These are the days of second-hand fantasies and antiquated hysteria.

But there are other sights in this city that I think are much more interesting. Not the least of which are those storefront temples of dubious denomination. There's one on Third and Snoville called the Church of the True Dividing Light, not to be mistaken, I presume, with that false light which dazzles so many searching eyes. Oddly enough, I've yet to see any light at all shining through the windows of this gray dwarfish building, and I always look for some sort of illumination as I ride by. I tell you, no one worships this city as I do. Especially its witticisms of proximity, one strange thing next to another, adding up to a greater strangeness. One of the more grotesque examples of this phenomenon occurs when you observe that a little shop whose display window features a fabulous array of prosthetic devices is right next-door to Marv's Second Hand City. Then there are those places – you've noticed them, I'm sure – that are freakishly suggestive in a variety of ways. One of them is that pink and black checkerboard box on Bender Boulevard that calls itself Bill's Bender Lounge, where a garish marquee advertises Nightly Entertainment. And if you stare at that legend long enough, the word "Nightly" will begin to connote more than the interval between dusk and dawn. Soon this simple word becomes truly evocative, as if it were code for the most exotic and unspeakable entertainments of the infinite night. And speaking of entertainment, I should cite that establishment whose owner, no doubt an epicure of musical comedy, gave it the title of Guys and Dolls, Inc. What a genius of vulgarity, considering that this business is devoted solely to the sale and repair of mannikins. Or is it really a front for a bordello of dummies? No offense intended, Rosalie.

I could go on – I still haven't mentioned Miss Wanda's Wigs or a certain hotel that boasts a "Bath in Every Room" – but maybe you're becoming a bit bored. Yes, I can understand what you mean when you say you don't notice that stuff after a while. The mind becomes dull and complacent. I know. Sometimes I get that way myself. But it seems that just when I'm comfortably mired in complacency, some good jolt comes along.

Maybe I'm sitting in my car, waiting for a red light to change. A derelict, drunk or brain-diseased or both, comes up to my defenseless vehicle and pounds on my windows – with both fists, like so – and demands a cigarette. He touches his ragged lips with scissored fingers to convey his meaning, having left speech behind him long ago. A cigarette? Indeed! The traffic signal changes and I drive on, watching the bum's half-collapsed form shrinking in my rearview mirror. But somehow I've taken him on as a passenger, a ghostly shape sitting cozily beside me and raving about all kinds of senseless and fascinating things, the autobiography of confusion. And in a little while I'm back on the lookout once more.

Touching story, don't you   Yes, I suppose it is getting a bit late and we haven't made much progress. Your apartment? I think that would be fine. No, nothing else in mind as far as places go. Yours is okay. Where is it, though? No kidding? That's the old Temple Towers with a new cognito. Excellent, our ride will take us through the neighborhood in the shadow of the brewery. What floor of the building do you live on? Well, a veritable penthouse, an urban aerie. The loftier the better, I say.

Shall we go, then? My car is parked right out front.

I hope it hasn't decided to rain. Nope, it's a beautiful night. But look, that's my car where that cop is standing. Just stay calm. I certainly won't say anything if you don't. You're not, by chance, a vice officer in disguise, are you, Rosiecrantz? You wouldn't betray this unsuspecting Hamlet. A simple "no" would have been sufficient. If you use that kind of language again I'll turn you in to the cops right now, and then we can see what sort of arrest record you've accumulated in your brilliant career. Silence, that's good. Just let me do the talking. Here goes.

Hi, officer. Yeah, that's my car. It's parked okay, isn't it? Geez, that's a relief. For a second I thought – My driver's license? Sure thing. Here you go. Beg pardon? Yeah, I guess I am a little far from home. But I work real close to here. I'm a stockbroker, here's my card. You know, I've been in the business for some time now, and I can almost tell just by the look of a guy if he's got something invested in the market. I'd bet that you have. See there, I knew I was right. Doesn't matter if you're just small-time. Listen, have you been in touch with an investment counsellor lately? Well, you should. There's a lot going on. People talk about inflation, recession, depression. Forget it. If you know where to put your finances, I mean really know, it doesn't matter if it's Friday the thirteenth and the streets are bloody with corporate corpses.

Smart advice is what you need. It's all anyone needs. For

example – and I tell you this just to make a point – there's an outfit right in this city, not a half-mile from here in fact, by the name of Lochmyer Laboratories. They've been working on a new product and are just about ready to market it. 'Course I don't understand the whole technical end of it, but I know for sure that it's going to revolutionize the field of – what d'you call it – psychopharmaceutics. Revolutionize it the way tranquilizers did in the Fifties. It'll be bigger than tranquilizers. Bigger than LSD. You know what I mean? That's the kind of thing you got to know.

That's right, officer, Lochmyer Laboratories. And they're on the New York Exchange. Good outfit all around. I own stock in it myself. What tip, hell? Hey, you don't have to thank me. Beg pardon? A tip for me? Well, now that you mention it, probably there are better neighborhoods for a man like me to be frequenting. I guess you probably *won't* be seeing me around here anymore. I appreciate that, officer. I'll remember. And you remember Loch Lab. Right, then. 'Night to you.

Wait for his car to turn the corner, Rosie, before getting in mine. We'll let the lawman maintain the illusion that his warning has set me straight with regard to the dangers of this seamy area and your seamy self. He looked at you like an old friend. Could have been trouble for both of us. You're a smart girl to have sat at my table tonight. I think my briefcase impressed him, don't you? Okay, we can get in the car now.

Yes, I did get us out of a touchy situation with that cop. But I hope when you just mentioned my *B.S.* apropos of that scene with the policeman, you were referring to the Bachelor of Science degree I received when I was sixteen years old. This is your last warning about unclean idioms. Now roll down your window and let's air your words out of this car as we drive. And as far as my deceiving that fine officer goes – I actually didn't. No, I'm not really a stockbroker. I told you the truth about being in chemicals. And I told that mole-eyed patrolman the truth when I advised him to put his money in Lochmyer Lab, for we *are* about to market a new mind medicine that should make our investors as pleased as amphetamine addicts at an all-night coffee shop. How did I know he owned stock in the first place? That is strange, isn't it? I guess I was just lucky. This is just my lucky night – and yours too.

You don't much like the *policía*, do you, Rrrosa? Yes, of course I can blame you. Without them, where would all of us outlaws be? What would we have? Only a lawless paradise . . . and paradise is a bore. Violence without violation is only a noise heard by no one, the most horrendous sound in the universe. No, I realize you don't have anything to do with violence. I didn't mean to imply you did. Yes, I can drop you off back at the bar when we've finished at your apartment. Of course.

Right now let's just enjoy the ride. What do you mean "so what's to enjoy"? Can't you see we're nearing the brewery? Look, there's its beer-golden sign, advertising the alchemical quest to transmute base ingredients into liquid gold. *Alchemical*, Rosetta. And I'm not referring to that shoddy firm of Allied Chem. Just look around at these hollowed-out houses, these seedy stores, each one of them a sacred site of the city, a shrine, if you will. You won't? You've seen it all a million times? A slum is a slum is a slum, eh? Always the same. *Always?*

Never.

What about when it's raining and the brown bricks of these old places start to drip and darken? And the smoke-gray sky is the smoky mirror of your soul. You give a lightning blink at a row of condemned buildings, starkly outlining them. And do they blink back at you? Or does that happen only in another type of storm, when windows are slyly browed with city-soiled clumps of snow. Was it under such conditions that you first thought of all the cold and dark places in the universe, all the clammy basements and gloomy attics of creation? Maybe you didn't want to think about those places, but you couldn't help yourself at the time. Another time you could have. No two times are the same. No two lives are alike: you have yours and others have theirs. And when you're traveling through these streets with some stranger, you have to contend with the way someone else sees things, the way you now must deal with my 20-20 visions and I with your blasé nearsightedness. Are these the same gutted houses you saw last night, or even a second ago? Or are they like the fluxing clouds that swirl above the chimneys and trees, and then pass on?

The alchemical transmutations are infinite and continuous, working all the time like slaves in the Great Laboratory. Tell me you can't perceive their work, especially in this part of the city. Especially where the glamor and sanity of former days wears a new mask of rats and rot, where an old style is transformed by time into a parody of itself which no man could foresee, where greater and greater schisms are forever developing between past shapes and future shapelessness, and finally where the evolution toward ultimate diversity can be glimpsed as if in a magic mirror.

This is, of course, the *real* alchemy, as you've probably gathered, and not that other kind which theorized that everything was struggling toward an auric perfection. Lead into gold, lower matter into higher spirit. No, it's not like that. Just the opposite, in point of fact. Please don't put that hunk of gum in your mouth; throw it out the window, now! As I was saying, everything is just variation without a theme. Oh, perhaps there is some solid and unchanging ideal, shining very dimly and very far off. Scientifically, I suppose, we should allow for that improbability. But to reach that ideal would mean a hopeless stroll along the path to hypothetically higher worlds. And on the way our ideas become feverish and confused. What begins as a solitary truth soon proliferates like malignant cells in the body of a dream, a body whose true outline remains unknown. Perhaps, then, we should be grateful to the whims of chemistry, the caprices of circumstance, and the enigmas of personal taste for giving us such an array of strictly local realities and desires.

No, I didn't always think this freaky, as you put it. But I can tell you almost precisely when I began to see the truth of things. I was a callow freshman in college, even callower than most, given my precocious progress. One day something seemed to change in my chemistry, as I like to think of it. It was quite horrible for a while. Eventually, though, I realized that the alteration was from a false chemistry to a true one. Yes, that's when I decided to pursue the subject as my career, my calling. But that's a story in itself, and here we are now at your apartment tower.

Please don't slam the car door the way you were about to. No need to draw attention to our presence. You're right, there's really no one around to be attentive anyway. The local street vermin seem to have withdrawn into their holes. Very good: "But their holes are not their vessels," indeed. Not the hole of man but the whole man is the true vessel, as some pompous sage might have said. And the *right* vessel is the whole point of the thing, for the best vessel will ultimately take the shape of its contents.

Never mind what I'm talking about. I just like to talk, as you may have noticed. Oops, almost forgot my briefcase. Wouldn't want to leave it unattended in this neighborhood, isn't that right? You're smiling about my briefcase, aren't you, Maryrose? You think you know something again. Well, go ahead and think that if you like. Everybody likes to think he has inside information. That policeman, for example. You could see how pleased he was to instantly become a man of knowledge, even if it's only by way of a knowledgeable tip on the stock market. Everybody wants to know the secret truth, *scientia arcana*, the real dope.

Maybe I do have some dope in my case. Then again, maybe it's just an empty prop, a leather vessel with a void inside. But you already know that I work for a dope company. You were thinking that, weren't you? Well, let's go up to your place and find out.

Cozy little lobby you have here; but I'm afraid the atmosphere is doing strange things to that pot of ferns over there. Of course I know they're artificial. Which only means that Nature, one of the Great Chemists, made them at one remove, that's all. Here, this elevator seems to be working, though a little noisily. After you, Lady R. The twenty-second floor if I remember right, and I always do. Uh, I believe there's to be no smoking in this elevator, if you don't mind. Thank you. And here we are. I'll bet your place is down this way. See, I *am* always right. Isn't that funny? Yes, I'm coming, I'm coming.

Well, your apartment has a very nice door. No, you're wrong. There's no such thing as "just like all the others." Yours is quite different, can't you see that? And tonight your door is visibly different from any other time you've ever seen it. I'm not just being egoistical about my unique presence at your threshold this evening. Do you see what I mean? Well, I'm sorry if you feel I've been lecturing you all night. I was a pedagogue once, which I suppose is obvious. It's just that there are some important things I must impart to you, my little rosebud, before we're through. Okay? Now, let's go in and see what kind of view you have from up here.

Keep the ceiling light off please, so that I don't have to look at a double of this dour room reflected in your window. One of your dim lamps should give us all the light we need. There, that's fine. You do have a good view of the city from this height. I think it's perfect, not too far up. I live in a mere two-story house myself and being up here makes me dizzily realize what I'm missing. From this lofty keep I could nightly observe the city and its constant mutations. A different city every night. Yes, Rosie, I have to say you're right – sarcastic tone and all – the city is indeed also a vessel. And it's one that obediently takes the shape of very strange contents. The Great Chemists are working out unfathomable formulae down there. Look at those lights outlining the different venues and avenues below, look at their lines and interconnections. They're like a skeleton of something . . . the skeleton of a dream, the hidden framework ready at any moment to shift its structure to support a new shape. The Great Chemists are always dreaming new things and risking that they may wake up while doing so. Should that ever happen you can be assured there will be hell to pay.

My imagination? No, I don't think it's *vivid* at all. On the contrary, it's not nearly potent enough. My poor imaginative faculties have always needed . . . extensions. That's why I'm here with you. You're smiling again, or rather you're *smirking*. Funny word, smirk. Rather like an extraterrestrial surname. Simon Smirk. How do you think that sounds?

Yes, maybe we are wasting too much time. But of course we'll have to endure just one more delay while I rummage around in my briefcase and remove what you've been waiting for. So you hope it's good dope, eh? Well, you'll have a chance to find out, since you seem so anxious to become a vessel yourself for my chemicals. No, stay seated just where you are please. There's no reason for you to glimpse every little secret I've got in here. All you're interested in seeing is one squat little bottle screwed tightly closed with a black cap . . . and here it is!

Yes, it does look like a bottle of powdered light. That's very observant. What is it? I thought you would know by now. Here, hold out your hand and you can have a closer look. Just a little powdery mound in the middle of your sweaty palm, about one brainful to be precise. Doesn't it look like pulverized diamonds? It glitters, yes it does. I don't blame you for thinking it might be dangerous to snort, or whatever else you imagine you're supposed to do with it. But by watching your hand very closely you'll see that you don't have to do anything at all.

See, it dissolved right into your palm. Disappeared completely, except for a few stray grains. But don't worry about them. Calm down, the burning will soon go away. There's no point in trying to rub the drug off your hand. It's in your system now. And it certainly won't help to get excited, nor are threats of any use to you. Please remain seated in that chair.

Can you feel any effects yet? I mean besides the fact that you're no longer able to move your arms or legs. That's just the beginning of this nightly entertainment. You see my glittering powder has now made possible a very interesting relationship between us. Between you and me, my red red rose. The drug has rendered you fantastically sensitive to the shaping influence of a certain form of energy, namely that which is being generated by me, or rather *through* me. To put it romantically, I'm now dreaming you. That's really the only way I can explain it that you might understand. Not dreaming *about* you, like some old love song. I'm *dreaming* you. Your arms and legs don't respond to your brain's commands because I'm dreaming of someone who is as still as a statue. I hope you can appreciate how remarkable this is.

Damn! I suppose that was your attempt to scream. You really

are terrified, aren't you? Just to be safe, perhaps I'd better dream of someone who hasn't anything to scream with. There, that should do it. You do look strange, though, like that. But we've only just begun. These minor tricks are child's play and I'm sure don't impress you in the least. Soon I'll show you that I can really make an impression, once I put my mind to it.

Is there something in your eyes? Yes, I can see there is. A question. Right now you would like to ask, if only you still had the means to do so, what's to become of old Rosie? It's only fair that you should know.

We are presently coming into perfect tune with each other, my dreams and my dream girl. You are about to become the flesh and blood kaleidoscope of my imagination. In the latter stages of this game anything might happen. Your form will know no limits of variety, for now the Great Chemists themselves are working through me. Soon I will put my dreaming in the hands of greater forces, and I'm sure there will be some surprises for both of us. That is one thing which never changes.

Nevertheless, there is still a problem with this process. It's not really perfect, certainly not marketable, as we say in the pill business. And wouldn't that be boring if it were perfect? What I mean to say is that under the stress of such diverse and alien metamorphoses, the original structure of the object somehow breaks down in a way even I don't understand. The consequence of the thing is simple: you can never be as you once were. I'm very sorry. You'll have to remain in whatever curious incarnation you take on at the dream's end. Which should rattle the wits of whoever is unfortunate enough to find you. But don't worry, you will not live long after I leave here. And by then you will have experienced god-like powers of proteation which I myself cannot hope to know, no matter how intimately I may try.

And now I think we can proceed with what has been your destiny all along. Are you ready? I am entirely ready and by degrees am giving myself over to those forces which, with any luck, I will never completely comprehend. Can you feel us both being caught up in the great web of delirium? Can you feel the fevers of this chemist? The power of my dreaming, my dreaming, my dreaming, my . . .

Now Rose of madness – Bloom!

DRINK TO ME ONLY
WITH LABYRINTHINE
EYES

Everyone at the party comments on them. They ask if I had them altered in some way, suggest that I've tucked some strange crystallized lenses under my eyelids. I tell them no, that I was born with these singular optic organs; they're not from some optometrist's bag of tricks, not the result of surgical mayhem. Of course they find this hard to believe, especially when I tell them I was also born with the full powers of a master hypnotist . . . and from there I rapidly evolved, advancing into a mesmeric wilderness untrod before or since by any others of my calling. No, I wouldn't say *business* or *profession*, I would have to say *calling*. What else do you call it when you're destined from birth, marked by fate's stigmata? At this point they smile politely, saying that they really enjoyed the show and that I certainly am good at what I do. I tell them how grateful I am for the opportunity to perform for such fancy persons in such a fancy house. Unsure to what extent I'm just kidding them, they nervously twirl the stems of their champagne glasses, the beverage sparkling and the crystal twinkling under a chandelier's kaleidoscopic blaze. Despite all the beauty, power, and prestige socializing in this rather baroque room tonight, I think they know how basically ordinary they all are. They are very impressed by me and my assistant, who have been asked to mingle with the guests and amuse them in whatever way we can. One gentleman with a flushed face looks across the room at my assistant, guzzling his drink as he does so. "Would you like to meet her," I ask. "You bet," he replies. They all do; they all want to know you, my somnambule.

Earlier in the evening we presented our show to these lovely people. I instructed the host of the party to serve no alcohol before our performance, and to arrange the furniture of this wonderfully ornate room in a way that would allow everyone a perfect view of us on our little platform. He complied obediently, of course. He also conceded to my request for payment in advance. Such an agreeable man, giving in to the will of another so readily.

At the start of the show I am alone before a silent audience. All illumination is cancelled except a single spotlight which I have set up on the floor exactly two point two meters from the stage. The spotlight focuses on a pair of metronomes, their batons sweeping back and forth in perfect unison like windshield wipers in the rain: smoothly back and smoothly forth, back and forth, back and forth. And at the tip of each baton is a luminous replica of each of my eyes swaying left and right in full view of everyone, while my voice speaks to them from a shadowy edge of the stage. First I give a brief lecture on hypnosis, its name and nature. After that I say: "Now, Ladies and Gentlemen, please direct your attention to that tall black cabinet with the stunning gold embellishments running riot upon its surface. Within stands the most beautiful creature you have ever laid eyes on. She is everything you can imagine in the way of physical perfection. Everything. And just for you she is already in the deepest trance. You *will* see her." There is a dramatic pause during which my eyes fix upon that beast of a congregation, keeping my control. Then I look back toward the cabinet and softly utter the simple but strategic words: "Darling, you may come out now."

The trick door opens, seemingly of its own will. Suddenly the audience emits a quiet gasp, and for a second I panic. Then there is applause, reassuring me that everything is all right, that they like the thing they see within the cabinet. What they see is standing upright inside, almost as tall as the cabinet itself. She is wearing a tiny outfit entirely of sequins, a vulgar costume whose rampant glitter somehow transcends the cliché, resurrecting its vaudevillian soul. Her gaze is fixed on an infinity slightly above the heads of everyone. "Darling?" I say invitingly. At this pre-arranged signal she begins to totter within the box. Finally she teeters into a forward fall, straight down toward the hard surface of the stage. At the last moment I rush over and catch her rigid and unflinching figure before it hits. There is applause while I restore her to a vertical position.

Now begins the performance proper, which is a regimented array of the usual mesmerian gimmicks. I place the somnambule's hypnotically stiffened body horizontally between two chairs and ask some behemoth from the audience to come up and sit on her. The man is only too glad to do this. Then I command the somnambule to become inhumanly limp, after which I stuff her into a small box which resembles a coffin. (And inwardly I titter at my tasteless joke.) Next I fire a gun loaded with blanks straight at her, not six inches from her face, and she doesn't wince one bit. We perform a few other routines in defiance of death and pain, afterward moving on to the memory tricks. In one of them I have everybody in the audience call out in turn his or her full name and birthdate. Then my somnambule repeats this information when requested at random to do so by individual audience members. She gets all the names right – and of course everyone is amazed – but she systematically fails to reply with the right dates. Instead she forecasts a future occasion which never coincides with the birthdate she was given. Some of the years of the dates she offers are in distant posterity and some disturbingly near. I express astonishment at my somnambule's behavior, explaining to the audience that portentous fortune-telling is not normally part of the show. I apologize for this ominous display of clairvoyance and vow to make it up to them with an unbelievably diverting finale. A blare of heavenly horns would not be inappropriate at this point.

I signal my assistant to move to the precise center of the stage. Here she positions herself with legs outspread to form an upside-down V out of her lower body. Another signal from me, and her arms rise slowly until they are stretched outward to their furthest limit, fingertips tensely straining for that extra millimeter or so. A final signal commands her nodding head to lift fully erect upon the muscle-knotted column of her neck, eyes glaring out at the audience. The eyes beyond the edge of the stage glare back at her with the same gaze. "Now," I admonish them with poised palm, "there must be total silence. This means no coughs, no sniffs, no clearing of throats." And they obey this unreasonable command; their bodies are silent, for I am their master. They are a noiseless maze of flesh. "Ladies and Gentlemen," I continue, "you are about to see something that I need not tout with tawdry preliminaries. My assistant is now in the deepest possible trance. The particles of her being are obeisant to forces beyond mundane existence, beyond life, death, and so on and so forth. At my instruction she will begin an astounding metamorphosis – entirely through the power of hypnotic energy – which will reveal to you one of the multitudinous unseen facets of the human diamond. Nothing more need be said. My dear, you may commence your change of form, code name: Sarah McFinn."

There she stands – arms, legs, towering head – my five-pointed somnambule: a star. "Already you can see the glowing," I tell the audience. "She begins to luminesce; she begins to effloresce; and now she approaches such radiance that up here on stage I am nearly blinded. But there is no pain, there is anything but eyesore." No one in the audience is even squinting, I notice, for the beams from her body – this labyrinth of light! – are dream beams without physical properties. "Keep watching," I shout at them, pointing to the human luminary. "Are those snow-white wings you see sprouting beyond the horizon of her shoulders? Have the slender lengths of her arms, her legs, her neck all turned to a quivering, angelified alabaster? Is she not the very image of celestiality discarnate?"

But I cannot sustain the moment. The light fades in the eyes of the audience, growing dimmer by the second, and my assistant collapses back into an earthly incarnation. I am exhausted. What's worse, all our efforts seem to have been wasted, for the audience answers this spectacle with only perfunctory applause. I can hardly believe it, but the finale fell flat. They don't understand. They actually like all the mock-death and bogus-pain stuff better. These are what fascinates them. Bah. Double bah.

"Thank you, Ladies and Gentlemen," I say when the lights come back on and the meager applause dies entirely. "I hope my beautiful assistant and I haven't bored you too much this evening. You do look a little sleepy, as if you've been lulled into a trance yourselves. Which is not such a bad feeling, is it? Sinking deep into a downy darkness, resting your souls on pillows stuffed with soft shadows. But our host informs me that things will liven up very soon. Certainly you will awake when a little chime commands you to do so. Remember, it's wake-up time when you hear the chime," I repeat. "And now I believe we can prosecute this evening's festivities."

I help my assistant down from the platform and we mix with the rest of the partiers. Drinks are served and the noise level in the room rises several decibels. The party's populus begins to coagulate into groups here and there. I separate myself from a boisterous congregation surrounding my assistant and me, but nobody seems to notice. They are entranced with my sequined somnambule. She dazzles them – a sun at the center of a drab galaxy, her costume catching the light of that monstrous chandelier winking with a thousand eyes. Everyone seems to be trying to command her attention; but she just smiles, so vacant and full of grace, not even sipping the drink some lucky person was allowed to place in her slender hand. They are transfixed, just like lady spiders during the mating ritual. After all, didn't I tell them that my lanky hypnotizee was their very own vision of fleshly perfection? And perfection is master! Or at least one's idea of it.

But I too have my admirers. One dark-suited bore asks me if hypnosis can help him stop drinking; another inquires if I can show him and his partners the way to undiscovered realms of wealth. I hand them each a business card with a cloud-gray pearl finish, on which is printed a non-existent phone number and a phony address in a real city. As for the name: Cosimo Fanzago. What else would one expect from a performing mesmerist extraordinaire. I have other cards with names like Gaudenzio Ferrari and Johnny Tiepolo printed on them. Nobody's caught on yet. But am I not as much an artist as they were?

And while I am being accosted by people who need cures or aids for their worldliness, I am watching you, dear somnambule. Watching you waltz about this remarkable room. It is not like the other rooms in this great house. Someone really let Fancy have its wild way in here. It harkens back to a time, centuries ago, when your somnambulating predecessors did their sleepwalking act for high society. You fit in so well with this room of leftover rococo. It's a delight to see you make your way about the irregular circumference of this room, where the wall undulates in gentle peaks and hollows, its surface sinewed with a maze of chinoiserie. The serpentine pattern makes it difficult to distinguish the wall's recesses from its protrusions. Some of the guests shift their weight wallwards and find themselves leaning on air, stumbling sideways like comedians from an old movie. But you, my perfect sleepwalker, have no trouble; you lean at the right times and in the right places. And your eyes play beautifully to whatever camera focuses on you; indeed, you take so many of your cues from others that one might suspect you of having no life of your own. Let's sincerely hope not!

Now I watch as you are encouraged to be seated in an elegant chair of blinding brocade, its delicate arms the texture of cartilage and its color like some powdery disc in a woman's cosmetics case. Your high heels make subtle points in the intricate scheme of the carpet, puncturing its arabesque flights of imagination. Now I watch as our host draws you over to the bar he has hospitably set up in this cornerless room. He waves his hand and indicates to you the many bottleshapes to choose from, shapes both *normale* and *baroque*. The baroquely shaped bottles are doing more interesting things with light and shadow than their normal brothers, and you select one of these with a gesture of robotic finesse. He pours two drinks while you watch, and while you watch I am watching you watch. Guiding you to another part of the room, he shows you a tableful of delicate figurines, each one caught in a paralyzed stance of some ancient dance. He places one of them in your hand, and you pass it back and forth before your unfocused eyes, as if trying to awaken yourself with this distraction of movement. But you never will, not without my help.

Now he directs you to a part of the room where there is soft music and dancing. But there are no windows in this room, only tall smoky mirrors, and as you pass from one end to the other you are caught between foggy looking-glasses facing their twins, creating endless files of somnambules in a false infinity beyond the walls. Then you dance with our host, though while he is gazing straightforwardly at you, you are gazing abstractly at the ceiling. O, that ceiling! In epic contrast to the capricious volutions of the rest of the room – designs tendriled to tenebrosity – the ceiling is a dark, chalky blue without a hint of flourish. In its purity it suggests a bottomless pool or an infinite sky wiped clean of stars. You are dancing in eternity, my quadrillioning mannequin. And the dance is indeed a long one, for another wants to cut in on our gracious host and become your partner. Then another. And another. They all want to embrace you; they are all taken in by your frigid elegance, your postures and poses like frozen roses. I am only waiting until everyone has had bodily contact with your powers of animal magnetism.

And while I watch and wait, I notice that we have an unexpected spectator looking down on us from above. Beyond the wide archway at the end of the room is a staircase leading to the second floor; and up there he is sitting, trying to glimpse all the grown-ups, his pajama-clad legs dangling between the Doric posts of the balustrade. I can tell he prefers the classic decor elsewhere predominating in this house. With moderate stealth I leave the main floor audience behind and pay a visit to the balcony, which I quite ignored during my performance earlier.

Creeping up the triple-tiered and white-carpeted stairway, I sit down on the floor beside the child. "Did you see my little show with the lady?" I ask him. He shakes his head horizontally, his mouth as tight as an unopened tulip. "Can you see the lady now? You know the one I mean." I take a shiny chrome-plated pen from the inside pocket of my coat and point down toward the room where the party is going on. At this distance the features of my sequined siren cannot be seen in any great detail. "Well, can you see her?" His head bobs on the vertical. Then I whisper: "And what do you think?" His two lips open and casually reply: "She . . . she's yucky." I breathe easier now. From this height she does indeed appear merely "yucky," but you can never know what the sharp sight of children may perceive. And it is certainly not my intention tonight to make any child's eyes roll the wrong way.

"Now listen closely to everything I say," I say in a very soft but not condescending tone, making sure the child's attention is held by my voice and by the gleaming pen on which his eyes are now focused. He is a good subject for a child, who usually have wandering eyes and minds. He agrees with me that he is feeling rather sleepy now, that bedtime is imminent. "And when you go back to your room, you will fall right to sleep and have wonderful dreams. You will not awaken until morning, *no matter what sounds you hear outside your door*. Understand?" He nods; he is a great nodder, this one. "Very good. And for being such an agreeable subject, I'm going to make you a present of this beautiful pen of sterling silver, which you will keep with you always as a reminder that nothing is what it seems to be. Do you know what I'm talking about?" His head moves slowly and gently up and down with the chilling appearance of deep wisdom. "All right, then. But before you go back to your room, I want you to tell me if there's a back stairway by which I may leave." His finger points down the hall and to the left. "Thank you, young man. Thank you very much. Now off to bed and to your wonderful dreams." He disappears into the Piranesian darkness at the end of the hallway.

For a moment I stand staring down into that merry room below, where the laughing and the dancing have reached their zenith. My fickle somnambule herself seems to be caught up in the party's web, and has forgotten all about her master. She's left me on the sidelines, a many-tendriled, mazy wallflower. But I'm not jealous; I can understand why they've taken you away from me. They simply can't help themselves, now can they? I told them how beautiful and perfect you were, and they can't resist you, my love.

Unfortunately they failed to appreciate the best part of you, preferring to lose themselves in the labyrinth of your grosser illusions. Didn't I show our well-behaved audience an angelized version of you? And you saw their reaction. They were bored and just sat in their seats like a bunch of stiffs. Of course, what can you expect? They wanted the death stuff, the pain stuff. All that flashy junk. They wanted cartwheels of agonized passion; somersaults into fires of doom; nosedives, if you will, into the frenzied pageant of vulnerable flesh. They wanted a tangible *thrill*.

And now that their own miniature pageant seems to have reached its peak, I think the time is right to awaken this mob from its hypnotic slumber and thrill the daylights out of them. It is time for the chime.

There is indeed a back stairway just where the boy indicated, one which leads me to a back hallway, back rooms, and finally a back door. And all these backways lead me to a vast yard where a garden is silhouetted beneath the moon and a small wood sways in the distance. A thick lawn pads my footsteps as I work my way around to the fine facade of this house.

I am standing on the front porch now, just behind its tall columns and beneath a lamp hanging at the end of a long brazen chain. I pause for a moment, savoring each voluptuous second. The serene constellations above wink knowingly. But not even these eyes are deep enough to outgaze me, to deceive the deceiver, illude the illusionist. To tell the truth, I am a very bad mesmeric subject, unable to be drawn in by Hypnos' Heaven. For I know how easily one can be led past those shimmering gates, only to have a trap door spring open once you are inside. Then down you go! I would rather be the attendant loitering outside Mesmer's Maze than its deluded victim bumbling about within.

It is said that death is a great awakening, an emergence from the trance of life. Ha, I have to laugh. Death is the consummation of mortality and – to let out a big secret – only heightens mortal susceptibilities. Of course, it takes a great master to pry open a pair of postmortem eyes once they are sewn tightly closed by Mr. D. And even afterward there is so little these creatures are good for. As conversationalists they are incredibly vacant; the things they tell you are no more than sweet nullities. But there is not much else you can do with them, they are so hideous and smell to high heaven. So mostly we just talk. Sometimes, however, I recruit them for my show, if I can manage to get their awkward forms out of the mausoleum, hospital, morgue, medical school, or funeral emporium I have deviously insinuated my way into. But there is one great problem: *You just can't make them beautiful*. One is not a sorcerer!

But perhaps one is a mental prestidigitator, an unusually adept whammy artist. One may make an audience think them beautiful, mistake them for spellbinding, snake-eyed charmers. One *can* do this at least, and loves to.

Even now I hear them still laughing, still dancing, still making a fuss over my charismatic doll of the dead. We showed them what you might be, O Seraphita, now let's show them what you really are. I have only to press this glowing little button of a doorbell to sound the chime which will awaken them, to send the toll rolling throughout the house. Then they'll see. They'll see the sepulchral wounds: your eyes recessed in their sockets, sunken into mouths – those labyrinthine pits! They'll wake up and find their nice dancing clothes all clotted with putrescent goo. And wait'll they get a sniff of that stiff. They *will* be amazed.

EYE OF THE LYNX

No architectural go-betweens divided the doorway – a side entrance off a block of diverse but connected buildings – from the sidewalk. The sidewalk itself was conjugally flush with the curb that bordered a street which in turn radiated off a boulevard of routine clamor, and all of this was enveloped by December's musty darkness. Sidewalk doorway, doorway sidewalk. I don't want to make too much of the matter, except to say that this peculiarity, if it was one, made an impression on me: there was no physical introduction to the doorway, surely not in the form of a little elevated slab of cement, certainly not even a single stair of stone. No structure of any kind prefaced the door. And it was recessed into the building itself with such deliberate shallowness that it almost looked painted directly onto the wall. I looked over at the traffic light above the intersection; it was amber going on red. I looked back at the door. The sidewalk seemed to slip right under it, urging one to step inside. So I did, after noting that the wall around the doorway was done up, somewhat ineptly, like a castle tower flanked by toothy merlons.

Inside I was immediately greeted by a reception committee of girls very professionally lounging in what looked like old church pews along an old wall. The narrow vestibule in which I found myself scintillated with a reddish haze that seemed not so much light as electric vapor. In the far upper corner of this entranceway a closed circuit camera was bearing down on us all, and I wondered how the camera's eye would translate that redly dyed room into the bluish hues of a security monitor. Not that it was any of my business. We might all be electronically meshed into a crazy purpurean tapestry, and that would have been just fine.

A fair-haired girl in denim slacks and leather jacket stood up and approached me. In the present light her blandness was actually more a murky tomato soup or greasy ketchup than fresh strawberry. She delivered a mechanical statement that began "Welcome to the House of Chains," and went on and on, spelling out various services and specific terms and finally concluding with a legal disclaimer of some carefully phrased sort. "Yes, yes," I said. "I've read the ads, the ones set in that spikey Gothic type, the ones that look like a page out of an old German bible. I've come to the right place, haven't I?"

"Sure you have," I thought to myself. "Sure you have," echoed the blonde with blood-dyed hair. "What will it be tonight?" I inwardly asked me. "What will it be tonight?" she asked aloud. "Do you see anything you like?" we both asked me at the same time. From my expression and casual glances somewhere beyond the claustrophobic space of that tiny foyer, she could see right away that I didn't see anything, or at least that I wanted her to think I didn't. We were on the same infra-red wavelength.

We stood there for a moment while she took a long delicious sip from a can of iced tea, pretending with half-closed eyes that it was the best thing she'd ever washed her insides with. Then she pushed a button next to an intercom on the wall behind her and turned her head to whisper some words, though still keeping those violent eyes hooked on mine.

And what did those eyes tell me? They told me of her life as she lived it in fantasy: a Gothic tale of a baronness deprived of her title and inheritance by a big man with bushy eyebrows, which he sometimes sprinkles with glitter. (She once dreamed that he did.) And now this high-born lady spends much of her time haunting second-hand shops, trying to reclaim her aristocratic accoutrements and various articles of her wardrobe which were dispersed at auction by the glitter-browed man who came out of the forest one spring when she was away visiting a Carmelite nunnery. So far she's done pretty well for herself, managing to assemble many items that for her are charged with sentiment. Her collection includes several dresses in her favorite shade of monastic black. Each of them tapers in severely under the bustline, while belling-out below the waist. A bib-like bodice buttons in her ribs, ascending to her neck where a strip of dark velvet is seized by a pearl brooch. At her wrist: a frail chain from which dangles a heart-shaped locket, a whirlpooling lock of golden hair inside. She wears gloves, of course, long and powdery pale. And tortuous hats from a mad milliner, with dependent veils like the fine cloth screen in a confessional, delicate flags of mourning repentance. But she prefers her enveloping hoods, the ones that gather with innumerable folds at the shoulders of heavy capes lined in satin that shines like a black sun. Capes with deep pockets and generous inner pouches for secreting precious souvenirs, capes with silk strings that tie about her neck, capes with weighted hems which nonetheless flutter weightlessly in midnight gusts. She loves them dearly.

Just so is she attired when the glitter-browed villain peers in her apartment window, accursing the casement and her dreams. What can she do but shrink with terror? Soon she is only doll-size in dark doll's costume. Nevertheless, quivering bones and feverish blood are the stuffings of this doll, its entrails tickled by fear's funereal plume. It flies to a corner of the room and cringes within enormous shadows, sometimes dreaming there throughout the night – of carriage wheels rioting in a lavender mist or a pearly fog, of nacreous fires twitching beyond the margins of country roads, of cliffs and stars. Then she awakes and pops a mint into her mouth from an unravelled roll on the nightstand, afterwards smoking half a cigarette before crawling out of bed and grimacing in the light of late afternoon.

"C'mon," she said after releasing the button of the intercom. "I think I can help you."

"But I thought you couldn't leave the reception area," I explained, almost apologetically. "Of course, if I'd known . . ."

"C'mon," she repeated with both hands in her jacket pockets. And her loud heels led me out of that room where every face wore a fake blush.

We walked though a pair of swinging doors which met in the middle and were bound like books, imitation leather tightly stretched across their broad boards and thick spines. Title page:

House of Chains: A Romance in Red Decorated with Divers Woodcuts

Page one: Deep into December, as the winds of winter howled beyond the walls, two children, one blond and the other dark, found themselves in the heart of a great castle in the heart of a gloomy forest. The central chamber of the castle, as is a heart's wont, glowed with a warm red light, though the surrounding masonry was of damp gray stone. A great many people of the court capered about, traveling aloft or below by means of sundry stairways, ingressing and egressing through the queerly shaped portals of shadowed corridors (which seemed everywhere), and thronging here and there as in the curious bazaars of oriental scenes. Uncouth voices and harsh music fell upon the children's ears.

Decoration opposite opening page: Two children, one blond

and the other not; passing through a tunnel of tangled forest which looks as if it's about to descend and devour them both. The girl, open mouthed, is pointing with her left hand while holding onto her brother with the right; the boy, all eyes, seems to be gazing in every direction at once, amazed at the pair's wondrous incarceration.

"Can I get the ninety-eight cent tour," I asked my hostess. "I'm from out of town. We don't have anything like this where I come from. I'm paying for this, right?"

Half of her mouth found it possible to smirk. "Sure," she said, drawing out the word well past its normal duration. She moved in a couple of false directions before guiding me toward some metal steps which clanged as we descended into a blur of crimson shadows. The vicious vapor followed us downstairs, of course, tagging along like an insanely devoted familiar.

Surprisingly enough, there was a window in the vaguely institutional basement of the House of Chains (I was beginning to enjoy that name), but it was composed of empty panes looking out upon a phony landscape. Pictured were vast regions of volcanic desolation towered over by prehistoric mountains which poked into a dead-end darkness. The scene was illuminated by a low-watt bulb. I felt a bit like a child peeking into a department store model of Santa's workshop, but I can't say it didn't create a mood.

"Nice painting," I said to my companion. "Kind of spooky, don't you think?" I looked at her for a reply to my patter, but no counter-patter was forthcoming. She simply stared at me as if I'd just told a joke she didn't get.

"There's not much down here," she finally said. "Just a couple of hallways that don't go anywhere and a bunch of rooms, most of them locked. If you want to see something spooky, go to the end of that hall and open the door on the right."

I faithfully followed her instructions. On the door handle hung a rather large animal collar at the end of a chain leash. The chain jingled a little when I pushed open the door. The red light in the hallway barely allowed me to see inside, but there was little to see anyway except a small, empty room. Its floor was bare cement and there was straw laid down upon it. The smell was terrific.

"Well?" she asked when I returned down the hallway.

"It's a start," I answered, winking the subtlest possible wink. We just stood for a moment gazing at each other in a light the color of fresh meat. Then she led me back upstairs.

"Where did you say you're from?" she asked as that noisy stairway amplified our footsteps into reverberant dungeonlike echoes.

"It's a real small place," I replied. "About a hundred miles outstate. It's not even on the maps."

"And you've never been to a place like this before?"

"Uh-uh, never."

She stopped at the top of the stairs. "Then before we go any further," she said, "I want to give you some advice and tell you to go back where you came from."

I just looked at her, shaking my head slowly and insolently.

"Okay, then. Let's go."

We went.

And there was much to see on the way – a Punch and Judy panorama which was staged between the chasmical folds of a playhouse curtain of rich inky red, and getting redder every passing second. Each scene flipped by like a page in a storybook: that frozen stage where the players are stiffened with immortality and around which the only thing that stirs is the reader's roving eye.

Locked doors were no obstacle.

Behind one, where every wall of the room was painted with heavy black bars from floor to ceiling, the Queen of the Singing Kingdom – riding crop raised high – sat atop her magic flying leopard, which unfortunately had been recently transformed into a human. And, sadly, the animal had lost one of its paws. What good fortune that it could still fly! But did it want to? Or did it prefer to lumber lamely around its cage, with the Queen herself growing out of its back like a Siamese twin, her royal blood and his beast's now flowing together, tributaries from distant worlds mingling in a hybrid harmony. The animal was so pleased that it yowled a tune as the Queen beat time upon its flanks with her stinging crop. Sing, leopard, sing!

Behind another door, one with a swastika splashed negligently on its front in such a way that the paint had dripped from every appendage of the spidery symbol, was a scene similar to the previous. Inside, some colored lights were angled down upon the floor, where a very small man, his hunchback possibly artificial, knelt with head bowed low. His hands were lost in a pair of enormous gloves with shapeless fingers which lolled around like ten drunken jacks-in-the-box. One of the numb fingers was trapped beneath the pointy toe at the base of a lofty boot. See the funny clown! Or rather *jester* in a jingly cap. His ringed eyes patiently gazed upwards into the darkness, attentive to the hollow voice hurling anger from on high. The voice was playing up the moral disparity between its proudly booted self and that humiliated freak upon the floor, contrasting its warrior's leaping delights with the fool's dragging sack of amusements. *But couldn't the stooping hunchback's fun be beautiful too?* his eyes whispered with their elliptical mouths. *But couldn't—* Silence! Now the little monkey was going to get it.

Behind still another door, which had no distinguishing marks, a single candle glowed through red glass, just barely keeping the room out of total blackness. It was hard to tell how many were in there, more than a couple, less than a horde. They were all wearing the same gear, little zippers and big zippers like silver stitches scarring their outfits. One very little one had an eyelash caught in it, I could tell that much. For the rest of it, they might as well have been human shadows that merged softly with one another, proclaiming threats of ultimate mayhem and wielding oversized straight razors. But although these gleaming blades were always potently poised, they never came down. It was only make-believe, just like everything else I had seen.

The next door, and for me the last, was at the end of an exhausting climb in what must have been a tower.

"Here's where you get your money's worth, mister," said my date, blind to the signs of apprehension – clutching my coat, lightly pawing my cheek – I was beginning to exhibit like an insecure artist about to reveal his unseen canvasses.

"Show me the worst," I said, eyeing the undersized door before us.

The situation here was as transparent as the others. Only this time it wasn't pet leopards, pathetic clowns, or paranoid shadows. It was, in fact, two new characters: a wicked witch and her assistant in the form of an enchanted puppet. The clumsy little creature, due to an incorrigibly mischievous temperament, had behaved badly. Now the witch was in the process, which she had down to perfection, of putting him back in line. She swept across the room, her dark dress swirling like a maelstrom, her hideous face sunken into an abundant hood. Behind her a stained-glass window shone with all the excommunicated tints of corruption. By the light of this infernal rainbow of wrinkled cellophane, she collared her naughty assistant and chained him hands and feet to a formidable-looking stone wall, which buckled aluminum-like when he collapsed against it. She angled down her hooded face and whispered into his wooden ear.

"Do you know what I do with little puppets who've been bad?" she inquired. "Do you?"

The puppet trembled a bit and would have beamed bright with perspiration had he been made of flesh and not wood.

"I'll tell you what I do," the witch continued half-sweetly. "I make them touch the fire. I burn them from the legs up."

Then, surprisingly, the puppet smiled.

"And what will you do," the puppet asked, "with all those old dresses, gloves, veils, and capes when I'm gone? What will you do in your low-rent castle with no one to stare, his brow of glittering silver, into the windows of your dreams?"

Perhaps the puppet was perspiring after all, for his brow was now glistening with tiny flecks of starlight.

The witch stepped back and whipped off her black hood, exposing blond hair beneath it. She wanted to know how I knew about all that stuff, which she had never revealed to anyone. She accused me of peeping-tomism, of breaking and entering, and of illicit curiosity in general.

"Let me out of these chains and I'll tell you all about myself," I shouted.

"Forget it," she answered. "I'm going to get someone to throw you out of here."

"Then I'll just have to release myself," I said more calmly.

The manacles opened around my ankles, my wrists, and the chains fell away.

"You can't pretend," I continued as I approached her, "that there isn't something familiar about me. After all we've meant to each other, after all we've done together, over and over and over. You're not bored, are you? I hate to think what that would mean . . . for both of us. You've been cooped up here in this silly place too long. For someone like you, that can be deadly. You've always known you were special, haven't you? That someday – and it was always just around the corner, wasn't it? – great things were going to happen, great things that didn't quite have a name yet. But they were there, as real as the velvet embrace of your favorite cape, the one with the silver chain that draws its curtainy wings together at your bosom. As real as the tall candles you love to light during storms, and which you drunkenly knocked over once, burning your right hand. No, don't cover up the scar, I'm sure no one's noticed it before now. You love those storms, don't you, with their chains of raindrops whipping against your windows. All that craving for noise and persecution. All that beautiful craziness! The storms: your eyes stared into their eyes, and into mine.

"But now you're in danger of losing all that, which is why I showed up tonight. You've got to get out of this tinsellated side-show. This is for hicks, this is small time. You can do better than this. I can take you places where the stories of tortuous romance and the storms never end. I'll take you there. Please, don't back away from me. There's nowhere to go and your eyes tell me you want the same things I do. If you're worried about the hardships of traveling to strange faraway places, don't! You're almost there now. Just fall into my arms, into my heart, into— There, that was easy, wasn't it?"

Afterward I retraced my steps down stairways and through corridors of scarlet darkness. "Goodnight, everybody!" I said to the girls in the reception room. Back out on the street, I paused and looked at that peculiar door again. I could now see the logic of doing away with gratuitous barriers between one place and another, between those on the outside and those within. Bring down the walls! But watch out for escapees.

Actually she made only a single attempt. It wasn't serious, though. A drunk I passed on the sidewalk saw an arm shoot out at him from underneath my shirt, projecting chest-high at a perfect right angle to the rest of me. He staggered over, shook the hand with a jolly vigor, and then proceeded on his way. And I proceeded on mine, once I'd got her safely back inside her fabulous prison, a happy captive of my heart. We fled down the sidewalk. We breathed the cold of that winter night. We were one forever.

At the corner the amber traffic light had finally burst into a glorious red as my old flame and I approached the ultimate intersection of our flesh . . . as well as our dreams.

THE CHRISTMAS EVES
OF AUNT ELISE:
A TALE OF POSSESSION
IN OLD GROSSE POINTE

We pronounced her name with a distinct "Z" sound – *Remember, Jack, remember* – the way some people slur Missus into Mizzuz or for Christmas say Chrizmuzz. It was at her remarkable home in Grosse Pointe that she insisted our family, both its wealthy and its unwealthy side, celebrate each Christmas Eve in a style that exuded the traditional, the old-fashioned, the antique. Actually, Aunt Elise constituted the wealthy side of the family all on her own. Her husband had died many years before, leaving his wife with a prosperous real estate business but no children. Not surprisingly, Aunt Elise undertook the ownership and management of the firm with phenomenal success, perpetuating our heirless uncle's family name on for-sale signs planted in front lawns all over the state. But what was Uncle's *first* name, a young nephew or niece sometimes wondered. Or, as it was more than once put by one of us children: "Where's *Uncle* Elise?" To which the rest of us answered in unison: "He's at his ease," a response we learned from none other than our widowed aunt herself.

Aunt Elise was without husband or offspring of her own, true enough. But she loved all the ferment of big families, and every holiday season she possessed as much in relations both young and no longer young as she did in her real estate returns, her tangible and intangible assets and investments, and her abundant hard cash. Her house was something of an Elizabethan country manor in style while remaining modest, even relatively miniature, in scale. It fit very nicely – when it existed – into a claustrophobic cluster of trees on some corner acreage a few steps uphill from Lake Shore Drive, profiling rather than facing the lake itself. A rather dull exterior of soot-gray stones somewhat camouflaged the old place in its woodland hideaway; until one caught sight of its diamond-paned windows – kept brilliant by the personal attention of Aunt Elise herself, no less – and one realized that a house in fact existed where before there seemed to be only shadowed emptiness.

Around Christmastime these many-faceted windows took on a candied glaze in the pink, blue, green, and other-colored lights strung about their perimeters. More often in the old days – *Remember them, Jack* – a thick December fog rolled off the not-yet-frozen lake and those kaleidoscopic windows would throw their spectrums into the softening mist. This, to my child's senses, was the image and atmosphere defining the winter holiday: a serene congregation of colors whose confused murmurings divulged to this world rumors of strange and solemn services that were concurrently taking place in another. This was the celebration, this the festival. Why did we leave it all behind us, leave it outside? And as I was guided up the winding front walk toward the house, a parent's hand in either of mine, I always stopped short, pulling Mom and Dad back like a couple of runaway horses, and for a brief, futile moment refused to go inside.

After my first Christmas – chronologically my fifth – I knew what happened inside the house, and year after year there was little change either in the substance or surface details of the program. For those from large families, this scene is a little too familiar to bother describing. Perhaps even lifelong orphans are jaded to it. Still, there are others to whom depictions of the unusual uncles, the loveable grandparents, and the common run of cousins will always be fresh and dear; those who delight in multiple generations of characters crowding the page, who are warmed by the feel of their paper flesh. I tell you they share these desires with my Aunt Elise, and her spirit is in them.

She always occupied and dominated, for the duration of these Christmas Eves, the main room of her house. This room I never saw except as a fantasy of ornamentation, an hallucinatorium in holiday dress. Right now I can only hope to portray a few of its highlights. First of all holly, both fresh and artificial, hung down the walls from wherever it was possible to hang – from the frames of paintings, from the stained-wood shelves of a thousand gewgaws, even from the velvety embossed pattern of the wallpaper itself, intertwining with its vegetable swirls and flourishes, if my memory sees this accurately. And from fixtures above, including a chandelier delicately sugared with tiny Italian lights, down came

gardens of mistletoe in mid-air. The huge fireplace blazed with
a festive inferno, and before its cinder-spitting hearth was a
protective screen, at either end of which stood a pair of thick
brass posts; and over the crown of each post – whose shape and
design I never glimpsed – were two puppet Santas, slipped on like
socks and drooping a little to one side, their mittens outstretched in
readiness to give someone a tiny, angular hug. In a corner, the one
beside the front window, a sturdy evergreen was somewhere
hidden beneath every imaginable type of dangling, roping, or
blinking decoration, as well as being dolled up with ridiculous
satin bows in pastel shades, lovingly tied by human hands. The
same hands did their work on the presents beneath the tree, and
year after year these seemed, like everything else in the room, to be
in exactly the same place, as if the gifts of last Christmas had never
been opened, quickening in me the nightmarish sense of a ritual
forever reenacted without hope of escape. (Somehow I am still
possessed by this same feeling of entrapment, and after all these
years.) My own present was always at the back of that horde of
packages, almost against the wall behind the tree. It was tied up
with a pale purple ribbon and covered with pale blue wrapping
paper upon which little bears in infants' sleeping gowns dreamed
of more pale blue presents which, instead of more bears, had little
boys dreaming upon them. I spent much of a given Christmas Eve
sitting near this gift of mine, mostly to find refuge from the others
rather than to wonder at the thing inside. It was always something
in the way of underwear, nightwear, or socks, never the nameless
marvel which I fervently hoped to receive from my obscenely well-
heeled aunt. Nobody seemed to mind that I sat on the other side of
the room from where most of them congregated to talk or sing
carols to the music of an ancient organ, which Aunt Elise played
with her back to her audience, and to me.

Slee – eep in heav – enly peace.

"That was very good," she said without turning around. As
usual the sound of her voice led you to expect that any moment she
would clear her throat of some sticky stuff which was clinging to its
insides. Instead she switched off the electric organ, after which
gesture some of the gathering, dismissed, left for other parts of the
house.

"We didn't hear Old Jack singing with us," she said, turning to
look across the room where I was seated in a large chair beside a
fogged window. On that occasion I was about twenty or twenty-
one, home from school for Christmas. I had drunk quite a bit of
Aunt Elise's holiday punch, and felt like answering: "Who cares if

you didn't hear Old Jack singing, you old bat?" But instead I simply stared her way, drunkenly taking in her features, with prejudice, for the family scrapbook of my memory: tight-haired head (like combed wires), calm eyes of someone in an old portrait (someone long gone), high cheekbones highly colored (less rosily than like a rash), and the prominent choppers of a horse charging out of nowhere in a dream. I had no worry about my future ability to recall these features, even though I had secretly vowed this would be the last Christmas Eve I would view them. So I could afford to be tranquil in the face of Aunt Elise's taunts that evening. Anyway, further confrontation between the two of us was aborted when some of the children began clamoring for one of their aunt's stories. "And this time a *true* story, Auntie. One that really happened."

"All right," she answered, adding that "maybe Old Jack would like to come over and sit with us."

"Too old for that, thank you. Besides, I can hear you just fine from—"   "Well," she began before I'd finished, "let me think a moment. There are so many, so *many*. Anyhow, here's one of them. This happened before any of you were born, a few winters after I moved into this neighborhood with your uncle. I don't know if you ever noticed, but a little ways down the street there's an empty lot where there should be, used to be, a house. You can see it from the front window over there," she said, pointing to the window beside my chair. I let my eyes follow her finger out that window and, through the fog, I witnessed the empty lot of her story.

"There was once a house on that lot, a beautiful old house with more floors and more windows than this one, more of everything. The house was lived in by a very old man who never went out and who never invited anyone to visit him, at least no one that I ever noticed. And after the old man died, what do you think happened to the house?"

"It disappeared," answered some of the children, jumping the gun.

"In a way, I suppose it did disappear. Actually what happened was that some men came and tore the house down brick by brick, shingle by shingle. I think the old man who lived there must have been very mean to want that to happen to his house after he died."

"How do you know he wanted it?" I interjected, trying to spoil her assumption.

"What other sensible explanation is there?" Aunt Elise answered. "Anyhow," she went on, "I think that the old man just couldn't stand the thought of anyone else living in the house and being happy there, because surely he wasn't. But maybe there was also another reason," said Aunt Elise, drawing out these last words and torturing them at length with her muddled vocal system. The children sitting on the carpet before her listened with a new intentness, while the blazing logs seemed to start up a little more noisily in the fireplace.

"Maybe by destroying his house, making it disappear, the old man thought he was taking it with him into the other world. People who have lived alone for a very long time often think and do very strange things," she emphasized, though I'm sure no one except me thought to apply this final statement to the storyteller herself. *Tell everything, Jack.* She went on:

"Now what would lead a person to such conclusions about the old man, you may wonder? Did something strange happen with him and his house, after both of them were gone? I'll tell you, because one night, yes, something did happen.

"One night – a foggy winter's night like this one, oh my little children – someone came walking down this exact street and paused at the property line of the house of the old man who was now dead. This someone was a young man whom many people had seen wandering around here off and on for some years. I myself, I tell you, once confronted him and asked him what business he had with us and with our homes, because that's what he seemed most interested in. Anywho, this young man called himself an an-tee-quarian, and he said he was very interested in old things, particularly old houses. And he had a very particular interest in that strange old house of the old man. A number of times he had asked if he could look around inside, but the old man always refused. Most of the time the house was dark and seemed as if no one was home, even though someone always was.

"Imagine the young man's surprise, then, when he now saw not a dark empty place, no, but a place of bright Christmas lights shining all fuzzy through the fog. Could this be the old man's house? Lit up with these lights? Yes, it could, because there was the old man himself standing at the window with a rather friendly look on his face. At least for him it was. So, one last time, the young man thought he would try his luck with the old house. He rang the bell and the front door slowly opened wide. The old man didn't say anything, but merely stepped back and allowed the other to enter. Finally the young antiquarian would be able to study the inside of the house to his heart's content. Along the way, in narrow halls and long-abandoned rooms, the old man stood silently beside his guest, smiling all the time."

"I can't imagine how you know this part of your *true* story, Aunt Elise," I interrupted.

"Aunt Elise knows," asserted one of my little cousins just to shut me up, saving my aunt the trouble. She went on:

"After the young man had looked all around the house, both men sat down in the deep comfortable chairs of the front parlor and talked a while about the house. But it wasn't too long before that smile on the old man's face, that quiet little smile, began to bother his visitor in a peculiar way. At last the young man claimed he had to go, glancing down at the watch he had drawn from his pocket. And when he looked up again . . . the old man was gone. This startled the young man for a moment. He checked the nearby rooms and hallways for his host, calling "sir, sir" because he never found out the old man's name. And though he could have been in a dozen different places, the owner of the house didn't seem to be anywhere in particular that the young man could see. So the antiquarian decided just to leave without saying goodbye or thank you or anything like that.

"But he didn't get as far as the front door when he stopped dead in his tracks because of what he saw through the front window. There seemed to be no street anymore, no street lamps or sidewalks, not even any houses, besides the one he was in, of course. There was only the fog and some horrible, tattered shapes wandering aimlessly within it. The young man could hear them crying. What was this place, and where had the old house taken him? He didn't know what to do except stare out the window. And when he saw the face reflected in the window, he thought for a second that the old man had returned and was standing behind him again, smiling his quiet smile.

"But then the young man realized that this was now his own face, and, like those terrible, ragged creatures lost in the fog, he too began to cry.

"After that night, no one around here ever saw the young man again, just as no one has ever seen the house that was torn down. At least no one has yet!

"Well, did you like that story, children?"

I felt tired, more tired than I'd ever been in my life. I barely had the strength, it seemed, to push myself out of the chair into which I'd sunk down so deep. I brushed up against bodies and shuffled slowly under the stares of remote faces. Where was I going? Was I in want of another drink? Did I have to find a bathroom for my old body? No, none of these served as my motive.

It could almost have been hours later that I was walking down a foggy street. The fog formed impenetrable white walls around me, narrow corridors leading nowhere and rooms without windows. I didn't walk very far before realizing I could go no farther.

But finally I did see something. What I saw was simply a cluster of Christmas lights, innocent colors beaming against the fog. But what could they have signified that they should seem so horrible to me? Why did this peaceful vision of inaccessible and hazy wonder, which possessed such marvelous appeal in my childhood, now strike me with all the terror of the impossible? The colors bled into the fog and were sopped up as if by a horrible gauze which drank the blood of rainbows. These were not the colors I had loved, this could not be the house. But it was, for there at the window stood its owner, and the sight of her thin smiling face crippled my body and my brain.

Then I remembered: Aunt Elise was dead now and her house, at the instruction of her will, had been dismantled brick by brick, shingle by shingle.

"Uncle Jack, wake up," urged young voices at close range, though technically, being an only child, I was not their uncle. More accurately, I was just a friendly elder member of the family who'd nodded off in a chair. It was Christmas Eve, and as usual I had had a little too much to drink.

"We're gonna sing carols, Uncle Jack," said the voices again. Then they went away.

I went away too, retrieving my overcoat from the bedroom where it lay buried in a communal grave under innumerable other overcoats. Everyone else was singing songs to the strumming of guitars in the living room. (I liked their bland music infinitely better than the rich, rotting vibrations of Aunt Elise's cathedral-esque keyboard of Christmas Eves past.) Foregoing all rituals of departure, I slipped quietly out the back door in the kitchen.

Though I do not remember very much about it, I must have gone to Grosse Pointe, to the empty land on which my aunt's house once stood. So many things I can remember so clearly from long ago – and at my age – but not this thing. *Leave out nothing, Jack. Remember.* I must have gone to Grosse Pointe, to the open land on which my aunt's house once stood. But I do not remember what it was like that Christmas Eve. *Remember, Jack.* How thick the fog must have been, if there was fog and not merely a slow descent of snow, or nothing. Would those old lights be there? *You* shall *remember.*

But I must have gone to Grosse Pointe that night, I must have gone there. Because what I do remember is this: standing before the door of a house which no longer existed. And then seeing that door begin to open in a slow, monumental sweep, receding with all the ponderous labor of a clock's barely budging hands. Another hand also moved with a monstrous languor, as it reached out and laid itself upon me. Then her face looked into mine, and the last thing I remember is that great, gaping smile, and the words: "Merry Christmas, Old Jack!"

Oh, I'll never forget the look on his face when I said these words. I had him at last, him and his every thought, all the pretty pictures of his mind. Those weeping demons, those souls forever lost to happiness, came out of the fog and took away his body. He was one of them now, crying like a baby! But I have kept the best part, all his beautiful memories, all those lovely times we had — the children, the presents, the colors of those nights! Anyhow, they are mine now. Tell us of those years, Old Jack, the years that were never yours. They were always mine, and now I have them to play with like toys according to my will. Oh, how nice, how nice and lovely to have my little home. How nice and lovely to live in a land where it's always dead with darkness, and where it's always alive with lights! And where it will always, forever after, be just like Christmas Eve.

THE LOST ART OF TWILIGHT

I have painted it, tried to at least. Oiled it, watercolored it, smeared it upon a mirror which I positioned to rekindle the glow of the real thing. And always in the abstract. Never actual sinking suns in spring, autumn, winter skies; never a sepia light descending over the trite horizon of a lake, not even the particular lake I like to view from the great terrace of my massive old mansion. But these *Twilights* of mine were not merely abstraction, which after all is just a matter of technique, a method for keeping out the riff-raff of the real world. Other painterly abstractionists may claim that nothing is represented by their canvasses, and probably nothing is: a streak of iodine red is just a streak of iodine red, a patch of flat black equals a patch of flat black. But pure color, pure light, pure lines and their rhythms, pure form in general all means much more than that. The others have only *seen* their dramas of shape and shade; I – and it is impossible to insist on this too strenuously – I have *been* there. And my twilight abstractions did in fact represent some reality, some-where, sometime: a zone formed by palaces of soft and sullen color standing beside seas of scintillating pattern and beneath sadly radiant skies; a zone in which the visitor himself is transformed into a formal essence, a luminous presence, free of substances – a citizen of the abstract. And a zone (I cannot sufficiently amplify my despair on this point, so I will not try) that I will never know again.

Only a few weeks ago I was sitting out on the terrace, watching the early autumn sun droop into the above-mentioned lake, talking to Aunt T. Her heels clomped with a pleasing hollowness on drab flagstones. Silver-haired, she was attired in a gray suit, a big bow flopping up to her lower chins. In her left hand was a long envelope, neatly caesarianed, and in her right hand the letter it had contained, folded in sections like a triptych.

"They want to see you," she said, gesturing with the letter. "They want to come here."

"I don't believe it," I said and skeptically turned in my chair to watch the sunlight stretching in long cathedral-like aisles across the upper and lower levels of the lawn.

"If you would only read the letter," she insisted.

"It's in French, no? Can't read."

"Now that's not true, to judge by those books you're always stacking in the library."

"Those happen to be art books. I just look at the pictures."

"You like pictures, André" she asked in her best matronly ironic tone. "I have a picture for you. Here it is: they *are* going to be allowed to come here and stay with us as long as they like. There's a family of them, two children and the letter also mentions an unmarried sister. They're travelling all the way from Aix-en-Provence to visit America, and while on their trip they want to see their only living blood relation here. Do you understand this picture? They know who you are and, more to the point, where you are."

"I'm surprised they would want to, since they're the ones—"

"No, they're not. They're from your *father's* side of the family. The Duvals," she explained. "They do know all about you but say," Aunt T. here consulted the letter for a moment, "that they are *sans préjugé*."

"The generosity of such creatures freezes my blood. Phenomenal scum. Twenty years ago these people do what they did to my mother, and now they have the gall, the *gall*, to say they aren't prejudiced against *me*."

Aunt T. gave me a warning hrumph to silence myself, for just then Rops walked out onto the terrace bearing a tray with a slender glass set upon it. I dubbed him Rops because he, as much as his artistic namesake, never failed to give me the charnel house creeps.

He cadavered over to Aunt T. and served her her afternoon cocktail.

"Thank you," she said, taking the glass of cloudy stuff.

"Anything for you, sir?" he asked, now holding the tray over his chest like a silver shield.

"Ever see me have a drink, Rops," I asked back. "Ever see me—"

"André, behave. That'll be all, thank you."

Rops left our sight in a few bony strides. "You can continue your rant now," said Aunt T. graciously.

"I'm through. You know how I feel," I replied and then looked away toward the lake, drinking in the dim mood of the twilight in the absence of normal refreshment.

"Yes, I do know how you feel, and you've always been wrong. You've always had these romantic ideas of how you and your mother, rest her soul, have been the victims of some monstrous injustice. But nothing is the way you like to think it is. They were not backward peasants who, we should say, *saved* your mother. They were wealthy, sophisticated members of her own family. And they were not superstitious, because what they believed about your mother was the truth."

"True or not," I argued, "they believed the unbelievable – they acted on it – and that I call superstition. What reason could they possibly—"

"What *reason?* I have to say that at the time you were in no position to judge reasons, considering that we knew you only as a slight swelling inside your mother's body. But I was actually there. I saw the 'new friends' she had made, that 'aristocracy of blood,' as she called it, in contrast to her own people's hard-earned wealth. But I don't judge her, I never have. After all, she had just lost her husband – your father was a good man and it's a shame you never knew him – and then to be carrying his child, the child of a dead man . . . She was frightened, confused, and she ran back to her family and her homeland. Who can blame her if she started acting irresponsibly. But it's a shame what happened, especially for your sake."

"You are indeed a comfort, *Auntie*," I said with now regrettable sarcasm.

"Well, you have my sympathy whether you want it or not. I think I've proven that over the years."

"Indeed you have," I agreed, and somewhat sincerely.

Aunt T. poured the last of her drink down her throat and a little drop she wasn't aware of dripped from the corner of her mouth, shining in the crepuscular radiance like a pearl.

"When your mother didn't come home one evening – I should say *morning* – everyone knew what had happened, but no one said anything. Contrary to your ideas about their superstitiousness, they actually could not bring themselves to believe the truth for some time."

"It was good of all of you to let me go on developing for a while, even as you were deciding how to best hunt my mother down."

"I will ignore that remark."

"I'm sure you will."

"We did not *hunt* her down, as you well know. That's another of your persecution fantasies. She came to us, now didn't she? Scratching at the windows in the night—"

"You can skip this part, I already—"

"—swelling full as the fullest moon. And that was strange, because you would actually have been considered a dangerously premature birth according to normal schedules; but when we followed your mother back to the mausoleum of the local church, where she lay during the daylight hours, she was carrying the full weight of her pregnancy. The priest was shocked to find what he had living, so to speak, in his own backyard. It was actually he, and not so much any of your mother's family, who thought we should not allow you to be brought into the world. And it was his hand that ultimately released your mother from the life of her new friends, and immediately afterward she began to deliver, right in the coffin in which she lay. The blood was terrible. If we did—"

"It's not necessary to— "

"—hunt down your mother, you should be thankful that I was among that party. I had to get you out of the country that very night, back to America. I—"

At that point she could see that I was no longer listening, was gazing with a distracted intensity on the pleasanter anecdotes of the setting sun. When she stopped talking and joined in the view, I said:

"Thank you, Aunt T., for that little bedtime story. I never tire of hearing it."

"I'm sorry, André, but I wanted to remind you of the truth."

"What can I say? I realize I owe you my life, such as it is."

"That's not what I mean. I mean the truth of what your mother became and what you now are."

"I am nothing. Completely harmless."

"That's why we must let the Duvals come and stay with us. To show them that the world has nothing to fear from you, because that's what I believe they're actually coming to see. That's the message they'll carry back to your family in France."

"You really think that's why they're coming?"

"I do. They could make quite a bit of trouble for you, for us."

I rose from my chair as the shadows of the failing twilight deepened. I went and stood next to Aunt T. against the stone balustrade of the terrace, and whispered:

"Then let them come."

II

I am an offspring of the dead. I am descended from the deceased. I am the progeny of phantoms. My ancestors are the illustrious multitudes of the defunct, grand and innumerable. My lineage is longer than time. My name is written with embalming fluid in the book of death. A noble name is mine.

In the immediate family, the first to meet his maker was my own maker: he rests in the tomb of the unknown father. But while the man did manage to sire me, he breathed his last breath in this world before I drew my first. He was felled by a single stroke, his first and last. In those final moments, so I'm told, his erratic and subtle brainwaves made strange designs across the big green eye of the EEG monitor. The same doctor who told my mother that her husband was no longer among the living also informed her, on the very same day, that she was pregnant. Nor was this the only poignant coincidence in the lives of my parents. Both of them belonged to wealthy families from Aix-en-Provence in southern France. However, their first meeting took place not in the old country but in the new, at the American university they each happened to be attending. And so two neighbors crossed a cold ocean to come together in a mandatory science course. When they compared notes on their common backgrounds, they knew it was destiny at work. They fell in love with each other and with their new homeland. The couple later moved into a rich and prestigious suburb (which I will decline to mention by name or state, since I still reside there and, for reasons that will eventually become apparent, must do so discreetly). For years the couple lived in contentment, and then my immediate male forbear died just in time for fatherhood, becoming the appropriate parent for his son-to-be.

Offspring of the dead.

But surely, one might protest, I was born of a living mother; surely upon arrival in this world I turned and gazed into a pair of glossy maternal eyes. Not so, as I think is evident from my earlier conversation with dear Aunt T. Widowed and pregnant, my mother had fled back to Aix, to the comfort of family estates and secluded living. But more on this in a moment. Meanwhile I can no longer suppress the urge to say a few things about my ancestral hometown.

Aix-en-Provence, where I was born but never lived, has many personal, though necessarily second-hand associations for me.

However, it is not just a connection between Aix and my own life that maintains such a powerful grip on my imagination, a lifelong *idée fixe* which actually has more to do with a few unrelated facts in the history of the region. Two pieces of historical data, to be exact. Separate centuries, indeed epochs, play host to these data, and they likewise exist in entirely different realms of mood, worlds apart in implication. Nevertheless, from a certain point of view they can impress one as inseparable opposites. The first one is as follows: in the seventeenth century there occurred the spiritual possession by divers demons of the nuns belonging to the Ursuline convent at Aix. Excommunication was soon in coming for the tragic sisters, who had been seduced into assorted blasphemies by the like of Grésil, Sonnillon, and Vérin. De Plancy's *Dictionnaire infernal* respectively characterizes these demons, in the words of an unknown translator, as "the one who glistens horribly like a rainbow of insects; the one who quivers in a horrible manner; and the one who moves with a particular creeping motion." There also exist engravings of these kinetically and chromatically weird beings, unfortunately static and in black and white. Can you believe it? What people are these – so stupid and profound – that they could devote themselves to such nonsense? Who can fathom the science of superstition? (For, as an evil poet once scribbled, superstition is the reservoir of all truths.) This, then, is one side of my imaginary Aix. The other side, and the second historical datum I offer, is simply the birth in 1839 of Aix's most prominent citizen: Cézanne. His figure haunts the landscape of my brain, wandering about the Provençal countryside in search of his pretty pictures.

These, then, are the two aspects of my personal Aix. Together they fuse into a single image, as grotesque and coherent as a pantheon of gargoyles amid the splendor of a medieval church.

Such was the world to which my mother re-emigrated some decades ago, this Notre Dame world of horror and beauty. It's no wonder that she was seduced into the society of those beautiful strangers, who promised her an escape from the world of mortality where shock and suffering had taken over, driving her into exile. I understood from Aunt T. that it all began at a summer party on the estate grounds of Ambroise and Paulette Valraux. The Enchanted Wood, as this place was known to the *hautes classes* in the vicinity. The evening of the party was as perfectly temperate as the atmosphere of dreams, which one rarely notices to be either sultry or frigid. Lanterns were hung high up in the lindens, guide-lights leading to a heard-about heaven. A band played.

It was a mixed crowd at the party. And as usual there were

present a few persons whom nobody seemed to know, exotic strangers whose elegance was their invitation. Aunt T. did not pay much attention to them at the time, and her account is rather sketchy. One of them danced with my mother, having no trouble coaxing the widow out of social retirement. Another with labyrinthine eyes whispered to her by the trees. Alliances were formed that night, promises made. Afterward my mother began going out on her own to rendezvous after sundown. Then she stopped coming home. Térèse – nurse, confidante, and personal maid whom my mother had brought back with her from America – was hurt and confused by the cold snubs she had lately received from her mistress. My mother's family was elaborately reticent about the meaning of her recent behavior. ("And in her condition, *mon Dieu!*") Nobody knew what measures to take. Then some of the servants reported seeing a pale, pregnant woman lurking outside the house after dark.

Finally a priest was taken into the family's confidence. He suggested a course of action which no one questioned, not even Térèse. They lay in wait for my mother, righteous soulhunters. They followed her drifting form as it returned to the mausoleum when daybreak was imminent. They removed the great stone lid of the sarcophagus and found her inside. *"Diabolique,"* one of them exclaimed. There was some question about how many times and in what places she should be impaled. In the end they pinned her heart with a single spike to the velvet bed on which she lay. But what to do about the child? What would it be like? A holy soldier of the living or a monster of the dead. (Neither, you fools!) Fortunately or unfortunately, I've never been sure which, Térèse was with them and rendered their speculations academic. Reaching into the bloodied matrix, she helped me to be born. I was now heir to the family fortune, and Térèse took me back to America. She was extremely resourceful in this regard, arranging with a sympathetic and avaricious lawyer to become the trustee of my estate. This required a little magic act with identities. It required that Térèse, for reasons of her own which I've never questioned, be promoted from my mother's maid to her posthumous sister. And so my Aunt T. was christened, born in the same year as I.

Naturally all this leads to the story of my life, which has no more life in it than story. It's not for the cinema, it is not for novels; it wouldn't even fill out a single lyric of modest length. It might make a piece of modern music: a slow, throbbing drone like the lethargic pumping of a premature heart. Best of all, though, would be the depiction of my life story as an abstract painting: a twilight world, indistinct around the edges and without center or focus; a bridge without banks, tunnel without openings; a crepuscular existence pure and simple. No heaven or hell, only a quiet haven between life's hysteria and death's tenacious darkness. (And you know, what I most loved about twilight is the sense, as one looks down the dimming west, not that it is some fleeting transitional moment, but that there's actually nothing before or after it: *that that's all there is.*) My life never had a beginning, so naturally I thought it would never end. Naturally, I was wrong.

Well, and what was the answer to those questions hastily put by the monsters who stalked my mother? Was my nature to be souled humanness or soulless vampirism? The answer: none of the above. I existed between two worlds and had little claim upon the assets or liabilities of either. Neither living nor dead, unalive or undead, not having anything to do with such tedious polarities, such tiresome opposites, which ultimately are no more different from each other than a pair of imbecilic monozygotes. I said no to life and death. No, Mr. Springbud. No, Mr. Worm. Without ever saying hello or goodbye, I merely avoided their company, scorned their gaudy invitations.

Of course, in the beginning Aunt T. tried to care for me as if I were a normal child. (Incidentally, I can perfectly recall every moment of my life from birth, for my existence took the form of one seamless moment, without forgettable yesterdays or expectant tomorrows). She tried to give me normal food, which I always regurgitated. Later she prepared for me a sort of puréed meat, which I ingested and digested, though it never became a habit. And I never asked her what was actually in that preparation, for Aunt T. wasn't afraid to use money, and I knew what money could buy in the way of unusual food for an unusual infant. I suppose I did become accustomed to similar nourishment while growing within my mother's womb, feeding on a potpourri of blood types contributed by the citizens of Aix. But my appetite was never very strong for physical food.

Stronger by far was my hunger for a kind of transcendental fare, a feasting of the mind and soul: the astral banquet of Art. There I fed. And I had quite a few master chefs to plan the menu. Though we lived in exile from the world, Aunt T. did not overlook my education. For purposes of appearance and legality, I have earned diplomas from some of the finest private schools in the world. (These, too, money can buy.) But my real education was even more private than that. Tutorial geniuses were well paid to visit our home, only too glad to teach an invalid child of nonetheless exceptional promise.

Through personal instruction I scanned the arts and sciences. Yes, I learned to quote my French poets,

> *Gaunt immortality in black and gold,*
> *Wreathed consoler hideous to behold.*
> *The beautiful lie of a mother's womb,*
> *The pious trick – for it is the tomb!*

but mostly in translation, for something kept me from ever attaining more than a beginner's facility in that foreign tongue. I did master, however, the complete grammar, every dialect and idiom of the French *eye*. I could read the inner world of Redon (who was almost born an American) – his *grand isolé* paradise of black. I could effortlessly comprehend the outer world of Manet and the Impressionists – that secret language of light. And I could decipher the impossible worlds of the surrealists – those twisted arcades where brilliant shadows are sewn to the rotting flesh of rainbows.

I remember in particular a man by the name of Raymond, who taught me the rudimentary skills of the artist in oils. I recollect vividly showing him a study I had done of that sacred phenomenon I witnessed each sundown. Most of all I recall the look in his eyes, as if they beheld the rising of a curtain upon some terribly involved outrage. He abstractedly adjusted his delicate spectacles, wobbling them around on the bridge of his nose. His gaze shifted from the canvas to me and back again. His only comment was: "The shapes, the colors are not supposed to lose themselves that way. Something . . . no, impossible." Then he asked to be permitted use of the bathroom facilities. At first I thought this gesture was meant as a symbolic appraisal of my work. But he was quite in earnest and all I could do was give him directions to the nearest chamber of convenience in a voice of equal seriousness. He walked out of the room with the first two fingers of his right hand pressing upon the pulse in his left wrist. And he never came back.

Such is a thumbnail sketch of my half-toned existence: twilight after twilight after twilight. And in all that blur of time I but occasionally, and then briefly, wondered if I too possessed the same potential for immortality as my undead mother before her life was aborted and I was born. It is not a question that really bothers one who exists beyond, below, above, between – triumphantly *outside* – the clashing worlds of human fathers and enchanted mothers.

I did wonder, though, how I would explain, that is *conceal*, my unnatural mode of being from my visiting relatives. Despite the hostility I showed toward them in front of Aunt T., I actually desired that they should take a good report of me back to the real world, if only to keep it away from my own world in the future. For days previous to their arrival, I came to think of myself as a certain stock character in Gothic stories: the stranger in a strange castle of a house, that shadowy figure whom the hero travels over long distances to encounter, a dark soul hiding his horrors. In short, a medieval geek perpetrating strange deeds in secret sanctums. I expected they would soon have the proper image of me as all impotence and no impetus. And that would be that.

But never did I anticipate being called upon to face the almost forgotten realities of vampirism – the taint beneath the paint of the family portrait.

III

The Duval family, and unmarried sister, were arriving on a night flight which we would meet at the airport. Aunt T. thought this would suit me fine, considering my tendency to sleep most of the day and arise with the setting sun. But at the last minute I suffered an acute seizure of stage fright. "The *crowds*," I appealed to Aunt T. She knew that crowds were the world's most powerful talisman against me, as if it had needed any at all. She understood that I would not be able to serve on the welcoming committee, and Rops' younger brother Gerald, a good seventy-five if he was a day, drove her to the airport alone. Yes, I promised Aunt T., I would be sociable and come out to meet everyone as soon as I saw the lights of the big black car floating up our private drive.

But I wasn't and I didn't. I took to my room and drowsed before a television with the sound turned off. As the colors danced in the dark, I submitted more and more to an anti-social sleepiness. Finally I instructed Rops, by way of the estate-wide intercom, to inform Aunt T. and company that I wasn't feeling very well and needed to rest. This, I figured, would be in keeping with the façade of a harmless valetudinarian, and a perfectly normal one at that. A night-sleeper. Very good, I could hear them saying to their souls. And then, I swear, I actually turned off the television and slept real sleep in real darkness.

But things became less real at some point deep into the night. I must have left the intercom open, for I heard little metallic voices emanating from that little metallic square on my bedroom wall. In my state of quasi-somnolence it never occurred to me that I could simply get out of bed and make the voices go away by switching off that terrible box. And terrible it indeed seemed. The voices spoke a foreign language, but it wasn't French, as one might have suspected. Something more foreign than that. Perhaps a cross between a madman talking in his sleep and the sonar screech of a bat. I heard the voices chattering and chattering with each other until I fell soundly asleep once more. And their dialogue had ended before I awoke, for the first time in my life, to the bright eyes of morning.

The house was quiet. Even the servants seemed to have duties that kept them soundless and invisible. I took advantage of my wakefulness at that early hour and prowled unnoticed about the old place, figuring everyone else was still in bed after their long and somewhat noisy night. The four rooms Aunt T. had set aside for our guests all had their big panelled doors closed: a room for the mama and papa, two others close by for the kids, and a chilly chamber at the end of the hall for the maiden sister. I paused a moment outside each room and listened for the revealing songs of slumber, hoping to know my relations better by their snores and whistles and monosyllables grunted between breaths. But they made none of the usual racket. They hardly made any sounds at all, though they echoed one another in making a certain noise that seemed to issue from the same cavity. It was a kind of weird wheeze, a panting from the back of the throat, the hacking of a tubercular demon. Having had an earful of strange cacophonies the night before, I soon abandoned my eavesdropping without regret.

I spent the day in the library, whose high windows I noticed were designed to allow a maximum of natural reading light. However, I drew the drapes on them and kept to the shadows, finding morning sunshine not everything it was said to be. But it was difficult to get much reading done. Any moment I expected to hear foreign footsteps descending the doubled-winged staircase, crossing the black and white marble chessboard of the front hall, taking over the house. Nevertheless, despite my expectations, and to my increasing sense of unease, the family never appeared.

Twilight came and still no mama and papa, no sleepy-eyed son or daughter, no demure sister remarking with astonishment at the inordinate length of her beauty sleep. And no Aunt T., either. They must've had quite a time the night before, I thought. But I didn't mind being alone with the twilight. I undraped the three west windows, each of them a canvas depicting the same scene in the sky. My private *Salon d'Automne*.

It was an unusual sunset. Having sat behind opaque drapery all day, I had not realized that a storm was pushing in and that much of the sky was the precise shade of old suits of armor one finds in museums. At the same time, patches of brilliance engaged in a territorial dispute with the oncoming onyx of the storm. Light and darkness mingled in strange ways both above and below. Shadows and sunshine washed together, streaking the landscape with an unearthly study of glare and gloom. Bright clouds and black folded into each other in a no-man's land of the sky. The autumn trees took on the appearance of sculptures formed in a dream, their leaden-colored trunks and branches and iron-red leaves all locked in an infinite and unliving moment, unnaturally timeless. The gray lake slowly tossed and tumbled in a dead sleep, nudging unconsciously against its breakwall of numb stone. A scene of contradiction and ambivalence, a tragicomedic haze over all. A land of perfect twilight.

I was in exaltation: finally the twilight had come down to earth, and to me. I had to go out into this rare atmosphere, I had no choice. I left the house and walked to the lake and stood on the slope of stiff grass which led down to it. I gazed up through the trees at the opposing tones of the sky. I kept my hands in my pockets and touched nothing, except with my eyes.

Not until an hour or more had elapsed did I think of returning home. It was dark by then, though I don't recall the passing of the twilight into evening, for twilight suffers no ostentatious finales. There were no stars visible, the storm clouds having moved in and wrapped up the sky. They began sending out tentative drops of rain. Thunder mumbled above and I was forced back to the house, cheated once again by the night.

In the front hall I called out names in the form of questions. Aunt T.? Rops? Gerald? M. Duval? Madame? Everything was silence. Where was everyone? I wondered. They couldn't still be asleep. I passed from room to room and found no signs of occupation. A day of dust was upon all surfaces. Where were the domestics? At last I opened the double doors to the dining room. Was I late for the supper Aunt T. had planned to honor our visiting family?

It appeared so. But if Aunt T. sometimes had me consume the forbidden fruit of flesh and blood, it was never directly from the branches, never the sap taken warm from the tree of life itself. Yet here were spread the remains of just such a feast. It was the ravaged body of Aunt T., though they'd barely left enough on her bones for identification. The thick white linen was clotted like an unwrapped bandage. "Rops!" I shouted. "Gerald, somebody!" But I knew the servants were no longer in the house, that I was alone.

Not quite alone, of course. This soon became apparent to my twilight brain as it dipped its way into total darkness. I was in the company of five black shapes which stuck to the walls and soon began flowing along their surface. One of them detached itself and moved toward me, a weightless mass which felt icy when I tried to sweep it away and put my hand right through the thing. Another followed, unhinging itself from a doorway where it hung down. A third left a blanched scar upon the wallpaper where it clung like a slug, pushing itself off to join the attack. Then came the others descending from the ceiling, dropping onto me as I stumbled in circles and flailed my arms. I ran from the room but the things had me closely surrounded. They guided my flight, heading me down hallways and up staircases. Finally they cornered me in a small room, a dusty little place I had not been in for years. Colored animals frolicked upon the walls, blue bears and yellow rabbits. Miniature furniture was draped with graying sheets. I hid beneath a tiny elevated crib with ivory bars. But they found me and closed in.

They were not driven by hunger, for they had already feasted. They were not frenzied with a murderer's bloodlust, for they were cautious and methodical. This was simply a family reunion, a sentimental gathering. Now I understood how the Duvals could afford to be *sans préjugé*. They were worse than I, who was only a half-breed, hybrid, a mere mulatto of the soul: neither a blood-warm human nor a blood-drawing devil. But they – who came from an Aix on the map – were the purebreds of the family.

And they drained my body dry.

IV

When I regained awareness once more, it was still dark and there was a great deal of dust in my throat. Not actually dust, of course, but a strange dryness I had never before experienced. And there was another new experience: hunger. I felt as if there were a chasm of infinite depth within me, a great abyss which needed to be filled – flooded with oceans of blood. I was one of them now, reborn into a hungry death. Everything I had shunned in my impossible, blasphemous ambition to avoid living and dying, I now had become. A sallow, ravenous thing. A beast with a hundred stirring hungers. André of the graveyards.

The five of them had each drunk from my body by way of five separate fountains. But the wounds had nearly sealed by the time I awoke in the blackness, owing to the miraculous healing capabilities of the dead. The upper floors were all in shadow now, and I made my way toward the light coming from downstairs. An impressionistic glow illuminated the wooden banister at the top of the stairway, where I emerged from the darkness of the second floor, and this sight inspired in me a terrible ache of emotion I'd never known before: a feeling of loss, though of nothing I could specifically name, as if somehow the deprivation lay in my future.

As I descended the stairs I saw that they were already waiting to meet me, standing silently upon the black and white squares of the front hall. Papa the king, mama the queen, the boy a knight, the girl a dark little pawn, and a bitchy maiden bishop standing behind. And now they had my house, my castle, to complete the pieces on their side. On mine there was nothing.

"Devils," I screamed, leaning hard upon the staircase rail. "Devils," I repeated, but they still appeared horribly undistressed, perhaps uncomprehending of my outburst. "*Diables,*" I reiterated in their own loathsome tongue.

But neither was French their true language, as I found out when they began speaking among themselves. I covered my ears, trying to smother their voices. They had a language all their own, a style of speech well-suited to dead vocal organs. The words were breathless, shapeless rattlings in the back of their throats, parched scrapings at the mausoleum portal. Arid gasps and dry gurgles were their dialects. These grating intonations were especially disturbing as they emanated from the mouths of things that had at least the form of human beings. But worst of all was my realization that I understood perfectly well what they were saying.

The boy stepped forward, pointing at me while looking back and speaking to his father. It was the opinion of this wine-eyed and rose-lipped youth that I should have suffered the same end as Aunt T. With an authoritative impatience the father told the boy that I was to serve as a sort of tour guide through this strange new land, a native who could keep them out of such difficulties as foreign visitors sometimes get into. Besides, he grotesquely concluded, *I was one of the family.* The boy was incensed and coughed out an incredibly foul characterization of his father. The things he said could only have been conveyed by that queer hacking patois, which suggested feelings and relationships of a nature incomprehensible outside of the world it mirrors with disgusting perfection. It is the discourse of hell on the subject of sin.

An argument ensued, and the father's composure turned to an infernal rage. He finally subdued his son with bizarre threats that have no counterparts in the language of ordinary malevolence. After the boy was silenced he turned to his aunt, seemingly for comfort. This woman of chalky cheeks and sunken eyes touched the boy's shoulder and easily drew him toward her with a single finger, guiding his body as if it were a balloon, weightless and toy-like. They spoke in sullen whispers, using a personal form of address that hinted at a long-standing and unthinkable allegiance between them.

Apparently aroused by this scene, the daughter now stepped forward and used this same mode of address to get my attention. Her mother abruptly gagged out a single syllable at her. What she called her daughter might possibly be imagined, but only with reference to the lowliest sectors of the human world. Their own words, their choking rasps, carried the dissonant overtones of another world altogether. Each perverse utterance was a rioting opera of evil, a choir shrieking psalms of intricate blasphemy and enigmatic lust.

"I will not become one of you," I *thought* I screamed at them. But the sound of my voice was already so much like theirs that the words had exactly the opposite meaning I intended. The family suddenly ceased bickering among themselves. My outburst had consolidated them. Each mouth, cluttered with uneven teeth like a village cemetery overcrowded with battered gravestones, opened and smiled. The expression on their faces told me something about my own. They could see my growing hunger, see deep down into the dusty catacomb of my throat which cried out to be anointed with bloody nourishment. They knew my weakness.

Yes, they could stay in my house. (*Famished.*)

Yes, I could make arrangements to cover up the disappearance of the servants, for I am a wealthy man and know what money can buy. (*Please, my family, I'm famished.*)

Yes, their safety could be insured and their permanent asylum perfectly feasible. (*Please, I'm famishing to dust.*)

Yes, yes, yes. I agreed to everything; everything would be taken care of. (*To dust!*)

But first I begged them, for heaven's sake, to let me go out into the night.

Night, night, night, night. Night, night, night.

Now twilight is an alarm, a noxious tocsin which rouses me to an
endless eve. There is a sound in my new language for that
transitory time of day preceding the dark hours. The sound
clusters together curious shades of meaning and shadowy impressions, none of which belong to my former conception of an abstract
paradise: the true garden of unearthly delights. The new twilight is
a violater, desecrator, stealthy graverobber; death-bell, life-knell,
curtain-raiser; banshee, siren, howling she-wolf. And the old
twilight is dead. I am even learning to despise it, just as I am
learning to love my eternal life and eternal death. Nevertheless, I
wish them well who would attempt to destroy my precarious
immortality, for my rebirth has taught me the torment of beginnings, while the idea of endings has assumed in my thoughts a
tranquil significance. And I cannot deny those who would avenge
the exsanguinated souls of my past and future. Yes, past and
future. Endings and beginnings. In brief, Time now exists,
measured like a perpetual holiday consisting only of midnight
revels. I once had an old family from an old world, and now I have
new ones. A new life, a new world. And this world is no longer one
where I can languidly gaze upon rosy sunsets, but another in
which I must fiercely draw a full-bodied blood from the night.

Night . . . after night . . . after night.

THE TROUBLES OF
DR. THOSS

When Alb Indys first heard the name of Dr. Thoss, he had some difficulty locating its speaker, or even discerning how many voices had spoken it. Initially the words seemed to emanate from an old radio in another apartment, for Alb Indys had no such device of his own. But he finally realized that this name had been uttered, in a rather harsh voice, just outside the corner window, and only window, of his room. After spending the night, not unusually, walking the floor or slumping wide-eyed in his only chair, he had been in bed since morning. Now, at mid-afternoon, he remained unslept and was still attired in pale gray pajamas. Bolstered by huge pillows, he was sitting up against the headboard. Upon his lap rested a drawing book filled with stiff sheets of paper, very white. A bottle of black ink was in reach on the sidetable next to his bed, and a shapely black pen with a sharp silvery nib was held tightly in his right hand. That Alb Indys was at that moment busy with a pen-and-ink rendering of the window, along with the empty chair beside it, was perhaps the chief reason that, very vaguely, he had overheard the words spoken beyond it.

He gave the drawing book a somewhat rough toss farther down the bed, where it fell against a lump swelling in the blankets: more than likely the creation of a wadded pair of trousers or an old shirt, possibly both, given the habits of Alb Indys. The window was partly open and, walking over to it without steadiness, he discreetly pushed it out a little more. They should have been just below the window, those speakers whom Alb Indys wished would go on speaking. He remembered hearing a voice say, "It's going to be the end of someone's troubles," or words to that effect, with the name of Dr. Thoss figuring in the discussion. The name was unfamiliar to him and gave rise to an enthusiasm that had much less to do with hope, which Alb Indys tried to keep at a minimum, than it did with pure nervous expectancy: the anticipation of new and unknown possibilities. But the talking had stopped, and just as he was becoming interested in this doctor. Where were they, those two? He was sure there were two, though there might have been a third. How could so many have simply vanished?

When he fully extended the window casement, Alb Indys saw no one on the street. He stretched forward for a better look and strands of blond hair, almost white, fell across his face, and then by a sudden salty breeze were blown back, thin and loose. It was not a very brilliant day, not one of excess activity. A few silhouettes and shadows maneuvered in the dimness on the other side of unreflecting windows. The stones of the street, so sparkling and picturesque for those enjoying a holiday here, succumbed to dullness out of season. Alb Indys fixed on one of them which looked dislodged in the pavement, imagining he heard it working itself free, creaking around in its stony cradle. But the noise was that of metal hinges squeaking somewhere in the wind. He quickly found them, his hearing made keen by insomnia. They were attached to a wooden sign hung outside the uppermost window of an old building. The structure ascended in peaks and slants and ledges piled over ledges into the gray sky, until at its highest, turreted point swung the sign. Alb Indys could never clearly make out its four capital letters so far above, though he had gazed up at them a thousand times. (And how often it seemed that something gazed back at him from that high window.) But a radio station need not be a visual presence in an old resort town, only an aural landmark, a voice for vacationers signalling the "sound beside the sea."

Alb Indys closed the window and returned to his thin-lined representation of it. Though he began the picture in the middle of a sleepless night, he did not copy the constellations beyond the window panes, keeping the drawing unmarred by any artistic suggestion of those star-filled hours. Nothing was in the window but the pure whiteness of the page, the pale abyss of unshut eyes. After making a few more marks on the picture, completing it, he signed his work very neatly in the lower right-hand corner. This page would later be put in one of the large portfolios which lay stacked upon a desk across the room.

What else was contained in these portfolios? Two sorts of things, two types of artwork which between them described the nature and limits of Alb Indys's pictorial talents. The first type included such scenes as the artist had recently executed: images drawn from his immediate surroundings, an immediacy that extended no farther than the sights observable in his own room. This was not his first study of the window, the subject he most often returned to and always in the same plain style. Sometimes he sat in the chair beside the window and portrayed his bed, lumpy and unmade, with occasional attention to the sidetable (noting each nick that blemished its original off-white surface) and the undecorated lamp which stood upon it (recording each chip that pocked its glassy smoothness). The desk-side of the room also received its fair share of treatments: the wall at that end of the room was the most tempting of the four, in itself a subtle canvas that had been painted and pitted and painted again, coated and repeatedly scraped of infinitesimal, seatown organisms, leaving it shrivelled and pasty and incurably damp. No pictures were hung to patch either this or any other wall of the room, though a tall bookcase obscured who knows what unseen worlds behind it. Transitory compositions – a flung shoe leaning toe-up against a bedpost, a dropped glove which hazard endowed with a pointing index finger – formed the remaining examples of this first type of drawing in which the artist indulged.

And the second type? Was it more interesting than the first? Perhaps, though not where the imagination is concerned; because Alb Indys had none whatever, or at least none that he could readily make use of. Whenever he tried to form a picture of something, anything, in his imagination, all he saw was a blank: a new page with nothing on it, or perhaps a very old page that had retained the nothingness of its original mintage. Once he nearly had a vision of something, a few specks flying across a fuzzy background of white snow in a white sky – and there was a garbled voice which he had not intentionally conjured. But it all fizzled out after a few seconds into a silent stretch of emptiness. This artistic handicap, however, was anything but a frustration or a disappointment to Alb Indys. He did not often test the powers of his imagination, for he somehow knew that there was as much to be lost as gained in doing so. In any case, there were other ways to make a picture, and we have already seen one of them, not a very unusual one. Here now is another.

This second method was a type of artistic forgery, though it might just as well be described by the term which Alb Indys himself preferred – collaboration. And who were his collaborators? In many instances, there was no way of knowing: anonymous penmen, mostly, of illustrations in very old books and periodicals, ones entirely forgotten. His shelves were full of them, dark and massive, their worn covers incredibly tender to the touch. French, Flemish, German, Swedish, Russian, Polish, any cultural source of published material would do as long as its pictures spoke the language of dark lines and vacant spaces. In fact, the more disparate the origins of these images, the better they served his purpose: because Alb Indys liked to take a century-old engraving of a subarctic landscape, studiously plagiarize its manner of suggesting icy mountains and a vast stretch of frozen whiteness; then select an equally old depiction of a cathedral in a town he had never heard of, painstakingly transport it stone by stone deep into the glacial wasteland; and finally, from still older pages, transcribe with all possible fidelity an unknown artist's conception of assorted devils and demons, making them dance down from the ice-mad mountains and invade the helpless cathedral. This was the typical process and product of his work with collaborators, who Alb Indys thought were actually in collaboration with one another and not with him at all. He was merely the inheritor of lost images; he was their resurrector, their invoker, their medium, and under his careful eye and steady hand there took place a mingling of artistic forms, their disparate anatomies tumbling out of the years to create the nightmare of his art. And it seemed perfectly natural to Alb Indys that, like everything else, even the most inviolable or obscure phenomena eventually find their way from good dreams into bad, or from bad dreams into the wholly abysmal.

At the moment he was working on a new collaboration, but all he had as yet was its barest beginnings: a sickle-shaped scar of moon, a common enough image which Alb Indys wanted to remove from one black sky and fix in another. Its relocation could have provided him with a way to waste the rest of the afternoon. However, the commotion outside the window earlier had upset the pace of his day and given it a new rhythm. Almost any event could do this to an insomniac's delicate routine, so as yet there was no reason to contemplate the exceptional. An appearance by his landlord, whether rent-hungry or merely casual, sometimes altered his course for weeks to come. Before, his thoughts were of nothing, genuinely; but now old preoccupations had become stirred up and sharpened in his awareness. Was there anything special about this doctor, this Thoss? Alb Indys could not help wondering. Was he like the others, or was he a doctor who would hear, really hear you? Not one had yet heard him, not one had offered him a remedy worth the name.

If there was a new doctor who had set up practice in the seaside town, Alb Indys could encounter none of the man's cures, either real or pretended, by staying at home. He needed to find some things out for himself, make inquiries, get out into the world. When was the last time he had had a good meal? Perhaps that would be a way to begin, and afterward he could take it from there. One could always get acceptable food at the place right around the corner, no reason to fear they were going to give him poison! Good, he thought. And after he ate he might have a nice walk for himself, gain some advantage from the fresh air and scenery of this town. After all, many people came here for vaguely therapeutic reasons, believing there were medicines dispensed by the very mood of the town's quaint streets and its sea-licked landscape. It might even happen that his maladies would disappear of their own accord, leaving him with no need for this doctor, this Thoss.

He dressed himself in dark, heavy clothes and made sure to lock the door behind him. But he had forgot to shut the window properly and a breeze edged in, disturbing the pages of the drawing book on his bed, fluttering them against that lump in the blankets.

At the restaurant Alb Indys found a small table in a quiet, comfortable corner, where he sat facing the rear wall and an empty chair. He ordered something to eat from a large board, nicely lettered, which was propped up on an easel at the front of the room. Because of his distance from this board, and a certain atmospheric dimness of the place, only a single word in bold letters was easily readable.

"Fish," he had said.

"Fish of the day?"

"Yes," he had answered, mechanically and without a trace of the anticipation he thought he might feel.

But despite his enduring lack of interest in daily meals, he did not regret this outing. A little lamp attached to the wall next to him, its light muffled by a grayish shade of some coarse fabric, created a slightly nocturnal ambiance. If he kept his gaze fixed upon a certain knotty plank in the wall, at a point just above the empty chair opposite him, everything peripheral to his left eye's vision faded into a dark fog, while the little lamp to his right cast an island of illumination upon the table before him, instilling the illusion that he was lost in some glowing and isolated corner of an endless night. But he could not sustain the illusion: the state of mild delight into which he fooled himself faded, while shapes around him sharpened.

Yet without this sharpening would he have noticed the newspaper someone had left behind on the seat of that empty chair? Messily bunched and repeatedly creased, it was still a welcome sight to his eyes. At this point he needed something of this kind, something to peruse in the rich glow of the lamp that was guiding him through an artificial night, preparing him for the authentic one in which he would have to face the unpredictable verdict which either terminated or terribly elongated his wakefulness. He reached for the pages, rustled them, unfolded and refolded them like an arrangement of bedcovers. His eyes followed dark letters across ruddy paper, and at last his mind was out of its terrible school for a while. When the food arrived he made way for the plate, building a nest of print and pictures around it: advertisements for the town's shops and businesses, weather forecasts, happenings on the west shore, and a feature article entitled "THE REAL STORY OF DR. THOSS – Local Legend Revived." A brief note explained that the article, written some years ago, was periodically reprinted when interest in the subject seemed, for one reason or another, newly aroused. Alb Indys paused over his meal for a moment and smiled, feeling disappointed and slightly relieved at the same time. It now appeared that he had been inspired by a misunderstanding, by imaginary consultations with a legendary doctor and his fictitious cures.

Who, then? What? When and why? His name, according to the article, may indeed have been that of a real doctor, one who lived either in the distant past or whose renown was imported, by recollection and rumor, from a distant place. A number of people associated him with the following vague but poignant tragedy: an excellent physician, and a most respected figure in the community, was psychically deranged one night by some incident of indefinite character; afterward he continued to make use of his training in physic but in a wholly new fashion, in a different key altogether from that of his former practice. This went on for some time before, violently, he was stopped. Decapitation, drowning in the nearby sea, or both were the prevailing conclusions to the real doctor's legend. Of course, the particulars vary, as do those of a second, and more widely circulated, version.

This variant Dr. Thoss was a recluse of the witch-days, less a doctor of medicine than one deeply schooled at forbidden universities of the supernatural. Or was he naturally a very wise man who was simply misunderstood? Histories of the period are unhelpful in resolving such questions. No definite misbehavior is attributed to him, except perhaps that of keeping an unpleasant little companion. The creature, according to most who know *this* Thossian legend, is said to possess the following traits: it is smallish, "no bigger than a man's head"; shrivelled and rotting, as if with disease or decomposition; speaks in a rough voice; and moves about by means of numerous appendages of special qualities, called "miracle claws" by some. There was good reason, the article went on, to put this abbreviated marvel at the center of this legend, for the creature may not have been merely a diabolical companion of Dr. Thoss but the mysterious doctor himself. Was his tale, then, a cautionary one, illustrating what happened to those who, either from evil or benevolent motives, got "into trouble" with the supernatural? Or was Dr. Thoss *itself* intended to serve as no more than an agent of spectral hideousness, a bogie for children and the secluded campfire? Ultimately the point of the legend is unclear, the article asserted, beyond evoking a certain uneasiness in those of superactive imagination.

But an even greater obscurity surrounded one last morsel of lore concerning who the doctor was and what he was about. It related to the way his name had come to be employed by certain people and under certain circumstances. Not the place for a scholarly inquest into regional expressions, the article merely cited an example, one that no doubt was already familiar to many of the newspaper's readers. This particular usage was based on the idea – and the following verb must be stressed – of "*feeding* one's troubles to the sea (or 'wind') and Dr. Thoss," as if this figure – whatever its anatomical or metaphysical identity – were some kind of eater of others' suffering. A concluding note invited readers to submit whatever smatterings they could to enlarge upon this tiny daub of local color.

End of the real story of Dr. Thoss.

Alb Indys had read the article with interest and appetite, more than he ever hoped to have, and he now pushed both crumpled newspaper and decimated meal away from him, sitting for a moment in blurry reflection on both. The surface of the old table, jaundiced by the little lamp above it, somehow seemed to be decaying in its grain, dissolving into a putrid haze. Possibly his attention had simply wandered too far when he heard, or thought he heard, a strange utterance. And it was delivered in a distorted, dry-throated voice, as though transmitted by garbled shortwave. "Yes, my name is Thoss," the voice had said. "I am a doctor."

"Excuse me, will there be anything else you'd like to order?"

Shaken back to life, Alb Indys declined further service, paid his bill, and left. On his way out, for no defensible reason, he scrutinized every face in the room. But none of them could have said it, he assured himself.

In any case, the doctor was now exposed as only a phantasm of local superstition. Or was he? To be perfectly honest about it, Alb

Indys had to credit the nonexistent healer with some part of his present well-being. How he had eaten, and every bit! True, it was not much of a day – the town was a tomb and the sky its vault – but for him a secret sun was glowing somewhere, he could feel it. And there were hours remaining before it had to set, hours. He walked to the end of the street where it dipped down a steep hill and the sidewalk ended in a flight of old stone stairs that had curving grins sliced into them. He continued walking to the edge of town, and then down a narrow road which led to one of the few places he could abide outside his own room.

Alb Indys approached the old church from the graveyard side and, as he closed in, only the great hexagonal peak, hornlike, could be seen projecting above the brown-leafed trees. Surrounding the graveyard was a barrier of thin black bars, with a thicker bar connecting them through the middle, spinelike. There was no gate, and the road he was on freely entered the church grounds. To his left and right were headstones and monuments, little marble slabs and golden plaques. They formed a forest of memorials, clumps of crosses and groves of gravestones. Some of them were very small and oddly shaped, and so loosened by time that they almost seemed to rock back and forth in the wind. But could one of them have just now fallen down entirely? Something was missing that had been there before, seemingly had sunk or slid away. Alb Indys watched for a moment, then proceeded toward the church. When he reached the edge of the graveyard he turned around, surveying not only the stones themselves but also the spaces between them. And the wind was pulling at his fine pale locks.

Standing in full view of the church, Alb Indys could not resist elevating his gaze to the height of that spire which rose from a square central tower whose four corners put out four lesser points. This great structure – with its dark, cowl-shaped windows and broken roman-numeraled clock – was buttressed by two low-roofed transepts which squatted and slanted on either side of it. Beneath the cloud-filled sky the church was an even shade of grayish white, unblemished by shadows. And from behind the church, where pale scrubby grasses edged toward a steep descent into sand and sea, came the sound of tossing waves, a hissing sound which Alb Indys perceived as somehow dry and electronic.

As always, there was no one else in the church at this time of day (and with hours remaining of it). Everything was very simple inside, very solemn and quiet and serenely lighted. The dark-paned windows along either wall confused all time, bending dawns into twilights, suspending minutes in eternity. Alb Indys slid into a pew at the back and rested his hands at his sides. His eyes were fixed on the distant apse, where everything – pillars, pictures, pulpit – appeared as an unfocused fragment of itself, folded within shadows that seemed to be the creation of dark hours. But his insomnia was not at issue here: suffering and transgressions alike were reprieved in this place that shut out time. He followed each moment as it tried to move past him: each was smothered by the stillness, and he watched them die. "But trouble feeds in the wind and hides in the window," he drowsily said to himself from somewhere inside his now dreaming brain.

Suddenly everything seemed wrong and he wanted to leave, but he could not leave because someone was speaking from the pulpit. Yes, a pulpit in such a large, such an enormous, church would be equipped with its microphone, but then why whisper in such confused language and so rapidly, like a single voice trying to be more? What were the voices saying now? No, he would rather not hear, because now everything was happening that he wished would not happen, and it was so late at night, and with so many hours left to sleep, finally to sleep for hours and hours, he would not be able to get away in time. If he could only move, just turn his head a little. And if he could only get his eyes to open and see what was wrong. The voices kept repeating without fading, multiplying in the fantastically spacious church. Then, with an effort sufficient to move the earth itself, he managed to turn his head just enough to look out a window in the east transept. And without even opening his tightly closed eyelids, he saw what was in the window. But he suddenly awoke for an entirely different reason, because finally he understood what the voices were saying. They said they were a doctor, and their name was—

Alb Indys had to get home, even if all the way there the sound of the sea was hissing behind him like a broken radio, and even if the wind rushed by his ears like breaking waves of air. There was not much daylight left and tonight, of all nights, he did not want to catch anything, did not want to be caught, that is, in the damp and chill of an off-season sundown. What misjudgements he had made that day, what mistakes, there was no question about it. And what a doctor to call upon to treat one's troubles . . .

An eternity of sleeplessness was to be preferred, if those were the dreams sleep had in waiting. Gratefully he would hold on to his old troubles, with the permission of the world, the wind, and the legendary Dr. Thoss.

And when Alb Indys reached his room, he was thinking about a gleaming crescent moon ready to be placed in a new scene, and he was thankful to have some project, any project, to fill the hours of that night. Exhausted, he threw his dark coat in a heap on the floor, then sat down on the bed to remove his shoes. He was holding the second one in his hand when he turned and, for some reason, began to contemplate that lump he had left in the bed-covers. Without reasoning why, he elevated the shoe directly above this shapeless swelling, held it aloft for a few moments, then let it drop straight down. The lump collapsed with a little poof, as if it had been an old hat with no head inside, or a magician's silk scarf that only seemed to have a plump white dove hidden under it. Enough of this for one day, Alb Indys thought sleepily, there was work he could be doing.

But when he picked up the drawing book of stiff clean pages from where he had earlier abandoned it on the bed, he saw that the work he intended to do had, by some miracle, already been done. He looked at the drawing of the window, the drawing he had finished off earlier that day with his meticulous signature. Was it only because he was so tired that he could not recall darkening those window panes and carving that curved scar of moon behind them? Could he have forgotten about scoring that bone-white cicatrix into the flesh of night? But he was holding that particular moon in reserve for one of his "collaborations" and this was *not* one of those. This belonged to that other type of drawing: he only penned, in these, what was enclosed within the four-walled frame of his room, never anything outside it. Then why did he ink in this night and this moon, and with the collaboration of what other artistic hand? If only he were not so drained by chronic insomnia, all those lost dreams hissing in his head, perhaps he could have thought more clearly about it. His dozing brain might even have noticed another change in the picture, for something now squatted in the chair which formerly had been unoccupied. But there was too much sleep to catch up on, and, as the sun went out in the window, Alb Indys shut his eyes languorously and lay down upon his bed.

And he never would have wakened that night, which seemed as white as winter, if it had not been for the noise. The window was lit up by a silvery blade of moon. It brightened the chair, whose two thin arms had other arms overhanging each of them, flexing slowly in the room's stillness. White night, white noise. As if speaking in static, the parched, crackling voice repeatedly said: *I am a doctor.* Then the occupant of the chair hopped gracefully onto the bed with a single thrust of its roundish body, and its claws began their work, delivering the sleeper to his miraculous remedy . . .

It was the landlord who eventually found him, though there was considerable difficulty identifying what lay on the bed. A rumor spread throughout the seaside town about a swift and terrible disease, something that perhaps one of the vacationers had brought in. But no other trouble was reported. Much later, the entire incident was confused by preposterous elaborations, which had the effect of relegating all of its horrors to the doubtful realm of regional legend.

MASQUERADE OF A DEAD SWORD: A TRAGEDIE

When the world uncovers some dark disguise
Embrace the darkness with averted eyes.
Psalms of the Silent

I Faliol's Rescue

No doubt the confusions of carnival night were to blame, in some measure, for many unforeseen incidents. Every violation of routine order was being perpetrated by the carousing mob, their cries of celebration providing the upper voices to a strange droning pedal point which seemed to be sustained by the night itself. Having declared their town an enemy of silence, the citizens of Soldori took to the streets; there they conspired against solitude and, to accompanying gyrations of squealing abandon, sabotaged monotony. Even the duke, a cautious man and one not normally given to those gaudy agendas of his counterparts in Lynnese or Daranzella, was now holding an extravagant masquerade, if only as a strategic concession to the little patch of world under his rule. Of all the inhabitants of the Three Towns, the subjects of the Duke of Soldori – occasionally to the duke's own dismay – were the most loving of amusement. In every quarter of this principality, frolicking celebrants combed the night for a new paradise, and were as likely to find it in a blood-match as in a song. All seemed anxious, even frantic to follow blindly the entire spectrum of diversion, to dawdle about the lines between pain and pleasure, to obscure their vision of both past and future.

So perhaps three well-drunk and boar-faced men seated in a roisterous hostelry could be excused for not recognizing Faliol, whose colors were always red and black. But this man, who had just entered the thickish gloom of that drinking house, was attired in a craze of colors, none of them construed to a pointed effect. One might have described this outfit as motley gone mad. Indeed, perhaps what lay beneath this fool's patchwork were the familiar blacks and reds that no other of the Three Towns – neither those who were dandies, nor those who were sword-whores (however golden their hearts), nor even those who, like Faliol himself, were both – would have dared to parody. But these notorious colors were now buried deep within a rainbow of rags which were tied about the man's arms, legs, and at every other point of his person, seeming to hold him together like torn strips hurriedly applied to the storm-fractured joists of a sagging roof. Before he had closed the door of that cave-like room behind him, the draft rushing in from the street made his ragged livery come alive like a mass of tattered flags flapping in a calamitous wind.

But even had he not been cast as a tatterdemalion, there was still so much else about Faliol that was unlike his former self. His sword, a startling length of blade to be pulled along by this ragman, bobbed about unbuckled at his left side. His dagger, whose sheath bore a mirror of polished metal (which now seemed a relic of more dandified days), was strung loosely behind his left shoulder, ready to fall at any moment. And his hair was trimmed monkishly close to the scalp, leaving little reminder of a gloriously hirsute era. But possibly the greatest alteration, the greatest problem and mystery of Faliol's travesty of his own image, was the presence on his face of a pair of . . . spectacles. And owing that the glass of these spectacles was unevenly blemished, as though murky currents flowed beneath their brittle surface, the eyes behind them were obscured.

Still, there remained any number of signs by which a discerning scrutiny could have identified the celebrated Faliol. For as he moved toward a seat adjacent to the alcove where the booming-voiced trio was ensconsed, he moved with a scornful, somehow involuntary assuredness of which no reversals of fate could completely unburden him. And his boots, though their fine black leather had gone gray with the dust of roads that a zealous equestrian such as Faliol would never have trod, still jangled with a few of those once innumerable silver links from which dangled small, agate-eyed medallions, ones exactly like that larger, onyx-eyed medallion which in other days hung from a silver chain around his lean throat. The significance of this particular ornament was such that Faliol – though often questioned, but never twice by the same inquisitor – avoided revelations of any kind.

Now, however, no medallion of any kind was displayed upon

Faliol's chest; and since he had lost or renounced the inkish eye of onyx, he had acquired two eyes of shadowed glass. Each lens of the spectacles reflected, like twin moons, the glow of the lantern above the place where Faliol seated himself. As if unaware that he was not settled in some cloistered cell of lucubration, he removed from somewhere within his shredded clothes a small book having the words *Psalms of the Silent* written in raised letters upon its soft, worn cover. And the cover was black, while the letters were the red of autumn leaves.

"Faliol, a scholar?" someone whispered in the crowded depths of the room, while another added: "And a scholar of his own grief, so I've heard."

Faliol unfixed the tiny silver clasp and opened the book somewhere toward its middle, where a thin strip of red velvet cloth, one the same shade as the letters upon the cover of the book, marked his place. And if there had been a miniature mirror bound in place of the book's left-hand leaf, Faliol could have seen three thuggish men gazing mutely, not to say thoughtfully, in his direction. Moreover, if there had been a second mirror set at the same angle on the book's right-hand leaf, he could also have noticed a fourth pair of eyes spying on him from the other side of the hostelry's engrimed window panes.

But there were only long, stem-looking letters written – to be precise handwritten, in Faliol's own hand – upon the opposing leaves of the book. Thus Faliol could not have seen either of these parties who, for reasons separate or similar, were observing him. He saw only two pale pages elegantly dappled by the words of somber verses. Then a shadow passed across these pages, and another, and another.

The three men were now standing evenly spaced before Faliol, though he continued to read as if they were not present. He read until the lantern above was extinguished, its stump of tallow snuffed out by the middleman's hugely knuckled stumps of flesh. Clasping his book closed, Faliol replaced it within the rags around his heart and sat perfectly still. The three men seemed to watch in a trance of ugsome hilarity at this slowly and solemnly executed sequence of actions. The face at the windowpanes merely pressed closer to witness what, in its view, was a soundless scene.

Some harsh words appeared to be addressed to the man in rags by the three men standing before him. The first of them splashed some ale in the spectacled face, as did the second man from his enormous tankard. Then more ale – this time expectorated – was received by the victim as the third man's contribution to what became quite a lengthy series of petty torments. But Faliol remained silent and as motionless as possible, thereby expressing an attitude of mind and body which seemed only to provoke further the carnival-mad souls of the three Soldorians. As the moments passed, the men waxed more cruel and their torments more inventive. Finally, they jostled a bloody-mouthed Faliol out of his seat, two of them pinioned him against the planks of the wall, someone snatched his spectacles . . .

Two blue eyes were suddenly revealed: they firmly clenched themselves closed, then reopened as if bursting out of black depths and into the light. Faliol's mouth stretched wide to let out a perfectly silent scream or one beyond human hearing – the scream of a mute under torture. But very soon his features relaxed, while his ragged chest began pumping up and down with an even rhythm.

The one who had taken Faliol's spectacles had turned away and his clumsy fingers were fiddling with delicate silver stems, fumbling with two shadowy lenses that were more precious than he knew. Thus amused and diverted, he did not perceive that Faliol was terrifying both of his companions out of their wits, that they had loosened their grasp on him, and that he had drawn his dagger from its shoulder-sheath.

"Where—" he started to shout to his loutish comrades as they ran bleeding from the hostelry's horror. Then he turned about-face to feel Faliol's sword against his greasy leather doublet. He saw, he must have seen, that the blade was unclean but very sharp; and he must have felt it scrape playfully against the chain-mail vest concealed beneath his doublet's sorry cover. Soon Faliol was lowering his blade until it reached the spot where the vest's protection no longer protected. "Now put them on, that you might see," he quietly instructed the giant with the pair of tiny toy spectacles. "Put . . . them . . . on," he said in a calm, dead voice.

The giant, his lip-licking tongue visibly parched, obeyed the command.

Everyone in the room leaned closer to see the giant in dark spectacles, and so did the well-groomed face at the hostelry window. Most of the men laughed – drunkenly and anonymously – but a few remained silent, if they did not in fact become silent, at this sight. "And a scholar of the wildest folly, too," someone whispered. Faliol himself grinned like a demon, his eyes widening at his work. After a few moments he returned his sword to its sheath, and even so the giant held his transfixed position. Faliol put away his dagger, and the giant did not budge a hair. A hopeless paralytic, he stood with arms hanging limp and thick at his enormous flanks, slightly trembling. The giant's face was extraordinarily pale, his grizzled cheeks like two mounds of snow that had been sown with ashes. Above them, circles of glass gleamed like two black suns.

All laughter had ceased by now, and many turned away from the unwonted spectacle. The giant's meaty lips were opening and closing, very slowly and very much in the manner of a dying fish gasping in the dry air. But the giant, having worn Faliol's own eyes, was not dying in his body: only his mind was a corpse. "The wildest folly," whispered the same voice.

Gently, almost contritely, Faliol removed the spectacles from the face of the grotesque idol, though he waited until he was outside the hostelry before replacing them on his own.

"Sir," called a voice from the shadows of the street. Faliol paused, but only as if considering the atmosphere of the night and not necessarily in response to an unknown accoster. "Please allow me to identify myself with the name Streldone. My messenger spoke with you in Lynnese? Good, that is a blessing. Here is my coach, so that we need not talk in all this confusion," he said, gesturing toward the jerking shadows of that carnival night. And when the coach began moving down streets on the circumference of the festivities, this expensively attired man – though he was just barely more than a youth – continued to speak to a silent Faliol.

"I was informed that you had arrived in Soldori not long ago, and have been following you since, waiting for a discreet moment to approach you. Of course you were aware of my presence," he said, pausing to scan Faliol's expressionless face. "Well, but this is all something I know nothing about. In any event, how unfortunate that you were forced to reveal yourself back in that sty of a drinking house. But I suppose you couldn't allow yourself to undergo much more of that treatment merely for the sake of anonymity. No harm done, I'm sure."

"And I am sure," Faliol replied in a monotone, "that three very sad men would disagree with you."

The young man laughed briefly at what he understood to be a witticism. "In any event, their kind will have their throats wrapped in the red cord sooner or later. The duke is quite severe when it comes to the lawlessness of others. Which brings me to what I require of you tonight, assuming that we need not bargain over the terms my messenger proposed to you in Lynnese. Very well," said Streldone, though obviously he had been prepared to haggle over the matter. But he left no pause which might have been filled with the second thoughts of this hired sword, who looked and acted more like one of the clockwork automatons which performed their mechanical routines high above the town square of Soldori. Thus, with a slow turn of his head and a set movement of his hand, Faliol received the jeweled pouch containing one-half his payment. Streldone promised that the other portion would follow upon the accomplishment of their night's work, as he now portrayed its reasons and aims.

It seemed there was a young woman of a noble and wealthy family, a young woman whom Streldone loved and who loved him in return. At least she loved him to the point of accepting his proposal of marriage and cleaving to his vision of their future as two who would be one. But there was also another, a man who called himself, or who was called, Wynge. Streldone referred to him thereafter as the Sorcerer, by way of further severing his adversary from the dignity of an authentic name. As Streldone explained the situation, the Sorcerer had appropriated the young woman for himself. This unnatural feat was achieved, Streldone hated to say, not only with the compliance of the young woman's father, but also through the powerful offices of the Duke of Soldori himself. Both men, according to Streldone, had been persuaded in this affair because the Sorcerer had promised to supply them, by means of alchemical transmutations of base metals into gold and silver, with an unending source of riches to finance their wars and undertakings of ambition. Without bothering to embellish the point, Streldone declared that his beloved, in their present state of separation, were two of the most wretched beings in all the world and two of the most deserving of assistance in their struggle to be reunited. And tonight Faliol must help untangle them from the taut, controlling strings of the Sorcerer and his compatriots in evil.

"Do I have your attention, sir?" Streldone abruptly asked.

Faliol vouchsafed his understanding of the matter by repeating to its last detail Streldone's account of his plight.

"Well, I am glad to know that your wits really are in order, however distracted you may seem. In any event, tonight the Sorcerer is attending the duke's masquerade at the palace. She will be with him. Help me steal her back, so that we may both escape from Soldori, and I will fill the empty part of that pouch."

Faliol asked if Streldone had possessed the foresight to have brought along a pair of costumes to enable their entrance to the masquerade. Streldone, somewhat vainly, produced from the shadows of the coach two such costumes, one that was appropriate to a knight of the old days and the other that of a court jester of the same period. Faliol reached out for the wildly patterned costume with the jeering mask.

"But I am afraid," said Streldone, "that I intended that costume for myself. The other is more suited to allow your sword—"

"No sword will be needed," Faliol assured his nervous companion. "This will be everything," he added, holding the hook-nosed fool's face opposite his own.

They were now traveling in the direction of the palace, and Soldori's carnival began to thicken about the wheels of Streldone's coach. Gazing upon the nocturnal confusion, Faliol's eyes were as dark and swirled with shadows as the raving night itself.

II The Story of the Spectacles

His eyes fixed and clouded as a blind man's, the mage sat before a small circular table upon which a single wax taper burned in its plain silver stick. Illuminated by the modest flame, the surface of the table was inlaid with esoteric symbols, a constellation of designs which reduced essential forces of existence to a few, rather picturesque, patterns. But the mage was not occupied with these. He was simply listening to someone who was raving in the shadows of that most secret chamber. The hour was late and the night was without a moon: the narrow window behind the beardless, pallid face of the mage was a solid sheet of blackness gleaming in the candlelight. Every so often someone would move before this window, his hands running through his thick dark hair as he spoke, or tried to speak. Occasionally he would move toward the candleflame, and a glimpse could be caught of his fine attire in blacks and reds, his shining blue eyes, his fevered face. Calmly, the mage listened to the man's wild speech.

"Not *if* I have become mad but of what my madness consists is the knowledge I seek from you. And please understand that I have no hopes, only a searing curiosity to riddle the corpse of my dead soul. As for the assertion that I have always been engaged in deeds which one might deem mad, I would be obliged to answer – Yes, countless deeds, countless mad games of flesh and steel. Having confessed that, I would also avow that these were *sanctioned* provocations of chaos, known in some form to the body of the world and even blessed by it, if the truth be spoken. But I have provoked another thing, a new madness which arrives from a world that is on the wrong side of light, a madness that is unsanctioned and without the seal of our natural selves. It is a forbidden madness, a saboteur from outside the body of known laws. And as you know, I have been the subject of its sabotage.

"Since the madness began working its destruction, I have become an adept of every horror which can be thought or sensed or dreamed. In my dreams – have I not told you of them? – there are scenes of slaughter without purpose, without constraint, and without end. I have crept through dense forests not of trees but of tall pikes planted in the earth; and upon each of them a crudely formed head has been fixed. These heads all wear faces which would forever blind the one who saw them anywhere but in a dream. And they follow my movements not with earthly eyes but with shadows rolling in empty sockets. Sometimes the heads speak as I pass through their hideous ranks, telling me things I cannot bear to hear. Nor can I shut out their words, and I listen until I have learned the horrors of each brutal head. And the voices from their ragged mouths, so clear, so precise to my ears, that every word is a bright flash in my dreaming brain, a brilliant new coin minted for the treasure houses of hell. At the end of my mad dream the heads make an effort to . . . laugh, creating a blasphemous babble which echoes throughout that terrible forest. And when I awaken I find myself standing on some hillside where I have never been, and for a moment the night continues to reverberate with fading laughter.

"But did I say that I awoke? If I did, then that is only one more madness among many. For to awaken, as I once understood this miracle, means to reinherit a world of laws which for a time were lost, to rise into the light of the world as one falls into the darkness of dream. But for me there is no sense of breaking through the envelope of sleep, that delicate membrane which excludes merely a single universe while containing countless more. It seems that I remain a captive of these dreams, these visions. For when that one leaves off this one begins, each giving way to the other like a labyrinth of connected rooms which will never lead to freedom beyond their strange walls. And for all that I can know, I am even now the inhabitant of such a room, and at any moment – I beg forgiveness, wise man – you may begin to disembowel weeping children before my eyes and smear their entrails upon the floor so that in them you may read my future, a future without escape from those heads, that hillside, and from what comes after.

"There is a citadel in which I am a prisoner and which holds within it a type of school, a school of torture. Ceremonial stranglers, their palms grooved by the red cord, stalk the corridors of this place or lie snoring in its shadows, dreaming of perfect throats. Artists of mayhem curse softly as their mutilated canvasses prematurely expire of their elegant lacerations. And somewhere the master carnefex, the supreme inquisitor waits as I am dragged across crude, incredibly crude floors and am presented to his rolling, witless eyes. Then my arms, my legs, everything is shackled, and I am screaming to die while the Torture of the Question . . ."

"Enough," said the mage without raising his voice.

"Enough," the madman repeated. "And so have I said numberless times. But there is no end, there is no hope. And this endless, hopeless torment incites me with a desire to turn its power on others, even to dream of turning it on all. To see the world drown in oceans of agony is the only vision which now brings me any relief from my madness, from a madness which is *not of this world*."

"Though neither is it of any other world," said the mage in the same quiet voice.

'But I have also had visions of butchering the angels," replied the madman, as if to argue the absolute hopelessness of his mania.

"You have envisioned precisely what you believe you have not envisioned. But how could you have known this, when it is the nature of what you have seen – this *anima mundi* of the oldest philosophers and alchemists – to deceive and to pose as the soul of another world, not the soul of the world we know? There is only one world and one soul of that world, which appears in beauty or in boredom or in madness according to how deeply *anima mundi* has revealed itself to you. It is something which is not there when you look and there again when you look away."

"You speak as if it were a god or demon."

"There is no other or truer way. Like god or demon, it is an assemblage of ourselves though not of ourselves alone. But no further words now," finished the mage.

He then instructed the madman to seat himself at the table of arcane designs and to wait there with his eyes calmly closed. And for what remained of that moonless night the mage worked secretly in another part of his house, returning to the wretched dreamer just before dawn. In one of his hands was the product of his labors: a pair of strangely darkened spectacles, as if they had shadows sealed within them.

"Do not open your unhappy eyes, my friend, but listen to my words. I know the visions you have known, for they are visions I was born to know. There are eyes within our eyes, and when these others open all becomes confusion and horror. The meaning of my long life consists of the endeavor to seize and settle these visions, until my natural eyes themselves have altered in accordance with them. Now, for what reasons I cannot say, *anima mundi* has revealed itself to you in its most savage aspect; which is to say, its secret face. Thus, your life will never again be as you have known it. All the pleasures of the past are now defiled, all your hopes violated beyond hope. There are things which only madmen fear because only madmen may truly conceive of them. Your world is presently black with the scars of madness, but you must make it blacker still in order to find any soundness or peace. You have seen both too much and not enough. Through the shadow-fogged lenses of these spectacles, you will be blinded so that you may see with greater sight. Through their darkly clouded glass the lesser madness of *anima mundi* will diffuse into the infinite, all-penetrating vision of things in which madness is the sole substance and thereby becomes absent and meaningless for its very ubiquity and absolute meaning. But what would murder another man's mind will bring yours peace, while making you a puppet of peace rather than its prince.

"Henceforth, all things will be in your eyes a distant play of shadows that fretfully strive to impersonate something real, ghosts that clamor to pass themselves as flesh, masks that desperately flit about to conceal the stillness of the void behind them – henceforth, all things will be reduced in your eyes to their inconsequential essence. And all that once shined for you – the steel, the stars, the eyes of another – will lose its luster and take its place among the other shadows. All will be dulled in the power of your vision, which will give you to see that the greatest power, the only power, is to care for nothing.

"Please know that this is the only way I may help you, for my life has taught me that no single soul may be restored where there is no hope of restoring the soul of the world itself. One final word: you must never be without these spectacles or your furies will return to you. There, now you may open your eyes."

Faliol sat very still for some time. At first he did not notice that one of the mage's own eyes was closed, covered by a sagging eyelid. What at last he saw this and perceived the sacrifice, he said, "And how may I serve you, wise man?"

In the window behind the two seated figures, the dull light of dawn was grappling with the darkness of the past night, with the shadows that seemed almost to be clinging to the window's glass, or were sealed within it.

III   Anima Mundi

While the revelers in the streets of Soldori remedied their dis-
contents by throwing off the everyday face of orthodoxy, those
attending the masquerade at the duke's palace found their
deliverance by donning other faces, other bodies, and perhaps
other souls. The anonymity of that night – no unmasking was
expected to be held – enabled a multitude of sins against taste,
from the most subtle to the most grotesque indiscretions. The
society of the court had transformed itself into a race of gods or
monsters, competing at once with the brightest and highest of stars
and the strangest of the world's lower creatures. Many would
undoubtedly spend the succeeding days or weeks in darkened
rooms behind closed doors, so that the effects their disguises had
wrought on their bodies might be known to none. For a few rare
spirits, this by necessity would be their last appearance in the eyes
of the court before a final seclusion. All were quite clearly arrayed
as if something unparalleled, and possibly conclusive, was to occur
that night. Musicians played in several of the palace's most
sumptuous and shimmering halls, glittering glasses were filled
by fountains of unnaturally colored wine, and maskers swarmed
about like living gargoyles freed from the cathedral's stone. All, or
nearly all, were straining from some unheard of antic, suffering the
pleasures of expectancy.

But as the hours passed, hopes dissolved. The duke – in essence a
simple man, even a dull one – took no initiative to unloose the
abundant possibilities of the masquerade; and, as if secretly aware
of these perilous directions, he restrained the efforts of others to
pursue them, to digress from the night's steadily unwinding course.
No coaxing could sway him: he allowed several odd witticisms to
pass unacknowledged, and he feigned that certain dubious suggestions and proposals were obscure to his mind. Unnourished by any
source in the duke's own nature, every attempt at innovation
curled at its colourful edges and died. The initial strangeness of the
masked gathering went stale: voices began to sound as though they
were transacting business of some tedious sort, and even the sight of
a jester, albeit one with darkness within the eyes of his mask,
offered no special merriment to this sullen assembly.

Accompanying the jester, who made no lively movements, was a
knight out of armor, dressed in radiant blues and golds, a
crusader's cross emblazoned upon his chest, and over his face a
white silk mask of blandly noble expression. The odd duo pro-

gressed from room to dazzling, crowded room of the palace, as if they were negotiating a thick wood in search of something or someone. The knight appeared nervous, his hand too obviously ready to go for the sword at his side, his head patrolling with skittish alertness the bizarre world around him. The jester, on the other hand, was altogether more composed and methodical, and with excellent reason: he knew, as the knight did not, that their purpose was not a difficult one, especially as they would enjoy the complicity of Wynge himself, whom the knight had called the Sorcerer and whom the jester addressed as a wise man mage. Had Faliol not been invited to Soldori by a certain messenger who served two masters? And was not Wynge eager to release himself from the unhappy girl who had sought his advice in a certain matter (such innocence he could hardly believe still existed in the world) and who became a pawn in her father and the duke's game? For himself he was unconcerned, but they had also placed the girl's fate in his hands. Once she was out of the scene, these two men, both emulous of a god's glory, would lose the power with which they manipulated the mage, whose retorts and formulas they wanted to provide them with magical riches. Under the present circumstances, the knight might easily regain his beloved, and the jester would finally make good a debt, settling the price he owed for a pair of spectacles.

The two characters paused at the hugely arched entrance to the last, and most intimate, of the masquerade's many rooms. Pulling at the knight's golden sleeve, the jester angled his pointed, sneering muzzle toward a costumed pair in the far corner. These distant figures were impersonating two monarchs of the old days, a king and queen in ancient robes and stoles and many-horned crowns.

"How can you be sure that they are the ones?" whispered the knight to the buffoon at his side.

"Boldly approach and take her hand. You will be sure, but say nothing until you have led yourselves back through these rooms and to freedom."

"But the Sorcerer," objected the knight. "He could have us both executed."

"All is safe. While I engage him as the king's jester, you will make off with the queen. Trust that what I tell is true."

"I do trust you," said the knight, as he surreptitiously stuffed a jeweled pouch twice the size of the first into the belt of the jester.

The two characters separated and merged with the murmuring crowd. A few moments later, the jester arrived first at their destination. From a distance he seemed to speak a few words into the king's ear and then suddenly leaped back to play the fool before him, hopping about wildly. The knight bowed before the queen and then without ostentation led her away to other rooms. Although her masked face smothered all expression, the manner in which she placed her hand upon his appeared to reveal her knowledge of the knight's identity. After they had gone, the jester ceased his antics and approached the stern and statue-like king.

"I shall watch the duke's men around us, who may have been watching you, wise man."

"And I shall see that our two little babes find their way through the forest," replied the mock-monarch, who abruptly strode off.

But that was not part of your design, thought Faliol. And neither was the pseudo-king's playful voice that of the solemn mage. The dark eyes of the jester's mask followed the movements of the imposter, until he passed through the hugely arched entrance and became lost in the dreamlike throng of the next room. Faliol had just started in pursuit when a strange commotion in another part of the palace swiftly conveyed its anxieties and rumors through all the rooms of the masquerade.

But now that something unheard of had finally occurred, it seemed neither to delight nor relieve any of those same souls who had wished for a unique happening on that carnival night.

The disturbance originated in the centermost room of that labyrinth of rooms composing the arena of the masquerade. To the surrounding as well as the peripheral rooms, including the one in which Faliol was now caught by the crushing crowd, there first traveled sounds of sudden amusement. These were quickly transformed, however, into ambiguous outbursts of surprise, even shock. Finally, the uproar took on the character of intense horror – all voices in alarm and confusion, all movements alarmed and confused. Word passed rapidly, though less and less reliably, from mouth to mouth, room to room. Something terrible had happened, something which had begun, or was initially perceived, as a fabulous hoax. No one knew exactly how it was possible, but there suddenly appeared in the midst of the most populated room some outlandish spectacle: two gruesome figures whose costumes went far beyond anything previously displayed at the masque. Someone said they were most closely akin to giant leeches or worms, for they did not walk upright but writhed along the floor. Another had heard that the creatures possessed countless tiny legs, and thus more properly resembled centipedes of some type. Still others contributed further characteristics – many-taloned claws, reptilian tails, near-human faces – which made up the composition of the fantastic beasts. But whatever may have been the initial reaction to these, presumably artificial, creatures – at some point they inspired the crowd with unreasoning panic. And however the subsequent actions may have transpired, the consequence was that these bizarre intruders were hacked and torn and trampled beyond recognition by the frenzied, nightmarish gathering.

Tragically, once the massacre was accomplished, it was not the slaughtered remains of two uncanny monsters that the masqueraders – their masks removed – looked down upon. Instead, it was two of their own – a knight and queen of the old days – whose blood was spreading across the intricate designs of the palace floor. Their bodies, once so far from each other, were now all but indistinguishable.

Throwing off his jester's face, Faliol worked himself near enough to the scene to confirm the horror with his own shaded eyes, merely to confirm it. For the image delivered to his mind immediately took its place among the seamless and unending flow of hellish eidola which constituted *anima mundi* and which, in his vision, was a monotonous tapestry of the terrible ceaselessly unfurling itself in the faintest tones of shadowy gray. Thus, the appalling tableau he now witnessed was neither more nor less sinister in his sight than any other which the world might show him.

"Look again, Fa-fa-faliol," said a voice behind him, as a forceful boot propelled him within inches of the carnage.

But why was everything painted so brilliantly now, when a moment ago it seemed so dull, so unspectacular? Why did every piece of severed flesh quiver with color? And even more vividly than their red-smeared forms did the horrible fates of these unhappy beings affect Faliol's mind and feelings. He had been hired to save them and he could do . . . nothing. His thoughts were now careening wildly through crimson corridors within him, madly seeking solutions but falling at every turn into blind corners and flailing hopelessly against something immovable, impossible. He pressed his hands over his face, hoping to blacken the radiant scene. But everything remained invincibly there before his eyes – everything save his spectacles.

Now the duke's voice broke the brief lull of the dazed and incredulous assembly. It shouted orders, demanded answers. It proclaimed the ruler's prophetic misgivings concerning the masquerade and its dangers: he had long known that something of this nature might occur, and had done what he could to prevent its coming to pass. On the spot, he outlawed all future occasions of this kind and called for arrests and interrogations, the Torture of the

Question to be liberally implemented. Exodus was instantaneous – the palace became a chaos of fleeing freaks.

"Faliol!" called a voice that sounded too clear, within all the confusion, to have its origin outside his own mind. "I have what you're looking for. They're with me now, right here in my hand, not lost forever."

When Faliol turned around, he saw the masked king standing some distance away, unmolested by the frantic mob. The king's hand was holding out the spectacles, as if they were the dangling head of a conquered foe. Fighting his way toward the unknown persecutor, Faliol continued to remain several steps behind him as he was led by this demon through all the rooms where the masquerade once flourished, and then deeper into the palace. At the end of a long silent corridor, the gaudy, flapping train of a royal robe disappeared into a doorway. Faliol followed the fluttering bait and at last entered a dim chamber with a single window, before which stood the mummer in a sparkling silk mask. The spectacles were still held by the velvet fingers of a tightly gloved hand. Watching as the dark lenses flashed in the candle-light, Faliol's eyes burned as much with questions as with madness.

"Where is the mage?" he demanded.

"The mage is no more. Quickly, what else?"

"Who are you?"

"Wasted question, you know who I am. What else?"

"What are you?"

"Another one like the other. Say I'm a sorcerer, very well?"

"And you killed the mage as you did the others."

"The others? How could you have not heard that rattling pantomime, all those swords and swift feet? Didn't you hear that there was a pair of leviathan leeches, or something in that way, menacing the guests? True, I had a hand in the illusion, but *my* hand contained no gouging blade. A shambles, you saw it with your own eyes."

"In their fate you saw your own future. Even a sorcerer may be killed."

"Agreed, even a sorcerer with three eyes, or two eyes, or one."

"Who are you to have destroyed the mage?"

"In fact, he destroyed himself – an heroic act, I'm sure – some days ago. And he did it before *my* own eyes, as if in spite. As for myself, I confess that I'm disappointed to be so far beneath your recognition. We have met previously, please remember. But it was many years past, and I suppose you became forgetful as well as dim-sighted once you put those pieces of glass over your eyes. You see why the mage had to be stopped. He ruined you as a madman, as *my* madman.

"But you might recall that you had another career before the madness took you, did you not? Buh-buh-brave Faliol. Don't you remember how you were made that way? Don't you wish to remember that you were Faliol the dandy before we met on the road that day? It was I – in my role as a charmseller – who outfitted you with that onyx-eyed amulet which you once wore around your neck, and which made you the skillful mercenary you once were. That you loved to be.

"And how everyone else loved you that way: to see a weakling transformed into a man of strength and of steel is the stuff of public comment, of legend, of the crowd's *amusement*. And how much more do they love to witness the reverse of this magical process: to see the mighty laid low, the lord of the sword made mad. This was the little drama I had planned. You were supposed to be *my* madman, Faliol, not the placid fool of that magician – a real lost soul of torments in red and black, not a pathetic monk chanting silent psalms in pale breaths. Don't you understand? It was that Wynge, or whatever his name was, who ruined you, who undid all my schemes for your tragic and colorful history. Because of him I had to change my plans and chase you down to this place. Blame him, if anyone, for the slaughter of those innocents and for what you are about to suffer. You know my ways, we are not strangers."

"No, demon horror, we are not. You are indeed the foul thing the wise man described to me, all the dark powers which we cannot understand but can only hate."

"Powers? At least the magician spoke of me as a being, albeit a type of god or demon. But I might even be regarded as a person of sorts, someone who is just like everybody else, but not quite like anyone. I honor him for his precise vision, as far as it went. But you're wrong to contend that no one understands me; and as for hating the one who stands before you – nothing, in truth, could be farther from truth. Listen, do you hear those brawling voices in the streets beyond the window. Those are not voices filled with hate. In fact, they could not possibly hold a greater love for me. And reciprocally I love them, every one of them: all I do is for them. Did you think that my business was the exceptional destinies of heroes and magicians, of kings and queens, saints and sinners, of all the so-called great? Such extravagant freaks come and go, they are puppets who dance before the eternal eyes of my true children. Only in these multitudes do I live, and through their eyes I see my own glory."

"You see but your own foulness."

"No, the foulness is yours alone to see, Faliol. You see something that, for them, truly does not exist. This is a privileged doom reserved for creatures such as yourself. A type of consolation."

"You have said enough."

"Liar! You know that you wish my speech to go on, because you fear what will happen when I stop speaking. But I haven't said what I came here to say, or rather to ask. You know the question, don't deny it, Faliol. The one you dreamed in those dreams that were not dreams. The torture of the question you dreaded to hear asked, and dreaded more to have answered."

"Demon!"

"What is the face of the soul of the world?"

"No, it is not a face . . . it is only—"

"Yes, Faliol, it is *this* face," said the masked figure as it peeled away its mask. "But why have you hidden your eyes that way, Faliol? And why have you fallen to your knees? Don't you appreciate the vision I've shown you? Could you ever have imagined that your life would lead you into the presence of such a sight? Your spectacles cannot save you now, now that you have seen. They are only so much glinting glass – there, listen to how they crunch into smaller and smaller fragments upon the fine, cool marble of the floor. No more spectacles, no more magic, no more magician. And I think, too, no more Faliol. Can you understand what I'm telling you now, jester? Well, what have you got to say? Nothing? How black your madness must be to make you so rude a buffoon. How black. But see, even though you cannot, how I've provided these escorts to show you the way back to the carnival, which is where a fool belongs. And be sure that you make my favorite little children laugh, or I will punish you. Yes, I can still punish you, Faliol. A living man can always be punished, so remember to be good. I will be watching. I am always watching. Farewell, then, fool."

A glazen-eyed guard on either side of him, Faliol was dragged from the duke's palace and given to the crowd which still rioted in the streets of Soldori. And the crowd embraced the mad, sightless jester, hoisting his jingling form upon their shoulders and shaking him like a toy as they carried him along. In its scheme to strangle silence forever, Soldori's unruled populus bellowed a robust refrain to Faliol's sickly moans. And his blind eyes gazed up at an onyx-black night which they could not see, which his vanished mind could no longer comprehend.

But there must have been some moment, however brief, in

which Faliol regained his old enlightenment and which allowed him to accomplish such a crucial and triumphant action. Was it solely by his own sleeping strength, fleetingly aroused, that he attained his greatest prize? If not, then what power could have enabled his trembling hands to reach so deeply into those haggard sockets, and with a gesture brave and sure dig out the awful seeds of his suffering? However it was done, the deed was done well. For as Faliol perished his face was flushed with a crimson glory.

And the crowd fell silent, and a new kind of confusion spread among them – those heads which were always watching – when it was found that what they were bearing through the streets of Soldori was only Faliol's victorious corpse.

DR. VOKE AND
MR. VEECH

There is a stairway. It climbs crooked up the side of total
darkness. Yet its outlines are visible, like a scribble of lightning engraved upon a black sky. And though standing unsup-
ported, it does not fall. Nor does it end its jagged ascent until it has
reached the obscure loft where Voke, the recluse, has cloistered
himself. Someone named Cheev is making his way up the stairway,
which seems to trouble him somehow. Though the angular
scaffolding as a whole is secure enough, Cheev appears hesitant
to place his full weight on the individual steps. A victim of vague
misgivings, he ascends in weird mincing movements. Every so
often he looks back over his shoulder at the stairs he has just
stepped upon, as if expecting to see the imprints of his soles there,
as if the stairs are not made of solid wood but molded of soft clay.
But the stairs are unchanged.

Cheev is wearing a long, brightly colored coat. The huge
splinters on the railing of the stairway sometimes snag his bulky
sleeves. They also snag his bony hands, but Cheev is more
exasperated by the destruction of expensive cloth than undear
flesh. While climbing, he sucks at a small puncture in his forefinger
to keep from staining his coat with blood. At the seventeenth stair
above the seventeenth, and last, landing – he trips. The long tails of
the coat become tangled between Cheev's legs and there is a
ripping sound as he falls. At the end of his patience, Cheev
removes the coat and flings it over the side of the stairway into
the black abyss. Cheev's arms and legs are very thin.

There is only a single door at the top of the stairs. Behind it is
Voke's loft, which appears to be a cross between a playroom and a
place of torture. No doubt Cheev notices this when, with five
widely splayed fingers pushing against the door, he enters.

The darkness and silence of the great room are compromised
only by noisy jets of blue-green light flickering spasmodically along
the walls. But for the most part the room lies buried in shadows.

Even its exact height is uncertain, since above the convulsive illumination almost nothing can be seen by even the sharpest pair of eyes, never mind Cheev's squinting little slits. Part of the lower cagework of the crisscrossing rafters is visible, but the ceiling is entirely obscured, if in fact Voke's sanctum has been provided with one.

Somewhere above the gritty floor, more than a few life-size dolls hang suspended by wires which gleam and look gummy like wetted strands of a spider web. But none of the dolls is seen in whole: the long-beaked profile of one juts into the light; the shiny satin legs of another find their way out of the upper dimness; a beautifully pale hand glows in the distance; while much closer the better part of a harlequin dangles into view, cut off at the neck by blackness. Much of the inventory of this vast room appears only as parts and pieces of objects which manage to push their way out of the smothering dark. Upon the grainy floor, a long low box thrusts a corner of itself into the scene, showing off reinforced edges of bright metal strips plugged with heavy bolts. Pointed and strangely shaped instruments bloom out of the loam of shadows; they are crusted with . . . age. A great wheel appears at quarterphase in the room's night. Other sections, appendages, and gear-works of curious machines complicate this immense gallery.

As Cheev progresses through the half-light, he is suddenly halted by a metal arm with a soft black handle. He backs off and continues to shuffle through the chamber, grinding sawdust, sand, perhaps pulverized stars underfoot. The dismembered limbs of dolls and puppets are strewn about the floor, drained of their stuffings. Posters, signs, billboards, and leaflets of various sorts are scattered around like playing cards, their bright words disarranged into nonsense. Countless other objects, devices, and leftover goods stock the room, more than one could possibly take notice of. But they are all, in some way, like those which have been described. One wonders, then, how they could all add up to such an atmosphere of . . . isn't *repose* the word? Yes, but a certain kind of repose: the repose of ruin.

"Voke," Cheev calls out. "Doctor, are you here?"

Within the darkness ahead a tall rectangle suddenly appears, like a ticket-seller's booth at a carnival. The lower part is composed of wood and the upper part of glass; its interior is lit up by an oily red glare. Slumped forward on its seat inside the booth, as if asleep, is a well-dressed dummy: nicely-fitting black jacket and vest with bright silver buttons, a white high-collar shirt with silver cufflinks, and a billowing cravat which displays a pattern of moons and stars. Because his head is forwardly inclined, the dummy's only feature of note is the black sheen of its painted hair.

Cheev approaches the booth a little cautiously. He fails to notice, or considers irrelevant, the inanimate character of the figure inside. Through a semi-circular opening in the glass, Cheev slides his hand into the booth, apparently with the intention of giving the dummy's arm a shake. But before his own arm creeps very far toward its goal, several things occur in succession: the dummy casually lifts its head and opens its eyes . . . it reaches out and places its wooden hand on Cheev's hand of flesh . . . and its jaw drops open to dispense a mechanical laugh – yah-ha-ha-ha-ha, yah-ha-ha-ha-ha.

Wresting his hand away from the lurid dummy, Cheev staggers backward a few chaotic steps. The dummy continues to give forth its mocking laughter, which flaps its way into every niche of the evil loft and flies back as peculiar echoes. The dummy's face is vacant and handsome; its eyes roll like mad marbles. Then, from out of the shadows behind the dummy's booth, steps a figure that is every bit as thin as Cheev, though much taller. His outfit is not unlike the dummy's, but the clothes hang on him, and what there is left of his sparse hair falls like old rags across his bone-white scalp.

"Did you ever wonder, Mr. Veech," Voke begins, parading slowly toward his guest while holding one side of his coat like the train of a gown, "did you ever wonder what it is that makes the animation of a wooden dummy so horrible to see, not to mention to hear. Listen to it, I mean really listen. Ya-ha-ha-ha-ha: a stupid series of sounds that becomes excruciatingly eloquent when uttered by the Ticket Man. They are a species of poetry that sings what should not be sung, that speaks what should not be spoken. But what in the world is it laughing about. Nothing, it would seem. No clear motives or impulses make the dummy laugh, and yet it does! Ya-ha-ha-ha-ha, just as pure and as evil as can be.

" 'What is this laughter for?' you might be wondering, Mr. Veech. It seems to be for your ears alone, doesn't it? It seems to be directed at every nameless secret of your being. It seems . . . knowing. And it is knowing, but in another way from what you suppose, in another direction entirely. It is not you the dummy knows, it is only itself. The question is not: 'What is the laughter for,' not at all. The question is: 'Where does it come from?' This is the thing of real horror, in fact. The dummy terrorizes you, while he is really the one in terror.

"Think of it: *wood waking up.* I can't put it any clearer than that. And let's not forget the paint for the hair and lips, the glass for the eyes. These too are aroused from a sleep that should never have been broken; these too are now part of a tingling network of dummy-nerves, alive and aware in a way we cannot begin to imagine. This is something too painful for tears and so the dummy laughs in your face, trying to give vent to an evil that was no part of his old home of wood and paint and glass. But this evil is now the very essence of its new home – our world, Mr. Veech. This is what is so horrible about the laughing Ticket Man. Go to sleep now, dummy. There, he has his nice silence back. Be glad I didn't make one that screams, Mr. Veech. And be glad the dummy is, after all, just a device.

"Well, to what do I owe your presence here today. It is day, isn't it, or very close to it?"

"Yes, it is," replies Cheev.

"Good, I like to keep abreast of things. What's your latest?" Voke inquires, proceeding to saunter slowly about and admiring the clutter of his loft.

Cheev leans back against a vague mound of indefinable objects and stares at the floor. He sounds drowsy. "I wouldn't have come here, but I didn't know what else to do. How can I tell you? The past days and nights, especially the nights, like icy hells. I suppose I should say that there is someone . . ."

"Whom you have taken a liking to," Voke finishes.

"Yes, but then there is someone else . . ."

"Who is somehow an obstacle, someone whose existence helps to insure that your nights will be frosty ones. This seems very straightforward. Tell me, what is her name, the first someone?"

"Prena," answers Cheev after some hesitation.

"And his, the second."

"Lamm, but why do you need their names to help me?"

"Their names, like your name, and mine for that matter, are of no actual importance. I was just maintaining a polite interest in your predicament, nothing more. As for helping you, that assumes I have some control over this situation, which thankfully I don't."

"But I thought," stammers Cheev, "the loft, your devices, you seem to have a certain . . . knowledge."

"Like the dummy's knowledge? You shouldn't have depended on it. Now you just have one more disappointment to contend with. One more pain. But listen, can't you just stick it out? For one reason or another, you could end up forgetting all about this Prena, this Lamm; you might come to realize that they are merely two shadows sewn together by their own delirium. It's something to consider. Anything can happen in this world of ours."

"I can't wait any more, Doctor," says Cheev in a nervous, shadowy voice.

"Well, you know what they say: Something is no worse than something or other with your own shadow. I forget exactly how it goes."

"I am my own shadow," Cheev replies.

"Yes, I can see that. Listen now, let us speak hypothetically for a moment. Are you familiar with the Street of Wavering Peaks? I know it has a more common name, but I like to call it that because of all those tall, slanty houses."

Cheev nods to indicate that he too knows the street.

"Well – and I promise nothing, remember, I make no pledges or vows – but if you can somehow manage to bring both of your friends through that street tonight, I think there might be a solution to your problem, if you really want one. Do you mind what form the solution takes?"

Cheev timidly turns his head side to side, meaning he does not mind.

"You really are serious, aren't you?"

Cheev says nothing in reply. Voke shrugs and gradually fades back to his point of origin within the deepest shadows of the room. The red light in the booth of the Ticket Man also fades like a setting sun, until the only color left in the room is the ultramarine of the flames burning on the walls. Cheev continues to gaze into the upper reaches of the loft for a few more moments, as if he can already see the slender rooftops of the houses in the Street of Wavering Peaks.

By night, façades of the houses on either side of this narrow street are fused, as if cut from a single piece of very old cardboard. Bonded by shadows and plastered together by moonlight, one house undulates into the next. Aside from their foundations and a few floors with shuttered windows, they are all roof. Splendidly they rise into the night, often reaching fantastic altitudes. At angles determined by an unknown system of forces and fixed forever on destiny's tilt, they fall into and across the sky.

Tonight the sky is a swamp of murky clouds glowing in the false fire of the moon. From the direction of the street's arched entranceway, three approaching figures are preceded by three elongated shadows. One figure walks ahead, leading the way but lacking the proper gestures of knowledge and authority. Behind are the shapes of a man and a woman, side by side with only a slice of evening's soft radiance between them.

Toward the end of the street, the leading figure stops and the other two catch up with him. They are now all three standing outside one of the loftiest of the peaked houses. This house appears also to serve as a business of some kind, since a large sign, which swings a little in the wind and is muddled by shadows, displays a painted picture of the goods or services sold there: a pair of tongs, or something similar, laying crosswise upon what is perhaps a poker, or some other lengthy implement. But the business is closed for the night and the shutters are secured. A round attic window high above seems to be no more than an empty socket, though from the street – where the three figures have assumed the tentative postures of somnambulists – it is difficult to tell exactly what things are like up there. And now a fog begins to cut off their gaze from the upper regions of the Street of Wavering Peaks.

Cheev looks vaguely distressed, apparently unsure just how much longer they should loiter in this place. Not being privy to what is supposed to occur, if anything, what action should he take? All he can do at the moment is stall. But everything is soon brought to a conclusion, very quickly yet without a sense of haste or violence.

One moment Cheev is drowsily conversing with his two companions, both of them looking sternly suspicious at this point; the next moment it is as if they are two puppets who have been whisked upwards on invisible strings, into the fog and out of sight. It all happens so suddenly that they do not make a sound, though a little later there are faint, hollow screams from high above. Cheev has fallen to his knees and is covering his face with his bony hands.

Two went up, but only one comes down, suspended a few inches from the ground and swinging a little in the wind. Cheev uncovers his eyes and looks at the thing. Yes, there is only one, but this one has too many . . . there is too much of everything on this body. Two faces sharing a single head, two mouths that have fallen silent forever with parted lips. The thing continues to hang in the air even after Cheev has completely collapsed on the Street of Wavering Peaks.

Voke's next meeting with Cheev is as unexpected as the last one. There is a disturbance in the loft, and the rigid recluse lugs his bones out of the shadows to investigate. What he sees is Cheev and the Ticket Man both screaming with laughter. Their cachinnations stir up the stagnant air of the loft; they are two maniac twins crying and cackling with a single voice.

"What's going on here, Mr. Veech?" demands Voke.

Cheev ignores him and continues his laughing duet with the dummy. Even after Voke touches the booth and says, "Go to sleep, dummy," Cheev still laughs all by himself, as if he too is an automaton without control over his actions. Voke knocks Cheev to the floor, which seems to hit the right mechanism to shut off his voice. At least he is quiet for a few moments. Then he raises his eyes from the floor and glares up at Voke.

"Why did you have to do that to them?" he asks with a deeply stricken reproachfulness. His voice is rough from all that laughter; it sounds like grinding machinery.

"I'm not going to pretend I don't know what you're talking about. I have heard about what happened, not that I should care. But you can't hold me responsible, Mr. Veech. I never leave my loft, you know that. However, you're perfectly free to go, if you go now. Haven't you caused me enough trouble! "

"Why did it have to happen like that?" Cheev protests.

"How should I know? You said you didn't mind what form the solution to your problem took. Besides, I think it all worked out for the best. Those two were making a fool of you, Mr. Veech. They wanted each other and now they have each other, so to speak, while you are free to move on to your next disaster. Wait one moment, I know what's bothering you," says Voke with sudden enlightenment. "You're distressed because it all ended up with *their* demise and not yours. Death is always the best thing, Mr. Veech, but who would have thought you could appreciate such a view? I've underestimated you, no doubt about it. My apologies."

"No," screams Cheev, quivering like a sick animal. Voke now becomes excited.

"No? Noooo? What is the matter with you, young friend? Why do you set me up for these disappointments? I've had quite enough without your adding to the heap. Take a lesson from the Ticket Man here. Do you see him whining? No, he is silent, he is still. A dummy's silence is the most soothing silence of all, and his stillness is the perfect stillness of the unborn. He could be making a fuss, but he isn't. And it is precisely his lack of action, his unfulfilled nature that makes him the ideal companion, my only true friend it seems. Deadwood, I adore you. Look at how his hands rest upon his lap in empty prayer. Look at the noble bearing of his collapsed and powerless limbs. Look at his numb lips muttering nothing, and look at those eyes – how they gaze on and on forever!"

Voke takes a closer look at the dummy's eyes, and his own begin to lower with dark intentness. He leans against the booth for the closest possible scrutiny, his hands adhering to the glass as if by the force of some powerful suction. Inside the booth, the dummy's eyes have changed. They are now dripping little drops of blood, which appear black in the red haze surrounding him.

Voke pulls himself away from the booth and turns to Cheev.

"You've been *tampering* with him!" he bellows as best he can.

Cheev blinks a few leftover tears of false laughter out of his eyes, and his lips form a true smile. "I didn't do a thing," he whispers mockingly. "Don't blame me for your troubles!"

Voke seems to be momentarily paralyzed with outrage, though his face is twisted by a thousand thoughts of action. Cheev apparently is aware of the danger and his eyes search throughout the room, possibly for a means of escape or for a weapon to use against his antagonist. He fixes on something and begins to move toward it in a crouch.

"Where do you think you're going?" says Voke, now liberated from the disabling effects of his rage.

Cheev is trying to reach something on the floor that is the approximate size and shape of a coffin. Only one corner of the long black box sticks out of the shadows into the bluish green glare of the loft. A thick strip of gleaming silver edges the object and is secured to it with silvery bolts.

"Get away from there," shouts Voke as Cheev stoops over the box, fingering its lid.

But before he can open it, before he can make another move, Voke makes his.

"I've done my best for you, Mr. Veech, and you've given me nothing but grief. I've tried to deliver you from the fate of your friends . . . but now I deliver you *to* it. Join them, *Cheev.*"

At these words, Cheev's body begins to rise in a puppet's hunch, then soars up into the tenebrous rafters and beyond, transported by unseen wires. His arms and legs twitch uncontrollably during the elevation, and his screams . . . fade.

But Voke pays no attention to his victim's progress. His baggy clothes flapping hysterically, he rushes to the object so recently threatened with violation. He drags it toward an open spot on the floor. The light from the walls, ghastly and oceanic, shines on the coffin's silky black surface. Voke is on his knees before the coffin, tenderly testing its security with his fingertips. As if each accumulated moment of deliberation were a blasphemy, he suddenly lifts back the lid.

Laid out inside is a young woman whose beauty has been unnaturally perpetuated by a fanatic of her form. Voke gazes for some time at the corpse, then finally says: "Always the best thing, my dear. Always the best thing."

He is still kneeling before the coffin as his features begin to undergo the ravages of various, obviously conflicting, phases of feeling. Eyes, mouth, the whole facial structure is called upon to perform gruesome acrobatics of expression. Ultimately an impossible task is relieved or avoided by laughter: the liberating laughter of an innocent derangement, of a virgin madness. Voke rises to his feet by the powers of his idiotic hilarity. He begins to move about in a weird dance – hopping and bouncing and bobbing. His laughter grows worse as he gyres aimlessly, and his gestures become more convulsive. Through complete lack of attention, or perhaps by momentarily regaining it, Voke makes his way out of the loft and is now laughing into the dark abyss beyond the precarious railing at the top of the crooked stairway. His final laugh seems to stick in his throat; he goes over the railing and falls without a sound, his baggy clothes flapping uselessly.

Thus the screams you now hear are not those of the plummeting Voke. Neither are they the screams of Cheev, who is long gone, nor the supernatural echoes of Prena and Lamm's cries of horror. These screams, the ones from beyond the door at the top of the stairs, belong only to a dummy who now feels warm drops of blood sliding thickly over his lacquered cheeks, and who has been left – alone and alive – in the shadows of an abandoned loft. And his eyes are rolling like mad marbles.

DR. LOCRIAN'S ASYLUM

Years passed and no one in our town, no one I could name, allotted a single word to that great ruin which marred the evenness of the horizon. Nor was mention made of that darkly gated patch of ground closer to the town's edge. Even in days more remote, few things were said about these sites. Perhaps someone would propose tearing down the old asylum and razing the burial-ground where no inmate had been interred for a generation or more; and perhaps a few others, swept along by the moment, would nod their heart's assent. But the resolution always remained poorly formed, very soon losing its shape entirely, its impetus dying a gentle death in the gentle old streets of our town.

Then how can I explain that sudden turn of events, that overnight conversion which set our steps toward that hulking and decayed edifice, trampling its graveyard along the way? In answer, I propose the existence of a secret movement, one conducted in the souls of the town's citizens, and in their dreams. Conceived thus, the mysterious conversion loses some of its mystery: one need only accept that we were all haunted by the same revenant, that certain images began to establish themselves deep within each of us and became part of our hidden lives. Finally, we resolved that we could no longer live as we had been.

When the idea of positive action first arose, the residents of the humble west end of town were the most zealous and impatient. For it was they who had suffered the severest unease, living as they did in close view of the wild plots and crooked headstones of that crowded strip of earth where mad minds had come to be shut away for eternity. But we all shared the burden of the crumbling asylum itself, which seemed to be visible from every corner of town – from the high rooms of the old hotel, from the quiet rooms of our houses, from streets obscured by morning mist or twilight haze, and from my own shop whenever I looked out its front window. The setting sun would always be half-hidden by that massive silhouette, that huge broken headstone of some unspeakable grave. But more disturbing than our own view of the asylum was the idiotic gaze that it seemed to cast back at us, and through the years certain shamefully superstitious persons actually claimed to have seen mad-eyed and immobile figures staring out from the asylum's windows on nights when the moon shone with unusual brightness and the dark sky above the town appeared to contain more than its usual share of stars. Although few people spoke of such experiences, almost everyone had seen other sights at the asylum that no one could deny. And what strange things were brought to mind because of them; all over town vague scenes were inwardly envisioned.

As children, most of us had paid a visit at some time to that forbidden place, and later we carried with us memories of our somber adventures. Over the years we came to compare what we experienced, compiling this knowledge of the asylum until it became unseemly to augment it further.

By all accounts that old institution was a chamber of horrors, if not in its entirety then at least in certain isolated corners. It was not simply that a particular room attracted notice for its atmosphere of desolation: the gray walls pocked like sponges, the floor filthied by the years entering freely through broken windows, and the shallow bed withered after supporting so many nights of futile tears and screaming. There was something more.

Perhaps one of the walls to such a room would have built into it a sliding panel, a long rectangular slot near the ceiling. And on the other side would be another room, an unfurnished room which seemed never to have been occupied. But leaning against one wall of this other room, directly below the sliding panel, would be some long wooden sticks; and mounted at the ends of these sticks would be horrible little puppets.

Another room might be completely bare, yet its walls would be covered with pale fragments of weird funereal scenes. By removing some loose floorboards at the center of the room, one would discover several feet of earth piled upon an old, empty coffin. And then there was a very special room, a room I had visited myself, that was located on the uppermost floor of the asylum and contained a great windowless skylight. Positioned under that opening upon the heavens, and fixed securely in place, stood a long table with huge straps hanging from its sides.

There may have been other rooms of a strange type which memory has forbidden to me. But somehow none of them was singled out for comment during the actual dismantling of the asylum, when most of us were busy heaving the debris of years through great breaches we had made in the asylum's outer walls, while some distance away the rest of the town witnessed the wrecking in a cautious state of silence. Among this group was Mr. Harkness Locrian, a thin and large-eyed old gentleman whose silence was not like that of the others.

Perhaps we expected Mr. Locrian to voice opposition to our project, but he did not do so at any stage of the destruction. Although no one, to my knowledge, suspected him of preserving any morbid sentiment for the old asylum, it was difficult to forget that his grandfather had been the director of the Shire County Sanitarium during its declining years and that his father had closed down the place under circumstances that remained an obscure episode in the town's history. If we spoke very little about the asylum and its graveyard, Mr. Locrian spoke of them not at all. This reticence, no doubt, served only to strengthen in our minds the intangible bond which seemed to exist between him and the awful ruin that sealed the horizon. Even I, who knew the old man better than anyone else in the town, regarded him with a degree of circumspection. Outwardly, of course, I was courteous to him, even friendly; he was, after all, the oldest and most reliable patron of my business. And not long after the demolition of the asylum was concluded, and the last of its former residents' remains had been exhumed and hastily cremated, Mr. Locrian paid me a visit.

At the very moment he entered the shop, I was examining some books which had just arrived for him by special order. But even if I had grown jaded to such coincidences following years of dealing in books, which have some peculiarity about them that breeds events of this nature, there was something unpleasant about this particular freak of timing.

"Afternoon," I greeted. "You know, I was just looking over . . ."

"I see," he said, approaching the counter where tiers of books left very little open space. As he glanced at these new arrivals – hardly interested, it seemed – he slowly unbuttoned his overcoat, a bulky thing which made his head appear somewhat small for his body. How easily I can envision him on that day. And even now his voice sounds clear in my memory, a voice that was far too quiet for the old man's harshly brilliant eyes. After a few moments he turned and casually began to wander about the shop, as if seeking out observers who might be secluded among its stacks. He rounded a corner and momentarily left my view. "So at last it's done," he said. "Something of a feat, a striking page of local history."

"I suppose it is," I answered, watching as Mr. Locrian traversed the rear aisle of the shop, appearing and disappearing as he passed by several rows of shelves.

"Without doubt it is," he replied, proceeding straight down the aisle in front of me. Finally reaching the counter behind which I stood, he placed his hands upon it, leaned forward, and asked: "But what has been achieved, what has really changed?"

The tone of voice in which he posed this question was both sardonic and morose, carrying undesirable connotations that echoed in all the remote places where truth had been shut up and abandoned like a howling imbecile. Nonetheless, I held to the lie.

"If you mean that there's very little difference now, I would have to agree. Only the removal of an eyesore. That was all we intended to do. Simply that."

Then I tried to draw his attention to the books that had arrived for him, but I was coldly interrupted when he said: "We must be walking different streets, Mr. Crane, and seeing quite different faces, hearing different voices in this town. Tell me," he asked, suddenly animated, "did you ever hear those stories about the sanitarium? What some people saw in its windows? Perhaps you yourself were one of them."

I said nothing, which he might have accepted as a confirmation that I was one of those people. He continued:

"And isn't there much the same feeling now, in this town, as there was in those stories? Can you admit that the days and nights are much worse now than they were . . . before? Of course, you may tell me that it's just the moodiness of the season, the chill, the dour afternoons you observe through your shop window. On my way here, I actually heard some people saying such things. They also said other things which they didn't think I could hear. Somehow everyone seems to know about these books of mine, Mr. Crane."

He did not look at me while delivering this last remark, but began to pace slowly from one end of the counter to the other, then back again.

"I'm sorry, Mr. Locrian, if you feel that I've violated some confidence. I never imagined that it would make any difference."

He paused in his pacing and now gazed at me with an expression of almost paternal forgiveness.

"Of course," he said in his earlier, quiet voice. "But things are very different now, will you allow that?"

". . . Yes," I conceded.

"But no one is sure exactly in what way they are different."

"No," I agreed.

"Did you know that my grandfather, *Doctor* Harkness Locrian, was buried in that graveyard?"

Feeling a sudden surprise and embarrassment, I replied: "I'm sure if you had said something." But it was as if I were the one who had said nothing at all, nothing that would deter him from what he had come to tell me.

"Is this safe to sit in?" he asked, pointing to an old chair by the front window. And beyond the window, unobstructed, the pale autumn sun was sinking down.

"Yes, help yourself," I said, noticing some passers-by who had noticed Mr. Locrian and looked oddly at him.

"My grandfather," Mr. Locrian continued, "felt at home with his lunatics. You may be startled to hear such a thing. Although the house that is now mine was once his, he did not spend his time there, not even to sleep. It was only after they closed down the sanitarium that he actually became a resident of his own home, which was also the home of myself and my parents, who now had charge of the old man. Of course, you probably don't remember . . .

"My grandfather passed his final years in a small upstairs room overlooking the outskirts of town, and I recall seeing him day after day gazing through his window at the sanitarium . . ."

"I had no idea," I interjected. "That seems rather—"

"Please, before you are led to think that his was merely a sentimental attachment, however perverse, let me say that it was no such thing. His feelings with respect to the sanitarium were in fact quite incredible, owing to the manner in which he had used his authority at that place. I found out about this when I was still very young, but not so young that I could not understand the profound conflict that existed between my father and grandfather. I disregarded my parents' admonitions that I not spend too much time with the old man, succumbing to the mystery of his presence. And one afternoon he revealed himself.

"He was gazing through the window and never once turned to face me. But after we had sat in silence for some time, he started to whisper something. 'They questioned,' he said. 'They accused. They complained that no one in that place ever became well.' Then he smiled and began to elaborate. 'What things had they seen,' he hissed, 'to give them such . . . wisdom? They did not look into the faces,' no, he did not say 'faces' but 'eyes.' Yes, he said, ' . . . did not look into the *eyes* of those beings, the eyes that reflected the lifeless beauty of the silent, staring universe itself.'

"Those were his words. And then he talked about the voices of the patients under his care. He whispered, and I quote, that 'the wonderful music of those voices spoke the supreme delirium of the planets as they go round and round like bright puppets dancing in the blackness.' In the wandering words of those lunatics, he told me, the ancient mysteries were restored.

"Like all true mysteriarchs," Mr. Locrian went on, "my grandfather desired a knowledge that was unspoken and unspeakable. And every volume of the strange library he left to his heirs attests to this desire. As you know, I have added to this collection in my own way, as did my father. But our reasons were not those of the old doctor. At his sanitarium, Dr. Locrian had done something very strange, something that perhaps only he possessed both the knowledge and the impulse to do. It was not until many years later that my father attempted to explain everything to me, as I now am attempting to explain it to you.

"I have said that my grandfather was and always had been a mysteriarch, never a philanthropist of the mind, not a restorer of wounded psyches. In no way did he take a therapeutic approach with the inmates at the sanitarium. He did not view them as souls that were possessed, either by demons or by their own painful histories, but as beings who held a strange alliance with other orders of existence, who contained within themselves a particle of something eternal, a golden speck of magic which he thought might be enlarged. Thus, his ambition led him not to relieve his patients' madness, but to *exasperate* it – to let it breathe with a life of its own. And this he did in certain ways that wholly eradicated what human qualities remained in these people. But sometimes that peculiar magic he saw in their eyes would seem to fade, and then he would institute his 'proper treatment,' which consisted of putting them through a battery of hellish ordeals intended to loosen their attachment to the world of humanity and to project them further into the absolute, the realm of the 'silent, staring universe' where the ultimate insanity of the infinite void might work a rather paradoxical cure. The result was something as pathetic as a puppet and as magnificent as the stars, something at once dead and never dying, a thing utterly without destiny and thus imperishable, possessing that abysmal absence of mind, that infinite vacuity which is the essence of all that is immortal. And somehow, in his last days, my grandfather used this same procedure on himself, reaching into spaces beyond death.

"I know this to be true, because one night late in my childhood, I awoke and witnessed the proof. Leaving my bed, I walked down the moonlit hallway, feeling irresistibly drawn toward the closed door of my grandfather's room. Stopping in front of that door, I turned its cold handle and slowly pushed back its strange nocturnal mass. Peeking timidly into the room, I saw my grandfather sitting before the window in the bright moonlight. My curiosity must have overcome my horror, for I actually spoke to this specter. 'What are you doing here, Grandfather?' I asked. And without turning away from the window, he slowly and tonelessly replied: 'We are doing just what you see.' Of course, what I saw was an old man who belonged in his grave, but who was now staring out his window across to the windows at the sanitarium, where others who were not human stared back.

"When I fearfully alerted my parents to what I had seen, I was surprised that my father responded not with disbelief but with anger: I had disobeyed his warnings about my grandfather's room. Then he revealed the truth just as I now reveal it to you, and year after year he reiterated and expanded upon this secret learning: why that room must always be kept shut and why the sanitarium must never be disturbed. You may not be aware that an earlier effort to destroy the sanitarium was aborted through my father's intervention. He was far more attached than I could ever be to this town, which ceased to have a future long ago. How long has it been since a new building was added to all the old ones? This place would have crumbled in time. The natural course of things would have dismantled it, just as the asylum would have disappeared had it been left alone. But when all of you took up those implements and marched toward the old ruin, I felt no desire to interfere. You have brought it on yourselves," he complacently ended.

"And what is it we have done?" I asked in a cold voice, now suppressing a mysterious outrage.

"You are only trying to preserve what remains of your mind's peace. You know that something is very wrong in this town, that you should never have done what you did, but still you cannot draw any conclusion from what I have told you."

"With all respect, Mr. Locrian, how can you imagine that I believe anything you've told me?"

He laughed weakly. "Actually, I don't. As you say, how could I? Without being somewhat mad, that is. But in time you will. And then I will tell you more things, things you will not be able to keep yourself from believing."

As he pushed himself up from the chair by the window, I asked: "Why tell me anything? Why did you come here today?"

"Why? Because I thought that perhaps my books had arrived, let me just take them like that. And also because everything is finished now. The others," he shrugged, ". . . hopeless. You are the only one who could understand. Not now, but in time."

And now I do understand what the old man told me as I never could on that autumn day some forty years ago.

It was toward the end of that same sullen day, in the course of a bleak twilight, that they began to appear. Like figures quietly emerging from the depths of memory, they struggled in the shadows and slowly became visible. But even if the transition had been subtle, insidiously graduated, it did not long go unnoticed. By nightfall they were distractingly conspicuous throughout the town, always framed in some high window of the structures they occupied: the rooms above the shops in the heart of the town, the highest story of the old hotel, the empty towers of civic buildings, the lofty turrets and grand gables of the most distinguished houses, and the attics of the humblest homes.

Their forms were as softly luminous as the autumn constellations in the black sky above, their faces glowing with the same fixed expression of placid vacuity. And the attire of these apparitions was grotesquely suited to their surroundings. Buried many years before in antiquated clothes of a formal and funereal cut, they seemed to belong to the dying town in a manner its living members could not emulate. For the streets of the town now lost what life was left in them and became the dark corridors of a museum where these waxen nightmares had been put on exhibition.

In daylight, when the figures in the windows took on a dull wooden appearance that seemed less maddening, some of us ventured into those high rooms. But nothing was ever found on the other side of *their* windows, nothing save a tenantless room which no light would illuminate and which sooner or later inspired any living occupant with a demented dread. By night, when it seemed we could hear them erratically tapping on the floors above us, their presence in our homes drove us out into the streets. Day and night we became sleepless vagrants, strangers in our own town. Eventually we may have ceased to recognize one another. But one name, one face was still known to all – that of Mr. Harkness Locrian, whose gaze haunted each one of us.

It was undoubtedly in his house that the fire began which mindlessly consumed every corner of the town. There were attempts made to oppose its path, but they were half-hearted and soon abandoned. For the most part we stood in silence, vacantly staring as the flames burned their way up to the high windows where spectral figures posed like portraits in their frames.

Ultimately these demons were exorcized, their windows left empty. But only after the town had been annulled by the holocaust.

Nothing more than charred wreckage remained. Afterward it was reported that one of our citizens had been taken by the fire, though none of us inquired into the exact circumstances under which old Mr. Locrian met his death.

There was, of course, no effort made to recover the town we had lost: when the first snow fell that year, it fell upon ruins grown cold and dreadful. But now, after the passing of so many years, it is not the ashen rubble of that town which haunts each of my hours; it is that one great ruin in whose shadow my mind has been interned.

And if they have kept me in this room because I speak to faces that appear at my window, then let them protect this same room from violations after I am gone. For Mr. Locrian has been true to his promise; he has told me of certain things when I was ready to hear them. And he has other things to tell me, secrets surpassing all insanity. Commending me to an absolute cure, he will have immured another soul within the black and boundless walls of that eternal asylum where stars dance forever like bright puppets in the silent, staring void.

THE SECT OF THE
IDIOT

The primal chaos, Lord of All . . . the blind idiot god – Azathoth.
Necronomicon

The extraordinary is a province of the solitary soul. Lost the very moment the crowd comes into view, it remains within the great hollows of dreams, an infinitely secluded place that prepares itself for your arrival, and for mine. Extraordinary joy, extraordinary pain – the fearful poles of the world that both menaces and surpasses this one. It is a miraculous hell towards which one unknowingly wanders. And its gate, in my case, was an old town – whose allegiance to the unreal inspired my soul with a holy madness long before my body had come to dwell in that incomparable place.

Soon after arriving in the town – whose identity I must allow to remain secret, along with my own – I was settled in a high room overlooking the ideal of my dreams through diamond panes. How many times had I already lingered before a figmentation of these windows through which I now gazed truly upon the old town? Having roamed its streets in reverie, I could finally become enveloped by their sensual visions.

I discovered an infinite stillness on foggy mornings, miracles of silence on indolent afternoons, and the strangely flickering tableau of neverending nights. A sense of serene enclosure was conveyed by every aspect of the old town. There were balconies, railed porches, and jutting upper stories of shops and houses that created intermittent arcades over sidewalks. Colossal roofs overhung entire streets and transformed them into the corridors of a single structure containing an uncanny multitude of rooms. And these fantastic crowns were echoed below by lesser roofs that drooped above windows like half-closed eyelids and turned each narrow doorway into a magician's cabinet harboring deceptive depths of shadow.

It is difficult to explain, then, how the old town also conveyed a sense of endlessness, of proliferating unseen dimensions, at the same time that it served as the very image of a claustrophobe's nightmare. Even the infinite nights above the great roofs of the town seemed merely the uppermost level of an earthbound estate, at most a musty old attic in which the stars were useless heirlooms and the moon a dusty trunk of dreams. And this paradox was precisely the source of the town's enchantment. I imagined the heavens themselves as part of an essentially interior decor. By day: heaps of clouds like dustballs floated across the empty rooms of the sky. By night: a fluorescent map of the cosmos was painted upon a great black ceiling. How I desired to live forever in this domain of medieval autumns and mute winters, serving out my sentence of life among all the visible and invisible wonders I had only dreamed about from so far away.

But no existence, however visionary, is without its trials and traps. After only a few days in the old town, I had been made acutely sensitive by the solitude of the place and by the solitary manner of my life. Late one afternoon I was relaxing in a chair beside those kaleidoscopic windows, when there was a knock at the door. It was only the faintest of knocks, but so unexpected was this elementary event, and so developed was my sensitivity, that it seemed like some unwonted upheaval of atmospheric forces, a kind of cataclysm of empty space, an earthquake in the invisible. Hesitantly I walked across the room and stood before the door, which was only a simple brown slab without molding around its frame. I opened it.

"Oh," said the little man waiting in the hallway outside. He had neatly groomed silver hair and strikingly clear eyes. "This is embarrassing. I must have been given the wrong address. The handwriting on this note is such chaos," he said, looking at the crumpled piece of paper in his hand. "Ha! Never mind, I'll go back and check."

However, the man did not immediately leave the scene of his embarrassment; instead, he pushed himself upwards on the points of his tiny shoes and stared over my shoulder into my room. His entire body, compact as it was in stature, seemed to be in a state of concentrated excitement. Finally he said, "Beautiful view from your room," and he smiled a very tight little smile.

"Yes, it is," I replied, glancing back into the room and not really knowing what to think. When I turned around the man was gone.

For a few startled moments I did not move. Then I stepped into the hallway and gazed up and down its dim length. It was not very wide, nor did it extend a great distance before turning a windowless corner. All the doors to the other rooms were closed, and not the slightest noise emerged from any of them. At last I heard what sounded like footsteps descending flights of stairs on the floors below, faintly echoing through the silence, speaking the quiet language of old rooming houses. I felt relieved and returned to my room. The rest of the day was uneventful, though somewhat colored by a whole spectrum of imaginings. And that night I experienced a very strange dream, the culmination, it seemed, of both my lifetime of dreaming and of my dreamlike sojourn in the old town. Certainly my view of the town was thereafter dramatically transformed. And yet, despite the nature of the dream, this change was not immediately for the worse.

In the dream I occupied a small dark room, a high room whose windows looked out on a maze of streets which unravelled beneath an abyss of stars. But although the stars were spread across a great reaching blackness, the streets below were bathed in a stale gray dimness which suggested neither night nor day nor any natural phase between them. Gazing out the window, I felt that cryptic proceedings were taking place in secluded corners of this scene, vague observances without any kind of reality to them. There seemed to be special cause for me to worry about certain things that were happening in one of the other high rooms of the town, a particular room whose location was nevertheless unknown to me. I had the idea that a peculiar correspondence existed between the activities in that room and my own life, but at the same time I felt infinitely removed from them: what transpired in the other room in no sense concerned my personal fate, yet somehow would profoundly affect it. I seemed to be an unseen speck lost in the convolutions of strange schemes. And it was this very remoteness from the designs of my dream universe, this feeling of fantastic homelessness amid a vast alien order, that was the source of unnameable terrors. I was no more than an irrelevant parcel of living tissue caught in a place I should not be, threatened with being snared in some great dredging net of doom, an incidental shred of flesh pulled out of its element of light and into an icy blackness. In the dream nothing supported my existence, which I felt at any moment might be horribly altered or simply . . . ended. In the profoundest meaning of the expression, my life was of *no matter*.

But still I could not keep my attention from straying into that other room, sensing what elaborate plots were evolving there. I thought I could see indistinct figures occupying that spacious chamber, a place furnished with only a few chairs of extremely odd design and commanding a dizzying view of the starry blackness. The great round moon of the dream created sufficient illumination for the night's purposes, painting the walls of the mysterious room a deep aquatic blue; the stars, unneeded and ornamental, presided as lesser lamps over this gathering and its nocturnal offices.

As I observed this scene – though not "bodily" present, as is the way with dreams – it became my conviction that certain rooms offered a marvelous solitude for such functions or festivities. Their atmosphere, that intangible quality which exists apart from its composing elements of shape and shade, was of a dreamy cast, a state in which time and space had become deranged: a few moments there might count as centuries or millenia, and the tiniest niche might encompass a universe. Nevertheless, at the same time this atmosphere seemed no different from that of the old rooms, the high and lonely rooms I had known in waking life, even if *this* room appeared to border on the voids of astronomy and its windows opened onto the infinite outside. And I found myself speculating that, if the room itself was not one of a unique species, perhaps it was the occupants that had introduced the singular element.

Although each of them was completely draped in a massive cloak, the manner in which this material descended in strange foldings to the floor, and the unusual structure of the chairs in which these creatures were seated, betrayed an oddness that inspired my curiosity and my terror. I could not help wondering what these robes might conceal. Who were these beings, so unnaturally shaped? With their tall, angular chairs arranged in a circle, they appeared to be leaning in every direction, like unsettled monoliths. It was as if they were assuming postures that were mysteriously symbolic, locking themselves in patterns hostile to mundane analysis. In like fashion, their heads inclined in a skewed relationship to the rest of their lofty forms, nodding in ways heretical to terrestrial anatomy. And they whispered almost incessantly, for I can think of no more precise word to describe the soft buzzing which seemed to serve them as speech. Or was it the suspension of this sound that conveyed their unknown messages to one another, those infrequent but remarkable silences which terrified me far more than the alien murmur?

But the dream offered another detail which possibly related to the mode of communication among these whispering figures who sat in stagnant moonlight. For projecting out of the bulky sleeves dangling at each figure's side were thin and delicate appendages that appeared to have withered away, wilted claws bearing numerous talons that tapered off into drooping tentacles. And all of these stringy digits seemed to be working together with lively and unceasing agitation.

At first sight of these gruesome gestures I felt myself about to awaken, to carry back into the world a sense of terrible enlightenment without sure meaning or possibility of expression in any language except the whispered vows of this eerie sect. But I remained longer in this dream, far longer than was natural. I witnessed the insect-like nervousness of those shrivelled mandibles, the brittle excitement of these members which seemed to be revealing an intolerable knowledge, some ultimate disclosure concerning the order of things. Such movements suggested an array of hideous analogies: the spinning legs of spiders, the greedy rubbing of a fly's spindly feelers, the rippling of a lizard's tongue or the twitching of its tail. But my cumulative sensation in the dream was only partially involved with what I would call the *triumph of the grotesque*; for much greater was a quite different perception, one accompanied by a bizarre elation tainted with nausea. This revelation – in keeping with the style of certain dreams – was complicated and exact, allowing no ambiguities or confusions to comfort the dreamer. And what was imparted to my witnessing mind was the vision of a world in a trance: a hypnotized parade of beings sleepwalking to the odious manipulations of their whispering masters, those hooded freaks *who were themselves among the hypnotized*. For there was a power superseding theirs, a power which they served and from which they merely emanated, something which was beyond the universal hypnosis by virtue of its very mindlessness, its awesome idiocy. These cloaked masters, in turn, partook in some measure of godhood, passively presiding as enlightened zombies over the multitudes of the entranced, that frenetic domain of the human sphere.

And it was at this place in my dream that I came to believe that there obtained a terrible intimacy between myself and those whispering effigies of chaos whose existence I dreaded for its very remoteness from mine. Had these beings, for some grim purpose comprehensible only to themselves, allowed me to intrude upon their infernal wisdom? Or was my unwanted access to such putrid arcana merely the outcome of some loathsome fluke in the universe of atoms, a chance intersection among the demonic elements of which all creation is composed? But the truth was notwithstanding in the face of these insanities; whether by calculation or accident, I was the victim of the unknown. And I finally succumbed to an ecstatic horror at this insufferable insight.

On waking, it seemed that I had carried back with me a tiny, jewel-like particle of this horrific ecstasy, and, by some alchemy of association, this darkly crystalline substance infused its magic into my image of the old town.

Although I formerly believed myself to be the consummate knower of the town's secrets, the following day was one of unforeseen discovery. The streets that I looked upon that motionless morning were filled with new secrets and seemed to lead me to the very essence of the extraordinary. And a previously unknown element appeared to have emerged in the composition of the town, one that must have been hidden within its most obscure quarters. I mean to say that, while these quaint, archaic facades still put on all the appearance of a dreamlike repose, there now existed, in my sight, evil stirrings beneath this surface. The town had more wonders than I knew, a secreted cache of blasphemous offerings. Yet somehow this formula of deception, of corruption in disguise, served to intensify the town's most attractive aspects: a wealth of unsuspected sensations was now provoked by a few slanting rooftops, a low doorway, or a narrow backstreet. The mist spreading evenly through the town early that morning was luminous with dreams.

The whole day I wandered in a fevered exaltation throughout the old town, seeing it as if for the first time. I scarcely stopped a moment to rest, and I am sure I did not pause to eat. By late afternoon I might also have been suffering from a strain on my nerves, for I had spent many hours nurturing a rare state of mind in which the purest euphoria was invaded and enriched by chaotic currents of fear. Each time I rounded a streetcorner or turned my head to catch some beckoning sight, the darkest tremors were inspired by the hybrid spectacle I witnessed – splendid scenes broken with malign shadows, the lurid and the lovely forever lost in each other's embrace. And when I passed under the arch of an old street and gazed up at the towering structure before me, I was nearly overwhelmed.

My recognition of the place was immediate, though I had never viewed it from my present perspective. And suddenly it seemed I was no longer outside in the street and staring upwards, but was looking down from the room just beneath that peaked roof. It was the highest room on the street, and no window from any of the other houses could see into it. The building itself, like some of those surrounding it, seemed to be empty, perhaps abandoned. I contemplated several ways by which I could force entry, but none of these methods was needed: the front door, contrary to my initial observation, was slightly ajar.

The place was indeed abandoned, stripped of furnishings and fixtures, its desolate, tunnel-like hallways visible only in the sickly light that shone through unwashed, curtainless windows. Identical windows also appeared on the landing of each section of the staircase that climbed up through the central part of the house like a crooked spine. I stood in a near cataleptic awe of the world I had wandered into, this decayed paradise. It was a place of strange atmospherics of infinite melancholy and unease, the everlasting residue of some cosmic misfortune. I ascended the stairs with a solemn, mechanical intentness, stopping only when I had reached the top and found the door to a certain room.

And even at the time, I asked myself: could I have entered this room with such unhesitant resolve if I truly expected to find something extraordinary within it? Was it ever my intention to confront the madness of the universe, or at least my own? I had to confess that although I had accepted the benefits of my dreams and fancies, I did not profoundly believe in them. At the deepest level I was their doubter, a thorough skeptic who had indulged a too-free imagination, and perhaps a self-made lunatic.

To all appearances the room was unoccupied. I noted this fact without the disappointment born of real expectancy, but also with a strange relief. Then, as my eyes adjusted to the confusing twilight of the room, I saw the circle of chairs.

They were as strange as I had dreamed, more closely resembling devices of torture than any type of practical or decorative object. Their tall backs were slightly bowed and covered with a coarse hide unlike anything I had ever beheld; the arms were like blades and each had four semicircular grooves cut into it that were spaced evenly across its length; and below were six jointed legs jutting outwards, a feature which transformed the entire piece into some crablike thing with the apparent ability to scuttle across the floor. If, for a stunned moment, I felt the idiotic impulse to install myself in one of these bizarre thrones, I quickly extinguished this desire upon observing that the seat of each chair, which at first appeared to be composed of a smooth and solid cube of black glass, was in fact only an open cubicle filled with a murky liquid which quivered strangely when I passed my hand over its surface. And as I did this I could feel my entire arm tingle in a way which sent me stumbling backward to the door of that horrible room and which made me loathe every atom of flesh gripping the bones of that limb. I turned around to exit but was stopped by a figure standing in the doorway.

Although I had previously met the man, he now seemed to be someone quite different, someone openly sinister rather than merely enigmatic. When he had disturbed me the day before, I could not have suspected his alliances: his manner had been unusual but very polite, and he had offered no reason to question his sanity. Now he appeared to be no more than a malignant puppet of madness. From the twisted stance he assumed in the doorway to the vicious and imbecilic expression that possessed the features of his face, he was a thing of strange degeneracy. Before I could back away from him, he took my trembling hand. "Thank you for coming to visit," he said in a voice that was a parody of his former politeness. He pulled me close to him; his eyelids lowered and his mouth widely grinned, as if he were enjoying a pleasant breeze on a warm day. And then he said, "They want you with them on their return. They want their chosen ones."

Nothing can describe what I felt on hearing these words which could only have meaning in a nightmare. Their implications were a quintessence of hellish delirium, and at that instant all the world's wonder turned suddenly to dread. I tried to free myself from the madman's grasp, shouting at him to let go of my hand. "*Your* hand?" he shouted back at me. Then he began to repeat the phrase over and over, laughing as if some sardonic joke had reached a conclusion within the depths of his lunacy. In his foul merriment he weakened, and I escaped. As I rapidly descended the many stairs of the old building, his laughter pursued me as hollow reverberations which filled the shadowy edifice.

And that freakish, echoing laughter remained with me as I wandered dazed in darkness, trying to flee my own thoughts and sensations. Gradually the terrible sounds that filled my brain subsided, but they were now replaced by a new terror – the whispering of strangers whom I passed on the streets of the old town. And no matter how low they spoke or how quickly they silenced one another with embarrassed throat-clearings and stern looks, their words reached my ears in fragments that I was able to reconstruct because of their frequent repetition. The most common terms were *deformity* and *disfigurement*. If I had not been so distraught I might have approached these persons with a semblance of politeness, cleared my own throat, and said, "I beg your pardon, but I could not help overhearing . . . And what exactly did you mean, if I may ask, when you said . . ." But I discovered for myself what those words meant – *how terrible, poor man* – when I returned to my room and stood before the mirror on the wall, holding my head in balance with a supporting hand on either side.

For only one of those hands was mine.

The other belonged to them.

Life is the nightmare that leaves its mark upon you in order to prove that it is, in fact, real. And to suffer a solitary madness seems the joy of paradise when compared to the extraordinary condition in which one's own madness merely echoes that of the world outside. I have been lured away by dreams; all is nonsense now.

Let me write, while I still am able, that the transformation has not limited itself. I now find it difficult to continue this manuscript with either hand; these twitching tentacles can barely grasp the pen, and I am losing the will to push a shrivelled paw across this page. While I have put myself at a great distance from the old town, its influence is undiminished. In these matters there is a terrifying freedom from the laws of space and time. I am bound by greater laws, strange powers that are at their work as I look helplessly on.

In the interest of others, I have taken precautions to conceal my identity and the precise location of a horror which cannot be helped; yet, I have also taken pains to reveal, as if with malicious intent, the existence and nature of those same horrors. Ultimately, neither my motives nor my actions are of any consequence: they are both well known to the things that whisper in the highest room of an old town. They know what I write and why I am writing it. Perhaps they are even guiding my pen by means of a hand that is an extension of their own. And if I ever desired to see what lay beneath those dark robes, I will soon be able to satisfy this curiosity with only a glance in my mirror.

I must return to the old town, for now my home can be nowhere else. But my manner of passage to that place cannot be the same, and when I enter again that world of dreams it will be by way of a threshold which no human being has ever crossed . . . nor ever shall.

THE GREATER FESTIVAL
OF MASKS

There are only a few houses in the district where Noss begins his excursions. Nonetheless, they are spaced in such a way that suggests some provision has been made to accommodate a greater number of them, like a garden from which certain growths have been removed or have yet to appear. It even seems to Noss that these hypothetical houses, the ones now absent, may at some point change places with those which can be seen, in order to enrich the lapses in the landscape and give the visible a rest within nullity. And of these houses now stretching high or spreading low there will remain nothing to be said, for they will have entered the empty spaces, which are merely blank faces waiting to gain features. Such are the declining days of the festival, when the old and the new, the real and the imaginary, truth and deception, all join in the masquerade.

But even at this stage of the festival some have yet to take a large enough interest in tradition to visit one of the shops of costumes and masks. Until recently Noss was among this group, for reasons neither he nor anyone else could clearly explain. Now, however, he is on his way to a shop whose every shelf is crammed and flowing over, even at this late stage of the festival, with costumes and masks. In the course of his little journey, Noss keeps watching as buildings become more numerous, enough to make a street, many narrow streets, a town. He also observes numerous indications of the festival season. These signs are sometimes subtle, sometimes blatant in nature. For instance, not a few doors have been kept ajar, even throughout the night, and dim lights are left burning in empty rooms. On the other hand, someone has ostentatiously scattered a bunch of filthy rags in a certain street, shredded rags that are easily disturbed by the wind and twist gaily about. But there are many other gestures of festive abandonment: a hat, all style mangled out of it, has been jammed into the space where a board is missing in a high fence; a poster stuck to a crumbling wall has been diagonally torn in half, leaving a scrap of face fluttering at its edges; and into strange pathways of caprice revelers will go, but to have *shorn* themselves in doorways, to have littered the shadows with such wiry clippings and tumbling fluff. Reliquiae of the hatless, the faceless, the tediously groomed. And Noss passes it all by with no more, if no less, than a glance.

His attention appears more sharply awakened as he approaches the center of the town, where the houses, the shops, the fences, the walls are more, much more . . . close. There seems barely enough space for a few stars to squeeze their bristling light between the roofs and towers above, and the outsized moon – not a familiar face in this neighborhood – must suffer to be seen only as a fuzzy anonymous glow mirrored in silvery windows. The streets are more tightly strung here, and a single one may have several names compressed into it from end to end. Some of the names may be credited less to deliberate planning, or even the quirks of local history, than to an apparent need for the superfluous, as if a street sloughed off its name every so often like an old skin, the extra ones insuring that it would not go completely nameless. Perhaps a similar need could explain why the buildings in this district exhibit so many pointless embellishments: doors which are elaborately decorated yet will not budge in their frames; massive shutters covering blank walls behind them; enticing balconies, well-railed and promising in their views, but without any means of entrance; stairways that enter dark niches . . . and a dead end. These structural adornments are mysterious indulgences in an area so pressed for room that even shadows must be shared. And so must other things. Backyards, for example, where a few fires still burn, the last of the festival pyres. For in this part of town the season is still at its peak, or at least the signs of its termination have yet to appear. Perhaps revelers hereabouts are still nudging each other in corners, hinting at preposterous things, coughing in the middle of jokes. Here the festival is not dead. For the delirium of this rare celebration does not radiate out from the center of things, but seeps inward from remote margins. Thus, the festival may have begun in an isolated hovel at the edge of town, if not in some lonely residence in the woods beyond. In any case, its agitations have now reached the heart of this dim region, and Noss has finally resolved to visit one of the many shops of costumes and masks.

A steep stairway leads him to a shrunken platform of a porch, and a little slot of a door puts him inside the shop. And indeed its shelves *are* crammed and flowing over with costumes and masks. The shelves are also very dark and mouth-like, stuffed into silence by the wardrobes and faces of dreams. Noss pulls at a mask that is over-hanging the edge of one shelf – a dozen fall down upon him. Backing away from the avalanche of false faces, he looks at the sardonically grinning one in his hand.

"Excellent choice," says the shopkeeper, who steps out from behind a long counter in the rearguard of shadows. "Put it on and let's see. Yes, my gracious, this is excellent. You see how your entire face is well-covered, from the hairline to just beneath the chin and no farther. And at the sides it clings snugly. It doesn't pinch, am I right?" The mask nods in agreement. "Good, that's how it should be. Your ears are unobstructed – you have very nice ones, by the way – while the mask holds on to the sides of the head. It is comfortable, yet secure enough to stay put and not fall off in the heat of activity. You'll see, after a while you won't even know you're wearing it! The holes for the eyes, nostrils, and mouth are perfectly placed for your features; no natural function is inhibited, that is a must. And it looks so good on you, especially up close, though I'm sure also at a distance. Go stand over there in the moonlight. Yes, it was made for you, what do you say? I'm sorry, what?"

Noss walks back toward the shopkeeper and removes the mask.

"I said alright, I suppose I'll take this one."

"Fine, there's no question about it. Now let me show you some of the other ones, just a few steps this way."

The shopkeeper pulls something down from a high shelf and places it in his customer's hands. What Noss now holds is another mask, but one that somehow seems to be . . . impractical. While the other mask possessed every virtue of conformity with its wearer's face, this mask is neglectful of such advantages. Its surface forms a strange mass of bulges and depressions which appear unaccommodating at best, possibly pain-inflicting. And it is so much heavier than the first one.

"No," says Noss, handing back the mask, "I believe the other will do."

The shopkeeper looks as if he is at a loss for words. He stares at Noss for many moments before saying: "May I ask a personal question? Have you lived, how shall I say this, *here* all your life?"

The shopkeeper is now gesturing beyond the thick glass of the shop's windows.

Noss shakes his head in reply.

"Well, then there's no rush. Don't make any hasty decisions. Stay around the shop and think it over, there's still time. In fact, it would be a favor to me. I have to go out for a while, you see, and if you could keep an eye on things I would greatly appreciate it. You'll do it, then? Good. And don't worry," he says, taking a large hat from a peg that poked out of the wall, "I'll be back in no time, no time at all. If someone pays us a visit, just do what you can for them," he shouts before closing the front door behind him.

Now alone, Noss takes a closer look at those outlandish masks the shopkeeper had just shown him. While differing in design, as any good assortment of masks must, they all share the same impracticalities of weight and shape, as well as having some very oddly placed apertures for ventilation, and too many of them. Outlandish indeed! Noss gives these new masks back to the shelves from which they came, and he holds on tightly to the one that the shopkeeper had said was so perfect for him, so practical in every way. After a vaguely exploratory shuffle about the shop, Noss finds a stool behind the long counter and there falls asleep.

It seems only a few moments later that he is awakened by some sound or other. Collecting his wits, he gazes around the dark shop, as if searching for the source of hidden voices which are calling to him. Then the sound returns, a soft thudding sound behind him and far off into the shadowy rooms at the rear of the shop. Hopping down from the stool, Noss passes through a narrow doorway, descends a brief flight of stairs, passes through another doorway, ascends another brief flight of stairs, walks down a short and very low hallway, and at last arrives at the back door. It rumbles again once or twice.

"Just do what you can for them," Noss remembers. But he looks uneasy. On the other side of that door there is only a tiny plot of ground surrounded by a high fence.

"Why don't you come around the front?" he shouts through the door. But there is no reply, only a request.

"Please bring five of those masks to the other side of the fence. That's where we are now. There's a fire, you'll see us. Well, can you do this or not?"

Noss leans his head into the shadows by the wall: one side of his face is now in darkness while the other is indistinct, blurred by a strange glare which is only an impostor of true light. "Give me a moment, I'll meet you there," he finally replies. "Did you hear me?"

There is no response from the other side. Noss turns the door handle, which is unexpectedly warm, and through a thread-like crack peers out into the backyard. There is nothing to be seen except a square of blackness surrounded by the tall wooden slabs of the fence, and a few thin branches twisting against a pale sky. But whatever signs of pranksterism Noss perceives or is able to fabricate to himself, there is no defying the traditions of the festival, even if one can claim to have merely adopted this town and its seasonal practices, however *rare* they may be. For innocence and excuses are not harmonious with the spirit of this fabulously infrequent occasion. Therefore, Noss retrieves the masks and brings them to the rear door of the shop. Cautiously, he steps out.

When he reaches the far end of the yard – a much greater distance from the shop than it had seemed – he sees a faint glow of fire through the cracks in the fence. There is a small door with clumsy black hinges and only a hole for a handle. Setting the five masks aside for a moment, Noss squats down and peers through the hole. On the other side of the fence is a dark yard exactly like the one on his side, save for the fire burning upon the ground. Gathered around the blaze are several figures – five, perhaps four – with hunched shoulders and spines curving toward the light of the flames. They are all wearing masks which at first seem securely fitted to their faces. But, one by one, these masks appear to loosen and slip down, as if each is losing hold upon its wearer. Finally, one of the figures pulls his off completely and tosses it into the fire, where it curls and shrinks into a wad of bubbling blackness. The others follow this action when their time comes. Relieved of their masks, the figures resume their shrugging stance. But the light of the fire now shines on four, yes four, smooth and faceless faces.

"These are the wrong ones, you little idiot," says someone who is standing in the shadows by the fence. And Noss can only stare dumbly as a hand snatches up the masks and draws them into the darkness. "We have no more use for *these!*" the voice shouts.

Noss runs in retreat toward the shop, the five masks striking his narrow back and falling face-up on the ground. For he has gained a glimpse of the speaker in the shadows and now understands why *those* masks are no good to them now.

Once inside the shop, Noss leans upon the long counter to catch his breath. Then he looks up and sees that the shopkeeper has returned.

"There were some masks I brought out to the fence. They were the wrong ones," he says to the shopkeeper.

"No trouble at all," the other replies. "I'll see that the right ones are delivered. Don't worry, there's still time. And how about you, then?"

"Me?"

"And the masks, I mean."

"Oh, I'm sorry to have bothered you in the first place. It's not at all what I thought . . . That is, maybe I should just—"

"Nonsense! You can't leave now, you see. Let me take care of everything. Listen to me, I want you to go to a place where they know how to handle cases like this, at times like this. You're not the only one who is a little frightened tonight. It's right around the corner, this – no, *that* way, and across the street. It's a tall gray building, but it hasn't been there very long so watch you don't miss it. And you have to go down some stairs around the side. Now will you please follow my advice?"

Noss nods obediently.

"Good, you won't be sorry. Now go straight there. Don't stop for anyone or anything. And here, don't forget these," the shopkeeper reminds Noss, handing him an unmatching pair of masks. "Good luck!"

Though there doesn't seem to be anyone or anything to stop for, Noss does stop once or twice and dead in his tracks, as if someone behind him has just called his name. Then he thoughtfully caresses his chin and his smooth cheeks; he also touches other parts of his face, frantically, before proceeding toward the tall gray building. By the time he reaches the stairway at the side of the building, he cannot keep his hands off himself. Finally Noss puts on one of the masks – the sardonically grinning one. But somehow it no longer fits him the way it once did. It keeps slipping, little by little, as he descends the stairs, which look worn down by countless footsteps, bowed in the middle by the invisible tonnage of time. Yet Noss remembers the shopkeeper saying that this place hadn't been here very long.

The room at the bottom, which Noss now enters, also looks very old and is very . . . quiet. At this late stage of the festival the room is crowded with occupants who do nothing but sit silently in the shadows, with a face here and there reflecting the dull light. These faces are horribly simple; they have no expression at all, or very slight expressions and ones that are strange. But they are finding their way back, little by little, to a familiar land of faces. And the process, if the ear listens closely, is not an entirely silent one. Perhaps this is how a garden would sound if it could be heard growing in the dead of night. It is that soft creaking of new faces breaking through old flesh. And they are growing very nicely. At length, with a torpid solemnity, Noss removes the old mask and tosses it away. It falls to the floor and lies there grinning in the dim glow of that room, fixed in an expression that, in days to come, many will find strange and wonder at.

For the old festival of masks has ended, so that a greater festival may begin. And of the old time nothing will be said, because nothing will be known. But the old masks, false souls, will find something to remember, and perhaps they will speak of those days when they are alone behind doors that do not open, or in the darkness at the summit of stairways leading nowhere.

THE MUSIC OF THE MOON

With considerable interest, and some disquiet, I listened while a small pale man named Tressor told of his experience, his mild voice barely breaking the silence of a moonlit room. It seems he was one of those who could not sleep, and so he often spent this superfluous time walking until daybreak, exchanging his natural rest for those nocturnal visions which our city will disclose to certain eyes. And who can resist such enchantment, even with the knowledge that it is really a secret evil which gilds our world with wonders, while this same evil may ultimately ruin both these wonders and our world. Above all, this paradox may pertain to the ones who find no rest in their beds.

But to gaze up and glimpse some unusual shape loping across steep roofs with a bewildering agility might be compensation for many nights of sleepless hells. Or to hear a nearly sensible murmuring, by moonlight, in one of our narrow streets, and to follow these whispers through the night without ever being able to close in on them, yet without their ever fading in the slightest degree – this very well might relieve the wearing effects of a monotonous torment. And what if most of these incidents remain inconclusive, and what if they are left as merely enticing episodes, undocumented and underdeveloped? May they not still serve their purpose? And how many has our city *saved* in this manner, staying their hands from the knife, the rope, or the poison vial? However, as Tressor's story was an exaggeration, a heightened as well as embellished version of such vague adventures, I was not surprised that its outcome was more than normally conclusive, if what I believe has happened to him is true.

During one of his blank nights of insomnia, he had wandered into the older section of town where there is unreserved activity at all hours. But Tressor was only interested in exhausting, not engaging those hours, in using them up with as little pain as possible. Thus, he gave no more than modest scrutiny to the character standing by the steps of a rotten old building, except to note that this man was roughly his own stature and that he seemed to be loitering to no special purpose, his hands buried deep in the huge pouches of his overcoat and his eyes gazing upon the passersby with a look of profound patience. The building outside of which he stood was itself a rather plain structure, one notable only for its windows, the way some faces are distinctive solely by virtue of an interesting pair of eyes. These windows were not the slender rectangles of most of the other buildings along the street, but were in the shape of half-circles divided into several slice-shaped panes. And in the moonlight they seem to shine in a particularly striking way, though possibly this is merely an effect of contrast to the surrounding area, where a few clean pieces of glass will inevitably draw attention to themselves. I cannot say for certain which may be upheld as the explanation.

In any case, Tressor was passing by this building, the one with those windows, when the man standing by the steps shoved something at him, leaving it in his grasp. And as he did so, he looked straight and deep into poor Tressor's eyes, which Tressor was quick to lower and fix upon the object in his hand. What had been given to him was a small sheet of paper, and further down the street Tressor paused by a lamp-post to read the thin lines of tiny letters. Printed in black ink on one side of a coarse, rather gummy grade of pulp, the handbill announced an evening's entertainment later that same night at the building he had just passed. Tressor looked back at the man who had handed him this announcement, but he was no longer standing in his place. And for a moment this seemed very odd, for despite his casual, even restful appearance of waiting for no one and for nothing, this man did seem to have been somehow attached to that particular spot outside the building, and now his sudden absence caused Tressor to feel . . . confused.

Once again Tressor scanned the page in his hand, absent-mindedly rubbing it between his thumb and fingers. It did have a strange texture, like ashes mixed with grease. Soon, however, he began to feel that he was giving the matter too much thought; and, as he resumed his insomniac meandering, he flung the sheet aside. But before it reached the pavement, the handbill was snatched out of the air by someone walking very swiftly in the opposite direction. Glancing back, Tressor found it difficult to tell which of the other pedestrians had retrieved the paper. He then continued on his way.

But later that night, desperate for some distraction which mere walking seemed no longer able to provide him, he returned to the building whose windows were shining half-circles.

He entered through the front door, which was unlocked and unattended, proceeding through silent, empty hallways. Along the walls were lamps in the form of dimly glowing spheres. Turning a corner, Tressor was suddenly faced with a black abyss, within which an unlighted stairway began to take shape as his eyes grew accustomed to the greater dark. After some hesitation he went up the stairs, playing a brittle music upon the old planks. From the first landing of the stairway he could see the soft lights above, and rather than turning back he ascended toward them. The second floor, however, much resembled the first, as did the third and all the succeeding floors. Reaching the heights of the building, Tressor began to roam around once again, even opening some of the doors.

But most of the rooms behind these doors were dark and empty, and the moonlight that shone through the perfectly clear windows fell upon bare, dust-covered floors and plain walls. Tressor was about to turn around and leave that place for good, when he spotted at the end of the last hallway a door with a faint yellow aura leaking out at its edges. He walked up to this door, which was slightly opened, and cautiously pushed it back.

Peering into the room, Tressor saw the yellowish globe of light which hung from the ceiling. Scanning slowly down the walls, he spied small, shadowlike things moving in corners and along the floor molding – the consequences of inept housekeeping, he concluded. Then he saw something by the far wall which made him quickly withdraw back into the hallway. What he had glimpsed were the dark outlines of four strangely shaped figures leaning upon the wall, the tallest of which was nearly as tall as he was and the smallest, far smaller. But once out in the hallway, he found these images had become clearer in his mind. He now felt almost sure of their true nature, although I have to confess that I could not imagine what they might have been until he spoke the keyword: "cases."

Venturing back into the room, Tressor stood before the closed cases which in all likelihood belonged to a quartet of musicians. They looked very old and were bound like books in some murky cloth. Tressor ran his fingers along this material, then before long began fingering the tarnished metal latches of the violin case. But he suddenly stopped when he saw a group of shadows rising on the wall in front of him.

"Why have you come in here?" asked a voice which sounded both exhausted and malicious.

"I saw the light," answered Tressor without turning around, still crouching over the violin case. Somehow the sound of his own voice echoing in that empty room disturbed him more than that of his interrogator, though he could not at the moment say why this was. He counted four shadows on the wall, three of them tall and trim, and the fourth somewhat smaller but with an enormous, misshapen head.

"Stand up," ordered the same voice as before. Tressor stood up. "Turn around."

Tressor slowly turned around. And he was relieved to see standing before him three rather ordinary-looking men and a woman whose head was enveloped by pale, ragged clouds of hair. Moreover, among the men was the one who had given Tressor the handbill earlier that night. But he now seemed to be much taller than he had been outside in the street.

"You handed me the paper," Tressor reminded the man as if trying to revive an old friendship. And again his voice sounded queer to him as it reverberated in that empty room.

The tall man looked to his companions, surveying each of the other three faces in turn, as though reading some silent message in their expressionless features. Then he removed a piece of paper from inside his coat.

"You mean this," he said to Tressor.

"Yes, that's it."

They all smiled gently at him, and the tall man said, "Then you're in the wrong place. You should be one floor up. But the main stairway won't take you to it. There's another, smaller flight of stairs in the back hallway. You should be able to see it. Are your eyes good?"

"Yes."

"Good as they look?" asked one of the other men.

"I can see very well, if that's what you mean."

"Yes, that's exactly what we mean," said the woman.

Then the four of them stepped back to make a path for Tressor, two on either side of him, and he started to walk from the room.

"There are already some people upstairs for the concert," said the tall man as Tressor reached the door. "We will be up shortly – to play!"

"Yes . . . yes . . . yes," muttered the others as they began fumbling with the dark cases containing their instruments.

"*Their* voices," thought Tressor, "not my voice."

As Tressor later explained it to me, the voices of the musicians, unlike his own, made no echoes of any kind in the empty room.

Nevertheless, Tressor went to find the stairway, which at first looked like an empty shaft of blackness in the corner of the back hall. Guided by the fragile railing that twisted in a spiral, he reached the uppermost level of the old building. And there the hallways were much narrower than those below, mere passageways lit by spherical lamps which were caked with dust and no longer appeared at even intervals. There were also fewer doors, and these could be better found by touch than by sight. But Tressor's eyes were very good, as he claimed, and he found the room where a number of people were already gathered, true to the musicians' claim.

I can imagine that it was not easy for Tressor to decide whether or not to go through with what he had started that night. If the inability to sleep sometimes leads a sufferer into strange or perilous consolations, Tressor still retained enough of a daylight way of thought to make a compromise. He did not enter the room where he saw people slumped down in seats scattered about, the black silhouettes of human heads visible only in the moonlight which poured through the pristine glass of those particular windows. Instead, he hid in the shadows farther down the hallway. And when the musicians arrived upstairs, burdened with their instruments, they filed into the moonlit room without suspecting Tressor's presence outside. The door closed behind them with a click that did not echo in the narrow hallway.

For a few moments there was only silence, a purer silence than Tressor had ever known, like the silence of a dark, lifeless world. Then sound began to enter the silence, but so inconspicuously that Tressor could not tell when the absolute silence had ended and an embellished silence had begun. Sound became music, slow and muffled music in the soft darkness, somewhat muted as it passed through the intervening door. At first there seemed to be only a single note wavering alone in a universe of darkness and silence, coaxing its hearers to an understanding of its subtle voice, to sense its secrets and perhaps to hear the unheard. The single note then burst into a shower of tones, proliferating harmonies, and at that exact moment a second note began to follow the same course; then another note, and another. There was now more music than could possibly be contained by that earlier silence, expansive as it may have seemed. Soon there was no space remaining for silence, or perhaps music and silence became confused, indistinguishable from each other, as colors may merge into whiteness. And at last, for Tressor, that interminable sequence of wakeful nights, each a mirror to the one before it and the one to follow, was finally broken.

When Tressor awoke, the light of a quiet gray dawn filled the narrow hallway where he lay hunched between peeling walls. Recalling in a moment the events of the previous night, he scrambled to his feet and began walking toward the room whose door was still closed. He put his ear up to the rough wood but heard no sounds on the other side. In his mind a memory of wonderful music rose up and then quickly faded. As before, the music sounded muffled to him, diminished in its power because he had been too fearful to enter the room where the music was played. But he entered it now.

And he was surprised to see the audience still in their seats, which were all facing four empty chairs and four abandoned instruments of varying size. The musicians themselves were nowhere in sight.

The spectators were all dressed in white, hooded robes woven of some gauzy material, almost like ragged shrouds wrapped tightly around them. They were very quiet and very still, perhaps sleeping that profound sleep from which Tressor had just risen. Tressor felt a strange fear of this congregation, strange because he also sensed that they were completely helpless and no more capable of voluntary action than a roomful of abandoned dolls. As his eyes became sharper in the grayish twilight of the room, the robes worn by these paralyzed figures began to look more and more like bandages of some kind, a heavy white netting which bound them securely. "But they were not bandages, or robes, or shrouds," Tressor finally told me. "They were webs, thick layers of webs which I first thought covered everyone's entire body."

But this was only how it appeared to Tressor from his perspective behind the mummified audience. For as he moved along the outer edge of the terrible gathering, progressing toward the four empty chairs at the front of the room, he saw that each stringy white cocoon was woven to expose the face of its inhabitant. And he also saw that the expressions on these faces were very similar, and that they might almost have been described as serene, if only those faces had been whole. But none of them seemed to have any eyes: the crowd was faced in the same direction to witness a spectacle it could no longer see, gazing at nothing with bleeding sockets. All save one of them, as Tressor finally discovered.

At the end of a rather chaotic row of chairs in the back of the room, one member of the dead audience stirred in his seat. As

Tressor slowly approached this figure, with vague thoughts of rescue in his mind, he noticed that its eyelids were shut. Without delaying for an instant, he began tearing at the webs which imprisoned the victim, speaking words of hope as he worked at the horrible mesh. But then the closed eyelids of the bound figure popped open and looked around, ultimately focusing on Tressor.

"You're the only one," said Tressor, laboring at the webby bonds.

"Shhhh," said the other, "I'm waiting."

Tressor paused in confusion, his fingers tangled with a gruesome stuff which felt sticky and abrasive, intolerably strange to touch.

"They might return," insisted Tressor, even though he was not entirely sure whom he meant by "they."

"They *will* return," answered the other's soft but excited voice. "With the moon they will return with their wonderful music."

Appalled by this enigma, fearful of things he could not name, Tressor began to back away. And I suspect that from within a number of those hollow sockets, four of them to be exact, the tiny eyes of strange creatures were watching him as he fled that horrible room.

Afterward Tressor visited me night after night to tell me about the music, until it seemed I could almost hear it myself and could tell his story as my own. Soon he talked only about the music, as he recalled hearing it somewhat dulled by a closed door. When he tried to imagine what it would be like to have heard the music, as he phrased it, "in the flesh," it was obvious that he had forgotten the fate of those who did hear it in this way. His voice became more and more faint as the music grew louder and clearer in his mind. Then one night Tressor stopped coming to visit me.

And now it seems that I am the one who cannot sleep, especially when I see the moon hovering above our city – the moon all pale and fat, glaring down on us from within its gauzy webs of clouds. And how can I rest beneath its enchanting gaze? How difficult it is to keep myself from straying into a certain section of town as night after night I wander strange streets alone.

THE JOURNAL OF
J.P. DRAPEAU

Introduction

It was late and we had been drinking. My friend, a poet who can become very excitable at times, looked across the table at me. Then he revived a pet grievance of his as though I had not heard it all before.

"Where is the writer," he began, "who is unstained by any habits of the human, who would be the ideal of everything alien to living, and whose own eccentricity, in its darkest phase, would turn in on itself to form increasingly more complex patterns of strangeness? Where is the writer who has remained his entire life in some remote dream that he inhabited from his day of birth, if not long before? Where is the writer from some mist-shrouded backwater of the earth – the city of Bruges itself, that withered place which some dreamer has described as 'a sumptuous corpse of the Middle Ages that sings to itself from innumerable bell-towers and lays bony bridges across the black veins of its old canals.'

"But perhaps our writer's home would have to be an even older, more decaying Bruges in some farther, more obscure Flanders . . . the one envisioned by Breughel and by Ensor. Where is the writer who was begotten by two passionate masks in the course of those macabre festivities called *kermesse*? Who was abandoned to develop in his own way, left to a lonely evolution in shadowed streets and beside sluggish canals. Who was formed by the dreams around him as much as those within him, and who filled himself with strange learning. Where is this writer, the one whose entangled hallucinations could only be accommodated by the most intimate of diaries? And this diary, this journal of the most unnecessary man who ever lived, would be a record of the most questionable experiences ever known, and the most beautiful."

"Of course, there is no such writer," I replied. "But there's always Drapeau. Out of anyone I could name, he most nearly meets, if I may say, those rather *severe* prerequisites of yours. Living the whole of his life in Bruges, keeping those notebooks of his, and he—"

But my friend the poet only moaned in despair:

"Drapeau, always Drapeau."

Excerpts from the journal

April 31, 189–

I have noticed that certain experiences are allowed to languish in the corners of life, are not allowed to *circulate* as freely as others. My own, for example. Since childhood, not one day has passed in which I have failed to hear the *music of graveyards*. And yet, to my knowledge, never has another soul on earth made mention of this phenomenon. Is the circulation of the living so poor that it cannot carry these dead notes? It must be a mere trickle!

December 24, 189–

Two tiny corpses, one male and the other female, live in that enormous closet in my bedroom. They are also very old, but still they are quick enough to hide themselves whenever I need to enter the closet to get something. I keep all my paraphernalia in there, stuffed into trunks or baskets and piled quite out of reach. I can't even see the floor or the walls any longer, and only if I hold a light high over my head can I study the layers of cobwebs floating about near the ceiling. After I close the door of the closet, its two miniature inhabitants resume their activities. Their voices are only faint squeaks which during the day hardly bother me at all. But sometimes I am kept awake far into the night by those interminable conversations of theirs.

May 31, 189–

After serving out the hours of a night in which sleep was absolutely forbidden, I went out for a walk. I had not gone far when I became spectator to a sad scene. Some yards ahead of me on the street, an old man was being forcibly led from a house by two other men. They had him in restraints and were delivering him to a waiting vehicle. Laughing hysterically, the man was apparently destined for the asylum. As the struggling trio reached the street, the eyes of the laughing man met my own. Suddenly he stopped laughing. Then, in a burst of resistance, he broke free of his escorts, ran toward me, and fell right into my arms. Since his own were so tightly bound, I had to hold up his full weight.

"Never tell them what it means," he said frantically, almost weeping.

"How can I tell them what I don't know?"

"Swear!" he demanded.

But by then his pursuers had caught up with him. As they dragged him off he began laughing just as before, and the peals of his laughter, in the early morning quiet, were soon devoured by the pealing of several church bells. Poor lunatic. This was one of the most malignant conspiracies I had ever witnessed; the bells, I mean. (They are everywhere.) This was also what made me decide that I had better keep the madman's secret after all.

August 1, 189–

As a child I maintained some very strange notions. For instance, I used to believe that during the night, while I slept, witches and monkeys removed parts of my body and played games with them, hiding my arms and legs, rolling my head across the floor. Of course I abandoned this belief as soon as I entered school, but not until much later did I discover the truth about it. After assimilating many facts from various sources and allowing them to mingle in my mind, I realized something. It happened one night as I was crossing a bridge that stretched over a narrow canal. (This was in a part of town fairly distant from where I live.) Pausing for a moment, as I usually do when crossing one of these bridges, I gazed not down into the dark waters of the canal, as I also usually do, but upwards through the branches of overhanging trees. It was those stars, I knew that now: certain of them had been promised specific parts of my body; in the darkest hours of the night, when one is unusually sensitive to such things, I could – and still can, though just barely – feel the force of these stars tugging away at various points, eager for the moment of my death when each of them might carry off that part of me which is theirs by right. Of course a child would misinterpret this experience. And how often I have found that every superstition has its basis in truth.

October 9, 189–

Last night I visited one of the little theaters and stood at the back for a while. Onstage was a magician, shiny black hair parted straight down the middle, with full prestidigitorial regalia about him: a long box to his left (moons and stars), a tall box to his right (oriental designs), and before him a low table covered with a red velvet cloth littered with divers objects. The audience, a full house, applauded wildly after each illusion. At one point the magician divided the various sections of his assistant into separate boxes, which he then proceeded to move to distant areas of the stage, while the dismembered hands and feet continued to wiggle about and a decapitated head laughed loudly. The audience was at great pains to express its amusement. "Isn't it incredible!" exclaimed a man standing beside me. "If you say so," I replied, and then headed for the exit, realizing that for me such things simply do not hold much interest.

November 1, 189–
From the earliest days of man there has endured the conviction that there is an order of existence which is entirely strange to him. It does indeed seem that the strict order of the visible world is only a semblance, one providing certain gross materials which become the basis for subtle *improvisations* of invisible powers. Hence, it may appear to some that a leafless tree is not a tree but a signpost to another realm; that an old house is not a house but a thing possessing a will of its own; that the dead may throw off that heavy blanket of earth to walk in their sleep, and in ours. And these are merely a few of the infinite variations on the themes of the natural order as it is usually conceived.

But is there *really* a strange world? Of course. Are there, then, two worlds? Not at all. There is only our own world and it alone is alien to us, intrinsically so by virtue of its lack of mysteries. If only it actually were deranged by invisible powers, if only it were susceptible to *real* strangeness, perhaps it would seem more like a home to us, and less like an empty room filled with the echoes of this dreadful improvising. To think that we might have found comfort in a world suited to *our* nature, only to end up in one so resoundingly strange!

January 1, 189–
There is a solitary truth which, whether for good or ill I don't know, cannot yet be expressed on this earth. This is very strange, since everything – outward scenes as much as inward ones – suggests this truth and like some fantastic game of charades is always trying to coax the secret into the open. The eyes of certain crudely fashioned dolls are especially suggestive. And distant laughter. In rare moments I feel myself very close to setting it down in my journal, just as I would any other revelation. It would only be a few sentences, I'm sure. But whenever I feel them

beginning to take shape in my mind, the page before me will not welcome my pen. Afterward I become fatigued with my failure and suffer headaches that may last for days. At these times I also tend to see odd things reflected in windows. Even after a full week has passed I may continue to wake up in the middle of the night, the silence of my room faintly vibrant with a voice that cries out to me from another universe.

March 30, 190–

Out of sheer absent-mindedness I had stared at my reflection in the mirror a little too deeply. I should say that that mirror has been hanging from that wall for more years, I would guess, than I have been on this earth. It's no surprise, then, that sooner or later it should get the edge on me. Up to a certain point there were no problems to speak of: there were only my eyes, my nose, my mouth, and that was that. But then it began to seem that those eyes were regarding me, rather than I them; that that mouth was about to speak things I had no notion of. Finally, I realized that an entirely different creature was hiding behind my face, making it wholly unrecognizable to me. Let me say that I spent considerable time reshaping my reflection into what it should be.

Later, when I was out walking, I stopped dead on the street. Ahead of me, standing beneath a lamp hanging from an old wall, was the outline of a figure of my general size and proportions. He was looking the other way but very stiffly and very tense, as if waiting anxiously for the precise moment when he would suddenly twist about-face. If that should happen, I knew what I would see: my eyes, my nose, my mouth, and behind those features a being strange beyond all description. I retraced my steps back home and went immediately to bed.

But I couldn't sleep. All night long a greenish glow radiated from the mirror in triumph.

No Date

I had just finished a book* in which there is an old town strung with placid meandering canals. I closed the book and went over to the window. This is an old town, if medieval counts as old, strung with placid meandering canals. The town in the book is often mist shrouded. This town is often mist shrouded. That town has close crumbling houses, odd arching bridges, innummerable church towers, and narrow twisting streets that end in queer little courtyards. So has this one, needless to say. And the infinitely

* Possibly the novel *Bruges-la-morte* (1892) by Georges Rodenbach. (T.L.)

hollow sounding of the bells in the book, at early morning and sullen twilight, is the same as your sounding bells, my lovely town. Thus, I pass easily between one town and the other, pleasantly confusing them.

O my storybook town, strange as death itself, I have made your mysteries mine, mine yours, and have suffered a few brief chapters in your sumptuous history of decay. I have studied your most obscure passages and found them as dark as the waters of your canals.

My town, my storybook, myself, how long we have held on! But it seems we will have to make up for this endurance and each, in our turn, will disappear. Every brick of yours, every bone of mine, every word in our book – everything gone forever. Everything, perhaps, except the sound of those bells, haunting an empty mist through an eternal twilight.

VASTARIEN

Within the blackness of his sleep a few lights began to glow like candles in a cloistered cell. Their illumination was unsteady and dim, issuing from no definite source. Nonetheless, he now discovered many shapes beneath the shadows: tall buildings whose rooftops nodded groundward, wide buildings whose facades seemed to follow the curve of a street, dark buildings whose windows and doorways tilted like badly hung paintings. And even if he found himself unable to fix his own location in this scene, he knew where his dreams had delivered him once more.

Even as the warped structures multiplied in his vision, crowding the lost distance, he possessed a sense of intimacy with each of them, a peculiar knowledge of the spaces within them and of the streets which coiled themselves around their mass. Once again he knew the depths of their foundations, where an obscure life seemed to establish itself, a secret civilization of echoes flourishing among groaning walls. Yet upon his probing more extensively into such interiors, certain difficulties presented themselves: stairways that wandered off-course into useless places; caged elevators that urged unwanted stops on their passengers; thin ladders ascending into a maze of shafts and conduits, the dark valves and arteries of a petrified and monstrous organism.

And he knew that every corner of this corroded world was prolific with choices, even if they had to be made blindly in a place where clear consequences and a hierarchy of possibilities were lacking. For there might be a room whose shabby and soundless decor exudes a desolate serenity which at first attracts the visitor, who then discovers certain figures enveloped in plush furniture, figures that do not move or speak but only stare; and, concluding that these weary mannikins have exercised a bizarre indulgence in repose, the visitor must ponder the alternatives: to linger or to leave?

Eluding the claustral enchantments of such rooms, his gaze now roamed the streets of this dream. He scanned the altitudes beyond the high sloping roofs: there the stars seemed to be no more than silvery cinders which showered up from the mouths of great chimneys and clung to something dark and dense looming above, something that closed in upon each black horizon. It appeared to him that certain high towers nearly breached this sagging blackness, stretching themselves nightward to attain the farthest possible remove from the world below. And toward the peak of one of the highest towers he spied vague silhouettes that moved hectically in a bright window, twisting and leaning upon the glass like shadow-puppets in the fever of some mad dispute.

Through the mazy streets his vision slowly glided, as if carried along by a sluggish draft. Darkened windows reflected the beams of stars and streetlamps; lighted windows, however dim their glow, betrayed strange scenes which were left behind long before their full mystery could overwhelm the dreaming traveller. He wandered into thoroughfares more remote, soaring past cluttered gardens and crooked gates, drifting alongside an expansive wall that seemed to border an abyss, and floating over bridges that arched above the black purling waters of canals.

Near a certain street corner, a place of supernatural clarity and stillness, he saw two figures standing beneath the crystalline glaze of a lamp ensconsed high upon a wall of carved stone. Their shadows were perfect columns of blackness upon the livid pavement; their faces were a pair of faded masks concealing profound schemes. And they seemed to have lives of their own, with no awareness of their dreaming observer, who wished only to live with these specters and know *their* dreams, to remain in this place where everything was transfixed in the order of the unreal.

Never again, it seemed, could he be forced to abandon this realm of beautiful shadows.

Victor Keirion awoke with a brief convulsion of his limbs, as if he had been chaotically scrambling to break his fall from an imaginary height. For a moment he held his eyes closed, hoping to preserve the dissipating euphoria of the dream. Finally he blinked once or twice. Moonlight through a curtainless window allowed him the image of his outstretched arms and his somewhat twisted hands. Releasing his awkward hold on the edge of the sheeted mattress, he rolled onto his back. Then he groped around until his fingers found the cord dangling from the light above the bed. A small, barely furnished room appeared.

He pushed himself up and reached toward the painted metal nightstand. Through the spaces between his fingers he saw the pale gray binding of a book and some of the dark letters tooled upon its cover: V, S, R, N. Suddenly he withdrew his hand without touching the book, for the magical intoxication of the dream had died, and he feared that he would not be able to revive it.

Freeing himself from the coarse bedcovers, he sat at the edge of the mattress, elbows resting on his legs and hands loosely folded. His hair and eyes were pale, his complexion rather grayish, suggesting the color of certain clouds or that of long confinement. The single window in the room was only a few steps away, but he kept himself from approaching it, from even glancing in its direction. He knew exactly what he would see at that time of night: tall buildings, wide buildings, dark buildings, a scattering of stars and lights, and some lethargic movement in the streets below.

In so many ways the city outside the window was a semblance of that other place, which now seemed impossibly far off and inaccessible. But the likeness was evident only to his inner vision, only in the recollected images he formed when his eyes were closed or out of focus. It would be difficult to conceive of a creature for whom *this* world – its bare form seen with open eyes – represented a coveted paradise.

Now standing before the window, his hands tearing into the pockets of a papery bathrobe, he saw that something was missing from the view, some crucial property that was denied to the stars above and the streets below, some unearthly essence needed to save them. The word *unearthly* reverberated in the room. In that place and at that hour, the paradoxical absence, the missing quality, became clear to him: it was the element of the unreal.

For Victor Keirion belonged to that wretched sect of souls who believe that the only value of this world lies in its power – at certain times – to suggest another world. Nevertheless, the place he now surveyed through the high window could never be anything but the most gauzy phantom of that other place, nothing save a shadowy mimic of the anatomy of that great dream. And although there were indeed times when one might be deceived, isolated moments when a gift for disguise triumphs, the impersonation could never be perfect or lasting. No true challenge to the rich unreality of Vastarien, where every shape suggested a thousand others, every sound disseminated everlasting echoes, every word founded a world. No horror, no joy was the equal of the abysmally vibrant sensations known in this place that was elsewhere, this spellbinding retreat where all experiences were interwoven to compose fantastic textures of feeling, a fine and dark tracery of limitless patterns. For everything in the unreal points to the infinite, and everything in Vastarien was unreal, unbounded by the tangible lie of existing. Even its most humble aspects proclaimed this truth: what door, he wondered, in any other world could imply the abundant and strange possibilities that belonged to the entrancing doors in the dream?

Then, as he focused his eyes upon a distant part of the city, he recalled a particular door, one of the least suggestive objects he had ever confronted, intimating little of what lay beyond.

It was a rectangle of smudged glass within another rectangle of scuffed wood, a battered thing lodged within a brick wall at the bottom of a stairway leading down from a crumbling street. And it pushed easily inward, merely a delicate formality between the underground shop and the outside world. Inside was an open room vaguely circular in shape, unusual in seeming more like the lobby of an old hotel than a bookstore. The circumference of the room was composed of crowded bookshelves whose separate sections were joined to one another to create an irregular polygon of eleven sides, with a long desk standing where a twelfth would have been. Beyond the desk stood a few more bookshelves arranged in aisles, their monotonous length leading into shadows. At the furthest point from this end of the shop, he began his circuit of the shelves, which appeared so promising in their array of old and ruddy bindings, like remnants of some fabulous autumn.

Very soon, however, the promise was betrayed and the mystique of the Librairie de Grimoires, in accord with his expectations, was stripped away to reveal, in his eyes, a side-show of charlatanry. For this disillusionment he had only himself to blame. Moreover, he could barely articulate the nature of the discrepancy between what he had hoped to find and what he actually found in such places. Aside from this hope, there was little basis for his belief that there existed some other arcana, one of a different kind altogether from that proffered by the books before him, all of which were sodden with an obscene reality, falsely hermetic ventures which consisted of circling the same absurd landscape. The other worlds portrayed in these books inevitably served as annexes of this one; they were impostors of the authentic unreality which was the only realm of redemption, however gruesome it might appear. And it was this *terminal* landscape that he sought, not those rituals of the "way" that never arrives, heavens or hells that are mere pretexts for circumnavigating the real and revelling in it. For he dreamed of strange volumes that turned away from all earthly light to become lost in their own nightmares, pages that preached a nocturnal salvation, a liturgy of shadows, catechism of phantoms. His absolute: to dwell among the ruins of reality.

And it seemed to surpass all probability that there existed no precedent for this dream, no elaboration of this vision into a word, a delirious bible that would be the blight of all others – a scripture that would begin in apocalypse and lead its disciple to the wreck of all creation.

He had, in fact, come upon passages in certain books that approached this ideal, hinting to the reader – almost admonishing him – that the page before his eyes was about to offer a view from the abyss and cast a wavering light on desolate hallucinations. *To become the wind in the dead of winter*, so might begin an enticing verse of dreams. But soon the bemazed visionary would falter, retracting the promised scene of a shadow kingdom at the end of all entity, perhaps offering an apologetics for this lapse into the unreal. The work would then once more take up the universal theme, disclosing its true purpose in belaboring the most futile and profane of all ambitions: power, with knowledge as its drudge. The vision of a disastrous enlightenment, of a catastrophic illumination, was conjured up in passing and then cast aside. What remained was invariably a metaphysics as systematically trivial and debased as the physical laws it purported to transcend, a manual outlining the path to some hypothetical state of absolute glory. What remained *lost* was the revelation that nothing ever known has ended in glory; that all which ends does so in exhaustion, in confusion, and debris.

Nevertheless, a book that contained even a false gesture toward his truly eccentric absolute might indeed serve his purpose. Directing the attention of a bookseller to selected contents of such books, he would say: "I have an interest in a certain subject area, perhaps you will see . . . that is, I wonder, do you know of other, what should I say, *sources* that you would be able to recommend for my . . ."

Occasionally he was referred to another bookseller or to the owner of a private collection. And ultimately he would be forced to realize that he had been grotesquely misunderstood when he found himself on the fringe of a society devoted to some strictly demonic enterprise.

The very bookshop in which he was now browsing represented only the most recent digression in a search without progress. But he had learned to be cautious and would try to waste as little time as possible in discovering if there was anything hidden for him here. Certainly not on the shelves which presently surrounded him.

"Have you seen our friend?" asked a nearby voice, startling him somewhat. Victor Keirion turned to face the stranger. The man was rather small and wore a black overcoat; his hair was also black and fell loosely across his forehead. Besides his general appearance, there was also something about his presence that made one think of a crow, a scavenging creature in wait. "Has he come out of his hole?" the man asked, gesturing toward the empty desk and the dark area behind it.

"I'm sorry, I haven't seen anyone," Keirion replied. "I only now noticed you."

"I can't help being quiet. Look at these little feet," the man said, pointing to a highly polished pair of black shoes. Without thinking, Keirion looked down; then, feeling duped, he looked up again at the smiling stranger.

"You look very bored," said the human crow.

"I'm sorry?"

"Never mind. I can see that I'm bothering you." Then the man walked away, his coat flapping slightly, and began browsing some distant bookshelves. "I've never seen you in here before," he said from across the room.

"I've never been in here before," Keirion answered.

"Have you ever read this?" the stranger asked, pulling down a book and holding up its wordless black cover.

"Never," Keirion replied without so much as glancing at the book. Somehow this seemed the best action to take with this character, who appeared to be foreign in some indefinable way, intangibly alien.

"Well, you must be looking for something special," continued the other man, replacing the black book on its shelf. "And I know what that's like, when you're looking for something very special. Have you ever heard of a book, an extremely special book, that is not . . . yes, that is not *about* something, but actually is that something?"

For the first time the obnoxious stranger had managed to intrigue Keirion rather than annoy him. "That sounds . . . ," he started to say, but then the other man exclaimed:

"There he is, there he is. Excuse me."

It seemed that the proprietor – that mutual friend – had finally made his appearance and was now standing behind the desk, looking toward his two customers. "My friend," said the crow-man as he stepped with outstretched hand over to the smoothly bald and softly fat gentleman. The two of them briefly shook hands; they whispered for a few moments. Then the crow-man was invited

behind the desk, and – led by the heavy, unsmiling bookseller –
made his way into the darkness at the back of the shop. In a distant
corner of that darkness the brilliant rectangle of a doorway
suddenly flashed into outline, admitting through its frame a
large, twoheaded shadow.

Left alone among the worthless volumes of that shop, Victor
Keirion felt the sad frustration of the uninvited, the abandoned.
More than ever he had become infected with hopes and curiosities
of an indeterminable kind. And he soon found it impossible to
remain outside that radiant little room the other two had entered,
and on whose threshold he presently stood in silence.

The room was a cramped bibliographic cubicle within which
stood another cubicle formed by free-standing bookcases, creating
four very narrow aisleways in the space between them. From the
doorway he could not see how the inner cubicle might be entered,
but he heard the voices of the others whispering within. Stepping
quietly, he began making his way along the perimeter of the room,
his eyes voraciously scanning a wealth of odd-looking volumes.

Immediately he sensed that something of a special nature
awaited his discovery, and the evidence for this intuition began
to build. Each book that he examined served as a clue in this
delirious investigation, a cryptic sign which engaged his powers of
interpretation and imparted the faith to proceed. Many of the
works were written in foreign languages he did not read; some
appeared to be composed in ciphers based on familiar characters
and others seemed to be transcribed in a wholly artificial cryptography. But in every one of these books he found an oblique
guidance, some feature of more or less indirect significance: a
strangeness in the typeface, pages and bindings of uncommon
texture, abstract diagrams suggesting no orthodox ritual or occult
system. Even greater anticipation was inspired by certain illustrated plates, mysterious drawings and engravings that depicted
scenes and situations unlike anything he could name. And such
works as *Cynothoglys* or *The Noctuary of Tine* conveyed schemes so
bizarre, so remote from known texts and treatises of the esoteric
tradition, that he felt assured of the sense of his quest.

The whispering grew louder, though no more distinct, as he
edged around a corner of that inner cubicle and anxiously noted
the opening at its far end. At the same time he was distracted, for
no apparent reason, by a small grayish volume leaning within a
gap between larger and more garish tomes. The little book had
been set upon the highest shelf, making it necessary for him to
stretch himself, as if on an upright torture rack, to reach it. Trying

not to give away his presence by the sounds of his pain, he finally secured the ashen-colored object – as pale as his own coloring – between the tips of his first two fingers. Mutely he strained to slide it quietly from its place; this act accomplished, he slowly shrunk down to his original stature and looked into the book's brittle pages.

It seemed to be a chronicle of strange dreams. Yet somehow the passages he examined were less a recollection of unruled visions than a tangible incarnation of them, not mere rhetoric but the thing itself. The use of language in the book was arrantly unnatural and the book's author unknown. Indeed, the text conveyed the impression of speaking for itself and speaking only to itself, the words flowing together like shadows that were cast by no forms outside the book. But although this volume appeared to be composed in a vernacular of mysteries, its words did inspire a sure understanding and created in their reader a visceral apprehension of the world they described, existing inseparable from it. Could this truly be the invocation of Vastarien, that improbable world to which those gnarled letters on the front of the book alluded? And was it a world at all? Rather the unreal essence of one, all natural elements purged by an occult process of extraction, all days distilled into dreams and nights into nightmares. Each passage he entered in the book both enchanted and appalled him with images and incidents so freakish and chaotic that his usual sense of these terms disintegrated along with everything else. Rampant oddity seemed to be the rule of the realm; imperfection became the source of the miraculous – wonders of deformity and marvels of miscreation. There was horror, undoubtedly. But it was a horror uncompromised by any feeling of lost joy or thwarted redemption; rather, it was a deliverance by damnation. And if Vastarien was a nightmare, it was a nightmare transformed in spirit by the utter absence of refuge: nightmare made normal.

"I'm sorry, I didn't see that you had drifted in here," said the bookseller in a high thin voice. He had just emerged from the inner chamber of the room and was standing with arms folded across his wide chest. "Please don't touch anything. And may I take that from you?" The right arm of the bookseller reached out, then returned to its former place when the man with the pale eyes did not relinquish the merchandise.

"I think I would like to purchase it," said Keirion. "I'm sure I would, if . . ."

"Of course, if the price is reasonable," finished the bookseller. "But who knows, you might not be able to understand how valuable these books can be. That one . . ." he said, removing a little pad and pencil from inside his jacket and scribbling briefly. He ripped off the top sheet and held it up for the would-be buyer to see, then confidently put away all writing materials, as if that would be the end of it.

"But there must be some latitude for bargaining," Keirion protested.

"I'm afraid not," answered the bookseller. "Not with something that is the only one of its kind, as are many of these volumes. Yet that one book you are holding, that single copy . . ."

A hand touched the bookseller's shoulder and seemed to switch off his voice. Then the crow-man stepped into the aisleway, his eyes fixed upon the object under discussion, and asked: "Don't you find that the book is somewhat . . . difficult?"

"Difficult," repeated Keirion. "I'm not sure . . . If you mean that the language is strange, I would have to agree, but—"

"No," interjected the bookseller, "that's not what he means at all."

"Excuse us for a moment," said the crow-man.

Then both men went back into the inner room, where they whispered for some time. When the whispering ceased, the bookseller came forth and announced that there had been a mistake. The book, while something of a curiosity, was worth a good deal less than the price earlier quoted. The revised evaluation, while still costly, was nevertheless within the means of this particular buyer, who agreed at once to pay it.

Thus began Victor Keirion's preoccupation with a certain book and a certain hallucinated world, though to make a distinction between these two phenomena ultimately seemed an error: the book, indeed, did not merely describe that strange world but, in some obscure fashion, was a true composition of the thing itself, its very form incarnate.

Each day thereafter he studied the hypnotic episodes of the little book; each night, as he dreamed, he carried out shapeless expeditions into its fantastic topography. To all appearances it seemed he had discovered the summit or abyss of the unreal, that paradise of exhaustion, confusion, and debris where reality ends and where one may dwell among its ruins. And it was not long before he found it necessary to revisit that twelve-sided shop, intending to question the obese bookseller on the subject of the book and unintentionally learning the truth of how it came to be sold.

When he arrived at the bookstore, sometime in the middle of a grayish afternoon, Victor Keirion was surprised to find that the door, which had opened so freely on his previous visit, was now firmly locked. It would not even rattle in its frame when he nervously pushed and pulled on the handle. Since the interior of the store was lighted, he took a coin from his pocket and began tapping on the glass. Finally, someone came forward from the shadows of the back room.

"Closed," the bookseller pantomimed on the other side of the glass.

"But . . ." Keirion argued, pointing to his wristwatch.

"Nevertheless," the wide man shouted. Then, after scrutinizing the disappointed patron, the bookseller unlocked the door and opened it far enough to carry on a brief conversation. "And what is it I can do for you. I'm closed, so you'll have to come some other time if—"

"I only wanted to ask you something. Do you remember the book that I bought from you not long ago, the one—"

"Yes, I remember," replied the bookseller, as if quite prepared for the question. "And let me say that I was quite impressed, as of course was . . . the other man."

"Impressed?" Keirion repeated.

"Flabbergasted is more the word in his case," continued the bookseller. "He said to me, 'The book has found its reader,' and what could I do but agree with him?"

"I'm afraid I don't understand," said Keirion.

The bookseller blinked and said nothing. After a few moments he reluctantly explained: "I was hoping that by now you would understand. He hasn't contacted you? The man who was in here that day?"

"No, why should he?"

The bookseller blinked again and said: "Well, I suppose there's no reason you need to stand out there. It's getting very cold, don't you feel it?" Then he closed the door and pulled Keirion a little to one side of it, whispering: "There's just one thing I would like to tell you. I made no mistake that day about the price of that book. And it was the price – in full – which was paid by the other man, don't ask me anything else about him. That price, of course, minus the small amount that you yourself contributed. I didn't cheat anyone, least of all *him*. He would have been happy to pay even more to get that book into your hands. And although I'm not exactly sure of his reasons, I think you should know that."

"But why didn't he simply purchase the book for himself?" asked Keirion.

The bookseller seemed confused. "It was of no use to him. Perhaps it would have been better if you hadn't given yourself away when he asked you about the book. How much you knew."

"But I don't know anything, apart from what I've read in the book itself. I came here to find—"

"—Nothing, I'm afraid. You're the one who should be telling me, very impressive. But I'm not asking, don't misunderstand. And there's nothing more I can tell you, since I've already violated every precept of discretion. This is such an exceptional case, though. Very impressive, if in fact you are the reader of that book."

Realizing that, at best, he had been led into a dialogue of mystification, and possibly one of lies, Victor Keirion had no regrets when the bookseller held the door open for him to leave.

But before very many days, and especially nights, had passed he learned why the bookseller had been so impressed with him, and why the crowlike stranger had been so generous: the bestower of the book who was blind to its mysteries. In the course of those days, those nights, he learned that the stranger had given only so that he might possess the thing he could gain in no other way, that he was reading the book with borrowed eyes and stealing its secrets from the soul of its rightful reader. At last it became clear what was happening to him throughout those strange nights of dreaming.

On each of those nights the shapes of Vastarien slowly pushed through the obscurity of his sleep, a vast landscape emerging from its own profound slumber and drifting forth from a place without name or dimension. And as the crooked monuments became manifest once again, they seemed to expand and soar high above him, drawing his vision toward them. Progressively the scene acquired nuance and articulation; steadily the creation became dense and intricate within its black womb: the streets were sinuous entrails winding through that dark body, and each edifice was the jutting bone of a skeleton hung with a thin musculature of shadows.

But just as his vision reached out to embrace fully the mysterious and jagged form of the dream, it all appeared to pull away, abandoning him on the edge of a dreamless void. The landscape was receding, shrinking into the distance. Now all he could see was a single street bordered by two converging rows of buildings. And at the opposite end of that street, rising up taller than the buildings themselves, stood a great figure in silhouette. This looming colossus made no movement or sound but firmly dominated the horizon where the single remaining street seemed to end. From th position the towering shadow was absorbing all other shapes its own, which gradually was gaining in stature as the landscape withdrew and diminished. And the outline of this titanic figure appeared to be that of a man, yet it was also that of a dark and devouring bird.

Although for several nights Victor Keirion managed to awake before the scavenger had thoroughly consumed what was not its own, there was no assurance that he would always be able to do so and that the dream would not pass into the hands of another. Ultimately, he conceived and executed the act that was necessary to keep possession of the dream he had coveted for so long.

Vastarien, he whispered as he stood in the shadows and moonlight of that bare little room, where a massive metal door prevented his escape. Within that door a small square of thick glass was implanted so that he might be watched by day and by night. And there was an unbending web of heavy wire covering the window which overlooked the city that was not Vastarien. Never, chanted a voice which might have been his own. Then more insistently: *never, never, never . . .*

When the door was opened and some men in uniforms entered the room, they found Victor Keirion screaming to the raucous limits of his voice and trying to scale the thick metal mesh veiling the window, as if he were dragging himself along some unlikely route of liberation. Of course, they pulled him to the floor; they stretched him out upon the bed, where his wrists and ankles were tightly strapped. Then through the doorway strode a nurse who carried a slender syringe crowned with a silvery needle.

During the injection he continued to scream words which everyone in the room had heard before, each outburst developing the theme of his unjust confinement: how the man he had murdered was using him in a horrible way, a way impossible to explain or make credible. The man could not read the book – there, that book – and was stealing the dreams which the book had spawned. *Stealing my dreams,* he mumbled softly as the drug began to take effect. *Stealing my . . .*

The group remained around the bed for a few moments, silently ˙ng at its restrained occupant. Then one of them pointed to the ˷nd initiated a conversation now familiar to them all.

ˋ should we do with it? It's been taken away enough times ˋ then there's always another that appears."

ˋe's no point to it. Look at these pages – nothing, ˌtten anywhere."

"So why does he sit reading them for hours? He does nothing else."

"I think it's time we told someone in authority."

"Of course, we could do that, but what exactly would we say? That a certain inmate should be forbidden from reading a certain book? That he becomes violent?"

"And then they'll ask why we can't keep the book away from him or him from the book? What should we say to that?"

"There would be nothing we could say. Can you imagine what lunatics we would seem? As soon as we opened our mouths, that would be it for all of us."

"And when someone asks what the book means to him, or even what its name is . . . what would be our answer?"

As if in response to this question, a few shapeless groans arose from the criminally insane creature who was bound to the bed. But no one could understand the meaning of the word or words that he uttered, least of all himself. For he was now far from his own words, buried deep within the dreams of a place where everything was transfixed in the order of the unreal; and whence, it truly seemed, he would never return.

PART 2
Grimscribe

THE LAST FEAST OF HARLEQUIN

1.

My interest in the town of Mirocaw was first aroused when I heard that an annual festival was held there which promised to include, to some extent, the participation of clowns among its other elements of pageantry. A former colleague of mine, who is now attached to the anthropology department of a distant university, had read one of my recent articles ("The Clown Figure in American Media," *Journal of Popular Culture*), and wrote to me that he vaguely remembered reading or being told of a town somewhere in the state that held a kind of "Fool's Feast" every year, thinking that this might be pertinent to my peculiar line of study. It was, of course, more pertinent than he had reason to think, both to my academic aims in this area and to my personal pursuits.

Aside from my teaching, I had for some years been engaged in various anthropological projects with the primary ambition of articulating the significance of the clown figure in diverse cultural contexts. Every year for the past twenty years I have attended the pre-Lenten festivals that are held in various places throughout the southern United States. Every year I learned something more concerning the esoterics of celebration. In these studies I was an eager participant – along with playing my part as an anthropologist, I also took a place behind the clownish mask myself. And I cherished this role as I did nothing else in my life. To me the title of Clown has always carried connotations of a noble sort. I was an adroit jester, strangely enough, and had always taken pride in the skills I worked so diligently to develop.

I wrote to the State Department of Recreation, indicating what information I desired and exposing an enthusiastic urgency which came naturally to me on this topic. Many weeks later I received a tan envelope imprinted with a government logo. Inside was a pamphlet that catalogued all of the various seasonal festivities of which the state was officially aware, and I noted in passing that there were as many in late autumn and winter as in the warmer seasons. A letter inserted within the pamphlet explained to me that, according to their voluminous records, no festivals held in the town of Mirocaw had been officially registered. Their files, nonetheless, could be placed at my disposal if I should wish to research this or similar matters in connection with some definite project. At the time this offer was made I was already laboring under so many professional and personal burdens that, with a weary hand, I simply deposited the envelope and its contents in a drawer, never to be consulted again.

Some months later, however, I made an impulsive digression from my responsibilities and, rather haphazardly, took up the Mirocaw project. This happened as I was driving north one afternoon in late summer with the intention of examining some journals in the holdings of a library at another university. Once out of the city limits the scenery changed to sunny fields and farms, diverting my thoughts from the signs that I passed along the highway. Nevertheless, the subconscious scholar in me must have been regarding these with studious care. The name of a town loomed into my vision. Instantly the scholar retrieved certain records from some deep mental drawer, and I was faced with making a few hasty calculations as to whether there was enough time and motivation for an investigative side trip. But the exit sign was even hastier in making its appearance, and I soon found myself leaving the highway, recalling the roadsign's promise that the town was no more than seven miles east.

These seven miles included several confusing turns, the forced taking of a temporarily alternate route, and a destination not even visible until a steep rise had been fully ascended. On the descent another helpful sign informed me that I was within the city limits of Mirocaw. Some scattered houses on the outskirts of the town were the first structures I encountered. Beyond them the numerical highway became Townshend Street, the main avenue of Mirocaw.

The town impressed me as being much larger once I was within its limits than it had appeared from the prominence just outside. I saw that the general hilliness of the surrounding countryside was also an internal feature of Mirocaw. Here, though, the effect was different. The parts of the town did not look as if they adhered very well to one another. This condition might be blamed on the irregular topography of the town. Behind some of the old stores in the business district, steeply roofed houses had been erected on a

sudden incline, their peaks appearing at an extraordinary elevation above the lower buildings. And because the foundations of
these houses could not be glimpsed, they conveyed the illusion of
being either precariously suspended in air, threatening to topple
down, or else constructed with an unnatural loftiness in relation to
their width and mass. This situation also created a weird distortion
of perspective. The two levels of structures overlapped each other
without giving a sense of depth, so that the houses, because of their
higher elevation and nearness to the foreground buildings, did not
appear diminished in size as background objects should. Consequently, a look of flatness, as in a photograph, predominated in
this area. Indeed, Mirocaw could be compared to an album of old
snapshots, particularly ones in which the camera had been upset in
the process of photography, causing the pictures to develop on an
angle: a cone-roofed turret, like a pointed hat jauntily askew,
peeked over the houses on a neighboring street; a billboard
displaying a group of grinning vegetables tipped its contents
slightly westward; cars parked along steep curbs seemed to be
flying skyward in the glare-distorted windows of a five-and-ten;
people leaned lethargically as they trod up and down sidewalks;
and on that sunny day the clock tower, which at first I mistook
for a church steeple, cast a long shadow that seemed to extend an
impossible distance and wander into unlikely places in its
progress across the town. I should say that perhaps the dishar-
monies of Mirocaw are more acutely affecting my imagination in
retrospect than they were on that first day, when I was primarily
concerned with locating the city hall or some other center of
information.

I pulled around a corner and parked. Sliding over to the other
side of the seat, I rolled down the window and called to a passerby:
"Excuse me, sir," I said. The man, who was shabbily dressed and
very old, paused for a moment without approaching the car.
Though he had apparently responded to my call, his vacant
expression did not betray the least awareness of my presence,
and for a moment I thought it just a coincidence that he halted on
the sidewalk at the same time I addressed him. His eyes were
focused somewhere beyond me with a weary and imbecilic gaze.
After a few moments he continued on his way and I said nothing to
call him back, even though at the last second his face began to
appear dimly familiar. Someone else finally came along who was
able to direct me to the Mirocaw City Hall and Community
Center.

The city hall turned out to be the building with the clock tower.

Inside I stood at a counter behind which some people were working at desks and walking up and down a back hallway. On one wall was a poster for the state lottery: a jack-in-the-box with both hands grasping green bills. After a few moments, a tall, middle-aged woman came over to the counter.

"Can I help you?" she asked in a neutral, bureaucratic voice.

I explained that I had heard about the festival – saying nothing about being a nosy academic – and asked if she could provide me with further information or direct me to someone who could.

"Do you mean the one held in the winter?" she asked.

"How many of them are there?"

"Just that one."

"I suppose, then, that that's the one I mean." I smiled as if sharing a joke with her.

Without another word, she walked off into the back hallway. While she was absent I exchanged glances with several of the people behind the counter who periodically looked up from their work.

"There you are," she said when she returned, handing me a piece of paper that looked like the product of a cheap copy machine. *Please Come to the Fun*, it said in large letters. *Parades*, it went on, *Street Masquerade, Bands, The Winter Raffle*, and *The Coronation of the Winter Queen*. The page continued with the mention of a number of miscellaneous festivities. I read the words again. There was something about that imploring little "please" at the top of the announcement that made the whole affair seem like a charity function.

"When is it held? It doesn't say when the festival takes place."

"Most people already know that." She abruptly snatched the page from my hands and wrote something at the bottom. When she gave it back to me, I saw "Dec. 19–21" written in blue-green ink. I was immediately struck by an odd sense of scheduling on the part of the festival committee. There was, of course, solid anthropological and historical precedent for holding festivities around the winter solstice, but the timing of this particular event did not seem entirely practical.

"If you don't mind my asking, don't these days somewhat conflict with the regular holiday season? I mean, most people have enough going on at that time."

"It's just tradition," she said, as if invoking some venerable ancestry behind her words.

"That's very interesting," I said as much to myself as to her.

"Is there anything else?" she asked.

"Yes. Could you tell me if this festival has anything to do with clowns? I see there's something about a masquerade."

"Yes, of course there are some people in . . . costumes. I've never been in that position myself . . . that is, yes, there are clowns of a sort."

At that point my interest was definitely aroused, but I was not sure how much further I wanted to pursue it. I thanked the woman for her help and asked the best means of access to the highway, not anxious to retrace the labyrinthine route by which I had entered the town. I walked back to my car with a whole flurry of half-formed questions, and as many vague and conflicting answers, cluttering my mind.

The directions the woman gave me necessitated passing through the south end of Mirocaw. There were not many people moving about in this section of town. Those that I did see, shuffling lethargically down a block of battered storefronts, exhibited the same sort of forlorn expression and manner as the old man from whom I had asked directions earlier. I must have been traversing a central artery of this area, for on either side stretched street after street of poorly tended yards and houses bowed with age and indifference. When I came to a stop at a streetcorner, one of the citizens of this slum passed in front of my car. This lean, morose, and epicene person turned my way and sneered outrageously with a taut little mouth, yet seemed to be looking at no one in particular. After progressing a few streets farther, I came to a road that led back to the highway. I felt delectably more comfortable as soon as I found myself traveling once again through the expanses of sun-drenched farmlands.

I reached the library with more than enough time for my research, and so I decided to make a scholarly detour to see what material I could find that might illuminate the winter festival held in Mirocaw. The library, one of the oldest in the state, included in its holdings the entire run of the Mirocaw *Courier*. I thought this would be an excellent place to start. I soon found, however, that there was no handy way to research information from this newspaper, and I did not want to engage in a blind search for articles concerning a specific subject.

I next turned to the more organized resources of the newspapers for the larger cities located in the same county, which incidentally shares its name with Mirocaw. I uncovered very little about the town, and almost nothing concerning its festival, except in one general article on annual events in the area that erroneously attributed to Mirocaw a "large Middle-Eastern community" which every spring hosted a kind of ethnic jamboree. From what I had already observed, and from what I subsequently learned, the citizens of Mirocaw were solidly midwestern-American, the probable descendants in a direct line from some enterprising pack of New Englanders of the last century. There was one brief item devoted to a Mirocavian event, but this merely turned out to be an obituary notice for an old woman who had quietly taken her life around Christmastime. Thus, I returned home that day all but empty-handed on the subject of Mirocaw.

However, it was not long afterward that I received another letter from the former colleague of mine who had first led me to seek out Mirocaw and its festival. As it happened, he rediscovered the article that caused him to stir my interest in a local "Fool's Feast." This article had its sole appearance in an obscure festschrift of anthropology studies published in Amsterdam twenty years ago. Most of these papers were in Dutch, a few in German, and only one was in English: "The Last Feast of Harlequin: Preliminary Notes on a Local Festival." It was exciting, of course, finally to be able to read this study, but even more exciting was the name of its author: Dr. Raymond Thoss.

2.

Before proceeding any further, I should mention something about Thoss, and inevitably about myself. Over two decades ago, at my alma mater in Cambridge, Mass., Thoss was a professor of mine. Long before playing a role in the events I am about to describe, he was already one of the most important figures in my life. A striking personality, he inevitably influenced everyone who came in contact with him. I remember his lectures on social anthropology, how he turned that dim room into a brilliant and profound circus of learning. He moved in an uncannily brisk manner. When he swept his arm around to indicate some common term on the blackboard behind him, one felt he was presenting nothing less than an item of fantastic qualities and secret value. When he replaced his hand in the pocket of his old jacket this fleeting magic was once again stored away in its well-worn pouch, to be retrieved at the sorcerer's discretion. We sensed he was teaching us more than we could possibly learn, and that he himself was in possession of greater and deeper knowledge than he could possibly impart. On one occasion I summoned up the audacity to offer an interpretation – which was somewhat opposed to his own –

regarding the tribal clowns of the Hopi Indians. I implied that personal experience as an amateur clown and special devotion to this study provided me with an insight possibly more valuable than his own. It was then he disclosed, casually and very obiter dicta, that he had actually acted in the role of one of these masked tribal fools and had celebrated with them the dance of the *kachinas*. In revealing these facts, however, he somehow managed not to add to the humiliation I had already inflicted upon myself. And for this I was grateful to him.

Thoss's activities were such that he sometimes became the object of gossip or romanticized speculation. He was a fieldworker par excellence, and his ability to insinuate himself into exotic cultures and situations, thereby gaining insights where other anthropologists merely collected data, was renowned. At various times in his career there had been rumors of his having "gone native" à la the Frank Hamilton Cushing legend. There were hints, which were not always irresponsible or cheaply glamorized, that he was involved in projects of a freakish sort, many of which focused on New England. It is a fact that he spent six months posing as a mental patient at an institution in western Massachussetts, gathering information on the "culture" of the psychically disturbed. When his book *Winter Solstice: The Longest Night of a Society* was published, the general opinion was that it was disappointingly subjective and impressionistic, and that, aside from a few moving but "poetically obscure" observations, there was nothing at all to give it value. Those who defended Thoss claimed he was a kind of super-anthropologist: while much of his work emphasized his own mind and feelings, his experience had in fact penetrated to a rich core of hard data which he had yet to disclose in objective discourse. As a student of Thoss, I tended to support this latter estimation of him. For a variety of tenable and untenable reasons, I believed Thoss capable of unearthing hitherto inaccessible strata of human existence. So it was gratifying at first that this article entitled "The Last Feast of Harlequin" seemed to uphold the Thoss mystique, and in an area I personally found captivating.

Much of the content of the article I did not immediately comprehend, given its author's characteristic and often strategic obscurities. On first reading, the most interesting aspect of this brief study – the "notes" encompassed only twenty pages – was the general mood of the piece. Thoss's eccentricities were definitely present in these pages, but only as a struggling inner force which was definitely contained – incarcerated, I might say – by the somber rhythmic movements of his prose and by some gloomy references he occasionally called upon. Two references in particular shared a common theme. One was a quotation from Poe's "The Conqueror Worm," which Thoss employed as a rather sensational epigraph. The point of the epigraph, however, was nowhere echoed in the text of the article save in another passing reference. Thoss brought up the well-known genesis of the modern Christmas celebration, which of course descends from the Roman Saturnalia. Then, making it clear he had not yet observed the Mirocaw festival and had only gathered its nature from various informants, he established that it too contained many, even more overt, elements of the Saturnalia. Next he made what seemed to me a trivial and purely linguistic observation, one that had less to do with his main course of argument than it did with the equally peripheral Poe epigraph. He briefly mentioned that an early sect of the Syrian Gnostics called themselves "Saturnians" and believed, among other religious heresies, that mankind was created by angels who were in turn created by the Supreme Unknown. The angels, however, did not possess the power to make their creation an erect being and for a time he crawled upon the earth like a worm. Eventually, the Creator remedied this grotesque state of affairs. At the time I supposed that the symbolic correspondences of mankind's origins and ultimate condition being associated with worms, combined with a year-end festival recognizing the winter death of the earth, was the gist of this Thossian "insight," a poetic but scientifically valueless observation.

Other observations he made on the Mirocaw festival were also strictly etic; in other words, they were based on second-hand sources, hearsay testimony. Even at that juncture, however, I felt Thoss knew more than he disclosed; and, as I later discovered, he had indeed included information on certain aspects of Mirocaw suggesting he was already in possession of several keys which for the moment he was keeping securely in his own pocket. By then I myself possessed a most revealing morsel of knowledge. A note to the "Harlequin" article apprised the reader that the piece was only a fragment in rude form of a more wide-ranging work in preparation. This work was never seen by the world. My former professor had not published anything since his withdrawal from academic circulation some twenty years ago. Now I suspected where he had gone.

For the man I had stopped on the streets of Mirocaw and from whom I tried to obtain directions, the man with the disconcertingly lethargic gaze, had very much resembled a superannuated version of Dr. Raymond Thoss.

3.

And now I have a confession to make. Despite my reasons for being enthusiastic about Mirocaw and its mysteries, especially its relationship to both Thoss and my own deepest concerns as a scholar – I contemplated the days ahead of me with no more than a feeling of frigid numbness and often with a sense of profound depression. Yet I had no reason to be surprised at this emotional state, which had little relevance to the outward events in my life but was determined by inward conditions that worked according to their own, quite enigmatic, seasons and cycles. For many years, at least since my university days, I have suffered from this dark malady, this recurrent despondency in which I would become buried when it came time for the earth to grow cold and bare and the skies heavy with shadows. Nevertheless, I pursued my plans, though somewhat mechanically, to visit Mirocaw during its festival days, for I superstitiously hoped that this activity might diminish the weight of my seasonal despair. In Mirocaw would be parades and parties and the opportunity to play the clown once again.

For weeks in advance I practiced my art, even perfecting a new feat of juggling magic, which was my special forte in foolery. I had my costumes cleaned, purchased fresh makeup, and was ready. I received permission from the university to cancel some of my classes prior to the holiday, explaining the nature of my project and the necessity of arriving in the town a few days before the festival began, in order to do some preliminary research, establish informants, and so on. Actually, my plan was to postpone any formal inquiry until after the festival and to involve myself beforehand as much as possible in its activities. I would, of course, keep a journal during this time.

There was one resource I did want to consult, however. Specifically, I returned to that outstate library to examine those issues of the Mirocaw *Courier* dating from December two decades ago. One story in particular confirmed a point Thoss made in the "Harlequin" article, though the event it chronicled must have taken place after Thoss had written his study.

The Courier story appeared two weeks after the festival had ended for that year and was concerned with the disappearance of a woman named Elizabeth Beadle, the wife of Samuel Beadle, a hotel owner in Mirocaw. The county authorities speculated that this was another instance of the "holiday suicides" which seemed to occur with inordinate seasonal regularity in the Mirocaw region. Thoss documented this phenomenon in his "Harlequin" article, though I suspect that today these deaths would be neatly categorized under the heading "seasonal affective disorder". In any case, the authorities searched a half-frozen lake near the outskirts of Mirocaw where they had found many successful suicides in years past. This year, however, no body was discovered. Alongside the article was a picture of Elizabeth Beadle. Even in the grainy microfilm reproduction one could detect a certain vibrancy and vitality in Mrs. Beadle's face. That an hypothesis of "holiday suicide" should be so readily posited to explain her disappearance seemed strange and in some way unjust.

Thoss, in his brief article, wrote that every year there occurred changes of a moral or spiritual cast which seemed to affect Mirocaw along with the usual winter metamorphosis. He was not precise about its origin or nature but stated, in typically mystifying fashion, that the effect of this "subseason" on the town was conspicuously negative. In addition to the number of suicides actually accomplished during this time, there was also a rise in treatment of "hypochondriacal" conditions, which was how the medical men of twenty years past characterized these cases in discussions with Thoss. This state of affairs would gradually worsen and finally reach a climax during the days scheduled for the Mirocaw festival. Thoss speculated that given the secretive nature of small towns, the situation was probably even more intensely pronounced than casual investigation could reveal.

The connection between the festival and this insidious subseasonal climate in Mirocaw was a point on which Thoss did not come to any rigid conclusions. He did write, nevertheless, that these two "climatic aspects" had had a parallel existence in the town's history as far back as available records could document. A late nineteenth-century history of Mirocaw County speaks of the town by its original name of New Colstead, and castigates the townspeople for holding a "ribald and soulless feast" to the exclusion of normal Christmas observances. (Thoss comments that the historian had mistakenly fused two distinct aspects of the season, their actual relationship being essentially antagonistic.) The "Harlequin" article did not trace the festival to its earliest appearance (this may not have been possible), though Thoss emphasized the New England origins of Mirocaw's founders. The festival, therefore, was one imported from this region and could reasonably be extended at least a century; that is, if it had not been brought over from the Old World, in which case its roots would become indefinite until further research could be done. Surely Thoss's allusion to the Syrian Gnostics suggested the latter possibility could not entirely be ruled out.

But it seemed to be the festival's link to New England that nourished Thoss's speculations. He wrote of this patch of geography as if it were an acceptable place to end the search. For him, the very words "New England" seemed to be stripped of all traditional connotations and had come to imply nothing less than a gateway to all lands, both known and suspected, and even to ages beyond the civilized history of the region. Having been educated partly in New England, I could somewhat understand this sentimental exaggeration, for indeed there are places that seem archaic beyond chronological measure, appearing to transcend relative standards of time and achieving a kind of absolute antiquity which cannot be logically fathomed. But how this vague suggestion related to a small town in the Midwest I could not imagine. Thoss himself observed that the residents of Mirocaw did not betray any mysteriously primitive consciousness. On the contrary, they appeared superficially unaware of the genesis of their winter merrymaking. That such a tradition had endured through the years, however, even eclipsing the conventional Christmas holiday, revealed a profound awareness of the festival's meaning and function.

I cannot deny that what I had learned about the Mirocaw festival did inspire a trite sense of fate, especially given the involvement of such an important figure from my past as Thoss. It was the first time in my academic career that I knew myself to be better suited than anyone else to discern the true meaning of scattered data, even if I could only attribute this special authority to chance circumstances.

Nevertheless, as I sat in that library on a morning in mid December I doubted for a moment the wisdom of setting out for Mirocaw rather than returning home, where the more familiar *rite de passage* of winter depression awaited me. My original scheme was to avoid the cyclical blues the season held for me, but it seemed this was also a part of the history of Mirocaw, only on a much larger scale. My emotional instability, however, was exactly what qualified me most for the particular fieldwork ahead, though I did not take pride or consolation in the fact. And to retreat would have been to deny myself an opportunity that might never offer itself again. In retrospect, there seems to have been no fortuitous resolution to the decision I had to make. As it happened, I went ahead to the town.

4.

Just past noon, on December 18, I started driving toward Mirocaw. A blur of dull, earthen-colored scenery extended in every direction. The snowfalls of late autumn had been sparse, and only a few white patches appeared in the harvested fields along the highway. The clouds were gray and abundant. Passing by a stretch of forest, I noticed the black, ragged clumps of abandoned nests clinging to the twisted mesh of bare branches. I thought I saw black birds skittering over the road ahead, but they were only dead leaves and they flew into the air as I drove by.

I approached Mirocaw from the south, entering the town from the direction I had left it on my visit the previous summer. This took me once again through that part of town which seemed to exist on the wrong side of some great invisible barrier dividing the desirable sections of Mirocaw from the undesirable. As lurid as this district had appeared to me under the summer sun, in the thin light of that winter afternoon it degenerated into a pale phantom of itself. The frail stores and starved-looking houses suggested a borderline region between the material and nonmaterial worlds, with one sardonically wearing the mask of the other. I saw a few gaunt pedestrians who turned as I passed by, though seemingly not *because* I passed by, making my way up to the main street of Mirocaw.

Driving up the steep rise of Townshend Street, I found the sights there comparatively welcoming. The rolling avenues of the town were in readiness for the festival. Streetlights had their poles raveled with evergreen, the fresh boughs proudly conspicuous in a barren season. On the doors of many of the businesses on Townshend were holly wreaths, equally green but observably plastic. However, although there was nothing unusual in this traditional greenery of the season, it soon became apparent to me that Mirocaw had quite abandoned itself to this particular symbol of Yuletide. It was garishly in evidence everywhere. The windows of stores and houses were framed in green lights, green streamers hung down from storefront awnings, and the beacons of the Red Rooster Bar were peacock green floodlights. I supposed the residents of Mirocaw desired these decorations, but the effect was one of excess. An eerie emerald haze permeated the town, and faces looked slightly reptilian.

At the time I assumed that the prodigious evergreen, holly wreaths, and colored lights (if only of a single color) demonstrated an emphasis on the vegetable symbols of the Nordic Yuletide, which would inevitably be muddled into the winter festival of any northern country just as they had been adopted for the Christmas season. In his "Harlequin" article Thoss wrote of the pagan aspect of Mirocaw's festival, likening it to the ritual of a fertility cult, with probable connections to chthonic divinities at some time in the past. But Thoss had mistaken, as I had, what was only part of the festival's significance for the whole.

The hotel at which I had made reservations was located on Townshend. It was an old building of brown brick, with an arched doorway and a pathetic coping intended to convey an impression of neoclassicism. I found a parking space in front and left my suitcases in the car.

When I first entered the hotel lobby it was empty. I thought perhaps the Mirocaw festival would have attracted enough visitors to at least bolster the business of its only hotel, but it seemed I was mistaken. Tapping a little bell, I leaned on the desk and turned to look at a small, traditionally decorated Christmas tree on a table near the entranceway. It was complete with shiny, egg-fragile bulbs; miniature candy canes; flat, laughing Santas with arms wide; a star on top nodding awkwardly against the delicate shoulder of an upper branch; and colored lights that bloomed out of flower-shaped sockets. For some reason this seemed to me a sorry little piece.

"May I help you?" said a young woman arriving from a room adjacent to the lobby.

I must have been staring rather intently at her, for she looked away and seemed quite uneasy. I could hardly imagine what to say to her or how to explain what I was thinking. In person she immediately radiated a chilling brilliance of manner and expression. But if this woman had not committed suicide twenty years before, as the newspaper article had suggested, neither had she aged in that time.

"Sarah," called a masculine voice from the invisible heights of a stairway. A tall, middle-aged man came down the steps. "I thought you were in your room," said the man, whom I took to be Samuel Beadle. Sarah, not Elizabeth, Beadle glanced sideways in my direction to indicate to her father that she was conducting the business of the hotel. Beadle apologized to me, and then excused the two of them for a moment while they went off to one side to continue their exchange.

I smiled and pretended everything was normal, while trying to

remain within earshot of their conversation. They spoke in tones
that suggested their conflict was a familiar one: Beadle's over-
protective concern with his daughter's whereabouts and Sarah's
frustrated understanding of certain restrictions placed upon her.
The conversation ended, and Sarah ascended the stairs, turning
for a moment to give me a facial pantomime of apology for the
unprofessional scene that had just taken place.

"Now, sir, what can I do for you?" Beadle asked, almost
demanded.

"Yes, I have a reservation. Actually, I'm a day early, if that
doesn't present a problem." I gave the hotel the benefit of the
doubt that its business might have been secretly flourishing.

"No problem at all, sir," he said, presenting me with the
registration form, and then a brass-colored key dangling from a
plastic disc bearing the number 44.

"Luggage?"

"Yes, it's in my car."

"I'll give you a hand with that."

While Beadle was settling me in my fourth-floor room it seemed
an opportune moment to broach the subject of the festival, the
holiday suicides, and perhaps, depending upon his reaction, the
fate of his wife. I needed a respondent who had lived in the town
for a good many years and who could enlighten me about the
attitude of Mirocavians toward their season of sea-green lights.

"This is just fine," I said about the clean but somber room.
"Nice view. I can see the bright green lights of Mirocaw just fine
from up here. Is the town usually all decked out like this? For the
festival, I mean."

"Yes, sir, for the festival," he replied mechanically.

"I imagine you'll probably be getting quite a few of us out-of-
towners in the next couple of days."

"Could be. Is there anything else?"

"Yes, there is. I wonder if you could tell me something about the
festivities."

"Such as . . ."

"Well, you know, the clowns and so forth."

"Only clowns here are the ones that're . . . well, picked out, I
suppose you would say."

"I don't understand."

"Excuse me, sir. I'm very busy right now. Is there anything
else?"

I could think of nothing at the moment to perpetuate our
conversation. Beadle wished me a good stay and left.

I unpacked my suitcases. In addition to regular clothing I had also brought along some of the items from my clown's wardrobe. Beadle's comment that the clowns of Mirocaw were "picked out" left me wondering exactly what purpose these street masqueraders served in the festival. The clown figure has had so many meanings in different times and cultures. The jolly, well-loved joker familiar to most people is actually but one aspect of this protean creature. Madmen, hunchbacks, amputees, and other abnormals were once considered natural clowns; they were elected to fulfil a comic role which could allow others to see them as ludicrous rather than as terrible reminders of the forces of disorder in the world. But sometimes a cheerless jester was required to draw attention to this same disorder, as in the case of King Lear's morbid and honest fool, who of course was eventually hanged, and so much for his clownish wisdom. Clowns have often had ambiguous and sometimes contradictory roles to play. Thus, I knew enough not to brashly jump into costume and cry out, "Here I am again!"

That first day in Mirocaw I did not stray far from the hotel. I read and rested for a few hours and then ate at a nearby diner. Through the window beside my table I watched the winter night turn the soft green glow of the town into a harsh and almost totally new color as it contrasted with the darkness. The streets of Mirocaw seemed to me unusually busy for a small town at evening. Yet it was not the kind of activity one normally sees before an approaching Christmas holiday. This was not a crowd of bustling shoppers loaded with bright bags of presents. Their arms were empty, their hands shoved deep in their pockets against the cold, which nevertheless had not driven them to the solitude of their presumably warm houses. I watched them enter and exit store after store without buying; many merchants remained open late, and even the places that were closed had left their neons illuminated. The faces that passed the window of the diner were possibly just stiffened by the cold, I thought; frozen into deep frowns and nothing else. In the same window I saw the reflection of my own face. It was not the face of an adept clown; it was slack and flabby and at that moment seemed the face of someone less than alive. Outside was the town of Mirocaw, its streets dipping and rising with a lunatic severity, its citizens packing the sidewalks, its heart bathed in green: as promising a field of professional and personal challenge as I had ever encountered – and I was bored to the point of dread. I hurried back to my hotel room.

"Mirocaw has another coldness within its cold," I wrote in my journal that night. "Another set of buildings and streets that exists behind the visible town's facade like a world of disgraceful back alleys." I went on like this for about a page, across which I finally engraved a big "X". Then I went to bed.

In the morning I left my car at the hotel and walked toward the main business district a few blocks away. Mingling with the good people of Mirocaw seemed like the proper thing to do at that point in my scientific sojourn. But as I began laboriously walking up Townshend (the sidewalks were cramped with wandering pedestrians), a glimpse of someone suddenly replaced my haphazard plan with a more specific and immediate one. Through the crowd and about fifteen paces ahead was my goal.

"Dr. Thoss," I called.

His head almost seemed to turn and look back in response to my shout, but I could not be certain. I pushed past several warmly wrapped bodies and green-scarved necks, only to find that the object of my pursuit appeared to be maintaining the same distance from me, though I did not know if this was being done deliberately or not. At the next corner, the dark-coated Thoss abruptly turned right onto a steep street which led downward directly toward the dilapidated south end of Mirocaw. When I reached the corner I looked down the sidewalk and could see him very clearly from above. I also saw how he managed to stay so far ahead of me in a mob that had impeded my own progress. For some reason the people on the sidewalk made room so that he could move past them easily, without the usual jostling of bodies. It was not a dramatic physical avoidance, thought it seemed nonetheless intentional. Fighting the tight fabric of the throng, I continued to follow Thoss, losing and regaining sight of him.

By the time I reached the bottom of the sloping street the crowd had thinned out considerably, and after walking a block or so farther I found myself practically a lone pedestrian pacing behind a distant figure that I hoped was still Thoss. He was now walking quite swiftly and in a way that seemed to acknowledge my pursuit of him, though really it felt as if he were leading me as much as I was chasing him. I called his name a few more times at a volume he could not have failed to hear, assuming that deafness was not one of the changes to have come over him; he was, after all, not a young man, nor even a middle-aged one any longer.

Thoss suddenly crossed in the middle of the street. He walked a few more steps and entered a signless brick building between a liquor store and a repair shop of some kind. In the "Harlequin" article Thoss had mentioned that the people living in this section of

Mirocaw maintained their own businesses, and that these were patronized almost exclusively by residents of the area. I could well believe this statement when I looked at these little sheds of commerce, for they had the same badly weathered appearance as their clientele. The formidable shoddiness of these buildings notwithstanding, I followed Thoss into the plain brick shell of what had been, or possibly still was, a diner.

Inside it was unusually dark. Even before my eyes made the adjustment I sensed that this was not a thriving restaurant cozily cluttered with chairs and tables – as was the establishment where I had eaten the night before – but a place with only a few disarranged furnishings, and very cold. It seemed colder, in fact, than the winter streets outside.

"Dr. Thoss?" I called toward a lone table near the center of the long room. Perhaps four or five were sitting around the table, with some others blending into the dimness behind them. Scattered across the top of the table were some books and loose papers. Seated there was an old man indicating something in the pages before him, but it was not Thoss. Beside him were two youths whose wholesome features distinguished them from the grim weariness of the others. I approached the table and they all looked up at me. None of them showed a glimmer of emotion except the two boys, who exchanged worried and guilt-ridden glances with each other, as if they had just been discovered in some shameful act. They both suddenly burst from the table and ran into the dark background, where a light appeared briefly as they exited by a back door.

"I'm sorry," I said diffidently. "I thought I saw someone I knew come in here."

They said nothing. Out of a back room others began to emerge, no doubt interested in the source of the commotion. In a few moments the room was crowded with these tramp-like figures, all of them gazing emptily in the dimness. I was not at this point frightened of them; at least I was not afraid they would do me any physical harm. Actually, I felt as if it was quite within my power to pummel them easily into submission, their mousy faces almost inviting a succession of firm blows. But there were so many of them.

They slid slowly toward me in a worm-like mass. Their eyes seemed empty and unfocused, and I wondered a moment if they were even aware of my presence. Nevertheless, I was the center upon which their lethargic shuffling converged, their shoes scuffing softly along the bare floor. I began to deliver a number of hasty inanities as they continued to press toward me, their weak and unexpectedly odorless bodies nudging against mine. (I understood now why the people along the sidewalks seemed to instinctively avoid Thoss.) Unseen legs became entangled with my own; I staggered and then regained my balance. This sudden movement aroused me from a kind of mesmeric daze into which I must have fallen without being aware of it. I had intended to leave that dreary place long before events had reached such a juncture, but for some reason I could not focus my intentions strongly enough to cause myself to act. My mind had been drifting farther away as these slavish things approached. In a sudden surge of panic I pushed through their soft ranks and was outside.

The open air revived me to my former alertness, and I immediately started pacing swiftly up the hill. I was no longer sure that I had not simply imagined what had seemed, and at the same time did not seem, like a perilous moment. Had their movements been directed toward a harmful assault, or were they trying merely to intimidate me? As I reached the green-glazed main street of Mirocaw I really could not determine what had just happened.

The sidewalks were still jammed with a multitude of pedestrians, who now seemed more lively than they had been only a short time before. There was a kind of vitality that could only be attributed to the imminent festivities. A group of young men had begun celebrating prematurely and strode noisily across the street at midpoint, obviously intoxicated. From the laughter and joking among the still sober citizens I gathered that, mardi-gras style, public drunkenness was within the traditions of this winter festival. I looked for anything to indicate the beginnings of the Street Masquerade, but saw nothing: no brightly garbed harlequins or snow-white pierrots. Were the ceremonies even now in preparation for the coronation of the Winter Queen? "The Winter Queen," I wrote in my journal. "Figure of fertility invested with symbolic powers of revival and prosperity. Elected in the manner of a high school prom queen. Check for possible consort figure in the form of a representative from the underworld."

In the pre-darkness hours of December 19 I sat in my hotel room and wrote and thought and organized. I did not feel too badly, all things considered. The holiday excitement which was steadily rising in the streets below my window was definitely infecting me. I forced myself to take a short nap in anticipation of a long night. When I awoke, Mirocaw's annual feast had begun.

5.

Shouting, commotion, carousing. Sleepily I went to the window and looked out over the town. It seemed all the lights of Mirocaw were shining, save in that section down the hill which became part of the black void of winter. And now the town's greenish tinge was even more pronounced, spreading everywhere like a great green rainbow that had melted from the sky and endured, phosphorescent, into the night. In the streets was the brightness of an artificial spring. The byways of Mirocaw vibrated with activity: on a nearby corner a brass band blared; marauding cars blew their horns and were sometimes mounted by laughing pedestrians; a man emerged from the Red Rooster Bar, threw up his arms, and crowed. I looked closely at the individual celebrants, searching for the vestments of clowns. Soon, delightedly, I saw them. The costume was red and white, with matching cap, and the face painted a noble alabaster. It almost seemed to be a clownish incarnation of that white-bearded and black-booted Christmas fool.

This particular fool, however, was not receiving the affection and respect usually accorded to a Santa Claus. My poor fellow-clown was in the middle of a circle of revelers who were pushing him back and forth from one to the other. The object of this abuse seemed to accept it somewhat willingly, but this little game nevertheless appeared to have humiliation as its purpose. "Only clowns here are the ones that're picked out," echoed Beadle's voice in my memory. "Picked *on*" seemed closer to the truth.

Packing myself in some heavy clothes, I went out into the green gleaming streets. Not far from the hotel I was stumbled into by a character with a wide blue and red grin and bright baggy clothes. Actually he had been shoved into me by some youths outside a drugstore.

"See the freak," said an obese and drunken fellow. "See the freak fall."

My first response was anger, and then fear as I saw two others flanking the fat drunk. They walked toward me and I tensed myself for a confrontation.

"This is a disgrace," one said, the neck of a wine bottle held loosely in his left hand.

But it was not to me they were speaking; it was to the clown, who had been pushed to the sidewalk. His three persecutors helped him up with a sudden jerk and then splashed wine in his face. They ignored me altogether.

"Let him loose," the fat one said. "Crawl away, freak. Oh, he flies!"

The clown trotted off, becoming lost in the throng.

"Wait a minute," I said to the rowdy trio, who had started lumbering away. I quickly decided that it would probably be futile to ask them to explain what I had just witnessed, especially amid the noise and confusion of the festivities. In my best jovial fashion I proposed we all go someplace where I could buy them each a drink. They had no objection and in a short while we were all squeezed around a table in the Red Rooster.

Over several drinks I explained to them that I was from out of town, which pleased them no end for some reason. I told them there were things I did not understand about their festival.

"I don't think there's anything to understand," the fat one said. "It's just what you see."

I asked him about the people dressed as clowns.

"Them? They're the freaks. It's their turn this year. Everyone takes their turn. Next year it might be mine. Or *yours*," he said, pointing at one of his friends across the table. "And when we find out which one you are—"

"You're not smart enough," said the defiant potential freak.

This was an important point: the fact that individuals who played the clowns remain, or at least attempted to remain, anonymous. This arrangement would help remove inhibitions a resident of Mirocaw might have about abusing his own neighbor or even a family relation. From what I later observed, the extent of this abuse did not go beyond a kind of playful roughhousing. And even so, it was only the occasional group of rowdies who actually took advantage of this aspect of the festival, the majority of the citizens very much content to stay on the sidelines.

As far as being able to illuminate the meaning of this custom, my three young friends were quite useless. To them it was just amusement, as I imagine it was to the majority of Mirocavians. This was understandable. I suppose the average person would not be able to explain exactly how the profoundly familiar Christmas holiday came to be celebrated in its present form.

I left the bar alone and not unaffected by the drinks I had consumed there. Outside, the general merrymaking continued. Loud music emanated from several quarters. Mirocaw had fully transformed itself from a sedate small town to an enclave of Saturnalia within the dark immensity of a winter night. But Saturn is also the planetary symbol of melancholy and sterility, a clash of opposites contained within that single word. And as I wandered half-drunkenly down the street, I discovered that there was a conflict within the winter festival itself. This discovery indeed appeared to be that secret key which Thoss withheld in his study of the town. Oddly enough, it was through my unfamiliarity with the outward nature of the festival that I came to know its true nature.

I was mingling with the crowd on the street, warmly enjoying the confusion around me, when I saw a strangely designed creature lingering on the corner up ahead. It was one of the Mirocaw clowns. Its clothes were shabby and nondescript, almost in the style of a tramp-type clown, but not humorously exaggerated enough. The face, though, made up for the lackluster costume. I had never seen such a strange conception for a clown's counte-nance. The figure stood beneath a dim streetlight, and when it turned its head my way I realized why it seemed familiar. The thin, smooth, and pale head; the wide eyes; the oval-shaped features resembling nothing so much as the skull-faced, screaming creature in that famous painting (memory fails me). This clownish imitation rivalled the original in suggesting stricken realms of abject horror and despair: an inhuman likeness more proper to something under the earth than upon it.

From the first moment I saw this creature, I thought of those inhabitants of the ghetto down the hill. There was the same nauseating passivity and languor in its bearing. Perhaps if I had not been drinking earlier I would not have been bold enough to take the action I did. I decided to join in one of the upstanding traditions of the winter festival, for it annoyed me to see this morbid impostor of a clown standing up. When I reached the corner I laughingly pushed myself into the creature – "Whoops!" – who stumbled backward and ended up on the sidewalk. I laughed again and looked around for approval from the festivalers in the vicinity. No one, however, seemed to appreciate or even acknowl-edge what I had done. They did not laugh with me or point with amusement, but only passed by, perhaps walking a little faster until they were some distance from this streetcorner incident. I realized instantly I had violated some tacit rule of behavior, though I had thought my action well within the common prac-tice. The idea occurred to me that I might even be apprehended and prosecuted for what in any other circumstances was certainly a criminal act. I turned around to help the clown back to his feet, hoping to somehow redeem my offense, but the creature was gone. Solemnly I walked away from the scene of my inadvertent crime and sought other streets away from its witnesses.

Along the various back avenues of Mirocaw I wandered,

pausing exhaustedly at one point to sit at the counter of a small sandwich shop that was packed with customers. I ordered a cup of coffee to revive my overly alcoholed system. Warming my hands around the cup and sipping slowly from it, I watched the people outside as they passed the front window. It was well after midnight but the thick flow of passersby gave no indication that anyone was going home early. A carnival of profiles filed past the window and I was content simply to sit back and observe, until finally one of these faces made me start. It was that frightful little clown I had roughed up earlier. But although its face was familiar in its ghastly aspect, there was something different about it. And I wondered that there should be two such hideous freaks.

Quickly paying the man at the counter, I dashed out to get a second glimpse of the clown, who was now nowhere in sight. The dense crowd kept me from pursuing this figure with any speed, and I wondered how the clown could have made its way so easily ahead of me. Unless the crowd had instinctively allowed this creature to pass unhindered through its massive ranks, as it did for Thoss. In the process of searching for this particular freak, I discovered that interspersed among the celebrating populous of Mirocaw, which included the sanctioned festival clowns, there was not one or two, but a considerable number of these pale, wraith-like creatures. And they all drifted along the streets unmolested by even the rowdiest of revelers. I now understood one of the taboos of the festival. These other clowns were not to be disturbed and should even be avoided, much as were the residents of the slum at the edge of town. Nevertheless, I felt instinctively that the two groups of clowns were somehow identified with each other, even if the ghetto clowns were not welcome at Mirocaw's winter festival. Indeed, they were not simply part of the community and celebrating the season in their own way. To all appearances, this group of melancholy mummers constituted nothing less than an entirely independent festival – a festival within a festival.

Returning to my room, I entered my suppositions into the journal I was keeping for this venture. The following are excerpts:

There is a superstitiousness displayed by the residents of Mirocaw with regard to these people from the slum section, particularly as they lately appear in those dreadful faces signifying their own festival. What is the relationship between these simultaneous celebrations? Did one precede the other? If so, which? My opinion at this point – and I claim no conclusiveness for it – is that Mirocaw's winter festival is the later manifestation, that it appeared after the festival of those depressingly pallid clowns, in order to cover it up or mitigate its effect. The holiday suicides come to mind, and the subclimate Thoss wrote about, the disappearance of Elizabeth Beadle twenty years ago, and my own experience with this pariah clan existing outside yet within the community. Of my own experience with this emotionally deleterious subseason I would rather not speak at this time. Still not able to say whether or not my usual winter melancholy is the cause. On the general subject of mental health, I must consider Thoss's book about his stay in a psychiatric hospital (in western Mass., almost sure of that. Check on this book & Mirocaw's New England roots). The winter solstice is tomorrow, albeit sometime past midnight (how blurry these days and nights are becoming!). It is, of course, the day of the year in which night hours surpass daylight hours by the greatest margin. Note what this has to do with the suicides and a rise in psychic disorder. Recalling Thoss's list of documented suicides in his article, there seemed to be a recurrence of specific family names, as there very likely might be for any kind of data collected in a small town. Among these names was a Beadle or two. Perhaps, then, there is a genealogical basis for the suicides which has nothing to do with Thoss's mystical subclimate, which is a colorful idea to be sure and one that seems fitting for this town of various outward and inward aspects, but is not a conception that can be substantiated.

One thing that seems certain, however, is the division of Mirocaw into two very distinct types of citizenry, resulting in two festivals and the appearance of similar clowns – a term now used in an extremely loose sense. But there is a connection, and I believe I have some idea of what it is. I said before that the normal residents of the town regard those from the ghetto, and especially their clown figures, with superstition. Yet it's more than that: there is fear, perhaps a kind of hatred – the particular kind of hatred resulting from some powerful and irrational memory. What threatens Mirocaw I think I can very well understand. I recall the incident earlier today in that vacant diner. "Vacant" is the appropriate word here, despite its contradiction of fact. The congregation of that half-lit room formed less a presence than an absence, even considering the oppressive number of them. Those eyes that did not or could not focus on anything, the pining lassitude of their faces, the lazy march of their feet. I was spiritually drained when I ran out of there. I then understood why these people and their activities are avoided.

I cannot question the wisdom of those ancestral Mirocavians who began the tradition of the winter festival and gave the town a pretext for celebration and social intercourse at a time when the consequences of brooding isolation are most severe, those longest and darkest days of the solstice. A mood of Christmas joviality obviously would not be sufficient to counter the menace of this season. But even so, there are still the suicides of individuals who are somehow cut off, I imagine, from the vitalizing activities of the festival.

It is the nature of this insidious subseason that seems to determine the outward forms of Mirocaw's winter festival: the optimistic greenery in a period of gray dormancy; the fertile promise of the Winter Queen; and, most interesting to my mind, the clowns. The bright clowns of Mirocaw who are treated so badly; they appear to serve as substitute figures for those dark-eyed mummers of the slums. Since the latter are feared for some power or influence they possess, they may still be symbolically confronted and conquered through their counterparts, who are elected for precisely this function. If I am right about this, I wonder to what extent there is a conscious awareness among the town's populace of this indirect show of aggression. Those three young men I spoke with tonight did not seem to possess much insight beyond seeing that there was a certain amount of robust fun in the festival's tradition. For that matter, how much awareness is there on the *other side* of these two antagonistic festivals? Too horrible to think of such a thing, but I must wonder if, for all their apparent aimlessness, those inhabitants of the ghetto are not the only ones who know what they are about. No denying that behind those inhumanly limp expressions there seems to lie a kind of obnoxious intelligence.

Now I realize the confusion of my present state, but as I wobbled from street to street tonight, watching those oval-mouthed clowns, I could not help feeling that all the merry-making in Mirocaw was somehow allowed only by their sufferance. This I hope is no more than a fanciful Thossian intuition, the sort of idea that is curious and thought-provoking without ever seeming to gain the benefit of proof. I know

my mind is not entirely lucid, but I feel that it may be possible
to penetrate Mirocaw's many complexities and illuminate the
hidden side of the festival season. In particular I must look for
the significance of the other festival. Is it also some kind of
fertility celebration? From what I have seen, the tenor of this
"celebrating" sub-group is one of anti-fertility, if anything.
How have they managed to keep from dying out completely
over the years? How do they maintain their numbers?

But I was too tired to formulate any more of my sodden speculations. Falling onto my bed, I soon became lost in dreams of streets
and faces.

6.

I was, of course, slightly hung over when I woke up late the next
morning. The festival was still going strong, and blaring music
outside roused me from a nightmare. It was a parade. A number of
floats proceeded down Townshend, a familiar color predominating. There were theme floats of pilgrims and Indians, cowboys and
Indians, and clowns of an orthodox type. In the middle of it all was
the Winter Queen herself, freezing atop an icy throne. She waved
in all directions. I even imagined she waved up at my dark
window.

In the first few groggy moments of wakefulness I had no
sympathy with my excitation of the previous night. But I discovered that my former enthusiasm had merely lain dormant, and
soon returned with an even greater intensity. Never before had my
mind and senses been so active during this usually inert time of
year. At home I would have been playing lugubrious old records
and looking out the window quite a bit. I was terribly grateful in a
completely abstract way for my commitment to a meaningful
mania. And I was eager to get to work after I had had some
breakfast at the coffee shop.

When I got back to my room I discovered the door was
unlocked. And there was something written on the dresser mirror. The writing was red and greasy, as if done with a clown's
make-up pencil – my own, I realized. I read the legend, or rather I
should say *riddle*, several times: "What buries itself before it is
dead?" I looked at it for quite a while, very shaken at how
vulnerable my holiday fortifications were. Was this supposed to
be a warning of some kind? A threat to the effect that if I persisted

in a certain course I would end up prematurely interred? I would have to be careful, I told myself. My resolution was to let nothing deter me from the inspired strategy I had conceived for myself. I wiped the mirror clean, for it was now needed for other purposes.

I spent the rest of the day devising a very special costume and the appropriate face to go with it. I easily shabbied up my overcoat with a torn pocket or two and a complete set of stains. Combined with blue jeans and a pair of rather scuffed-up shoes, I had a passable costume for a derelict. The face, however, was more difficult, for I had to experiment from memory. Conjuring a mental image of the screaming pierrot in that painting (*The Scream*, I now recall), helped me quite a bit. At nightfall I exited the hotel by the back stairway.

It was strange to walk down the crowded street in this gruesome disguise. Though I thought I would feel conspicuous, the actual experience was very close, I imagined, to one of complete invisibility. No one looked at me as I strolled by, or as they strolled by, or as we strolled by each other. I was a phantom – perhaps the ghost of festivals past, or those yet to come.

I had no clear idea where my disguise would take me that night, only vague expectations of gaining the confidence of my fellow specters and possibly in some way coming to know their secrets. For a while I would simply wander around in that lackadaisical manner I had learned from them, following their lead in any way they might indicate. And for the most part this meant doing almost nothing and doing it silently. If I passed one of my kind on the sidewalk there was no speaking, no exchange of knowing looks, no recognition at all that I was aware of. We were there on the streets of Mirocaw to create a presence and nothing more. At least this is how I came to feel about it. As I drifted along with my bodiless invisibility, I felt myself more and more becoming an empty, floating shape, seeing without being seen and walking without the interference of those grosser creatures who shared my world. It was not an experience completely without interest or even pleasure. The clown's shibboleth of "here we are again" took on a new meaning for me as I felt myself a novitiate of a more rarified order of harlequinry. And very soon the opportunity to make further progress along this path presented itself.

Going the opposite direction, down the street, a pickup truck slowly passed, gently parting a sea of zigging and zagging celebrants. The cargo in the back of this truck was curious, for it was made up entirely of my fellow sectarians. At the end of the block the truck stopped and another of them boarded it over the back gate. One block down I saw still another get on. Then the, truck made a U-turn at an intersection and headed in my direction.

I stood at the curb as I had seen the others do. I was not sure the truck would pick me up, thinking that somehow they knew I was an imposter. The truck did, however, slow down, almost coming to a stop when it reached me. The others were crowded on the floor of the truck bed. Most of them were just staring into nothingness with the usual indifference I had come to expect from their kind. But a few actually glanced at me with some anticipation. For a second I hesitated, not sure I wanted to pursue this ruse any further. At the last moment, some impulse sent me climbing up the back of the truck and squeezing myself in among the others.

There were only a few more to pick up before the truck headed for the outskirts of Mirocaw and beyond. At first I tried to maintain a clear orientation with respect to the town. But as we took turn after turn through the darkness of narrow country roads, I found myself unable to preserve any sense of direction. The majority of the others in the back of the truck exhibited no apparent awareness of their fellow passengers. Guardedly, I looked from face to ghostly face. A few of them spoke in short whispered phrases to others close by. I could not make out what they were saying but the tone of their voices was one of innocent normalcy, as if they were not of the hardened slum-herd of Mirocaw. Perhaps, I thought, these were thrill-seekers who had disguised themselves as I had done, or, more likely, initiates of some kind. Possibly they had received prior instructions at such meetings as I had stumbled onto the day before. It was also likely that among this crew were those very boys I had frightened into a precipitate exit from that old diner.

The truck was now speeding along a fairly open stretch of country, heading toward those higher hills that surrounded the now distant town of Mirocaw. The icy wind whipped around us, and I could not keep myself from trembling with cold. This definitely betrayed me as one of the newcomers among the group, for the two bodies that pressed against mine were rigidly still and even seemed to be radiating a frigidity of their own. I glanced ahead at the darkness into which we were rapidly progressing.

We had left all open country behind us now, and the road was enclosed by thick woods. The mass of bodies in the truck leaned into one another as we began traveling up a steep incline. Above us, at the top of the hill, were lights shining somewhere within the woods. When the road levelled off, the truck made an abrupt turn, steering into what looked like a great ditch.

There was an unpaved path, however, upon which the truck proceeded toward the glowing in the near distance.

This glowing became brighter and sharper as we approached it, flickering upon the trees and revealing stark detail where there had formerly been only smooth darkness. As the truck pulled into a clearing and came to a stop, I saw a loose assembly of figures, many of which held lanterns that beamed with a dazzling and frosty light. I stood up in the back of the truck to unboard as the others were doing. Glancing around from that height I saw approximately thirty more of those cadaverous clowns milling about. One of my fellow passengers spied me lingering in the truck and in a strangely high-pitched whisper told me to hurry, explaining something about the "apex of darkness". I thought again about this solstice night; it was technically the longest period of darkness of the year, even if not by a very significant margin from many other winter nights. Its true significance, though, was related to considerations having little to do with either statistics or the calendar.

I went over to the place where the others were forming into a tighter crowd, which betrayed a sense of expectancy in the subtle gestures and expressions of its individual members. Glances were now exchanged, the hand of one lightly touched the shoulder of another, and a pair of circled eyes gazed over to where two figures were setting their lanterns on the ground about six feet apart. The illumination of these lanterns revealed an opening in the earth. Eventually the awareness of everyone was focused on this roundish pit, and as if by prearranged signal we all began huddling around it. The only sounds were those of the wind and our own movements as we crushed frozen leaves and sticks underfoot.

Finally, when we had all surrounded this gaping hole, the first one jumped in, leaving our sight for a moment but then reappearing to take hold of a lantern which another handed him from above. The miniature abyss filled with light, and I could see it was no more than six feet deep. One of its walls opened into the mouth of a tunnel. The figure holding the lantern stooped a little and disappeared into the passage.

Each of us, in turn, dropped into the darkness of this pit, and every fifth one took a lantern. I kept to the back of the group, for whatever subterranean activities were going to take place, I was sure I wanted to be on their periphery. When only about ten of us remained on the ground above, I maneuvered to let four of them precede me so that as the fifth I might receive a lantern. This was exactly how it worked out, for after I had leaped to the bottom of the hole a light was ritually handed down to me. Turning about-face, I quickly entered the passageway. At that point I shook so with cold that I was neither curious nor afraid, but only grateful for the shelter.

I entered a long, gently sloping tunnel, just high enough for me to stand upright. It was considerably warmer down there than outside in the cold darkness of the woods. After a few moments I had sufficiently thawed out so that my concerns shifted from those of physical comfort to a sudden and justified preoccupation with my survival. As I walked I held my lantern close to the sides of the tunnel. They were relatively smooth as if the passage had not been made by manual digging but had been burrowed by something which left behind a clue to its dimensions in the tunnel's size and shape. This delirious idea came to me when I recalled the message that had been left on my hotel room mirror: "What buries itself before it is dead?"

I had to hurry along to keep up with those uncanny spelunkers who preceded me. The lanterns ahead bobbed with every step of their bearers, the lumbering procession seeming less and less real the farther we marched into that snug little tunnel. At some point I noticed the line ahead of me growing shorter. The processioners were emptying out into a cavernous chamber where I, too, soon arrived. This area was about thirty feet in height, its other dimensions approximating those of a large ballroom. Gazing into the distance above made me uncomfortably aware of how far we had descended into the earth. Unlike the smooth sides of the tunnel, the walls of this cavern looked jagged and irregular, as though they had been gnawed at. The earth had been removed, I assumed, either through the tunnel from which we had emerged, or else by way of one of the many other black openings that I saw around the edges of the chamber, for possibly they too led back to the surface.

But the structure of this chamber occupied my mind a great deal less than did its occupants. There to meet us on the floor of the great cavern was what must have been the entire slum population of Mirocaw, and more, all with the same eerily wide-eyed and oval-mouthed faces. They formed a circle around an altar-like object which had some kind of dark, leathery covering draped over it. Upon the altar, another covering of the same material concealed a lumpy form beneath.

And behind this form, looking down upon the altar, was the only figure whose face was not greased with makeup.

He wore a long snowy robe that was the same color as the wispy hair berimming his head. His arms were calmly at his sides. He made no movement. The man I once believed would penetrate great secrets stood before us with the same professorial bearing that had impressed me so many years ago, yet now I felt nothing but dread at the thought of what revelations lay pocketed within the abysmal folds of his magisterial attire. Had I really come here to challenge such a formidable figure? The name by which I knew him seemed itself insufficient to designate one of his stature. Rather I should name him by his other incarnations: god of all wisdom, scribe of all sacred books, father of all magicians, thrice great and more – rather I should call him *Thoth*.

He raised his cupped hands to his congregation and the ceremony was underway.

It was all very simple. The entire assembly, which had remained speechless until this moment, broke into the most horrendous high-pitched singing that can be imagined. It was a choir of sorrow, of shrieking delirium, and of shame. The cavern rang shrilly with the dissonant, whining chorus. My voice, too, was added to the congregation's, trying to blend with their maimed music. But my singing could not imitate theirs, having a huskiness unlike their cacophonous keening wail. To keep from exposing myself as an intruder I continued to mouth their words without sound. These words were a revelation of the moody malignancy which until then I had no more than sensed whenever in the presence of these figures. They were singing to the "unborn in paradise," to the "pure unlived lives." They sang a dirge for existence, for all its vital forms and seasons. Their ideals were those of darkness, chaos, and a melancholy half-existence consecrated to all the many shapes of death. A sea of thin, bloodless faces trembled and screamed with perverted hopes. And the robed, guiding figure at the heart of all this – elevated over the course of twenty years to the status of high priest – was the man from whom I had taken so many of my own life's principles. It would be useless to describe what I felt at that moment and a waste of the time I need to describe the events which followed.

The singing abruptly stopped and the towering white-haired figure began to speak. He was welcoming those of the new generation – twenty winters had passed since the "Pure Ones" had expanded their ranks. The word "pure" in this setting was a violence to what sense and composure I still retained, for nothing could have been more foul than what was to come. Thoss – and I employ this defunct identity only as a convenience – closed his sermon and drew closer to the dark-skinned altar. Then, with all the flourish of his former life, he drew back the topmost covering. Beneath it was a limp-limbed effigy, a collapsed puppet sprawled upon the slab. I was standing toward the rear of the congregation and attempted to keep as close to the exit passage as I could. Thus, I did not see everything as clearly as I might have.

Thoss looked down upon the crooked, doll-like form and then out at the gathering. I even imagined that he made knowing eye-contact with myself. He spread his arms and a stream of continuous and unintelligible words flowed from his moaning mouth. The congregation began to stir, not greatly but perceptibly. Until that moment there was a limit to what I believed was the evil of these people. They were, after all, only that. They were merely morbid, self-tortured souls with strange beliefs. If there was anything I had learned in all my years as an anthropologist it was that the world is infinitely rich in strange ideas, even to the point where the concept of strangeness itself had little meaning for me. But with the scene I then witnessed, my conscience bounded into a realm from which it will never return.

For now was the transformation scene, the culmination of every harlequinade.

It began slowly. There was increasing movement among those on the far side of the chamber, from where I stood. Someone had fallen to the floor and the others in the area backed away. The voice at the altar continued its chanting. I tried to gain a better view but there were too many of them around me. Through the mass of obstructing bodies I caught only glimpses of what was taking place.

The one who had swooned to the floor of the chamber seemed to be losing all former shape and proportion. I thought it was a clown's trick. They were clowns, were they not? I myself could make four white balls transform into four black balls as I juggled them. And this was not my most astonishing feat of clownish magic. And is there not always a sleight-of-hand inherent in all ceremonies, often dependent on the transported delusions of the celebrants? This was a good show, I thought, and giggled to myself. The transformation scene of Harlequin throwing off his fool's facade. O God, Harlequin, do not move like that! Harlequin, where are your arms? And your legs have melted together and begun squirming upon the floor. What horrible, mouthing umbilicus is that where your face should be? *What is it that buries itself before it is dead?* The almighty serpent of wisdom – the Conqueror Worm.

It now started happening all around the chamber. Individual members of the congregation would gaze emptily – caught for a moment in a frozen trance – and then collapse to the floor to begin the sickening metamorphosis. This happened with ever-increasing frequency the louder and more frantic Thoss chanted his insane prayer or curse. Then there began a writhing movement toward the altar, and Thoss welcomed the things as they curled their way to the altar-top. I knew now what lax figure lay upon it.

This was Kora and Persephone, the daughter of Ceres and the Winter Queen: the child abducted into the underworld of death. Except this child had no supernatural mother to save her, no living mother at all. For the sacrifice I witnessed was an echo of one that had occurred twenty years before, the carnival feast of the preceding generation – O *carne vale!* Now both mother and daughter had become victims of this subterranean sabbath. I finally realized this truth when the figure stirred upon the altar, lifted its head of icy beauty, and screamed at the sight of mute mouths closing around her.

I ran from the chamber into the tunnel. (There was nothing else that could be done, I have obsessively told myself.) Some of the others who had not yet changed began to pursue me. They would have caught up to me, I have no doubt, for I fell only a few yards into the passage. And for a moment I imagined that I too was about to undergo a transformation, but I had not been prepared as the others had been. When I heard the approaching footsteps of my pursuers I was sure there was an even worse fate facing me upon the altar. But the footsteps ceased and retreated. They had received an order in the voice of their high priest. I too heard the order, though I wish I had not, for until then I had imagined that Thoss did not remember who I was. It was that voice which taught me otherwise.

For the moment I was free to leave. I struggled to my feet and, having broken my lantern in the fall, retraced my way back through cloacal blackness.

Everything seemed to happen very quickly once I emerged from the tunnel and climbed up from the pit. I wiped the reeking greasepaint from my face as I ran through the woods and back to the road. A passing car stopped, though I gave it no other choice except to run me down.

"Thank you for stopping."

"What the hell are you doing out here?" the driver asked.

I caught my breath. "It was a joke. The festival. Friends thought it would be funny . . . Please drive on."

My ride let me off about a mile out of town, and from there I could find my way. It was the same way I had come into Mirocaw on my first visit the summer before. I stood for a while at the summit of that high hill just outside the city limits, looking down upon the busy little hamlet. The intensity of the festival had not abated, and would not until morning. I walked down toward the welcoming glow of green, slipped through the festivities unnoticed, and returned to the hotel. No one saw me go up to my room. Indeed, there was an atmosphere of absence and abandonment throughout that building, and the desk in the lobby was unattended.

I locked the door to my room and collapsed upon the bed.

7.

When I awoke the next morning I saw from my window that the town and surrounding countryside had been visited during the night by a snowstorm, one which was entirely unpredicted. The snow was still falling on the now deserted streets of Mirocaw. The festival was over. Everyone had gone home.

And this was exactly my own intention. Any action on my part concerning what I had seen the night before would have to wait until I was away from the town. I am still not sure it will do the slightest good to speak up like this. Any accusations I could make against the slum populace of Mirocaw would be resisted, as well they should be, as unbelievable. Perhaps in a very short while none of this will be my concern.

With packed suitcases in both hands I walked up to the front desk to check out. The man behind the desk was not Samuel Beadle, and he had to fumble around to find my bill.

"Here we are. Everything all right?"

"Fine," I answered in a dead voice. "Is Mr. Beadle around?"

"No, I'm afraid he's not back yet. Been out all night looking for his daughter. She's a very popular girl, being the Winter Queen and all that nonsense. Probably find she was at a party somewhere."

A little noise came out of my throat.

I threw my suitcases in the back seat of my car and got behind the wheel. On that morning nothing I could recall seemed real to me. The snow was falling and I watched it through my windshield, slow and silent and entrancing. I started up my car, routinely glancing in my rear view mirror. What I saw there is now vividly framed in my mind, as it was framed in the back window of my car when I turned to verify its reality.

In the middle of the street behind me, standing ankle-deep in snow, was Thoss and another figure. When I looked closely at the other I recognized him as one of the boys whom I surprised in that diner. But he had now taken on a corrupt and listless resemblance to his new family. Both he and Thoss stared at me, making no attempt to forestall my departure. Thoss knew that this was unnecessary.

I had to carry the image of those two dark figures in my mind as I drove back home. But only now has the full weight of my experience descended upon me. So far I have claimed illness in order to avoid my teaching schedule. To face the normal flow of life as I had formerly known it would be impossible. I am now very much under the influence of a season and a climate far colder and more barren than all the winters in human memory. And mentally retracing past events does not seem to have helped; I can feel myself sinking deeper into a velvety white abyss.

At certain times I could almost dissolve entirely into this inner realm of awful purity and emptiness. I remember those invisible moments when in disguise I drifted through the streets of Mirocaw, untouched by the drunken, noisy forms around me: untouchable. But instantly I recoil at this grotesque nostalgia, for I realize what is happening and what I do not want to be true, though Thoss proclaimed it was. I recall his command to those others as I lay helplessly prone in the tunnel. They could have apprehended me, but Thoss, my old master, called them back. His voice echoed throughout that cavern, and it now reverberates within my own psychic chambers of memory.

"He is one of us," it said. "He has *always* been one of us."

It is this voice which now fills my dreams and my days and my long winter nights. I have seen you, Dr. Thoss, through the snow outside my window. Soon I will celebrate, alone, that last feast which will kill your words, only to prove how well I have learned their truth.

To the memory of H. P. Lovecraft

THE SPECTACLES IN
THE DRAWER

1.

Last year at this time, perhaps on this very day, Plomb visited me at my home. He always seemed to know when I had returned from my habitual travelling and always appeared uninvited on my doorstep. Although this former residence of mine was pathetically run-down, Plomb seemed to regard it as a kind of castle or fortress, always gazing up at its high ceilings as if he were witnessing its wonders for the first time. That day – a dim one, I think   hc did not fail to do the same. Then we settled into one of the spacious though sparsely furnished rooms of my house.

"And how were your travels?" he asked, as if only in the spirit of polite conversation. I could see by his smile – an emulation of my own, no doubt – that he was glad to be back in my house and in my company. I smiled too and stood up. Plomb, of course, stood up along with me, almost simultaneously with my own movements.

"Shall we go then?" I said. *What a pest*, I thought.

Our footsteps tapped a moderate time on the hard wooden floor leading to the stairway. We ascended to the second floor, which I left almost entirely empty, and then up a narrower stairway to the third floor. Although I had led him along this route several times before, I could see from his wandering eyes that, for him, every tendrilled swirl of wallpaper, every cobweb fluttering in the corners above, every stale draft of the house composed a suspenseful prelude to our destination. At the end of the third-floor hall there was a small wooden stairway, no more than a ladder, that led to an old storeroom where I kept certain things which I collected.

It was not by any means a spacious room, and its enclosed atmosphere was *thickened*, as Plomb would have emphasized, by its claustrophobic arrangement of tall cabinets, ceiling-high shelves, and various trunks and crates. This is simply how things worked out over a period of time. In any case, Plomb seemed to favor this state of affairs. "Ah, the room of secret mystery," he said. "Where all your treasures are kept, all the raw wonders cached away."

These treasures and wonders, as Plomb called them, were, I suppose, remarkable from a certain point of view. Plomb loved to go through all the old objects and articles, gathering together a lapful of curios and settling down on the dusty sofa at the center of this room. But it was the new items, whenever I returned from one of my protracted tours, that always took precedence in Plomb's hierarchy of wonders. Thus, I immediately brought out the double-handled dagger with the single blade of polished stone. At first sight of the ceremonial object, Plomb held out the flat palms of his hands, and I placed this exotic device upon its rightful altar. "Who could have made such a thing?" he asked, though rhetorically. He expected no answer to his questions and possibly did not really desire any. And of course I offered no more elaborate an explanation than a simple smile. But how quickly, I noticed, the magic of that first fragment of "speechless wonder," as he would say, lost its initial surge of fascination. How fast that glistening fog, which surrounded only him, dispersed to unveil a tedious clarity. I had to move faster.

"Here," I said, my arm searching the shadows of an open wardrobe. "This should be worn when you handle that sacrificial artifact." And I threw the robe about his shoulders, engulfing his smallish frame with a cyclone of strange patterns and colors. He admired himself in the mirror attached inside the door of the wardrobe. "Look at the robe in the mirror," he practically shouted. "The designs are all turned around. How much stranger, how much better." While he stood there glaring at himself, I relieved him of the dagger before he had a chance to do something careless. This left his hands free to raise themselves up to the dust-caked ceiling of the room, and to the dark gods of his imagination. Gripping each handle of the dagger, I suddenly elevated it above his head, where I held it poised. In a few moments he started to giggle, then fell into spasms of sardonic hilarity. He stumbled over to the old sofa and collapsed upon its soft cushions. I followed, but when I reached his prostrate form it was not the pale-blue blade that I brought down upon his chest – it was simply a book, one of many I had put before him. His peaked legs created a lectern on which he rested the huge volume, propping it securely as he began turning the stiff crackling pages. The sound seemed to absorb him as much as the sight of a language he could not even name let alone comprehend.

"The lost grimoire of the Abbot of Tine," he giggled. "Transcribed in the language of —"

"A wild guess," I interjected. "And a wrong one."

"Then the forbidden *Psalms of the Silent*. The book without an author."

"Without a living author, if you will recall what I told you about it. But you're very wide of the mark."

"Well, suppose you give me a hint," he said with an impatience that surprised me. "Suppose—"

"But wouldn't you prefer to guess at its wonders, Plomb?" I suggested encouragingly. Some moments of precarious silence passed.

"I suppose I would," he finally answered, and to my relief. Then I watched him gorge his eyes on the inscrutable script of the ancient volume.

In truth, the mysteries of this Sacred Writ were among the most genuine of their kind, for it had never been my intention to dupe my disciple – as he justly thought of himself – with false secrets. But the secrets of such a book are not absolute: once they are known, they become relegated to a lesser sphere, which is that of the knower. Having lost the prestige they once enjoyed, these former secrets now function as tools in the excavation of still deeper ones which, in turn, will suffer the same corrosive fate. And this is the fate of all true secrets. Eventually the seeker may conclude – either through insight or sheer exhaustion – that this ruthless process is neverending, that the mortification of one mystery after another has no terminus beyond that of the seeker's own extinction. And how many still remain susceptible to the search? How many pursue it to the end of their days with undying hope of some ultimate revelation? Better not to think in precise terms just how few the faithful are. More to the present point, it seems that Plomb was one of their infinitesimal number. And it was my intention to reduce that number by one.

The plan was simple: to feed Plomb's hunger for mysterious sensations to the point of nausea . . . and beyond. The only thing to survive would be a gutful of shame and regret for a defunct passion.

As Plomb lay upon the sofa, ogling that stupid book, I moved toward a large cabinet whose several doors were composed of a tarnished metal grillwork framed by darkest wood. I opened one of these doors and exposed a number of shelves cluttered with books and odd objects. Upon one shelf, resting there as sole occupant, was a very white box. It was no larger, as I mentally envision it, than a modest jewelry case. There were no markings on the box, except the fingerprints, or rather thumbprints, smearing its smooth white surface at its opposing edges and halfway along its length. There were no handles or embellishments of any kind; not even, at first sight, the thinnest of seams to indicate the level at which the lower part of the box met the upper part, or perhaps give away the existence of a drawer. I smiled a little at the mock intrigue of the object, then gripped it from either side, gently, and placed my thumbs precisely over the fresh thumbprints. I applied pressure with each thumb, and a shallow drawer popped open at the front of the box. As hoped, Plomb had been watching me as I went through these meaningless motions.

"What do you have there?" he asked.

"Patience, Plomb. You will see," I answered while delicately removing two sparkling items from the drawer: one a small and silvery knife which very much resembled a razor-sharp letter opener, and the other a pair of old-fashioned wire-rimmed spectacles.

Plomb laid aside the now-boring book and sat up straight against the arm of the sofa. I sat down beside him and opened up the spectacles so that the stems were pointing toward his face. When he leaned forward, I slipped them on. "They're only plain glass," he said with a definite tone of disappointment. "Or a very weak prescription." His eyes rolled about as he attempted to scrutinize what rested upon his own face. Without saying a word, I held up the little knife in front of him until he finally took notice of it. "Ahhhh, " he said, smiling. "There's more to it." "Of course there is," I said, gently twirling the steely blade before his fascinated eyes. "Now hold out your palm, just like that. Good, good. You won't even feel this, completely harmless. Now," I instructed him, "keep watching that tiny red trickle.

"Your eyes are now fused with those fantastic lenses, and your sight is one with its object. And what exactly is that object? Obviously it is everything that fascinates, everything that has power over your gaze and your dreams. You cannot even conceive the wish to look away. And even if there are no simple images to see, nonetheless there is a vision of some kind, an infinite and overwhelming scene expanding before you. And the vastness of this scene is such that even the dazzling diffusion of all the known universes cannot convey its wonder. Everything is so brilliant, so great, and so alive: landscapes without end that are rolling with life, landscapes that are themselves alive. Unimaginable diversity of form and motion, design and dimension. And each detail is perfectly crystalline, from the mammoth shapes lurching in outline against endless horizons to the minutest cilia wriggling in an obscure oceanic niche. Even this is only a mere fragment of all that there is to see and to know. There are labyrinthine astronomies, discrete systems of living mass which yet are woven together by a complex of intersections, at points mingling in a way that mutually affects those systems involved, yielding instantaneous evolutions, constant transformations of both appearance and essence. You are witness to all that exists or ever could exist. And yet, somehow concealed in the shadows of all that you can see is something that is not yet visible, something that is beating like a thunderous pulse and promises still greater visions: all else is merely its membrane enclosing the ultimate thing waiting to be born, preparing for the cataclysm which will be both the beginning and the end. To behold the prelude to this event must be an experience of unbearable anticipation, so that hope and dread merge into a new emotion, one corresponding perfectly to the absolute and the wholly unknown. The next instant, it seems, will bring with it a revolution of all matter and energy. But the seconds keep passing, the experience grows more fascinating without fulfilling its portents, without extinguishing itself in revelation. And although the visions remain active inside you, deep in your blood – you now awake."

Pushing himself up from the sofa, Plomb staggered forward a few steps and wiped his bloodied palm on the front of his shirt, as if to wipe away the visions. He shook his head vigorously once or twice, but the spectacles remained secure.

"Is everything all right?" I asked him.

Plomb appeared to be dazzled in the worst way. Behind the spectacles his eyes gazed dumbly, and his mouth gaped with countless unspoken words. However, when I said, "Perhaps I should remove these for you," his hand rose toward mine, as if to prevent me from doing so. But his effort was half-hearted. Folding their wire stems one across the other, I replaced them back in their box. Plomb now watched me, as if I were performing some ritual of great fascination. He seemed to be still composing himself from the experience.

"Well?" I asked.

"Dreadful," he answered. "But . . ."

"But?"

"But I . . ."

"You?"

"What I mean is – where did they come from?"

"Can't you imagine that for yourself?" I countered. And for a moment it seemed that in this case, too, he desired some simple answer, contrary to his most hardened habits. Then he smiled rather deviously and threw himself down upon the sofa. His eyes glazed over as he fabricated an anecdote to his fancy.

"I can see you," he said, "at an occultist auction in a disreputable quarter of a foreign city. The box is carried forward, the spectacles taken out. They were made several generations ago by a man who was at once a student of the Gnostics and a master of optometry. His ambition: to construct a pair of artificial eyes that would allow him to bypass the obstacle of physical appearances and glimpse a far-off realm of secret truth whose gateway is within the depths of our own blood."

"Remarkable," I replied. "Your speculation is so close to truth itself that the details are not worth mentioning for the mere sake of vulgar correctness."

In fact, the spectacles belonged to a lot of antiquarian rubbish I once bought blindly, and the box was of unknown, or rather unremembered, origin – just something I had lying around in my attic room. And the knife, a magician's prop for efficiently slicing up paper money and silk ties.

I carried the box containing both spectacles and knife over to Plomb, holding it slightly beyond his reach. I said, "Can you imagine the dangers involved, the possible nightmare of possessing such 'artificial eyes'?" He nodded gravely in agreement. "And you can imagine the restraint the possessor of such a gruesome artifact must practice." His eyes were all comprehension, and he was sucking a little at his slightly lacerated palm. "Then nothing would please me more than to pass the ownership of this obscure miracle on to you, my dear Plomb. I'm sure you will hold it in wonder as no one else could."

And it was exactly this wonder that it was my malicious aim to undermine, or rather to expand until it ripped itself apart. For I could no longer endure the sight of it.

As Plomb once again stood at the door of my home, holding his precious gift with a child's awkward embrace, I could not resist asking him the question. Opening the door for him, I said, "By the way, Plomb, have you ever been hypnotized?"

"I . . ." he answered.

"You," I prompted.

"No," he said. "Why do you ask?"

"Curiosity," I replied. "You know how I am. Well, good-night, Plomb."

And I closed the door behind the most willing subject in the world, hoping it would be some time before he returned. "If ever," I said aloud, and the words echoed in the hollows of my home.

2.

But it was not long afterward that Plomb and I had our next confrontation, though the circumstances were odd and accidental. Late one afternoon, as it happens, I was browsing through a shop that dealt in second-hand merchandise of the most pathetic sort. The place was littered with rusty scales that once would have given your weight for a penny, cock-eyed bookcases, dead toys, furniture without style or substance, grotesque standing ashtrays late of some hotel lobby, and a hodgepodge of old-fashioned fixtures. For me, however, such decrepit bazaars offered more diversion and consolation than the most exotic marketplaces, which so often made good on their strange promises that mystery itself ceased to have meaning. But my second-hand seller made no promises and inspired no dreams, leaving all that to those more ambitious hucksters who trafficked in such perishable stock in trade. At the time I could ask no more of a given gray afternoon than to find myself in one of these enchantingly desolate establishments.

That particular afternoon in the second-hand shop brought me a brief glimpse of Plomb in a second-hand manner. The visual transaction took place in a mirror that leaned against a wall, one of the many mirrors that seemed to constitute a specialty of the shop. I had squatted down before this rectangular relic, whose frame reminded me of the decorated borders of old books, and wiped my bare hand across its dusty surface. And there, hidden beneath the dust, was the face of Plomb, who must have just entered the shop and was standing a room's length away. While he seemed to recognize immediately the reverse side of me, his expression betrayed the hope that I had not seen him. There was shock as well as shame upon that face, and something else besides. And if Plomb had approached me, what could I have said to him? Perhaps I would have mentioned that he did not look very well or that it appeared he had been the victim of an accident. But how could he explain what had happened to him except to reveal the truth that we both knew and neither would speak? Fortunately, this scene was to remain in its hypothetical state, because a moment later he was out the door.

I cautiously approached the front window of the shop in time to see Plomb hurrying off into the dull, unreflecting day, his right hand held up to his face. "It was only my intention to cure him," I mumbled to myself. I had not considered that he was incurable, nor that things would have developed in the way they did.

3.

And after that day I wondered, eventually to the point of obsession, what kind of hell had claimed poor Plomb for its own. I knew only that I had provided him with a type of toy: the subliminal ability to feast his eyes on an imaginary universe in a rivulet of his own blood. The possibility that he would desire to magnify this experience, or indeed that he would be capable of such a feat, had not seriously occurred to me. Obviously, however, this had become the case. I now had to ask myself how much farther could Plomb's situation be extended. The answer, though I could not guess it at the time, was presented to me in a dream.

And it seemed fitting that the dream had its setting in that old attic storeroom of my house, which Plomb once prized above all other rooms in the world. I was sitting in a chair, a huge and enveloping chair which in reality does not exist but in the dream directly faces the sofa. No thoughts or feelings troubled me, and I had only the faintest sense that someone else was in the room. But I could not see who it was, because everything appeared so dim in outline, blurry and grayish. There seemed to be some movement in the region of the sofa, as if the enormous cushions themselves had become lethargically restless. Unable to fathom the source of this movement, I touched my hand to my temple in thought. This was how I discovered that I was wearing a pair of spectacles with circular lenses connected to wiry stems. I thought to myself: "If I remove these spectacles I will be able to see more clearly." But a voice told me not to remove them, and I recognized that voice. "Plomb," I said. And then something moved, like a man-shaped shadow, upon the sofa. A climate of dull horror began to invade my surroundings. "Even if your trip is over," I said deliriously, "you have nothing to show for it." But the voice disagreed with me in sinister whispers that made no sense but seemed filled with meaning. I would indeed be shown things, these whispers might have said. Already I was being shown things, astonishing things – mysteries and marvels beyond anything I had ever suspected. And suddenly all my feelings, as I gazed through the spectacles, were proof of that garbled pronouncement. They were feelings of a peculiar nature which, to my knowledge, one experiences only in dreams: sensations of infinite expansiveness and ineffable meaning that have no place elsewhere in our lives. But although these monstrous, astronomical emotions suggested wonders of incredible magnitude and character, I saw nothing through those magic lenses except this: the obscure shape in the shadows before me as its outline grew clearer and clearer to my eyes. Gradually I came to view what appeared to be a mutilated carcass, something of a terrible rawness, a torn and flayed thing whose every laceration could be traced in crystalline sharpness. The only thing of color in my grayish surroundings, it twitched and quivered like a gory heart exposed beneath the body of the dream. And it made a sound like hellish giggling. Then it said: "I am back from my trip," in a horrible, piercing voice.

It was this simple statement that inspired my efforts to tear the spectacles from my face, even though they now seemed to be part of my flesh. I gripped them with both hands and flung them against the wall, where they shattered. Somehow this served to exorcise my tormented companion, who faded back into the grayness. Then I looked at the wall and saw that it was running red where the spectacles had struck. And the broken lenses that lay upon the floor were bleeding.

To experience such a dream as this on a single occasion might very well be the stuff of a haunting, lifelong memory, something that perhaps might even be cherished for its unfathomable depths of feeling. But to suffer over and over this same nightmare, as I soon found was my fate, leads one to seek nothing so much as a cure to kill the dream, to reveal all its secrets and thus bring about a selective amnesia.

At first I looked to the sheltering shadows of my home for deliverance and forgetfulness, the sobering shadows which at other times had granted me a cold and stagnant peace. I tried to argue myself free of my nightly excursions, to discourse these visions away, lecturing the walls *contra* the prodigies of a mysterious world. "Since any form of existence," I muttered, "since any form of existence is by definition a conflict of forces, or it is nothing at all, what can it possibly matter if these skirmishes take place in a world of marvels or one of mud? The difference between the two is not worth mentioning, or none. Such distinctions are the work of only the crudest and most limited perspectives, the sense of mystery and wonder foremost among them. Even the most esoteric ecstasy, when it comes down to it, requires the prop of vulgar pain in order to stand up as an experience. Having acknowledged the truth, however provisional, and the reality, if subject to mutation, of all the strange things in the universe – whether known, unknown, or merely suspected – one is left with no recourse than to conclude that none of them makes any difference, that such marvels change nothing: our experience remains *the same*. The gallery of human sensations that existed in prehistory is identical to the one that faces each life today, that will continue to face each new life as it enters this world . . . and then looks beyond it."

And thus I attempted to reason my way back to self-possession. But no measure of my former serenity was forthcoming. On the contrary, my days as well as my nights were now poisoned by an obsession with Plomb. Why had I given him those spectacles! More to the point, why did I allow him to retain them? It was time to take back my gift, to confiscate those little bits of glass and twisted metal that were now harrowing the wrong mind. And since I had succeeded too well in keeping him away from my door, I would have to be the one to approach his.

4.

But it was not Plomb who answered the rotting door of that house which stood at the street's end and beside a broad expanse of empty field. It was not Plomb who asked if I was a newspaper journalist or a policeman before closing that gouged and filthy door in my face when I replied that I was neither of those persons. Pounding on that wobbling door, which seemed about to crumble under my fist, I summoned the sunken-eyed man a second time to ask if this in fact was Mr. Plomb's address. I had never visited him at his home, that hopeless little box in which he lived and slept and dreamed.

"Was he a relative?"

"No," I answered.

"A friend. You're not here to collect a bill, because if that's the case . . ."

For the sake of simplicity I interjected that, yes, I was a friend of Mr. Plomb.

"Then how is it you don't know?"

For the sake of my curiosity I said that I had been away on a trip, as I often was, and had my own reasons for notifying Mr. Plomb of my return.

"Then you don't know anything," he stated flatly.

"Exactly," I replied.

"It was even in the newspaper. And they asked me about him."

"Plomb," I confirmed.

"That's right," he said, as if he had suddenly become the custodian of a secret knowledge.

Then he waved me into the house and led me through its ugly, airless interior to a small storage room at the back. He reached along the wall inside the room, as if he wanted to avoid entering it, and switched on the light. Immediately I understood why the hollow-faced man preferred not to go into that room, for Plomb had renovated that tiny space in a very strange way. Each wall, as well as the ceiling and floor, was a mosaic of mirrors, a shocking galaxy of redundant reflections. And each mirror was splattered with sinister droplets, as if someone had swung several brushfuls of paint from various points throughout the room, spreading dark stars across a silvery firmament. In his attempt to exhaust or exaggerate the visions to which he had apparently become enslaved, Plomb had done nothing less than multiplied these visions into infinity, creating oceans of his own blood and enabling himself to see with countless eyes. Entranced by such aspiration, I gazed at the mirrors in speechless wonder. Among them was one I remembered looking into some days – or was it weeks? – before.

The landlord, who did not follow me into the room, said something about suicide and a body ripped raw. This news was of course unnecessary, even boring. But I was overwhelmed at Plomb's ingenuity: it was some time before I could look away from that gallery of glass and gore. Only afterward did I fully realize that I would never be rid of the horrible Plomb. He had broken through all the mirrors, projected himself into the eternity beyond them.

And even when I abandoned my home, with its hideous attic storeroom, Plomb still followed me in my dreams. He now travels with me to the ends of the earth, initiating me night after night into his unspeakable wonders. I can only hope that we will not meet in another place, one where the mysteries are always new and dreams never end. Oh, Plomb, will you not stay in that box where they have put your riven body?

FLOWERS OF THE ABYSS

I must whisper my words in the wind, knowing somehow that they will reach you who sent me here. Let this misadventure, like the first rank scent of autumn, be carried back to you, my good people. For it was you who decided where I would go, you who wished I come here and to him. And I agreed, because the fear that filled your voices and lined your faces was so much greater than your words could explain. I feared your fear of him: the one whose name we did not know, the one whom we saw but who never spoke, the one who lived far from town in that ruined house which long ago had seen the passing of the family Van Livenn.

I was chosen to unravel his secrets and find what malice or indifference he harbored toward our town. I should be the one, you said. Was I not the teacher of the town's child-citizens, the one who had knowledge that you had not and who might therefore see deeper into the mystery of our man? That was what you said, in the shadows of our church where we met that night; but what you thought, whether you knew it or not, was that he has no children of his own, no one, and so many of his hours are spent walking through those same woods in which lives the stranger. It would seem quite natural if I happened to pass the old Van Livenn house, if I happened to stop and perhaps beg a glass of water for a thirsty walker of the woods. But these simple actions, even then, seemed an extraordinary adventure, though none of us confessed to this feeling. Nothing to fear, you said. And so I was chosen to go alone.

You have seen the house and how, approaching it from the road that leads out of town, it sprouts suddenly into view – a pale flower amid the dark summer trees, now a ghostly flower at autumn. At first this is how it appeared to my eyes. (Yes, my eyes, think about them, good people: dream about them.) But as I neared the house, its greyish-white planks, bowed and buckled and oddly spotted, turned the pallid lily to a pulpy toadstool. Surely the house has played this trick on some of you, and all of you have seen it at one time or another: its roof of rippling shingles shaped like scales from some great fish, sea-green and sparkling in the autumn sun; its two attic gables with parted windows that come to a point like the tip of a tear, but do not gleam like tears; its sepulcher-shaped doorway at the top of rotted wooden stairs, where there is barely a place for one to stand. And as I stood among the shadows outside that door, I heard hundreds of raindrops running up the steps behind me, as the air went cold and the skies gained shadows of their own. The light rain spotted the empty, ashen plot nearby the house, watering the barren ground where a garden might have blossomed in the time of the Van Livenns. What better excuse for my imposing upon the present owner of this house? Shelter me, stranger, from the icy autumn storm, and from a fragrance damp and decayed.

He responded promptly to my rapping, without suspicious movements of the ragged curtains, and I entered his dark home. There was no need for explanation; he had already seen me walking ahead of the clouds. And you, good people, have already seen him, at one time or another: his lanky limbs like vaguely twisted branches; his lazy expressionless face; the colorless rags which are easier to see as tattered wrappings than as parts of even the poorest wardrobe. But his voice, that is something none of you has ever heard. Although shaken at how gentle and musical it sounded, I was even less prepared for the sense of frightening distances created by the echo of his hollow words.

"It was just such a day as this when I saw you the first time out there in the woods," he said, looking out at the rain. "But you did not come near to the house."

He had also seen me on other occasions, and our introduction to each other appeared to have already been made long before. I removed my coat, which he took and placed on a very small wooden chair beside the front door. Extending a long crooked arm and wide hand toward the interior, he welcomed me into his home.

But somehow he himself did not seem at home there, even then. And nothing seemed to belong to him, though there was little enough in that house to be possessed by anyone. Apart from the two old chairs in which we sat down and the tiny misshapen table between them, the few other objects I could see appeared to have been brought together only by accident or default, as if a child had put all the odd, leftover furnishings of her dollhouse into an odd, leftover room. A huge trunk lying in the corner, its great tarnished lock sprung open and its heavy straps falling loosely to the floor, would have looked much less sullen buried away in an attic or a cellar. And that miniature chair by the door, with an identical twin fallen on its back near the opposite wall, belonged in a child's room, but a child whom one could not imagine as still living, even as a dim memory in the most ancient mind. The tall bookcase by the shuttered window would have seemed in keeping, if only those cracked pots, bent boots, and other paraphernalia foreign to bookcases had not been stuffed among its battered volumes. A large bedroom bureau stood against one wall, but that would have seemed misplaced in any room: the hollows of its absent drawers were deeply webbed with disuse. All of these things seemed to me wracked by their own history of transformation, culminating in the metamorphoses of decay. And there was a thick dreamy smell that permeated the room, inspiring the sense that invisible gardens of pale growths were even then budding in the dust and dirty corners everywhere around me. But not everything was visible, to my eyes.

The only light in the house was provided by two lamps that burned on either side of a charred mantle over the fireplace. Behind each of these lamps was an oval mirror in an ornate frame, and the reflected light of their quivering wicks threw our shadows onto the wide bare wall at our backs. And while the two of us were sitting still and silent, I saw those other two fidgeting upon the wall, as if wind-blown or perhaps undergoing some subtle torture.

"I have something for you to drink," he said. "I know how far it is to walk from the town."

And I did not have to feign my thirst, good people, for it was such that I wanted to swallow the storm, which I could hear beyond the door and the walls but could only see as a brilliance occasionally flashing behind the curtains or shining needle-bright between the dull slats of the shutters.

In the absence of my host I directed my eyes to the treasures of his house and made them my own. There was something I had not yet seen, somehow I knew this. But what I was looking for was not yet to be seen, which I did not know. I was sent to spy and so everything around me appeared suspicious. Can you see it, through my eyes? Can you peek into those cobwebbed corners or scan the titles of those tilting books? Yes; but can you now, in the maddest dream of your lives, peer into places that have no corners and bear no names? This is what I tried to do: to see beyond the ghoulish remnants of the good Van Livenns, who were now merely dead; to see beyond this haunted stage of hysterical actors, who in their panics pretend to feel what we, good people, pretend not to feel. And so I had to turn corners inside-out with my eyes and to read the third side of a book's page, seeking in futility to gaze at what I could then touch with none of my senses. It remained something shapeless and nameless, dampish and submerged, something swamplike and abysmal which opposed the pure cold of the autumn storm outside.

When he returned he carried with him a dusty green bottle and a sparkling glass, both of which he set upon that little table between our chairs. I took up the bottle and it felt warm in my hand. Expecting some thickish dark liquid to gush from the bottle's neck, I was surprised to see only the clearest water, and strangely the coolest, pouring into the glass. I drank and for a few moments was removed to a world of frozen light that lived within the cool water.

In the meantime he had placed something else upon the table. It was a small music box, like a miniature treasure chest, made of some dark wood which looked as if it had the hardness of a jewel. This object, I felt, was very old. Slowly, he drew back the cover of the box and sat back in his chair. I held both hands around that cold glass and listened to the still colder music. The crisp little notes that arose from the box were like stars of sound coming out in the twilight shadows and silence of the house. The storm had ended, leaving the world outside muffled by wetness. Within those closed rooms, which might now have been transported to the brink of a chasm or deep inside the earth, the music glimmered like infinitesimal flakes of light in that barren decor of dead days. Neither of us appeared to be breathing and even the shadows behind our chairs were charmed with enchanted immobility. Everything held for a moment to allow the wandering music from the box to pass on toward some unspeakably wondrous destination. I tried to follow it – through the yellowish haze of the room and deep into the darkness that pressed against the walls, and then deeper into the darkness between the walls, then through the walls and into the unbordered red spaces where those silvery tones ascended and settled as true stars. There I could have stretched out forever and lost myself in the soothing mirrors of infinity. But even then something was stirring, irrupting like a disease, poking its horribly colored head through the cool blackness . . . and chasing me back to my body.

"Were you able to see the garden out in the yard?" he asked. I replied that I had seen nothing except a blank slate of dirt. He nodded slowly and then, good people, he softly began.

"Do I look surprised that you will not admit what you saw? But I'm not. Of course you did, you saw them in the garden. Please don't go on shaking your head, don't hide behind a vacant stare. You are not the only one who has passed this house. Almost everyone from the town has gone by, at one time or another, but no one will talk about it. Every one of you has seen them and carries their image with him. But you are the only one to come and see me about it, whether you think you have or not. It's foolish to be amazed, but I am. Because in itself this can only be a small terror, among the vastness of all terrible things. And if this small thing stops your speech, even within yourself, what would the rest of it do to you?

"No, I have no business talking to you this way. Don't listen to me, forget what I said. Be silent, shhhh. Work in silence and think only in silence and do all things silently. Be courageous and silent. Now go. I am not here, the family who gave this house its name are not here, no one is here. But you are here, and the others, I didn't mean—Don't listen to me! Go now."

He had sprung forward in his chair. After a few moments – of silence – he again fell into a slouch. I stayed; was I not sent, by you, to learn everything you could not?

"Your eyes," he said, "are practicing another kind of silence, a hungry silence, the wrong kind. If that is what you want, it makes no difference to me. You see how I live: shadows and silence, leaving things as I find them because I have no reason to disturb them. But there are things that I have known, even though I never wished to know them and cannot give them a name. Now I will tell you one of them. This is about those things you saw in the garden.

"I did not find them while in this body, that I know. Whenever I fall asleep, or sometimes if I'm sitting very still, I may move on to a different place. And sometimes I return to where I was and sometimes I do not. I have to smile because that could be all there is to say about me, about my life or lives, I can't be sure. But I could say something about those other places and about the things I have seen there. In one of these places I found the flowers – and why should I not call them that, since they now dwell in a garden? Almost everything was dark in the place where I found the flowers. But it wasn't dark as a house is sometimes dark or as the woods are dark because of thick trees keeping out the light. It was dark only because there was nothing *to keep out the darkness*. How do I know this? I know because I could see with more than my eyes – I could see with the darkness itself. With the darkness I saw the darkness. And it was immensity without end around me, and I believe within me. It was unbroken expansion, dark horizon meeting dark horizon. But there were also things within the darkness, within me and outside of me, so that if I reached out to touch them across a universe of darkness, I also reached deep inside of this body. But all I could feel were the flowers themselves: to touch them was like touching light and touching colors and a thousand kinds of bristling and growing shapes. It was a horrible feeling, to touch them. In all that darkness which gave me breath and let me see with itself, these things squirmed and fought against me. I cannot explain why they were there, but it sickened me that anything had to be there and more so because it was these flowers, which were like a great mass of maimed things writhing upon the shore of a beautiful dark sea.

"I don't think I meant to bring any of them back with me. When I found that I had, I quickly buried them. They broke through the earth that same night, and I thought they would come after me. But I don't think they care about that or about anything. I think they like being where they are now, buried and not buried. You have seen yourself how they twist and dance, almost happily. They are horrible things without reason."

After these words he recoiled, for a moment, into silence. Now it was dark outside, beyond the curtains and the shutters. The lamps upon the mantle shone with a piercing light that cut shadows out of the cloth of blackness around us. Why, good people, was I so astonished that this phantom before me could walk across the room and actually lift one of the lamps, and then carry it toward the back hallway of the house? He paused, turned, and gestured for me to rise from my chair.

"Now you will see them better, even in the darkness." I rose and followed.

We walked quietly from the house, as if we were two children sneaking away for a night in the woods. The lamplight skimmed across the wet grass behind the house and then paused where the yard ended and the woods began, fragrant and wind-blown. The light moved to the left and I moved with it, toward that area which I – and you, good people – admit only as a great unsodded grave.

"Look at them twisting in the light," he said when the first rays fell on a convulsing tangle of shapes, like the radiant entrails of hell. But the shapes quickly disappeared into the darkness and out of view, pulling themselves from the rainsoftened soil. "They retreat from this light. And you see how they return to their places when the light is withdrawn."

They closed in again like parted waters rushing to remerge. But these were corrupt waters whose currents had congealed and diversified into creaturely forms no less horrible than if the cool air itself were strung with sticky and pumping veins, hung with working mouths.

"I want to be in there," I said. "Move the light as close as you can to the garden."

He stepped to the very edge, as I stepped farther still toward that retreating flood of tendriled slime, those aberrations of the abyss. When I was deep into their mesh, I whispered behind me: "Don't lose the light, or they will cover again the ground I am standing on. I can see them perfectly now. How on earth? The spectacle itself. I can see them with the darkness, I can touch *their* light. I don't need the other, but for heaven's sake don't take it away."

He did not, good people, for I heard him say, "It was not I" when the light went out. No, it was not you, evil stranger; it was only the wind. It came down from the trees and swept across us who are in the garden. And the wind now carries my words to you, good people. I cannot be there to guide you, but you know now what must be done, to me and to this horrible house. Please, one last word to stir your sleep. I remember screaming to the stranger:

Bring back the light. They are drawing me into themselves. My eyes can see everything in the darkness. Can you hear what they are doing? Can you hear?

"What is it?" whispered one of the many awakening voices in the dark bedrooms of the town.

"I said, 'Can you hear them outside'?"

A nightgowned figure rose from the bed and moved as a silhouette to the window. Down in the street was a mob carrying lights and rapping on doors for those still dreaming to join them. Their lamps and lanterns bobbed in the darkness, and the fires of their torches flickered madly. Clusters of flame shot up into the night.

And though the people of the town said not a word to one another, they knew where they were going and what they would do to free their fellow citizen from the madman who had taken him and from the wickedness they knew would one day come from the ruined house of the Van Livenns. And though their eyes saw nothing but the wild destruction that lay ahead, buried like a forgotten dream within each one of them was a perfect picture of other eyes and of the unspeakable shape in which they now lived, and which now had to be murdered.

NETHESCURIAL

The Idol and the Island

I have uncovered a rather wonderful manuscript, *the letter began*. It was an entirely fortuitous find, made during my day's dreary labors among some of the older and more decomposed remains entombed in the library archives. If I am any judge of antique documents, and of course I am, these brittle pages date back to the closing decades of the last century. (A more precise estimate of age will follow, along with a photocopy which I fear will not do justice to the delicate, crinkly script, nor to the greenish black discoloration the ink has taken on over the years.) Unfortunately there is no indication of authorship either within the manuscript itself or in the numerous and tedious papers whose company it has been keeping, none of which seem related to the item under discussion. And what an item it is – a real storybook stranger in a crowd of documentary types, and probably destined to remain unknown.

I am almost certain that this invention, though at times it seems to pose as a letter or journal entry, has never appeared in common print. Given the bizarre nature of its content, I would surely have known of it before now. Although it is an untitled "statement" of sorts, the opening lines were more than enough to cause me to put everything else aside and seclude myself in a corner of the library stacks for the rest of the afternoon.

So it begins: "In the rooms of houses and beyond their walls – beneath dark waters and across moonlit skies – below earth mound and above mountain peak – in northern leaf and southern flower – inside each star and the voids between them – within blood and bone, through all souls and spirits – among the watchful winds of this and the several worlds – behind the faces of the living and the dead . . ." And there it trails off, a quoted fragment of some more ancient text. But this is certainly not the last we will hear of this all-encompassing refrain!

As it happens, the above string of phrases is cited by the narrator in reference to a certain *presence*, more properly an omnipresence, which he encounters on an obscure island located at some unspecified northern latitude. Briefly, he has been summoned to this island, which appears on a local map under the name of Nethescurial, in order to rendezvous with another man, an archaeologist who is designated only as Dr. N— and who will come to know the narrator of the manuscript by the self-admitted alias of "Bartholomew Gray" (they don't call 'em like that anymore). Dr. N—, it seems, has been occupying himself upon that barren, remote, and otherwise uninhabited isle with some peculiar antiquarian rummagings. As Mr. Gray sails toward the island he observes the murky skies above him and the murky waters below. His prose style is somewhat plain for my taste, but it serves well enough once he approaches the island and takes surprisingly scrupulous notice of its eerie aspect: contorted rock formations; pointed pines and spruces of gigantic stature and uncanny movements; the masklike countenance of sea-facing cliffs; and a sickly, stagnant fog clinging to the landscape like a fungus.

From the moment Mr. Gray begins describing the island, a sudden enchantment enters into his account. It is that sinister enchantment which derives from a profound evil that is kept at just the right distance from us so that we may experience both our love and our fear of it in one sweeping sensation. Too close and we may be reminded of an omnipresent evil in the living world, and threatened with having our sleeping sense of doom awakened into full vigor. Too far away and we become even more incurious and complacent than is our usual state, and ultimately exasperated when an imaginary evil is so poorly evoked that it fails to offer the faintest echo of its real and all-pervasive counterpart. Of course, any number of locales may serve as the setting to reveal ominous truths; evil, beloved and menacing evil, may show itself anywhere precisely because it is everywhere and is as stunningly set off by a foil of sunshine and flowers as it is by darkness and dead leaves. A purely private quirk, nevertheless, sometimes allows the purest essence of life's malignity to be aroused only by sites such as the lonely island of Nethescurial, where the real and the unreal swirl freely and madly about in the same fog.

It seems that in this place, this far-flung realm, Dr. N— has discovered an ancient and long-sought artifact, a marginal but astonishing entry in that unspeakably voluminous journal of creation. Soon after landfall, Mr. Gray finds himself verifying the truth of the archaeologist's claims: that the island has been strangely molded in all its parts, and within its shores every manifestation of plant or mineral or anything whatever appears to have fallen at the mercy of some shaping force of demonic temperament, a genius loci which has sculpted its nightmares out of the atoms of the local earth. Closer inspection of this insular spot on the map serves to deepen the sense of evil and enchantment that had been lightly sketched earlier in the manuscript. But I refrain from further quotation (it is getting late and I want to wrap up this letter before bedtime) in order to cut straight through the epidermis of this tale and penetrate to its very bones and viscera. Indeed, the manuscript does seem to have an anatomy of its own, its dark green holography rippling over it like veins, and I regret that my paraphrase may not deliver it alive. Enough!

Mr. Gray makes his way inland, lugging along with him a fat little travelling bag. In a clearing he comes upon a large but unadorned, almost primitive house which stands against the fantastic backdrop of the island's wartlike hills and tumorous trees. The outside of the house is encrusted with the motley and leprous stones so abundant in the surrounding landscape. The inside of the house, which the visitor sees upon opening the unlocked door, is spacious as a cathedral but far less ornamented. The walls are white and smoothly surfaced; they also seem to taper inward, pyramid-like, as they rise from floor to lofty ceiling. There are no windows, and numerous oil lamps scattered about fill the interior of the house with a sacral glow. A figure descends a long staircase, crosses the great distance of the room, and solemnly greets his guest. At first wary of each other, they eventually achieve a degree of mutual ease and finally get down to their true business.

Thus far one can see that the drama enacted is a familiar one: the stage is rigidly traditional and the performers upon it are caught up in its style. For these actors are not so much people as they are puppets from the old shows, the ones that have told the same story for centuries, the ones that can still be very strange to us. Traipsing through the same old foggy scene, seeking the same old isolated house, the puppets in these plays always find everything new and unknown, because they have no memories to speak of and can hardly recall making these stilted motions countless times in the past. They struggle through the same gestures, repeat the same lines, although in rare moments they may feel a dim suspicion that this has all happened before. How like they are to the human race itself! This is what makes them our perfect representatives – this and the fact that they are handcarved in the image of maniacal victims who seek to share the secrets of their individual torments as their strings are manipulated by the same master.

The secrets which these two Punchinellos share are rather deviously presented by the author of this confession (for upon consideration this is the genre to which it truly belongs). Indeed, Mr. Gray, or whatever his name might be, appears to know much more than he is telling, especially with respect to his colleague the archaeologist. Nevertheless, he records what Dr. N— knows and, more importantly, what this avid excavator has found buried on the island. The thing is only a fragment of an object dating from antiquity. Known to be part of a religious idol, it is difficult to say which part. It is a twisted piece of a puzzle, one suggesting that the figure as a whole is intensely unbeautiful. The fragment is also darkened with the verdigris of centuries, causing its substance to resemble something like decomposing jade.

And were the other pieces of this idol also to be found on the same island? The answer is no. The idol seems to have been shattered ages ago, and each broken part of it buried in some remote place so that the whole of it might not easily be joined together again. Although it was a mere representation, the effigy itself was the focus of a great power. The ancient sect which was formed to worship this power seem to have been pantheists of a sort, believing that all created things – appearances to the contrary – are of a single, unified, and transcendent *stuff*, an emanation of a central creative force. Hence the ritual chant which runs "in the rooms of houses", et cetera, and alludes to the all-present nature of this deity – a most primal and pervasive type of god, one that falls into the category of "gods who eclipse all others", territorialist divinities whose claim to the creation purportedly supersedes that of their rivals. (The words of the famous chant, by the way, are the only ones to come down to us from the ancient cult and appeared for the first time in an ethnographical, quasi-esoteric work entitled *Illuminations of the Ancient World,* which was published in the latter part of the nineteenth century, around the same time, I would guess, as this manuscript I am rushing to summarize was written.) At some point in their career as worshipants of the "Great One God", a shadow fell upon the sect. It appears that one day it was revealed to them, in a manner both obscure and hideous, that the power to which they bowed was essentially evil in character and that their religious mode of pantheism was in truth a kind of pandemonism. But this revelation was not a surprise to all of the sectarians, since there seems to have been an internecine struggle which ended in slaughter. In any case, the anti-demonists prevailed, and they immediately rechristened their ex-deity to reflect its newly discovered essence in evil. And the name by which they henceforth called it was Nethescurial.

A nice turn of affairs: this obscure island openly advertises itself as the home of the idol of Nethescurial. Of course, this island is only one of several to which the pieces of the vandalized totem were scattered. The original members of the sect who had treacherously turned against their god knew that the power concentrated in the effigy could not be destroyed, and so they decided to parcel it out to isolated corners of the earth where it could do the least harm. But would they have brought attention to this fact by allowing these widely disseminated burial plots to bear the name of the pandemoniacal god? This is doubtful, just as it is equally unlikely that it was they who built those crude houses, temples of a fashion, to mark the spot where a particular shard of the old idol might be located by others.

So Dr. N— is forced to postulate a survival of the demonist faction of the sect, a cult that had devoted itself to searching out those places which had been transformed by the presence of the idol and might thus be known by their gruesome features. This quest would require a great deal of time and effort for its completion, given the global reaches where those splinters of evil might be tucked away. Known as the "seeking", it also involved the enlistment of outsiders, who in latter days were often researchers into the ways of bygone cultures, though they remained ignorant that the cause they served was still a living one. Dr. N— therefore warns his "colleague, Mr. Gray", that they may be in danger from those who carried on the effort to reassemble the idol and revive its power. The very presence of that great and crude house on the island certainly proved that the cult was already aware of the location of *this* fragment of the idol. In fact, the mysterious Mr. Gray, not unexpectedly, is actually a member of the cult in its modern incarnation; furthermore, he has brought with him to the island – bulky travelling bag, you know – all the other pieces of the idol, which have been recovered through centuries of seeking. Now he only needs the one piece discovered by Dr. N— to make the idol whole again for the first time in a couple of millenia.

But he also needs the archaeologist himself as a kind of sacrifice to Nethescurial, a ceremony which takes place later the same night in the upper part of the house. If I may telescope the ending for brevity's sake, the sacrificial ritual holds some horrific surprises for Mr. Gray (these people seem never to realize what they are getting themselves into), who soon repents of his evil practices and is driven to smash the idol to pieces once more. Making his escape from that weird island, he throws these pieces overboard, sowing the cold gray waters with the scraps of an incredible power. Later, fearing an obscure threat to his existence (perhaps the reprisal of his fellow cultists), he composes an account of a horror which is both his own and that of the whole human race.

End of manuscript.*

Now, despite my penchant for such wild yarns as I have just attempted to describe, I am not oblivious to their shortcomings. For one thing, whatever emotional impact the narrative may have lost in the foregoing precis, it certainly gained in coherence: the incidents in the manuscript are clumsily developed, important details lack proper emphasis, impossible things are thrown at the reader without any real effort at persuasion of their veracity. I do admire the fantastic principle at the core of this piece. The nature of that pandemoniac entity is very intriguing. Imagine all of creation as a mere mask for the foulest evil, an absolute evil whose reality is mitigated only by our blindness to it, an evil at the heart of things, existing "inside each star and the voids between them – within blood and bone – through all souls and spirits", and so forth. There is even a reference in the manuscript that suggests an analogy between Nethescurial and that beautiful myth of the Australian aborigines known as the Alchera (the Dreamtime, or Dreaming), a super-reality which is the source of all we see in the world around us. (And this reference will be useful in dating the manuscript, since it was toward the end of the last century that Australian anthropologists made the aboriginal cosmology known to the general public.) Imagine the universe as the dream, the feverish nightmare of a demonic demiurge. O Supreme Nethescurial!

The problem is that such supernatural inventions are indeed quite difficult to imagine. So often they fail to materialize in the mind, to take on a mental texture, and thus remain unfelt as anything but an abstract monster of metaphysics – an elegant or awkward schematic that cannot rise from the paper to touch us. Of course, we do need to keep a certain distance from such specters as Nethescurial, but this is usually provided by the medium of words as such, which ensnare all kinds of fantastic creatures before they can tear us body and soul. (And yet the words of this particular manuscript seem rather weak in this regard, possibly because they

---

* Except for the concluding lines, which reveal the somewhat extravagant, but not entirely uninteresting, conclusion of the narrator himself.

are only the drab green scratchings of a human hand and not the heavy mesh of black type.) But we do want to get close enough to feel the foul breath of these beasts, or to see them as prehistoric leviathans circling about the tiny island on which we have taken refuge. Even if we are incapable of a sincere belief in ancient cults and their unheard of idols, even if these pseudonymous adventurers and archaeologists appear to be mere shadows on a wall, and even if strange houses on remote islands are of shaky construction, there may still be a power in these things that threatens us like a bad dream. And this power emanates not so much from within the tale as it does from somewhere *behind* it, someplace of infinite darkness and ubiquitous evil in which we may walk unaware.

But never mind these night thoughts; it's only to bed that I will walk after closing this letter.

Postscript

Later the same night.

Several hours have passed since I set down the above description and analysis of that manuscript. How naive those words of mine now sound to me. And yet they are still true enough, from a certain perspective. But that perspective was a privileged one which, at least for the moment, I do not enjoy. The distance between me and a devastating evil has lessened considerably. I no longer find it so difficult to imagine the horrors delineated in that manuscript, for I have known them in the most intimate way. What a fool I seem to myself for playing with such visions. How easily a simple dream can destroy one's sense of safety, if only for a few turbulent hours. Certainly I have experienced all this before, but never as acutely as tonight.

I had not been asleep for long but apparently long enough. At the start of the dream I was sitting at a desk in a very dark room. It also seemed to me that the room was very large, though I could see little of it beyond the area of the desktop, at either end of which glowed a lamp of some kind. Spread out before me were many papers varying in size. These I knew to be maps of one sort or another, and I was studying them each in turn. I had become quite absorbed in these maps, which now dominated the dream to the exclusion of all other images. Each of them focused on some concatenation of islands without reference to larger, more familiar land masses. A powerful impression of remoteness and seclusion

was conveyed by these irregular daubs of earth fixed in bodies of
water that were unnamed. But although the location of the islands
was not specific, somehow I was sure that those for whom the maps
were meant already had this knowledge. Nevertheless, this secrecy
was only superficial, for no esoteric key was required to seek out the
greater geography of which these maps were an exaggerated
detail: they were all distinguished by some known language in
which the islands were named, different languages for different
maps. Yet upon closer view (indeed, I felt as if I were actually
journeying among those exotic fragments of land, tiny pieces of
shattered mystery), I saw that every map had one thing in
common: within each group of islands, whatever language was
used to name them, there was always one called Nethescurial. It
was as if all over the world this terrible name had been insinuated
into diverse locales as the only one suitable for a certain island. Of
course there were variant cognate forms and spellings, sometimes
transliterations, of the word. (How precisely I saw them!) Still,
with the strange conviction that may overcome a dreamer, I knew
these places had all been claimed in the name of Nethescurial and
that they bore the unique sign of something which had been buried
there – the pieces of that dismembered idol.

And with this thought, the dream reshaped itself. The maps
dissolved into a kind of mist; the desk before me became something
else, an altar of coarse stone, and the two lamps upon it flared up to
reveal a strange object now positioned between them. So many
visions in the dream were piercingly clear, but this dark object was
not. My impression was that it was conglomerate in form,
suggesting a monstrous whole. At the same time these outlines
which alluded to both man and beast, flower and insect, reptiles,
stones, and countless things I could not even name, all seemed to
be changing, mingling in a thousand ways that prevented any
sensible image of the idol.

With the upsurge in illumination offered by the lamps, I could
see that the room was truly of unusual dimensions. The four
enormous walls slanted toward one another and joined at a point
high above the floor, giving the space around me the shape of a
perfect pyramid. But I now saw things from an oddly remote
perspective: the altar with its idol stood in the middle of the room
and I was some distance away, or perhaps not even in the scene.
Then, from some dark corner or secret door, there emerged a file of
figures walking slowly toward the altar and finally congregating in
a half-circle before it. I could see that they were all quite skeletal in
shape, for they were identically dressed in a black material which

clung tightly to their bodies and made them look like skinny
shadows. They seemed to be actually bound in blackness from
head to foot, with only their faces exposed. But they were not, in
fact, faces – they were pale, expressionless, and identical masks.
The masks were without openings and bestowed upon their
wearers a terrible anonymity, an ancient anonymity. Behind
these smooth and barely contoured faces were spirits beyond all
hope or consolation except in the evil to which they would
willingly abandon themselves. Yet this abandonment was a highly
selective process, a ceremony of the chosen.

One of the white-faced shadows stepped forward from the
group, seemingly drawn forth into the proximity of the idol.
The figure stood motionless, while from within its dark body
something began to drift out like luminous smoke. It floated,
swirling gently, toward the idol and there was absorbed. And I
knew – for was this not my own dream? – that the idol and its
sacrifice were becoming one within each other. This spectacle
continued until nothing of the glowing, ectoplasmic haze remained
to be extracted, and the figure – now shrunken to the size of a
marionette – collapsed. But soon it was being lifted, rather
tenderly, by another from the group who placed the dwarfish
form upon the altar and, taking up a knife, carved deep into the
body, making no sound. Then something oozed upon the altar,
something thick and oily and strangely colored, darkly colored
though not with any of the shades of blood. Although the
strangeness of this color was more an idea than a matter of
vision, it began to fill the dream and to determine the final stage
of its development.

Quite abruptly, that closed, cavernous room dissolved into an
open stretch of land: open yet also cluttered with a bric-a-brac
topography whose crazed shapes were all of that single and sinister
color. The ground was as if covered with an ancient, darkened
mold and the things rising up from it were the same. Surrounding
me was a landscape that might once have been of stone and earth
and trees (such was my impression) but had been transformed
entirely into something like petrified slime. I gazed upon it
spreading before me, twisting in the way of wrought iron tracery
or great overgrown gardens of writhing coral, an intricate lattice-
work of hardened mulch whose surface was overrun with a chaos of
little carvings, scabby designs that suggested a world of demonic
faces and forms. And it was all composed in that color which
somehow makes me think of rotted lichen. But before I exited in
panic from my dream, there was one further occurrence of this

color: the inkish waters washing upon the shores of the island around me.

As I wrote a few pages ago, I have been awake for some hours now. What I did not mention was the state in which I found myself after waking. Throughout the dream, and particularly in those last moments when I positively identified that foul place, there was an unseen presence, something I could feel was circulating within all things and unifying them in an infinitely extensive body of evil. I suppose it is nothing unusual that I continued to be under this visionary spell even after I left my bed. I tried to invoke the gods of the ordinary world – calling them with the whistle of a coffee pot and praying before their icon of the electric light – but they were too weak to deliver me from that other whose name I can no longer bring myself to write. It seemed to be in possession of my house, of every common object inside and the whole of the dark world outside. Yes – lurking among the watchful winds of this and the several worlds. Everything seemed to be a manifestation of this evil and to my eyes was taking on its aspect. I could feel it also emerging in myself, growing stronger behind this living face that I am afraid to confront in the mirror.

Nevertheless, these dream-induced illusions now seem to be abating, perhaps driven off by my writing about them. Like someone who has had too much to drink the night before and swears off liquor for life, I have forsworn any further indulgence in weird reading matter. No doubt this is only a temporary vow, and soon enough my old habits will return. But certainly not before morning!

The Puppets in the Park

Some days later, and quite late at night.

Well, it seems this letter has mutated into a chronicle of my adventures Nethescurialian. See, I can now write that unique nomen with ease; furthermore, I feel almost no apprehension in stepping up to my mirror. Soon I may even be able to sleep in the way I once did, without visionary intrusions of any kind. No denying that my experiences of late have tipped the scales of the strange. I found myself just walking restlessly about – impossible to work, you know – and always carrying with me this heavy dread in my solar plexus, as if I had feasted at a banquet of fear and the meal would not digest. Most strange, since I have been loath to take nourishment during this time. How could I put anything into my mouth, when everything looked the way it did? Hard enough to touch a doorknob or a pair of shoes, even with the protection of the gloves. I could feel every damn thing squirming, not excluding my own flesh. And I could also *see* what was squirming beneath every surface, my vision penetrating through the usual armor of objects and discerning the same gushing *stuff* inside whatever I looked upon. It was that dark color from the dream, I could identify it clearly now. Dark and greenish. How could I possibly feed myself? How could I even bring myself to settle very long in one spot? So I kept on the move. And I tried not to look too closely at how everything, *everything* was crawling within itself and making all kinds of shapes inside there, making all kinds of faces at me. (Yet it was really all the same face, everything gorged with that same creeping stuff.) There were also sounds that I heard, voices speaking vague words, voices that came not from the mouths of the people I passed on the street but from the very bottom of their brains, garbled whisperings at first and then so clear, so eloquent.

This rising wave of chaos reached its culmination tonight and then came crashing down. But my timely maneuvering, I trust, has put everything right again.

Here, now, are the terminal events of this nightmare as they occurred. (And how I wish I were not speaking figuratively, that I was in fact only in the world of dreams or back in the pages of books and old manuscripts.) This conclusion had its beginning in the park, a place that is actually some distance from my home, so far had I wandered. It was already late at night, but I was still walking about, treading the narrow asphalt path that winds through that island of grass and trees in the middle of the city. (And somehow it seemed I had already walked in this same place on this same night, that this had all happened to me before.) The path was lit by globes of light balanced upon slim metal poles; another glowing orb was set in the great blackness above. Off the path the grass was darkened by shadows, and the trees swishing overhead were the same color of muddied green.

After walking some indefinite time along some indefinite route, I came upon a clearing where an audience had assembled for some late-night entertainment. Strings of colored lights had been hung around the perimeter of this area and rows of benches had been set up. The people seated on these benches were all watching a tall, illuminated booth. It was the kind of booth used for puppet shows, with wild designs painted across the lower part and a curtained opening at the top. The curtains were now drawn back and two clownish creatures were twisting about in a glary light which emanated from inside the booth. They leaned and squawked and awkwardly batted each other with soft paddles they were hugging in their soft little arms. Suddenly they froze at the height of their battle; slowly they turned about and faced the audience. It seemed the puppets were looking directly at the place I was standing behind the last row of benches. Their misshapen heads tilted, and their glassy eyes stared straight into mine.

Then I noticed that the others were doing the same: all of them had turned around on the benches and, with expressionless faces and dead puppet eyes, held me to the spot. Although their mouths did move, they were not silent. But the voices I heard were far more numerous than was the gathering before me. These were the voices I had been hearing as they chanted confused words in the depths of everyone's thoughts, fathoms below the level of their awareness. The words still sounded hushed and slow, monotonous phrases mingling like the sequences of a fugue. But now I could understand these words, even as more voices picked up the chant at different points and overlapped one another, saying, "In the rooms of houses . . . across moonlit skies . . . through all souls and spirits . . . behind the faces of the living and the dead."

I find it impossible to say how long it was before I was able to move, before I backed up toward the path, all those multitudinous voices chanting everywhere around me and all those many-colored lights bobbing in the wind-blown trees. Yet it seemed only a single voice I heard, and a single color I saw, as I found my way home, stumbling through the greenish darkness of the night.

I knew what needed to be done. Gathering up some old boards from my basement, I piled them into the fireplace and opened the flue. As soon as they were burning brightly, I added one more thing to the fire: a manuscript whose ink was of a certain color. Blessed with a saving vision, I could now see whose signature was on that manuscript, whose hand had really written those pages and had been hiding in them for a hundred years. The author of that narrative had broken up the idol and drowned it in deep waters, but the stain of its ancient patina had stayed upon him. It had invaded the author's crabbed script of blackish green and survived there, waiting to crawl into another lost soul who failed to see what dark places he was wandering into. How I knew this to be true! And has this not been proved by the color of the smoke that rose from the burning manuscript, and keeps rising from it?

I am writing these words as I sit before the fireplace. But the flames have gone out and still the smoke from the charred paper hovers within the hearth, refusing to ascend the chimney and disperse itself into the night. Perhaps the chimney has become blocked. Yes, this must be the case, this must be true. Those other things are lies, illusions. That mold-colored smoke has not taken on the shape of the idol, the shape that cannot be seen steadily and whole but keeps turning out so many arms and heads, so many eyes, and then pulling them back in and bringing them out again in other configurations. That shape is not drawing something out of me and putting something else in its place, something that seems to be bleeding into the words as I write. And my pen is not growing bigger in my hand, nor is my hand growing smaller, smaller . . .

See, there is no shape in the fireplace. The smoke is gone, gone up the chimney and out into the sky. And there is nothing in the sky, nothing I can see through the window. There is the moon, of course, high and round. But no shadow falls across the moon, no churning chaos of smoke that chokes the frail order of the earth, no shifting cloud of nightmares enveloping moons and suns and stars. It is not a squirming, creeping, smearing shape I see upon the moon, not the shape of a great deformed crab scuttling out of the black oceans of infinity and invading the island of the moon, crawling with its innumerable bodies upon all the spinning islands of inky space. That shape is not the cancerous totality of all creatures, not the oozing ichor that flows within all things. *Nethescurial is not the secret name of the creation.* It is not in the rooms of houses and beyond their walls . . . beneath dark waters and across moonlit skies . . . below earth mound and above mountain peak . . . in northern leaf and southern flower . . . inside each star and the voids between them . . . within blood and bone, through all souls and spirits . . . among the watchful winds of this and the several worlds . . . behind the faces of the living and the dead.

I am not dying in a nightmare.

THE DREAMING IN
NORTOWN

1.

There are those who require witnesses to their doom. Not content with a solitary perdition, they seek an audience worthy of the spectacle – mind to remember the stages of their downfall or perhaps only a mirror to multiply their abject glory. Of course, other motives may figure in this scheme, ones far too tenuous and strange for mortal reminiscence. Yet there exists a memoir of dreams in which I may recall an old acquaintance by the name of Jack Quinn (an alias that closely echoes nymic truth). For it was he who sensed my peculiar powers of sympathy and, employing a rather contrary stratagem, engaged them. This all began, according to my perspective, late one night in the decaying and spacious apartment which Quinn and I shared and which was located in that city – or, more precisely, in a certain region *within* it – where we attended the same university.

I was asleep. In the darkness a voice was calling me away from my ill-mapped world of dreams. Then something heavy weighed down the edge of the mattress and a slightly infernal aroma filled the room, an acrid combination of tobacco and autumn nights. A small red glow wandered in an arc toward the apex of the seated figure and there glowed even brighter, faintly lighting the lower part of a face. Quinn was smiling, the cigar in his mouth smoking in the darkness. He remained silent for a moment and crossed his legs beneath his long threadbare overcoat, an ancient thing that was wrapped loosely around him like a skin about to be sloughed. So many pungent Octobers were collected in that coat. It is the events of this month that I am remembering.

I assumed he was drunk, or perhaps still in the remote heights or depths of the artificial paradise he had been exploring that night. When Quinn finally spoke, it was definitely with the stumbling words of a returning explorer, a stuporous and vaguely awed voice. But he seemed more than simply drug-entranced.

He had attended a meeting, he said, speaking the word in an

odd way which seemed to expand its significance. Of course there were others at this gathering, people who to me remained simply "those others". It was a kind of philosophical society, he told me. The group sounded colourful enough: midnight assemblies, the probable use of drugs, and participants in the grip of strange mystical ecstasies.

I got out of bed and switched on the light. Quinn was a chaotic sight, his clothes more crumpled than usual, his face flushed, and his long red hair intricately tangled.

"And exactly where did you go tonight?" I asked with the measure of true curiosity he seemed to be seeking. I had the distinct idea that Quinn's activities of that evening had occurred in the vicinity of Nortown (another pseudonym, of course, as are all the names in this narrative), where the apartment we shared was located. I asked him if they had.

"And perhaps in other places," he answered, laughing a little to himself as he meditated upon the gray end of his cigar. "But you might not understand. Excuse me, I have to go to bed."

"As you wish," I replied, leaving aside all complaints about this nocturnal intrusion. He puffed on his cigar and went to his room, closing the door behind him.

This, then, was the beginning of Quinn's ultimate phase of esoteric development. And until the final night, I actually saw very little of him during that most decisive episode of his life. We were pursuing different courses of study in our graduate school days – I in anthropology and he in . . . it troubles me to say I was never entirely sure of his academic program. In any case, our respective timetables seldom intersected. Nonetheless, Quinn's daily movements, at least the few I was aware of, did invite curiosity. There was a general tenor of chaos that I perceived in his behavior, a quality which may or may not make for good company but which always offers promise of the extraordinary.

He continued to come in quite late at night, always entering the apartment with what seemed a contrived noisiness. After that first night he did not overtly confide his activities to me. The door to his room would close, and immediately afterward I would hear him collapse on the old springs of his mattress. It seemed he did not undress for bed, perhaps never even removed the overcoat which was becoming shabbier and more crumpled day by day. My sleep temporarily shattered, I passed this wakeful time by eavesdropping on the noises in the next room. There was a strange catalogue of sounds which either I had never noticed before or which were somehow different from the usual nightly din: low moans emanating from the most shadowy chasms of dream; sudden intakes of breath like the suction of a startled gasp; and abrupt snarls and snorts of a bestial timbre. The whole rhythm of his sleep betrayed expressions of unknown turmoil. And sometimes he would violate the calm darkness of the night with a series of staccato groans followed by a brief vocal siren that made me bolt up suddenly in my bed. This alarming sound surely carried the entire audible spectrum of nightmare-inspired terror . . . but there were also mingling overtones of awe and ecstasy, a willing submission to some unknown ordeal.

"Have you finally died and gone to hell?" I shouted one night through his bedroom door. The sound was still ringing in my ears.

"Go back to sleep," he answered, his low-pitched voice still speaking from the deeper registers of somnolence. The smell of a freshly lit cigar then filtered out of his bedroom.

After these late-night disturbances, I would sometimes sit up to watch the dun colors of dawn stirring in the distance outside my eastern window. And as the weeks went by that October, the carnival of noise going on in the next room began to work its strange influence upon my own sleep. Soon Quinn was not the only one in the apartment having nightmares, as I was inundated by a flood of eidetic horrors that left only a vague residue upon waking.

It was throughout the day that fleeting scenes of nightmare would suddenly appear to my mind, brief and vivid, as though I had mistakenly opened a strange door somewhere and, after inadvertently seeing something I should not have, quickly closed it once again with a reverberating slam. Eventually, however, my dream-censor himself fell asleep, and I recalled in total the elusive materials of one of those night-visions, which returned to me painted in scenes of garishly vibrant colors.

The dream took place at a small public library in Nortown where I sometimes retreated to study. On the oneiric plane, however, I was not a studious patron of the library but one of the librarians – the only one, it seemed, keeping vigil in that desolate institution. I was just sitting there, complacently survey-ing the shelves of books and laboring under the illusion that in my idleness I was performing some routine but very important function. This did not continue very long – nothing does in dreams – though the situation was one that already seemed interminable.

What shattered the status quo, initiating a new phase to the dream, was my discovery that a note scrawled upon a slip of paper had been left on the well-ordered surface of my desk. It was a request for a book and had been submitted by a library patron whose identity I puzzled over, for I had not seen anyone put it there. I fretted about this scrap of paper for many dream-moments: had it been there even before I sat down at the desk and had I simply overlooked it? I suffered a disproportionate anxiety over this possible dereliction. The imagined threat of a reprimand of some strange nature terrorized me. Without delay I phoned the back room to have the person on duty there bring forth the book. But I was truly alone in that dream library and no one answered what was to my mind now an emergency appeal. Feeling a sense of urgency in the face of some imaginary deadline, and filled with a kind of exalted terror, I snatched up the request slip and set out to retrieve the book myself.

In the stacks I saw that the telephone line was dead, for it had been ripped from the wall and lay upon the floor like the frayed end of a disciplinary whip. Trembling, I consulted the piece of paper I carried with me for the title of the book and call-number. No longer can I remember that title, but it definitely had some-thing to do with the name of the city, suburb of a sort, where Quinn's and my apartment was located. I proceeded to walk down a seemingly endless aisle flanked by innumerable smaller aisles between the lofty bookshelves. Indeed, they were so lofty that when I finally reached my destination I had to climb a high ladder to reach the spot where I could secure the desired book. Mounting the ladder until my shaking hands gripped the highest rung, I was at eye level with the exact call-number I was seeking, or some forgotten dream-glyphs which I took to be these letters and digits. And like these symbols, the book I found is now hopelessly unmemorable, its shape, color, and dimensions having perished on the journey back from the dream. I may have even dropped the book, but that was not important.

What was important, however, was the dark little slot created when I withdrew the book from its rank on the shelf. I peered in, somehow knowing I was supposed to do this as part of the book-retrieving ritual. I gazed deeper . . . and the next phase of the dream began.

The slot was a window, perhaps more of a crack in some dream-wall or a slit in the billowing membrane that protects one world against the intrusion of another. Beyond was something of a landscape – for lack of a more suitable term – which I viewed through a narrow rectangular frame. But this landscape had no earth and sky that hinged together in a neat line at the horizon, no floating or shining objects above to echo and balance their earthbound countershapes below. This landscape was an infinite expanse of depth and distance, a never-ending morass deprived of all coherence, a state of strange existence rather than a chartable locus, having no more geographical extension than a mirage or a rainbow. There was definitely something before my vision, elements that could be distinguished from one another but impossible to fix in any kind of relationship. I experienced a prolonged gaze at what is usually just a delirious glimpse, the way one might suddenly perceive some sidelong illusion which disappears at the turn of the head, leaving no memory of what the mind had deceptively seen.

The only way I can describe the visions I witnessed with even faint approximation is in terms of other scenes which might arouse similar impressions of tortuous chaos: perhaps a festival of colors twisting in blackness, a tentacled abyss that alternately seems to glisten moistly as with some horrendous dew, then suddenly dulls into an arid glow, like bone-colored stars shining over an extra-terrestrial desert. The vista of eerie disorder that I observed was further abetted in its strangeness by my own feelings about it. They were magnified dream-feelings, those encyclopedic emotions which involve complexities of intuition, sensation, and knowledge impossible to express. My dream-emotion was indeed a monstrous encyclopedia, one that described a universe kept under infinite wraps of deception, a dimension of disguise.

It was only at the end of the dream that I saw the colors or colored shapes, molten and moving shapes. I cannot remember if I felt them to be anything specific or just abstract entities. They seemed to be the only things active within the moody immensity I stared out upon. Their motion somehow was not pleasant to watch – a bestial lurching of each color-mass, a legless pacing in a cage from which they might escape at any moment. These phantasms introduced a degree of panic into the dream sufficient to wake me.

Oddly enough, though the dream had nothing to do with my roommate, I woke up calling his name repeatedly in my dream-distorted voice. But he did not answer the call, for he was not home at the time.

I have reconstructed my nightmare at this point for two reasons. First, to show the character of my inner life during this time; second, to provide a context in which to appreciate what I found the next day in Quinn's room.

When I returned from classes that afternoon, Quinn was nowhere to be seen, and I took this opportunity to research the nightmares that had been visiting our apartment in Nortown.

Actually I did not have to pry very deeply into the near-fossilized clutter of Quinn's room. Almost immediately I spied on his desk something that made my investigation easier, this something being a spiral notebook with a cover of mock marble. Switching on the desklamp in that darkly curtained room, I looked through the first few pages of the notebook. It seemed to be concerned with the sect Quinn had become associated with some weeks before, serving as a kind of spiritual diary. The entries were Quinn's meditations upon his inward evolution and employed an esoteric terminology which must remain largely undocumented, since the notebook is no longer in existence. Its pages, as I recall them, outlined Quinn's progress along a path of offbeat enlightenment, a tentative peering into what might have been merely symbolic realms.

Quinn seemed to have become one of a jaded philosophical society, a group of arcane deviates. Their *raison d'être* was a kind of mystical masochism, forcing initiates toward feats of occult daredevilry – "glimpsing the inferno with eyes of ice", to take from the notebook a phrase that was repeated often and seemed a sort of chant of power. As I suspected, hallucinogenic drugs were used by the sect, and there was no doubt that they believed themselves communing with strange metaphysical venues. Their chief aim, in true mystical fashion, was to transcend common reality in the search for higher states of being, but their stratagem was highly unorthodox, a strange detour along the usual path toward *positive* illumination. Instead, they maintained a kind of blasphemous fatalism, a doomed determinism which brought them face to face with realms of obscure horror. Perhaps it was this very obscurity that allowed them the excitement of their central purpose, which seemed to be a precarious flirting with personal apocalypse, the striving for horrific dominion over horror itself.

Such was the subject matter of Quinn's notebook, all of it quite interesting. But the most intriguing entry was the last, which was brief and which I can recreate nearly in full. In this entry, like most of the others, Quinn addressed himself in the second person with various snatches of advice and admonishment. Much of it was unintelligible, for it seemed to be obsessed almost entirely with regions alien to the conscious mind. However, Quinn's words did have a certain curious meaning when I first read them, and more so later on. The following, then, exemplifies the manner of his notes to himself:

So far your progress has been faulty but inexorable. Last night you saw the zone and now know what it is like – wobbling glitter, a field of colorous venoms, the glistening inner skin of deadliest nightshade. Now that you are actually nearing the plane of the zone, awake! Forget your dainty fantasies and learn to move like the eyeless beast you must become. Listen, feel, *smell* for the zone. Dream your way through its marvelous perils. You know what the things from there may do to you with their dreaming. Be aware. Do not stay in one place for very long these next few nights. This will be the strongest time. Get out (perhaps into the great night-light of Nortown) – wander, tramp, tread, somnambulate if you must. Stop and watch but not for very long. Be mindlessly cautious. Catch the entrancing fragrance of fear – and prevail.

I read this several times, and each time its substance seemed to become less the "fantasies" of an overly imaginative sectarian and more a strange reflection of matters by now familiar to me. Thus, I seemed to be serving my purpose, for the sensitivity of my psyche had allowed a subtle link to Quinn's spiritual pursuits, even in their nuances of mood. And judging from the last entry in Quinn's notebook, the upcoming days were crucial in some way, the exact significance of which may have been entirely psychological. Nevertheless, other possibilities and hopes had crossed my mind. As it happened, the question was settled the following night over the course of only a few hours. This post-meridian adventure – somehow inevitably – took place amid the dreamy and debased nightlife of Nortown.

2.

Of course, Nortown has never really been considered a suburb, for its city limits lie not somewhere on the periphery of that larger city where Quinn and I attended the university, but entirely within its boundaries. For the near-indigent student the sole attraction of this area is the inexpensive housing it offers in a variety of forms, even if the accommodations are not always the most appealing. However, in the case of Quinn and myself, the motives may have differed, for both of us were quite capable of appreciating the hidden properties and possibilities of the little city. Because of Nortown's peculiar proximity to the downtown area of a large urban center it absorbed much of the big city's lurid glamor, only on a smaller scale and in a concentrated way. Of course, there were a multitude of restaurants with bogusly exotic cuisines as well as a variety of nightspots, of bizarre reputation and numerous establishments that existed in a twilight realm with regard to their legality.

But in addition to these second-rate epicurean attractions, Nortown also offered less earthly interests, however ludicrous the form they happened to take. The area seemed a kind of spawning ground for marginal people and movements. (I believe that Quinn's fellow sectarians – whoever they may have been – were either residents or habitues of the suburb.) Along Nortown's seven blocks or so of bustling commerce, one may see storefront invitations to personalized readings of the future or private lectures on the spiritual foci of the body. And if one looks up while walking down certain streets, there is a chance of spying second-floor windows with odd symbols pasted upon them, cryptic badges whose significance is known only to the initiated. In a way difficult to analyze, the mood of these streets was reminiscent of that remarkable dream I have previously described – the sense of dim and disordered landscapes was evoked by every sordid streetcorner of that city within a city.

Not the least of Nortown's inviting qualities is the simple fact that many of its businesses are active every hour of the day and night. Which was probably one reason why Quinn's activities gravitated to this place. And now I knew of at least a few particular nights that he planned to spend treading the sidewalks of Nortown.

Quinn left the apartment just before dark. Through the window I watched him walk around to the front of the building and then proceed up the street toward Nortown's business district. I followed when he seemed a safe distance ahead of me. I supposed that if my plan to chart Quinn's movements for the evening was going to fail, it would do so in the next few minutes. Of course, it was reasonable to credit Quinn with an extra sense or two which would alert him to my scheme. All the same, I was not wrong to believe I was merely conforming to Quinn's unspoken wish for a spectator to his doom, a chronicler of his demonic quest. And everything proceeded smoothly as we arrived in the more heavily trafficked area of Nortown, approaching Carton, the suburb's main street.

Up ahead, the high buildings of the surrounding metropolis towered behind and above Nortown's lower structures. In the distance a pale sun had almost set, highlighting the peaks of the larger city's skyline. The valleyed enclave of Nortown now lay in this skyline's shadows, a dwarfish replica of the enveloping city. And this particular dwarf was of the colorfully clothed type suitable for entertaining jaded royalty; the main street flashed comic colors from an electric spectrum, dizzily hopping foot to foot in its attempt to conquer the nameless boredom of the crowds along the sidewalks. The milling crowds – unusual for a chilly autumn evening – made it easier for me to remain inconspicuous, though more difficult to shadow Quinn.

I almost lost him for a moment when he left the ranks of some sluggish pedestrians and disappeared into a little drugstore on the north side of Carton. I stopped farther down the block and window-shopped for second-hand clothes until he came out onto the street again. Which he did a few minutes later, holding a newspaper in one hand and stuffing a flat package of cigars inside his overcoat with the other. I saw him do this in the light flooding out of the drugstore windows, for by now it was nightfall.

Quinn walked a few more steps and then crossed at midstreet. I saw that his destination was only a restaurant with a semi-circle of letters from the Greek alphabet painted on the front windows. Through the window I could see him take a seat at the counter inside and spread out his newspaper, ordering something from the waitress who stood with pad in hand. For at least a little while he would be easy to keep track of. Not that I simply wanted to observe Quinn go in and out of restaurants and drugstores the rest of the night. I had hoped that his movements would eventually become more revealing. But for the moment I was gaining practice at being his shadow.

I watched Quinn at his dinner from inside a Middle-Eastern import store located across the street from the restaurant. I could observe him easily through the store's front display window. Unfortunately I was the only patron of this musty place, and three times a bony, aged woman asked if she could help me. "Just looking," I said, taking my eyes from the window momentarily and glancing around at a collection of assorted trinkets and ersatz Arabiana. The woman eventually went and stood behind a merchandise counter, where she kept her right hand tenaciously out of view. For possibly no reason at all I was becoming very nervous among the engraved brass and ruggy smells of that store. I decided to return to the street, mingling along the crowded but strangely quiet sidewalks.

After about a half-hour, at approximately quarter to eight, Quinn came out of the restaurant. From down the street and on the opposite side I watched him fold up the newspaper he was carrying and neatly dispose of it in a nearby mailbox. Then, a recently lit cigar alternating between hand and mouth, he started north again. I let him walk half a block or so before I crossed the street and began tailing him once more. Although nothing manifestly unusual had yet occurred, there now seemed to be a certain promise of unknown happenings in the air of that autumn night.

Quinn continued on his way through the dingy neon of Nortown's streets. But he now seemed to have no specific destination. His stride was less purposeful than it had been; he no longer looked expectantly before him but gawked aimlessly about the scene, as if these surroundings were unfamiliar or had altered in some way from the condition of previous visits. The overcoated and wild-haired figure of my roommate gave me the impression he was overwhelmed by something around him. He looked up toward the roof-ledges of buildings as though the full weight of the black autumn sky were about to descend. Absent-mindedly he nudged into a few people and at some point lost hold of his cigar, scattering sparks across the sidewalk.

Quinn turned at the next corner, where Carton intersected with a minor sidestreet. There were only a few places alive with activity in this area, which led into the darker residential regions of Nortown. One of these places was a building with a stairway leading below the street level. From a safe position of surveillance I saw Quinn go down this stairway into what I assumed was a bar or coffee house of some sort. Innocent as it may have been, my imagination impulsively populated that cellar with patrons of fascinating diversity and strangeness. Suppressing my fantasies, I confronted the practical decision of whether or not to follow Quinn inside and risk shattering his illusion of a lonely mystic odyssey. I also speculated that perhaps he was meeting others in this place, and possibly I would end up following multiple cultists, penetrating their esoteric activities, such as they may have been. But after I had cautiously descended the stairway and peered through the smeary panes of the window there, I saw Quinn sitting in a distant corner . . . and he was alone.

"Like peeping in windows?" asked a voice behind me. "Windows are the eyes of the soulless," said another. This twosome looked very much like professors from the university, though not those familiar to me from the anthropology department. I followed these distinguished academics into the bar, thereby making a less obvious entrance than if I had gone in alone.

The place was dark and crowded and much larger than it looked from outside. I sat at a table by the door and at a strategic remove from Quinn, who was seated behind a half-wall. some distance away. The decor around me looked like that of an unfinished basement or a storage room. There were a great number of flea-market antiquities hanging from the walls, and dangling from the ceiling were long objects that resembled razor strops. After a few moments a rather vacant-looking girl walked over and stood silently near my table. I did not immediately notice that she was just a waitress, so unconvivial was her general appearance and manner.

At some point during the hour or so that I was allowed to sit there nursing my drink, I discovered that if I leaned forward as far as possible in my chair, I could catch a glimpse of Quinn on the other side of the half-wall. This tactic now revealed to me a Quinn in an even greater state of agitated wariness than before. I thought he would have settled down to a languid series of drinks, but he did not. In fact, there was a cup of coffee, not liquor, sitting at his elbow. Quinn seemed to be scrutinizing every inch of the room for something. His nervous glances once nearly focused on my own face, and from then on I became more discreet.

A little later on, not long before Quinn's and my exit, a girl with a guitar wandered up onto a platform against one wall of the room. As she made herself comfortable in a chair on the platform and tuned her guitar, someone switched on a single spotlight on the floor. I noticed that attached to the front of the spotlight was a movable disc divided into four sections: red, blue, green, and transparent. It was now adjusted to shine only through the transparent section.

The entertainer gave herself no introduction and started singing a song after lethargically strumming her guitar for a moment or so. I did not recognize the piece, but I think any song would have sounded strange as rendered by that girl's voice. It was the gloomy and unstudied voice of a feeble-minded siren locked away somewhere and wailing pitifully to be set free. That the song was intended as mournful I could not doubt. It was, however, a very foreign and disorienting kind of mournfulness, as if the singer had eavesdropped on some exotic and grotesque rituals for her inspiration.

She finished the song. After receiving applause from only a single person somewhere in the room, she started into another number which sounded no different from the first. Then, about a minute or so into the weird progress of this second song, something happened – a moment of confusion – and seconds later I found myself back on the streets.

What happened was actually no more than some petty mischief.

While the singer was calling feline-like to the lost love of the song's verses, someone sneaked up near the platform, grabbed the disc attached to the front of the spotlight, and gave it a spin. A wild kaleidoscope ensued; the swarming colors attacked the singer and those patrons at nearby tables. The singing continued, its languishing tempo off-sync with the speedy reds, blues, and greens. There was something menacing about the visual disorder of those colors gleefully swimming around. And then, for a brief moment, the colorful chaos was eclipsed when a silhouette hurriedly stumbled past, moving between my table and the singer on the platform. I almost missed seeing who it was, for my eyes were averted from the general scene. I let him make it out the door, which he seemed to have some trouble opening, before dashing from the place myself.

When I emerged from the stairway onto the sidewalk, I saw Quinn standing at the corner on Carton. He had paused to light a cigar, rather frenetically striking several matches that would not stay lit in the autumn wind. I kept my place in the shadows until he proceeded on his way up the street.

We walked a few blocks, brief in length but ponderously decorated with neon signs streaming across the night. I was diverted by the sequentially lit letters spelling out E-S-S-E-N-C-E LOUNGE, LOUNGE, LOUNGE; and I wondered what secrets were revealed to those anointed by the priestesses of Medea's Massage.

Our next stop was a short one, though it also threatened the psychic rapport Quinn and I had been so long in establishing. Quinn entered a bar where a sign outside advertised for persons who desired work as professional dancers. I let a few moments pass before following Quinn into the place. But just as I stepped within the temporarily blinding darkness of the bar, someone shouldered me to one side in his haste to leave. Fortunately I was standing in a crowd of men waiting for seats inside, and Quinn did not seem to take note of me. In addition, his right hand – with cigar – was visoring his eyes or perhaps giving his brow a quick massage. In any case, he did not stop but charged past me and out the door. As I turned to follow him in his brusque exit, I noticed the scene within the bar, particularly focusing on a stage where a single figure gyred about – clothed in flashing colors. And gazing briefly on this chaotic image, I recalled that other flurrying chaos at the underground club, wondering if Quinn had been disturbed by this second confrontation with a many-hued phantasmagoria, this flickering and disorderly rainbow of dreams. Certainly he seemed

to have been repulsed in some way, causing his furious exit. I
exited more calmly and resumed my chartings of Quinn's nocturnal voyage.

He next visited a number of places into which, for one reason or
another, I was wary to follow. Included among these stops was a
bookstore (not an occult one), a record shop with an outdoor
speaker that blared madness into the street, and a lively amusement arcade, where Quinn remained for only the briefest moment.
Between each of these diversions Quinn appeared to be getting
progressively more, I cannot say frantic, but surely . . . watchful.
His once steady stride was now interrupted by half-halts to glance
into store windows, frequent hesitations that betrayed a multitude
of indecisive thoughts and impulses, a faltering uncertainty in
general. His whole manner of movement had changed, its aspects
of rhythm, pace, and gesture adding up to a character-image
radically altered from his former self. At times I could even have
doubted that this was Jack Quinn if it had not been for his
unmistakable appearance.

Perhaps, I thought, he had become subliminally aware of
someone being always at his back, and that, at this point in his
plummet to an isolated hell, he no longer required a companion or
could not tolerate a voyeur of his destiny. But ultimately I had to
conclude that the cause of Quinn's disquiet was something other
than a pair of footsteps trailing behind him. There was something
else that he seemed to be seeking, searching out clues in the brick
and neon landscape, possibly in some signal condition or circumstance from which he could derive guidance for his movements
that frigid and fragrant October night. But I do not think he
found, or could properly read, whatever sign it was he sought.
Otherwise the consequences might have been different.

The reason for Quinn's lack of alertness had much to do with his
penultimate stop that evening. The time was close to midnight. We
had worked our way down Carton to the last block of Nortown's
commercial area. Here, also, were the northern limits of the
suburb, beyond which lay a stretch of condemned buildings
belonging to the surrounding city. This part of the suburb was
similarly blighted in ways both physical and atmospheric. On
either side of the street stood a row of attached buildings of
sometimes dramatically varying height. Many of the businesses
on this block were equipped with no outside lights or were not
using the ones they had. But the lack of outward illumination
seldom signified that these places were not open for business, at
least judging by the comings and goings on the sidewalks outside

the darkened shops, bars, small theaters, and other establishments. Casual pedestrian traffic at this end of the suburb had seemingly diminished to certain determined individuals of specific taste and destination. Street traffic too was reduced, and there was something about those few cars left parked at the curbs that gave them a look of abandonment, if not complete immobility.

Of course, I am sure those cars, or most of them, were capable of motion, and it was only the most pathetic of fallacies that caused one to view them as sentient things somehow debilitated by their broken-down surroundings. But I think I may have been dreaming on my feet for a few seconds: sounds and images seemed to come to me from places outside the immediate environment. I stared at an old building across the street – a bar, perhaps, or a nameless club of some exclusive membership – and for a moment I received the impression that it was sending out strange noises, not from within its walls but from a far more distant source, as if it were transmitting from remote dimensions. And these noises had a visible aspect too, a kind of vibration in the night air, like static that one could see, sparkling in the darkness. But all the while there was just an old building and nothing more than that. I stared a little longer and the noises faded into confused voicey echoes, the sparkling became dull and disappeared, the connection lost, and the place fully resumed its decrepit reality.

The building looked much too intimate in size to afford concealment, and I perceived a certain privacy in its appearance that made me feel a newcomer would have been awkwardly noticeable. Quinn, however, had unhesitantly gone inside. I suppose it would have been helpful to observe him in there, to see what sort of familiarity he had with this establishment and its patrons. But all I know is that he remained in there for just less than an hour. During part of that time I waited at a counter stool in a diner down the street.

When Quinn finally came out he was drunk, observably so. This surprised me, because I had assumed that he intended to maintain the utmost control of his faculties that evening. The coffee I saw him drinking at that underground club seemed to support this assumption. But somehow Quinn's intentions to hold on to his sobriety, if he had such intentions to begin with, had been revised or forgotten.

I had positioned myself farther down the street by the time he reappeared, but there was much less need for caution now. It was ridiculously easy to remain unnoticed behind a Quinn who could barely see the pavement he walked upon. A police car with flashing lights passed us on Carton, and Quinn exhibited no awareness of it. He halted on the sidewalk, but only to light a cigar. And he seemed to have a difficult time performing this task in a wind that turned his unbuttoned overcoat into a wild-winged cape flapping behind him. It was this wind, as much as Quinn himself, that led the way to our final stop where a few last lights relieved the darkness on the very edge of Nortown.

The lights were those of a theater marquee. And it was also here that we caught up with the revolving beacons of the patrol car. Behind it was another vehicle, a large luxury affair that had a deep gash in its shiny side. Not far away along the curb was a No Parking sign that was creased into an L shape. A tall policeman was inspecting the damaged city property, while the owner of the car that had apparently done the deed was standing by. Quinn gave only a passing glance at this tableau as he proceeded into the theater. A few moments later I followed him, but not before hearing the owner of that disfigured car tell the patrolman that something brightly colored had suddenly appeared in his headlights, causing him to swerve. And whatever it was had subsequently vanished.

Stepping into the theater, I noted that it must have been a place of baroque elegance in former days, though now the outlines of the enscrolled molding above were blurred by grayish sediment and the enormous chandelier was missing some of its parts and all of its glitter. The glass counter on my right had been converted, probably long ago, from a refreshment bar to a merchandise stand, pornographic magazines and other things having replaced the snacks.

I walked through one of a long line of doors and stood around for a while in the hallway behind the auditorium. Here a group of men were talking and smoking, dropping their cigarettes onto the floor and stepping them out. Their voices almost drowned out the austere soundtrack of the film that was being shown, the sound emanating from the aisle entrances and humming unintelligibly in the back walls. I looked into the film-lit auditorium and saw only a few moviegoers scattered here and there in the worn seats of the theater, mostly sitting by themselves. By the light of the film I located Quinn within the sparse audience. He was sitting very close to the screen in a front-row seat next to some curtains and an exit sign.

He seemed to be dozing in his seat rather than watching the film, and I found it a simple matter to position myself a few rows behind him. By that time, however, I found myself losing some of the resolve to remain attentive when Quinn himself appeared to have lost much of his earlier intensity, and the momentum of that night was running down. In the darkness of the theater I nodded, and then slept, much as it seemed Quinn had already done.

I did not sleep for long, no more than a few minutes, but this time I definitely dreamed. There was no nightmarish scenery in this dream, no threatening scenarios. Only darkness . . . darkness and a voice. The voice was that of Quinn. He was calling out to me from a great distance, a distance that did not seem a matter of physical space but one of immeasurable and alien dimensions. His words were distorted, as if passing through some medium that was misshaping them, turning human sounds into a beastlike rasping – the half-choking and half-shrieking voice of a thing being slowly and methodically wounded. First he called my name several times in the wild modulations of a coarse scream. Then he said, as well as I can remember: "Stopped watching for them . . . fell asleep . . . where are you . . . help us . . . they're dreaming too . . . they're dreaming . . . shaping things with their dreams . . ."

I awoke and the first thing I saw was what seemed a great shapeless mass of color, which was only the giant images of the film. My eyes focused and I looked down the rows toward Quinn. He seemed to be slumped over very low in his seat or was nodding somehow, the top of his head much too near his shoulders. A mound of movement struggled on the other side of the seat, emerging sideways into the aisle. I could see it easily, its faint luminosity at first appearing to my vision as a reflection of the colors flickering erratically on the movie screen. But because of the diminished size and strange proportions, I could not be sure if it was Quinn or someone else. The bottom of his overcoat dragged along the floor, its sleeves hanging loose and handless, its collar caving in. The thing fought to take each awkward step, as if it did not have full control of its motion, like a marionette jerking this way and that way as it labors forth. Its glow seemed to be gaining in radiance now, a pulsing opalescent aura that crawled or flowed all around the lumbering dwarf.

I might still be in a dream, I reminded myself. This might be a distorted after-vision, a delirious blend of images derived from nightmare, imagination, and that enormous stain of colors at the front of the dark auditorium in which I had just awakened. I tried to collect myself, to focus upon the thing that was disappearing behind that thick curtain beneath the lighted exit sign.

I followed, passing through the opening in the frayed and velvety curtain. Beyond the curtain was a cement stairway leading up to the metal door that was now swinging closed. Halfway up the stairs I saw a familiar shoe which must have been lost in Quinn's frantic yet retarded haste. Where was he running and from what? These were my only thoughts now, without consideration of the pure strangeness of the situation. I had abandoned all connections to any guiding set of norms by which to judge reality or unreality, and merely accepted everything. However, all that was needed to shatter this acceptance waited outside – something of total unacceptability, an ascent upon the infinite and rickety scaffold of estrangement. After I stepped out the door at the top of the stairs, I discovered that the previous events of that night had only served as a springboard into other realms, a point of departure from a world now diminishing with a furious velocity behind me.

The area outside the theater was unlit but nonetheless was not dark. Something was shining in a long narrow passageway between the theater and an adjacent building. This was where he had gone. Illumination was there, and sounds.

From around the corner's edge a grotesque light was trickling out, the first intimations of an ominous sunrise over a dark horizon. I dimly recognized this colored light, though not from my waking memory. It grew more intense, now pouring out in weird streams from beyond the solid margin of the building. And the more intense it grew, the more clearly I could hear the screaming voice that had called out to me in a dream. I shouted his name, but the swelling colored brightness was a field of fear which kept me from making any move toward it. It was no amalgam of colors comparable to anything in mortal experience. It was as if all natural colors had been mutated into a painfully lush iridescence by some prism fantastically corrupted in its form; it was a rainbow staining the sky after a poison deluge; it was an aurora painting the darkness with a blaze of insanity, a blaze that did not burn vigorously but shimmered with an insect-jeweled frailness. And, in actuality, it was nothing like these color-filled effusions, which are merely a feeble means of partially fixing a reality uncommunicable to those not initiated to it, a necessary resorting to the makeshift gibberish of the mystic isolated by his experience and left without a language to describe it.

The entire experience was temporally rather brief, though its unreal quality made it seem of an indefinite duration – the blink of an eye or an eon. Suddenly the brightness ceased flowing out from the other side of the wall, as if some strange spigot had been abruptly turned off somewhere. The screaming had also stopped. I stood in the silence and moonlit darkness behind the theater. Immediately I rushed around the corner of the building, but everything was now hopelessly safe, beyond rescue or recovery.

There was, in fact, nothing there. Nothing to relieve my sense of doubt as to what exactly had happened. (Though not a mere novitiate of the unreal, I have had my moments of dazed astonishment.) But perhaps there was one thing. On the ground was a burnt-out patch of earth, a shapeless and bare spot that was deprived of the weeds and litter that covered the surrounding area. Possibly it was only a place from which some object had recently been removed, spirited off, leaving the earth beneath it vacant and dead. For a moment, when I first looked at the spot, it seemed to twinkle with a faint luminosity. Possibly I only imagined its outline as being that of a human silhouette, though one contorted in such a way that it might also have been mistaken for other things, other shapes. In any case, whatever had been there was now gone.

And around this barren little swatch of ground was only trash: newspapers mutilated by time and the elements; brown bags reduced by decay to their primal pulp; thousands of cigarette butts; and one item of debris that was almost new and had yet to have any transformations worked upon it. It was a thin book-like box. I picked it up. There were still two fresh cigars in it.

3.

I do not recall making my way back to the apartment that night, but I woke up there the next morning. When I saw the sunlight shafting through my bedroom window, the enormous divide between night and day seemed comfortingly unbridgeable. Then I realized I had fallen asleep with all my clothes on and the connection was made once again. I jumped out of bed and stumbled over to my roommate's room, which of course was empty. For a moment I had entertained the protective thought that I had dreamed the events of the night before. Or perhaps dream merely overlapped reality in certain places – props and stage sets from one having been deceptively transferred in my memory to the other. On another hand, maybe everything I recalled was just one dream mingling with its own kind, all of it lacking any point of contact with real facts and experiences, whatever they might finally be.

One fact, however, was later established: Quinn never returned to the apartment. After a few days I reported him as missing to the Nortown police. Before doing this I destroyed the notebook in his room, for in a fit of paranoia I thought the police would find it in the course of their investigations and then ask some rather uncomfortable questions. I did not want to explain to them things that they simply would not believe, especially activities indulged in that final night. This would only have erroneously cast suspicion upon myself. Fortunately, the Nortown authorities are notoriously lax in their official functions. As it turned out, the police asked very few questions and never came around to the apartment.

After Quinn's disappearance I immediately began looking for another apartment. And although my roommate was gone, the strange dreams continued during my last days at the old residence. But these dreams were different in some particulars. The general backdrop was much the same nightmare expanse, but now I viewed it from some mysterious distance outside the dream. It was actually more like watching a film than dreaming, and they did not seem to be my own dreams at all. Perhaps these were Quinn's leftover visions or terrors still haunting the apartment, for he played the dreams' central role. Perhaps it was in these dreams that I continued to follow Quinn beyond the point at which I lost him. For at that point I imagined him as already starting to change, and in my last dreams he changed further.

He no longer bore any resemblance to my former roommate, though with dreamlike omniscience I knew it was he. His shape kept changing, or rather was deliberately being changed by those kaleidoscopic beasts. Playing out a scene from some Boschian hell, the tormenting demons encircled their victim and were *dreaming* him. They dreamed him through a hideous series of grotesque transfigurations, maliciously altering the screaming mass of the damned soul. They were dreaming things out of him and dreaming things into him. Finally, the purpose of their transformations became apparent. They were torturing their victim through a number of stages which would ultimately result in his becoming one of them, fulfilling his most fearful and obsessive vision. I no longer recognized him but saw that there was now one more glittering beast that took its place with the others and frolicked among them.

This was the last dream I had before leaving the apartment. There have been no others – at least none that have troubled my own sleep. I cannot say the same for that of my new roommate,

who rages in his slumber night after night. Once or twice he has
attempted to communicate to me his strange visions and the
company into which they have led him. But he can see that I
myself am not afflicted with the same disease of dreams. Perhaps he
will never suspect that I am now its carrier.

THE MYSTICS OF MUELENBURG

If things are not what they seem and we are forever reminded that this is the case – then it must also be observed that enough of us ignore this truth to keep the world from collapsing. Though never exact, always shifting somewhat, the *proportion* is crucial. For a certain number of minds are fated to depart for realms of delusion, as if in accordance with some hideous timetable, and many will never be returning to us. Even among those who remain, how difficult it can be to hold the focus sharp, to keep the picture of the world from fading, from blurring in selected zones and, on occasion, from sustaining epic deformations over the entire visible scene.

I once knew a man who claimed that, overnight, all the solid shapes of existence had been replaced by cheap substitutes: trees made of flimsy posterboard, houses built of colored foam, whole landscapes composed of hair-clippings. His own flesh, he said, was now just so much putty. Needless to add, this acquaintance had deserted the cause of appearances and could no longer be depended on to stick to the common story. Alone he had wandered into a tale of another sort altogether; for him, all things now participated in this nightmare of nonsense. But although his revelations conflicted with the lesser forms of truth, nonetheless he did live in the light of a greater truth: that all is unreal. Within him this knowledge was vividly present down to his very bones, which had been newly simulated by a compound of mud and dust and ashes.

In my own case, I must confess that the myth of a natural universe – that is, one that adheres to certain continuities whether we wish them or not – was losing its grip on me and was gradually being supplanted by a hallucinatory view of creation. Forms, having nothing to offer except a mere suggestion of firmness, declined in importance; fantasy, that misty domain of pure meaning, gained in power and influence. This was in the days when esoteric wisdom seemed to count for something in my mind, and I would willingly have sacrificed a great deal in its pursuit. Hence, my interest in the man who called himself Klaus Klingman; hence, too, that brief yet profitable association between us, which came about through channels too twisted to recall.

Without a doubt, Klingman was one of the illuminati and proved this many times over in various psychic experiments, particularly those of the seance type. For those outside scientific circles, I need only mention the man who was severally known as Nemo the Necromancer, Marlowe the Magus, and Master Marinetti, each of whom was none other than Klaus Klingman himself. But Klingman's highest achievement was not a matter of public spectacle and consisted entirely of this private triumph: that he had attained, by laborious effort, an unwavering acceptance of the spectral nature of things, which to him were neither what they seemed to be nor were they quite anything at all.

Klingman lived in the enormous upper story of a warehouse that had been part of his family's legacy to him, and there I often found him wandering amidst a few pieces of furniture and the cavernous wasteland of dim and empty storage space. Collapsing into an ancient armchair, reposing far beneath crumbling rafters, he would gaze beyond the physical body of his visitor, his eyes surveying remote worlds and his facial expression badly disorganized by dreams and large quantities of alcohol. "Fluidity, always fluidity," he shouted out, his voice carrying through the expansive haze around us, which muted daylight into dusk. The embodiment of his mystic precepts, he appeared at any given moment to be on the verge of an amazing disintegration, his particular complex of atoms ready to go shooting off into the great void like a burst of fireworks.

We discussed the dangers – for me and for the world – of adopting a visionary program of existence. "The chemistry of things is so delicate," he warned. "And this word chemistry, what does it mean but a mingling, a mixing, a gushing together? Things that people fear." Indeed, I had already suspected the hazards of his company, and, as the sun was setting over the city beyond the great windows of the warehouse, I became afraid. With an uncanny perception of my feelings, Klingman pointed at me and bellowed:

"The worst fear of the race – yes, the world suddenly transformed into a senseless nightmare, horrible dissolution of things. Nothing compares, even oblivion is a sweet dream. You understand why, of course. Why this peculiar threat. These brooding psyches, all the busy minds everywhere. I hear them buzzing like flies in the blackness. I see them as glow worms flitting in the blackness. They are struggling, straining every second to keep the sky above them, to keep the sun in the sky, to keep the dead in the earth – to keep all things, so to speak, *where they belong*. What an undertaking! What a crushing task! Is it any wonder that they are all tempted by a universal voice, that in some dark street of the mind a single voice whispers to one and all, softly hissing, and says: 'Lay down your burden.' Then thoughts begin to drift, a mystical magnetism pulls them this way and that, faces start to change, shadows speak . . . sooner or later the sky comes down, melting like wax. But as you know, everything has not yet been lost: absolute terror has proved its security against this fate. Is it any wonder that these beings carry on the struggle at whatever cost?"

"And you?" I asked.

"I?"

"Yes, don't you shoulder the universe in your own way?"

"Not at all," he replied, smiling and sitting up in his chair as on a throne. "I am a lucky one, parasite of chaos, maggot of vice. Where I live is nightmare, thus a certain nonchalance. In a previous life, you know, I may actually have been at Muelenburg before it was lost in the delirium of history. Who can say? Smothered by centuries now. But *there* was an opportunity, a moment of distraction in which so much was nearly lost forever, so many lost in that medieval gloom, catastrophe of dreams. How their minds wandered in the shadows even as their bodies were seemingly bound to narrow rutted streets and apparently safeguarded by the spired cathedral which was erected between 1365 and 1399. A rare and fortuitous juncture when the burden of the heavens was heaviest – so much to keep in its place – and the psyche so ill-developed, so easily taxed and tempted away from its labors. But they knew nothing about that, and never could. They only knew the prospect of absolute terror."

"In Muelenburg", I said, hoping to draw his conversation outward before it twisted further into itself. "You said the cathedral."

"*I see* the cathedral, the colossal vault above, the central aisle stretching out before us. The woodcarvings leer down from dark corners, animals and freaks, men in the mouths of demons. Are you taking notes again? Fine, then take notes. Who knows what you will remember of all this? Or will memory help you at all? In any case we are already there, sitting among the smothered sounds of

the cathedral. Beyond the jeweled windows is the town in twilight."

Twilight, as Klingman explained and I must paraphrase, had
come upon Muelenburg somewhat prematurely on a certain day
deep into the autumn season. Early that afternoon, clouds had
spread themselves evenly above the region surrounding the town,
withholding heaven's light and giving a dull appearance to the
landscape of forests, thatched farmhouses, and windmills standing
still against the horizon. Within the high stone walls of Muelenburg itself, no one seemed particularly troubled that the narrow
streets – normally so cluttered with the pointed shadows of peaked
roofs and jutting gables at this time of day – were still immersed in
a lukewarm dimness which turned merchants' brightly colored
signs into faded artifacts of a dead town and which made faces look
as if they were fashioned in pale clay. And in the central square –
where the shadow from the clock-tower of the town hall at times
overlapped those cast by the twin spires of the cathedral on the one
hand, or the ones from high castle turrets looming at the border of
the town on the other – there was only grayness undisturbed.

Where were the minds of the townspeople? How had they ceased
paying homage to the ancient order of things? And when had the
severing taken place that sent their world drifting on strange
waters?

For some time they remained innocent of the disaster, going
about their ways as the ashen twilight lingered far too long, as it
encroached upon the hours that belonged to evening and suspended the town between day and night. Everywhere windows
began to glow with the yellow light of lamps, creating the illusion
that darkness was imminent. Any moment, it seemed, the natural
cycle would relieve the town of the prolonged dusk it had suffered
that autumn day. How well received the blackness would have
been by those who waited silently in sumptuous chambers or
humble rooms, for no one could bear the sight of Muelenburg's
twisting streets in that eerie, overstaying twilight. Even the
nightwatchman shirked his nocturnal routine. And when the
bells of the abbey sounded for the monks' midnight prayers, each
toll spread like an alarm throughout the town still held in the
strange luminousness of the gloaming.

Exhausted by fear, many shuttered their windows, extinguished
lamps, and retired to their beds, hoping that all would be made
right in the interval. Others sat up with a candle, enjoying the lost
luxury of shadows. A few, who were not fixed to the life of the town,

broke through the unwatched gate and took to the roads, all the
while gazing at the pale sky and wondering where they would go.

But whether they kept the hours in their dreams or in sleepless
vigils, all were disturbed by something in the spaces around them,
as if some strangeness had seeped into the atmosphere of their
town, their homes, and perhaps their souls. The air seemed heavier
somehow, resisting them slightly, and also seemed to be flowing
with things that could not be perceived except as swift, shadowlike
movement escaping all sensible recognition, transparent flight
which barely caressed one's vision.

When the clock high in the tower of the town hall proved that a
nightful of hours had passed, some opened their shutters, even
ventured into the streets. But the sky still hovered over them like an
infinite vault of glowing dust. Here and there throughout the town
the people began to gather in whispering groups. Appeals were
soon made at the castle and the cathedral, and speculations were
offered to calm the crowd. There was a struggle in heaven, some
had reasoned, which had influenced the gross reality of the visible
world. Others proposed a deception by demons or an ingenious
punishment from on high. A few, who met secretly in well-hidden
chambers, spoke in stricken voices of old deities formerly driven
from the earth who were now monstrously groping their way back.
And all of these explications of the mystery were true in their own
way, though none could abate the dread which had settled upon
the town of Muelenburg.

Submerged in unvarying grayness, distracted and confused by
phantasmal intrusions about them, the people of the town felt their
world dissolving. Even the clock in the town hall tower failed to
keep their moments from wandering strangely. Within such
disorder were bred curious thoughts and actions. Thus, in the
garden of the abbey an ancient tree was shunned and rumours
spread concerning some change in its twisted silhouette, something
flaccid and rope-like about its branches, until finally the monks
dowsed it with oil and set it aflame, their circle of squinting faces
bathing in the glare. Likewise, a fountain standing in one of the
castle's most secluded courtyards became notorious when its
waters appeared to suggest fabulous depths far beyond the natural
dimensions of its shell-shaped basin. The cathedral itself had
deteriorated into a hollow sanctuary where prayers were mocked
by queer movements among the carved figures in cornices and by
shadows streaming horribly in the twitching light of a thousand
candles.

Throughout the town, all places and things bore evidence to

striking revisions in the base realm of matter: precisely sculptured stone began to loosen and lump, an abandoned cart melded with the sucking mud of the street, and objects in desolate rooms lost themselves in the surfaces they pressed upon, making metal tongs mix with brick hearth, prismatic jewels with lavish velvet, a corpse with the wood of its coffin. At last the faces of Muelenburg became subject to changing expressions which at first were quite subtle, though later these divergences were so exaggerated that it was no longer possible to recapture original forms. It followed that the townspeople could no more recognize themselves than they could one another. All were carried off in the great torrent of their dreams, all spinning in that grayish whirlpool of indefinite twilight, all churning and in the end merging into utter blackness.

It was within this blackness that the souls of Muelenburg struggled and labored and ultimately awoke. The stars and high moon now lit up the night, and it seemed that their town had been returned to them. And so terrible had been their recent ordeal that of its beginning, its progress, and its termination, they could remember . . . nothing.

"Nothing?" I echoed.

"Of course," Klingman answered. "All of those terrible memories were left behind in the blackness. How could they bear to bring them back?"

"But your story," I protested. "These notes I've taken tonight."

"Privileged information, far off the main roads of historical record. You know that sooner or later each of them recollected the episode in detail. It was all waiting for them in the place where they had left it – the blackness which is the domain of death. Or, if you wish, that blackness of the old alchemists' magic powder."

I remembered the necromantic learning that Klingman had both professed and proven, but still I observed: "Then nothing can be verified, nothing established as fact."

"Nothing at all," he agreed, "except the fact that I am one with the dead of Muelenburg and with all who have known the great dream in all its true liquescence. They have spoken to me as I am speaking to you. Many reminiscences imparted by those old dreamers, many drunken dialogues I have held with them."

"Like the drunkenness of this dialogue tonight," I said, openly disdaining his narrative.

"Perhaps, only much more vivid, more real. But the yarn which you suppose I alone have spun has served its purpose. To cure you of doubt, you first had to be made a doubter. Until now, pardon my saying so, you have shown no talent in that direction. You believed every wild thing that came along, provided it had the least evidence whatever. Unparalleled credulity. But tonight you have doubted and thus you are ready to be cured of this doubt. And didn't I mention time and again the dangers? Unfortunately, you cannot count yourself among those forgetful souls of Muelenburg. You even have your mnemonic notes, as if anyone will credit them when this night is over. The time is right again, and it has happened more than once, for the grip to go slack and for the return of fluidity in the world. And later so much will have to be washed away, assuming a renascence of things. Fluidity, always fluidity."

When I left his company that night, abandoning the dead and shapeless hours I had spent in that warehouse, Klingman was laughing like a madman. I remember him slouched in that threadbare throne, his face all flushed and contorted, his twisted mouth wailing at some hilarious arcana known only to himself, the sardonic laughter reverberating in the great spaces of the night. To all appearances, some ultimate phase of dissipation had seized his soul.

Nevertheless, that I had underrated or misunderstood the powers of Klaus Klingman was soon demonstrated to me, and to others. But no one else remembers that time when the night would not leave and no dawn appeared to be forthcoming. During the early part of the crisis there were sensible, rather than apocalyptic, explanations proffered everywhere: blackout, bizarre meteorological phenomena, an eclipse of sorts. Later, these myths became useless and ultimately unnecessary.

For no one else recalls the hysteria that prevailed when the stars and the moon seemed to become swollen in the blackness and to cast a lurid illumination upon the world. How many horrors await in that blackness to be restored to the memories of the dead. For no one else living remembers when everything began to change, no one else with the possible exception of Klaus Klingman.

In the red dawn following that gruesomely protracted night, I went to the warehouse. Unfortunately the place was untenanted, save by its spare furnishings and a few empty bottles. Klingman had disappeared, perhaps into that same blackness for which he seemed to have an incredible nostalgia. I, of course, make no appeals for belief. There can be no belief where there is no doubt. There cannot be something where there is no nothing. This is far from secret knowledge, as if such knowledge could change anything. This is only how it seems, and seeming is everything.

IN THE SHADOW OF
ANOTHER WORLD

Many times in my life, and in many different places, I have found myself walking at twilight down streets lined with gently stirring trees and old silent houses. On such lulling occasions things seem firmly situated, quietly settled and exceedingly present to the natural eye: over distant rooftops the sun abandons the scene and casts its last light upon windows, watered lawns, the edges of leaves. In this drowsy setting both great things and small achieve an intricate union, apparently leaving not the least space for anything else to intrude upon their visible domain. But other realms are always capable of making their presence felt, hovering unseen like strange cities disguised as clouds or hidden like a world of pale specters within a fog. One is besieged by orders of entity that refuse to articulate their exact nature or proper milieu. And soon those well-aligned streets reveal that they are, in fact, situated among bizarre landscapes where simple trees and houses are marvelously obscured, where everything is settled within the depths of a vast, echoing abyss. Even the infinite sky itself, across which the sun spreads its expansive light, is merely a blurry little window with a crack in it – a jagged fracture beyond which one may see, at twilight, what occupies and envelops a vacant street lined with gently stirring trees and old silent houses.

On one particular occasion I followed a tree-lined street past all the houses and continued until it brought me to a single house a short distance from town. As the road before me narrowed into a bristling path, and the path ascended in a swerving course up the side of a hump in the otherwise even landscape, I stood before my day's destination.

Like other houses of its kind (I have seen so many of them outlined against a pale sky at dusk), this one possessed the aspect of a mirage, a chimerical quality that led one to doubt its existence. Despite its dark and angular mass, its peaks and porches and worn wooden steps, there was something improperly tenuous about its substance, as if it had been constructed of illicit materials – dreams and vapor posing as solid matter. And this was not the full extent of its resemblance to a true chimera, for the house seemed to have acquired its present form through a fabulous conglomeration of properties: conceivably, it had not been forever limited to a single nature and function. Might it not have been a survival of the world's prehistory, a great beast unearthed by time and the elements? There seemed to be the appearance of petrified flesh in its rough outer surfaces, and it was very simple to imagine an inner framework not of beams and boards, but rather of gigantic bones. The chimneys and shingles, windows and doorways were thus the embellishments of a later age which had misunderstood the real essence of this ancient monstrosity, transforming it into a motley and ludicrous thing. Little wonder, then, that in shame it would attempt to reject its reality and pass itself as only a shadow on the horizon, a thing of nightmarish beauty that aroused impossible hopes.

As in the past, I looked to the unseen interior of the house to be the focus of unknown . . . celebrations. It was my wishful conviction that the inner world of the house participated, after its own style, in a kind of ceremonious desolation – that translucent festivals might be glimpsed in the corners of certain rooms and that the faraway sounds of mad carnivals filled certain hallways at all hours of the day and night. I am afraid, however, that a peculiar feature of the house prevented full indulgence in the usual anticipations. This feature was a turret built into one side of the house and rising to an unusual height beyond its roof, so that it looked out upon the world as a lighthouse, diminishing the aspect of introspection that is vital to such structures. And near the cone-roofed peak of this turret, a row of large windows appeared to have been placed, as a later modification, around its entire circumference. But if the house was truly employing its windows to gaze outward more than within, what it saw was nothing. For all the windows of the three ample stories of the house, as well as those of the turret and that small octagonal aperture in the attic, were shuttered closed.

This was, in fact, the state in which I expected to find the house, since I had already exchanged numerous letters with Raymond Spare, the present owner.

"I was expecting you much sooner," Spare said on opening the door. "It's almost nightfall and I was sure you understood that only at certain times . . ."

"My apologies, but I'm here now. Shall I come in?"

Spare stepped aside and gestured theatrically toward the interior of the house, as if he were presenting one of those dubious spectacles that had earned him a substantial livelihood. It was out of an instinct for mystification that he had adopted the surname of the famed visionary and artist, even claiming some blood or spiritual kinship with this great eccentric. But tonight I was playing the skeptic, as I had in my correspondence with Spare, so that I might force him to earn my credence. There would have been no other way to gain his invitation to witness the phenomena that, as I understood from sources other than the illusionistic Spare, were well worth my attention. And he was so deceptively mundane in appearance, which made it difficult to keep in mind his reputation for showmanship, his gift for fantasmic histrionics.

"You have left everything as he had it before you?" I asked, referring to the deceased former owner whose name Spare never disclosed to me, though I knew it all the same. But that was of no importance.

"Yes, very much as it was. Excellent housekeeper, all things considered."

Spare's observation was regrettably true: the interior of the house was immaculate to the point of being suspect. The great parlor in which we now sat, as well as those other rooms and hallways that receded into the house, exuded the atmosphere of a plush and well-tended mausoleum where the dead are truly at rest. The furnishings were dense and archaic, yet they betrayed no oppressive awareness of other times, no secret conspiracies with departed spirits, regardless of the unnatural mood of twilight created by fastidiously clamped shutters which admitted none of nature's true twilight from the outside world. The clock that I heard resonantly ticking in a nearby room caused no sinister echoes to sound between dark, polished floors and lofty, uncob-webbed ceilings. Absent was all fear or hope of encountering a malign presence in the cellar or an insane shadow in the attic. Despite a certain odd effect created by thaumaturgic curios appearing on a shelf, as well as a hermetic chart of the heavens nicely framed and hanging upon a wall, no hint of hauntedness was evoked by either the surfaces or obscurities of this house.

"Quite an *innocent* ambiance," said Spare, who displayed no special prowess in voicing this thought of mine.

"Unexpectedly so. Was that part of his intention?"

Spare laughed. "The truth is that this *was* his original intention, the genesis of what later occupied his genius. In the beginning . . ."

"A spiritual wasteland?"

"Exactly," Spare confirmed.

"Sterile but . . . safe."

"You understand, then. His reputation was for risk not retreat. But the notebooks are very clear on the suffering caused by his fantastic gifts, his incredible *sensitivity*. He required spiritually antiseptic surroundings, yet was hopelessly tempted by the visionary. Again and again in his notebooks he describes himself as 'overwhelmed' to the point of madness. You can appreciate the irony."

"I can certainly appreciate the horror," I replied.

"Of course, well . . . tonight we will have the advantage of his unfortunate experience. Before the evening advances much further I want to show you where he worked."

"And the shuttered windows?" I asked.

"They are *very much* to the point," he answered.

The workshop of which Spare had spoken was located, as one might have surmised, in the uppermost story of the turret in the westernmost part of the house. This circular room could only be reached by climbing a twisting and tenuous stairway into the attic, where a second set of stairs led up into the turret. Spare fumbled with the key to the low wooden door, and soon we had gained entrance.

The room was definitely what Spare had implied: a workshop, or at least the remains of one. "It seems that toward the end he had begun to destroy his apparatus, as well as some of his work," Spare explained as I stepped into the room and saw the debris everywhere. Much of the mess consisted of shattered panes of glass that had been colored and distorted in strange ways. A number of them still existed intact, leaning against the curving wall or lying upon a long work table. A few were set up on wooden easels like paintings in progress, the bizarre transformations of their surfaces left unfinished. These panes of corrupted glass had been cut into a variety of shapes, and each had affixed to it – upon a little card – a scribbled character resembling an oriental ideograph. Similar symbols, although much larger, had been inscribed into the wood of the shutters that covered the windows all around the room.

"A symbology that I cannot pretend to understand," Spare admitted, "except in its function. Here, see what happens when I remove these labels with the little figures squiggled on them."

I watched as Spare went about the room stripping the misshapen glyphs from those chromatically deformed panels of glass. And it was not long before I noticed a change in the general character of the room, a shift in atmospherics as when a clear day is suddenly complicated by the shadowy nuances of clouds. Previously the circular room had been bathed in a twisted kaleidoscope of colors as the simple lights around the room diffused through the strangely tinted windowpanes; but the effect had been purely decorative, an experience restricted to the realm of aesthetics, with no implications of the spectral. Now, however, a new element permeated the round chamber, partially and briefly exposing qualities of quite a different order in which the visible gave way to the truly visionary. What formerly had appeared as an artist's studio, however eccentric, was gradually inheriting the transcendent aura of a stained-glass cathedral, albeit one that had suffered some obscure desecration. In certain places upon the floor, the ceiling, and the circular wall broken by the shuttered windows, in select regions of the room which I perceived through those prismatic lenses, vague forms seemed to be struggling toward visibility, freakish outlines laboring to gain full embodiment. Whether their nature was that of the dead or the demonic – or possibly some peculiar progeny generated by their union – I could not tell. But whatever class of creation they seemed to occupy at the time, it was certain that they were gaining not only in clarity and substance, but also in size, swelling and surging and expanding their universe toward an eclipse of this world's vision.

"Is it possible," I said, turning to Spare, "that this effect of magnification is solely a property of the medium through which . . ."

But before I could complete my speculation, Spare was rushing about the room, frantically replacing the symbols on each sheet of glass, dissolving the images into a quivering translucence and then obliterating or masking them altogether. The room lapsed once again into its former state of iridescent sterility. Then Spare hastily ushered me back to the ground floor, the door to the turret room standing locked behind us.

Afterward he served as my guide through the other, less crucial rooms of the house, each of which was sealed by dark shutters and all of which shared in the same barren atmosphere – the aftermath of a strange exorcism, a purging of the grounds which left them neither hallowed nor unholy, but had simply turned them into a pristine laboratory where a fearful genius had practiced his science of nightmares.

We passed several hours in the small, lamplit library. The sole window of that room was curtained, and I imagined that I saw the night's darkness behind the pattern. But when I put my hand upon that symmetrical and velvety design, I felt only a hardness on the other side, as if I had touched a coffin beneath its pall. It was this barrier that made the world outside seem twice darkened, although I knew that when the shutters were opened I would be faced with one of the clearest nights ever seen.

For some time Spare read to me passages from the notebooks whose simple cryptography he had broken. I sat and listened to a voice that was accustomed to speaking of miracles, a well-practiced tout of mystical freakshows. Yet I also detected a certain conviction in his words, which is to say that his delivery was flawed by dissonant overtones of fear.

"We sleep," he read, "among the shadows of another world. These are the unshapely substance inflicted upon us and the prime material to which we give the shapes of our understanding. And though we create what is seen, yet we are not the creators of its essence. Thus nightmares are born from the impress of ourselves on the life of things unknown. How terrible these forms of specter and demon when the eyes of the flesh cast light and mold the shadows which are forever around us. How much more terrible to witness their true forms roaming free upon the land, or in the most homely rooms of our houses, or frolicking through that luminous hell which in madness we have named the heavens. Then we truly waken from our sleep, but only to sleep once more and shun the nightmares which must ever return to that part of us which is hopelessly dreaming."

After witnessing some of the phenomena which had inspired this hypothesis, I could not escape becoming somewhat entranced with its elegance, if not with its originality. Nightmares both within and around us had been integrated into a system that seemed to warrant admiration. However, the scheme was ultimately no more than terror recollected in tranquility, a formula reflecting little of the mazy trauma that had initiated these speculations. Should it be called revelation or delirium when the mind interposes itself between the sensations of the soul and a monstrous mystery? Truth was not an issue in this matter, nor were the mechanics of the experiment (which, even if faulty, yielded worthy results), and in my mind it was faithfulness to the mystery and its terror that was paramount, even sacred. In this the theoretician of nightmares had failed, fallen on the lucid blade of theories that, in the end, could not save him. On the other hand, those wonderful symbols that Spare was at a loss to illuminate, those crude and cryptic designs, represented a genuine power against the mystery's madness, yet could not be explained by the most esoteric analysis.

"I have a question," I said to Spare when he had closed the volume he held on his lap. "The shutters elsewhere in the house are not painted with the signs that are on those in the turret. Can you enlighten me?"

Spare led me to the window and drew back the curtains. Very cautiously he pulled out one of the shutters just far enough to expose its edge, which revealed that something of a contrasting color and texture composed a layer between the two sides of the dark wood.

"Engraved upon a panel of glass placed inside each shutter," he explained.

"And the ones in the turret?" I asked.

"The same. Whether the extra set of symbols there are precautionary or merely redundant . . ."

His voice had faded and then stopped, though the pause did not seem to imply any thoughtfulness on Spare's part.

"Yes," I prompted, "precautionary or redundant."

For a moment he revived. ". . . that is, whether the symbols were an added measure against . . ."

It was at this point that Spare mentally abandoned the scene, following within his own mind some controversy or suspicion, a witness to a dramatic conflict being enacted upon a remote and shadowy stage.

"Spare," I said in a somewhat normal voice.

"Spare," he repeated, but in a voice that was not his own, a voice that sounded more like the echo of a voice than natural speech. And for a moment I asserted my pose of skepticism, placing none of my confidence in Spare or in the things he had thus far shown me, for I knew that he was an adept of pasteboard visions, a medium whose hauntings were of mucilage and gauze. But how much more subtle and skilful were the present effects, as though he were manipulating the very atmosphere around us, pulling the strings of light and shadow.

"The clearest light is now shining," he said in that hollow, tremulous voice. "Now light is flowing in the glass," he spoke, placing his hand upon the shutter before him. "Shadows gathering against . . . against . . ."

And it seemed that Spare was not so much pulling the shutter away from the window as trying to push the shutter closed while it slowly opened further and further, allowing a strange radiance to leak gradually into the house. It also appeared that he finally gave up the struggle and let another force guide his actions. "Flowing together in me," he repeated several times as he went from window to window, methodically opening the shutters like a sleepwalker performing some obscure ritual.

Ransoming all judgment to fascination, I watched him pass through each room on the main floor of the house, executing his duties like an old servant. Then he ascended a long staircase, and I heard his footsteps traversing the floor above, evenly pacing from one side of the house to the other. He was now a nightwatchman making his rounds in accordance with a strange design. The sound of his movements grew fainter as he progressed to the next floor and continued to perform the services required of him. I listened very closely as he proceeded on his somnambulistic course into the attic. And when I heard the echoes of a distant door as it slammed shut, I knew he had gone into that room in the turret.

Engrossed in the lesser phenomenon of Spare's suddenly altered behavior, I had momentarily overlooked the greater one of the windows. But now I could no longer ignore those phosphorescent panes which focused or reflected the incredible brilliance of the sky that night. As I reiterated Spare's circuit about the main floor, I saw that each room was glowing with the superlunary light that was outlined by each window frame. In the library I paused and approached one of the windows, reaching out to touch its wrinkled surface. And I felt a lively rippling in the glass, as if there truly was some force flowing within it, an uncanny sensation that my tingling fingertips will never be able to forget. But it was the scene beyond the glass that finally possessed my attention.

For a few moments I looked out only upon the level landscape that surrounded the house, its open expanse lying desolate and pale beneath the resplendent heavens. Then, almost inconspicuously, different scenes or fragments of scenes began to intrude upon the outside vicinity, as if other geographies of the earth were being superimposed upon the local one, composing a patchwork of images that might seem to have been the hallucinated tableaux of some cosmic tapestry.

The windows – which, for lack of a more accurate term, I must call *enchanted* – had done their work. For the visions they offered were indeed those of a haunted world, a multi-faceted mural portraying the marriage of insanity and metaphysics. As the images clarified, I witnessed all the intersections which commonly remain unseen to earthly sight, the conjoining of planes of entity which should exclude each other and should no more be mingled than is flesh with the unliving objects that surround it. But this is precisely what took place in the scenes before me, and it appeared there existed no place on earth that was not the home of a spectral ontogeny. All the world was a pageant of nightmares. . . .

Sunlit bazaars in exotic cities thronged with faces that were transparent masks for insect-like countenances; moonlit streets in antique towns harbored a strange-eyed slithering within their very stones; dim galleries of empty museums sprouted a ghostly mold that mirrored the sullen hues of old paintings; the land at the edge of oceans gave birth to a new evolution transcending biology and remote islands offered themselves as a haven for these fantastic forms having no analogy outside of dreams; jungles teemed with beast-like shapes that moved beside the sticky luxuriance as well as through the depths of its pulpy warmth; deserts were alive with an uncanny flux of sounds which might enter and animate the world of substance; and subterranean landscapes heaved with cadaverous generations that had sunken and merged into sculptures of human coral, bodies heaped and unwhole, limbs projecting without order, eyes scattered and searching the darkness.

My own eyes suddenly closed, shutting out the visions for a moment. And during that moment I once again became aware of the sterile quality of the house, of its "innocent ambiance". It was then that I realized that this house was possibly the only place on earth, perhaps in the entire universe, that had been cured of the plague of phantoms that raged everywhere. This achievement, however futile or perverse, now elicited from me tremendous admiration as a monument to Terror and the stricken ingenuity it may inspire.

And my admiration intensified as I pursued the way that Spare had laid out for me and ascended a back staircase to the second floor. For on this level, where room followed upon room through a maze of interconnecting doors which Spare had left open, there seemed to be an escalation in the optical power of the windows, thus heightening the threat to the house and its inhabitants. What had appeared, through the windows of the floor below, as scenes in which spectral monstrosities had merely intruded upon orthodox reality, were now magnified to the point where that reality underwent a further eclipse: the other realm became dominant and pushed through the cover of masks, the concealment of stones, spread its moldy growths at will, generating apparitions of the most feverish properties and intentions, erecting formations that enshadowed all familiar order.

By the time I reached the third floor, I was somewhat prepared for what I might find, granted the elevating intensity of the visions to which the windows were giving increasingly greater force and focus. Each window was now a framed phantasmagoria of churning and forever changing shapes and colors, fabulous depths and distances opening to the fascinated eye, grotesque transfigurations that suggested a purely supernatural order, a systemless cosmogony reeling with all the caprice of the immaterial. And as I wandered through those empty and weirdly lucent rooms at the top of the house, it seemed that the house itself had been transported to another universe.

I have no idea how long I may have been enthralled by the chaotic fantasies imposing themselves upon the unprotected rooms of my mind. But this trance was eventually interrupted by a commotion emanating from an even higher room – the very crown of the turret and, as it were, the cranial chamber of that many-eyed beast of a house. Making my way up the narrow, spiralling stairs to the attic, I found that there, too, Spare had unsealed the octagonal window, which now seemed the gazing eye of some god as it cast forth a pyrotechnic craze of colors and gave a frenzied life to shadows. Through this maze of illusions I followed the voice which was merely a vibrating echo of a voice, the counterpart in sound to the swirling sights around me. I climbed the last stairway to the door leading into the turret, listening to the reverberant words that sounded from the other side.

"Now the shadows are moving in the stars as they are moving within me, within all things. And their brilliance must reach throughout all things, all the places which are created according to the essence of these shadows and of ourselves . . . *This house is an abomination, a vacuum and a void. Nothing must stand against . . . against . . .*"

And with each repetition of this last word it seemed that a struggle was taking place and that the echoing alien voice was fading as the tones of Spare's natural voice was gaining dominance. Finally, Spare appeared to have resumed full possession of himself. Then there was a pause, a brief interim during which I considered a number of doubtful strategies, anxious not to misuse this moment of unknown and extravagant possibilities. Was it merely the end of life that faced one who remained in that room? Could the experience that had preceded the disappearance of that other visionary, under identical circumstances, perhaps be worth the strange price one would be asked to pay? No occult theories, no arcane analyses, could be of any use in making my decision, nor justly serve the sensations of those few seconds, when I stood gripping the handle of that door, waiting for the impulse or accident that would decide everything. All that existed for the moment was the irreducible certainty of nightmare.

From the other side of the door there now came a low, echoing laughter, a sound which became louder as the laughing one approached. But I was not moved by this sound and did nothing except grip the door handle more tightly, dreaming of the great shadows in the stars, of the strange visions beyond the windows, and of an infinite catastrophe. Then I heard a soft scraping noise at my feet; looking down, I saw several small rectangles projecting from under the door, fanned out like a hand of cards. My only action was to stoop and retrieve one of them, to stare in endless wonderment at the mysterious symbol which decorated its face. I counted the others, realizing that none had been left attached to the windows within the room in the turret.

It was the thought of what effect these windows might have, now that they had been stripped of their protective signs and stood in the full glare of starlight, that made me call out to Spare, even though I could not be sure that he still existed as his former self. But by then the hollow laughter had stopped, and I am sure that the last voice I heard was that of Raymond Spare. And when the voice began screaming – *the windows*, it said, *pulling me into the stars and shadows* – I could not help trying to enter the room. But now that the impetus for this action had arrived, it proved to be useless for both Spare and myself. For the door was securely locked, and Spare's voice was fading into nothingness.

I can only imagine what those last few moments were like among all the windows of that turret room and among alien orders of existence beyond all definition. That night, it was to Spare alone that such secrets were confided; he was the one to whom it fell – by some disaster or design – to be among the elect. Such privileged arcana, on this occasion at least, were not to be mine. Nevertheless, it seemed at the time that some fragment of this experience might be salvaged. And to do this, I believed, was a simple matter of abandoning the house.

My intuition was correct. For as soon as I had gone out into the night and turned back to face the house, I could see that its rooms were no longer empty, no longer the pristine apartments I had lamented earlier that evening. As I had thought, these windows were for looking in as well as out. And from where I stood, the sights were now all inside the house, which had become an edifice possessed by the festivities of another world. I remained there until morning, when a cold sunlight settled the motley phantasms of the night before.

Years later I had the opportunity to revisit the house. As expected, I found the place bare and abandoned: every one of its window frames was empty and there was not a sign of glass anywhere. In the nearby town I discovered that the house had also acquired a bad reputation. For years no one had gone near it. Wisely avoiding the enchantments of hell, the citizens of the town have kept to their own little streets of gently stirring trees and old silent houses. And what more can they do in the way of caution? How can they know what it is their houses are truly nestled among? They cannot see, nor even wish to see, that world of shadows with which they consort every moment of their brief and innocent lives. But often, perhaps during the visionary time of twilight, I am sure they have sensed it.

THE COCOONS

Early one morning, hours before sunrise, I was awakened by Dr. Dublanc. He was standing at the foot of my bed, lightly tugging on the covers. For a moment I was convinced, in my quasi-somnolent state, that a small animal was prancing about on the mattress, performing some nocturnal ritual unknown to higher forms of life. Then I saw a gloved hand twitching in the glow of the streetlight outside my window. Finally I identified the silhouette, shaped by a hat and overcoat, of Dr. Dublanc.

I switched on the bedside lamp and sat up to face the well-known intruder. "What's wrong?" I asked as if in protest.

"My apologies," he said in a polite yet unapologetic tone. "There is someone I want you to meet. I think it might be beneficial for you."

"If that's what you say. But can't it wait? I haven't been sleeping well as it is. Better than anyone you should know that."

"Of course I know. I also know other things," he asserted, betraying his annoyance. "The gentleman I want to introduce to you will be leaving the country very soon, so there is a question of timing."

"All the same . . ."

"Yes, I know – your nervous condition. Here, take these."

Dr. Dublanc placed two egg-shaped pills in the palm of my hand. I put them to my lips and then swallowed a half-glass of water that was on the nightstand. I set down the empty glass next to my alarm clock, which emitted a soft grinding noise due to some unknown mutations of its internal mechanism. My eyes became fixed by the slow even movement of the second hand, but Dr. Dublanc, in a quietly urgent voice, brought me out of my trance.

"We should really be going. I have a taxi waiting outside."

So I hurried, thinking that I would end up being charged for this excursion, cab fare and all.

Dr. Dublanc had left the taxi standing in the alley behind my apartment building. Its headlights beamed rather weakly in the blackness, scarcely guiding us as we approached the vehicle. Side by side, the doctor and I proceeded over uneven pavement and through blotched vapors emerging from the fumaroles of several sewer covers. But I could see the moon shining between the close rooftops, and I thought that it subtly shifted phases before my eyes, bloating a bit into fullness. The doctor caught me staring.

"It's not going haywire up there, if that's what is bothering you."

"But it seemed to be changing."

With a growl of exasperation, the doctor pulled me after him into the cab.

The driver appeared to have been stilled into a state of dormancy. Yet Dr. Dublanc was able to evoke a response when he called out an address to the hack, who turned his thin rodent face toward the back seat and glared briefly. For a time we sat in silence as the taxi proceeded through a monotonous passage of unpeopled avenues. At that hour the world on the other side of my window seemed to be no more than a mass of shadows wavering at a great distance. The doctor touched my arm and said, "Don't worry if the pills I gave you seem to have no immediate effect."

"I trust your judgement," I said, only to receive a doubtful glance from the doctor. In order to revive my credibility, I told him what was actually on my mind: the matter of who I would be meeting, and why.

"A former patient of mine," he answered bluntly, for it was apparent that at this point he was prepared to assume an open manner with me. "Not to say that some unfortunate aspects do not still exist in his case. For certain reasons I will be introducing him to you as 'Mr. Catch', though he's also a doctor of sorts – a brilliant scientist, in fact. But what I want you to see are just some films he has made in the course of his work. They are quite remarkable. Not to deny those unfortunate aspects I mentioned . . . yet very intriguing. And possibly beneficial – to you, I mean. Possibly most beneficial. And that's all I can say at the moment."

I nodded as if in comprehension of this disclosure. Then I noticed how far we had gone, almost to the opposite end of the city, if that was possible in what seemed a relatively short period of time. (I had forgotten to wear my watch, and this negligence somewhat aggravated my lack of orientation.) The district in which we were now traveling was of the lowest order, a landscape without pattern or substance, especially as I viewed it by moonlight.

There might be an open field heaped with debris, a devastated plain where bits of glass and scraps of metal glittered, though perhaps a solitary house remained in this wasteland, an empty skeletal structure scraped of its flesh. And then, turning a corner, one left behind this lunar spaciousness and entered a densely tangled nest of houses, the dwarfish and the great all tightly nestled together and all eaten away, disfigured. Even as I watched them through the taxi's windows they appeared to be carrying on their corruption, mutating in the dull light of the moon. Roofs and chimneys elongated toward the stars, dark bricks multiplied and bulged like tumors upon the facades of houses, entire streets twisted themselves along some unearthly design. Although a few windows were filled with light, however sickly, the only human being I saw was a derelict crumpled at the base of a traffic sign.

"Sorry, doctor, but this may be too much."

"Just hold on to yourself," he said, "we're almost there. Driver, pull into that alley behind those houses."

The taxi joggled as we made our way through the narrow passage. On either side of us were high wooden fences beyond which rose so many houses of such impressive height and bulk, though of course they were still monuments to decay. The cab's headlights were barely up to the task of illuminating the cramped little alley, which seemed to become ever narrower the further we proceeded. Suddenly the driver jerked us to a stop to avoid running over an old man slouched against the fence, an empty bottle lying at his side.

"This is where we get out," said Dr. Dublanc. "Wait here for us, driver."

As we emerged from the taxi I pulled at the doctor's sleeve, whispering about the expense of the fare. He replied in a loud voice, "You should worry more about getting a taxi to take us back home. They keep their distance from this neighborhood and rarely answer the calls they receive to come in here. Isn't that true, driver?" But the man had returned to that dormant state in which I first saw him. "Come on," said the doctor. "He'll wait for us. This way."

Dr. Dublanc pushed back a section of the fence that formed a kind of loosely hinged gate, closing it carefully behind us after we passed through the opening. On the other side was a small backyard, actually a miniature dumping ground where shadows bulged with refuse. And before us, I assumed, stood the house of Mr. Catch. It seemed very large, with an incredible number of bony peaks and dormers outlined against the sky, and even a weathervane in some vague animal-shape that stood atop a ruined turret grazed by moonlight. But although the moon was as bright as before, it appeared to be considerably thinner, as if it had been worn down just like everything else in that neighborhood.

"It hasn't altered in the least," the doctor assured me. He was holding open the back door of the house and gesturing for me to approach.

"Perhaps no one's home," I suggested.

"Not at all – the door's unlocked. You see how he's expecting us?"

"There don't appear to be any lights in use."

"Mr. Catch likes to conserve on certain expenses. A minor mania of his. But in other ways he's quite extravagant. And by no means is he a poor man. Watch yourself on the porch – some of these boards are not what they once were."

As soon as I was standing by the doctor's side he removed a flashlight from the pocket of his overcoat, shining a path into the dark interior of the house. Once inside, that yellowish swatch of illumination began flitting around in the blackness. It settled briefly in a cobwebbed corner of the ceiling, then ran down a blank battered wall and jittered along warped floor moldings. For a moment it revealed two suitcases, quite well used, at the bottom of a stairway. It slid smoothly up the stairway banister and flew straight to the floors above, where we heard some scraping sounds, as if an animal with long-nailed paws was moving about.

"Does Mr. Catch keep a pet?" I asked in a low voice.

"Why shouldn't he? But I don't think we'll find him up there."

We went deeper into the house, passing through many rooms which fortunately were unobstructed by furniture. Sometimes we crushed bits of broken glass underfoot; once I inadvertently kicked an empty bottle and sent it clanging across a bare floor. Reaching the far side of the house, we entered a long hallway flanked by several doors. All of them were closed and behind some of them we heard sounds similar to those being made on the second floor. We also heard footsteps slowly ascending a stairway. Then the last door at the end of the hallway opened, and a watery light pushed back some of the shadows ahead of us. A round-bodied little man was standing in the light, lazily beckoning to us.

"You're late, you're very late," he chided while leading us down into the cellar. His voice was high-pitched yet also quite raspy. "I was just about to leave."

"My apologies," said Dr. Dublanc, who sounded entirely sincere on this occasion. "Mr. Catch, allow me to introduce —"

"Never mind that Mr. Catch nonsense. You know well enough

what things are like for me, don't you, doctor? So let's get started, I'm on a schedule now."

In the cellar we paused amid the quivering light of candles, dozens of them positioned high and low, melting upon a shelf or an old crate or right on the filth-covered floor. Even so, there was a certain lack of definition among the surrounding objects, but I could see that an old-fashioned film projector had been set up on a table toward the center of the room, and a portable movie screen stood by the opposite wall. The projector was plugged into what appeared to be a small electrical generator humming on the floor.

"I think there are some stools or whatnot you can sit on," said Mr. Catch as he threaded the film around the spools of the projector. Then for the first time he spoke to me directly. "I'm not sure how much the doctor has explained about what I'm going to show you. Probably very little."

"Yes, and deliberately so," interrupted Dr. Dublanc. "If you just roll the film I think my purpose will be served, with or without explanations. What harm can it do?"

Mr. Catch made no reply. After blowing out some of the candles to darken the room sufficiently, he switched on the projector, which was a rather noisy mechanism. I worried that whatever dialogue or narration the film might contain would be drowned out between the whirring of the projector and the humming of the generator. But I soon realized that this was a silent film, a cinematic document that in every aspect of its production was thoroughly primitive, from its harsh light and coarse photographic texture to its nearly unintelligible scenario.

It seemed to serve as a visual record of scientific experiment, a laboratory demonstration in fact. The setting, nevertheless, was anything but clinical – a bare wall in a cellar which in some ways resembled, yet was not identical to, the one where I was viewing this film. And the subject was human: a shabby, unshaven, and unconscious derelict who had been propped up against a crude grayish wall. Not too many moments passed before the man began to stir. But his movements were not those of awakening from a deep stupor; they were only spasmodic twitchings of some energy which appeared to *inhabit* the old tramp. A torn pant leg wiggled for a second, then his chest heaved, as if with an incredible sigh. His left arm, no his right arm, flew up in the air and immediately collapsed. Soon his head began to wobble and it kept on wobbling, even though its owner remained in a state of profound obliviousness.

Something was making its way through the derelict's scalp,

rustling among the long greasy locks of an unsightly head. Part of it finally poked upwards – a thin sticklike thing. More of them emerged, dark wiry appendages that were bristling and bending and reaching for the outer world. At the end of each was a pair of slender snapping pincers. What ultimately broke through that shattered skull, pulling itself out with a wriggling motion of its many newborn arms, was approximately the size and proportions of a spider monkey. It had tiny translucent wings which fluttered a few times, glistening but useless, and was quite black, as if charred. Actually the creature seemed to be in an emaciated condition. When it turned its head toward the camera, it stared into the lens with malicious eyes and seemed to be chattering with its beaked mouth.

I whispered to Dr. Dublanc: "Please, I'm afraid that —"

"Exactly," he hissed back at me. "You are always afraid of the least upset in the order of things. You need to face certain realities so that you may free yourself of them."

Now it was my turn to give the doctor a skeptical glance. Yet I certainly realized that he was practicing something other than facile therapeutics. And even then our presence in that cellar – that cold swamp of shadows in which candles flickered like fireflies – seemed to be as much for Dr. Dublanc's benefit as it was for mine, if "benefit" is the proper word in this case.

"Those pills you gave me . . ."

"Shhh. Watch the film."

It was almost finished. After the creature had hatched from its strange egg, it proceeded very rapidly to consume the grubby derelict, leaving only a collection of bones attired in cast-off clothes. Picked perfectly clean, the skull leaned wearily to one side. And the creature, which earlier had been so emaciated, had grown rather plump with its feast, becoming bloated and meaty like an overfed dog. In the final sequence, a net was tossed into the scene, capturing the gigantic vermin and dragging it off camera. Then whiteness filled the screen and the film was flapping on its reel.

"Apparently Mr. Catch has left us," said the doctor, noticing that I remained under the spell of what I had just seen. Taking advantage of the moment, he tried to lend a certain focus or coloration to this experience. "You must understand," he continued, "that the integrity of material forms is only a prejudice, at most a point of view. This is not to mention the *substance* of those forms, which is an even more dubious state of affairs. That the so-called anatomy of a human being might burst forth as a fantastic insect should be no cause for consternation. I know that it may seem that in the past I've attempted to actually bolster your prejudices about a clockwork world of sunrise schedules and lunar routines. But this insistence has only had a paradoxical effect, just like certain drugs that in some people induce a reaction quite the opposite of the norm. All of my assurances have made you more confirmed in your suspicions that things are not *bolted down*, so to speak. And no more is that thing which we call the mind. We can both learn a great deal from Mr. Catch. Of course, I still recognize that there remain some unfortunate aspects to his case – there was only so much I could do for him – but nonetheless I think that he has gained rare and invaluable knowledge, the consequences notwithstanding.

"His research had taken him into areas where, how should I say, where the shapes and levels of phenomena, the multiple planes of natural existence, revealed their ability to establish new relationships with one another . . . to become interconnected, as it were, in ways that were never apparent. At some point everything became a blur for him, a sort of pandemonium of forces, a phantasmagoria of possibilities which he eagerly engaged. We can have no idea of the tastes and temptations that may emerge or develop in the course of such work . . . a curious hedonism that could not be controlled. Oh, the vagaries of omnipotence, breeder of indulgence. Well, Mr. Catch retreated in panic from his own powers, yet he could not put the pieces back as they had been: unheard of habits and responses had already ingrained themselves into his system, seemingly forever. The worst sort of slavery, no doubt, but how persuasively he spoke of the euphorias he had known, the infinitely diverse sensations beyond all common understanding. It was just this understanding that I required in order to free him of a life that, in its own fashion, had become as abysmal and problematic as your own – except he is at the opposite pole. Some middle ground must be established, some balance. How well I understand that now! This is why I have brought you two together. This is the only reason, however it may seem to you."

"It seems to me," I replied, "that Mr. Catch is no longer available."

Dr. Dublanc emitted the shadow of a laugh. "Oh, he's still in the house. You can be sure of that. Let's take a look upstairs."

He was, in fact, not far at all. Stepping into that hallway of closed doors at the top of the cellar stairs, we saw that one of those doors was now partially open and the room beyond it was faintly aglow. Without announcing us, Dr. Dublanc slowly pushed back the door until we could both see what had happened inside.

It was a small unfurnished room with a bare wooden floor upon which a candle had been fixed with its own drippings. The candlelight shone dimly on the full face of Mr. Catch, who seemed to have collapsed in a back corner of the room, lying somewhat askew. He was sweating, though it was cold in the room, and his eyes were half-closed in a kind of languorous exhaustion. But something was wrong with his mouth: it seemed to be muddied and enlarged, sloppily painted into a clown's oversized grin. On the floor beside him were, to all appearances, the freshly ravaged remains of one of those creatures in the film.

"You made me wait too long!" he suddenly shouted, opening his eyes fully and straightening himself up for a moment before his posture crumbled once again. He then repeated this outburst: "You couldn't help me and now you make me wait too long."

"It was in order to help you that I came here," the doctor said to him, yet all the time fixing his eyes on the mutilated carcass on the floor. When he saw that I had observed his greedy stare he regained himself. "I'm trying to help both of you the only way you can be helped. Show him, Mr. Catch, show him how you breed those amazing individuals."

Mr. Catch groped in his pants pocket, pulled out a large handkerchief, and wiped off his mouth. He was smiling a little idiotically, as if intoxicated, and worked himself to his feet. His body now seemed even more swollen and bulbous than before, really not quite human in its proportions. After replacing his handkerchief in one pocket, he reached down into the other, feeling around for some moments. "It's so simple," he explained in a voice that had become placid. And it was with a kind of giddy pride that he finally said, "Oh, here they are," and held out his open hand toward me. In the thick pad of his palm I could see two tiny objects that were shaped like eggs.

I turned abruptly to the doctor. "The pills you gave me."

"It was the only thing that could be done for you. I've tried so hard to help you both."

"I had a suspicion," said Mr. Catch, now reviving himself from his stupefaction. "I should never have brought you into this. Don't you realize that it's difficult enough without involving your own patients. The derelicts are one thing, but this is quite another. Well, my suitcases are packed. It's your operation now, doctor. Let me by, time to go."

Mr. Catch maneuvered himself from the room, and a few

moments later the sound of a door being slammed echoed throughout the house. The doctor kept close watch on me, waiting for some reaction, I suppose. Yet he was also listening very intently to certain sounds emanating from the rooms around us. The noise of restless skittering was everywhere.

"You understand, don't you?" asked the doctor. "Mr. Catch isn't the only one who has waited too long . . . far too long. I thought by now the pills would have had their effect."

I went into my pocket and removed the two little eggs which I had failed to swallow earlier. "I can't claim that I ever had much faith in your methods," I said. Then I tossed the pills at Dr. Dublanc who, speechless, caught them. "You won't mind if I return home by myself."

Indeed, he was relieved to see me go. As I traced my way back through the house I heard him running about and opening door after door, saying, "There you are, you beauties. There you are."

Although the doctor himself was now hopeless, I think that in some manner he had effected a cure in my case, however ephemeral it may have been. For during those first few moments on that hazy morning, when the taxi edged out of the alley and passed through that neighborhood of gnawed houses, I felt myself attain the middle ground Dr. Dublanc spoke of – the balancing point between an anxious flight from the abyss and the temptation to plunge into it. There was a great sense of escape, as if I could exist serenely outside the grotesque ultimatums of creation, an entranced spectator casting a clinical gaze at the chaotic tumult both around and within him.

But the feeling soon evaporated. "Could you go a little faster?" I said to the driver when it began to seem to me that we were making no progress in leaving that district behind: things again appeared to be changing, ready to burst forth from their sagging cocoons and take on uncertain forms. Even the pale morning sun seemed to be wavering from its proper proportions.

At the end of the ride, I was content to pay the extraordinary fare and return to my bed. The following day I started looking for a new doctor.

THE NIGHT SCHOOL

Instructor Carniero was holding class once again.

I discovered this fact on my return from a movie theater. It was late and I thought, "Why not take a short cut across the grounds of the school?" How much trouble this alternate route would save me was not precisely clear. Nevertheless, I suddenly felt that if I left the street I was walking along, which was lighted well enough, and proceeded across the grounds of the school, which were vast and dark, I would truly be taking a short cut. Besides, the night was actually quite cold, and when I looked down the front of my overcoat I saw that the single remaining button holding it together had become loose and possibly would not last much longer. So a short cut, taken on a very cold night, appeared entirely in order. In fact, any other course of action seemed unthinkable to me.

I entered the school grounds as if they were only a great park located in the midst of surrounding streets. The trees were set close and from the edge of the grounds I could not see the school hidden within them. *Look up here,* I almost heard someone say to me. I did look and saw that the branches overhead were without leaves; through their intertwining mesh the sky was fully visible. How bright and dark it was at the same time. *Bright* with a high, full moon shining among the spreading clouds, and *dark* with the shadows mingling within those clouds – a slowly flowing mass of mottled shapes, a kind of unclean outpouring from the black sewers of space.

I noticed that in one place these clouds were leaking down into the trees, trickling in a narrow rivulet across the wall of the night. But it was really smoke, dense and dirty, rising up to the sky. A short distance ahead, and well into the thickly wooded grounds of the school, I saw the spastic flames of a small fire among the trees. By the smell, I guessed that someone was burning refuse. Then I could see the misshapen metal drum spewing smoke, and the figures standing behind the firelight became visible to me, as I was to them.

"Class has resumed," one of them called out. "He's come back after all."

I knew these were others from the school, but their faces would not hold steady in the flickering light of the fire that warmed them. They seemed to be smudged by the smoke, greased by the odorous garbage burning in that dark metal drum, its outer surface almost glowing from the heat and flaking off in places.

"Look there," said another member of the group, pointing deeper into the school grounds. The massive outline of a building occupied the distance, a few of its windows sending a dim light through the trees. From the roof of the building a number of smokestacks stood out against the pale sky.

A wind rose up, droning loudly around us and breathing a noisy life into the fire in the decaying metal drum. I tried to shout above the confusion of sounds. "Was there an assignment?" I cried out. When I repeated the question, they only seemed to shrug. I left them hunched around the fire, assuming they would be along. The wind died and I could hear someone say the word "maniac," which was not spoken, I realized, either to me or about me.

Instructor Carniero, in his person, was rather vague to my mind. I had not been in the class very long before some disease – a terribly serious affliction, one of my classmates hinted – had caused his absence. So what remained, for me, was no more than the image of a slender gentleman in a dark suit, a gentleman with a darkish complexion and a voice thick with a foreign accent. "He's a Portuguese," one of the other students told me. "But he's lived almost everywhere." And I recalled a particular refrain spoken by that soft and heavy voice. "Look up here," he would say, usually singling out one of us who had not been attending to those diagrams he was incessantly creating on the blackboard. A few members of the class never needed to be called to attention in this manner, a certain small group who had been longtime students of the instructor and without distraction scrutinized the unceasing series of diagrams he would design upon the blackboard and then erase, only to construct again, with slight variation, a moment later.

Although I cannot claim that these often complex diagrams were not directly related to our studies, there were always extraneous elements within them which I never bothered to transcribe into my own notes for the class. They were a strange array of abstract symbols, frequently geometric figures altered in some way: various polygons with asymmetrical sides, trapezoids whose sides did not meet, semicircles with double or triple slashes across them, and many other examples of a deformed or corrupted scientific notation. These signs appeared to be primitive in essence, more relevant to magic than mathematics. The instructor marked them in an extremely rapid hand upon the blackboard, as if they were the words of his natural language. In most cases they formed a border around the perimeter of a strictly technical diagram, enclosing it and sometimes, it seemed, transforming its sense. Once a student actually questioned him regarding this apparently superfluous embellishment of the diagrams. Why did Instructor Carniero subject us to these bewildering symbols? "Because," he answered, "a true instructor must share everything."

As I proceeded across the grounds of the school, I felt certain changes had occurred since I was last there. The trees looked different somehow, even in the faint moonlight which shone through their bare branches. They had become so much thinner than I remembered, emaciated and twisted like broken bones that had never healed properly. Their bark seemed to be peeling away in soft layers, because it was not only fallen leaves I trudged through on my way to the school building, but also something like dark rags, strips of decomposed material. Even the clouds upon which the moon cast its glow were thin or rotted, unraveled by some process of degeneration in the highest atmosphere of the school grounds. There was also a scent of corruption, an enchanting fragrance really – like the mulchy rot of autumn or early spring – that I thought was emerging from the earth as I disturbed the strange debris strewn over it. But I noticed that this odor became more pungent as I approached the yellowish light of the school, and strongest as I finally reached the old building itself.

It was a four-story structure of dark scabby bricks that had been patched together in another era, a time so different that it might be imagined as belonging to an entirely alien history, one composed solely of nights well advanced, an after-hours history. How difficult it was to think of this place as if it had been constructed in the usual manner. Far easier to credit some fantastic legend that it had been erected by a consort of demons during the perpetual night of its past, and that its materials were absconded from other architectures, all of them defunct: ruined factories, crumbling prisons, abandoned orphanages, mausoleums long out of use. The school was indeed a kind of freakish growth in a dumping ground, a blossom of the cemetery or the cesspool. Here it was that Instructor Carniero, who had been everywhere, held his class.

On the lower floors of the building a number of lights were in use, weak as guttering candles. The highest story was blacked out, and I noticed that many of the windows were broken. Nevertheless, there was sufficient light to guide me into the school, even if the main hallway could hardly be seen to its end. And its walls appeared to be tarred over with something which exuded the same smell that filled the night outside the school. Without touching these walls, I used them to navigate my way into the school, following several of the greater and lesser hallways that burrowed throughout the building. Room after room passed on either side of me, their doorways filled with darkness or sealed by wide wooden doors whose coarse surfaces were pocked and peeling. Eventually I found a classroom where a light was on, though it was no brighter than the swarthy illumination of the hallway.

When I entered the room I saw that only some of the lamps were functioning, leaving certain areas in darkness while others were smeared with the kind of greasy glow peculiar to old paintings in oil. A few students were seated at desks here and there, isolated from one another and silent. By no means was there a full class, and no instructor stood at the lectern. The blackboard displayed no new diagrams but only the blurred remnants of past lessons.

I took a desk near the door, looking at none of the others as they did not look at me. In one of the pockets of my overcoat I turned up a little stub of a pencil but could find nothing on which to take notes. Without any dramatic gestures, I scanned the room for some kind of paper. The visible areas of the room featured various items of debris without offering anything that would allow me to transcribe the complex instructions and diagrams demanded by the class. I was reluctant to make a physical search of the shelves set into the wall beside me because they were very deep and from them drifted that same heady fragrance of decay.

Two rows to my left sat a man with several thick notebooks stacked on his desk. His hands were resting lightly on these notebooks, and his spectacled eyes were fixed on the empty lectern, or perhaps on the blackboard beyond. The space between the rows of desks was very narrow, so I was able to lean across the unoccupied desk that separated us and speak to this man who seemed to have a surplus of paper on which one could take notes, transcribe diagrams, and, in short, do whatever scribbling was demanded by the instructor of the class.

"Pardon me," I whispered to the staring figure. In a single, sudden movement, his head turned to face me. I remembered his pocked complexion, which had obviously grown worse since our class last met, and the eyes that squinted behind heavy lenses. "Do you have any paper you could share with me?" I asked, and was somehow surprised when he shifted his head toward his notebooks and began leafing through the pages of the topmost one. As he performed this action, I explained that I was unprepared for the class, that only a short time before did I learn it had resumed. This happened entirely by chance. I was coming home from a movie theater and decided to take a short cut across the school grounds.

By the time I was finished illuminating my situation, the other student was searching through his last notebook, the pages of which were as solidly covered with jottings and diagrams as the previous ones. I observed that his notes were different from those I had been taking for Instructor Carniero's course. They were far more detailed and scrupulous in their transcriptions of those strange geometric figures which I considered only as decorative intrusions in the instructor's diagrams. Some of the other students' notebook pages were wholly given over to rendering these figures and symbols to the exclusion of the diagrams themselves.

"I'm sorry," he said. "I don't seem to have any paper I could share with you."

"Well, could you tell me if there was an assignment?"

"That's very possible. You can never tell with this instructor. He's a Portuguese, you know. But he's been all over and knows everything. I think he's out of his mind. The kind of thing he's been teaching should have gotten him into trouble somewhere, and probably did. Not that he ever cared what happened to him, or to anyone else. That is, those that he could influence, and some more than others. The things he said to *us*. The lessons in measurement of cloacal forces. Time as a flow of sewage. The excrement of space, scatology of creation. The voiding of the self. The whole filthy integration of things and the nocturnal *product*, as he called it. Drowning in the pools of night . . ."

"I'm afraid I don't recall those concepts," I interrupted.

"You were new to the class. To tell the truth, it didn't seem you were paying attention. But soon enough he would have gotten through to you. Told you to look up there," he said, pointing to the blackboard. "You remember that much, don't you? He was very captivating, the instructor. And always ready for anything."

"I thought that he recovered from the sickness that caused his absence, that he was back teaching."

"Oh, he's back. He was always ready. But somewhere he must have made some enemies. Did you know that the class is now being held in another part of the school? I couldn't tell you where, since I haven't been with Instructor Carniero as long as some of the others. To tell the truth, I don't care where it's being held. Isn't it enough that we're here, in this room?"

I had little idea how to answer this question and understood almost nothing of what the man had been trying to explain to me. It did seem clear, or at least very possible, that the class had moved to a different part of the school. But I had no reason to think that the other students seated elsewhere in the room would be any more helpful on this point than the one who had now turned his spectacled face away from me. Wherever the class was being held, I was still in need of paper on which to take notes, transcribe diagrams, and so forth. This could not be accomplished by staying in that room where everyone and everything was degenerating into the surrounding darkness.

For a time I wandered about the hallways on the main floor of the school, keeping clear of the walls which certainly were thickening with a dark substance, an odorous sap with the intoxicating potency of a thousand molting autumns or the melting soil of spring. The stuff was running from top to bottom down the walls, leaking from above and dulling the already dim light in the hallways.

I began to hear echoing voices coming from a distant part of the school I had never visited before. No words were decipherable, but it sounded as if the same ones were being repeated in a more or less constant succession of cries that rang hollow in the halls. I followed them and along the way met up with someone walking slowly from the opposite direction. He was dressed in dirty workclothes and almost blended in with the shadows which were so abundant in the school that night. I stopped him as he was about to shuffle straight past me. Turning an indifferent gaze in my direction was a pair of yellowish eyes set in a thin face with a coarse, patchy complexion. The man scratched at the left side of his forehead and some dry flakes of skin fell away. I asked him:

"Could you tell me where Instructor Carniero is holding class tonight?"

He looked at me for some moments, and then pointed a finger at the ceiling. "Up there," he said.

"On which floor?"

"The top one," he answered, as if a little amazed at my ignorance.

"There are a lot of rooms on that floor," I said.

"And every one of them his. Nothing to be done about that. But I have to keep the rest of this place in some kind of condition. I don't see how I can do that with him up there." The man glanced around at the stained walls and let out a single, wheezing laugh.

"It only gets worse. Starts to get to you if you go up any further. Listen. Hear the rest of them?" Then he groaned with disgust and went on his way. But before he was entirely out of view he looked over his shoulder and shouted to me. "There's another one you might see. A new one. Just so you'll know."

But by that point I felt that any knowledge I had amassed – whether or not it concerned Instructor Carniero and his night classes – was being taken away from me piece by piece. The man in dirty workclothes had directed me to the top floor of the school. Yet I remembered seeing no light on that floor when I first approached the building. The only thing that seemed to occupy that floor was an undiluted darkness, a darkness far greater than the night itself, a consolidated darkness, something clotted with its own density. "The nocturnal *product*," I could hear the spectacled student reminding me in a hollow voice. "Drowning in the pools of night."

What could I know about the ways of the school? I had not been in attendance very long, not nearly long enough, it seemed. I felt myself a stranger to my fellow students, especially since they revealed themselves to be divided in their ranks, as though among the initiatory degrees of a secret society. I did not know the coursework in the way some of the others seemed to know it and in the spirit that the instructor intended it to be known. My turn had not yet come to be commanded by Instructor Carniero to look up at the hieroglyphs of the blackboard and comprehend them fully. So I did not understand the doctrines of a truly *septic* curriculum, the science of a spectral pathology, philosophy of absolute disease, the metaphysics of things sinking into a common disintegration or rising together, flowing together, in their dark rottenness. Above all, I did not know the instructor himself: the places he had been . . . the things he had seen and done . . . the experiences he had embraced . . . the laws he had ignored . . . the troubles he had caused . . . the enemies he had made. The fate that he had incurred, gladly, upon himself and others. And of course I could not know anything of that "new one" about whom the man in the dirty workclothes had warned me, the one who may have also been an instructor, after a fashion – the instructor's instructor . . . and his accommodating enemy.

I was close to a shaft of stairways leading to the upper floors of the school. The voices became louder, though not more distinct, as I approached the stairwell. The first flight of stairs seemed very long and steep and badly defined in the dim light of the hallway. The landing at the top of the stairs was barely visible for the poor light and unreflecting effluvia that here moved even more thickly down the walls. But it did not appear to possess any real substance, no sticky surface or viscous texture as one might have supposed, only a kind of density like heavy smoke, filthy smoke from some smoldering source of expansive corruption. It carried the scent of corruption as well as the sight, only now it was more potent with the nostalgic perfume of autumn decay or the feculent muskiness of a spring thaw.

As I reached the first landing of the stairway, I nearly overlooked the figure standing motionless in a corner. This was certainly the newcomer to the school whose presence had been foretold to me. He was almost naked and his skin was of a darkness, an excremental darkness, that made him blend into the obscurity of the stairwell. His face was leathery and deeply lined, incredibly old, while the hair surrounding it was stringy and had been hung with objects that looked like tiny bones and teeth. They were tied up within long strands of hair and jangled in the darkness. Around the neck of this figure was a rope or thin strap which was strung with little skulls, dismembered claws, and whole withered bodies of creatures I could not name. Although I stood for some moments quite near to the ancient savage, he took no notice of me. His large, fierce eyes stared upwards, fixed upon the heights of the stairwell. His thin peeling lips were alive with a silent language, mouthing words without sound. But I could not read his speech and so turned away from him.

I climbed another flight of stairs, which ascended in the opposite direction from the first, and reached the second floor. Each of the four stories of the school had two flights of stairs going in opposite directions between them, with a narrow landing that intervened before one could complete the ascent to a new floor. The second floor was not as well-lighted as the one below, and the walls there were even worse: their surface had been wholly obscured by that smoky blackness which seeped down from above, the blackness so richly odorous with the offal of worlds in decline or perhaps with the dark compost of those about to be born, the great rottenness in which all things are founded, the fundament of wild disease.

On the stairs that led up to the third floor I saw the first of them – a young man who was seated on the lower steps of this flight and who had been one of the instructor's most assiduous students. He was absorbed in his own thoughts and did not acknowledge me until I spoke to him.

"*The class?*" I said, stressing the words into a question.

He gazed at me calmly. "The instructor suffered a terrible

disease, a great disease." This was all he said. Then he returned within himself and would not respond.

There were others, similarly positioned higher on the stairs or squatting on the landing. The voices were still echoing in the stairwell, chanting a blurred phrase in unison. But the voices did not belong to any of these students, who sat silent and entranced amid the litter of pages torn from their voluminous notebooks. Pieces of paper with strange symbols on them lay scattered everywhere like fallen leaves. They rustled as I walked through them toward the stairs leading to the highest story of the school.

The walls in the stairwell were now swollen with a blackness that was the very face of a plague – pustulant, scabbed, and stinking terribly. It was reaching to the edges of the floor, where it drifted and churned like a black fog. Only in the moonlight that shone through a hallway window could I see anything of the third floor. I stopped there, for the stairs to the fourth were deep in blackness. Only a few faces rose above it and were visible in the moonlight. One of them was staring at me, and, without prompting, spoke.

"The instructor suffered a terrible disease. But he is holding class again. He could suffer anything and did not shun enemies. He had been everywhere. Now he is in a new place, somewhere he has not been." The voice paused and the interval was filled by the many voices calling and crying from the total blackness that prevailed over the heights of the stairwell and buried everything beneath it like tightly packed earth in a grave. Then the single voice said: "The instructor died in the night. You see? He is with the night. You hear the voices? They are with him. All of them are with him and he is with the night. The night has spread itself within him, the disease of the night has spread its blackness. He who has been everywhere may go anywhere with the spreading disease of the night. Listen. The Portuguese is calling to us."

I listened and finally the voices became clear. *Look up here*, they said. *Look up here.*

The fog of blackness had now unfurled down to me and lay about my feet, gathering there and rising. For a time I could not move or speak or form any thoughts. Inside me, everything was becoming black. The blackness was quivering inside me, quivering everywhere and making everything black. It was holding me, and the voices were saying to me, "Look up here, look up here." And I began to look. But I was enduring something that I could never endure, that I was not prepared to endure. The blackness quivering inside me could not go on to its end. I could not remain where I was or look up to the place where the voices called out to me.

Then the blackness was no longer inside me, and I was no longer inside the school but outside of it, almost as if I had suddenly awakened there. Without looking back, I retraced my steps across the grounds of the school, forgetting about the short cut I had meant to take that night. I passed those students who were still standing around the fire burning in an old metal drum. They were feeding the bright flames with pages from their notebooks, pages scribbled to blackness with all those diagrams and freakish signs. Some of those among the group called out to me. "Did you see the Portuguese?" one of them shouted above the noise of the fire and the wind. "Did you hear anything about an assignment?" another voice cried out, and then I heard them all laughing among themselves as I made my way back to the streets I had left before entering the school grounds. I moved with such haste that the loose button on my overcoat finally came off by the time I reached the street outside the grounds of the school.

As I walked beneath the streetlights, I held the front of my overcoat together and tried to keep my eyes on the sidewalk before me. But I might have heard a voice bid me: "Look up here," because I did look, if only for a moment. Then I saw the sky was clear of all clouds, and the full moon was shining in the black pool of space. It was shining bright and blurry, as if coated with a luminous mold, floating like a lamp in the great sewers of the night.

THE GLAMOUR

It had long been my practice to wander late at night and often to attend movie theaters at this time. But something else was involved on the night I went to that theater in a part of town I had never visited before. A new tendency, a mood or penchant formerly unknown to me, seemed to lead the way. How difficult to say anything precise about this mood that overcame me, because it seemed to belong to my surroundings as much as to my self. As I advanced farther into that part of town I had never visited before, my attention was drawn to a certain aspect of things – a fine aura of fantasy radiating from the most common sights, places and objects that were both bluffed and brightened as they projected themselves into my vision.

Despite the lateness of the hour, there was an active glow cast through many of the shop windows in that part of town. Along one particular avenue, the starless evening was glazed by these lights, these diamonds of plate glass set within old buildings of dark brick. I paused before the display window of a toy store and was entranced by a chaotic tableau of preposterous excitation. My eyes followed several things at once: the fated antics of mechanized monkeys that clapped tiny cymbals or somersaulted uncontrollably; the destined pirouettes of a music-box ballerina; the grotesque wobbling of a newly sprung jack-in-the-box. The inside of the store was a Christmas-tree clutter of merchandise receding into a background that looked shadowed and empty. An old man with a smooth pate and angular eyebrows stepped forward to the front window and began rewinding some of the toys to keep them in ceaseless gyration. While performing this task he suddenly looked up at me, his face expressionless.

I moved down the street, where other windows framed little worlds so strangely picturesque and so dreamily illuminated in the shabby darkness of that part of town. One of them was a bakery whose window display was a gallery of sculptured frosting, a winter landscape of swirling, drifting whiteness, of snowy rosettes and layers of icy glitter. At the center of the glacial kingdom was a pair of miniature people frozen atop a many-tiered wedding cake. But beyond the brilliant arctic scene I saw only the deep blackness of an establishment that kept short hours. Standing outside another window nearby, I was uncertain if the place was open for business or not. A few figures were positioned here and there within faded lighting reminiscent of an old photograph, though it seemed they were beings of the same kind as the window dummies of this store, which apparently trafficked in dated styles of clothing. Even the faces of the mannikins, as a glossy light fell upon them, wore the placidly enigmatic expressions of a different time.

But in fact there actually were several places doing business at that hour of the night and in that part of town, however scarce potential customers appeared to be on this particular street. I saw no one enter or exit the many doors along the sidewalk; a canvas awning that some proprietor had neglected to roll up for the night was flapping in the wind. Nevertheless, I did sense a certain vitality around me and felt the kind of acute anticipation that a child might experience at a carnival, where each lurid attraction incites fantastic speculations, while unexpected desires arise for something which has no specific qualities in the imagination yet seems to be only a few steps away. Thus my mood had not abandoned me but only grew stronger, a possessing impulse without object.

Then I saw the marquee for a movie theater, something I might easily have passed by. For the letters spelling out the name of the theater were broken and unreadable, while the title on the marquee was similarly damaged, as though stones had been thrown at it, a series of attempts made to efface the words that I finally deciphered. The feature being advertised that night was called *The Glamour*.

When I reached the front of the theater I found that the row of doors forming the entrance had been barricaded by crosswise planks with notices posted upon them warning that the building had been condemned. This action was apparently taken some time ago, judging by the weathered condition of the boards that blocked my way and the dated appearance of the notices stuck upon them. In any case, the marquee was still illuminated, if rather poorly. So I was not surprised to see a double-faced sign propped up on the sidewalk, an inconspicuous little board that read: ENTRANCE TO THE THEATER. Beneath these words was an arrow pointing into an alleyway which separated the theater from the remaining buildings on the block. Peeking into this dark opening, this aperture in the otherwise solid facade of that particular street, I saw only a long, narrow corridor with a single light set far into its depths. The light shone with a strange shade of purple, like that of a freshly exposed heart, and appeared to be positioned over a doorway leading into the theater. It had long been my practice to attend movie theaters late at night – this is what I reminded myself. But whatever reservations I felt at the time were easily overcome by a new surge of the mood I was experiencing that night in a part of town I had never visited before.

The purple lamp did indeed mark a way into the theater, casting a kind of arterial light upon a door that reiterated the word "entrance." Stepping inside, I entered a tight hallway where the walls glowed a deep pink, very similar in shade to that little beacon in the alley but reminding me more of a richly blooded brain than a beating heart. At the end of the hallway I could see my reflection in a ticket window, and approaching it I noticed that those walls so close to me were veiled from floor to ceiling with what appeared to be cobwebs. These cobwebs were also strewn upon the carpet leading to the ticket window, wispy shrouds that did not scatter as I walked over them, as if they had securely bound themselves to the carpet's worn and shallow fiber, or were growing out of it like postmortem hairs on a corpse.

There was no one behind the ticket window, no one I could see in that small space of darkness beyond the blur of purple-tinted glass in which my reflection was held. Nevertheless, a ticket was protruding from a slot beneath the semi-circular cutaway at the bottom of the window, sticking out like a paper tongue. A few hairs lay beside it.

"Admission is free," said a man who was now standing in the doorway beside the ticket booth. His suit was well-fitted and neat, but his face appeared somehow in a mess, bristled over all its contours. His tone was polite, even passive, when he said, "The theater is under new ownership."

"Are you the manager?" I asked.

"I was just on my way to the rest room."

Without further comment he drifted off into the darkness of the theater. For a moment something floated in the empty space he left in the doorway – a swarm of filaments like dust that scattered or settled before I stepped through. And in those first few seconds inside, the only thing I could see were the words "rest room" glowing above a door as it slowly closed.

I manuevered with caution until my sight became sufficient to the dark and allowed me to find a door leading to the auditorium of the movie theater. But once inside, as I stood at the summit of a sloping aisle, all previous orientation to my surroundings underwent a setback. The room was illuminated by an elaborate chandelier centered high above the floor, as well as a series of light fixtures along either of the side walls. I was not surprised by the dimness of the lighting nor by its hue, which made shadows appear faintly bloodshot – a sickly, liverish shade that might be witnessed in an operating room where a torso lies open on the table, its entrails a palette of pinks and reds and purples . . . diseased viscera imitating all the shades of sunset.

However, my perception of the theater auditorium remained problematic not because of any oddities of illumination but for another reason. While I experienced no difficulty in mentally registering the elements around me – the separate aisles and rows of seats, the curtainflanked movie screen, the well-noted chandelier and wall lights – it seemed impossible to gain a sense of these features in simple accord with their appearances. I saw nothing that I have not described, yet . . . the roundbacked seats were at the same time rows of headstones in a graveyard; the aisles were endless filthy alleys, long desolate corridors in an old asylum, or the dripping passages of a sewer narrowing into the distance; the pale movie screen was a dust-blinded window in a dark unvisited cellar, a mirror gone rheumy with age in an abandoned house; the chandelier and smaller fixtures were the facets of murky crystals embedded in the sticky walls of an unknown cavern. In other words, this movie theater was merely a virtual image, a veil upon a complex collage of other places, all of which shared certain qualities that were projected into my vision, as though the things I saw were possessed by something I could not see.

But as I lingered in the theater auditorium, settling in a seat toward the back wall, I realized that even on the level of plain appearances there was a peculiar phenomenon I had not formerly observed, or at least had yet to perceive to its fullest extent. I am speaking of the cobwebs.

When I first entered the theater I saw them clinging to the walls and carpeting. Now I saw how much they were a part of the theater and how I had mistaken the nature of these long pale threads. Even in the hazy purple light, I could discern that they had penetrated into the fabric of the seats in the theater, altering the weave in its depths and giving it a slight quality of movement, the slow curling of thin smoke. It seemed the same with the movie screen, which might have been a great rectangular web, tightly woven and faintly in motion, vibrating at the touch of some unseen force. I thought: "Perhaps this subtle and pervasive *wriggling* within the theater may clarify the tendency of its elements to suggest other things and other places thoroughly unlike a simple theater auditorium, a process parallel to the ever-mutating images of dense clouds." All textures in the theater appeared similarly affected, without control over their own nature, but I could not clearly see as high as the chandelier. Even some of the others in the audience, which was small and widely scattered about the auditorium, were practically invisible to my eyes.

Furthermore, there may have been something in my mood that night, given my sojourn in a part of town I had never visited before, that influenced what I was able to see. And this mood had become steadily enhanced since I first stepped into the theater, and indeed from the moment I looked upon the marquee advertising a feature entitled *The Glamour*. Having at last found a place among the quietly expectant audience of the theater, I began to suffer an exacerbation of this mood. Specifically, I sensed a greater proximity to the point of focus for my mood that night, a tingling closeness to something quite literally *behind the scene*. Increasingly I became unconcerned with anything except the consummation or terminus of this abject and enchanting adventure. Consequences were evermore difficult to regard from my tainted perspective.

Therefore I was not hesitant when this focal point for my mood suddenly felt so near at hand, as close as the seat directly behind my own. I was quite sure this seat had been empty when I selected mine, that all the seats for several rows around me were unoccupied. And I would have been aware if someone had arrived to fill this seat directly behind me. Nevertheless, like a sudden chill announcing bad weather, there was now a definite presence I could feel at my back, a force of sorts that pressed itself upon me and inspired a surge of dark elation. But when I looked around, not quickly yet fully determined, I saw no occupant in the seat behind me, nor in any seat between me and the back wall of the theater. I continued to stare at the empty seat because my sensation of a vibrant presence there was unrelieved. And in my staring I perceived that the fabric of the seat, the inner webbing of swirling fibers, had composed a pattern in the image of a face – an old woman's face with an expression of avid malignance, floating amidst wild shocks of twisting hair. The face itself was a portrait of atrocity, a grinning image of lust for sites and ceremonies of mayhem. It was formed of those hairs stitching themselves together.

All the stringy, writhing cobwebs of that theater, as I now discovered, were the reaching tendrils of a vast netting of hairs. And in this discovery my mood of the evening, which had delivered me to a part of town I had never visited before and to that very theater, only became more expansive and defined, taking in scenes of graveyards and alleyways, reeking sewers and wretched corridors of insanity as well as the immediate vision of an old theater that now, as I had been told, was under new ownership. But my mood abruptly faded, along with the face in the fabric of the theater seat, when a voice spoke to me. It said:

"You must have seen her, by the looks of you."

A man sat down one seat away from mine. It was not the same person I had met earlier; this one's face was nearly normal, although his suit was littered with hair that was not his own.

"So did you see her?" he asked.

"I'm not sure what I saw," I replied.

He seemed almost to burst out giggling, his voice trembling on the edge of a joyous hysteria. "You would be sure enough if there had been a private encounter, I can tell you."

"Something was happening, then you sat down."

"Sorry," he said. "Did you know that the theater has just come under new ownership?"

"I didn't notice what the showtimes are."

"Showtimes?"

"For the feature."

"Oh, there isn't any feature. Not as such."

"But there must be . . . something," I insisted.

"Yes, there's something," he replied excitedly, his fingers stroking his cheek.

"What, exactly. And these cobwebs . . ."

But the lights were going down into darkness. "Quiet now," he whispered. "It's about to begin."

The screen before us was glowing a pale purple in the blackness, although I heard no sounds from the machinery of a movie projector. Neither were there any sounds connected with the images which were beginning to take form on the screen, as if a lens were being focused on a microscopic world. And in some way the movie screen might have been a great glass slide that projected to gigantic proportions a landscape of organism normally hidden from our sight. But as these visions coalesced and clarified, I recognized them as something I had already seen, more accurately *sensed*, in that theater. The images were appearing on the screen as if a pair of disembodied eyes was moving within venues of profound morbidity and degeneration. Here was the purest essence of those places I had felt were superimposing themselves on the genuinely tangible aspects of the theater, those graveyards, alleys, decayed corridors, and subterranean passages whose spirit had intruded on another locale and altered it. Yet the places now revealed on the movie screen were without an identity I could name: they were the fundament of the sinister and seamy regions which cast their spectral ambience on the reality of the theater but which were themselves merely the shadows, the superficial counterparts of a deeper, more obscure realm. Farther and farther into it we were being taken.

The all-pervasive purple coloration could now be seen as emanating from the labyrinth of a living anatomy: a compound of the reddish, bluish, palest pink structures, all of them morbidly inflamed and lesioned to release a purple light. We were being guided through a catacomb of putrid chambers and cloisters, the most secreted ways and waysides of an infernal land. Whatever these spaces may once have been, they were now habitations for ceremonies of a private sabbath. The hollows in their fleshy, gelatinous integuments streamed with something like moss, a fungus in thin strands that were threading themselves into translucent tissue and quivering beneath it like veins. It was the sabbath ground, secret and unconsecrated, but it was also the theater of an insane surgery. The hair-like sutures stitched among the yielding entrails, unseen hands designing unnatural shapes and systems, weaving a nest in which the possession would take place, a web wherein the bits and pieces of the anatomy could be consumed at leisure. There seemed to be no one in sight, yet everything was scrutinized from an intimate perspective, the viewpoint of that invisible surgeon, the weaver and webmaker, the old puppet-master who was setting the helpless creature with new strings and placing him under the control of a new owner. And through her eyes, entranced, we witnessed the work being done.

Then those eyes began to withdraw, and the purple world of the organism receded into purple shadows. When the eyes finally emerged from where they had been, the movie screen was filled with the face and naked chest of a man. His posture was rigid, betraying a state of paralysis, and his eyes were fixed, yet strikingly alive. "She's showing us," whispered the man who was sitting nearby me. "She has taken him. He cannot feel who he is any longer, only her presence within him."

This statement, at first sight of the possessed, seemed to be the case. Certainly such a view of the situation provided a terrific stimulus to my own mood of the evening, urging it toward culmination in a type of degraded rapture, a seizure of panic oblivion. Nonetheless, as I stared at the face of the man on the screen, he became known to me as the one I encountered in the vestibule of the theater. The recognition was difficult, however, because his flesh was now even more obscured by the webs of hair woven through it, thick as a full beard in spots. His eyes were also quite changed and glared out at the audience with a ferocity that suggested he indeed served as the host of great evil. But all the same, there was something in those eyes that belied the fact of a complete transformation – an awareness of the bewitchment and an appeal for deliverance. Within the next few moments, this observation assumed a degree of substance.

For the man on the movie screen regained himself, although briefly and in limited measure. His effort of will was evident in the subtle contortions of his face, and his ultimate accomplishment was modest enough: he managed to open his mouth in order to scream. Of course no sound was projected from the movie screen, which only played a music of images for eyes that would see what should not be seen. Thus, a disorienting effect was created, a sensory dissonance which resulted in my being roused from the mood of the evening, its spell over me echoing to nothingness. Because the scream that resonated in the auditorium had originated in another part of the theater, a place beyond the auditorium's towering back wall.

Consulting the man who was sitting near me, I found him oblivious to my comments about the scream within the theater. He seemed neither to hear nor see what was happening around him and what was happening to him. Long wiry hairs were sprouting from the fabric of the seats, snaking low along their arms and along every part of them. The hairs had also penetrated into the cloth of the man's suit, but I could not make him aware of what was happening. Finally I rose to leave, because I could feel the hairs tugging to keep me in position. As I stood up they ripped away from me like stray threads pulled from a sleeve or pocket.

No one else in the auditorium turned away from the man on the movie screen, who had lost the ability to cry out and relapsed into a paralytic silence. Proceeding up the aisle I glanced above at a rectangular opening high in the back wall of the theater, the window-like slot from which images of a movie are projected. Framed within this aperture was the silhouette of what looked like an old woman with long and wildly tangled hair. I could see her eyes gazing fierce and malignant at the purple glow of the movie screen. And from these eyes were sent forth two shafts of the purest purple light that shot through the darkness of the auditorium.

Exiting the theater the way I had come in, it was not possible to ignore the words "rest room", so brightly were they now shining. But the lamp over the side door in the alley was dead; the sign reading ENTRANCE TO THE THEATER was gone. Even the letters spelling out the name of the feature that evening had been taken down. So this had been the last performance. Henceforth the theater would be closed to the public.

Also closed, if only for the night, were all the other businesses along that particular street in a part of town I had never visited before. The hour was late, the shop windows were dark. But how sure I was that in each one of those dark windows I passed was the even darker silhouette of an old woman with glowing eyes and a great head of monstrous hair.

THE LIBRARY OF
BYZANTIUM

Father Sevich's visit

In whatever corner of our old house I happened to find myself, I could always sense the arrival of a priest. Even in the most distant rooms of the upper floors, those rooms which had been closed up and which were forbidden to me, I would suddenly experience a very certain feeling. The climate of my surroundings then became inexplicably altered in a manner at first vaguely troublesome and afterward rather attractive. It was as if a new presence had invaded the very echoes of the air and had entered into the mellow afternoon sunlight which fell in stripes and squares across the dark wooden floors and upon the pale contortions of the ancient wallpaper. All around me invisible games had begun. My earliest philosophy regarding the great priestly tribe was therefore not a simple one by any means; rather, it comprised a thick maze of propositions, a labyrinthine layering of systems in which abstract dread and a bizarre sort of indebtedness were forever confronting each other.

In retrospect, the prelude to Fr. Sevich's visit seems to me as crucial, and as introductory to later events, as the visit itself; so I have no qualms about lingering upon these lonely moments. For much of that day I had been secluded in my room, intently pursuing a typical activity of my early life and in the process badly ravaging what previously had been a well-made bed. Having sharpened my pencil innumerable times, and having worn down a thick gray eraser into a stub, I was ready to give myself up as a relentless failure. The paper itself seemed to defy me, laying snares within its coarse texture to thwart my every aim. Yet this rebellious mood was a quite recent manifestation: I had been allowed to fill in nearly the entire scene before this breakdown in relations between myself and my materials.

The completed portion of my drawing was an intense impression of a monastic fantasy, evoking the cloistral tunnels and the vaulted penetralia without attempting a guide-book representation of them. Nevertheless, the absolute precision of two specific elements in the picture was very much on my mind. The first of these was a single row of columns receding in sharp perspective, a diminishing file of rigid sentinels starkly etched into the surrounding gloom. The second element was a figure who had hidden himself behind one of these columns and was peering out of the shadows at something frightful beyond the immediate scene. Only the figure's face and a single column-clutching hand were to be rendered. The hand I executed well enough, but when it came to the necessary features of fear which needed to be implanted on that countenance – there was simply no way to capture the desired effect. My wish was to have every detail of the unseen horror clearly readable in the facial expression of the seer himself, a maddening task and, at the time, a futile one. Every manipulation of my soft-pointed pencil betrayed me, masking my victim with a series of completely irrelevant expressions. First it was misty-eyed wonder, and then a kind of cretinous bafflement. At one point the gentleman appeared to be smiling in an almost amiable way at his imminent doom.

Thus, one may comprehend how easily I succumbed to the distraction of Fr. Sevich's visit. My pencil stopped dead on the paper, my eyes began to wander about, checking the curtains, the corners, and the open closet for something that had come to play hide-and-seek with me. I heard footsteps methodically treading down the long hallway and stopping at my bedroom door. My father's voice, muffled by solid wood, instructed me to make an appearance downstairs. There was a visitor.

My frustrations of that afternoon must have disadvantaged me somewhat, because I completely fell into the trap of expectation: that is, I believed our caller was only Fr. Orne, who often dropped by and who served as a kind of ecclesiastical familiar of our family. But when I descended the stairs and saw that strange black cloak drooping down from the many-pegged rack beside the front door, and when I saw the wide-brimmed hat of the same color hanging beside it like an age-old companion, I realized my error.

From the parlor came the sound of soft conversation, the softest part of which was supplied by Fr. Sevich himself, whose speaking voice was no more than a sleepy whisper. He was seated, quite fairly, in one of our most expansive armchairs, toward which destination my mother maneuvered me as soon as I entered the room. During the presentation I was silent, and for a few suspenseful moments afterward continued to remain so. Fr. Sevich thought that I was fascinated into muteness by his fancy walking stick, and he said as much. At that moment the priest's voice was infiltrated, to my amazement, by a foreign accent I had not previously noticed. He handed his cane over to me for examination, and I hefted the formidable length of wood a few times. However, the real source of my fascination lay not in his personal accessories, but in the priest's own person, specifically in the chalky-looking texture of his very round face.

Invited to join the afternoon gathering, I was seated in a chair identical to the one supporting Fr. Sevich's bulk, and angled slightly toward it. But my alliance to this group was in body only: I contributed not a word to the ensuing conversation, nor did I understand those words that now filled the parlor with their drowsy music. My concentration on the priest's face had wholly exiled me from the world of good manners and polite talk. It was not just the pale and powdery cast of his complexion, but also a certain emptiness, a look of incompleteness that made me think of some unfinished effigy in a toymaker's workshop. The priest smiled and squinted and performed several other common manipulations, none of which resulted in a true facial expression. Something vital to expression was missing, some essential spirit in which all expressions are born and evolve toward their unique destiny. And, to put it graphically, his flesh simply did not have the appearance of flesh.

At some point my mother and father found an excuse to leave me alone with Fr. Sevich, presumably to allow his influence to have a free reign over me, so that his sacerdotal presence might not be adulterated by the profanity of theirs. This development was in no way surprising, since it was my parents' secret hope that someday my life would take me at least as far as seminary school, if not beyond that into the purple-robed mysteries of priesthood.

In the first few seconds after my parents had abandoned the scene, Fr. Sevich and I looked each other over, almost as if our previous introduction had counted for naught. And soon a very interesting thing happened: Fr. Sevich's face underwent a change, one in favor of the soul which had formerly been interred within his most obscure depths. Now, from out of that chalky tomb emerged a face of true expression, a masterly composition of animated eyes, living mouth, and newly flushed cheeks. This transformation, however, must have been achieved at a certain cost; for what his face gained in vitality, the priest's voice lost in volume. His words now sounded like those of a hopeless invalid, withered things reeking of medicines and prayers. What their exact topic of discourse was I'm not completely sure, but I do recall that my drawings were touched upon. Fr. Orne, of course, was already familiar with these fledgling works, and it seemed that something in their pictorial nature had caused him to mention them to his colleague who was visiting us from the old country. Something had caused Fr. Orne to single my pictures out, as it were, among the sights of his parish.

Fr. Sevich spoke of those scribblings of mine in a highly circuitous and rarefied fashion, as if they were a painfully delicate subject which threatened a breach in our acquaintanceship. I did not grasp what constituted his tortuous and subtle interest in my pictures, but this issue was somewhat clarified when he showed me something: a little book he was carrying within the intricate folds of his clerical frock.

The covering of the book had the appearance of varnished wood, all darkish and embellished with undulating grains. At first I thought that this object would feel every bit as brittle as it looked, until Fr. Sevich actually placed it in my hands and allowed me to discover that its deceptive binding was in fact extremely supple, even slippery. There were no words on the front of the book, only two thin black lines which intersected to create a cross. On closer examination, I observed that the horizontal beam of the cross had, on either end, squiggly little extensions resembling tiny hands. And the vertical beam appeared to widen at its vertex into something like a little bulb, so that the black decoration formed a sort of stickman.

At Fr. Sevich's instruction, I randomly opened the book and thumbed over several of its incredibly thin pages, which were more like layers of living tissue than dead pulp. There seemed to be an infinite number of them, with no possibility of ever reaching the beginning or the end of the volume merely by turning over the pages one by one. The priest warned me to be careful and not to harm any of these delicate leaves, for the book was very old, very fragile, and unusually precious.

The language in which the book was written resisted all but imaginary identifications by one who was as limited in years and learning as I was then. Even now, memory will not permit me to improve upon my initial speculation that the book was composed in some exotic tongue of antiquity. But its profusion of pictures alleviated many frustrations and illuminated the darkness of the book's secret symbols. In these examples of the art of the woodcut,

I could almost read that collection of sermons, of prayers and homilies, every one of which devoted itself with a single-minded insistence to wearing away at a single theme: *salvation through suffering*.

It was this chamber of sacred horrors that Fr. Sevich believed would catch my eye and my interest. How few of us, he explained, really understood the holy purpose of such images of torment, the divine destiny toward which the paths of anguish have always led. The production, and even the mere contemplation, of these missals of blessed agony was one of the great lost arts, he openly lamented. Then he began to tell me about a certain library in the old country, but my attention was already wandering along its own paths, and my eye was inextricably caught by the dense landscape of these old woodcuts. One scene in particular appeared exemplary of the book's soul.

The central figure in this illustration was bearded and emaciated, with his head bowed, hands folded, and knees bent. Contracted in an attitude of prayerful pleading, he seemed to be suspended in mid-air. All around this bony ascetic were torturing demons, surprisingly effective owing to, or perhaps despite, the artist's brutal technique and the sparseness of precise detail. An exception to this general rule of style was a single squatting devil whose single eye had clusters of perfect little eyes growing out of it; and each of the smaller eyes had its own bristling lashes that sprouted like weeds, an explosion of minute grotesquerie. (And now that I reflect on the matter, all of the illustrations that I saw contained at least one such exception.) The ascetic's own eyes were the focus of his particular form: stark white openings in an otherwise dark face, with two tiny pupils rolling deliriously heavenward. But what was it about the transports written on this face which inspired in me the sense of things other than fear, or pain, or even piety? In any event, I did find inspiration in this terrible scene, and tried to make an imprint of it upon the photographic plates of my memory.

With a tight grip of my index finger and thumb, I was holding the page on which this woodcut was reproduced when Fr. Sevich unexpectedly snatched the book out of my hands. I looked up, not at the priest but at my mother and father now returning to the parlor after their brief and calculated absence. Fr. Sevich was gazing in the same direction, while blindly stashing the little book back in its place; so he must not have noticed the thin leaf which was loosely draped over my fingers and which I immediately concealed between my legs. At any rate, he said nothing about the mishap. And at the time I could not imagine that any power on earth could perceive the loss of a single page from the monstrously dense and prodigious layers of that book. Certainly I was safe from the eyes of Fr. Sevich, which had once again become as dull and expressionless as the plaster complexion of his face.

Shortly thereafter the priest had to be on his way. With fascination I watched as he assembled himself in our foyer, donning his cloak, his huge hat, propping himself with his walking stick. Before leaving, he invited us all to visit him in the old country, and we promised to do so should our travels ever take us to that part of the world. While my mother held me close to her side, my father opened the door for the priest. And the sunny afternoon, now grown windy and overcast, received him.

Father Sevich's return

The stolen woodcut from the priest's prayerbook was not the solution I thought it would be. Although I suspected that it possessed certain inspirational powers, a modest fund of moral energy, I soon found that the macabre icon withheld its blessings from outsiders. Perhaps I should have been more deeply acquainted with the secretive nature of sacred objects, but I was too infatuated with all the marvelous lessons I believed it could teach – above all, how I might provide my faceless man in the monastery with a countenance of true terror. However, I learned no such lessons and was forced to leave my figure in an unfinished state, a ridiculously empty slate which I remained unable to embellish with the absolute horror of an off-stage atrocity. But the picture, I mean the one in the prayerbook, did have another and unsuspected value for me.

Since I had already established a spiritual rapport with Fr. Sevich, I could not obstruct a certain awareness of his own mysteries. He soon became connected in my mind with unarticulated narratives of a certain kind, stories in the rough, and ones potentially epic, even cosmic, in scope. Without a doubt there was an aura of legend about him, a cycle of mute, incredible lore; and I resolved that his future movements merited my closest possible attention. Such a difficult undertaking was made infinitely easier due to my possession of that single and very thin page torn from his prayerbook.

I kept it with me at all times, protectively enclosed in some wrapping tissue I borrowed from my mother. The initial results were soon in coming, but at the same time they were not entirely successful, considering the expense of this rather prodigal burst of psychic effort. Hence, the early scenes were highly imperfect, visions easily dispersed, fragmentary, some quite near to nonsense. Among them was a visit Fr. Sevich paid another family, a morose vignette in which the anemic priest seemed to have grown pale to the point of translucency.

And the others involved were even worse: some of them had barely materialized or were visible only as a sort of anthropomorphic mist. There was considerable improvement when Fr. Sevich was alone or in the presence of only one other person. A lengthy conversation with Fr. Orne, for example, was projected in its totality; but, as in an improperly lighted photographic scene, the substance of every shape had been watered down into an eerie lividity. Also, given the nature of these visionary endeavors, the entire meeting transpired in dead silence, as if the two clergymen were merely pantomiming their parts.

And in all phases of activity, Fr. Sevich remained the model visitor from a foreign diocese, laying no new ground for scandal since his brief, though infinitely promising, visit with my parents and me. Perhaps the only occasions on which he threatened to live up to this promise, this pledge to incarnate some of those abstract myths that his character suggested to my imagination, took place during his intervals of absolute privacy. In the most unconscious hours of darkness, when the rest of the rectory's population was in slumber, Fr. Sevich would leave the austere comforts of his bed and, seating himself at a window-facing desk, would pour over the contents of a certain book, turning page after page and stopping every so often to mouth some of the strange words inscribed upon them. Somehow these were the sentences of his own mysterious biography, a chronicle of truly unspeakable things. In the formation of the priest's lips as he mimed the incantations of a dead language, in the darting movements of his tongue between rows of immaculate teeth, one could almost chart the convoluted chronology of this foreign man. How alien is the deepest life of another: the unbelievable beginnings, the unimaginably elaborate developments; and the incalculable eons which prepare, which foretell, the multiform phenomena of a few score years! Much of what Fr. Sevich had endured in his allotted span could already be read on his face. But something still remained to be revealed in his features, something which the glowing lamp resting upon the desk, joined by the light of every constellation in the visible universe, was struggling to illuminate.

When Fr. Sevich returned to his homeland, I lost all touch with his life's whereabouts, and soon my own life collapsed back into established routine. After that weary and fruitless summer had passed, it was time for me to begin another year of school, to encounter once again the oppressive mysteries of the autumn season. But I had not entirely forgotten my adventure with Fr. Sevich. At the height of the fall semester we began to draw pumpkins with thick orange crayons whose points were awkwardly blunt, and with dull scissors we shaped black cats from the formless depths of black paper. Succumbing to a hopeless urge for innovation I created a man-shaped silhouette with my paper and scissors. The just proportions of my handiwork even received compliments from the nun who served as our art instructor. But when I trimmed the figure with a tiny white collar and gave it a crudely screaming mouth – there was outrage and there was punishment. Without arguing a happy sequence of cause and effect between this incident and what followed, it was not long afterward that the school season, for me, became eventful with illness. And it was during this time of shattered routine, as I lay three days and nights dripping with fever, that I regained my hold, with a visionary grasp that reached across the ocean between us, on the curious itinerary of Fr. Sevich.

With hat and cloak and walking stick, the old priest was hobbling along rather briskly, and alone, down the narrow, nocturnal streets of some very old town in the old country. It was a fairy-tale vision to which not even the most loving illustrator of medieval legends could do justice. Fortunately, the town itself – the serpentine lanes, the distorted glow of streetlamps, the superimposed confusion of pointed roofs, the thinnest blade of moon which seemed to belong to this town as it belonged to no other place on earth – does not require any protracted emphasis in this memoir. Although it did not give away its identity, either in name or location, the town still demanded a designation of some kind, some official title, however much in error it might be. And of all the names that had ever been attached to places of this world, the only one which seemed proper, in its delirious way, was an ancient name which, after all these years, seems no less fitting and no less ludicrous now than it did then. Unmentionably ludicrous, so I will not mention it.

Now Fr. Sevich was disappearing into a narrow niche between two dark houses, which led him to an unpaved lane bordered by low walls, along which he travelled in almost total blackness until the pathway opened into a small courtyard surrounded by high walls and lit by a single dull lamp at its center. He paused a moment to catch his breath, and when he gazed up at the night, as if to reconcile his course with the stars above, one could see his face sweating and shining in the jaundiced lamplight. Somewhere in the shadows that were draped and fluttering upon those high walls was an opening; passing through this doubtful gate, the old priest continued his incredible rambling about the darkest and most remote quarters of the old town.

Now he was descending a stairway of cut stone which led below the level of the town's streets; then a brief tunnel brought him to another stairway which burrowed in a spiral down into the earth and absolute blackness. Knowing his way, the priest ultimately emerged from this nowhere of blackness when he suddenly entered a vast circular chamber. The place appeared to be a tower sunken beneath the town and soaring to a great and paradoxical height. In the upper reaches of the tower, tiny lights glimmered like stars and threw down their illumination in a patternless weave of criss-crossing strands.

The subterranean structure, at whose center Fr. Sevich now stood, ascended in a series of terraces, each bordered by a shining balustrade made of some golden metal and each travelling the circumference of the inner chamber. These terraces multiplied into the upward distance, contracting in perspective into smaller and thinner circles, blurring together at some point and becoming lost in clouds of shadows that hovered far above. Each level was furthermore provided with numerous and regularly spaced portals, all of them dark, hinting at nothing of what lay beyond their unguarded thresholds. But one might surmise that if this was the library of which the priest spoke, if this was a true repository of such books as the one he had just removed from under his cloak, then those slender openings must have led to the archives of this fantastic athenaeum, suggesting nothing less than a bibliographic honeycomb of unknown expanse and complexity. Scanning the shadows about him, the priest seemed to be anticipating the appearance of someone in charge, someone entrusted with care of this institution. Then one of the shadows, one of the most sizeable shadows and the one closest to the priest, turned around . . . and three such caretakers now stood before him.

This triumvirate of figures seemed to share the same face, which was almost a caricature of serenity. They were attired very much like the priest himself, and their eyes were large and calm. When the priest held out the book to the one in the middle, a hand moved forward to take it, a hand as white as the whitest glove. The central figure then rested its other hand flat upon the front of the book, and then the figure to the left extended a hand which laid itself upon the first; then a third hand, belonging to the third figure, covered them both with its soft white palm and long fingers, uniting the three. The hands remained thus placed for some time, as if an invisible transference of fabulously subtle powers was occurring, something being given or received. The heads of the three figures slowly turned toward one another, and simultaneously there was a change in the atmosphere of the chamber streaked with the chaotic rays of underworld starlight. And if forced to name this new quality and point to its outward sign, one might draw attention to a certain look in the large eyes of the three caretakers, a certain expression of rarefied scorn or disgust.

They removed their hands from the book and placed them once again out of view. Then the caretakers turned their eyes upon the priest, who had already moved a few steps away from these indignant shadows. But as the priest began to turn his back on them, almost precisely at the mid-point of his pivot, he seemed to freeze abruptly in position, like someone who has just heard his name called out to him in some strange place far from home. However, he did not remain thus transfixed for very long, this statue poised to take a step which is forbidden to it, with its face as rigid and pale as a monument's stone. Soon his black, ankle-high shoes began to kick about as they left the solid ground. And when the priest had risen a little higher, well into the absolute insecurity of empty air, he lost hold of his walking stick; and it fell to the great empty expanse of the tower's floor, where it looked as small as a twig or a pencil. His wide-brimmed hat soon followed, settling crown-up beside the cane, as the priest began tossing and turning in the air like a restless sleeper, wrapping himself up in the dark cocoon of his cloak. Then the cloak was torn away, but not by the thrashing priest. Something else was up there with him, ascending the uncountable tiers of the tower, or perhaps many unseen things which tore at his clothes, at the sparse locks of his hair, at the interlocking fingers of his hands which were now folded and pressed to his forehead, as though in desperate prayer. And finally at his face.

Now the priest was no more than a dark speck agitating in the greater heights of the dark tower. Soon he was nothing at all. Below, the three figures had absconded to their refuge of shadows, and the vast chamber appeared empty once more. Then everything went black.

*   *   *

My fever grew worse over the course of several more days, and then late one night it suddenly, quite unexpectedly, broke. Exhausted by the ordeals of my delirium, I lay buried in my bed beneath heavy blankets, whose usually numerous layers had been supplemented according to the ministrations of my mother. Just a few moments before, or a few millennia, she had gone out of my room, believing that I was at last asleep. But I had not even come near to sleeping, no more than I approached a normal state of wakefulness. The only illumination in my room was the natural nightlight of the moon shining through the windows. Through half-closed eyes I focused on this light, suspecting strange things about it, until I finally noticed that all the curtains in my room had been tightly drawn, that the pale glow at the foot of my bed was an unnatural phosphorescence, an infernal aura or angelic halo beaming about the form of Fr. Sevich himself.

In my confusion I greeted him, trying to lift my head from its pillow but falling back in weakness. He showed no awareness of my presence, and for a second I thought – in the hellish wanderings of my fever – that *I* was the revenant, not he. Attempting to take a clearer account of things, I forced open my leaden eyelids with all the strength I could muster. As a reward for this effort, I witnessed with all possible acuity of my inward and outward vision the incorporeal grandeur of the specter's face. And in a moment unmeasurable by earthly increments of time, I grasped every detail, every datum and nuance of this visitor's life-history, the fantastic destiny which had culminated in the creation of this infinitely gruesome . . . visage: a visage grown rigid at the sight of unimaginable horrors, a visage petrified into spectral stone. And in that same moment, I felt that I too could see what this lost soul had seen.

Now, with all the force of a planet revolving its unspeakable tonnage in the blackness of space, the face turned on its terrible axis and, while it still appeared to have no apprehension of my existence, it spoke, as if to itself alone and to its solitary doom:

Not given back as it had been given, the law of the book is broken. The law . . . of the book . . . is broken.

The spectre had barely spoken the last resounding syllables of its strange pronouncement, when it underwent a change: before my eyes it began to shrivel like something thrown into a fire; without the least expression of anguish it crinkled into nothing, as if some invisible power had suddenly decided to dispose of its work, to crumple up an aborted exercise and toss it into oblivion. And it was then that I felt my own purposes at an intersection, a fortuitous crossroads, with that savage and unseen hand. But *I* would not scorn what I had seen. My health miraculously restored, I gathered together my drawing materials and stayed up the rest of that night recording the vision. At last I had the face I was seeking.

Postscriptum

Not long after that night, I paid a visit to our parish church. As this gesture was entirely self-initiated, my parents were free to interpret it as a sign of things to come, and no doubt they did so. The purpose of this act, however, was merely to collect a small bottle of holy water from the handsome metal cistern which dispensed this liquid to the public and which stood in the vestibule of the church. With apologies to my mother and father, I did not on this occasion actually enter the church itself. Gaining the priest-blessed solution, I hurried home, where I immediately unearthed – from the bottom of my dresser drawer – the folio torn from Fr. Sevich's book. Both items, prayerbook page and bottle of holy water, I took into the upstairs bathroom. I locked the door and placed the delicate little leaf in the bathroom sink, staring for a few moments at that wonderful woodcut. I wondered if one day I might make amends for my act of vandalism, perhaps by offering something of my own to a certain repository for such treasures in the old country. But then I recalled the fate of Fr. Sevich, which helped to chase the whole matter from my mind. From the uncorked bottle, I sprinkled the holy water over the precious page spread out at the bottom of the sink. For a few moments it sizzled, exactly as if I had poured a powerful acid on it, and gave off a not unpleasant vapor, an incense reeking of secret denial and privilege. Finally, it dissolved altogether. Then I knew that the game was over, the dream at an end. In the mirror above the sink I saw my own face smiling a smile of deep contentment.

MISS PLARR

It was spring, though still quite early in the season, when a young woman came to live with us. Her purpose was to manage the affairs of the household while my mother was suffering some vague ailment, lingering but not serious, and my father was away on business. She arrived on one of those misty, drizzling days which often prevailed during the young months of that particular year and which remain in my memory as the signature of this remarkable time. Since my mother was self-confined to her bed and my father absent, it was left for me to answer those sharp urgent rappings at the front door. How they echoed throughout the many rooms of the house, reverberating in the farthest corners of the upper floors.

Pulling on the curved metal door handle, so huge in my child's hand, I found her standing with her back to me and staring deep into a world of darkening mist. Her black hair glistened in the light from the vestibule. As she turned slowly around, my eyes were fixed upon that great ebony turban of hair, folded so elaborately into itself again and again yet in some way rebelling against this discipline, with many shiny strands escaping their bonds and bursting out wildly. Indeed, it was through a straggle of mist-covered locks that she first glared down at me, saying: "My name is . . ."

"I know," I said.

But at that moment it was not so much her name that I knew, despite my father's diligent recitations of it to me, as all the unexpected correspondences I sensed in her physical presence. For even after she stepped into the house, she kept her head slightly turned and glanced over her shoulder through the open door, watching the elements outside and listening with intense expectancy. By then this stranger had already gained a precise orientation amid the world's chaos of faces and other phenomena. Quite literally her place was an obscure one, lying somewhere deep within the peculiar mood of that spring afternoon when the natural gestures of the season had been apparently distanced and suppressed by an otherworldly desolation – seething luxuriance hidden behind dark battlements of clouds looming above a bare, practically hibernal landscape. And the sounds for which she listened also seemed remote and stifled, shut out by a mute and sullen twilight, smothered in that tower of stonegray sky.

However, while Miss Plarr appeared to reflect with exactitude all the signs and mannerisms of those days all shackled in gloom, her place in our household was still an uncertainty.

During the early part of her stay with us, Miss Plarr was more often heard than seen. Her duties, whether by instruction or her own interpretation, had soon engaged her in a routine of wandering throughout the echoing rooms and hallways of the house. Rarely was there an interruption in those footsteps as they sounded upon aged floorboards; day and night these gentle crepitations signaled the whereabouts of our vigilant housekeeper. In the morning I awoke to the movements of Miss Plarr on the floors above or below my bedroom, while late in the afternoon, when I often spent time in the library upon my return from school, I could hear the clip-clopping of her heels on the parquet in the adjacent room. Even late at night, when the structure of the house expressed itself with a fugue of noises, Miss Plarr augmented this decrepit music with her own slow pacing upon the stairs or outside my door.

One time I felt myself awakened in the middle of the night, though it was not any disturbing sounds that had broken my sleep. And I was unsure exactly what made it impossible for me to close my eyes again. Finally, I slid out of bed, quietly opened the door of my room a few inches, and peeped down the darkened hallway. At the end of that long passage was a window filled with the livid radiance of moonlight, and within the frame of that window was Miss Plarr, her entire form shaded into a silhouette as black as the blackness of her hair, which was all piled up into the wild shape of some night-blossom. So intently was she staring out the window that she did not seem to detect my observance of her. I, on the other hand, could no longer ignore the force of her presence.

The following day I began a series of sketches. These works first took form as doodles in the margins of my school books, but swiftly evolved into projects of greater size and ambition. Given the enigmas of any variety of creation, I was not entirely surprised that the images I had elaborated did not include the overt portrayal of Miss Plarr herself, nor of other persons who might serve by way of symbolism or association. Instead, my drawings appeared to illustrate scenes from a tale of some strange and cruel kingdom. Possessed by curious moods and visions, I depicted a bleak domain that was obscured by a kind of fog or cloud whose depths brought forth a plethora of incredible structures, all of them somehow twisted into aspects of bizarre savagery. From the matrix of this fertile haze was born a litter of towering edifices that combined the traits of castle and crypt, many-peaked palace and multi-chambered mausoleum. But there were also clusters of smaller buildings, warped offshoots of the greater ones, housing perhaps no more than a single room, an apartment of ominously skewed design, an intimate dungeon cell reserved for the most exclusive captivity. Of course, I betrayed no special genius in my execution of these fantasmal venues: my technique was as barbarous as my subject. And certainly I was unable to introduce into the menacing images any suggestion of certain sounds that seemed integral to their *proper* representation, a kind of aural accompaniment to these operatic stage sets. In fact, I was not able even to imagine these sounds with any degree of clarity. Yet I knew that they belonged in the pictures, and that, like the purely visible dimension of these works, their source could be found in the person of Miss Plarr.

Although I had not intended to show her the sketches, there was evidence that she had indulged in private viewings of them. They lay more or less in the open on the desk in my bedroom; I made no effort to conceal my work. And I began to suspect that their order was being disturbed in my absence, to sense a subtle disarrangement that was vaguely telling but not conclusive. Finally, she gave herself away. One gray afternoon, upon returning from school, I discovered a sure sign of Miss Plarr's investigations. For lying between two of my drawings, pressed like a memento in an old scrapbook, was a long black strand of hair.

I wanted to confront Miss Plarr immediately regarding her intrusion, not because I resented it in any way but solely to seize the occasion to approach this devious eccentric and perhaps draw closer to the strange sights and sounds she had brought into our household. However, at that stage of her term of employment she was no longer so easily located, having ceased her constant, noisy marauding and begun practicing more sedentary, even stealthy rituals.

Since there was no sign of her elsewhere in the house, I went directly to the room which had been set aside for her, and which I had previously respected as her sanctum. But as I slowly stepped up to the open doorway I saw that she was not there. After entering the room and rummaging about, I realized that she was not using it at all and perhaps had never settled in. I turned around to continue my search for Miss Plarr when I found her standing silently in the doorway and gazing into the room without fixing her eyes on anything, or any*one*, within it. I nevertheless appeared to be in a position of chastisement, losing all the advantage I earlier possessed over this invader of *my* sanctum. Yet there was no mention of either of these transgressions, despite what seemed our mutual understanding of them. We were helplessly drifting into an abyss of unspoken reproaches and suspicions. Finally, Miss Plarr rescued us both by making an announcement she had obviously been saving for the right moment.

"I have spoken with your mother," she declared in a strong voice, "and we have concluded that I should begin tutoring you in some of your . . . weaker school subjects."

I believe that I must have nodded, or offered some other gesture of assent. "Good," she said. "We will start tomorrow."

Then, rather quietly, she walked away, leaving her words to resound in the cavity of that unoccupied room – unoccupied, I may claim, since my own presence now seemed to have been eclipsed by the swelling shadow of Miss Plarr. Nonetheless, this extra-scholastic instruction did prove of immense value in illuminating what, at the time, was my weakest subject: Miss Plarr in general, with special attention to where she had made accommodations for herself in our household.

My tutorship was conducted in a room which Miss Plarr felt was especially suited to the purpose, though her reasoning may not have been readily apparent. For the place she had selected as her classroom was a small, remote attic located beneath the highest and westernmost roof of the house. The slanted ceiling of that room exposed to us its rotting beams like the ribbing of some ancient seagoing vessel that might carry us to unknown destinations. And there were cold drafts that eddied around us, opposing currents emanating from the warped frame in which a many-paned window softly rattled now and then. The light by which I was schooled was provided by overcast afternoons fading in that window, assisted by an old oil lamp which Miss Plarr had hung upon a nail in one of the attic rafters. (I still wonder where she unearthed this antique.) It was this greasy lamplight that enabled me to glimpse a heap of old rags which had been piled in a corner to form a kind of crude bedding. Nearby stood the suitcase Miss Plarr had arrived with.

The only furniture in this room was a low table, which served as my desk, and a small frail chair, both articles being relics of my early childhood and no doubt rediscovered in the course of my teacher's many expeditions throughout the house. Seated at the center of the room, I submitted to the musty pathos of my surroundings. "In a room such as this," Miss Plarr asserted, "one may learn certain things of the greatest importance." So I listened while Miss Plarr clomped noisily about, wielding a long wooden pointer which had no blackboard to point to. All considered, however, she did deliver a series of quite fascinating lectures.

Without attempting to render the exact rhetoric of her discourse, I remember that Miss Plarr was especially concerned with my development in subjects that often touched upon history or geography, occasionally broaching realms of philosophy and science. She lectured from memory, never once misstepping in her delivery of countless facts that had not reached me by way of the conventional avenues of my education. Yet these talks were nonetheless as meandering as her footsteps upon the cold floor of that attic room, and at first I was breathless trying to follow her from one point to the next. Eventually, though, I began to extract certain themes from her chaotic syllabus. For instance, she returned time and again to the earliest twitchings of human life, portraying a world of only the most rudimentary law but one so intriguingly advanced in what she called "visceral practices". She allowed that much of what she said in this way was speculative, and her discussions of later periods deferred to the restrictions, while also enjoying the explicitness, of accepted records. Hence, I was made intimate with those ancient atrocities which gained renown for a Persian monarch, with a century-old massacre in the Brazilian backlands, and with the curious methods of punishment employed by various societies often relegated to the margins of history. And in other flights of instruction, during which Miss Plarr might flourish her pointer in the air like an artist's paintbrush, I was introduced to lands whose chief feature was a kind of brutality and an air of exile – coarse and torturous terrains, deliriums of earth and sky. These included desolate mist-bound islands in polar seas, countries of barren peaks lacerated by unceasing winds, wastelands that consumed all sense of reality in their vast spaces, shadowed realms littered with dead cities, and sweltering hells of jungle where light itself is tinged with a bluish slime.

At some point, however, Miss Plarr's specialized curriculum, once so novel and engrossing, dulled with repetition. I started to fidget in my miniature seat; or my head would slump over my miniature desk. Then her words suddenly stopped, and she drew close to me, laying her rubber-tipped pointer across my shoulder. When I looked up I saw only those eyes glaring down at me, and that black bundle of hair outlined in the dismal light drifting through the attic like a glowing vapor.

"In a room such as this," she whispered, "one may also learn the *proper* way to behave."

The pointer was then pulled away, grazing my neck, and Miss Plarr walked over to the window. Outside were effervescent clouds of mist which hung down over trees and houses. The scene was held immobile by the mist as if captured within the murky depths of ice; everything appeared remote or hallucinatory, shadows bound to a misty shore. All was silence, and Miss Plarr gazed out at a world suspended in obscurity. But she was also listening to it.

"Do you know the sound of something that stings the air?" she asked, swinging her pointer lightly against herself. "You will know that sound if you do not act properly. Do you hear me?"

I understood her meaning and nodded my compliance. But at the same time I seemed to hear more than a teacher's switch as it came down upon a pupil's body. Sounds more serious and more strange intruded upon the hush of the classroom. They were faraway sounds lost in the hissing of rainy afternoons: great blades sweeping over great distances, expansive wings cutting through cold winds, long whips lashing in darkness. I heard other sounds, too, other things that were stinging the air in other places, sounds of things I heard but could never give explanation. These sounds grew increasingly louder. Finally, Miss Plarr dropped her pointer and put her hands over her ears.

"That will be all for today," she shouted.

And neither did she hold class on the following day, nor ever again resume my tutorship.

It seemed, however, that my lessons with Miss Plarr had continued their effect in a different form. Those afternoons in that attic must have exhausted something within me, and for a brief time I was unable to leave my bed. During this period I noticed that Miss Plarr was suffering a decline of her own, allowing the intangible sympathies which had already existed between us to become so much deeper and more entangled. To some extent it might be said that my own process of degeneration was following hers, much as my faculty of hearing, sensitized by illness, followed her echoing footsteps as they moved about the house. For Miss Plarr had reverted to her restless wandering, somehow having failed to settle herself into any kind of repose.

On her visits to my room, which had become frequent and were always unexpected, I could observe the phases of her dissolution on both the material and the psychic level. Her hair now hung loose about her shoulders, twisting itself in the most hideous ways like a dark mesh of nightmares, a foul nest in which her own suspicions were swarming. Moreover, her links to strictly mundane elements had become shockingly decayed, and my relationship with her was conducted at the risk of intimacy with spheres of a highly questionable order.

One afternoon I awoke from a nap to discover that all the drawings she had inspired me to produce had been torn to pieces and lay scattered about my room. But this primitive attempt at exorcism proved to have no effect, for in the late hours of that same night I found her sitting on my bed and leaning close to me, her hair brushing against my face. "Tell me about those sounds," she demanded. "You've been doing this to frighten me, haven't you?" For a while I felt she had slipped away altogether, severing our extraordinary bond and allowing my health to improve. But just as I seemed to be approaching a full recovery, Miss Plarr returned.

"I think that you're much better now," she said as she entered my room with a briskness that seemed to be an effort. "You can get dressed today. I have to do some shopping, and I want you to come along and assist me."

I might have protested that to go out on such a day would promise a relapse, for outside waited a heavy spring dampness and so much fog that I could see nothing beyond my bedroom window. But Miss Plarr was already lost to the world of wholesome practicalities, while her manner betrayed a hypnotic and fateful determination that I could not have resisted.

"As for this fog," she said, even though I had not mentioned it, "I think we shall be able to find our way."

Having a child's weakness for miracles, I followed Miss Plarr into that fog-smothered landscape. After walking only a few steps we lost sight of the house, and even the ground beneath our feet was submerged under layers of a pale floating web. But she took my hand and marched on as if guided by some peculiar vision.

And it was by her grasp that this vision was conducted into me, setting both of us upon a strange path. Yet as we progressed, I began to recognize certain shapes gradually emerging around us – that brood of dark forms which pushed through the fog, as if their growth could no longer be contained by it. When I tightened my grip on Miss Plarr's hand – which seemed to be losing its strength, fading in its substance – the vision surged toward clarity. With the aspect of some leviathan rising into view from the abyss, a monstrous world defined itself before our eyes, forcing its way through the surface of the fog, which now trailed in wisps about the structures of an immense and awful kingdom.

More expansive and intricate than my earlier, purely artistic imaginings, these structures sprung forth like a patternless conglomerate of crystals, angular and many-faceted monuments clustering in a misty graveyard. It was a dead city indeed, and all residents were entombed within its walls – or they were nowhere. There were streets of a sort which cut through this chaos of architecture, winding among the lopsided buildings, and yet it all retained an interlocking unity, much like a mountain range of wildly carved peaks and chasms and very much like the mountainous and murky thunderheads of a rainy season. Surely the very essence of a storm inhered in the jagged dynamism of these structures, a pyrotechnics that remained suspended or hidden, its violence a matter of suspicion and conjecture, suggesting a realm of atrocious potential – that infinite country which hovers beyond fogs and mists and gray heaping skies.

But even here something remained obscure, a sense provoked of rites or observances being enacted in concealment. And this peculiar sense was aroused by certain sounds, as of smothered cacophonous echoes lashing out in black cells and scourging the lengths of blind passages. Through the silence of the fog they gradually disseminated.

"Do you hear them?" asked Miss Plarr, though by then they had already risen to a conspicuous stridency. "There are rooms we cannot see where those sounds are being made. Sounds of something that stings the air."

Her eyes seemed to be possessed by the sight of these rooms she spoke of; her hair was mingling with the mist around us. Finally, she released her hold on my hand and drifted onward. There was no struggle: she had known for some time what loomed in the background of her wandering and what waited her approach. Perhaps she thought this was something she could pass on to others, or in which she might gain their company. But her company, her *proper* company, had all the time been preparing for her arrival elsewhere. Nevertheless, she had honored me as the heir of her visions.

The fog swept around her and thickened once again until there was nothing else that could be seen. After a few moments I managed to gain my geographical bearings, finding myself in the middle of the street only a few blocks from home.

*   *   *

Soon after the disappearance of Miss Plarr, our household was again established in its routine: my mother made a strong recovery from her pseudo-illness and my father returned from his business excursion. The hired girl, it seemed, had vacated the house without giving notice, a turn of events that caused little surprise in my mother. "Such a flighty creature," she said about our former housekeeper.

I supported this characterization of Miss Plarr, but offered nothing that might suggest the nature of her flight. In truth, no word of mine could possibly have brought the least clarity to the situation. Nor did I wish to deepen the mysteries of this episode by revealing what Miss Plarr had left behind in that attic room. For me this chamber was now invested with a dour mystique, and I revisited its drafty spaces on several occasions over the years. Especially on afternoons in early spring when I could not close my ears to certain sounds that reached me from beyond a gray mist or from skies of hissing rain, as if somewhere the tenuous forms of spirits were thrashing in a dark and forsaken world.

THE SHADOW AT THE
BOTTOM OF THE
WORLD

Before there occurred anything of a truly prodigious nature, the season had manifestly erupted with some feverish intent. This, at least, was how it appeared to us, whether we happened to live in town or somewhere outside its limits. (And traveling between town and countryside was Mr. Marble, who had been studying the seasonal signs far longer and in greater depth than we, disclosing prophecies that no one would credit at the time.) On the calendars which hung in so many of our homes, the monthly photograph illustrated the spirit of the numbered days below it: sheaves of cornstalks standing brownish and brittle in a newly harvested field, a narrow house and wide barn in the background, a sky of empty light above, and fiery leafage frolicking about the edges of the scene. But something dark, something abysmal always finds its way into the bland beauty of such pictures, something that usually holds itself in abeyance, some entwining presence that we always know is there. And it was exactly this presence that had gone into crisis, or perhaps had been secretly invoked by small shadowy voices calling out in the midst of our dreams. There came a bitter scent into the air, as of sweet wine turning to vinegar, and there was an hysteric brilliance flourished by the trees in town as well as those in the woods beyond, while along the roads between were the intemperate displays of thornapple, sumac, and towering sunflowers that nodded behind crooked roadside fences. Even the stars of chill nights seemed to grow delirious and take on the tints of an earthly inflammation. Finally, there was a moonlit field where a scarecrow had been left to watch over ground that had long been cleared yet would not turn cold.

Adjacent to the edge of town, the field allowed full view of itself from so many of our windows. It lay spacious beyond tilting fenceposts and under a bright round moon, uncluttered save for the peaked silhouettes of corn shocks and a manlike shape that stood fixed in the nocturnal solitude. The head of the figure was slumped forward, as if a groteque slumber had overtaken its straw-stuffed body, and the arms were slackly extended in a way that suggested some incredible gesture toward flight. For a moment it seemed to be an insistent wind which was flapping those patched-up overalls and fluttering the worn flannel of those shirt sleeves; and it would seem a forceful wind indeed which caused that stitched-up head to nod in its dreams. But nothing else joined in such movements: the withered leaves of the cornstalks were stiff and unstirring, the trees of the distant woods were in a lull against the clear night. Only one thing appeared to be living where the moonlight spread across that dead field. And there were some who claimed that the scarecrow actually raised its arms and its empty face to the sky, as though declaring itself to the heavens, while others thought that its legs kicked wildly, like those of a man who is hanged, and that they kept on kicking for the longest time before the thing collapsed and lay quiet. Many of us, we discovered, had been nudged from our beds that night, called as witnesses to this obscure spectacle. Afterward, the sight we had seen, whatever we believed its reason, would not rest within us but snatched at the edges of our sleep until morning.

And during the overcast hours of the following day we could not keep ourselves from visiting the place around which various rumors had hastily arisen. As pilgrims we wandered into that field, scrutinizing the debris of its harvest for augural signs, circling that scarecrow as if it were a great idol in shabby disguise, a sacred avatar out of season. But everything upon that land seemed unwilling to support our hunger for revelation, and our congregation was lost in fidgeting bemusement. (With the exception, of course, of Mr. Marble, whose eyes, we recall, were gleaming with illuminations he could not offer us in any words we would understand.) The sky had hidden itself behind a leaden vault of clouds, depriving us of the crucial element of pure sunlight which we needed to fully burn off the misty dreams of the past night. And a vine-twisted stone wall along the property line of the farm was the same shade as the sky, while the dormant vines themselves were as colorless as the stone they enmeshed like a strange network of dead veins. But this calculated grayness was merely an aspect of the scene, for the colors of the abundant woods along the margins of the landscape were undulled, as if those radiant leaves possessed some inner source of illumination or stood in contrast to some deeper shadow which they served to mask.

Such conditions no doubt impeded our efforts to come to terms with our fears about that particular field. Above all these manifestations, however, was the fact that the earth of those harvested acres, especially in the area surrounding the scarecrow, was unnaturally warm for the season. It seemed, in fact, that a late harvest was due. And some insisted that the odd droning noises that filled the air could not be blamed on the legions of local cicadas but indeed rose up from under the ground.

By the time of twilight, only a few stragglers remained in the field, among them the old farmer who owned this suddenly notorious acreage. We knew that he shared the same impulse as the rest of us when he stepped up to his scarecrow and began to tear the impostor to pieces. Others joined in the vandalism, pulling out handfuls of straw and stripping away the clothes until they had exposed what lay beneath them – the strange and unexpected sight.

For the skeleton of the thing should have been merely two crosswise planks. We verified this common fact with its maker, and he swore that no other materials had been used. Yet the shape that stood before us was of a wholly different nature. It was something black and twisted into the form of a man, something that seemed to have come up from the earth and grown over the wooden planks like a dark fungus, consuming the structure. There were now black legs that hung as if charred and withered; there was a head that sagged like a sack of ashes upon a meager body of blackness; and there were thin arms stretched out like knobby branches from a lightning-scorched tree. All of this was supported by a thick dark stalk which rose out of the earth and reached into the effigy like a hand into a puppet.

And even as that dull day was dimming into night, our vision was distracted by the profounder darkness of the thing which dangled so blackly in the dusk. Its composition appeared to be of the blackest earth, of earth that had gone stagnant somewhere in its depths, where a rich loam had festered into a bog of shadows. Soon we realized that each of us had fallen silent, entranced by a deep blackness which seemed to absorb our sight but which exposed nothing to scrutiny except an abyss in the outline of a man. Even when we ventured to lay our hands on that mass of darkness, we found only greater mysteries. For there was almost no tangible aspect to it, merely a hint of material sensation, barely the feel of wind or water. It seemed to possess no more substance than a few shifting flames, but flames of only the slightest warmth, black flames that have curled together to take on the molten texture of spoiled fruit. And there was a vague sense of circulation, as though a kind of serpentine life swirled gently within. But no one could stand to keep his hold upon it for long before stepping suddenly away.

"Damn the thing, it's not going to be rooted to my land," said the old farmer. Then he walked off toward the barn. And like the rest of us he was trying to rub something from the hand that had touched the shrivelled scarecrow, something that could not be seen.

He returned to us with an armory of axes, shovels, and other implements for uprooting what had grown upon his land, this eccentricity of the harvest. It would seem to have been a simple task: the ground was unusually soft all around the base of that black growth and its tenuous substance could hardly resist the wide blade of the farmer's ax. But when the old man swung and tried to split the thing like a piece of firewood, the blade would not cleave. The ax entered and was closed upon, as if sunk within a viscous mire. The farmer pulled at the handle and managed to dislodge the ax, but he immediately let it fall from his hands. "It was pulling back on me," he said in a low voice. "And you heard that sound." Indeed, the sound which had haunted the area all that day – like innumerable insects laughing – did seem to rise in pitch and intensity when the thing was struck.

Without a word, we began digging up the earth where that thick black stalk was buried. We dug fairly deep before the approaching darkness forced us to abandon our efforts. Yet no matter how far down we burrowed, it was not far enough to reach the bottom of that sprouting blackness. Furthermore, our attempts became hindered by a perverse reluctance, as in the instance of someone who is hesitant to have a diseased part of his own body cut away in order to keep the disease from spreading.

It was nearly pitch dark when we finally walked away from that field, for the clouds of that day had lingered to hide the moon. In the blackness our voices whispered various strategies, so that we might yet accomplish what we had thereto failed in doing. We whispered, although none of us would have said why he did so.

The great shadow of a moonless night encompassed the landscape, preserving us from seeing the old farmer's field and what was tenanted there. And yet so many of the houses in town were in vigil throughout those dark hours. Soft lights shone through curtained windows along the length of each street, where our trim wooden homes seemed as small as dollhouses beneath the dark rustling depths of the season. Above the gathered roofs hovered the glass globes of streetlamps, like little moons set inside the dense leaves of elms and oaks and maples. Even in the night, the light shining through those leaves betrayed the festival of colors seething within them, blazing auras which had not faded with the passing days, a plague of colors that had already begun to infect our dreams. This prodigy had by then become connected in our minds with that field just outside of town and the strange growth which there had taken root.

Thus, a sense of urgency led us back to that place, where we found the old farmer waiting for us as the frigid aurora of dawn appeared above the distant woods. Our eyes scanned the frost-powdered earth and studied every space among shadows and corn shocks spread out over the land, searching for what was no longer present in the scene. "It's gone back," the farmer revealed to us. "Gone into the earth like something hiding in its shell. Don't walk there," he warned, pointing to the mouth of a wide pit.

We gathered about the edge of this opening in the ground, gazing into its depths. Even full daybreak did not show us the bottom of that dark well. Our speculations were brief and useless. Some of us picked up the shovels lying nearby, as if to begin the long duty of filling in the great aperture. "No use in that," said the farmer. He then found a large stone and dropped it straight down the shaft. We waited and waited; we put our heads close to the hole and listened. But all we seemed to hear were remote, droning echoes, as of countless voices of insects chattering unseen. Finally, we covered the hazardous pit with some boards and buried the makeshift enclosure under a mound of soft dirt. "Maybe there'll be some change in the spring," someone said. But the old farmer only chuckled. "You mean when the ground warms up? Why do you think those leaves aren't falling the way they should?"

It was not long after this troubling episode that our dreams, which formerly had been the merest shadows and glimpses, swelled into full phase. Yet they must not have been dreams entirely, but also excavations into the season which had inspired them. In sleep we were consumed by the feverish life of the earth, cast among a ripe, fairly rotting world of strange growth and transformation. We took a place within a darkly flourishing landscape where even the air was ripened into ruddy hues and everything wore the wrinkled grimace of decay, the mottled complexion of old flesh. The face of the land itself was knotted with so many other faces, ones that were corrupted by vile impulses. Grotesque expressions were molding themselves into the darkish grooves of ancient bark and the whorls of withered leaf; pulpy, misshapen features peered out of damp furrows; and the crisp skin of stalks and dead seeds split into a multitude of crooked smiles. All was a freakish mask painted with russet, rashy colors – colors that bled with a virulent intensity, so rich and vibrant that things trembled with their own ripeness. But despite this gross palpability, there remained something spectral at the heart of these dreams. It moved in shadow, a presence that was in the world of solid forms but not of it. Nor did it belong to any other world that could be named, unless it was to that realm which is suggested to us by an autumn night when fields lay ragged in moonlight and some wild spirit has entered into things, a great aberration sprouting forth from a chasm of moist and fertile shadows, a hollow-eyed howling malignity rising to present itself to the cold emptiness of space and the pale gaze of the moon.

And it was to that moon we were forced to look for comfort when we awoke trembling in the night, overcome by the sense that another life was taking root within us, seeking its ultimate incarnation in the bodies we always dreamed were our own and inviting us into the depths of an extraordinary harvest. Certainly there was some relief when we began to discover, after many insecure hints and delvings, that the dreams were not a sickness restricted to solitary individuals or families but in fact were epidemic throughout the community. No longer were we required to disguise our uneasiness as we met on the streets under the luxuriant shadows of trees that would not cast off their gaudy foliage, the mocking plumage of a strange season. We had become a race of eccentrics and openly declared an array of curious whims and suspicions, at least while daylight allowed this audacity.

Honored among us was that one old fellow, well known for his oddities, who had anticipated our troubles weeks beforehand. As he wandered about town, wheeling the blade-sharpening grind-stone by which he earned his living, Mr. Marble had spoken of what he could "read in the leaves", as if those fluttering scraps of lush color were the pages of a secret book in which he perused gold and crimson hieroglyphs. "Just look at them," he urged passersby, "bleeding their colors like that. They should be bled dry, but now they're . . . making pictures. Something inside trying to show itself. They're as dead as rags now, look at them all limp and flapping. But something's still in there. Those pictures, do you see them?"

Yes, we saw them, though somewhat belatedly. And they were not seen only in the chromatic designs of those deathless leaves. They could show themselves anywhere, if always briefly. Upon a cellar wall there might appear an ill-formed visage among the damp and fractured stones, a hideous impersonation of a face infiltrating the dark corners of our homes. Other faces, leprous masks, would arise within the grain of panelled walls or wooden floors, spying for a moment before sinking back into the knotty shadows, withdrawing below the surface. And there were so many nameless patterns that might spread themselves across the boards of an old fence or the side of a shed, engravings all tangled and wizened like a subterranean craze of roots and tendrils, an underworld riot of branching convolutions, gnarled ornamentations. Yet these designs were not unfamiliar to us . . . for in them we recognized the same outlines of autumnal decay that illuminated our dreams.

Like the old visionary who sharpened knives and axes and curving scythes, we too could now read the great book of countless colored leaves. But still he remained far in advance of what was happening deep within us all. For it was he who manifested certain idiosyncrasies of manner that would have later appeared in so many others, whether they lived in town or somewhere outside its limits. Of course, he had always set himself apart from us by his waywardness of speech, his willingness to utter pronouncements of dire or delightful curiosity. To a child he might say: "The sight of the night can fly like a kite," while someone older would be told: "Doesn't have arms, but it knows how to use them. Doesn't have a face, but it knows where to find one."

Nevertheless, he plied his trade with every efficiency, pedalling the mechanism that turned the grindstone, expertly honing each blade and taking his pay like any man of business. Then, we noticed, he seemed to become distracted in his work. In a dull trance he touched metal implements to his spinning wheel of stone, careless of the sparks that flew into his face. Yet there was also a wild luminousness in his eyes, as of a diamond-bright fever burning within him. Eventually we found ourselves unable to abide his company, though we now attributed this merely to some upsurge in his perennial strangeness rather than to a wholly unprecedented change in his behavior. It was not until he no longer appeared on the streets of town, or anywhere else, that we admitted our fears about him.

And these fears necessarily became linked to the other disruptions of that season, those extravagant omens which were gaining force all around us. The disappearance of Mr. Marble coincided with a new phenomenon, one that finally became apparent in the twilight of a certain day when all of the clustering and tenacious foliage seemed to exude a vague phosphorescence. By nightfall this prodigy was beyond skepticism. The multicolored leaves were softly glowing against the black sky, creating an untimely nocturnal rainbow which scattered its spectral tints everywhere and dyed the night with a harvest of hues: peach gold and pumpkin orange, honey yellow and winy amber, apple red and plum violet. Luminous within their leafy shapes, the colors cast themselves across the darkness and were splattered upon our streets and our fields and our faces. Everything was resplendent with the pyrotechnics of a new autumn.

That night we kept to our houses and watched at our windows. It was no marvel, then, that so many of us saw the one who wandered that iridescent eve, who joined in its outbursts and celebrations. Possessed by the ecstasies of a dark festival, he moved in a trance, bearing in his hand that great ceremonial knife whose keen edge flashed a thousand glittering dreams. He was seen standing alone beneath trees whose colors shined upon him, staining his face and his tattered clothes. He was seen standing alone in the yards of our houses, a rigid scarecrow concocted from a patchwork of colors and shadows. He was seen stalking slow and rhythmically beside high wooden fences that were now painted with a quivering colored glow. Finally, he was seen at a certain intersection of streets at the center of town; but now, as we saw, he was no longer alone.

Confronting him in the open night were two figures whom none of us knew: a young woman and, held tightly by her side, a small boy. We were not unaccustomed to strangers walking the streets of our town, or even stopping by one of the surrounding farms – people who were passing through, some momentarily lost. And it was not too late in the evening for some travellers to appear, not really late at all. But they should not have been there, those two. Not on that night. Now they stood transfixed before a creature of whom they could have no conception, a thing that squeezed the knife in its hand the way the woman was now squeezing the small boy. We might have taken action but did not; we might have made an effort to help them. But the truth is that we wanted something to happen to them – we wanted to see them silenced. Such was our desire. Only then would we be sure that they could not tell what they knew. Our fear was not what those intruders might have learned about the trees that glowed so unnaturally in the night; or about the chattering noises that now began rising to a pitch of vicious laughter; or even about the farmer's field where a mound of dirt covered a bottomless hole. Our fear was what they might have known, what they must certainly have discovered, about *us*.

And we lost all hope when we saw the quaking hand that could not raise the knife, the tortured face that could only stare while those two terrible victims – the rightful sacrifice! – ran off to safety, never to be seen by us again. After that we turned back to our houses, which now reeked of moldering shadows, and succumbed to a dreamless sleep.

Yet at daybreak it became evident that something had indeed happened during the night. The air was silent, everywhere the earth was cold. And the trees now stood bare of leaves, all of which lay dark and withered upon the ground, as if their strangely deferred dying had finally overtaken them in a sudden rage of mortification. Nor was it long before Mr. Marble was discovered by an old farmer.

The corpse reposed in a field, stretched face-down across a mound of dirt and alongside the remains of a dismantled scarecrow. When we turned over the body we saw that its staring eyes were as dull as that ashen autumn morning. We also saw that its left arm had been slashed by the knife held in its right hand.

Blood had flowed over the earth and blackened the flesh of the suicide. But those of us who handled that limp, nearly weightless body, dipping our fingers into the dark wound, found nothing at all that had the feeling of blood. We knew very well, of course, what that shadowy blackness did feel like; we knew what had found its way into the man before us, dragging him down into its savage world. His dreams had always reached much deeper than ours. So we buried him deep in a bottomless grave.

PART 3
from *Noctuary*

THE MEDUSA

I

Before leaving his room Lucian Dregler transcribed a few stray thoughts into his notebook.

> The sinister, the terrible never deceive: the state in which they leave us is always one of enlightenment. And only this condition of vicious insight allows us a full grasp of the world, *all* things considered, just as a frigid melancholy grants us full possession of ourselves.

> We may hide from horror only in the heart of horror.

> Could I be so unique among dreamers, having courted the Medusa – my first and oldest companion – to the exclusion of all others? Would I have her respond to this sweet talk?

Relieved to have these fragments safely on the page rather than in some precarious mental notebook, where they were likely to become smudged or altogether effaced, Dregler slipped into an old overcoat, locked the door of his room behind him, and exited down a series of staircases at the back of his apartment building. An angular pattern of streets and alleys was his usual route to a certain place he now and then visited, though for time's sake – in order to *waste* it, that is – he chose to stray from his course at several points. He was meeting an acquaintance he had not seen in quite a while.

The place was very dark, though no more than in past experience, and much more populated than it first appeared to Dregler's eyes. He paused at the doorway, slowly but unsystematically removing his gloves, while his vision worked with the faint halos of illumination offered by lamps of tarnished metal, which were spaced so widely along the walls that the light of one lamp seemed barely to link up and propagate that of its neighbor. Gradually, then, the darkness sifted away, revealing the shapes beneath it: a beaming forehead with the glitter of wire-rimmed eyeglasses below, cigarette-holding and beringed fingers lying asleep on a table, shoes of shining leather which ticked lightly against Dregler's own as he now passed cautiously through the room. At the back stood a column of stairs coiling up to another level, which was more an appended platform, a little brow of balcony, than a section of the establishment proper. This level was caged in at its brink with a railing constructed of the same rather wiry and fragile material as the stairway, giving this area the appearance of a makeshift scaffolding. Rather slowly, Dregler ascended the stairs.

"Good evening, Joseph," Dregler said to the man seated at the table beside an unusually tall and narrow window. Joseph Gleer stared for a moment at the old gloves Dregler had tossed onto the table.

"You still have those same old gloves," he replied to the greeting, then lifted his gaze, grinning: "And that overcoat!"

Gleer stood up and the two men shook hands. Then they both sat down and Gleer, indicating the empty glass between them on the table, asked Dregler if he still drank brandy. Dregler nodded, and Gleer said "Coming up" before leaning over the rail a little ways and holding out two fingers in view of someone in the shadows below.

"Is this just a sentimental symposium, Joseph?" inquired the now uncoated Dregler.

"In part. Wait until we've got our drinks, so you can properly congratulate me."

Dregler nodded again, scanning Gleer's face without any observable upsurge in curiosity. A former colleague from Dregler's teaching days, Gleer had always possessed an open zest for minor intrigues, academic or otherwise, and an addiction to the details of ritual and protocol, anything preformulated and with precedent. He also had a liking for petty secrets, as long as he was among those privy to them. For instance, in discussions – no matter if the subject was philosophy or old films – Gleer took an obvious delight in revealing, usually at some advanced stage of the dispute, that he had quite knowingly supported some treacherously absurd school of thought. His perversity confessed, he would then assist, and even surpass, his opponent in demolishing what was left of his old position, supposedly for the greater glory of disinterested intellects everywhere. But at the same time, Dregler saw perfectly well what Gleer was up to. And though it was not always easy to play into Gleer's hands, it was this secret counter-knowledge that provided Dregler's sole amusement in these mental contests, for

Nothing that asks for your arguments is worth arguing, just as nothing that solicits your belief is worth believing. The real and the unreal lovingly cohabit *in our terror*, the only "sphere" that matters.

Perhaps secretiveness, then, was the basis of the two men's relationship, a flawed secretiveness in Gleer's case, a consummate one in Dregler's.

Now here he was, Gleer, keeping Dregler in so-called suspense. His eyes, Dregler's, were aimed at the tall narrow window, beyond which were the bare upper branches of an elm that twisted with spectral movements under the floodlights fixed high upon the outside wall. But every few moments Dregler glanced at Gleer, whose babylike features were so remarkably unchanged: the cupid's bow lips, the cookie-dough cheeks, the tiny gray eyes now almost buried within the flesh of a face too often screwed up with laughter.

A woman with two glasses on a cork-bottomed tray was standing over the table. While Gleer paid for the drinks, Dregler lifted his and held it in the position of a lazy salute. The woman who had brought the drinks looked briefly and without expression at toastmaster Dregler. Then she went away and Dregler, with false ignorance, said: "To your upcoming or recently passed event, whatever it may be or have been."

"I hope it will be for life this time, thank you, Lucian."

"What is this, quintus?"

"*Quartus*, if you don't mind."

"Of course, my memory is as bad as my powers of observation. Actually I was looking for something shining on your finger, when I should have seen the shine of your eyes. No ring, though, from the bride?"

Gleer reached into the open neck of his shirt and pulled out a length of delicate chainwork, dangling at the end of which was a tiny rose-colored diamond in a plain silver setting.

"Modern innovations," he said neutrally, replacing the chain and stone. "The moderns must have them, I suppose, but marriage is still marriage."

"Here's to the Middle Ages," Dregler said with unashamed weariness.

"And the middle-aged," refrained Gleer.

The men sat in silence for some moments. Dregler's eyes moved once more around that shadowy loft, where a few tables shared the light of a single lamp. Most of its dim glow backfired onto the wall, revealing the concentric coils of the wood's knotty surface. Taking a calm sip of his drink, Dregler waited.

"Lucian," Gleer finally began in a voice so quiet that it was nearly inaudible.

"I'm listening," Dregler assured him.

"I didn't ask you here just to commemorate my marriage. It's been almost a year, you know. Not that that would make any difference to you."

Dregler said nothing, encouraging Gleer with receptive silence.

"Since that time," Gleer continued, "my wife and I have both taken leaves from the university and have been traveling, mostly around the Mediterranean. We've just returned a few days ago. Would you like another drink? You went through that one rather quickly."

"No, thank you. Please go on," Dregler requested very politely.

After another gulp of brandy, Gleer continued. "Lucian, I've never understood your fascination with what you call the Medusa. I'm not sure I care to, though I've never told you that. But through no deliberate efforts of my own, let me emphasize, I think I can further your, I guess you could say, pursuit. You are still interested in the matter, aren't you?"

"Yes, but I'm too poor to afford Peloponnesian jaunts like the one you and your wife have just returned from. Was that what you had in mind?"

"Not at all. You needn't even leave town, which is the strange part, the real beauty of it. It's very complicated how I know what I know. Wait a second. Here, take this."

Gleer now produced an object he had earlier stowed away somewhere in the darkness, laying it on the table. Dregler stared at the book. It was bound in a rust-colored cloth and the gold lettering across its spine was flaking away. From what Dregler could make out of the remaining fragments of the letters, the title of the book seemed to be: *Electro-Dynamics for the Beginner*.

"What is this supposed to be?" he asked Gleer.

"Only a kind of passport, meaningless in itself. This is going to sound ridiculous – how I know it! – but you want to bring the book to this establishment," said Gleer, placing a business card upon the book's front cover, "and ask the owner how much he'll give you for it. I know you go to these shops all the time. Are you familiar with it?"

"Only vaguely," replied Dregler.

The establishment in question, as the business card read, was *Brothers' Books: Dealers in Rare and Antiquarian Books, Libraries and*

Collections Purchased, Large Stock of Esoteric Sciences and Civil War, No Appointment Needed, Member of Manhattan Society of Philosophical Bookdealers, Benjamin Brothers, Founder and Owner.

"I'm told that the proprietor of this place knows you by your writings," said Gleer, adding in an ambiguous monotone: "He thinks you're a real philosopher."

Dregler gazed at length at Gleer, his long fingers abstractly fiddling with the little card. "Are you telling me that the Medusa is supposed to be a book?" he said.

Gleer stared down at the table-top and then looked up. "I'm not telling you anything I do not know for certain, which is not a great deal. As far as I know, it could still be anything you can imagine, and perhaps already have. Of course you can take this imperfect information however you like, as I'm sure you will. If you want to know more than I do, then pay a visit to this bookstore."

"Who told you to tell me this?" Dregler calmly asked.

"It seems better if I don't say anything about that, Lucian. Might spoil the show, so to speak."

"Very well," said Dregler, pulling out his wallet and inserting the business card into it. He stood up and began putting on his coat. "Is that all, then? I don't mean to be rude but –"

"Why should you be any different from your usual self? But one more thing I should tell you. Please sit down. Now listen to me. We've known each other a long time, Lucian. And I know how much this means to you. So whatever happens, or doesn't happen, I don't want you to hold me responsible. I've only done what I thought you yourself would want me to do. Well, tell me if I was right."

Dregler stood up again and tucked the book under his arm. "Yes, I suppose. But I'm sure we'll be seeing each other. Good night, Joseph."

"One more drink," offered Gleer.

"No, good night," answered Dregler.

As he started away from the table, Dregler, to his embarrassment, nearly rapped his head against a massive wooden beam which hung hazardously low in the darkness. He glanced back to see if Gleer had noticed this clumsy mishap. And after merely a single drink! But Gleer was looking the other way, gazing out the window at the tangled tendrils of the elm and the livid complexion cast upon it by the floodlights fixed high upon the outside wall.

For some time Dregler thoughtlessly observed the wind-blown trees outside before turning away to stretch out on his bed, which was a few steps from the window of his room. Beside him now was a copy of his first book, *Meditations on the Medusa.* He picked it up and read piecemeal from its pages.

> The worshipants of the Medusa, including those who clog pages with "insights" and interpretations such as these, are the most hideous citizens of this earth – and the most numerous. But how many of them *know* themselves as such? Conceivably there may be an inner cult of the Medusa, but then again: who could dwell on the existence of such beings for the length of time necessary to round them up for execution?

> It is possible that only the dead are not in league with the Medusa. We, on the other hand, are her allies – but always against ourselves. How does one become her *companion*. . . and live?

> We are never in danger of beholding the Medusa. For that to happen she needs our consent. But a far greater disaster awaits those who know the Medusa to be gazing at them and long to reciprocate in kind. What better definition of a marked man: one who "has eyes" for the Medusa, whose eyes have a will and a fate of their own.

> Ah, to be a thing without eyes. What a break to be *born* a stone!

Dregler closed the book and then replaced it on one of the shelves across the room. On that same overcrowded shelf, leather and cloth pressing against cloth and leather, was a fat folder stuffed with loose pages. Dregler brought this back to the bed with him and began rummaging through it. Over the years the file had grown enormously, beginning as a few random memoranda – clippings, photographs, miscellaneous references which Dregler copied out by hand – and expanding into a storehouse of infernal serendipity, a testament of terrible coincidence. And the subject of every entry in this inadvertent encyclopaedia was the Medusa herself.

Some of the documents fell into a section marked "Facetious," including a comic book (which Dregler picked off a drugstore rack) that featured the Medusa as a benevolent superheroine who used her hideous powers only on equally hideous foes in a world without beauty. Others belonged under the heading of "Irrelevant," where was placed a three-inch strip from a decades-old sports page lauding the winning season of "Mr *(sic)* Medusa." There was also a meager division of the file which had no official designation, but which Dregler could not help regarding as items of "True Horror." Prominent among these was a feature article from a British scandal sheet: a photoless chronicle of a man's year-long suspicion that his wife was periodically possessed by the serpent-headed demon, a senseless little guignol which terminated with the wife's decapitation while she lay sleeping one night and the subsequent incarceration of a madman.

One of the least creditable subclasses of the file consisted of pseudo-data taken from the less legitimate propagators of mankind's knowledge: renegade "scientific" journals, occult-anthropology newsletters, and publications of various centers of sundry studies. Contributions to the file from periodicals such as *The Excentaur*, a back issue of which Dregler stumbled across in none other than Brothers' Books, were collectively categorized as "Medusa and Medusans: Sightings and Material Explanations." An early number of this publication included an article which attributed the birth of the Medusa, and of all life on Earth, to one of many extraterrestrial visitors, for whom this planet had been a sort of truckstop or comfort station en route to other locales in other galactic systems.

All such enlightening finds Dregler relished with a surly joy, especially those proclamations from the high priests of the human mind and soul, who invariably relegated the Medusa to a psychic underworld where she served as the image par excellence of romantic panic. But unique among the curiosities he cherished was an outburst of prose whose author seemed to follow in Dregler's own footsteps: a man *after his own heart.* "Can we be delivered," this writer rhetorically queried, "from the 'life force' as symbolized by Medusa? Can this energy, if such a thing exists, be put to death, crushed? Can we, in the arena of our being, come stomping out – gladiator-like – net and trident in hand, and, poking and swooping, pricking and swishing, *torment* this soulless and hideous demon into an excruciating madness, and, finally, annihilate it to the thumbs-down delight of our nerves and to our soul's deafening applause?" Unfortunately, however, these words were written in the meanest spirit of sarcasm by a critic who parodically reviewed Dregler's own *Meditations on the Medusa* when it first appeared twenty years earlier.

But Dregler never sought out reviews of his books, and the

curious thing, the amazing thing, was that this item, like all the other bulletins and ponderings on the Medusa, had merely fallen into his hands unbidden. (In a dentist's office, of all places.) Though he had read widely in the lore of and commentary on the Medusa, none of the material in his rather haphazard file was attained through the normal channels of research. None of it was gained in an official manner, none of it foreseen. In the fewest words, it was all a gift of unforeseen circumstances, strictly unofficial matter.

But what did this prove, exactly, that he continued to be offered these pieces to his puzzle? It proved nothing, exactly or otherwise, and was merely a side-effect of his preoccupation with a single subject. Naturally he would be alert to its intermittent cameos on the stage of daily routine. This was normal. But although these "finds" proved nothing, rationally, they always did suggest more to Dregler's imagination than to his reason, especially when he poured over the collective contents of these archives devoted to his oldest companion.

It was, in fact, a reference to this kind of imagination for which he was now searching as he lay on his bed. And there it was, a paragraph he had once copied in the library from a little yellow book entitled *Things Near and Far*. "There is nothing in the nature of things," the quotation ran, "to prevent a man from seeing a dragon or a griffin, a gorgon or a unicorn. Nobody as a matter of fact has seen a woman whose hair consisted of snakes, nor a horse from whose forehead a horn projected; though very early man probably did see dragons – known to science as pterodactyls – and monsters more improbable than griffins. At any rate, none of these zoological fancies violates the fundamental laws of the intellect; the monsters of heraldry and mythology do not exist, but there is no reason in the nature of things nor in the laws of the mind why they should not exist."

It was therefore in line with the nature of things that Dregler suspended all judgements until he could pay a visit to a certain bookstore.

II

It was late the following afternoon, after he emerged from daylong doubts and procrastinations, that Dregler entered a little shop squeezed between a gray building and a brown one. Nearly within arm's reach of each other, the opposing walls of the shop were solid with books. The higher shelves were attainable only by means of a very tall ladder, and the highest shelves were apparently not intended for access. Back numbers of old magazines – *Black-wood*'s, *The Spectator*, the London and American *Mercurys* – were stacked in plump, orderless piles by the front window, their pulpy covers dying in the sunlight. Missing pages from forgotten novels were stuck forever to a patch of floor or curled up in corners. Dregler noted page two-hundred-and-two of *The Second Staircase* at his feet, and he could not help feeling a sardonic sympathy for the anonymous pair of eyes confronting an unexpected dead end in the narrative of that old mystery. Then again, he wondered, how many thousands of these volumes had already been browsed for the last time. This included, of course, the one he held in his own hand and for which he now succumbed to a brief and absurd sense of protectiveness. Dregler blamed his friend Gleer for this subtle aspect of what he suspected was a farce of far larger and cruder design.

Sitting behind a low counter in the telescopic distance of the rear of the store, a small and flabby man with wire-rimmed eyeglasses was watching him. When Dregler approached the counter and lay the book upon it, the man – Benjamin Brothers – hopped alertly to his feet.

"Help you?" he asked. The bright tone of his voice was the formal and familiar greeting of an old servant.

Dregler nodded, vaguely recognizing the little man from a previous visit to his store some years ago. He adjusted the book on the counter, simply to draw attention to it, and said: "I don't suppose it was worth my trouble to bring this sort of thing here."

The man smiled politely. "You're correct in that, sir. Old texts like that, worth practically nothing to no one. Now down there in my basement," he said, gesturing toward a narrow doorway, "I've got literally thousands of things like that. Other things too, you know. The *Bookseller's Trade* called it 'Benny's Treasurehouse.' But maybe you're just interested in *selling* books today."

"Well, it seems that as long as I'm here . . ."

"Help yourself, Dr Dregler," the man said warmly as Dregler started toward the stairway. Hearing his name, Dregler paused and nodded back at the bookdealer; then he proceeded down the stairs.

Dregler now recalled this basement repository, along with the three lengthy flights of stairs needed to reach its unusual depths. The bookstore at street-level was no more than a messy little closet in comparison to the expansive disorder down below: a cavern of clutter, all heaps and mounds, with bulging tiers of bookshelves laid out according to no easily observable scheme. It was a universe constructed solely of the softly jagged brickwork of books. But if the Medusa was a book, how would he ever find it in this chaos? And if it was not, what other definite form could he expect to encounter of a phenomenon which he had avoided precisely defining all these years, one whose most nearly exact emblem was a hideous woman with a head of serpents?

For some time he merely wandered around the crooked aisles and deep niches of the basement. Every so often he took down some book whose appearance caught his interest, unwedging it from an indistinct mass of battered spines and rescuing it before years rooted to the same spot caused its words to mingle with others among the ceaseless volumes of "Benny's Treasurehouse," fusing them all into a babble of senseless, unseen pages. Opening the book, he leaned a threadbare shoulder against the towering, filthy stacks. And after spending very little time in the cloistered desolation of that basement, Dregler found himself yawning openly and unconsciously scratching himself, as if he were secluded in some personal sanctum.

But suddenly he became aware of this assumption of privacy which had instilled itself in him, and the feeling instantly perished. Now his sense of a secure isolation was replaced, at all levels of creaturely response, by its opposite. For had he not written that "personal well-being serves solely to excavate within your soul a chasm which waits to be filled by a landslide of dread, an empty mold whose peculiar dimensions will one day manufacture the shape of your *unique* terror?"

Whether or not it was the case, Dregler felt that he was no longer, or perhaps never was, alone in the chaotic treasurehouse. But he continued acting as if he were, omitting only the yawns and the scratchings. Long ago he had discovered that a mild flush of panic was a condition capable of *seasoning* one's more tedious moments. So he did not immediately attempt to discourage this, probably delusory, sensation. However, like any state dependent upon the play of delicate and unfathomable forces, Dregler's mood or intuition was subject to unexpected metamorphoses.

And when Dregler's mood or intuition passed into a new phase, his surroundings followed close behind: both he and the treasure-house simultaneously crossed the boundary which divides playful panics from those of a more lethal nature. But this is not to say that one kind of apprehension was more excusable than the other; they were equally opposed to the likings of logic. ("Regarding dread, intensity in itself is no assurance of validity.") So it meant nothing, necessarily, that the twisting aisles of books appeared to be tightening around the suspicious bibliophile, that the shelves now looked more conspicuously swollen with their soft and musty stock, that faint shufflings and shadows seemed to be frolicking like a fugue through the dust and dimness of the underground treasurehouse. Could he, as he turned the next corner, be led to see that which should not be seen?

The next corner, as it happened, was the kind one is trapped in rather than turns – a cul-de-sac of bookshelves forming three walls which nearly reached the rafters of the ceiling. Dregler found himself facing the rear wall like a bad schoolboy in punishment. He gazed up and down its height as if contemplating whether or not it was real, pondering if one could simply pass through it once one had conquered the illusion of its solidity. Just as he was about to turn and abandon this nook, something lightly brushed against his left shoulder. With involuntary suddenness he pivoted in this direction, only to feel the same airy caress now squarely across his back. Continuing counterclockwise, he executed one full revolution until he was standing and staring at someone who was standing and staring back at him from the exact spot where he, a mere moment before, had been standing.

The woman's high-heeled boots put her face at the same level as his, while her turban-like hat made her appear somewhat taller. It was fastened on the right side, Dregler's left, with a metal clasp studded with watery pink stones. From beneath her hat a few strands of straw-colored hair sprouted onto an unwrinkled forehead. Then a pair of tinted eyeglasses, then a pair of unlipsticked lips, and finally a high-collared coat which descended as a dark, elegant cylinder down to her boots. She calmly withdrew a pad of paper from one of her pockets, tore off the top page, and presented it to Dregler.

"Sorry if I startled you," it said.

After reading the note, Dregler looked up at the woman and saw that she was gently chopping her hand against her neck, but only a few times and merely to indicate some vocal disability. Laryngitis, wondered Dregler, or something chronic? He examined the note once again and observed the name, address, and telephone number of a company that serviced furnaces and air-conditioners. This, of course, told him nothing.

The woman then tore off a second pre-written message from the pad and pressed it into Dregler's already paper-filled palm, smiling at him very deliberately as she did so. (How he wanted to see what her eyes were doing!) She shook his hand a little before taking away hers and making a silent, scentless exit. So what was that reek Dregler detected in the air when he stared down at the note, which simply read: "Regarding M."

And below this word-and-a-half message was an address, and below that was a specified time on the following day. The handwriting was nicely formed, the most attractive Dregler had ever seen.

In the light of the past few days, Dregler almost expected to find still another note waiting for him when he returned home. It was folded in half and stuffed underneath the door to his apartment. "Dear Lucian," it began, "just when you think things have reached their limit of ridiculousness, they become more ridiculous still. In brief – we've been had! Both of us. And by my wife, no less, along with a friend of hers. (A blond-haired anthropology prof whom I think you may know, or know of; at any rate she knows you, or at least your writings, maybe both.) I'll explain the whole thing when we meet, which I'm afraid won't be until my wife and I get back from another "jaunt." (Eyeing some more islands, this time in the Pacific.)

"I was thinking that you might be skeptical enough not to go to the bookstore, but after finding you not at home I feared the worst. Hope you didn't have your hopes up, which I don't think has ever happened to you anyway. No harm done, in either case. The girls explained to me that it was a quasi-scientific hoax they were perpetrating, a recondite practical joke. If you think you were taken in, you can't imagine how I was. Unbelievable how real they made the whole ruse seem to me. But if you got as far as the bookstore, you know by now that the punchline to the joke was a pretty weak one. The whole point, as I was told, was merely to stir your interest just enough to get you to perform some mildly ridiculous act. I'm curious to know how Mr B. Bros. reacted when the distinguished author of *Meditations on the Medusa* and other ruminative volumes presented him with a hopelessly worthless old textbook.

"Seriously, I hope it caused you no embarrassment, and both of us, all *three* of us, apologize for wasting your time. See you soon, tanned and pacified by a South Sea Eden. And we have plans for making the whole thing up to you, that's a promise."

The note was signed, of course, by Joseph Gleer.

But Gleer's confession, though it was evident to Dregler that he himself believed it, was no more convincing than his "lead" on a Bookstore Medusa. Because this lead, which Dregler had not credited for a moment, led further than Gleer, who no longer credited it, had knowledge of. So it seemed that while his friend had now been placated by a false illumination, Dregler was left to suffer alone the effects of a true state of unknowing. And whoever was behind this hoax, be it a true one or false, knew the minds of both men very well.

Dregler took all the notes he had received that day, paper-clipped them together, and put them into a new section of his massive file. He tentatively labelled this section: "Personal Confrontations with the Medusa, Either Real or Apparent."

III

The address given to Dregler the day before was not too far for him to walk, restive peripatetic that he was. But for some reason he felt rather fatigued that morning, so he hired a taxi to speed him across a drizzle-darkened city. Settling into the spacious dilapidation of the taxi's back seat, he took note of a few things. Why, he wondered, were the driver's glasses, which every so often filled the rear-view mirror, even darker than the day? Did she make a practice of thus "admiring" all her passengers? And was this back-seat debris – the "L"-shaped cigarette butt on the door's armrest, the black apple core on the floor – supposed to serve as objects of *his* admiration?

Dregler questioned a dozen other things about that routine ride, that drenched day, and the city outside where umbrellas multiplied like mushrooms in the grayness, until he grew satisfied with his lack of a sense of well-being. Earlier he was concerned that his flow of responses that day would not be those of a man who was possibly about to confront the Medusa. He was apprehensive that he might look on this ride and its destination with lively excitement or as an adventure of some kind; in brief, he feared that his attitude would prove, to a certain extent, to be one of insanity. To be sane, he held, was either to be sedated by melancholy or activated by hysteria, two responses which are "always and equally warranted for those of *sound* insight." All others were irrational, merely symptoms of imaginations left idle, of memories out of work. And above these mundane responses, the only elevation allow-able, the only valid transcendence, was a sardonic one: a bliss that annihilated the visible universe with jeers of dark joy, a *mindful* ecstasy. Anything else in the way of "mysticism" was a sign of deviation or distraction, and a heresy to the obvious.

The taxi turned onto a block of wetted brownstones, stopping before a tiny streetside lawn overhung by the skeletal branches of two baby birch trees. Dregler paid the driver, who expressed no gratitude whatever for the tip, and walked quickly through the drizzle toward a golden-bricked building with black numbers – two-oh-two – above a black door with a brass knob and knocker. Reviewing the information on the crumpled piece of paper he took from his pocket, Dregler pressed the glowing bell-button. There was no one else in sight along the street, its trees and pavement fragrantly damp.

The door opened and Dregler stepped swiftly inside. A shabbily dressed man of indefinite age closed the door behind him, then asked in a cordially nondescript voice: "Dregler?" The philosopher nodded in reply. After a few reactionless moments the man moved past Dregler, waving once for him to follow down the ground-floor hallway. They stopped at a door that was directly beneath the main stairway leading to the upper floors. "In here," said the man, placing his hand upon the doorknob. Dregler noticed the ring, its rosewater stone and silver band, and the disjunction between the man's otherwise dour appearance and this comparatively striking piece of jewelry. The man pushed open the door and, without entering the room, flipped a lightswitch on the inside wall.

To all appearances it was an ordinary storeroom cluttered with a variety of objects. "Make yourself comfortable," the man said as he indicated to Dregler the way into the room. "Leave whenever you like, just close the door behind you."

Dregler gave a quick look around the room. "Isn't there anything else?" he asked meekly, as if he were the stupidest student of the class. "This is it, then?" he persisted in a quieter, more dignified voice.

"This is it," the man echoed softly. Then he slowly closed the door, and from inside Dregler could hear footsteps walking back down the hallway.

The room was an average understairs niche, and its ceiling tapered downward into a smooth slant where angular steps ascended upward on the other side. Elsewhere its outline was obscure, confused by bedsheets shaped like lamps or tables or small horses; heaps of rocking chairs and baby-chairs and other items of disused furniture; bandaged hoses that drooped like dead pythons from hooks on the walls; animal cages whose doors hung open on a single hinge; old paint cans and pale turps speckled like an egg; and a dusty light fixture that cast a gray haze over everything.

Somehow there was not a variety of odors in the room, each

telling the tale of its origin, but only a single smell pieced like a puzzle out of many: its complete image was dark as the shadows in a cave and writhing in a dozen directions over curving walls. Dregler gazed around the room, picked up some small object and immediately set it down again because his hands were trembling. He found himself an old crate to sit on, kept his eyes open, and waited.

Afterward he could not remember how long he had stayed in the room, though he did manage to store up every nuance of the eventless vigil for later use in his voluntary and involuntary dreams. (They were compiled into that increasingly useful section marked "Personal Confrontations with the Medusa," a section that was fleshing itself out as a zone swirling with red shapes and a hundred hissing voices.) Dregler recalled vividly, however, that he left the room in a state of panic after catching a glimpse of himself in an old mirror that had a hair-line fracture slithering up its center. And on his way out he lost his breath when he felt himself being pulled back into the room. But it was only a loose thread from his overcoat that had gotten caught in the door. It finally snapped cleanly off and he was free to go, his heart livened with dread.

Dregler never let on to his friends what a success that afternoon had been for him, not that he could have explained it to them in any practical way even if he desired to. As promised, they did make up for any inconvenience or embarrassment Dregler might have suffered as a result of, in Gleer's words, the "bookstore incident." The three of them held a party in Dregler's honor, and he finally met Gleer's new wife and her accomplice in the "hoax." (it became apparent to Dregler that no one, least of all himself, would admit it had gone further than that.) Dregler was left alone with this woman only briefly, and in the corner of a crowded room. While each of them knew of the other's work, this seemed to be the first time they had personally met. Nonetheless, they both confessed to a feeling of their prior acquaintance without being able, or willing, to substantiate its origins. And although plenty of mutually known parties were established, they failed to find any direct link between the two of them.

"Maybe you were a student of mine," Dregler suggested.

She smiled and said: "Thank you, Lucian, but I'm not as young as you seem to think."

Then she was jostled from behind ("Whoops," said a tipsy academic), and something she had been fiddling with in her hand ended up in Dregler's drink. It turned the clear bubbling beverage into a glassful of liquid rose-light.

"I'm so·sorry. Let me get you another," she said, and then disappeared into the crowd.

Dregler fished the earring out of the glass and stole away with it before she had a chance to return with a fresh drink. Later in his room he placed it in a small box, which he labelled: "Treasures of the Medusa."

But there was nothing he could prove, and he knew it.

IV

It was not many years later that Dregler was out on one of his now famous walks around the city. Since the bookstore incident, he had added several new titles to his works, and these had somehow gained him the faithful and fascinated audience of readers that had previously eluded him. Prior to his "discovery" he had been accorded only a distant interest in scholarly and popular circles alike, but now every little habit of his, not least of all his daily meanderings, had been turned by commentators into "typifying traits" and "defining quirks." "Dregler's walks," stated one article, "are a constitutional of the modern mind, urban journeys by a tortured Ulysses *sans* Ithaca." Another article offered this back-cover superlative: "the most baroque inheritor of Existentialism's obsessions."

But whatever fatuosities they may have inspired, his recent books – *A Bouquet of Worms, Banquet for Spiders*, and *New Meditations on the Medusa* – had enabled him to "grip the minds of a dying generation and pass on to them his pain." These words were written, rather uncharacteristically, by Joseph Gleer in a highly favorable review of *New Meditations* for a philosophical quarterly. He probably thought that this notice would revive his friendship with his old colleague, but Dregler never acknowledged Gleer's effort, nor the repeated invitations to join his wife and him for some get-together or other. What else could Dregler do? Whether Gleer knew it or not, he was now one of them. And so was Dregler, though his saving virtue was an awareness of this disturbing fact. And this was part of his pain.

"We can only live by leaving our 'soul' in the hands of the Medusa," Dregler wrote in *New Meditations*. "Whether she is an angel or a gargoyle is not the point. Each merely allows us a gruesome diversion from some ultimate catastrophe which would turn us to stone; each is a mask hiding the *worst* visage, a medicine that numbs the mind. And the Medusa will see to it that we are protected, sealing our eyelids closed with the gluey spittle of her snakes, while their bodies elongate and slither past our lips to devour us *from the inside*. This is what we must never witness, except in the imagination, where it is a charming sight. And in the word, no less than in the mind, the Medusa fascinates much more than she appalls, and haunts us just *this side* of petrification. On the other side is the unthinkable, the unheard-of, that-which-should-not-be: hence, the Real. This is what throttles our souls with a hundred fingers – somewhere, perhaps in that dim room which caused us to forget ourselves, that place where we left ourselves behind amid shadows and strange sounds – while our minds and words toy, like playful, stupid pets, with *diversions* of an immeasurable disaster. The tragedy is that we must steer so close in order to avoid this hazard. *We may hide from horror only in the heart of horror.*"

Now Dregler had reached the outermost point of his daily walk, the point at which he usually turned and made his way back to his apartment, that *other* room. He gazed at the black door with the brass knob and knocker, then glanced down the street at the row of porchlights and bay windows, which were glowing madly in the late dusk. Looking skyward, he saw the bluish domes of street lamps: inverted halos or open eyes. A light rain began to sprinkle down, nothing very troublesome. But in the next moment Dregler had already sought shelter in the welcoming brownstone.

He soon came to stand before the door of the room, keeping his hands deep in the pockets of his overcoat and away from temptation. Nothing had changed, he noticed, nothing at all. The door had not been opened by anyone since he had last closed it behind him on that hectic day years ago. And there was the proof, as he knew, somehow, it would be: that long thread from his coat still dangled from where it had been caught between door and frame. Now there was no question about what he would do.

It was to be a quick peek through a hand-wide crack, but enough to risk disillusionment and the dispersal of all the charming traumas he had articulated in his brain and books, scattering them like those peculiar shadows he supposed lingered in that room. And the voices – would he hear that hissing which heralded her presence as much as the flitting red shapes? He kept his eyes fixed upon his hand on the doorknob, turning it gently to nudge open the door. So the first thing he saw was the way it, his hand, took on a rosy dawn-like glow, then a deeper twilight crimson as it was bathed more directly by the odd illumination within the room.

There was no need to reach in and flick the lightswitch just inside. He could see quite enough as his vision, still exceptional, was further aided by the way a certain cracked mirror was positioned, giving his eyes a reflected entrance into the dim depths of the room. And in the depths of the mirror? A split-image, something fractured by a thread-like chasm that oozed up a viscous red glow. There was a man in the mirror; no, not a man but a mannikin, or a frozen figure of some kind. It was naked and rigid, leaning against a wall of clutter, its arms outstretching and reaching behind, as if trying to break a backwards fall. Its head was also thrown back, almost broken-necked; its eyes were pressed shut into a pair of well-sealed creases, two ocular wrinkles which had taken the place of the sockets themselves. And its mouth gaped so widely with a soundless scream that all wrinkles had been smoothed away from that part of the old face.

He barely recognized this face, this naked and paralyzed form which he had all but forgotten, except as a lurid figure of speech he once used to describe the uncanny condition of his soul. But it was no longer a charming image of the imagination. Reflection had given it charm, made it acceptable to sanity, just as reflection had made those snakes, and the one who wore them, picturesque and not petrifying. But no amount of reflection could have conceived seeing the thing itself, nor the state of being stone.

The serpents were moving now, coiling themselves about the ankles and wrists, the neck; stealthily entering the screaming man's mouth and prying at his eyes. Deep in the mirror opened another pair of eyes the color of wine-mixed water, and through a dark tangled mass they glared. The eyes met his, but not in a mirror. And the mouth was screaming, but made no sound. Finally, he was reunited, in the worst possible way, with the thing within the room.

Stiff inside of stone now, he heard himself think. *Where is the world, my words?* No longer any world, any words, there would only be that narrow room and its two inseparable occupants. Nothing other than that would exist for him, could exist, nor, in fact, had ever existed. In its own rose-tinted heart, his horror had at last found him.

CONVERSATIONS IN A
DEAD LANGUAGE

Conveniens vitae mors fuit ista suae.
Ovid

I

After changing out of his uniform, he went downstairs to search the kitchen drawers, rattling his way through cutlery and cooking utensils. Finally he found what he wanted. A carving knife, a holiday knife, the traditional blade he'd used over the years. Knifey-wifey.

First he carved out an eye, spearing the triangle with the point of his knife and neatly drawing the pulpy thing from its socket. Pinching the blade, he slid his two fingers along the blunt edge, pushing the eye onto the newspaper he'd carefully placed next to the sink. Another eye, a nose, a howling oval mouth. Done. Except for manually scooping out the seedy and stringy entrails and supplanting them with a squat little candle of the vigil type. Guide them, holy lantern, through darkness and disaster. To me. To meezy-weezy.

He dumped several bags of candy into a large potato chip bowl, fingering pieces here and there: the plump caramels, the tarty sour balls, the chocolate kisses for the kids. A few were test-chewed for taste and texture. A few more. Not too many, for some of his co-workers already called him Fatass, almost behind his back. And he would spoil the holiday dinner he had struggled to prepare in the little time left before dark. Tomorrow he'd start his diet and begin making more austere meals for himself.

At dark he brought the pumpkin out to the porch, placing it on a small but lofty table over which he'd draped a bedsheet no longer in normal use. He scanned the old neighborhood. Beyond the railings of other porches and in picture windows up and down the street glowed a race of new faces in the suburb. Holiday visitors come to stay the night, without a hope of surviving till the next day. All Souls Day. Father Mickiewicz was saying an early morning mass, which there would be just enough time to attend before going to work.

No kids yet. Wait. There we go, bobbing down the street: a scarecrow, a robot, and – what is it? – oh, a white-faced clown. Not the skull-faced thing he'd at first thought it was, pale and hollow-eyed as the moon shining frostily on one of the clearest nights he'd ever seen. The stars were a frozen effervescence.

Better get inside. They'll be coming soon. Waiting behind the glass of the front door with the bowl of candy under his arm, he nervously grabbed up palmsful of the sweets and let them fall piece by piece back into the bowl, a buccaneer revelling in his loot . . . a grizzled-faced pirate, eye-patch over an empty socket, a jolly roger on his cap with "x" marking the spot in bones, running up the front walk, charging up the wooden stairs of the porch, rubber cutlass stuffed in his pants.

"Trick or treat."

"Well, well, well," he said, his voice rising in pitch with each successive "well." "If it isn't Blackbeard. Or is it Bluebeard, I always forget. But you don't have a beard at all, do you?" The pirate shook his head shyly to say no. "Maybe we should call you Nobeard, then, at least until you start shaving."

"I have a moustache. Trick or treat, mister," the boy said, impatiently holding up an empty pillow case.

"You do have a nice moustache at that. Here you go, then," he said, tossing a handful of candy into the sack. "And cut a few throats for me," he shouted as the boy turned and ran off.

He didn't have to say those last words so loudly. Neighbors. No, no one heard. The streets are filled with shouters; tonight, one the same as another. Listen to the voices all over the neighborhood, music against the sounding board of silence and the chill infinity of autumn.

Here come some more. Goody.

Trick or treat: an obese skeleton, meat bulging under its painted-costume bones. How unfortunate, especially at his age. Fatass of the boneyard and the schoolyard. Give him an extra handful of candy. "Thanks a *lot*, mister." "Here, have more." Then the skeleton waddled down the porch steps, its image thinning out into the nullity of the darkness, candy-filled paper bag rattling away to a whisper.

Trick or treat: an overgrown baby, bibbed and bootied, with a complexion problem erupting on its pre-adolescent face. "Well, cootchie coo," he said to the infant as he showered its open bunting with candy. Baby sneered as it toddled off, pouchy diapers slipping down its backside, disappearing once again into the black from which it had momentarily emerged.

Trick or treat: midget vampire, couldn't be more than six years old. Wave to Mom waiting on the sidewalk. "*Very* scary. Your parents must be proud. Did you do all that make-up work yourself," he whispered. The little thing mutely gazed up, its eyes underlidded with kohl-dark smudges. It then used a tiny finger, pointy nail painted black, to indicate the guardian figure near the street. "Mom, huh? Does she like sourballs? Sure she does. Here's some for Mom and some more for yourself, nice red ones to suck on. That's what you scary vampires like, eh?" he finished, winking. Cautiously descending the stairs, the child of the night returned to its parent, and both proceeded to the next house, joining the anonymous ranks of their predecessors.

Others came and went. An extraterrestrial with a runny nose, a smelly pair of ghosts, an asthmatic tube of toothpaste. The parade thickened as the night wore on. The wind picked up and a torn kite struggled to free itself from the clutches of an elm across the street. Above the trees the October sky remained lucid, as if a glossy veneer had been applied across the night. The moon brightened to a teary gleam, while voices below waned. Fewer and fewer disguises perpetrated deception in the neighborhood. These'll probably be the last ones coming up the porch. Almost out of candy anyway.

Trick or treat. Trick or treat.

Remarkable, these two. Obviously brother and sister, maybe twins. No, the girl looks older. A winning couple, especially the bride. "Well, congratulations to the gride and broom. I know I said it backwards. That's because you're backwards, aren't you? Whose idea was that?" he asked, tossing candy like rice into the bag of the tuxedoed groom. What faces, so clear. Shining stars.

"Hey, you're the mailman," said the boy.

"Very observant. You're marrying a smart one here," he said to the groom.

"I saw you were, too," she replied.

"Course you did. You're sharp kids, both of you. Hey, you guys must be tired, walking around all night." The kids shrugged, unaware of the meaning of fatigue. "I know I am after delivering the mail up and down these streets. And I do that every day, except Sunday of course. Then I go to church. You kids go to church?" It seemed they did; wrong one, though. "You know, at our church we have outings and stuff like that for kids. Hey, I got an idea – "

A car slowed down on the street, its constabulary spotlight scanning between houses on the opposite side. Some missing Halloweeners maybe. "Never mind my idea, kids. Trick or treat," he said abruptly, lavishing candy on the groom, who immediately strode off. Then he turned to the bride, on whom he bestowed the entire remaining contents of the large bowl, conveying a scrupulously neutral expression as he did so. Was the child blushing, or was it just the light from the jack-o-lantern?

"C'mon, Charlie," his sister called from the sidewalk.

"Happy Halloween, Charlie. See you next year." Maybe around the neighborhood.

His thoughts drifted off for a moment. When he regained control the kids were gone, all of them. Except for imaginary ones, ideals of their type. Like that boy and his sister.

He left the candle burning in the jack-o-lantern. Let it make the most of its brief life. Tomorrow it would be defunct and placed out with the other refuse, an extinguished shell pressed affectionately against a garbage bag. Tomorrow . . . All Souls Day. Pick up Mother for church in the morning. Could count it as a weekly visit, holy day of obligation. Also have to remember to talk to Father M. about taking that kiddie group to the football game.

The kids. Their annual performance was now over, the make-up wiped away and all the costumes back in their boxes. After he turned off the lights downstairs and upstairs, and was lying in bed, he still heard "trick or treat" and saw their faces in the darkness. And when they tried to dissolve into the background of his sleepy mind . . . he brought them back.

II

"Ttrrrick or ttrrreat," chattered a trio of hacking, sniffing hoboes. It was much colder this year, and he was wearing the bluish-gray wool overcoat he delivered the mail in. "Some for you, you, and you," he said in a merely efficient tone of voice. The bums were not overly grateful for the handouts. They don't appreciate anything the way they used to. Things change so fast. Forget it, close the door, icy blasts.

Weeks ago the elms and red maples in the neighborhood had been assaulted by unseasonable frigidity and stripped to the bone.

Clouds now clotted up the sky, a murky purple ceiling through which no star shone. Snow was imminent.

Fewer kids observed the holiday this year, and of the ones who did a good number of them evidently took little pride in the imagination or lavishness of their disguises. Many were content to rub a little burnt cork on their faces and go out begging in their everyday clothes.

So much seemed to have changed. The whole world had become jaded, an inexorable machine of cynicism. Your mother dies unexpectedly, and they give you two days leave from your job. When you get back, people want to have even less to do with you than before. Strange how you can feel the loss of something that never seemed to be there in the first place. A dwarfish, cranky old woman dies . . . and all of a sudden there's a royal absence, as if a queen had cruelly vacated her throne. It was the difference between a night with a single fibrillating star in it and one without anything but smothering darkness.

But remember those times when she used to . . . No, *nihil nisi bonum*. Let the dead, et cetera, et cetera. Father M. had conducted an excellent service at the funeral home, and there was little point in ruining that perfect sense of finality the priest had managed to convey regarding the earthly phase of his mother's existence. So why bring her now into his thoughts? Night of the Dead, he remembered.

There were no longer very many emissaries of the deceased roaming the streets of the neighborhood. They had gone home, the ones who had left it in the first place. Might as well close up till next year, he thought. No, wait.

Here they are again, coming late in the evening as they did last year. Take off the coat, a sudden flash of warmth. The warming stars had returned, shining their true light once more. How they beamed, those two little points in the blackness. Their stellar intensity went right into him, a bright tightness. He was now grateful for the predominant gloom of this year's Halloween, which only exacerbated his present state of delight. That they were wearing the same costumes as last year was more than he could have hoped.

"Trick or treat," they said from afar, repeating the invocation when the man standing behind the glass door didn't respond and merely stood staring at them. Then he opened the door wide.

"Hello, happy couple. Nice to see you again. You remember me, the mailman?"

The children exchanged glances, and the boy said: "Yeah,

sure." The girl antiphonied with a giggle, enhancing his delight in the situation.

"Well, here we are one year later and you two are still dressed and waiting for the wedding to start. Or did it just get over with? At this rate you won't make any progress at all. What about next year? And the next? You'll never get any older, know what I mean? Nothing'll change. Is that okay with you?"

The children tried for comprehending nods but only achieved movements and facial expressions of polite bewilderment.

"Well, it's okay with me too. Confidentially, I wish things had stopped changing for me a long time ago. Anyway, how about some candy?"

The candy was proffered, the children saying "thaaank yooou" in the same way they said it at dozens of other houses. But just before they were allowed to continue on their way . . . he demanded their attention once more.

"Hey, I think I saw you two playing outside your house one day when I came by with the mail. It's that big white house over on Pine Court, isn't it?"

"Nope," said the boy as he carefully inched his way down the porch stairs, trying not to trip over his costume. His sister had impatiently made it to the sidewalk already. "It's red with black shutters. On Ash." Without waiting for a reaction to his answer he joined his sister, and side by side the bride and groom walked far down the street, for there didn't seem to be any other houses open for business nearby. He watched them become tiny in the distance, eventually disappear into the dark.

Cold out here, shut the door. There was nothing more to see; he had successfully photographed the encounter for the family album of his imagination. If anything, their faces glowed even brighter and clearer this year. Perhaps they really hadn't changed and never would. No, he thought in the darkness of his bedroom. Everything changes and always for the worst. But they wouldn't make any sudden transformations now, not in his thoughts. Again and again he brought them back to make sure they were the same.

He set his alarm clock to wake himself for early mass the next day. There was no one who would be accompanying him to church this year. He'd have to go alone.

Alone.

III

Next Halloween there was a premature appearance of snow, a thin foundation of whiteness that clung to the earth and trees, putting a pallid face on the suburb. In the moonlight it glittered, a frosty spume. This sparkling below was mirrored by the stars positioned tenuously in the night above. A monstrous mass of snowclouds to the west threatened to intervene, cutting off the reflection from its source and turning everything into a dull emptiness. All sounds were hollowed by the cold, made into the cries of migrating birds in a vacant November dusk.

Not even November yet and look at it, he thought as he stared through the glass of his front door. Very few were out tonight, and the ones who were found fewer houses open to them, closed doors and extinguished porchlights turning them away to roam blindly through the streets. He had lost much of the spirit himself, had not even set out a jack-o-lantern to signal his harbor in the night.

Then again, how would he have carried around such a weighty object with his leg the way it was now? One good fall down the stairs and he started collecting disability pay from the government, laid up for months in the solitude of his home.

He had prayed for punishment and his prayers had been answered. Not the leg itself, which only offered physical pain and inconvenience, but the other punishment, the solitude. This was the way he remembered being corrected as a child: sent into the basement, exiled to the cold stone cellar without the relief of light, save for that which hazed in through a dusty window-well in the corner. In that corner he stood, near as he could to the light. It was there that he once saw a fly twitching in a spider web. He watched and watched and eventually the spider came out to begin feasting on its prey. He watched it all, dazed with horror and sickness. When it was over he wanted to do something. He did. With a predatory stealth he managed to pinch up the little spider and pull it off its web. It tasted like nothing at all really, except a momentary tickle on his dry tongue.

"Trick or treat," he heard. And he almost got up to arduously cane his way to the door. But the Halloween slogan had been spoken somewhere in the distance. Why did it sound so close for a moment? Crescendoing echoes of the imagination, where far is near, up is down, pain pleasure. Maybe he should close up for the night. There seemed to be only a few kids playing the game this year. Only the most desultory stragglers remained at this point. Well, there was one now.

"Trick or treat," said a mild, failing little voice. Standing on the other side of the door was an elaborately garbed witch, complete with a warm black shawl and black gloves in addition to her black gown. An old broom was held in one hand, a bag in the other.

"You'll have to wait just a moment," he called through the door as he struggled to get up from the sofa with the aid of his cane. Pain. Good, good. He picked up a full bag of candy from the coffee table and was quite prepared to bestow its entire contents on the little lady in black. But then he recognized who it was behind the cadaver-yellow make-up. Watch it. Wouldn't want to do anything unusual. Play you don't know who it is. And do not say anything concerning red houses with black shutters. Nothing about Ash Street.

To make matters worse, there was the outline of a parent standing on the sidewalk. Insure the safety of the last living child, he thought. But maybe there were others, though he'd only seen the brother and sister. Careful. Pretend she's unfamiliar; after all, she's wearing a different get-up from the one she wore the past two years. Above all don't say a word about you know who.

And what if he should innocently ask where was her little brother this year? Would she say: "He was killed," or maybe, "He's dead," or perhaps just, "He's gone," depending on how the parents handled the whole affair. With any luck, he would not have to find out.

He opened the door just far enough to hand out the candy and in a bland voice said: "Here you go, my little witch." That last part just slipped out somehow.

"Thank you," she said under her breath, under a thousand breaths of fear and experience. So did it seem.

She turned away, and as she descended the porch steps her broom clunked along one step behind her. An old, frayed, throw-away broom. Perfect for witches. And the kind perfect for keeping a child in line. An ugly old thing kept in a corner, an instrument of discipline always within easy reach, always within a child's sight until the thing became a dream-haunting image. Mother's broom.

After the girl and her mother were out of sight, he closed the door on the world and, having survived a tense episode, was actually grateful for the solitude that only minutes ago was the object of his dread.

Darkness. Bed.

But he could not sleep, not to say he did not dream. Hypnagogic horrors settled into his mind, a grotesque succession of images resembling lurid frames from old comic strips. Impossibly distorted faces painted in garish colors frolicked before his mental eye, all entirely beyond his control. These were accompanied by a series of funhouse noises which seemed to emanate from some zone located between his brain and the moonlit bedroom around him. A drone of half-thrilled, half-horrified voices filled the background of his imagination, punctuated by super-distinct shouts which used his name as an excuse for sound. It was an abstract version of his mother's voice, now robbed of any sensual quality to identify it as such, remaining only a pure idea. The voice called out his name from a distant room in his memory. *Samuel*, it shouted with a terrible urgency of obscure origin. Then suddenly – *trick or treat*. The words echoed, changing in sense as they faded into silence: *trick or treat – down the street – we will meet – ashes, ashes*. No, not ashes but other trees. The boy walked behind some big maples, was eclipsed by them. Did he know a car was following him that night? Panic. Don't lose him now. Don't lose him. Ah, there he was on the other side. Nice trees. Good old trees. The boy turned around, and in his hand was a tangled web of strings whose ends extended up to the stars which he began working like kites or toy airplanes or flying puppets, staring up at the night and screaming for the help that never came. Mother's voice started shouting again; then the other voices mixed in, becoming a foul babbling unity of dead voices chattering away. Night of the Dead. All the dead conversed with him in a single voicey-woicey.

Trick or treat, it said.

But this didn't sound as if it were part of his delirium. The words seemed to originate from outside him, for their utterance served to disturb his half-sleep and free him of its terrible weight. Instinctively cautious of his lame leg, he managed to wrest himself from sweaty bedcovers and place both feet on the solid floor. This felt reassuring. But then:

Trick or treat.

It was outside. Someone on the front porch. "I'm coming," he called into the darkness, the sound of his own voice awakening him to the absurdity of what it had said. Had the months of solitude finally exacted their strange price from his sanity? Listen closely. Maybe it won't happen again.

Trick or treat. Trick or treat.

Trick, he thought. But he'd have to go downstairs to be sure. He imagined seeing a playfully laughing shape or shapes scurrying off into the darkness the moment he opened the door. He'd have to hurry, though, if he was to catch them at it. Damn leg, where's that cane. He next found his bathrobe in the darkness and draped it over his underclothed body. Now to negotiate those wicked stairs. Turn on the hallway light. No, that would alert them to his coming. Smart.

He was making it down the stairs in good time, considering the gloomy conditions he was working under. Neither this nor that nor gloom of night. Gloom of night. Dead of night. Night of the Dead.

With that odd sprightliness of cripples he ambled his way down the stairs, his cane always remaining a step ahead for support. Concentrate, he told his mind, which was starting to wander into strange places in the darkness. Watch out! Almost took a tumble that time. Finally he made it to the very bottom. A sound came through the wall from out on the front porch, a soft explosion it seemed. Good, they were still there. He could catch them and reassure his mind regarding the source of its fancies. The labor of walking down the stairs had left him rather hyperventilated and unsure about everything.

Trying to effect the shortest possible interval between the two operations, he turned the lock above the handle and pulled back the door as suddenly as he was able. A cold wind seeped in around the edges of the outer door, prowling its way past him and into the house. Out on the porch there was no sign of a boyish trickster. Wait, yes there was.

He had to turn on the porchlight to see it. Directly in front of the door a jack-o-lantern had been heaved forcefully down onto the cement, caving in its pulpy shell which had exploded into fragments lying here and there on the porch. He opened the outer door for a closer look, and a swift wind invaded the house, flying past his head on frigid wings. What a blast, close the door. Close the door!

"Little buggers," he said very clearly, an attempt to relieve his sense of disorder and delirium.

"Who, meezy-weezy?" said the voice behind him.

At the top of the stairs. A dwarfish silhouette, seemingly with something in its hand. A weapon. Well, he had his cane at least.

"How did you get in here, child?" he asked without being sure it really was a child, considering its strangely hybrid voice.

"Child yourself, sonny. No such things where I come from. No Sammy-Wammies either. I'm just in disguise."

"How did you get in?" he repeated, still hoping to establish a rational manner of entry.

"In? I was already in."

"Here?" he asked.

"No, not here. There-dee-dare." The figure was pointing out the window at the top of the stairs, out at the kaleidoscopic sky. "Isn't it a beauty? No children, no anything."

"What do you mean?" he inquired with oneiric inspiration, the normalcy of dream being the only thing that kept his mind together at this stage.

"Mean? I don't mean nothing, you meany."

Double negative, he thought, relieved to have retained contact with a real world of grammatical propriety. Double negative: two empty mirrors reflecting each other's emptiness to infinite powers, nothing cancelling out nothing.

"Nothing?" he echoed with an interrogative inflection.

"Yup, that's where you're going."

"How am I supposed to do that?" he asked, gripping his cane tightly, sensing a climax to this confrontation.

"How? Don't worry. You already made sure of how-wow-wow . . . TRICK OR TREAT!"

And suddenly the thing came gliding down through the darkness.

IV

He was found the next day by Father Mickiewicz, who had telephoned earlier after failing to see this clockwork parishioner appear as usual for early mass on All Souls Day. The door was wide open, and the priest discovered his body at the bottom of the stairs, its bathrobe and underclothes grotesquely disarranged. The poor man seemed to have taken another fall, a fatal one this time. Aimless life, aimless death: *Thus was his death in keeping with his life*, as Ovid wrote. So ran the priest's ad hoc eulogy, though not the one he would deliver at the deceased's funeral.

But why was the door open if he fell down the stairs? Father M. came to ask himself. The police answered this question with theories about an intruder or intruders unknown. Given the nature of the crime, they speculated on a revenge motive, which the priest's informal testimony was quick to contradict. The idea of revenge against such a man was far-fetched, if not totally meaningless. Yes, meaningless. Nevertheless, the motive was not robbery and the man seemed to have been beaten to death, possibly with his own cane. Later evidence showed that the corpse had been violated, but with an object much longer and more coarse than the cane originally supposed. They were now looking for something with the dimensions of a broomstick, probably a very old thing, splintered and decayed. But they would never find it in the places they were searching.

THE PRODIGY OF DREAMS

> I conceived my ideal leavetaking from this earth – a drama prepared by strange portents, swiftly developed by dreams and visions nurtured in an atmosphere of sublime dread, growing overnight like some gaudy fungus in a forgotten cellar. . .
>
> *The Travel Diaries of Arthur Emerson*

It seemed to Arthur Emerson that the swans, those perennial guests of the estate, had somehow become strange. Yet his knowledge of their natural behavior was vague, providing him with little idea of precisely how they had departed from habit or instinct. But he strongly sensed that there had indeed been such a departure, an imperceptible drifting into the peculiar. Suddenly these creatures, which had become as tedious to him as everything else, filled him with an astonishment he had not known in many years.

That morning they were gathered at the center of the lake, barely visible within a milky haze which hovered above still waters. For as long as he observed them, they did not allow themselves the slightest motion toward the grassy shores circling the lake. Each of them – there were four – faced a separate direction, as though some antagonism existed within their order. Then their sleek, ghostly forms revolved with a mechanical ease and came to huddle around an imaginary point of focus. For a moment their heads nodded slightly toward one another, bowing in wordless prayer; but soon they stretched their snaking necks in unison, elevated their orange and black bills toward the thick mist above, and gazed into its depths. There followed a series of haunting cries unlike anything ever heard on the vast grounds of that isolated estate.

Arthur Emerson now wondered if something he could not see was disturbing the swans. As he stood at the tall windows which faced the lake, he made a mental note to have Graff go down there and find out what he could. Possibly some unwelcome animal was now living in the dense woods nearby. And as he further considered the matter, it appeared that the numerous wild ducks, those brownish goblins that were always either visible or audible somewhere in the vicinity of the lake, had already vacated the area. Or perhaps they were only obscured by the unusually heavy mist of that singular morning.

Arthur Emerson spent the rest of the day in the library. At intervals he was visited by a very black cat, an aloof and somewhat phantasmal member of the small Emerson household. Eventually it fell asleep on a sunny window ledge, while its master wandered among the countless uncatalogued volumes he had accumulated over the past fifty years or so.

During his childhood, the collection which filled the library's dark shelves was a common one, and much of it he had given away or destroyed in order to provide room for other works. He was the only scholar in a lengthy succession of businessmen of one kind or another, the last living member of the old family; at his death, the estate would probably pass into the hands of a distant relative whose name and face he did not know. But this was not of any great concern to Arthur Emerson: resignation to his own inconsequence, along with that of all things of the earth, was a philosophy he had nurtured for some time, and with considerable success.

In his younger years he had travelled a great deal, these excursions often relating to his studies, which could be approximately described as ethnological bordering on the esoteric. Throughout various quarters of what now seemed to him a shrunken, almost claustrophobic world, he had attempted to satisfy an inborn craving to comprehend what *then* seemed to him an astonishing, even shocking existence. Arthur Emerson recalled that while still a child the world around him suggested strange expanses not subject to common view. This sense of the invisible often exerted itself in moments when he witnessed nothing more than a patch of pink sky above leafless trees in twilight or an abandoned room where dust settled on portraits and old furniture. To him, however, these appearances disguised realms of an entirely different nature. For within these imagined or divined spheres there existed a certain . . . confusion, a swirling, fluttering motion that was belied by the relative order of the seen.

Only on rare occasions could he enter these unseen spaces, and always unexpectedly. A striking experience of this kind took place in his childhood years and involved a previous generation of swans which he had paused one summer afternoon to contemplate from a knoll by the lake. Perhaps their smooth drifting and gliding upon the water had induced in him something like a hypnotic state. The ultimate effect, however, was not the serene catatonia of hypnosis, but a whirling flight through a glittering threshold which opened within the air itself, propelling him into a kaleidoscopic universe where space consisted only of multi-colored and ever-changing currents, as of wind or water, and where time did not exist.

Later he became a student of the imaginary lands hypothesized by legends and theologies, and he had sojourned in places which concealed or suggested unknown orders of existence. Among the volumes in his library were several of his own authorship, bibliographical shadows of his lifetime obsessions. His body of works included such titles as: *In the Margins of Paradise, The Forgotten Universe of the Vicoli*, and *The Secret Gods and Other Studies*. For many feverish years he was burdened with the sensation, an ancient one to be sure, that the incredible sprawl of human history was no more than a pathetically partial record of an infinitely vast and shadowed chronicle of universal metamorphoses. How much greater, then, was the feeling that his own pathetic history formed a practically invisible fragment of what itself was merely an obscure splinter of the infinite. Somehow he needed to excarcerate himself from the claustral dungeon cell of his life. In the end, however, he broke beneath the weight of his aspiration. And as the years passed, the only mystery which seemed worthy of his interest, and his amazement, was that unknown day which would inaugurate his personal eternity, that incredible day on which the sun simply would not rise, and forever would begin.

Arthur Emerson pulled a rather large book down from its high shelf and ambled toward a cluttered desk to make some notes for a work which would very likely be his last. Its tentative title: *Dynasties of Dust*.

Toward nightfall he suspended his labors. With much stiffness, he walked to the window ledge where the cat lay sleeping in the fading light of dusk. But its body seemed to rise and fall a little too vigorously for sleep, and it made a strange whistling sound rather than the usual murmuring purr. The cat opened its eyes and rolled sideways, as it often did when inviting a hand to stroke its glossy black fur. But as soon as Arthur Emerson laid his palm upon that smooth coat, his fingers were rapidly gnawed. The animal then leaped to the floor and ran out of the room, while Arthur Emerson watched his own blood trickling over his hand in a shapeless stain.

All that evening he felt restless, profoundly at odds with the atmosphere of each room he entered and then soon abandoned. He wandered the house, telling himself that he was in search of his ebony pet, in order to establish the terms of their misunderstanding. But this pretext would every so often dissolve, and it then became clear to Arthur Emerson that he searched for something less tangible than a runaway cat. These rooms, however high their ceilings, suffocated him with shadowy questions; his footsteps, echoing sharply down long gleaming corridors, sounded like clacking bones. The house had become a museum of mystery.

He finally gave up the search and allowed fatigue to guide him to his bedroom, where immediately he opened a window in the hope that something without a name would fly from the house. But he now discovered that it was not only the house which was swollen with mysteries; it was the very night itself. A nocturnal breeze began lifting the curtains, mingling with the air inside the room. Shapeless clumps of clouds floated with mechanical complacency across a stone gray sky, a sky which itself seemed shapeless rather than evenly infinite. To his left he saw that the inner surface of the open window reflected a strange face, his face, and he pushed the fear-stricken thing out into the darkness.

Arthur Emerson eventually slept that night, but he also dreamed. His dreams were without definite form, a realm of mist where twisted shadows glided, their dark mass shifting fluently. Then, through the queerly gathered and drifting clouds of mist, he saw a shadow whose dark monstrosity made the others seem shapely and radiant. It was a deformed colossus, a disfigured monument carved from the absolute density of the blackest abyss. And now the lesser shadows, the pale and meager shadows, seemed to join in a squealing chorus of praise to the greater one. He gazed at the cyclopean thing in a trance of horror, until its mountainous mass began to move, slowly stretching out some part of itself, flexing what might have been a misshapen arm. And when he awoke, scattering the bedcovers, he felt a warm breeze wafting in through a window which he could not remember having left open.

The next morning it became apparent that there would be no relief from the uncanny influences which still seemed to be lingering from the day before. All about the Emerson estate a terrific fog had formed, blinding the inhabitants of the house to most of the world beyond it. What few shapes remained visible – the closest and darkest trees, some rose bushes pressing against the windows – seemed drained of all earthly substance, creating a landscape both infinite and imprisoning, an estate of dream. Unseen in the fog, the swans were calling out like banshees down by the lake. And even Graff, when he appeared in the library attired in a bulky groundskeeper's jacket and soiled trousers, looked less like a man than like a specter of ill prophecy.

"Are you certain," said Arthur Emerson, who was seated at his desk, "that you have nothing to report about those creatures?"

"No sir," replied Graff. "Nothing."

There was, however, something else Graff had discovered, something which he thought the master of the house should see for himself. Together they travelled down several stairways leading to the various cellars and storage chambers beneath the house. On the way Graff explained that, as also ordered, he had searched for the cat, which had not been seen since last evening. Arthur Emerson only gazed at his man and nodded in silence, while inwardly muttering to himself about some strangeness he perceived in the old retainer. Between every few phrases the man would begin humming, or rather singing at the back of his throat in an entirely peculiar manner.

After making their way far into the dark catacombs of the Emerson house, they arrived at a remote room which seemed to have been left unfinished when the house had been erected so long ago. There were no lighting fixtures (except the one recently improvised by Graff), the stone walls were unplastered and unpainted, and the floor was of hard, bare earth. Graff pointed downward, and his crooked finger wandered in an arc through the sepulchral dimness of the room. Arthur Emerson now saw that the place had been turned into a charnel house for the remains of small animals: mice, rats, birds, squirrels, even a few young possums and raccoons. He already knew the cat to be an obsessive hunter, but it seemed strange that these carcasses had all been brought to this room, as if it were a kind of sanctum of mutilation and death.

While contemplating this macabre chamber, Arthur Emerson noticed peripherally that Graff was fidgeting with some object concealed in his pocket. How strange indeed the old servant had become.

"What have you got there?" Arthur Emerson asked.

"Sir?" Graff replied, as though his manual gyrations had proceeded without his awareness. "Oh, this," he said, revealing a metal gardening implement with four clawlike prongs. "I was doing some work outdoors; that is, I was intending to do so, if there was time."

"Time? On a day like this?"

Obviously embarrassed and at a loss to explain himself, Graff pointed the taloned tool at the decomposing carcasses. "None of the animals actually seem to have been eaten," he quietly observed, and that curious piping in his throat sounded almost louder than his words.

"No," Arthur Emerson agreed with some bewilderment. He then reached up to grasp a thick black extension cord which Graff had slung over the rafters; at the end of the cord was a light bulb which he tried to maneuver to more fully illuminate the room. Incautiously, perhaps, Arthur Emerson was thinking that there existed some method to the way the bodies of the slaughtered creatures were positioned across the entire floor. Graff's next remark approximated the unformed perception of his employer: "Like a trail of dominos winding round and round. But no true sense to it."

Arthur Emerson readily granted the apt analogy to a maze of dominos, but concerning the second of Graff's statements there suddenly appeared to be some doubt. For at that moment Arthur Emerson looked up and saw a queerly shaped stain, as if made by mold or moisture, upon the far wall.

"Shall I clean the place out?" asked Graff, raising the metal claw.

"What? No," decided Arthur Emerson as he gazed at the shapeless, groping horror that appeared to have crawled from his own dream and stained itself into the stone before him. "Leave everything exactly as it is," he ordered the old whistling servant.

Arthur Emerson returned to the library, and there he began to explore a certain shelf of books. This shelf comprised his private archives of handsomely bound travel diaries he had kept over the years. He withdrew one after another, paged through each volume, and then replaced it. Finally he found the one he wanted, which was the record of a visit to central and southern Italy made when he was a young man. Settling down at his desk, he leaned into the words before him. After reading only a few sentences he began to wonder who this strange lyrical creature, this ghost, might be. No doubt himself, but in some previous incarnation, some bizarre anterior life.

Spoleto (Ides of October)

What wonders dwell within the vicoli! How often can I celebrate those fabulous little thoroughfares which form a maze of magic and dreams, and how often can I praise the medieval hill towns of Umbria which are woven of such streets? Guiding one into courtyards, they are snug roads invented for the meanderings of sleepwalkers. One is embraced by the gray walls of high houses, one is nestled beneath their wood-beamed roofs and beneath innumerable arches which cut the monotonous day into a wealth of shadows and frame the stars at night within random curves and angles. Nightfall in the vicoli! Pale yellow lanterns awake like apparitions in the last moments of twilight, claiming the dark narrow lanes for their own, granting an enchanted but somewhat uneasy passage to those who would walk there. And last evening I found myself among these spirits.

Intoxicated as much by the Via Porta Fuga as by the wine I had drunk at dinner, I wandered across bridges, beneath arches and overhanging roofs, up and down battered stairways, past ivy-hung walls and black windows masked with iron grillwork. I turned a corner and glimpsed a small open doorway ahead. Without thinking, I looked inside as I passed, seeing only a tiny niche, not even a room, which must have been constructed in the space between two buildings. All I could clearly discern were two small candles which were the source and focus of a confusion of shadows. From inside a man's voice spoke to me in English: "A survival of the ancient world," said the voice, which carried the accent of a cultivated Englishman, sounding very bored and mechanical and very out of place in the circumstances. And I also must note a strange whistling quality in his words, as if his naturally low speaking voice were resonating with faintly high-pitched overtones. "Yes, sir, I am speaking to you," he continued. "A fragment of antiquity, a survival of the ancient world. Nothing to fear, there is no fee demanded."

He now appeared in the doorway, a balding and flabby middle-aged gentleman in a tattered, tieless suit – the image of his own weary voice, the voice of an exhausted fairgrounds huckster. His face, as it reflected the pale yellow light of the lantern beside the open doorway, was a calm face; but its calmness seemed to derive from a total despair of soul rather than from a serenity of mind. "I am referring to the altar of the god," he said. "However extensive your learning and your travels, that *one* is not among those deities you will have heard about; that one is not among those divinities you may have laughed about. It could be distantly related, perhaps, to those numina of Roman cesspools and sewage systems. But it is not a mere Cloacina, not a Mephitis or Robigo. In name, the god is known as Cynothoglys: the god without shape, the god of changes and confusion, the god of decompositions, the mortician god of both gods and men, the metamortician of all things. There is no fee demanded."

I remained where I stood, and then the man stepped out into the little vicolo in order to allow me a better view through the open doorway, into the candlelit room beyond. I could now see that the candles were shining on either side of a low slab, cheap candles that sent out a quivering haze of smoke. Between these tapers was an object which I could not define, some poor shapeless thing, perhaps the molten relic of a volcanic eruption at some distant time, but certainly not the image of an ancient deity. There seemed to be nothing and no one else inhabiting that sinister little nook.

I may now contend that, given the unusual circumstances described above, the wisest course of action would have been to mumble a few polite excuses and move on. But I have also described the spell which is cast by the vicoli, by their dimly glowing and twisted depths. Entranced by these dreamlike surroundings, I was thus prepared to accept the strange gentleman's offer, if only to enhance my feeling of intoxication with all the formless mysteries whose name was now Cynothoglys.

"But be solemn, sir. I warn you to be solemn." I stared at the man for a brief moment, and in that moment this urging of my solemnity seemed connected in some way to his own slavish and impoverished state, which I found it difficult to believe had always been his condition. "The god will not mock your devotions, your prayers," he whispered and whistled. "Nor will it be mocked."

Then, stepping through the little doorway, I approached the primitive altar. Occupying its center was a dark, monolithic object whose twisting shapelessness has placed it beyond simple analogies in my imagination. Yet there was something in its contours – a certain dynamism, like that of great crablike roots springing forth from the ground – which suggested more than mere chaos or random creation. Perhaps the following statement could be more sensibly attributed to the mood of the moment, but there seemed a definite power somehow linked to this gnarled effigy, a gloomy force which was disguised by its monumentally static appearance. Toward the summit of the mutilated sculpture, a crooked armlike appendage extended outward in a frozen grasp, as if it had held this position for unknown eons and at any time might resume, and conclude, its movement.

I drew closer to the contorted idol, remaining in its presence far longer than I intended. That I actually found myself mentally composing a kind of supplication tells more than I am presently able about my psychological and spiritual state last evening. Was it this beast of writhing stone or the spell of the vicoli which inspired my prayer and·determined its form? It was, I think, something which they shared, a suggestion of great things: great secrets and great sorrows, great wonders and catastrophes, great destinies, great doom, and a single great death. My own. Drugged by this inspiration, I conceived my ideal leavetaking from this earth – a drama prepared by strange portents, swiftly developed by dreams and visions nurtured in an atmosphere of sublime dread, growing overnight like some gaudy fungus in a forgotten cellar, and always with the awful hand of the mortician god working the machinery behind the scenes. Beasts and men would form an alliance with great Cynothoglys, the elements themselves would enter into the conspiracy, a muted vortex of strange forces all culminating in a spectral denouement, all converging to deliver me to the inevitable, but deliver me in a manner worthy of the most expansive and unearthly sensations of my life. I conceived the primal salvation of tearing flesh, of seizure by the god and the ecstatic rending of the frail envelope of skin and sinew. And as others only sink into their deaths – into mine I would soar.

But how could I have desired this to be? I now wonder, fully sober following my debauch of dreams. Perhaps I am too repentant of my prayer and try to reassure myself by my very inability to give it a rational place in the history of the world. The mere memory of my adventure and my delirium, I expect, will serve to carry me through many of the barren days ahead, though only to abandon me in the end to a pathetic demise of meaningless pain. By then I may have forgotten the god I encountered, along with the one who served him like a slave. Both seem to have disappeared from the vicoli, their temple standing empty and abandoned. And now I am free to imagine that it was not I who came to the vicoli to meet the god, but the god who came to meet me.

After reading these old words, Arthur Emerson sat silent and solemn at his desk. Was it over for him, then? All the portents had appeared and all the functionaries of his doom were now assembled, both outside the library door – where the footfall of man and beast sounded – and beyond the library windows, where a horrible thing without shape had begun to loom out of the fog, reaching through the walls and windows as if they too were merely mist. Were a thousand thoughts of outrage and dread now supposed to rise within him at the prospect of this occult extermination? After all, he was about to have forced upon him that dream of death, that whim of some young adventurer who could not resist being granted a wish or two by a tourist attraction.

And now the crying of the swans had begun to sound from the lake and through the fog and into the house. Their shrieks were echoing everywhere, and he might have predicted as much. Would he soon be required to add his own shrieks to theirs, was it now time to be overcome by the wonder of the unknown and the majesty of fate; was this how it was *done* in the world of doom?

Risking an accusation of bad manners, Arthur Emerson failed to rise from his chair to greet the guest he had invited so long ago. "You are too late," he said in a dry voice. "But since you have taken the trouble. . ." And the god, like some obedient slave, descended upon its victim.

It was only at the very end that Arthur Emerson's attitude of incuriosity abandoned him. As he had guessed, perhaps even wished, his voice indeed became confused with the screaming of the swans, soaring high into the muffling fog.

MRS RINALDI'S ANGEL

From time to time during my childhood, the striking dreams that I nightly experienced would become brutally vivid, causing me to awake screaming.

The shouting done, I sank back into my bed in a state of super-enervation resulting from the bodiless adventures imposed upon my slumbering self. Yet my body was surely affected by this nocturnal regimen, exercised harshly by visions both crystalline and confused. This activity, however immaterial, only served to drain my reserves of strength and in a few moments stole from me the benefits of a full night's sleep. Nevertheless, while I was deprived of the privilege of a natural rest, there may also have been some profit gained: the awful opulence of the dream, a rich and swollen world nourished by the exhaustion of the flesh. The world, in fact, *as such*. Any other realm seemed an absence by comparison, at best a chasm in the fertile graveyard of life.

Of course my parents did not share my feelings on this subject. "What is *wrong* with him," I heard my father bellow from far down the hallway, his voice full of reproach. Shortly afterward my mother was by my side. "They seem to be getting worse," she would say. Then on one occasion she whispered, "I think it's time we did something about this problem."

The tone of her voice told me that what she had in mind was not the doctor's appointment so often urged by my father. Hers was a more dubious quest for a curative, though one which no doubt also seemed more appropriate to my "suffering." My mother was always prone to the enticements of superstition, and my troubled dreams appeared to justify an indulgence in unorthodox measures. Her shining and solemn gaze betrayed her own dreams of trafficking with esoteric forces, of being on familiar terms with specialists in a secret universe, entrepreneurs of the intangible.

"Tomorrow your father is leaving early on business. You stay home from school, and then we'll go and visit a woman I know."

Late the following morning, my mother and I went to a house in one of the outlying neighborhoods of town and were graciously invited to be seated in the parlor of the long-widowed Mrs Rinaldi. Perhaps it was only the fatigue my dreams had inflicted on me that made it so difficult to consolidate any lucid thoughts or feelings about the old woman and her remote house. Although the well-ordered room we occupied was flush with sunlight, this illumination somehow acted in the way of a wash over a watercolor painting, blurring the outline of things and subduing the clarity of surfaces. This obscurity was not dispersed even by the large and thickly shaded lamp Mrs Rinaldi kept lighted beside the small divan on which she and my mother sat. I was close to them in an old but respectably upholstered armchair, and yet their forms refused to come into focus, just as everything else in that room resisted definition. How well I knew such surroundings, those deep interiors of dream where everything is saturated with unreality and more or less dissolves under a direct gaze. I could tell how neatly this particular interior was arranged – pictures perfectly straight and tight against the walls, well-dusted figurines arranged along open shelves, lace-fringed tablecovers set precisely in place, and delicate silk flowers in slim vases of colored glass. Yet there was something so fragile about the balance of these things, as if they were all susceptible to sudden derangement should there be some upset, no matter how subtle, in the secret system which held them together. This volatility seemed to extend to Mrs Rinaldi herself, though in fact she may have been its source.

Casually examined, she appeared to present only the usual mysteries of old women who might be expected to speak with a heavy accent, whether or not they actually did so. She wore the carnal bulk and simple attire of a peasant race, and her calm manner indeed epitomized the peasant quietude of popular conception: her hands folded without tremor upon a wide lap and her eyes mildly attentive. But those eyes were so pale, as was her complexion and gauzy hair. It was as if some great strain had depleted her, and was continually depleting her, of the strong coloring she once possessed, draining her powers and leaving her vulnerable to some tenuous onslaught. At any moment during the time my mother was explaining the reason why we sought her help, Mrs Rinaldi might have degenerated before our eyes, might have finally succumbed to spectral afflictions she had spent so many years fending off, both for her own sake and for the sake of others. And still she might have easily been mistaken for just another old woman whose tidy parlor displayed no object or image that would betray her most questionable and perilous occupation.

"Missus," she said to my mother, though her eyes were on me,

"I would like to take your son into another room in this house. There I believe I may begin to help him."

My mother assented and Mrs Rinaldi escorted me down a hallway to a room at the back of the house. The room reminded me of a little shop of some kind, one that kept its merchandise hidden in dark cabinets along the walls, in great chests upon the floor, boxes and cases of every sort piled here and there. Nothing except these receptacles, this array of multiform exteriors, was exposed to view. The only window was tightly shuttered and a bare light bulb hanging overhead served as the only illumination.

There was nowhere to sit, only empty floor space; Mrs Rinaldi took my hand and stood me at the center of the room. After gazing rather sternly down at me for some moments, she proceeded to pace slowly around me.

"Do you know what dreams are?" she asked quietly, and then immediately began to answer her own question. "They are parasites – maggots of the mind and soul, feeding on the mind and soul as ordinary maggots feed on the body. And their feeding on the mind and soul in turn gnaws away at the body, which in turn again affects the mind and the soul, and so on until death. These things cannot be separated, nor can anything else. Because everything is terribly inseparable and affects every other thing. Even the most alien things are connected together with every other thing. And so if these dreams have no world of their own to nourish them, they may come into yours and possess it, exhaust it little by little each night. They use your world and use it up. They wear your face and the faces of things you know: things that are yours they use in ways that are theirs. And some persons are so easy for them to use, and they use them so hard. But they use everyone and have always used everyone, because they are from the old time, the time before all the worlds awoke from a long and helpless night. And these dreams, these things that are called dreams, are still working to throw us back into that great mad darkness, to exhaust each one of us in our lonely sleep and to use up everyone until death. Little by little, night after night, they take us away from ourselves and from the truth of things. I myself know very well what this can be like and what the dreams can do to us. They make us dance to their strange illusions until we are too exhausted to live. And they have found in you, child, an easy partner for their horrible dancing."

With these words Mrs Rinaldi not only revealed a side of herself quite different from the serene wise woman my mother had seen, but she also took me much deeper into things I had merely suspected until that day in the room where chests and strange boxes were piled up everywhere and great cabinets loomed along the walls, so many tightly closed doors and drawers and locked-up lids with so many things on the other side of them.

"Of course," she went on, "these dreams of yours cannot be wholly exorcised from your life, but only driven back so that they may do no *extraordinary* harm. They will still triumph in the end, denying us not just the restoration of nightly sleep. For ultimately they steal away the time which might have measured into immortality. They corrupt us in *every way*, abducting us from the ranks of angels we might have been or become, pure and calm and everlasting. It is because of them that we endure such a meager allotment of years, with all their foulness. This is all I can offer you, child, even if you may not understand what it means. For it is surely not meant that you should fall into the fullest corruption before your time."

Her speech concluded, Mrs Rinaldi stood before me, massive and motionless, her breathing now a bit labored. I confess that her theories intrigued me as far as I could comprehend them, for at the time her statements regarding the meaning and mechanisms of dream appeared to be founded on somewhat questionable assumptions, unnecessarily outlandish in their departures from the oldest orthodoxies of creation. Nonetheless, I decided not to resist whatever applications she chose to make of her ideas. On her side, she was scrutinizing my small form with some intensity, engaged in what seemed a psychic sizing up of my presence, as if she was seriously unsure whether or not it was safe to move on to the next step with me.

Apparently resolving her doubts, she shuffled over to a tall cabinet, unlocked its door with a key she had taken from a sagging pocket in her dress, and from within removed two items: a slim decanter half-filled with a dark red liquid, presumably wine, and a shallow wide-mouthed drinking glass. Carrying these objects back to me, she put out her right hand, in which she held the glass, and said: "Take this and spit into it." After I had done this, she poured some of the wine into the glass and then replaced the decanter in its cabinet, which she locked once again. "Now kneel down on the floor," she ordered. "Don't let anything spill out of the glass, and don't get up until I tell you to do so. I'm going to turn out the light."

Even in total darkness, Mrs Rinaldi maneuvered well about the room, her footsteps again moving away from me. I heard her opening another cabinet, or perhaps it was a large chest whose heavy lid she struggled to push back, its hinges grinding in the darkness. A slight draft crossed the room, a brief drifting current of air without scent and neither warm nor cold. Mrs Rinaldi then approached me, moving more slowly than she had before, as if bearing some weighty object. With a groan, she set it down, and I heard it scrape the floor inches from where I knelt, though I could not see what it was.

Suddenly a thin line of light scored the blackness, and I could see Mrs Rinaldi's old finger slowly lifting the lid of a long low box from which the luminousness emanated. The glowing slit widened as the lid was drawn back farther, revealing a pale brilliance that seemed confined wholly within the box itself, casting not the least glimmer into the room. The source of this light was a kind of incandescent vapor that curled about in a way that seemed to draw the room's darkness into its lustrous realm, which appeared to extend beyond the boundaries of the visible and made the box before me look bottomless. But I felt the bottom for myself when the whispering voice of Mrs Rinaldi instructed me to place the glass I was holding down into the box. So I offered the glass to that fluorescent mist, that churning vapor which was electrical in some way, scintillating with infinitesimal flashes of sharp light, sprinkled with shattered diamonds.

I expected to feel something as I put my hand in the shining box, easily setting the glass upon its shallow and quite solid bottom. But there was nothing at all to be felt, no sensation whatever – not even that of my own hand. There seemed to be a power to this prodigy, but it was a terribly quiescent power, a cataract of the purest light plummetting silently in the blackness of space. If it could have spoken it might have told, in a soft and reverberant voice, of the lonely peace of the planets, the uninhabited paradise of clouds, and an antiseptic infinity.

After I placed the glass of wine and spittle into the box, the light from within took on a rosy hue for just a moment, then resumed its glittering whiteness once again. It had taken the offering. Mrs Rinaldi whispered "amen," then carefully closed the lid upon the box, returning the room to blackness. I heard her replace the object in its tabernacle of storage, wherever that may have been. At last the lights came on.

"You can get up now," Mrs Rinaldi said. "And wipe off your knees, they're a little dirty."

When I finished brushing off my pants I found that Mrs Rinaldi was again scrutinizing me for tell-tale signs of some possible misunderstanding or perhaps misconduct that I might disclose to her. I imagined that she was about to say, "Do not ask what it was you saw in this room." But in actuality she said, "You will feel better now, but never try to guess what is in that box. Never seek to know more about it." She did not pause to hear any response I might have had to her command, for she was indeed a wise woman and knew that in matters such as these no casual oath of abstention can be trusted, all fine intentions notwithstanding.

As soon as we left Mrs Rinaldi's house, my mother asked me what had happened, and I described the ceremony in detail. Nevertheless, she remained at a loss for any simple estimate of what I had told her: while she expected that Mrs Rinaldi's methods might be highly unusual, she also knew her own son's imagination. Still, she was obliged to keep faith with the arcane processes that she herself had set in motion. So after I recounted the incidents that took place in that room, my mother only nodded silently, perhaps bewilderedly.

I should document that, for a certain period of time, my mother's faith in Mrs Rinaldi did not appear to have been misplaced. The very day of our visit to the old woman was for me the beginning of a unique phase of experience. Even my father noted the change in my nighttime habits, as well as a newfound characterology I exhibited throughout the day. "The boy does seem quieter now," he commented to my mother.

Indeed, I could feel myself approaching a serenity almost shameful in its expansiveness, one that submerged me in a placid routine of the most violent contrast to my former life. I slept straight through each night and barely ruffled my bedcovers. This is not to claim that my sleep was left completely untouched by dreams. But these were no more than ripples on great becalmed waters, pathetic gestures of something that was trying to bestir the immobility of a vast and colorless world. A few figures might appear, tremulous as smoke, but they were the merest invalids of hallucination, lacking the strength to speak or raise a hand against my terrible peace.

My daydreams were actually more interesting, while still being incredibly vague and without tension. Sitting quietly in the classroom at school, I often gazed out the window at clouds and sunlight, watching the way the sunlight penetrated the clouds and the way the clouds were filled with both sunlight and shadows. Yet no images or ideas were aroused by this sight, as they had been before. Only a vacant meditation took place, a musing without subject matter. I could feel something trying to emerge in my imagination, some wild and colorful drama that was being kept far away from me, as far away as those clouds, remaining entirely vaporous and empty of either sense or sensation. And if I tried to draw any pictures in my notebook, allowing my hand all possible freedom (in order to find out if it could feel and remember what I could not), I found myself sketching over and over the same thing: boxes, boxes, boxes.

Nonetheless, I cannot say that I was unhappy during this time. My nightmares and everything associated with them had been bled from my system, drained away as I slept. I had been purified of tainted substances, sponged clean of strangely tinted stains on my mind and soul. I felt the vapid joy of a lightened being, a kind of clarity which seemed in a way true and even virtuous. But this moratorium on every form of darkness could only last so long before the old impulses asserted themselves within me, moving out like a pack of famished wolves in search of the stuff that once fed them and would feed them again.

For a number of nights my dreams remained somewhat anemic and continued to present only the palest characters and scenes. Thus, they had been rendered too weak to use me as they had before, seizing, as they did, the contents of my life – my memories and emotions, all the paraphernalia of a private history – and working them in their way, giving form to things that had none of their own and thereby exhausting my body and soul. Mrs Rinaldi's theory of these parasites that have been called dreams was therefore accurate . . . as far as it went. But she had failed to consider, or perhaps refused to acknowledge, that the dreamer on his part draws something from the dream, gaining a store of experience otherwise impossible to obtain, hoarding the grotesque or banal enigmas of the night to try and fill out the great empty spaces of the day. And my dreams had ceased to perform this function, or at least were no longer adequate to my needs – that appetite I had discovered in myself for banqueting on the absurd and horrible, even the perfectly evil. It was this deprivation, I believe, which brought about the change in the nature of my dreaming.

Having such paltry sustenance on which to nourish my tastes – frail demons and insipid decors – I must have been thrown back upon my own consciousness . . . until finally I became fully aware of my dreaming state, an intensely lucid spelunker in the caves of sleep. Over the course of several nights, then, I noticed a new or formerly obscure phenomenon, something that existed in the distance of those bankrupt landscapes that I had started to explore. It was a kind of sickly mist that lingered about the horizon of each dream, exerting a definite magnetism, a tugging upon the austere scenes that it enveloped from all sides, even hovering high above like an animate sky, a celestial vault that glistened softly. Yet the dreams themselves were cast in the dullest tones and contained the most spare and dilapidated furnishings.

In the very last dream I had of this type, I was wandering amid a few widely scattered ruins that seemed to have arisen from some undersea abyss, all soft and pallid from their dark confinement. Like the settings of the other dreams, this one seemed familiar, though incomplete, as if I was seeing the decayed remnants of something I might have known in waking life. For those were *not* time-eaten towers rising around me, and at my feet there were not sunken strongboxes crumbling like rotten flesh. Instead, these objects were the cabinets and cases I remembered from that room in Mrs Rinaldi's house, except now this memory was degenerating, being dragged away little by little, digested by that mist which surrounded everything and nibbled at it. And the more closely I approached this mist, the more decomposed the scenery of the dream became, until it was consumed altogether and I could see nothing but that sparkling, swirling vapor.

It was only when I had entered this foggy void that the true sense of dream, the inherent dread of my visions, was restored to me. Here was a sort of reservoir into which the depths of my dreams were being directed, leaving only a shallow spillover that barely trickled through my nights. *Here, I* say, without knowing really what place or plane of being it was: some spectral venue, a vacant lot situated along the backstreet of sleep, an outpost of the universe itself . . . or perhaps merely the inside of a box hidden away in the house of an old woman, a box in which something existed in all its insensible purity, a cloudy ether free of tainted forms and knowledge, freely cleansing others with its sterile grace.

In any event, I sensed that the usual boundaries of my world of sleep had extended into another realm. And it was here, I found, that the lost dreams were fully alive *in their essence*. Consumed within that barren vapor which I had seen imbibe a mixture of my own saliva and the reddest wine, they lived in exile from the multitude of unwitting hosts whose experiences they had once used like a wardrobe for those eerie performances behind the curtain of sleep. These were the parasites which forced the sleeper into the dual role of both player and witness in the manipulations of his memories and his emotions, the ungranted abduction of his private history for those reckless revels called dreams. But here, in that prison of glittering purity, they had been reduced to their primordial state – dreams in abstraction, faceless and formless things from the old time that a very old woman had revealed to me. And although they had neither face nor form, none of the multitudinous disguises in which I had always known them, their presence was still quite palpable all around me, bearing down upon the richly laden lucidity I had brought with me into a place where I did not belong.

A struggle evolved as that angelic mist – agent of my salvation – held at bay the things that craved my mind and soul, my very consciousness. But rather than join in that struggle, I gave myself up to this ravenous siege, offering my awareness to what had none of its own, bestowing all the treasures of my life on this wasteland of abstractions.

Then the infinite whiteness itself was flooded with the colors of countless faces and forms, a blank sky suddenly dense with rainbows, until *everything* was so saturated with revels and thick with frenzy that it took on the utter blackness of the old time. And in the blackness I awoke, screaming for all the world.

The next day I was standing on Mrs Rinaldi's porch, watching as my mother repeatedly slammed the doorknocker without being able to summon the old woman. But something told us she was nevertheless at home, a shadow that we saw pass nervously behind the front window. At last the door opened for us, but whoever opened it stayed on the other side, saying: "Missus, take your child home. There is nothing more that can be done. I made a mistake with him."

My mother protested the recurrence of my "sickness," taking a step inside the house and pulling me along with her. But Mrs Rinaldi only said: "Do not come in here. It is not a fit place to visit, and I am not fit to be looked upon." From what I could observe of the parlor, it did seem that an essential change had occurred, as if the room's fragile balance had failed and the ever-threatening derangement of its order had finally been consummated. Everything in this interior seemed askew, distorted by some process of decay and twisted out of natural proportion. It was a room seen through a warped and strangely colored window.

And how much stranger this color appeared when Mrs Rinaldi suddenly showed herself, and I saw that her once-pale eyes and sallow face had taken on the same tint, a greenish glaze as of something both rotten and reptilian. My mother was immediately silenced by this sight. "Now will you leave me?" she said. "Even for myself there is nothing I can do any longer. You know what I am saying, child. All those years the dreams had been kept away. But you have *consorted* with them, I know you did. I have made a mistake with you. You let my angel be poisoned by the dreams which you could not deny. It *was* an angel, did you know that? It was pure of all thinking and pure of all dreaming. And you are the one who made it think and dream and now it is dying. And it is dying not as an angel, but as a demon. Do you want to see what it is like now?" she said, gesturing toward a door that led into the cellar of her house. "Yes, it is down there because it is not the way it was and could not remain where it was. It crawled away with its own body, the body of a demon. And it has its own dreams, the dreams of a demon. It is dreaming and dying of its dreams. And I am dying too, because all the dreams have come back."

Mrs Rinaldi then began to approach me, and the color of her eyes and her face seemed to deepen. That was when my mother grasped my arm to pull me quickly from the house. As we ran off I looked over my shoulder and saw the old woman raving in the open doorway, cursing me for a demon.

It was not long afterward that we learned of Mrs Rinaldi's death. True to her own diagnosis, the parasites were upon her, although local gossip told that she had been suffering for years from a cancer of some kind. There was also evidence that another inhabitant of the house survived the old woman for a short time. As it happened, several of my schoolmates reported to me their investigations after dark at the house of the "old witch," a place where I myself was forbidden by my parents to go. So I cannot claim that I observed with my own eyes what crept along the floor of that moonlit house, "like a pile of filthy rags," said one boy.

But I did dream about this prodigy; I even dreamed about its dreams as they dragged every shining angelic particle of this being into the blackness of the old time. Then all my bad dreams abated after a while, just as they always had and always would, using my world only at intervals and gradually dissolving my life into theirs.

THE TSALAL

1 Moxton's leavetaking

None of them could say how it was they had returned to the skeleton town. Some had reached the central cross streets, where a single traffic light, long dead, hung down like a dark lantern. There they paused and stood dumbstruck, scarecrows standing out of place, their clothes lying loose and worn about scrawny bodies. Others slowly joined them, drifting in from the outskirts or disembarking from vehicles weighted down with transportable possessions. Then all of them gathered silently together on that vast, gray afternoon.

They seemed too exhausted to speak and for some time appeared not to recognize their location among the surrounding forms and spaces. Their eyes were fixed with an insomniac's stare, the stigma of both monumental fatigue and painful attentiveness to everything in sight. Their faces were narrow and ashen, a few specks mingling with the dusty surface of that day and seeking to hide themselves within its pale hours. Opposing them was the place they had abandoned and to which they had somehow returned. Only one had not gone with them. He had stayed in the skeleton town, and now they had come back to it, though none of them could say how or why this had happened.

A tall, bearded man who wore a flat-brimmed hat looked up at the sky. Within the clouds was a great seeping darkness, the overflow of the coming night and of a blackness no one had ever seen. After a moment the man said, "It will be dark soon." His words were almost whispered and the effort of speaking appeared to take the last of his strength. But it was not simply a depleted vigor that kept him and the others from turning about and making a second exodus from the town.

No one could say how far they had gone before they reversed their course and turned back toward the place which they believed themselves to have abandoned forever. They could not remember what juncture or dead end they had reached that aborted the evacuation. Part of that day was lost to them, certain images and experiences hidden away. They could feel these things closeted somewhere in their minds, even if they could not call them to memory. They were sure they had seen something they should not remember. And so no one suggested that they set out again on the road that would take them from the town. Yet they could not accept staying in that place.

A paralysis had seized them, that state of soul known to those who dwell on the highest plane of madness, aristocrats of insanity whose nightmares confront them on either side of sleep. Soon enough the wrenching effect of this psychic immobility became far less tolerable than the prospect of simply giving up and staying in the town. Such was the case with at least one of these cataleptic puppets, a sticklike woman who said, "We have no choice. He has stayed in *his* house." Then another voice among them shouted, "He has stayed too long."

A sudden wind moved through the streets, flapping the garments of the weary homecomers and swinging the traffic light that hung over their heads. For a moment all the signals lit up in every direction, disturbing the deep gray twilight. The colors drenched the bricks of buildings and reflected in windows with a strange intensity. Then the traffic light was dark once more, its fit of transformation done.

The man wearing a flat-brimmed hat spoke again, straining his whispery voice. "We must meet together after we have rested."

As the crowd of thin bodies sluggishly dispersed there was almost nothing spoken among them. An old woman shuffling along the sidewalk did not address anyone in particular when she said, "Blessed is the seed that is planted forever in darkness."

Someone who had heard these words looked at the old woman and asked, "Missus, what did you say?" But the old woman appeared genuinely confused to learn she had said anything at all.

2 The one who stayed behind

In the house where a man named Ray Starns and a succession of others before him once resided, Andrew Maness ascended the stairway leading to the uppermost floor, and there entered a small room that he had converted to a study and a chamber of meditation. The window in this room looked out over the rooftops in the neighborhood to offer a fair view of Moxton's main street. He watched as everyone abandoned the town, and he watched them when they returned. Now far into the night, he was still watching after they had all retreated to their homes. And every one of these homes was brightly illuminated throughout the night, while Main Street was in darkness. Even the traffic light was extinguished.

He looked away from the window and fixed his eyes on a large book that lay open on his desk a few steps across the room. The pages of the book were brown and brittle as fallen leaves. "Your wild words were true," he said to the book. "My friends did not go far before they were sent trudging back. You know what made them come home, but I can only guess. So many things you have devoutly embellished, yet you offer nothing on this point. As you say, 'The last vision dies with him who beholds it. Blessed is the seed that is planted forever in darkness.' But the seed that has been planted still grows."

Andrew Maness closed the book. Written in dark ink upon its cover was the word TSALAL.

3 The power of a place

Before long everyone in Moxton had shut themselves in their houses, and the streets at the center of town were deserted. A few streetlights shone on the dull facades of buildings: small shops, a modest restaurant, a church of indefinite denomination, and even a movie theater, which no one had patronized for some weeks. Surrounding this area were clusters of houses that in the usual manner collect about the periphery of skeleton towns. These were structures of serene desolation that had settled into the orbit of a dead star. They were simple pinewood coffins, full of stillness, leaning upright against a silent sky. Yet it was this silence that allowed sounds from a fantastic distance to be carried into it. And the stillness of these houses and their narrow streets led the eye to places astonishingly remote. There were even moments when the entire veil of desolate serenity began to tremble with the tumbling colors of chaos.

Everything seems so unusual in the plainness of these neighborhoods that clutter the margins of a skeleton town. Often no mention is made of the peculiar virtues of such places by their residents. Even so, there may be a house that does not stand *along* one of those narrow streets but at its *end*. This house may even be somewhat different from the others in the neighborhood. Possibly it is taller than the other houses or displays a weathervane that spins in the wind of storms. Perhaps its sole distinguishing quality is that it has been long unoccupied, making it available as an empty vessel in which much of that magical desolation of narrow streets and coffin-shaped houses comes to settle and distill like an essence of the old alchemists. It seems part of a design – some great inevitability – that this house should exist among the other houses that clutch at the edges of a skeleton town. And the sense of this vast, all-encompassing design in fact arises within the spindly residents of the area when one day, unexpectedly, there arrives a red-headed man with the key to this particular house.

4 Memories of a Moxton childhood

Andrew Maness closed the book named TSALAL. His eyes then looked around the room, which had not seemed so small to him in the days when he and his father occupied the house, days too long ago for anyone else to recall with clarity. He alone was able to review those times with a sure memory, and he summoned the image of a small bed in the far corner of the room.

As a child he would lie awake deep into the night, his eyes wandering about the moonlit room that seemed so great to his doll-like self. How the shadows enlarged that room, opening certain sections of it to the black abyss beyond the house and beyond the blackness of night, reaching into a blackness no one had ever seen. During these moments things seemed to be changing all around him, and it felt as if he had something to do with this changing. The shadows on the pale walls began to curl about like smoke, creating a swirling murkiness that at times approached sensible shapes – the imperfect zoology of cloud-forms – but soon drifted into hazy nonsense. Smoky shadows gathered everywhere in the room.

It appeared to him that he could see what was making these shadows which moved so slowly and smoothly. He could see that simple objects around him were changing their shapes and making strange shadows. In the moonlight he could see the candle in its tarnished holder resting on the bedstand. The candle had burned quite low when he blew out its flame hours before. Now it was shooting upwards like a flower growing too fast, and it sprouted outward with tallowy vines and blossoms, waxy wings and limbs, pale hands with wriggling fingers and other parts he could not name. When he looked across the room he saw that something was moving back and forth upon the windowsill with a staggered motion. This was a wooden soldier which suddenly stretched out the claws of a crab and began clicking them against the window-panes. Other things that he could barely see were also changing in the room; he saw shadows twisting about in strange ways. Every-thing was changing, and he knew that he was doing something to make things change. But this time he could not stop the changes. It seemed the end of everything, the infernal apocalypse . . .

Only when he felt his father shaking him did he become aware that he had been screaming. Soon he grew quiet. The candle on his bedstand now burned brightly and was not as it had been a few moments before. He quickly surveyed the room to verify that nothing else remained changed. The wooden soldier was lying on the floor, and its two arms were fixed by its sides.

He looked at his father, who was sitting on the bed and still had on the same dark clothes he had worn when he held church services earlier that day. Sometimes he would see his father asleep in one of the chairs in the parlor or nodding at his desk where he was working on his next sermon. But he had never known his father to sleep during the night.

The Reverend Maness spoke his son's name, and the younger Andrew Maness focused on his father's narrow face, recognizing the crown of white hair, which yet retained a hint of red, and the oval-shaped spectacles reflecting the candle flame. The old man whispered to the boy, as if they were not alone in the house or were engaged in some conspiracy.

"Has it happened again, Andrew?" he asked.

"I did not want to make it happen," Andrew protested. "I was not by myself."

The Reverend Maness held up an open hand of silence and understanding. The glare of the candlelight on his spectacles concealed his eyes, which now turned toward the window beside his son's bed. "The mystery of lawlessness doth already work," he said.

"The Epistles," Andrew swiftly responded, as if the quote had been a question.

"Can you finish the passage?"

"Yes, I think I can," answered Andrew, who then assumed a solemn voice and recited: "Now there is one that restraineth, until he be taken out of the way; and then shall be revealed the lawless one, whom the Lord will slay and bring to nought."

"You know it well, that book."

"The Holy Bible," said Andrew, for it sounded strange to him not to name the book in the proper way.

"Yes, the Holy Bible. You should know its words better than you know anything else on earth. You should always have its words in mind like a magical formula."

"I do, Father. You have always told me that I should."

The Reverend Maness suddenly stood up from the bed and towering over his son shouted: "Liar! You did not have the words in your mind on this night. You could not have. You allowed the lawless one to do its work. *You* are the lawless one, but you must not be. You must become the other one, the *katechon*, the one who restrains."

"I'm sorry, Father," Andrew cried out. "Please don't be angry with me."

The Reverend Maness recovered his temper and again held up his open hand, the fingers of which interlocked and separated several times in what appeared to be a deliberate sequence of subtle gesticulations. He turned away from his son and slowly walked the length of the room. When he reached the window on the opposite side he stared out at the blackness that covered the town of Moxton, where he and his son had first arrived some years before. On the main street of the town the reverend had built a church; nearby, he had built a house. The silhouette of the church bell-tower was outlined against moonlit clouds. From across the room the Reverend Maness said to his son, "I built the church in town so that it would be seen. I made the church of brick so that it would endure."

Now he paced the floor in an attitude of meditation while his son looked on in silence. After some time he stood at the foot of his son's bed, glaring down as though he stood at the pulpit of his church. "In the Bible there is a beast," he said. "You know this, Andrew. But did you know that the beast is also within you? It lives in a place that can never see light. Yes, it is housed here, inside the skull, the habitation of the Great Beast. It is a thing so wonderful in form that its existence might be attributed to the fantastic conjurings of a sorcerer or to a visitation from a far, dark place which no one has ever seen. It is a nightmare that would stop our hearts should we ever behold it gleaming in some shadowy corner of our home, or should we ever – by terrible mischance – lay our hands upon the slime of its flesh. This must never happen, the beast must be kept within its lair. But the beast is a great power that reaches out into the world, a great maker of worlds that are as nothing we can know. And it may work changes on this world. Darkness and light, shape and color, the heavens and the earth – all may be changed by the beast, the great reviser of things seen and unseen, known and unknown. For all that we see and know are but empty vessels in which the beast shall pour a new tincture, therewith changing the aspect of the land, altering the shadows themselves, giving a strange color to our days and our nights, making the day *into* night, so that we dream while awake and can never sleep again. There is nothing more awful and nothing more sinful than such changes in things. Nothing is more grotesque than these changes. All changes in things are grotesque. The very possibility of changes in things is grotesque. And the beast is the author of all changes. You must never again consort with the beast!"

"Don't say that, Father!" Andrew screamed, the palms of his hands pressed to his ears in order to obstruct further words of judgment. Yet he heard them all the same.

"You are repentant, but still you do not read the book."

"I do read the book."

"But you do not have the words of the book always in your mind, because you are always reading other books that are forbidden to you. I have seen you looking at my books, and I know that you take them from my shelves like a thief. Those are books that should not be read."

"Then why do you keep them?" Andrew shouted back, knowing that it was evil to question his father and feeling a great joy in having done so. The Reverend Maness stepped around to the side of the bed, his spectacles flashing in the candlelight.

"I keep them," he said, "so that you may learn by your own will to renounce what is forbidden in whatever shape it may appear."

But how wonderful he found those books that were forbidden to him. He remembered seeing them for the first time cloistered on high shelves in his father's library, that small and windowless room at the very heart of the house the Reverend Maness had built. Andrew knew these books on sight, not only by the titles which had such words in them as Mystery, Haunted, Secret, and Shadow, but also by the characters that formed these words – a jagged script closely resembling the letters of his own Bible – and by the shades of their cloth bindings, the faded vestments of autumn twilights. He somehow knew these books were forbidden to him, even before the reverend had made this fact explicit to his son and caused the boy to feel ashamed of his desire to hold these books and to know their matter. He became bound to the worlds he imagined were revealed in the books, obsessed with what he conceived to be a cosmology of nightmares. And after he had wrongfully admitted himself to his father's library, he began to plot in detail the map of a mysterious universe – a place where the sun had passed from view, where towns were cold and dark, where mountains trembled with the monstrosities they concealed, woods rattled with secret winds, and all the seas were horribly calm. In his dreams of this universe, which far surpassed the darkest visions of any of the books he had read, a neverending night had fallen upon every imaginable landscape.

In sleep he might thus find himself standing at the rim of a great gorge filled with pointed evergreens, and in the distance were the peaks of hills appearing in black silhouette under a sky chaotic with stars. Sublime scenery of this type often recurred in those books forbidden to him, sometimes providing the subject for one of the engraved illustrations accompanying a narrative. But he had never read in any book what his dream showed him in the sky above the gorge and above the hills. For each of the bright, bristling stars would begin to loosen in the places where the blackness held them. They wobbled at first, and then they rolled over in their bed of night. Now it was the other side of the stars that he saw, which was unlike anything ever displayed to the eyes of the earth. What he could see resembled not stars but something more like the underside of large stones one might overturn deep in damp woods. They had changed in the strangest way, changed because everything in the universe was changing and could no longer be protected from the changes being worked upon them by something that had been awakened in the blackness, something that desired to remold everything it could see . . . and had the power to see all things. Now the faces of the stars were crawling with things that made them gleam in a way that stars had never gleamed before. And then these things he saw in his dream began to drip from the stars toward the earth, streaking the night with their gleaming trails.

In those nights of dreaming, all things were subject to forces that knew nothing of law or reason, and nothing possessed its own nature or essence but was only a mask upon the face of absolute darkness, a blackness no one had ever seen.

Even as a child he realized that his dreams did not follow the creation taught to him by his father and by *that book*. It was another creation he pursued, a counter-creation, and the books on the shelves of his father's library could not reveal to him what he desired to know of this other genesis. While denying it to his father, and often to himself, he dreamed of reading the book that was truly forbidden, the scripture of a deadly creation, one that would tell the tale of the universe in its purest sense.

But where could he find such a book? On what shelf of what library would it appear before his eyes? Would he recognize it when fortune allowed it to fall into his hands? Over time he became certain he would know the book, so often did he dream of it. For in the most unlikely visions he found himself in possession of the book, as though it belonged to him as a legacy. But while he held the book in dreams, and even saw its words with miraculous clarity, he could not comprehend the substance of a script whose meaning seemed to dissolve into nonsense. Never was he granted in these dreams an understanding of what the book had to tell him. Only as the most obscure and strangest sensations did it communicate with his mind, only as a kind of presence that invaded and possessed his sleep. On waking, all that remained was a euphoric terror. And it was then that objects around him would begin their transformations, for his soul had been made lawless by dreams and his mind was filled with the words of the wrong book.

5   The author of the book

"You knew it was hopeless," said Andrew Maness as he stood over the book that lay on the desk, glaring at the pages of old handwriting in black ink. "You told me to always read the right words and to always have them in my mind, but you knew I would read the wrong words. You knew what I was. You knew that such a being existed only to read the wrong words and to want to see those words written across the sky in a black script. Because you yourself were the author of the book. And you brought your son to the place where he would read your words. This town was the wrong place, and you knew it was the wrong place. But you told yourself it was the only place where what you had done . . . might be undone. Because you became afraid of what you and those others had done. For years you were intrigued by the greatest madness, the most atrocious secrets and schemes, and then you became afraid. What did you discover that could make you so afraid, you and the others who were always intrigued by the monstrous things you told of, that you sang of, in the book? You preached to me that all change is grotesque, that the very possibility of change is evil. Yet in the book you declare 'transformation as the only truth' – the only truth of the Tsalal, that one who is without law or reason. 'There is no nature to things,' you wrote in the book. 'There are no faces except masks held tight against the pitching chaos behind them.' You wrote that there is not true growth or evolution in the life of this world but only transformations of appearance, an incessant melting and molding of surfaces without underlying essence. Above all you pronounced that there is no salvation of any being because no beings exist as such, nothing exists to be saved – everything, everyone exists only to be drawn into the slow and endless swirling of mutations that we may see every second of our lives if we simply gaze through the eyes of the Tsalal.

"Yet these truths of yours that you kept writing in your book cannot be the reason you became afraid, for even while your voice is somber or trembling to speak of these things, your phrases are burdened with fascination and you are always marvelling at the grand mockery of the universal masquerade, the 'hallucination of lies that obscures the vision of all but the elect of the Tsalal.' It is something of which you will not speak or cannot speak that caused you to become afraid. What did you discover that you could not face without renouncing what you and those others had done, without running to this town to hide yourself in the doctrines of a church that you did not truly uphold? Did this knowledge, this discovery remain within you, at once alive and annihilated to your memory? Was it this that allowed you to prophesy that the people of Moxton would return to their town, yet prevented you from telling what phenomenon could be more terrible than the nightmare they had fled, those grotesque changes which had overtaken the streets and houses of this place?

"You knew this was the wrong place when you brought me here as a child. And I knew that this was the wrong place when I came home to this town and stayed here until everyone knew that I had stayed too long in this place."

6   The white-haired woman

Not long after Andrew Maness moved back to the town of Moxton, an old woman came up to him late one afternoon on the street. He was staring into the window of a repair shop that closed early. Corroded pieces of machinery were strewn before him, as if on display: the guts and bones of a defunct motor of some kind. His reverie was disturbed when the old woman said, "I've seen you before."

"That is possible, ma'am," he replied. "I moved into a house on Oakman a few weeks ago."

"No, I mean that I've seen you before that." He smiled very

slightly at the old woman and said, "I lived here for a time, but I didn't think anyone would remember."

"I remember the hair. It's red but kind of greenish too, yellow maybe."

"Discolored through the years," he explained.

"I remember it the way it was. And it's not much different now. My hair's white as salt."

"Yes, ma'am," he said.

"I told those damn fools I remembered. No one listens to me. What's your name?"

"My name, Mrs . . ."

"Spikes," she snapped.

"My name, Mrs Spikes, is Andrew Maness."

"Maness, Maness," she chanted to herself. "No, I don't think I know Maness. You're in the Starns house."

"It was in fact purchased from one of Mr Starns' family who inherited the house after he died."

"Used to be the Waterses lived there. Before them the Wellses. And before them the McQuisters. But that's getting to be before my time. Before the McQuisters is just too damn long to remember. Too damn long." She was repeating these words as she charged off down the street. Andrew Maness watched her thin form and salt-white hair recede and lose all color in the drab surroundings of the skeleton town.

7 Revelations of a unique being

For Andrew Maness, the world had always been divided into two separate realms defined by what he could only describe as a *prejudice of soul*. Accordingly he was provided with a dual set of responses that he would have to a given locale, so that he would know if it was a place that was right for him, or one that was wrong. In places of the former type there was a separation between his self and the world around him, an enveloping absence. These were the great empty spaces which comprised nearly the whole of the world. There was no threat presented by such places. But there were other places where it seemed a presence of some dreadful kind was allowed to enter, a force that did not belong to these places yet moved freely within them . . . and within him. It was precisely such places as this, and the presence within them, which came to preside over his life and determine its course. He had no choice, for this was the scheme of the *elect persons* who had generated him, and he was compelled to fall in with their design. He was in fact the very substance of their design.

His father knew that there were certain places in the world to which he must respond, even in his childhood, and which would cause him to undergo a second birth under the sign of the Tsalal. The Reverend Maness knew that the town of Moxton was among such places – outposts on the desolate borderlands of the real. He said that he had brought his son to this town so that the boy would learn to resist the presence he would feel here and elsewhere in the world. He said that he had brought his son to the right place, but he had in fact brought him to a place that was entirely wrong for the being that he was. And he said that his son should always fill his mind with the words of that book. But these words were easily silenced and usurped by those other words in those other books. His father seemed to entice him into reading the very books he should not have read. Soon these books provoked in Andrew Maness the sense of that power and that presence which may manifest itself in a place such as the town of Moxton. And there were other places where he felt that same presence. Following intuitions that grew stronger as he grew older, Andrew Maness would find such places by hazard or design.

Perhaps he would come upon an abandoned house standing shattered and bent in an isolated landscape – a raw skeleton in a boneyard. But this dilapidated structure would seem to him a temple, a wayside shrine to that dark presence with which he sought union, and also a doorway to the dark world in which it dwelled. Nothing can convey those sensations, the countless nuances of trembling excitement, as he approached such a decomposed edifice whose skewed and ragged outline suggested another order of existence, the truest order of existence, as though such places as this house were only wavering shadows cast down to earth by a distant, unseen realm of entity. There he would experience the touch of something outside himself, something whose will was confused with his own, as in a dream wherein one feels possessed of a fantastic power to determine what events will transpire and yet also feels helpless to control that power, which, *through* oneself, may produce the chaos of nightmare. This mingling of mastery and helplessness overwhelmed him with a black intoxication and suggested his life's goal: to work the great wheel that turns in darkness, and to be broken upon it.

Yet Andrew Maness had always known that his ambition was an echo of that conceived by his father many years before, and that the pursuit of this ambition had been consummated in his own birth.

8 Not much more than a century ago

"As a young man," the Reverend Maness explained to his son, who was now a young man himself, "I thought myself an adept in the magic of the old gods, a communicant of entities both demonic and divine. I did not comprehend for years that I was merely a curator in the museum where the old gods were on display, their replicas and corpses set up in the countless galleries of the *invisible* . . . and now the *extinct*. I knew that in past millennia these beings had always replaced one another as each of them passed away along with the worlds that worshipped them. This mirror-like succession of supreme monarchs may still seem eternal to those who have not sensed the great shadow which has always been positioned behind every deity or pantheon. Yet I was able to sense this shadow and see that it had eclipsed the old gods without in any way being one of their kind. For it was even older than they, the dark background against which they had forever carried on their escapades as best they could. But its emergence into the foreground of things was something new, an advent occurring not much more than a century ago. Perhaps this great blackness, this shadow, has always prevailed on worlds other than our own, places that have never known the gods of *order*, the gods of *design*. Even this world had long prepared for it, creating certain places where the illusion of a reality was worn quite thin and where the gods of order and design could barely breathe. Such places as this town of Moxton became fertile ground for this blackness no one had ever seen.

"Yes, it was not much more than a century ago that the people of this world betrayed their awareness of a new god that was not a god. Such an awareness may never be complete, never reach a true agony of illumination, except among an elect. I myself was slow in coming to it. The authenticity of my enlightenment may seem questionable and arbitrary, considering its source. Nonetheless, there is a tradition of revelation, an ancient protocol, by which knowledge of the unseen is delivered to us through inspired texts. And it is by means of these scriptures dictated from beyond that we of this world may discover what we have not and cannot experience in a direct confrontation. So it was with the Tsalal. But the book that I have written, and which I have named *Tsalal, is* not the revealed codex of which I am speaking. It is only a reflection, or rather a distillation, of those other writings in which I first detected the existence, the emergence, of the Tsalal itself.

"Of course, there have always been writings of a certain kind, a primeval lore which provided allusions to the darkness of creation and to monstrosities of every type, human and inhuman, as if there were a difference. Something profoundly dark and grotesque has always had a life in every language of this world, appearing at intervals and throwing its shadow for a moment upon stories that try to make sense of things, often confounding the most happy tale. And this shadow is never banished in any of these stories, however we may pretend otherwise. The darkness of the grotesque is an immortal enigma: in all the legends of the dead, in all the tales of creatures of the night, in all the mythologies of mad gods and lucid demons, there remains a kind of mocking nonsense to the end, a thick and resonant voice which calls out from the heart of these stories and declares: 'Still I am here.' And the idiot laughter of that voice – how it sounds through the ages! This laughter often reaches our ears through certain stories wherein this grotesque spirit itself has had a hand. However we have tried to ignore the laughter of this voice, however we have tried to overwhelm its words and protect ourselves by always keeping other words in our minds, it still sounds throughout the world.

"But it was not much more than a century ago that this laughter began to rise to a pitch. You have heard it yourself, Andrew, as you furtively made incursions into my library during your younger days, revelling in a Gothic feast of the grotesque. These books do not hold an arcane knowledge intended for the select few but were written for a world which had begun to slight the gods of order and design, to question their very existence and to exalt in the disorders of the grotesque. Both of us have now studied the books in which the Tsalal was being gradually revealed as the very nucleus of our universe, even if their authors remained innocent of the revelations they were perpetrating. It was from one of the most enlightened of this sect of Gothic storytellers that I took the name of that one. You recall, Andrew, the adventures of an Arthur Pym in a fantastic land where everything, people and landscape alike, is of a *perfect blackness* – the Antarctic country of Tsalal. This was among the finest evocations I had discovered of that blackness no one had ever seen, a literary unveiling of being without soul or substance, without meaning or necessity – not a universe of design and order but one whose sole principle was that of senseless transmutation. A universe of the grotesque. And from that moment it became my ambition to invoke what I now called the Tsalal, and ultimately to effect a worldly incarnation of the thing itself.

"Through the years I found there were others who had become entranced with an ambition so near to my own that we formed a league . . . the elect of the Tsalal. They too had been adepts of the old gods who had been made impotent or extinct by the emergence of that one, an inevitable advent which we were avid to hasten and lose ourselves in. For we had recognized the mask of our identities, and our only consolation for what we had lost, a perverse salvation, was to embrace the fatality of the Tsalal. Vital to this end was a woman upon whom was performed a ceremony of conception. And it was during these rites that we first came into the most intimate communion with that one, which moved within us all and worked the most wonderful changes upon so many things.

"None of us suspected how it would be when we gathered that last night. This all happened in another country, an older country. But it was nevertheless a place like this town of Moxton, a place where the appearances of this world seem to waver at times, hovering before one's eyes as a mere fog. This place was known among our circle as the Street of Lamps, which was the very heart of a district under the sign of the Tsalal. In recollection, the lamps seem only a quirk of scene, an accident of atmosphere, but at the time they were to us the eyes of the Tsalal itself. These sidewalk fixtures of radiant glass upheld by dark metal stems formed a dreamlike procession up and down the street, a spectacle of infinite pathos and mystery. One poet of the era called them 'iron lilies,' and another compared their jewel-like illumination to the yellow topaz. In a different language, and a different city, these devices – les réverbères, les becs de gaz – were also celebrated, an enigmatic sign of a century, a world, that was guttering out.

"It was in this street that we prepared a room for your birth and your nurturing under the sign of the Tsalal. There were few other residents in this ramshackle area, and they abandoned it some time before you were born, frightened off by changes that all of us could see taking place in the Street of Lamps. At first the changes were slight: spiders had begun laying webs upon the stones of the street and thin strands of smoke spun out from chimney stacks, tangling together in the sky. When the night of your birth arrived the changes became more intense. They were focused on the room in which we gathered to chant the invocation to the Tsalal. We incanted throughout the night, standing in a circle around the woman who had been the object of the ceremony of conception. Did I mention that she was not one of us? No, she was a gaunt denizen of the Street of Lamps whose body we appropriated some months before, an honorary member of our sect whom we treated very well during her term of captivity. As the moment of your birth drew closer she lay upon the floor of the ceremonial room and began screaming in many different voices. We did not expect her to survive the ordeal. Neither did we expect the immediate consequences of the incarnation we attempted to effect, the consummation of a bond between this woman and the Tsalal.

"We were inviting chaos into the world, we knew this. We had been intoxicated by the prospect of an absolute disorder. With a sense of grim exaltation we greeted the *intimations* of a universal nightmare – the ultimate point of things. But on that night, even as we invoked the Tsalal within that room, we came to experience a realm of the unreal hitherto unknown to us. And we discovered that it had never been our desire to lose ourselves in the unreal, not in the manner which threatened us in the Street of Lamps. For as you, Andrew, began to enter the world through this woman, so was the Tsalal also entering the world through this woman. She was now the *seed* of that one, her flesh radiant and swelling in the fertile ground of the unreal which was the Street of Lamps. We looked beyond the windows of that room, already contemplating our escape. But then we saw that there was no longer any street, nor any buildings along that street. All that remained were the streetlamps with their harsh yellow glow like rotten stars, endless rows of streetlamps that ascended into the all-encompassing blackness. Can you imagine: endless rows of streetlamps ascending into the blackness. Everything that sustained the reality of the world around us had been drained away. We noticed how our own bodies had become suddenly drawn and meager, while the body of that woman, the seed of the coming apocalypse, was becoming ever more swollen with the power and magic of the Tsalal. And we knew at that moment what needed to be done if we were ever to escape the unreality that had been sown in that place called the Street of Lamps."

9   A skeleton town

Even in the time of the McQuisters, which almost no one could remember very well, Moxton was a skeleton town. No building there had ever seemed new. Every crudded brick or faded board, every crusted shingle or frayed awning appeared to be handed down from the demise of another structure in another town, castoffs of a thriving center that had no use for worn out materials. The front windows of stores were cloudy with a confusion of reflected images from someplace else. Entire establishments might have been dumped off in Moxton, where buildings stood along the street like odd objects forgotten on a cellar shelf.

It was less a real town than the semblance of a town, a pasteboard backdrop to an old stage show, its outlines crudely stroked with an antique paintbrush unconcerned with the details of character and identity, lettering the names of streets and shops with senseless scribbles no one was ever meant to read. Everything that might have been real about the town had somehow become thwarted. Nothing flourished there, nothing made a difference by its presence or absence.

No business could do more than anonymously survive in Moxton. Even larger enterprises such as a dimestore or a comfortable hotel could not assert themselves but were forced to assume the same air of unreality possessed by lesser establishments: the shoe store whose tiny front window displayed merchandise long out of style, the clothes store where dust collected in the folds of garments worn by headless mannikins, the repair shop at which a good number of the items brought in were left unclaimed and lay corroding in every cranny of the place.

Many years ago a movie theater opened on the prominent corner of Webster and Main, decades before a traffic light had been hung over the intersection of these streets. A large neon sign with letters stacked in a vertical file spelled out the word RIVIERA. For a moment this word appeared in searing magenta against the Moxton twilight, calling up and down the street to everyone in the town. But by nightfall the glowing letters had been subdued, their glamor suffocating in a rarefied atmosphere where sights and sounds were drained of reality. The new movie theater now burned no more brightly than McQuister's Pharmacy across the street. Both of them were allotted a steady and modest patronage in a skeleton town that was no more enchanted with the one than the other.

Thus was the extent of Moxton's compromise with any manifestation of the real. For there are certain places that exist on the wayside of the real: a house, a street, even entire towns which have claims upon them by virtue of some nameless affinity with the most remote orders of being. They are, these places, fertile ground for the unreal and retain the minimum of immunity against exotic disorders and aberrations. Their concessions to a given fashion of reality are only placating gestures, a way of stifling it through limited acceptance. It was unnecessary, even perverse, to resist construction of the movie theater or the new church (founded in 1893 by the Rev. Andrew Maness). Such an action might imbue these things with an unwarranted measure of substance or power, and in a skeleton town there is little substance, while all power resides only in the unreal. The citizens of such a place are custodians of a rare property, a precious estate whose true owners are momentarily absent. All that remains before full proprietorship of the land may be assumed is the planting of a single seed and its nurturing over a sufficient period of time, an interval that has nothing to do with the hours and days of the world.

10   A plea in the past

As Andrew Maness grew older in the town of Moxton he watched his father submit to the despair and the wonder that he could not unmake the thing that he and those others had *incarnated*. On several occasions the reverend entered his son's room as the boy slept. With knife and ax and long-handled scythe he attempted to break the growing bond between his son and the Tsalal. In the morning young Andrew's bedroom would reek like a slaughter-house. But his limbs and organs were again made whole and a new blood flowed within them proving the reality of what had been brought into the world by his father and those other enthusiasts of that one.

There were times when the Reverend Maness, in a state of awe and desperation, awoke his son from dreams and made his appeal to the boy, informing him that he was reaching a perilous juncture in his development and begging him to submit to a peculiar ritual that would be consummated by Andrew's ruin.

"What ritual is this?" Andrew asked with a novitiate's excitation. But the reverend's powers of speech became paralyzed at this question and many nights would pass before he again broached the subject.

At last the Reverend Maness came into his son's room carrying a book. He opened the book to its final pages and began to read. And the words he read laid out a scheme for his son's destruction. These words were his own, the ultimate chapter in a great work he had composed documenting a wealth of revelations concerning the force or entity called the Tsalal.

Andrew could not take his eyes off the book and strained to hear every resonance of his father's reading from it, even if the ritual the old man spelled out dictated the atrocious manner of Andrew's death – the obliteration of the seed of the apocalypse which was called the Tsalal.

"Your formula for cancelling my existence calls for the participation of others," Andrew observed. "The elect of . . . that one."

"Tsalal," the Reverend Maness intoned, still captivated by an occult nomenclature.

"Tsalal," Andrew echoed. "My protector, my guardian of the black void."

"You are not yet wholly the creature of that one. I have tried to change what I could not. But you have stayed too long in this place, which was the wrong place for a being such as you. You are undergoing a second birth under the sign of the Tsalal. But there is still enough time if you will submit yourself to the ritual."

"I must ask you, Father: who will carry it out? Will there be a convocation of strangers in this town?"

After a painfully reflective pause, the reverend said: "There are none remaining who will come. They would be required to relive the events following your birth, the first time you were born."

"And my mother?" Andrew asked.

"She did not survive."

"But how did she die?"

"By the ritual," the Reverend Maness confessed. "At the ritual of your birth it became necessary to perform the ritual of death."

"Her death."

"As I told you before. This ritual had never been performed, or even conceived, prior to that night on which you were born. We did not know what to expect. But after a certain point, after seeing certain things, we acted in the correct manner, as if we had always known what needed to be done."

"And what needed to be done, Father?"

"It is all in this book."

"You have the book, but you're still lacking for those others. A congregation, so to speak."

"I have my congregation in this very town. They will do what needs to be done. To this you must submit yourself. To the end of your existence you must consent."

"And if I don't?"

"Soon," the Reverend Maness began, "the bond will be sealed between you and the other, that one which is all nightmare of grotesque metamorphoses behind the dream of earthly forms, that one which is the center of so-called entity and so-called essence. To the living illusions of the world of light will come a blackness no one has ever seen, a dawn of darkness. What you yourself have known of these things is only a passing glimpse, a flickering candleflame beside the conflagration which is to come. You have found yourself fascinated by those moments after you have been asleep, and awake to see how the things around you are affected in their form. You look on as they change in every freakish manner, feeling the power that changes them to be connected to your own being, conveying to you its magic through a delicate cord. Then the cord grows too thin to hold, your mind returns to you, and the little performance you were watching comes to an end. But you have already stayed long enough in this place to have begun a second birth under the sign of the Tsalal. The cord between you and that one is strong. Wherever you go, you will be found. Wherever you stay, there the changes will begin. *For you are the seed of that one.* You are just as the *luz,* the bone-seed of rabbinic prophecy: that sliver of every mortal self from which the whole body may be reconstructed and stand for judgement at the end of time. Wherever you stay, there the resurrection will begin. You are a fragment of the one that is without law or reason. The body that will grow out of you is the true body of all things. The changes themselves are the body of the Tsalal. The changes are the truth of all bodies, which we believe have a face and a substance only because we cannot see that they are always changing, that they are only fragile forms which are forever being shattered in the violent whirlpool of truth.

"This is how it will be for all your days: you will be drawn to a place that reveals the sign of the Tsalal – an aspect of the unreal, a forlorn glamor in things – and with your coming the changes will begin. These may go unnoticed for a time, affecting only very small things or greater things in subtle ways, a disruption of forms that you very well know. But other people will sense that something is wrong in that place, which may be a certain house or street or even an entire town. They will go about with uneasy eyes and become emaciated in their flesh, their very bones growing thin with worry, becoming worn down and warped just as the world around them is slowly stripped of whatever seemed real, leaving them famished for the sustenance of old illusions. Rumors will begin to pass among them about unpleasant things they believe they have seen or felt and yet cannot explain – a confusion among the lower creatures, perhaps, or a stone that seems to throb with a faint life. For these are the modest beginnings of the chaos that will ultimately consume the stars themselves, which may be left to crawl within that great blackness no one has ever seen. And by their proximity to your being they will know that you are the source of these changes, that *through your being* these changes radiate into the world. The longer you stay in a place, the worse it will become. If you leave such a place in time, then the changes can have no lasting power – the ultimate point will not have been reached, and it will be as the little performances of grotesquerie you have witnessed in your own room."

"And if I do stay in such a place?" asked Andrew.

"Then the changes will proceed toward the ultimate point. So long as you can bear to watch the appearances of things become degraded and confused, so long as you can bear to watch the people in that place wither in their bodies and minds, the changes will proceed toward their ultimate point – the disintegration of all apparent order, the birth of the Tsalal. Before that happens you must submit to the ritual of the ultimate point."

But Andrew Maness only laughed at his father's scheme, and the sound of this laughter almost shattered the reverend entirely. In a deliberately serious voice, Andrew said: "Do you really believe you will gain the participation of others?"

"The people of this town will do the work of the ritual," his father replied. "When they have seen certain things, they will do what must be done. Their hunger to preserve the illusions of their world will surpass their horror at what must be done to save it. But it will be your decision whether or not you will submit to the ritual which will determine the course of so many things in this world."

11 A meeting in Moxton

Everyone in the town gathered in the church that the Reverend Maness had built so many years ago. No others had succeeded the reverend, and no services had been held since the time of his pastorate. The structure had never been outfitted with electricity, but the illumination of numerous candles and oil lamps the congregation had brought supplemented the light of a grayish afternoon that penetrated the two rows of plain, peaked windows along either side of the church. In the corner of one of those windows a spider fumbled about in its web, struggling awkwardly with appendages that resembled less the nimble legs of the arachnid than they did an octet of limp tentacles. After several thrusts the creature reached the surface of a window pane and passed into the glass itself, where it began to move about freely in its new element.

The people of Moxton had tried to rest themselves before this meeting, but their haggard look spoke of a failure to do so. The entire population of the town barely filled a half dozen pews at the front of the church, although some were collapsed upon the floor and others shuffled restlessly along the center aisle. All of them appeared even more emaciated than the day before, when they had attempted to escape the town and unaccountably found themselves driven back to it.

"Everything has gotten worse since we returned," said one man, as if to initiate the meeting which had no obvious hope or purpose beyond collecting in a single place the nightmares of the people of Moxton. A murmur of voices rose up and echoed throughout the church. Several people spoke of what they had witnessed the night before, reciting a litany of grotesque phenomena that had prohibited sleep.

There was a bedroom wall which changed colors, turning from its normal rosy tint that was calm and pale in the moonlight to a quivering and luminescent green that rippled like the flesh of a great reptile. There was a little doll whose neck began to elongate until it was writhing through the air like a serpent, while its tiny doll's head whispered words that had no sense in them yet conveyed a profoundly hideous meaning. There were things no one had seen that made noises of a deeply troubling nature in the darkness of cellars or behind the doors of closets and cupboards. And then there was something that people saw when they looked through the windows of their houses toward the house where a man named Andrew Maness now lived. But when anyone began to describe what it was they saw in the vicinity of that house, which they called the McQuister house, their words became confused. They did see something and yet they saw nothing.

"I also saw what you speak of," whispered the tall, bearded man who wore a flat-brimmed hat. "It was a blackness, but it was not the blackness of the night or of shadows. It was hovering over the old McQuister place, or around it. This was something I had not seen in Moxton even since the changes."

"No, not in Moxton, not *in the town*. But you *have* seen it before. We have all seen it," said a man's voice that sounded as if it came from elsewhere in the church.

"Yes," answered the tall man, as if confessing a thing that had formerly been denied. "But we are not seeing it the way it might be seen, the way we had seen it when we were outside the town, when we tried to leave and could not."

"That was not blackness we saw then," said one of the younger women who seemed to be wresting an image from her memory. "It was something . . . something that wasn't blackness at all."

"There were different things," shouted an old man who suddenly stood up from one of the pews, his eyes fixed in a gaze of revelation. A moment later this vision appeared to dissolve, and he sat down again. But the eyes of others followed this vision, surveying the empty spaces of the church and watching the flickering lights of the many lamps and candles.

"There *were* different things," someone started to say, and then someone else completed the thought: "But they were all spinning and confused, all swirling together."

"Until all we could see was a great blackness," said the tall man, gaining his voice again.

A silence now overcame the congregation, and the words they had spoken seemed to be disappearing into this silence, once more drawing the people of Moxton back to the refuge of their former amnesia. But before their minds lost all clarity of recollection a woman named Mrs Spikes rose to her feet and from the last row of the church, where she sat alone, cried out, "Everything started with him, the one in the McQuister house."

"How long has it been?" one voice asked.

"Too long,' answered Mrs Spikes. "I remember him. He's older than I am, but he doesn't look older. His hair is a strange color."

"Reddish like pale blood," said one.

"Green like mold," said another. "Or yellow and orange like a candleflame."

"He lived in that house, that same house, a long time ago," continued Mrs Spikes. "Before the McQuisters. He lived with his father. But I can only remember the stories. I didn't see anything myself. Something happened one night. Something happened to the whole town. Their name was Maness."

"That is the name of the man who built this church," said the tall man. "He was the first clergyman this town had seen. And there were no others after him. What happened, Mrs Spikes?"

"It was too long ago for anyone to remember. I only know the stories. The reverend said things about his son, said the boy was going to do something and how people had to keep it from happening."

"What happened, Mrs Spikes? Try to remember."

"I'm trying. It was only yesterday that I started to remember. It was when we got back to town. I remembered something that the reverend said in the stories about that night."

"I heard you," said another woman. "You said, 'Blessed is the seed that is planted forever in darkness.' "

Mrs Spikes stared straight ahead and lightly pounded the top of the pew with her right hand, as though she were calling up memories in this manner. Then she said: "That's what he was supposed to have been saying that night, 'Blessed is the seed that is planted forever in darkness.' And he said that people had to do something, but the stories I heard when I was growing up don't say what he wanted people to do. It was about his son. It was something queer, something no one understood. But no one did anything that he wanted them to do. When they took him home, his son wasn't there, and no one saw that young man again. The stories say that the ones who brought the reverend to his house saw things there, but no one could explain what they saw. What everyone did remember was that late the same night the bells started ringing up in the tower of this church. That's where they found the reverend. He'd hung himself. It wasn't until the McQuisters moved into town that anyone would go near the reverend's house. Then it seemed no one could remember anything about the place."

"Just as we could not remember what happened only yesterday," said the tall man. "Why we came back to this place when it was the last place we wanted to be. The blackness we saw that was a blackness no one had ever seen. That blackness which was not a blackness but was all the colors and shapes of things darkening the sky."

"A vision!" said one old man who for many years had been the proprietor of McQuister's Pharmacy.

"Perhaps only that," replied the tall man.

"No," said Mrs Spikes. "It was something *he* did. It was like everything else that's been happening since he came here and stayed so long. All the little changes in things that kept getting worse. It's something that's been moving in like a storm. People have seen that it's in the town now, hanging over that house of his. And the changes in things are worse than ever. Pretty soon it's us that'll be changing."

Then there arose a chorus of voices among the congregation, all of them composing a conflict between "we must do something" and "what can be done?"

While the people of Moxton murmured and fretted in the light of lamps and candles, there was a gradual darkening outside the windows of the church. An unnatural blackness was overtaking the gray afternoon. And the words of these people also began to change, just as so many things had changed in that town. Within the same voices there mingled both keening outcries of fear and a low, muttering invocation. Soon the higher pitched notes in these voices diminished and then wholly disappeared as the deeper tones of incantation prevailed. Now they were all chanting a single word in hypnotic harmony: *Tsalal, Tsalal, Tsalal*. And standing at the pulpit was the one who was leading the chant, the man whose strangely shaded hair shone in the light of candles and oil lamps. At last he had come from his house where he had stayed too long. The bell in the tower began to ring, sounding in shattered echoes. The resonant cacophony of voices swelled within the church. For these were the voices of people who had lived so long in the wrong place. These were people of a skeleton town.

The figure at the pulpit lifted up his hands before his congregation, and they grew quiet. When he focused his eyes on an old woman sitting alone in the last row, she rose from her seat and walked to the double doors at the rear of the church. The man at the pulpit spread his arms wider, and the old woman pushed back each of the doors.

Through the open doorway was the main street of Moxton, but it was not as it had been. An encompassing blackness had descended and only the lights of the town could be seen. But these lights were now as endless as the blackness itself. The rows of yellowish streetlamps extended to infinity along an avenue of the abyss. Fragments of neon signs were visible, the vibrant magenta letters of the movie theater recurring again and again, as though reflected in a multitude of black mirrors. In the midst of the other lights hovered an endless succession of traffic signals that filled the blackness like multi-colored stars. All these bright remnants of the town, its broken pieces in transformation, were becoming increasingly dim and distorted, bleeding their radiance into the blackness that was consuming them, even as it freakishly multiplied the shattered images of the world, collecting them within its kaleidoscope of colors so dense and so varied that they lost themselves within a black unity.

The man who had built the church in which the people of Moxton were gathered had spoken of the ultimate point. This was now imminent. And as the moment approached, the gathering within the church moved toward the figure at the pulpit, who descended to meet them. They were far beyond their old fears, these skeleton people. They had attained the stripped bone of being, the last layer of an existence without name or description, without nature or essence: the nothingness of the blackness no one had ever seen . . . or would ever see. For no one had ever lived except as a shadow of the blackness of the Tsalal.

And their eyes looked to the one who was the incarnation of the blackness, and who had come to them to seal his bond with that other one. They looked to him for some word or gesture in order to bring to fulfilment that day which had turned into night. They looked to him for the thing that would bind them to the blackness and join them within the apocalypse of the unreal.

Finally, as if guided by some whim of the moment, he told them how to do what must be done.

12   What is remembered

The story that circulated in later years among the people of Moxton told how everyone had gathered in the church one afternoon during a big storm that lasted into the night. Unused for decades before this event, the church was strongly constructed and proved a suitable shelter. There were some who recalled that for weeks prior to this cataclysm a variety of uncommon effects had resulted from what they described as a season of strange weather in the vicinity of the town.

The details of this period remain unclear, as do memories of a man who briefly occupied the old McQuister place around the time of the storm. No one had ever spoken with him except Mrs Spikes, who barely recollected their conversation and who died of cancer not long after the biggest storm of the year. The house in which the man had lived was previously owned by relatives of Ray Starns, but the Starns people were no longer residents of Moxton. In any case, the old McQuister place was not the only untenanted house in the skeleton town, and there was no reason for people to concern themselves with it. Nor did anyone in Moxton give serious thought to the church once the storm had passed. The doors were once again secured against intruders, but no one ever tested these old locks which had been first put in place after the Reverend Maness hung himself in the church tower.

Had the people of the town of Moxton ventured beyond the doors of the church they might have found what they left behind following the abatement of the storm. Lying twisted at the foot of the pulpit was the skeleton of a man whose name no one would have been able to remember. The bones were clean. No bit of their flesh could be discovered either in the church or anywhere else in the town. Because the flesh was that of one who had stayed in a certain place too long. It was the seed, and now it had been planted in a dark place where it would not grow. They had buried his flesh deep in the barren ground of their meager bodies. Only a few strands of hair of an unusual color lay scattered upon the floor, mingling with the dust of the church.

MAD NIGHT OF ATONEMENT

A Future Tale

Once more from the beginning; once more until the end. You know who Dr Francis Haxhausen was and how his disappearance affected the scientific world. There was dismay and confusion when one of the leading scientists on earth withdrew from an active life of research. And there was doubt, even anxiety, when he could no longer be reached for consultation on this or that question of urgent relevance to his former colleagues, if not to the vast body of the human race. Ah, the human race. Pacing the floors of gleaming labs, the geniuses in their long white smocks fretted about the missing man of science: they bore the stigmata of worry upon their faces and their voices grew quiet, like voices heard in the shadows of a lonely church. Rumors multiplied, panicky speculations were the order of the day. But however troubled certain people had become in the absence of Dr Haxhausen, they were no less bothered by his sudden return from a strange retirement.

He was now quite a different man, shaking the hands of old friends and smiling with a warmth that was entirely out of character. "I've been travelling here and there," he explained, though he avoided elaborating on this statement. For a time everyone kept an eye on Dr Haxhausen, eager to witness a revelation of some kind, or at least some clue to suggest what had happened to him. And how nerve-wracking vigilance can be. It was not long, however, before the inevitable conclusion had to be drawn: the unfortunate man had lost his reason, gone mad from years of overwork in the service of his calling. But perhaps there still remained some pretext for hoping that the scientist would recover. After all, he managed to avoid the constraints which some, including members of his own family, attempted to place upon his movements. And certainly this was an achievement that hinted at the survival of some measure of his old genius. Indeed, Dr Haxhausen fought to preserve his freedom with very good reason, for he required a great deal of it – freedom, not reason – to pursue his plans for the future.

For almost a year he worked secretly, and alone, in an old, empty factory building located in an open field many miles from the nearest city. And into this building he brought a motley array of equipment – objects, devices, and machinery that belonged to quite different times and places, diverse worlds of human creation. There were of course the most modern machines and instruments of science, some of which had only come into being since Dr Haxhausen's disappearance. But there were also items of far earlier historical periods and a few imported from cultures that would not be considered very far along the path of technological progress. Thus, Dr Haxhausen unpacked several oddly shaped vessels decorated with strange glyphs and primitive images. And these clumsy vessels he rested upon a table among elegant containers of nearly invisible glass. Then he pieced together something that resembled a dirty drainspout or an old stovepipe. And he placed it, for the moment, upon the immaculate metal surface of a computer, which was the color and texture of an eggshell.

More exotic or antiquated paraphernalia were revealed slumbering in crates and boxes: cauldrons, retorts, masks with wide-open mouths, alembics, bellows of different sizes, crusted bells that rang with dead voices, and rusted tongs that squeaked when manipulated; a large hourglass, a small telescope, shining swords and dull knives, a long wooden pitchfork with two hornlike prongs and a tall staff with marvelously embellished headpiece; miniature bottles of very thick glass plugged with stoppers in the shape of human or animal heads, candles in ivory holders with curious carvings, bright beads, beautiful convex mirrors of perfect silver, golden chalices engraved with intricate designs and powerful phrases; huge books with brittle pages, a skull and some bones; doll-like figures made of dried vegetables, puppet-like figures made of wax and wood, and various little dummies composed of obscure materials. Finally, there was a shallow crate from which Dr Haxhausen removed a vaguely circular object that seemed to be a flat stone, but a stone that was translucent and mottled like an opal with a spectrum of soft hues. And all these things the scientist brought together within his dim and drafty laboratory: each, in his mind, would play its part in his design. Clearly his ideas about the practice of science had taken an incredible leap, though whether the direction was forward or backward remained to be seen.

For months he worked with a mechanical industriousness and without worry or doubt, as though following some foreordained plan of assured success. Slowly his invention began to take form out of the chaos of materials he had united in his experiment, a miscegenation that would give birth to a revolutionary artifact, a cross-bred assemblage of freakish novelty. And the result of his labors at last stood before him upon the cold and dusty floor of that factory, and he was pleased by the sight of it.

To the average eye, granted, Dr Haxhausen's invention might have appeared as no more than a bizarre scrapheap, a hybrid of some inscrutable fancy. Dense and unbeautiful, it branched out wildly in every direction, a mad foliage of ragged metal. And it seemed just barely, or not all, integrated into a whole. Through dark hollows within the chaotic tangle of the apparatus, the faces of dolls and puppets peeked out like malicious children in hiding. Incorporated into the body of the invention, their dwarfish forms mingled with its circuitry; these figures alone, by their very presence, might have bred doubts as to the validity of the scientist's creation. And, as must already be apparent, the eccentricities of the machine did not end with a few idiotic faces.

Nevertheless, there was a certain feature of the invention that did appear to suggest some definite purpose. This was the long black tube projecting from the midst of the debris, rising from it in the manner of a cobra set for the attack. But in place of the cobra's pair of fascinating eyes, this artificial serpent was equipped with a single cyclopean socket in which was fixed a smooth disc of beautifully blended colors. When Dr Haxhausen turned a dial on the remote control unit resting in his palm, the dark metallic beast reared back its head and, with a sinister grinding sound, directed its gaze up toward a grimy skylight. For years this window on the heavens had remained sealed. But that night, through the efforts of the inexhaustible scientist, it was opened. And the spectral light of a full moon shone down into the old factory, pouring its beams into the opalescent eye of Dr Haxhausen's machine. Later, when it seemed the beast was sated with its lunar nourishment, Dr Haxhausen confidently flicked a switch on the remote control unit. And the moonlight, which had been digested and transmuted in the bowels of the beast, was now given back to its source, spewing forth as a stream of lurid colors into the blackness, a harsh spectrum which one witness later described to authorities as an "awful rainbow quivering across the night." In the doctor's own description, this was called his Sacred Ray.

With the first stage of his project successfully completed, Dr

Haxhausen moved out of his secluded laboratory. His machine, along with other things, was loaded on a truck by some hired laborers. Thus, it could easily be transported from one place to another, to be exhibited before the eyes of any who would come to see it. And this is exactly what the scientist had in mind. Abandoning obscurity and breaking his silence, he once again allowed himself to be known to the world. Naturally there was a great deal of publicity, none of which was complimentary to the worth of the scientist's revelations, though some of which paid sad homage to the former glory of his delicate mind. But public reaction was of no concern to him. His task would in any case be carried out: the world was to be given notice, the annunciation made. So he continued to travel here and there: in rented halls and auditoriums of many cities, he demonstrated the powers of his machine and spread the word to those who would hear it.

"Good evening, ladies and gentlemen," he began a typical performance in a typically out-of-date movie theater in a typical town. Standing alone on stage, Dr Haxhausen was wearing an old dark suit; as if to simulate formal attire, he added a new bow tie. His hair was greased and combed but had been allowed to grow far too long to convey a well-groomed image. And his black-framed eyeglasses now seemed far too large on the face of a man who had lost so much weight in the past year or so. Their thick lenses glinted in the glare of the footlights, which cast Dr Haxhausen's gigantic and twisted shadow upon the threadbare curtain behind him.

"Some of you," he continued, "are perhaps aware of who I am and may have an idea of why I am here tonight. Others of you may be curious to discover the meaning of those handbills which have lately appeared around your town or possibly were intrigued by the marquee outside this theater which touts the 'World Famous Dr Haxhausen.' Like many important events in human history, my exhibition has been somewhat accurately reported as far as its superficial aspects are concerned, yet remains sadly misrepresented in its substance. Allow me at this point to disabuse you of a few false conceptions which may have affected your powers of judgment.

"First, I do not claim to be either the Almighty Himself or His incarnation come down to earth; nor, in fact, am I one or the other of these things. Second, I nevertheless do claim that in the course of my recent travels, what the world has called my 'disappearance,' I was granted certain revelations directly from the Creator and in no uncertain terms received an itinerary of action from this same source. Third, and last, I am indeed the scientist known as Francis

Henry Haxhausen and not, as can be conclusively proved, an imposter. As an appendix to my previous statements, I should say that my exhibition is not the absurd extravaganza of scientific farce some have portrayed it to be, but a simple agenda consisting of a brief lecture followed by a practical demonstration of a device I have recently constructed. At no point do I attempt, either as an illusion or in fact, to work permanent damage on the body or soul of any member of my audience. That would be contrary to the Creator's law and the truth of His nature. And that is all I have to state in the way of a preamble to what I hope you will find an entertaining and enlightening attraction.

"I would like to open my lecture with the following anecdote. There is a legend, and I hasten to underline the word legend, that I learned while I was travelling here and there. It seems there was a sorcerer, or an alchemist or something along those lines, who dreamed of transforming the world through the creation of an artificial man. This man, the sorcerer dreamed, would not be subject to the flaws and limitations of the former type, but would instead live through many lifetimes, accumulating the knowledge and wisdom it would one day use to serve and improve the human race. The sorcerer, like all dreamers of this kind, was intent upon his vision and not particularly concerned with its ramifications in a larger scheme of things. Thus, he set about employing all his thaumaturgical arts in the creation of his 'new man.' First, a physical form was made out of the simple materials of wood and wax, resulting in a grotesque thing rather like a gigantic ventriloquist's dummy. Next, the sorcerer practiced a secret chemistry and a hermetic linguistics to elevate this lifeless effigy into a rather admirable semblance of human life – fatefully admirable, I might add. Without wasting a moment glorying in his own achievement, uttering not a single word of self-praise, the sorcerer engaged his creature in a course of learning that would enable it to function and evolve toward its destiny after the sorcerer's death. However, it was not long after this regimen had begun that the Omnipotent One realized what the sorcerer was intending to do. And so it happened that the creature, strong and well-coordinated but still a child in its mind, was awakened in the dead of night by a voice that cursed it as a blasphemy and an abomination. The voice bid the creature to go to its foul maker in the attic where he had sequestered himself among evil books and impure devices. Confused and terrified, the creature ascended several stairways and entered the attic. And there he found the sorcerer, motionless and hung upon the wall like something in a puppet-maker's workshop, his dark robe grazing the dusty floor and his head drooping down. Acting on a mechanical impulse beyond dread or despair, the creature raised up his master's head and saw that it was now no more than wood and wax. The sight was a maddening one, and it did not take long for the creature to find the rope with which it hung itself from the rafters of the attic. Thus was concluded the judgment passed upon the house of the sorcerer."

There was a pause in the scientist's flow of words. Calmly, he pulled a handkerchief from the inner pocket of his coat and wiped his face, which was perspiring in the heat of the footlights. Then he briefly scanned the faces of his audience, many of which bore dumbfounded expressions, before resuming his lecture.

"Who can know the intentions of the Creator? That which is suited to human designs may not suit His. With these rather unquestionable premises in mind, what conclusions might be drawn from the example of the sorcerer? By way of exegesis, I would say that the sorcerer, in conceiving a creature of limitless promise for good and none for evil, had violated a mysterious law, transgressed against a secret truth. And how had he strayed from this law and this truth? Simply in this manner: he had failed to provide for the corruption of his creation, not merely as a possibility but as a fate. And it was precisely by this oversight that the sorcerer fell out of step with the Creator's own design. It is the vision of this Great Design that I have been privileged to see, and that is why I am here tonight. As a footnote, however, I should state that even before I was granted certain divine insights, I had already been travelling toward them, approaching their truth in the unconscious or accidental manner of great scientific discoveries. And I thus found myself somewhat in readiness to receive and accept the proffered vision.

"Let me explain that I have spent nearly all my life as a scientist in a methodically frantic pursuit of perfection, driven by the dream of utopia, by the idea that I indeed contributed to an earthly paradise *in the making*. But slowly, very slowly, I began to notice certain things. I noticed that there were mechanisms built into the system of reality that nullified all our advancements in this world, that rerouted them into a hidden laboratory where these so-called blessings were cancelled out altogether, if not converted into formulas for our collapse. I noticed that there were higher forces working against us and working through us at the same time. On the one hand, our vision has always been of creating a world of perpetual vitality, despite our grudging recognition of death's 'necessity.' On the other hand, all we have constructed is an elaborate facade to conceal our immortal traumas, a false front that hides the perennial ordeals of the human race. Oh, the human race. And I began to see that perfection has never been the point, that both the lost paradise of the past and the one sought in the future were merely convenient pretexts for our true destiny of . . . disintegration.

"As a scientist I have had the opportunity to observe the workings of the world at close quarters and over a relatively extended stretch of time, not to mention space. And after careful observation and painstaking verification I was forced to this conclusion: the world thrives on its faults and strives, by every possible means, to aggravate them, while at the same time to mask them like a congenital deformity. The signs are everywhere, though I could not always read them.

"But if vitality and perfection are not the aim of this world, what in heaven's name is? That, my dear ladies and gentlemen, is the thrust of the second part of my exhibition, consisting of more comments by myself, a demonstration of my machine, and an entertaining display of what I might describe as a *tableau mort*. While I prepare things backstage, there will be a brief intermission. Thank you."

Dr Haxhausen walked off the stage with sluggish dignity and, as soon as he was out of sight, the audience began chattering all at once, as if they had been simultaneously revived from a hypnotic trance. Most of them, in outrage, left the theater; some, however, stayed for the finale. And both reactions, as well as these relative proportions, were typical at each exhibition that Dr Haxhausen held. Those who prematurely left the performance were content to believe they had been witnesses to nothing more than the interior theater of a madman. The others, intellectuals or neurotic voyeurs, had convinced themselves that the former genius deserved a full hearing before the inevitable condemnation, while secretly dreading that something he had to show them would reverberate, however faintly, with truth.

"Ladies and gentlemen," said Dr Haxhausen, who seemed to reappear on stage out of nowhere. "Ladies and gentlemen," he repeated more quietly, and then fell silent for a rather extended moment. And no one was whispering in the audience; no one said a word.

"There are holy places in this world, and I have been to some of them. Places where the presence of something sacred can be felt like an invisible meteorology. Always these places are quiet, and often they are in ruins. The ones that are not already at some stage of dilapidation nonetheless display the signs and symptoms, the *promise* of coming decay. We feel a sense of divinity in ruined places, abandoned places – shattered temples on mountaintops, crumbling catacombs, islands where a stone idol stands almost faceless. We never have such feelings in our cities or even in natural settings where the flora and fauna are overly evident. This is why so much is atoned for in wintertime, when a numinous death descends on those chosen lands of our globe. Indeed, winter is not so much the holiest time as it is the holiest place, the visible *locus* of the divine. And after winter, spring; thus turns the carousel of our planet, and all the others. But need it turn forever? I think not. For the ultimate winter draws near, ladies and gentlemen: the cycle of seasons, so the Creator has told me, is about to stop.

"He first spoke to me on a night which I had spent wandering the tattered fringes of a city. It might have been a city like this one, or any city. What matters is the mute decrepitude I found there among a few condemned buildings and vacant lots gone wild. I had all but forgotten my own name, who I was and what world I belonged to. And they are not wrong who say that my reason perished in the radiant face of unattainable dreams for the future. False dreams, nightmares! And then, in that same place where I had travelled to hang myself, I heard a voice among the shadows and moonlight. It was not a peaceful voice or a consoling voice, but something like an articulate sigh, a fabulously eloquent moan. There was also a man-like shape slumped down in a corner of that sad room which I had chosen for my ultimate refuge. The legs of the figure lay bent like a cripple's upon the broken floor, the moonlight cutting across them and leaving the rest of the body in darkness – all except two eyes that shone like colored glass in the moonlight. And although the voice seemed to emanate from everything around me, I knew that it was the voice of that sad thing before me, which was the Creator's earthly form: a simple department store mannikin.

"I was the chosen one, It said. I would carry the message which, like every annunciation from on high, would be despised or ignored by mankind. Because I, at that moment, could clearly read the signs which had been present everywhere in the world since the beginning. I had already noted many of the hints and foreshadowings, the prophecies, and knew them as inspired clues the Creator had planted, prematurely revealing the nature of His world and its true destiny. And I felt the sacred aura radiated by the crumpled figure in the corner, and I understood the scripture of the Great Design.

"It was written in the hieroglyphics of humble things, things humble to the point of mockery. All the lonesome pathetic things, all the desolate dusty things, all the misbegotten things, ruined things, failed things, all the imperfect semblances and deteriorating remnants of what we arrogantly deign to call the Real, to call . . . Life. In brief, the entire realm of the unreal – wherein He abides – is what He loves like nothing in this world. And haven't we ourselves at some time come face to face with this blessed realm? Can you recall ever having travelled down a deserted road and coming upon something like an old fairground: a desolate assemblage of broken booths and sagging tents, all of which you glimpsed through a high arcing entranceway with colors like a rusted rainbow? Didn't it seem as if some great catastrophe had struck, leaving only lifeless matter to molder in silent anonymity? And were you sad to see a place of former gaiety lying in its grave? Did you attempt to revive it in your imagination, start up the dead machinery, and fill the midway once again with fresh colors and laughing faces? We have all done this, all attempted to resurrect the defunct. And this is precisely where we have separated ourselves from the law and the truth of the Creator. Were we in harmony with Him, our gaze would fall upon a thriving scene and perceive nothing there but ruins and the ghosts of puppets. These, ladies and gentlemen, are what delight His heart. This much He has confided to me.

"But the Creator's taste for the unreal has required something to be real in the first place, and then to wither into ruins, to fail gloriously. Hence – the World. Extend this premise to its logical conclusion and you have – curtain! – the Creator's Great Design." And as the curtain slowly began to rise, the scientist backed away and said in a giddy voice: "But please don't think that when everything caves in there won't still be *muuusic*."

The auditorium went black, and in the blackness arose a hollow and tuneless melody which wandered to the wheezing accompaniment of a concertina, a pathetic duet belonging to a world of low cabarets or second-rate carnivals. Then, on either side of the stage, a tall glass case lit up to reveal that the two atrocious musicians were in fact life-size automatons, one of which pumped and pulled the snaking bellows of a concertina with a rigid motion of his arms, while the other scraped back and forth across the strings of a violin. The concertina player had his head thrown back in a wooden howl of merriment; the violin player stared down in empty-eyed concentration at his instrument. And both appeared lost in a kind of mechanical rapture.

The rest of the stage area, both above and below, also seemed to be occupied entirely by imitations of the human image: puppets and marionettes were strung up at various elevations, relieved of their weight by fragile glistening threads; mannikins posed in a paralyzed leisure which looked at once grotesque and idyllic; other dummies and an odd assortment of dolls sat in miniature chairs here and there, or simply sprawled about the floorboards, sometimes propping each other back to back. But among these mock-people, as became evident the longer one gazed at the stage, were hidden real ones who, rather ably, imitated the imitations. (These were persons whom Dr Haxhausen recruited, at fair recompense, whenever he entered a new town.) And forming the only scenery beyond both the artificial and the genuine figures of life was a gigantic luminescent mural in shades of black and white. With photographic accuracy, the mural portrayed a desolate room which might have been an attic or an old studio, and which contained some pieces of nondescript debris strewn about. A single, frameless window set into the torn wall at the rear of the room looked out upon a landscape that was still more desolate than the room itself: earth and sky had merged into a gray and jagged scene.

"You see how things are, ladies and gentlemen. Whereas we have been dreaming so long of creating perfect life in the laboratory, the Creator holds sacred only the crude facsimile, which best echoes or expresses His own will. He has always been far ahead of us, envisioning a completed work at the end of history. And He has no more time to linger over the vital stage of universal evolution. Because no truth or life can exist in us as we are, for truth and life can only exist in the mind, the will of the Creator – and we have stubbornly made it our business to do nothing but oppose that mind, that will. We are simply the raw material for His beloved puppets, which reflect to perfection the truth of the Creator and are the ideal dwellers in His paradise of ruins. And after His chosen ones are triumphantly installed in that good place, the Creator has some wonderful stories to tell as a way to pass the hours of eternity.

"And we may be among those in paradise, this is the great news I bring to you tonight. We may take our place among the puppets, as the tableau you see before you will serve to demonstrate. For at the moment there are certain faces insinuated within this elect company that do not . . . *belong*, that stand out in an unpleasant way. How to bring them into the fold is the question. And the answer, if you will turn for a moment and direct your eyes toward the balcony, the answer – spotlight! – is the puppet machine."

Turning their heads as instructed, the audience saw the object which, under the sharp spotlight, seemed to be resting on nothing, as if secured to the darkness itself. Some of the more observant members of the audience noticed the shining waxen faces whose eyes looked back at them from within the bizarre contraption. Set in motion by the remote control device in Dr Haxhausen's coat pocket, the machine noisily elevated its stovepipe neck and pointed its single, iridescent eye at the figures upon the stage.

"Ladies and gentlemen, I mentioned earlier that winter is the sacred state of things, the season of the soul. But that is not to say that the definitive winter we are approaching will be without all the colors of the rainbow. For it is the frigid aurora of the Sacred Ray, the very eye of the Creator, that will bring about the wondrous conversion of all things. As you can see, the design is His own. And, by means of modern assembly techniques, a sufficient quantity may be produced to serve the world, bathing every one of us in the garish radiance of our destiny. The effects? If you just keep watching your fellows upon this stage.

"There. See how the shafts of color pour down upon this stark scene, overlaying surfaces with an uncanny kaleidoscopic tint. It is the old surfaces that must be stripped away and disposed of. Time to leap from that summit of illusion our world has achieved, a glorious plummet after so many centuries in which we *erred on the side of excellence*. When all the Creator had in mind was a third-rate sideshow of beatific puppetry. But our strainings for progress were not useless; they were simply mistaken as to their ultimate aim. For it is modern science itself which will enable us to realize the Creator's dream, and to unrealize all the rest. See for yourselves. Look what is happening to the flesh of these future puppets, and to their eyes: wax and wood and shining glass to replace the sad and cumbersome structures of biology."

In the audience a few low sounds propagated into a network of obscure whispers and murmurings. Faces leaned toward the spectacle of crazy puppets painted with light, Dr Haxhausen's *tableau mort*. Some persons betrayed their cautious temperaments by dropping down in their seats, expanding the distance between themselves and the stream of colors that flowed over their heads on its way to the stage. Dr Haxhausen continued to preach above the shapeless, droning music.

"Please do not concern yourselves that any lasting conversion is being worked upon the people in this exhibition. I told you earlier that I would do no such thing. In the absence of a willing heart, the conversion you have witnessed would be the greatest sin in the universe, the unpardonable sin. There. The Sacred Ray has been extinguished. Your friends are again as they once were. And I thank you for coming to see me. Good night."

When the curtain descended and the house lights came on, an elderly woman in the audience stood up and called out to Dr Haxhausen: "The Lord saith, 'And if the prophet be deceived when he has spoken a thing, I the Lord have deceived that prophet, and I will stretch out my hand upon him, and will destroy him from the midst of my people Israel'." Others simply laughed or shook their heads in disgust. But Dr Haxhausen remained silent, smiling placidly as the congregation filed out of the theater.

The scientist, it seemed, was truly mad.

A few remarks by way of an epilogue. Although certain people will attach themselves to virtually any innovation of a mystical nature, the prophecies of Dr Haxhausen never found a following. Soon the scientist himself lapsed in notoriety, save for an occasional blurb in some newspaper, a passing mention which often implied that Dr Haxhausen's later role as a crank doomsayer had, in the public mind, entirely eclipsed his former renown as a man of science. Finally, on a particular evening in December, as a sparse audience populated for the most part by boozy derelicts and noisy adolescents awaited the notorious exhibition in a dreary banquet hall, it seemed that another visionary's career was destined for oblivion. When the world famous hallucinator did not appear at the publicized time, someone took it upon himself to pull back the makeshift curtain of a makeshift stage. And there, gently swinging from the long sooty gibbet of his fantastic machine, hung Dr Haxhausen. Whether the cause of death should have been deemed murder or the more apparent one of suicide was never discovered. For something else happened that same winter night that threw all other events into the background.

But of course you know, ladies and gentlemen, what it was that happened. I can see by the glitter in your eyes, the flush on your waxen faces, that you remember well how the colors appeared in the sky that night, a fabulous aurora sent by the sun and reflected by the moon, so that all the world would be baptized at once by the spectral light of truth. Willing or not, your hearts had heard the voice of the creature you thought mad. But they would not listen; they never have. Why did you force this transgression of divine law? And why do you still gaze with your wooden hate from the ends of the earth? It was for you that I committed this last and greatest sin, all for you. When have you ever appreciated these gestures from on high! And for this act I must now exist in eternal banishment from the paradise in which you exalt. How beautiful is your everlasting ruin.

Oh, blessed puppets, receive My prayer, and teach Me to make Myself in *thy* image.

THE STRANGE DESIGN
OF MASTER RIGNOLO

It was well into evening and for some time Nolon had been seated at a small table in a kind of park. This was a long, thin stretch of land – vaguely triangular in shape, like a piece of broken glass – bordered by three streets of varying breadth, varying evenness of surface, and of varying stages of disintegration as each thoroughfare succumbed in its own way and in its own time to the subtle but continuous movements of the slumbering earth below. From the far end of the park a figure in a dark overcoat was approaching Nolon's table, and it appeared there was going to be a meeting of some sort.

There were other tables here and there, all of them unoccupied, but most of the park was unused ground covered with a plush, fuzzy kind of turf. In the moonlight this densely woven pile of vegetation turned a soft shade of aquamarine, almost radiant. Beyond the thinning trees, stars were bright but without luster, as if they were made of luminous paper. Around the park, a jagged line of high roofs, black and featureless, crossed the sky like the uneven teeth of an old saw.

Nolon was resting his hands at the edge of the small, nearly circular table. In the middle of the table a piece of candle flickered inside a misshapen bubble of green glass, and Nolon's face was bathed in a restless green glare. He too was wearing a dark overcoat, unbuttoned at the top to reveal a scarf of lighter shade stuffed inside it. The scarf was wrapped about Nolon's neck right to the base of his chin. Every so often Nolon glanced up, not to look at Grissul as he proceeded across the park, but to try and catch sight of something in that lighted window across the street: a silhouette which at irregular intervals slipped in and out of view. Above the window was a long, low roof surmounted by a board which appeared to be a sign or marquee. The lettering on this board was entirely unreadable, perhaps corroded by the elements or even deliberately effaced. But the image of two tall, thin bottles could still be seen, their slender necks angled festively this way and that.

Grissul sat down, facing Nolon at eye level.

"Have you been here long?" he asked.

Nolon calmly pulled out a watch from deep inside his coat. He stared at it for a few moments, tapped the glass once or twice, then gently pushed it back inside his coat.

"Someone must have known I was thinking about seeing you," Grissul continued, "because I've got a little story I could tell."

Nolon again glanced toward the lighted window across the street. Grissul noticed this and twisted his head around, saying, "Well, someone's there after all. Do you think tonight we could get, you know, a little service of some kind?"

"Maybe you could go over there yourself and see what our chances are," Nolon replied.

"All the same to me," Grissul insisted, twisting his head back to face Nolon. "I've still got my news."

"Is that specifically why this meeting is taking place?"

To this query Grissul returned a blank expression. "Not that I know of," he asserted. "As far as I'm concerned, we just met by chance."

"Of course," Nolon agreed, smiling a little. Grissul smiled back but with much less subtlety.

"So I was going to tell you," Grissul began, "that I was out in that field, the one behind those empty buildings at the edge of town where everything just slides away and goes off in all directions. And there's a marsh by there, makes the ground a little, I don't know, stringy or something. No trees, though, only a lot of wild grass, reeds, you know where I mean?"

"I now have a good idea," Nolon replied, a trifle bored or at least pretending to be.

"This was a little before dark that I was there. A little before the stars began to come out. I really wasn't planning to do anything, let me say that. I just walked some ways out onto the field, changed direction a few times, walked a ways more. Then I saw something through a blind of huge stalks of some kind, skinny as your finger but with these great spiky heads on top. And really very stiff, not bending at all, just sort of wobbling in the breeze. They might well have creaked, I don't know, when I pushed my way through to see beyond them. Then I knelt down to get a better look at what was there on the ground. I'm telling you, Mr Nolon, it was right *in* the ground. It appeared to be a part of it, like—"

"Mr Grissul, *what* appeared?"

Grissul remembered himself and found a tone of voice not so exhausting of his own strength, nor so wearing on his listener's patience.

"The face," he said, leaning back in his chair. "It was right there, about the size of, I don't know, a window or a picture hanging on a wall, except that it was in the ground and it was a big oval, not rectangular in any way. Just as if someone had partly buried a giant, or better yet, a giant's *mask*. Only the edges of the face seemed not so much buried as, well, *woven* I guess you would say, right into the ground. The eyes were closed, not *shut* closed – it didn't seem to be dead – but relaxed. The same with the lips, very heavy lips rubbing up against each other. Even complexion, ashy gray, and soft cheeks. They *looked* soft, I mean, because I didn't actually touch them in any way. I think it was asleep."

Nolon shifted slightly in his chair and looked straight into Grissul's eyes.

"Then come and see for yourself," Grissul insisted. "The moon's bright enough."

"That's not the problem. I'm perfectly willing to go along with you, whatever might be there. But for once I have other plans."

"Oh, other plans," repeated Grissul as if some deeply hidden secret had been revealed. "And what other plans would those be, Mr Nolon?"

"Plans of relatively long standing and not altered since made, if you can conceive of such a thing these days. Are you listening? Oh, I thought you nodded off. Well, Rignolo, that mysterious little creature, has made a rare move. He's asked if I would like to have a look around his studio. No one's ever been there that I know of. And no one's actually seen what he paints."

"No one that you know of," added Grissul.

"Of course. Until tonight, that is, a little while from now unless a change of plans is necessary. Otherwise I shall be the first to see what all that talk of his is about. It should really be worth the trouble, and I could invite you to come along."

Grissul's lower lip pushed forward a little. "Thank you, Mr Nolon," he said, "but that's more in your line. I thought when I told you about my observation this evening— "

"Of course, your observation is very interesting, extraordinary, Mr Grissul. But I think that that sort of thing can wait, don't you? Besides, I haven't told you anything of Rignolo's work."

"You can tell me."

"Landscapes, Mr Grissul. Nothing but landscapes. Exclusively his subject, a point he even brags about."

"That's very interesting, too."

"I thought you would say something like that. And you might be even more interested if you had ever heard Rignolo discourse on his canvasses. But . . . well, you can see and hear for yourself. What do you say, then? First Rignolo's studio and then straight out to see if we can find that old field again?"

They agreed that these activities, in this sequence, would not be the worst way to fill an evening.

As they got up from the table, Nolon had a last look at the window across the street. The light that once brightened it must have been put out during his conversation with Grissul. So there was no way of knowing whether or not someone was now observing them. Buttoning their overcoats as far as their scarfed necks, the two men walked in silence across the park upon which countless stars stared down like the dead eyes of sculptured faces.

"Don't just walk stepping everywhere," Rignolo told his visitors as they all entered the studio. He was a little out of breath from the climb up the stairs, wheezing his words, quietly muttering to himself, "This place, oh, this place." There was hardly a patch of floor that was not in some way cluttered over, so he need not have warned Nolon, or even Grissul. Rignolo was of lesser stature than his guests, virtually a dwarf, and so moved with greater freedom through that cramped space. "You see," he said, "how this isn't really a room up here, just a little closet that tried to grow into one, bulging out every which way and making all these odd niches and alcoves surrounding us, this shapeless gallery of *nooks*. There's a window around here, I suppose, under some of these canvasses. But those are what you're here for, not to look out some window that who knows where it is. Nothing to see out there, even so."

Rignolo then ushered his visitors through the shrunken maze composed of recesses of one sort or another, indicating to them a canvass here or there. Each somehow held itself to a wall or was leaning against one, as if with exhaustion. Having brought their attention to this or that picture, he would step a little to the side and allow them to admire his work, standing there like a polite but slightly bored curator of some seldom-visited museum, a pathetic figure attired in over-sized clothes of woven . . . dust. His small ovoid face was as lifeless as a mask: his skin had the same faded complexion as his clothes and was just as slack, flabby; his lips were the same color as his skin but more full and taut; his hair shot out in tufts from his head, uncontrolled, weedy; and his eyes showed too much white, having to all appearances rolled up halfway into his forehead, as if they were trying to peek under it.

While Nolon was gazing at one of Rignolo's landscapes, Grissul seemed unable to shake off a preoccupation with the artist himself, though he was obviously making the effort. But the more he tried to turn his attention away from Rignolo, the more easily it was drawn back to the flabby skin, the faded complexion, the undisciplined shocks of hair. Finally, Grissul gave a little nudge to Nolon and began to whisper something. Nolon looked at Grissul in a way that might have said, "Yes, I know, but have some sense of decorum in any case," then resumed his contemplation of Rignolo's excellent landscapes.

They were all very similar to one another. Given such titles as "*Glistening Marsh*," "*The Tract of Three Shadows*," and "*The Stars, the Hills*," they were not intended to resemble as much as *suggest* the promised scenes. A vague hint of material forms might emerge here and there, some familiar effect of color or outline, but for the most part they could be described as extremely remote in their perspective on tangible reality. Grissul, who was no stranger to some of the locales purportedly depicted in these canvasses, could very well have expressed the objection that these conglomerations of fractured mass, these whirlpools of distorted light, simply did not achieve their purpose, did not in fact deserve connection with the geographical subjects from which they took their titles. Perhaps it was Rignolo's intuition that just such a protest might be forthcoming that inspired – in the rapid, frantic voice of a startled sleeper – the following outburst:

"Think anything you like about these scenes, it's all the same to me. Whisper to each other, my hearing is wonderfully bad. Say that my landscapes do not invite one's eyes to pass into them and wander, let alone linger for the briefest moment. Nevertheless, that is exactly their purpose, and as far as I am concerned they are quite adequate to it, meticulously efficient. I have spent extraordinary lengths of *time* within the borders of each canvass, both as maker and as casual inhabitant, until the borders no longer exist for me and neither does . . . that other thing. Understand that when I say *inhabitant*, I do not in any way mean that I take my clumsy feet tromping up and down staircases of color, or that I stand this stunted body of mine upon some lofty ledge where I can play the master of all I see. There are no masters of these scenes and no seers, because bodies and their organs cannot function there – no place for them to go, nothing to survey with ordinary eyes, no thoughts to think for the mighty brain. And my thoroughfares will not take you from the doorstep of one weariness to the backdoor of another, and they cannot crumble, because they are burdened with nothing to convey – their travelers are already there, continuously arriving at infinite sites of the perpetually astonishing. Yet these sites are also a homeland, and nothing there will ever threaten to become strange. What I mean to say is that to *inhabit* my landscapes one must, in no figurative sense, grow into them. At best they are a paradise for sleepwalkers, but only those sleepwalkers who never rise to their feet, who forget their destination, and who may thus never reach that ultimate darkness beyond dreams, but may loiter in perpetuity in these lands of mine, which neighbor on nothingness and stand next door to endlessness. So you see, my critics, what we have in these little pictures is a living communion with the void, a vital annihilation and a thoroughly decorative eternity of—"

"All the same," Grissul interjected, "it does sound unpleasant."

"You're interfering," Nolon said under his breath.

"The old bag of wind," Grissul said under his.

"And just where do you see the unpleasantness? Where, show me. Nowhere, in my view. One cannot be unpleasant to one's self, one cannot be *strange* to oneself. I claim that all will be different when one is joined with the landscape. We need not go the way of doom when such a hideaway is so near at hand – a land of escape. For the initiated, each of those little swirls is a cove which one may enter into and become; each line – jagged or merely jittery – is a cartographer's shoreline which may be explored at all points at once; each crinkled wad of radiance is a star basking in its own light, and in yours. This, gentlemen, is a case of making the most of one's talent for pro-jec-tion. There indeed exist *actual* locales on which my pictures are based, I admit that. But these places keep their distance from the spectator: whereas my new landscapes make you feel at home, those old ones put you off, hold you at arm's length, and in the end throw you right out of the picture. That's the way it is out there – everything looks at you with strange eyes. But you can get around this intolerable situation, jump the fence, so to speak, and trespass into a world where you *belong* for a change. If my landscapes look unfamiliar to you, it is only because everything looks different from the other side. All this will be understood much more clearly when you have seen my masterwork. Step this way, please."

Nolon and Grissul glanced blankly at each other and then followed the artist up to a narrow door. Opening the door with a tiny key, Rignolo ushered his guests inside. It was a tight squeeze through the doorway.

"*Now this* place really is a closet," Grissul whispered to Nolon. "I don't think I can turn around."

"Then we'll just have to walk out of here backwards, as if there were something wrong with that."

The door slammed closed and for a moment there was no place on earth darker than that little room.

"Watch the walls," Rignolo called through the door.

"Walls?" someone whispered.

The first images to appear in the darkness were those crinkled wads of radiance Rignolo spoke of, except these were much larger, more numerous, and became more radiant than the others bound within their cramped little canvasses. And they emerged on all sides of the spectator, above and below as well, so that an irresistible conviction was instilled that the tiny gravelike room had expanded into a star-strewn corridor of night, the certainty created that one was suspended in space without practical means of remaining there. Reaching out for the solid walls, crouching on the floor, only brought confusion rather than relief from the sense of impossibility. The irregular daubs of brightness grew into great silver blotches, each of them ragged at its rim and glowing wildly. Then they stopped growing in the blackness, attaining some predesigned composition, and another kind of growing began: thin filaments of bluish light started sprouting in the spaces between those bulbous thistles of brilliance, running everywhere like cracks up and down a wall. And these threadlike, hairlike tendrils eventually spread across the blackness in an erratic fury of propagation, until all was webbed and stringy in the universal landscape. Then the webbing began to fray and grow shaggy, cosmic moss hanging in luminous clumps, beards. But the scene was not muddled, no more so, that is, than the most natural marsh or fen-like field. Finally, enormous stalks shot out of nowhere, quickly crisscrossed to form interesting and well-balanced patterns, and suddenly froze. They were a strange shade of green and wore burry crowns of a pinkish color, like prickly brains.

The scene, it appeared, was now complete. All the actual effects were displayed: *actual* because the one further effect was most likely an illusion. For it seemed that deep within the shredded tapestry of webs and hairs and stalks, something else had been woven, something buried beneath the marshy morass but slowly rising to the surface.

"Is that a face?" someone said.

"I can begin to see one too," said the other, "but I don't know if I want to see it. I don't think I can feel where I am now. Let's try not to look at those faces."

A series of cries from within the little room finally induced Rignolo to open the door, which sent Nolon and Grissul tumbling backwards into the artist's studio. They lay among the debris on the floor for some time. Rignolo swiftly secured the door, and then stood absolutely still beside it, his upturned eyes taking no interest in his visitors' predicament. As they regained their feet, a few things were quickly settled in low voices.

"Mr Nolon, I recognized the place that that room is supposed to be."

"I'm sure you did."

"And I'm also sure I know whose face it was that I saw tonight in that field."

"I think we should be going."

"What are you saying?" demanded Rignolo.

Nolon gestured toward a large clock high upon the wall and asked if that was the time.

"Always," replied Rignolo, "since I've never yet seen its hands move."

"Well, then, thank you for everything," said Nolon.

"We have to be *leaving*," added Grissul.

"Just one moment," Rignolo shouted as they were making their way out. "I know where you're going now. Someone, I won't say who, told me what you found in that field. I've done it, haven't I? You can tell me all about it. No, it's not necessary. I've put myself into the scene at last. The abyss with a decor, the ultimate flight! In short – survival in the very maw of oblivion. Oh, perhaps there's still some work to be done. But I've made a good start, haven't I? I've got my foot in the door, my face looking in the window. Little by little, then . . . forever. True? No, don't say anything. Show me where it is, I need to go there. I have a right to go."

Having no idea what sort of behavior a refusal might inspire in the maniacal Rignolo, not to mention possible reprisals from unknown parts, Nolon and Grissul respected the artist's request.

*　　*　　*

Into a scene which makes no sound, three figures arrive. Their silhouettes move with distinct, cautious steps across an open field, progressing slowly, almost without noticeable motion. Around them, crisscrossing shafts of tall grasses are entirely motionless, their pointed tips sharply outlined in the moonlight. *Above them, the moon is round and bright; but its brightness is of a dull sort, like the flat whiteness that appears in the spaces of complex designs embellishing the page of a book.*

The three figures, one of which is much shorter than the other two, have stopped and are standing completely still before a particularly dense clump of oddly shaped stalks. Now one of the taller figures has raised his arm and is pointing toward this clump of stalks, while the shorter figure has taken a step in the direction indicated. The two tall figures are standing together as the short one has all but disappeared into the dark, dense overgrowth. Only a single shoe, its toe angled groundward, remains visible. Then nothing at all.

The two remaining figures continue to stand in their places, making no gestures, their hands in the pockets of their long overcoats. They are staring into the blackness where the other one has disappeared. Around them, crisscrossing shafts of tall grasses; above them, the moon is round and bright.

Now the two figures have turned themselves away from the place where the other one disappeared. They are each slightly bent over and are holding their hands over their ears, as though to deafen themselves to something they could not bear. Then, slowly, almost without noticeable motion, they move out of the scene.

The field is empty once again. And now everything awakes with movement and sound.

*   *   *

After their adventure, Nolon and Grissul returned to the same table in that place they had met earlier that evening. But where they had left a bare table-top behind them, not considering the candleflame within its unshapely green bubble, there were at the moment two shallow glasses set out, along with a tall, if somewhat thin bottle placed between them. They looked at the bottle, the glasses, and each other methodically, as if they did not want to rush into anything.

"Is there still, you know, someone in the window across the street?" Grissul asked.

"Do you think I should look?" Nolon asked back.

Grissul stared at the table, allowing moments to accumulate, then said, "I don't care, Mr Nolon, I have to say that what happened tonight was very unpleasant."

"Something like that would have happened sooner or later," Nolon replied. "He was too much the dreamer, let's be honest. Nothing he said made any sense to speak of, and he was always saying more than he should. Who knows *who* heard what."

"I've never heard screaming like that."

"It's over," said Nolon quietly.

"But what could have happened to him?" asked Grissul, gripping the shallow glass before him, apparently without awareness of the move.

"Only he could know that for certain," answered Nolon, who mirrored Grissul's move and seemingly with the same absence of conscious intent.

"And why did he scream that way, why did he say it was all a trick, a mockery of his dreams, that 'filthy thing in the earth'? Why did he scream not to be 'buried forever in that strange, horrible mask'?"

"Maybe he became confused," said Nolon. Nervously, he began pouring from the thin bottle into each of their glasses.

"And then he cried out for someone to kill him. But that's not what he wanted at all, just the opposite. He was afraid to you-know-what. So why would he— "

"Do I really have to explain it all, Mr Grissul?"

"I suppose not," Grissul said very softly, looking ashamed. "He was trying to get away, to get away with something."

"That's right," said Nolon just as softly, looking around. "Because he wanted to escape from here without having to you-know-what. How would that look?"

"Set an example."

"Exactly. Now let's just take advantage of the situation and drink our drinks before moving on."

"I'm not sure I want to," said Grissul.

"I'm not sure we have any say in the matter," replied Nolon.

"Yes, but—"

"Shhh. Tonight's our night."

Across the street a shadow fidgeted in the frame of a lighted window. An evening breeze moved through the little park, and the green glow of a candleflame flickered upon two silent faces.

THE VOICE IN THE BONES

The blackness above was deep and unbroken. Rising toward it was a tower with a single opening which framed a pale, quivering light. The narrow aperture was fixed high within the darkness and was engulfed by its dense and voiceless unity. Below the tower was a scattering of other structures, while other lights emerged here and there in the lower darkness. One of these was a lamp set into a wall at the border of a fractured street. The lamp spread its glow upon the gray wall and upon two figures who stood motionless before it. No color in their tight, unblemished faces, no sign of breath under the dark covering of their forms: simple beings with long fingers and empty eyes. Yet their gaze was clearly focused on a building across that vacant street, rigidly directed toward a certain window there. Every so often someone would peer out along the very edge of that window, though he never looked for more than a moment before retreating out of sight. And he occupied a room where everything seemed to tremble with shadows.

The shadows moved slowly, obscuring so many of the objects within the room and appearing to change the outlines of the simplest furnishings. The room itself became altered in its dimensions. Over the course of slow transformations it pushed outward into a great abyss and squeezed inward to create a maze of strange black turnings. Every shape was imposing itself on another shape, breeding a chaos of overlapping patterns.

The occupant of the room remained on his guard in these surroundings. Now he saw something hiding inside a shadow moving along the woodwork by the window, using the shadow as a mask. He nudged his foot against the wall, which felt as if it softly gave way to his touch. But there was nothing in the shadow, or nothing any longer. And when he reached out slowly and pulled the dangling cord of a light, it was not illumination that filled the room but a voice.

"Mister Ha-ha!" it shrieked, echoing into many voices around him.

"Ha-ha," repeated a similar voice.

With lethargic caution he slid toward the window and peeked around the casement. He could not imagine that those keen and jagged voices belonged to the two figures across the street. He had never seen them open their mouths when they called out to him with some improvised name. They only stood firm and watchful by the high rough wall. He looked away.

"Mister Tick-tock!"

"Tick-tock, tick-tock."

He took another step, an intensely sluggish effort, and stood centered in the window frame. Now they would see him, now they would know. But the ones who had been so patient in their vigil had abandoned the scene. And shadows merged with fading echoes in the room.

Then there were new echoes for him to hear. Yet they did not lack definition or intent, as did so many of the sounds produced by the large building that contained him: a dull drawn-out crash or a brief crackling might come from anywhere without giving up its origin or identity. But these new sounds, these particular echoes, did not seek anonymity. And there was a focus, a center upon which they converged. Footsteps, the creak of a closing window or a slowly opening door, a fumbling among the objects of another room, all these noises spoke a strange language among the surrounding shadows and joined with them in a greater scheme.

He began moving from room to room in a laborious expedition and became a fugitive in a realm of twisted suppositions. A window might allow some glaze of illumination, a glassy luminescence, but he was often confused by certain deviations in the design of these rooms. Forced to turn an unseen corner, he was faced with a small door, and around its edges some thin lines of light alternately appeared and disappeared in the darkness. He opened the door. On the other side was a long low corridor with a row of small lamps that together blinked on and off along either wall. He stood and stared. For it seemed that something came into being during the intervals of darkness in the corridor, a swarm of obscure shapes that were but imperfectly dispersed by the returning light, gnarled specters that somehow belonged to the very walls and reached out with their shapeless limbs. He crouched and then crossed his arms upon his chest, so that his body would not touch anything which need not be touched. When the light next filled the corridor he ran across the floor and felt himself being thrust forward, strangely propelled by a power which was not his own and which he could not control. A railing caught him before he plunged down a stairwell reaching into the blackness below.

Yet these flights of stairs, which from above described a perfect vertical shaft, soon began to wander. They led him into unfamiliar regions of the building without offering a means of escape, only of retreat. And when he paused a moment to survey the dark and doorless world around him, he heard the echoing voices.

"Mister Fizzle," they shouted at him in unison.

He proceeded to descend the stairway and resigned himself to whatever destination it would lead him, always moving with that irresistible rapidity which had possessed his body and confused his thoughts. The echoes of other footsteps were now in pursuit. They appeared to catch up to him as small and barely visible objects, soft and irregular spheres that tumbled past him on the stairs and then faded before his eyes. Soon the others would be able to see him, soon they would reach him.

At last there came an end to the prodigious stairs, and he arrived at the abysmal fundament of the building. The ground upon which he now stood seemed to be of raw clay, cold and tallowy. Ahead of him was a crude passage, nearly a tunnel, which dripped with something that gave off a grayish glow. And there were other passages and also doors within the damp walls. It seemed he had no choice but to hide within one of these rooms. For upon that slippery ground he could no longer move with the same speed that had brought him there.

He turned down one passageway after another. By then the others were with him in those dim catacombs. It was time to take refuge behind one of the doors, each of which perfectly withheld the secret of whatever lay behind it.

The room in which he closed himself was lit by a dimmer light than that of the passages outside. It was an oily and erratic illumination which seemed to emerge from thick pools and patches of corruption that mottled the greasy clay of the floor. An atmosphere of filth and decay occupied the room, a rank presence that was the soul of slaughter. Indefinite in its dimensions, the chamber seemed to be a place of disposal for a kind of fleshy refuse. He was about to seek a more tolerable sanctuary when two figures stepped out of some dark recess within the room.

"Mister Thump," one of them said without the slightest movement of his thin mouth. So it was not they who spoke, but something else which spoke through them, something which practiced a strange ventriloquism.

When he turned to try and escape through the door, he found that it was stuck, jammed within its frame by shadows clogging its edges, oozing out like black suet.

"Thump, thump, thump," whispered the voices approaching him.

An interval of oblivion passed, and it was an entirely different room in which he awoke. This was a small, bare cubicle lit only by a peculiar radiance which shone through a narrow slot in the large, locked door. There were no windows in the room. The floor felt gritty and vaguely shifting, as if he were being supported by very loose sand. He lay against a wall in darkness, with only his thin legs projecting into the strip of light cast upon the floor.

A voice was whispering to him from somewhere. Slowly the words gained force, yet somehow they remained an abstract sound which merely flirted with messages, never really cohering. The voice seemed to be reaching him through the wall, for he was alone in that room. And still the tones were emphatic, even piercing, as if unaffected by the dulling interference of a barrier.

"Listen," the voice said. "Are you listening now? I am also a prisoner, but it is not the same for me. Things have changed in this place. I know that you wonder about those ones who brought you here, and about other things. Are you listening? Someone made them, you know. *He* is the one who made them, he could do such things. And he did something else, something that he is still doing. For he could never truly perish. Things have changed since he came to this place. He came here with strange dreams, and things began to change. He hid himself here and practiced his dreams. Bones and shadows, are you listening? Pale bones and black shadows. And now he is gone but he is not gone. I know my voice is not the same, if you are listening. It is only an echo now. I have heard so many voices, and how could I not become their echo? The echo of dreams, dreams of bones and shadows together. Do you know the shadows I mean? They draw you toward them, they take you into their blackness. But that is where you would go. Something in the very bones reaches out to the shadows and their blackness. He dreamed about this, and he practiced this dream. The bones themselves are only pale shadows, the dust of shadows. Where they are gathered, so are shadows gathered there. And they are dreamed together. These dreams have not gone from this place. Everything is the subject of shadows, everything serves them and their blackness. The bones are silent because the shadows have taken their voices. He dreamed about this. Now we are all servants of shadows, and they have taken voices from the bones to join with their blackness. The shadows have taken these voices now. And they are using them, listen to my words. Things have changed but everything continues as he dreamed it would be. Everything continues but is not the same. And are you . . ."

But the words were interrupted when the door groaned and swung slowly toward him, flooding his cell with a confusing radiance. In the open doorway were two figures which stood lean and dark and without features against the flaring incandescence. Yet they were not hindered by the brilliance and moved toward him with a mechanical efficiency. They positioned themselves on either side of his slouching form, then lifted him easily off the floor. He struggled awkwardly, at last gripping one of their pale hands and pulling on it. The skin slipped back from the wrist and bunched up like a glove; underneath was revealed a kind of stuffing composed of pale chips and slivers that cohered within a thick black paste.

They brought him out into the narrow circular corridor, where the brightness of a multitude of hanging lamps eliminated any suggestion of shadows. He noticed, as he hung in the grasp of the two servants, that the neighboring cell had its door wide open and was without an occupant. But when they began to proceed down the corridor there appeared to be something that moved upon the wall of that vacant cell, evading the light. They passed other cells, all of whose doors were open and all of which betrayed a stirring along the walls within that told him they were not wholly unoccupied.

His wordless escorts now pushed him through a peaked doorway cut into the gray inner wall of the corridor. On the other side was a stone stairway which twisted through the heart of the prison. He climbed the stairs slowly and stiffly with long-fingered hands guiding him. And now shadows appeared upon the bending wall, joining themselves into an unshapely creature, a chimerical guide that knew its way and led him to a place high above. There was no variation in the light around him, yet a sense of gradual darkening imposed itself on him with every ascending step. Now he was approaching some vast and massive source of the obscure, a great nexus of shadows, a birthplace and perhaps also a graveyard where things without substance waited, a realm of first and final dreams.

The stairs ended as they emerged through the floor at the center of a great room. And here a new species of illumination – a pale and grainy phosphorescence – could be seen spreading throughout the open space around them. This strange light appeared to emanate from several transparent vessels which were shaped like urns and had been randomly positioned upon the floor or atop objects various in size. Each of these containers seemed to be filled with a colorless, powdery substance from which a cold and gritty glow was sent forth. But this glow, this scintillating gloss, did not reveal the surfaces of the room as much as it coated them with another surface, transfiguring what lay beneath.

For in that troubled glare everything lost the density and presence it might have possessed. Wide and lofty cabinets seemed to waver, barely settled upon the uneven floor. The straight lines of tall shelves took on a slight tilt and threatened to disgorge the countless books so tenuously supported there. So many books were already scattered across the floor, their pages torn out and gathered in ragged heaps that might take themselves into the air at any moment. Located in a far section of the chamber was an armory of curious devices mounted upon the wall or suspended by wires, devices which could have been hallucinations, phantoms through which one's hand would pass on attempting to use them as they were designed to be used. And they seemed to have been designed for projects that involved rending and ripping, flaying and grinding. Yet all of these instruments apparently had lain idle for ages, displaying a corrosion which further removed them from their former substance and placed them in a category of phantasmal curiosities. Even the long low table about which these atrocious implements were congregated was dissolving with neglect.

Nevertheless, he was forced by his guardians to lie upon this coarse slab and be fettered by straps so decayed that he could easily tear them off. But the stern auxiliaries did not seem to be aware of the true condition of things: they continued to perform routine tasks that once may have had a purpose before being eclipsed by changes unknown to them.

Through the brittle haze of that room he watched his keepers as they went about some dutiful business, picking up obscure debris lying about the table, remnants of an undertaking long abandoned, or one no longer practiced in the same manner. This material they deposited in a large chest and locked it within. Then, with the studied automatism of pallbearers, they lifted the chest by its handles and carried it away, descending the stairs at the center of the room, their heavy feet scuffing the steps of that great prison tower. And echoes diminished in the depths below.

With the labored movements of a sleeper prematurely awakened, he turned himself from the table. And it was then he saw that the room was provided with a window, a single opening without glass. But so filled was this aperture with the blackness beyond that it seemed to be only a shadow painted upon the wall. He stepped slowly about the mounds of paper and other waste lying about the floor, careful of the deceptions of the room's fractured light, and leaned over the window's ledge. Far below he could see two tiny figures with a miniature box bobbing between them. They shrank farther into the quiet distance and finally disappeared into one of those dark hulking structures which were crowded together along narrow streets. So alike were these buildings that he could not keep his fix on the one they had entered, though he had his suspicions. Remaining at the window, he gazed into the great blackness above, which seemed to exert a strange magnetism, a tugging at the tower that rose so near to this mute and lightless firmament. After a few moments he turned away from the window. Now he was alone, with nothing to hold him to that place.

But as he moved toward the stairs to leave, he paused and scrutinized the piles of disjecta about him. Among this scattering of odds and ends there appeared to be something like bones or pieces of bones, broken leavings of some enterprise that had taken place here. And there was also such an abundance of jettisoned paper, pages dark with scribbling and sloughed off in the chaos of composition. Yet as he studied with greater intentness this mass of wild marks, he began to receive a few splinters of its theme, to read the wreckage of an unknown adventure. He seemed to see phrases, incantations, formulae, and almost to hear them spoken by a shattered voice. *The pact of bones and blackness,* the voice declaimed to him. *The collection of shadows . . . shadows binding bones . . . skeletons becoming shadows.* And he came to understand other things: *the land stripped of flesh . . . the reeking earth ripped clean and rising into the great blackness.* This reverberant discourse had made him its student, imparting theories and practice: *bones pummeled into purity . . . parts turned to brilliant particles . . . the shadows seeded with the voice of skulls . . . the many voices within eternal blackness . . . the tenebrous harmony.*

At last he turned his eyes from these words that were not words. Trying to draw away from them, he stumbled toward the stairs. But the voice which spoke these things continued to speak to him. It then became many voices speaking. Things had already begun to change. And now the stairs descended only into blackness, a blackness that was rising into the room as a great shadow around him. Shadows and their blackness and the voices they possessed. The one who had dreamed of bones and shadows – bones and shadows together – spoke in these voices and knew the name to speak, the name that would flay the flesh, the true name that called its bearer into the shadows as folds of blackness fell upon him and wrapped him in their shroud.

Now they had summoned him, now he was with them. Things had changed yet everything continued as before. And he cried out as the shadow sought his bones and as he felt his bones reaching into the blackness. Yet it was no longer his own voice that sounded in the tower, but the echoing clamor of strange shrieking multitudes.

PART 4
Teatro Grottesco and Other Tales

TEATRO GROTTESCO

The first thing I learned was that no one *anticipates* the arrival of the Teatro. One would not say, or even think, "The Teatro has never come to this city – it seems we're due for a visit," or perhaps, "Don't be surprised when you-know-what turns up, it's been years since the last time." Even if the city in which one lives is exactly the kind of place favored by the Teatro, there can be no basis for predicting its appearance. No warnings are given, no fanfare to announce that a Teatro season is about to begin, or that *another* season of that sort will soon be upon us. But if a particular city possesses what is sometimes called an "artistic underworld," and if one is in close touch with this society of artists, the chances are optimal for being among those who discover that things have already started. This is the most one can expect.

For a time it was all rumors and lore, hearsay and dreams. Anyone who failed to show up for a few days at the usual club or bookstore or special artistic event was the subject of speculation. But most of the crowd I am referring to lead highly unstable, even precarious lives. Any of them might pack up and disappear without notifying a single soul. And almost all of the supposedly "missing ones" were, at some point, seen again. One such person was a filmmaker whose short movie *Private Hell* served as the featured subject of a local one-night festival. But he was nowhere to be seen either during the exhibition or at the party afterwards. "Gone with the Teatro," someone said with a blasé knowingness, while others smiled and clinked glasses in a sardonic farewell toast.

But only a week later the filmmaker was spotted in one of the back rows of a pornographic theater. He later explained his absence by insisting he had been in the hospital following a thorough beating at the hands of some people he had been filming but who did not consent or desire to be filmed. This sounded plausible, given the subject matter of the man's work. Yet for some reason no one believed his hospital story, despite the evidence of bandages he was still required to wear. "It has to be the Teatro," argued a woman who always dressed in shades of purple and who was a good friend of the filmmaker. "*His* stuff and *Teatro* stuff," she said, holding up two crossed fingers for everyone to see.

But what was meant by "Teatro stuff?" This was a phrase I heard spoken by a number of persons, not all of them artists of a pretentious or self-dramatizing type. Certainly there is no shortage of anecdotes that have been passed around which purport to illuminate the nature and workings of this "cruel troupe," an epithet used by those who are too superstitious to invoke the Teatro Grottesco by name. But sorting out these accounts into a coherent *profile*, never mind their truth value, is another thing altogether.

For instance, the purple woman I mentioned earlier held us all spellbound one evening with a story about her cousin's roommate, a self-styled "visceral artist" who worked the night shift as a stock clerk for a supermarket chain in the suburbs. On a December morning, about an hour before sun-up, the artist was released from work and began his walk home through a narrow alley that ran behind several blocks of various stores and businesses along the suburb's main avenue. A light snow had fallen during the night, settling evenly upon the pavement of the alley and glowing in the light of a full moon which seemed to hover just at the alley's end. The artist saw a figure in the distance, and something about this figure, this winter-morning vision, made him pause for a moment and stare. Although he had a trained eye for sizing and perspective, the artist found this silhouette of a person in the distance of the alley intensely problematic. He could not tell if it was short or tall, or even if it was moving – either toward him or away from him – or was standing still. Then, in a moment of hallucinated wonder, the figure stood before him in the middle of the alley.

The moonlight illuminated a little man who was entirely unclothed and who held out both of his hands as if he were grasping at a desired object just out of his reach. But the artist saw that something was wrong with these hands. While the little man's body was pale, his hands were dark and were too large for the tiny arms on which they hung. At first the artist believed the little man to be wearing oversized mittens. His hands seemed to be covered by some kind of fuzz, just as the alley in which he stood was layered with the fuzziness of the snow that had fallen during the night. His hands looked soft and fuzzy like the snow, except that the snow was white and his hands were black.

In the moonlight the artist came to see that the mittens worn by this little man were actually something like the paws of an animal. It almost made sense to the artist to have thought that the little man's hands were actually paws which had only appeared to be two black mittens. Then each of the paws separated into long thin fingers that wriggled wildly in the moonlight. But they could not have been the fingers of a hand, because there were too many of them. And the hands were not paws, nor were the paws really mittens. And all of this time the little man was becoming smaller and smaller in the moonlight of that alley, as if he were moving into the distance far away from the artist who was hypnotized by this vision. Finally a little voice spoke which the artist could barely hear, and it said to him: "I cannot keep them away from me anymore, I am becoming so small and weak." These words suddenly made this whole winter-morning scenario into something that was too much even for the self-styled "visceral artist."

In the pocket of his coat the artist had a tool which he used for cutting open boxes at the supermarket. He had cut into flesh in the past, and, with the moonlight glaring upon the snow of that alley, the artist made a few strokes which turned that white world red. Under the circumstances what he had done seemed perfectly justified to the artist, even an act of mercy. The man was becoming so small.

Afterward the artist ran through the alley without stopping until he reached the rented house where he lived with his roommate. It was she who telephoned the police, saying there was a body lying in the snow at such and such a place and then hanging up without giving her name. For days, weeks, the artist and his roommate searched the local newspapers for some word of the extraordinary thing the police must have found in that alley. But nothing ever appeared.

"You see how these incidents are hushed up," the purple woman whispered to us. "The police know what is going on. There are even *special police* for dealing with such matters. But nothing is made public, no one is questioned. And yet, after that morning in the alley, my cousin and her roommate came under surveillance and were followed everywhere by unmarked cars. Because these special policemen know that it is artists, or highly artistic persons, who are *approached* by the Teatro. And they know whom to watch after something has happened. It is said that these police may be party to the deeds of that 'company of nightmares'."

But none of us believed a word of this Teatro anecdote told by the purple woman, just as none of us believed the purple woman's friend, the filmmaker, when he denied all innuendos that connected him to the Teatro. On the one hand, our imaginations had sided with this woman when she asserted that her friend, the creator of the short movie *Private Hell*, was somehow in league with the Teatro; on the other hand, we were mockingly dubious of the story about her cousin's roommate, the self-styled visceral artist, and his encounter in the snow-covered alley.

This divided reaction was not as natural as it seemed. Never mind that the case of the filmmaker was more credible than that of the visceral artist, if only because the first story was lacking the extravagant details which burdened the second. Until then we had uncritically relished all we had heard about the Teatro, no matter how bizarre these accounts may have been and no matter how much they opposed a verifiable truth or even a coherent portrayal of this phenomenon. As artists we suspected that it was in our interest to have our heads filled with all kinds of Teatro craziness. Even I, a writer of nihilistic prose works, savored the inconsistency and the flamboyant absurdity of what was told to me across a table in a quiet library or a noisy club. In a word, I delighted in the *unreality* of the Teatro stories. The truth they carried, if any, was immaterial. And we never questioned any of them until the purple woman related the episode of the visceral artist and the small man in the alley.

But this new disbelief was not in the least inspired by our sense of reason or reality. It was in fact based solely on fear; it was driven by the will to negate what one fears. No one gives up on something until it turns on them, whether or not that thing is real or unreal. In some way all of this Teatro business had finally worn upon our nerves; the balance had been tipped between a madness that intoxicated us and one that began to menace our minds. As for the woman who always dressed herself in shades of purple . . . we avoided her. It would have been typical of the Teatro, someone said, to use a person like that for their purposes.

Perhaps our judgement of the purple woman was unfair. No doubt her theories concerning the "approach of the Teatro" made us all uneasy. But was this reason enough to cast her out from that artistic underworld which was the only society available to her? Like many societies, of course, ours was founded on fearful superstition, and this is always reason enough for any kind of behavior. She had been permanently stigmatized by too closely associating herself with something unclean in its essence. Because even after her theories were discredited by a newly circulated Teatro tale, her status did not improve.

I am now referring to a story that was going around in which an artist was not *approached* by the Teatro but rather took the first step *toward* the Teatro, as if acting under the impulse of a sovereign will.

The artist in this case was a photographer of the I-am-a-camera type. He was a studiedly bloodless specimen who quite often, and for no apparent reason, would begin to stare at someone and to continue staring until that person reacted in some manner, usually by fleeing the scene but on occasion by assaulting the photographer, who invariably pressed charges. It was therefore not entirely surprising to learn that he tried to engage the services of the Teatro in the way he did, for it was his belief that this cruel troupe could be hired to, in the photographer's words, "utterly destroy someone." And the person he wished to destroy was his landlord, a small balding man with a mustache who, after the photographer had moved out of his apartment, refused to remit his security deposit, perhaps with good reason but perhaps not.

In any case, the photographer, whose name incidentally was Spence, made inquiries about the Teatro over a period of some months. Following up every scrap of information, no matter how obscure or suspect, the tenacious Spence ultimately arrived in the shopping district of an old suburb where there was a two-story building that rented space to various persons and businesses, including a small video store, a dentist, and, as it was spelled out on the building's directory, the Theatre Grottesco. At the back of the first floor, directly below a studio for dancing instruction, was a small suite of offices whose glass door displayed some stencilled lettering that read: T G VENTURES. Seated at a desk in the reception area behind the glass door was a young woman with long black hair and black-rimmed eyeglasses. She was thoroughly engrossed in writing something on a small blank card, several more of which were spread across her desk. The way Spence told it, he was undeterred by all appearances that seemed to suggest the Teatro, or Theatre, was not what he assumed it was. He entered the reception area of the office, stood before the desk of the young woman, and introduced himself by name and occupation, believing it important to communicate as soon as possible his identity as an artist, or at least imply as best he could that he was a highly artistic photographer, which undoubtedly he was. When the young woman adjusted her eyeglasses and asked, "How can I help you?" the photographer Spence leaned toward her and whispered, "I would like to enlist the services of the Teatro, or Theatre if you like." When the receptionist asked what he was planning, the photographer answered, "To utterly destroy someone." The young woman was absolutely unflustered, according to Spence, by this declaration. She began calmly gathering the small blank cards that were spread across her desk and, while doing this, explained that T G Ventures was, in her words, an "entertainment service." After placing the small blank cards to one side, she removed from her desk a folded brochure which outlined the nature of the business, which provided clowns, magicians, and novelty performances for a variety of occasions, their specialty being children's parties.

As Spence studied the brochure, the receptionist placidly sat with her hands folded and gazed at him from within the black frames of her eyeglasses. The light in that suburban office suite was bright but not harsh; the pale walls were incredibly clean and the carpeting, in Spence's description, was conspicuously new and displayed the exact shade of purple found in turnips. The photographer said that he felt as if he were standing in a mirage. "This is all a front," Spence finally said, throwing the brochure on the receptionist's desk. But the young woman only picked up the brochure and placed it back in the same drawer from which it had come. "What's behind that door?" Spence demanded, pointing across the room. And just as he pointed at that door there was a sound on the other side of it, a brief rumbling as if something heavy had just fallen to the floor. "The dancing classes," said the receptionist, her right index finger pointing up at the floor above. "Perhaps," Spence allowed, but he claimed that this sound that he heard, which he described as having an "abysmal resonance," caused a sudden rise of panic within him. He tried not to move from the place he was standing, but his body was overwhelmed by the impulse to leave that suite of offices. The photographer turned away from the receptionist and saw his reflection in the glass door. She was watching him from behind the lenses of black-framed eyeglasses, and the stencilled lettering on the glass door read backwards, as if in a mirror. A few seconds later Spence was outside the building in the old suburb. All the way home, he asserted, his heart was pounding.

The following day Spence paid a visit to his landlord's place of business, which was a tiny office in a seedy downtown building. Having given up on the Teatro, he would have to deal in his own way with this man who would not return his security deposit. Spence's strategy was to plant himself in his landlord's office and stare him into submission with a photographer's unnerving gaze. After he arrived at his landlord's rented office on the sixth floor of what was a thoroughly depressing downtown building, Spence seated himself in a chair looking across a filthy desk at a small balding man with a mustache. But the man merely looked back at the photographer. To make things worse, the landlord (whose name was Herman Zick), would lean towards Spence every so often and in a quiet voice say, "It's all perfectly legal, you know." Then Spence would continue his staring, which he was frustrated to find ineffective against this man Zick, who of course was not an artist, or even a highly artistic person, as were the usual victims of the photographer. Thus the battle kept up for almost an hour, the landlord saying, "It's all perfectly legal," and Spence trying to hold a fixed gaze upon the man he wished to utterly destroy.

Ultimately Spence was the first to lose control. He jumped out of the chair in which he was sitting and began to shout incoherently at the landlord. Once Spence was on his feet, Zick swiftly maneuvered around the desk and physically evicted the photographer from the tiny office, locking him out in the hallway. Spence said that he was in the hallway for only a second or two when the doors opened to the elevator that was directly across from Zick's sixth-floor office. Out of the elevator compartment stepped a middle-aged man in a dark suit and black-framed eyeglasses. He wore a full, well-groomed beard which, Spence observed, was slightly streaked with gray. In his left hand the gentleman was clutching a crumpled brown bag, holding it a few inches in front of him. He walked up to the door of the landlord's office and with his right hand grasped the round black doorknob, jiggling it back and forth several times. There was a loud click that echoed down the hallway of that old downtown building. The gentleman turned his head and looked at Spence for the first time, smiling briefly before admitting himself to the office of Herman Zick.

Again the photographer experienced that surge of panic he had felt the day before when he visited the suburban offices of T G Ventures. He pushed the down button for the elevator, and while waiting he listened at the door of the landlord's office. What he heard, Spence claimed, was that terrible sound that had sent him running out in the street from T G Ventures, that "abysmal resonance," as he defined it. Suddenly the gentleman with the well-groomed beard and black-rimmed glasses emerged from the tiny office. The door to the elevator had just opened, and the man walked straight past Spence to board the empty compartment. Spence himself did not get on the elevator but stood outside, helplessly staring at the bearded gentleman, who was still holding that small crumpled bag. A split second before the elevator doors slid closed, the gentleman looked directly at Spence and winked at him. It was the assertion of the photographer that this wink, executed from behind a pair of black-framed eyeglasses, made a mechanical clicking sound which echoed down the dim hallway.

Prior to his exit from the old downtown building, leaving by way of the stairs rather than the elevator, Spence tried the door to his landlord's office. He found it unlocked and cautiously stepped inside. But there was no one on the other side of the door.

The conclusion to the photographer's adventure took place a full week later. Delivered by regular post to his mail box was a small square envelope with no return address. Inside was a photograph. He brought this item to Des Esseintes' Library, a bookstore where several of us were giving a late-night reading of our latest literary efforts. A number of persons belonging to the local artistic underworld, including myself, saw the photograph and heard Spence's rather frantic account of the events surrounding it. The photo was of Spence himself staring stark-eyed into the camera, which apparently had taken the shot from inside an elevator, a panel of numbered buttons being partially visible along the righthand border of the picture. "I could see no camera," Spence kept repeating. "But that wink he gave me . . . and what's written on the reverse side of this thing." Turning over the photo Spence read aloud the following handwritten inscription: "The little man is so much littler these days. Soon he will know about the soft black stars. And your payment is past due." Someone then asked Spence what they had to say about all this at the offices of TG Ventures. The photographer's head swivelled slowly in exasperated negation. "Not there anymore," he said over and over. With the single exception of myself, that night at Des Esseintes' Library was the last time anyone saw Mr. Spence.

After the photographer ceased to show up at the usual meeting places and special artistic events, there were no cute remarks about his having "gone with the Teatro." We were all of us beyond that stage. I was perversely proud to note that a degree of philosophical maturity had now developed among those in the artistic underworld of which I was a part. There is nothing like fear to complicate one's consciousness, inducing previously unknown levels of reflection. Under such mental stress I began to organize my own thoughts and observations about the Teatro, specifically as this phenomenon related to the artists who seemed to be its sole objects of attention.

Whether or not an artist was approached by the Teatro or took the initiative to approach the Teatro himself, it seemed the effect was the same: the end of an artist's work. I myself verified this fact as thoroughly as I could. The filmmaker whose short movie *Private Hell* so many of us admired had, by all accounts, become a full-time dealer in pornographic videos, none of them his own productions. The self-named visceral artist had publicly called an end to those stunts of his which had gained him a modest underground reputation. According to his roommate, the purple woman's cousin, he was now managing the supermarket where he had formerly labored as a stock clerk. As for the purple woman herself, who was never much praised as an artist and whose renown effectively began and ended with the "cigar box assemblage" phase of her career, she had gone into selling real estate, an occupation in which she became quite a success. This roster of ex-artists could be extended considerably, I am sure of that. But for the purposes of this report or confession (or whatever else you would like to call it) I must end my list of no-longer-artistic persons with myself, while attempting to offer some insights into the manner in which the Teatro Grottesco could transform a writer of nihilistic prose works into a non-artistic, more specifically a *post-artistic* being.

It was after the disappearance of the photographer Spence that my intuitions concerning the Teatro began to crystalize and become explicit thoughts, a dubious process but one to which I am inescapably subject as a prose writer. Until that point in time, everyone tacitly assumed that there was an intimacy of *kind* between the Teatro and the artists who were either approached by the Teatro or who themselves approached this cruel troupe by means of some overture, as in the case of Spence, or perhaps by gestures more subtle, even purely noetic (I retreat from writing *unconscious*, although others might argue with my intellectual reserve). Many of us even spoke of the Teatro as a manifestation of super-art, a term which we always left conveniently nebulous. However, following the disappearance of the photographer, all knowledge I had acquired about the Teatro, fragmentary as it was, became configured in a completely new pattern. I mean to say that I no longer considered it possible that the Teatro was in any way related to a super-art, or to an art of any kind, quite the opposite in fact. To my mind the Teatro was, and is, a phenomenon intensely destructive of everything that I conceived of as art. Therefore, the Teatro was, and is, intensely destructive of all artists and even of highly artistic persons. Whether this destructive force is a matter of intention or is an epiphenomenon of some unrelated, perhaps greater design, or even if there exists anything like an intention or design on the part of the Teatro, I have no idea (at least none I can elaborate in comprehensible terms). Nonetheless, I feel certain that for an artist to encounter the Teatro there can be only one consequence: the end of that artist's work. Strange, then, that knowing this fact I still acted as I did.

I cannot say if it was I who approached the Teatro or vice versa, as if any of that stupidness made a difference. The important thing is that from the moment I perceived the Teatro to be a profoundly anti-artistic phenomenon I conceived the ambition to make my form of art, by which I mean my nihilistic prose writings, into an anti-*Teatro* phenomenon. In order to do this, of course, I required a penetrating knowledge of the Teatro Grottesco, or of some significant aspect of that cruel troupe, an insight of a deeply subtle, even dreamlike variety into its nature and workings.

The photographer Spence had made a great visionary advance when he intuited that it was in the nature of the Teatro to act on his request to utterly destroy someone (although the exact meaning of the statement "he will know about the soft black stars," in reference to Spence's landlord, became known to both of us only sometime later). I realized that I would need to make a similar leap of insight in my own mind. While I had already perceived the Teatro to be a profoundly anti-artistic phenomenon, I was not yet sure what in the world would constitute an anti-*Teatro* phenomenon, as well as how in the world I could turn my own prose writings to such a purpose.

Thus, for several days I meditated on these questions. As usual, the psychic demands of this meditation severely taxed my bodily processes, and in my weakened state I contracted a virus, specifically an *intestinal virus*, which confined me to my small apartment for a period of one week. Nonetheless, it was during this time that things fell into place regarding the Teatro and the insights I required to oppose this company of nightmares in a more or less efficacious manner.

Suffering through the days and nights of an illness, especially an intestinal virus, one becomes highly conscious of certain realities, as well as highly sensitive to the *functions* of these realities, which otherwise are not generally subject to prolonged attention or meditation. Upon recovery from such a virus, the consciousness of these realities and their functions necessarily fades, so that the once-stricken person may resume his life's activities and not be driven to insanity or suicide by the acute awareness of these most unpleasant facts of existence. Through the illumination of analogy, I came to understand that the Teatro operated in much the same manner as the illness from which I recently suffered, with the consequence that the person exposed to the Teatro-disease becomes highly conscious of certain realities and their functions, ones quite different of course from the realities and functions of an intestinal virus. However, an intestinal virus ultimately succumbs, in a reasonably healthy individual, to the formation of antibodies (or something of that sort). But the disease of the Teatro, I now understood, was a disease for which no counteracting agents, or antibodies, had ever been created by the systems of the individuals – that is, the *artists* – it attacked. An encounter with any disease, including an intestinal virus, serves to alter a person's mind, making it intensely aware of certain realities, but this mind cannot remain altered once this encounter has ended or else that person will never be able to go on living in the same way as before. In contrast, an encounter with the Teatro appears to remain within one's system and to alter a person's mind permanently. For the artist the result is *not* to be driven into insanity or suicide (as might be the case if one assumed a permanent mindfulness of an intestinal virus) but the absolute termination of that artist's work. The simple reason for this effect is that there are no antibodies for the disease of the Teatro, and therefore no relief from the consciousness of the realities which an encounter with the Teatro has forced upon an artist.

Having progressed this far in my contemplation of the Teatro – so that I might discover its nature or essence and thereby make my prose writings into an anti-Teatro phenomenon – I found that I could go no further. No matter how much thought and meditation I devoted to the subject I did not gain a definite sense of having revealed to myself the true realities and functions that the Teatro communicated to an artist and how this communication put an end to that artist's work. Of course I could vaguely imagine the species of awareness that might render an artist thenceforth incapable of producing any type of artistic efforts. I actually arrived at a fairly detailed and disturbing idea of such an awareness – a *world-awareness*, as I conceived it. Yet I did not feel I had penetrated the mystery of "Teatro-stuff." And the only way to know about the Teatro, it seemed, was to have an encounter with it. Such an encounter between myself and the Teatro would have occurred in any event as a result of the discovery that my prose writings had been turned into an anti-Teatro phenomenon: this would constitute an *approach* of the most outrageous sort to that company of nightmares, forcing an encounter with all its realities and functions. Thus it was not necessary, at this point in my plan, to have actually succeeded in making my prose writings into an anti-Teatro phenomenon. I simply had to make it known, falsely, that I had done so.

As soon as I had sufficiently recovered from my intestinal virus I began to spread the word. Every time I found myself among others who belonged to the so-called artistic underworld of this city I bragged that I had gained the most intense awareness of the Teatro's realities and functions, and that, far from finishing me off as an artist, I had actually used this awareness as inspiration for a series of short prose works. I explained to my colleagues that merely to exist – let alone create artistic works – we had to keep certain things from overwhelming our minds. However, I continued, in order to keep these things, such as the realities of an intestinal virus, from overwhelming our minds we attempted to deny them any voice whatever, neither a voice in our minds and certainly not a precise and clear voice in works of art. The voice of madness, for instance, is barely a whisper in the babbling history of art because its realities are themselves too maddening to speak of for very long . . . and those of the Teatro have no voice at all, given their imponderably grotesque nature. Furthermore, I said, the Teatro not only propagated an intense awareness of these things, these realities and functionings of realities, it was *identical* with them. And I, I boasted, had allowed my mind to be overwhelmed by all manner of Teatro stuff, while also managing to use this experience as material for my prose writings. "This," I practically shouted one day at Des Esseintes' Library, "is the super-art." Then I promised that in two days time I would give a reading of my series of short prose pieces.

Nevertheless, as we sat around on some old furniture in a corner of Des Esseintes' Library, several of the others challenged my statements and assertions regarding the Teatro. One fellow writer, a poet, spoke hoarsely through a cloud of cigarette smoke, saying to me: "No one knows what this Teatro stuff is all about. I'm not sure I believe it myself." But I answered that Spence knew what it was all about, thinking that very soon I too would know what he knew. "*Spence!*" said a woman in a tone of exaggerated disgust (she once lived with the photographer and was a photographer herself). "He's not telling us about anything these days, never mind the Teatro." But I answered that, like the purple woman and the others, Spence had been overwhelmed by his encounter with the Teatro, and his artistic impulse had been thereby utterly destroyed. "And *your* artistic impulse is still intact," she said snidely. I answered that, yes, it was, and in two days I would prove it by reading a series of prose works that exhibited an intimacy with the most overwhelmingly grotesque experiences and gave voice to them. "That's because you have no idea what you're talking about," said someone else, and almost everyone supported this remark. I told them to be patient, wait and see what my prose writings revealed to them. "Reveal?" asked the poet. "Hell, no one even knows why it's called the Teatro Grottesco." I did not have an answer for that, but I repeated that they would understand much more about the Teatro in a few days, thinking to myself that within this period of time I would have either succeeded or failed in my attempt to provoke an encounter with the Teatro and the matter of my nonexistent anti-Teatro prose writing would be immaterial.

On the very next day, however, I collapsed in Des Esseintes' Library during a conversation with a different congregation of artists and highly artistic persons. Although the symptoms of my intestinal virus had never entirely disappeared I had not expected to collapse the way I did and ultimately to discover that what I thought was an intestinal virus was in fact something far more serious. As a consequence of my collapse, my unconscious body ended up in the emergency room of a nearby hospital, the kind of place where borderline indigents like myself always end up – a backstreet hospital with dated fixtures and a staff of sleepwalkers.

When I next opened my eyes it was night. The bed in which they had put my body was beside a tall paned window that reflected the dim fluorescent light fixed to the wall above my bed, creating a black glare in the windowpanes that allowed no view of anything beyond them but only a broken image of myself and the room around me. There was a long row of these tall paned windows and several other beds in the ward, each of them supporting a sleeping body that, like mine, was damaged in some way and therefore had been committed to that backstreet hospital.

I felt none of the extraordinary pain that had caused me to collapse in Des Esseintes' Library. At that moment, in fact, I could feel nothing of the experiences of my past life: it seemed I had always been an occupant of that dark hospital ward and always would be. This sense of estrangement from both myself and everything else made it terribly difficult to remain in the hospital bed where I had been placed. At the same time I felt uneasy about any movement *away* from that bed, especially any movement that would cause me to approach the open doorway which led into a half-lighted backstreet hospital corridor. Compromising between my impulse to get out of my bed and my fear of moving away from the bed and approaching that corridor, I positioned myself so that I was sitting on the edge of the mattress with my bare feet grazing the cold linoleum floor. I had been sitting on the edge of that mattress for quite a while before I heard the voice out in the corridor.

The voice came over the public address system, but it was not a particularly loud voice. In fact I had to strain my attention for several minutes simply to discern the peculiar qualities of the voice and to decipher what it said. It sounded like a child's voice, a sing-songy voice full of taunts and mischief. Over and over it repeated the same phrase – *paging Dr. Groddeck, paging Dr. Groddeck.* The voice sounded incredibly hollow and distant, garbled by all kinds of interference. *Paging Dr. Groddeck*, it giggled from the other side of the world.

I stood up and slowly approached the doorway leading out into the corridor. But even after I had crossed the room in my bare feet and was standing in the open doorway, that child's voice did not become any louder or any clearer. Even when I actually moved out into that long dim corridor with its dated lighting fixtures, the voice that was calling Dr. Groddeck sounded just as hollow and distant. And now it was as if I were in a dream in which I was walking in my bare feet down a backstreet hospital corridor, hearing a crazy voice that seemed to be eluding me as I moved past the open doorways of innumerable wards full of damaged bodies. But then the voice died away, calling to Dr. Groddeck one last time before fading like the final echo in a deep well. At the same moment that the voice ended its hollow outcrying, I paused somewhere toward the end of that shadowy corridor. In the absence of the mischievous voice I was able to hear something else, a sound like quiet, wheezing laughter. It was coming from the room just ahead of me along the right hand side of the corridor. As I approached this room I saw a metal plaque mounted at eye-level on the wall, and the words displayed on this plaque were these: Dr. T. Groddeck.

A strangely glowing light emanated from the room where I heard that quiet and continuous wheezing laughter. I peered around the edge of the doorway and saw that the laughter was coming from an old gentleman seated behind a desk, while the strangely glowing light was coming from a large globular object positioned on top of the desk directly in front of him. The light from this object – a globe of solid glass, it seemed – shone on the old gentleman's face, which was a crazy-looking face with a neatly clipped beard that was pure white and a pair of spectacles with slim rectangular lenses resting on the bridge of a slender nose. When I stood in the doorway of that office, the eyes of Dr. Groddeck did not gaze up at me but continued to stare into the strange, shining globe and at the things that were inside it.

What were these things inside the globe that Dr. Groddeck was looking at? To me they appeared to be tiny star-shaped flowers evenly scattered throughout the glass, just the thing to lend a mock-artistic appearance to a common paperweight. Except that these flowers, these spidery chrysanthemums, were pure black. And they did not seem to be firmly fixed within the shining sphere, as one would expect, but looked as if they were floating in position, their starburst of petals wavering slightly like tentacles. Dr. Groddeck appeared to delight in the subtle movements of those black appendages. Behind rectangular spectacles his eyes rolled about as they tried to take in each of the hovering shapes inside the radiant globe on the desk before him.

Then the doctor slowly reached down into one of the deep pockets of the lab coat he was wearing, and his wheezing laughter grew more intense. From the open doorway I watched as he carefully removed a small paper bag from his pocket, but he never even glanced at me. With one hand he was now holding the crumpled bag directly over the globe. When he gave the bag a little shake, the things inside the globe responded with an increased agitation of their thin black arms. He used both hands to open the top of the bag and quickly turned it upside down.

From out of the bag something tumbled onto the globe, where it seemed to stick to the surface. It was not actually adhering to the surface of the globe, however, but was sinking into the interior of the glass. It squirmed as those soft black stars inside the globe gathered to pull it down to themselves. Before I could see what it was that they had captured and surrounded, the show was over. Afterward they returned to their places, floating slightly once again within the glowing sphere.

I looked at Dr. Groddeck and saw that he was finally looking back at me. He had stopped his asthmatic laughter, and his eyes were staring frigidly into mine, completely devoid of any readable meaning. Yet somehow these eyes provoked me. Even as I stood in the open doorway of that hideous office in a backstreet hospital, Dr. Groddeck's eyes provoked in me an intense outrage, an astronomical resentment of the position I had been placed in. Even as I had consummated my plan to encounter the Teatro and experience its most devastating realities and functions (in order to turn my prose works into an anti-Teatro phenomenon) I was outraged to be standing where I was standing and resentful of the staring eyes of Dr. Groddeck. No matter if I had approached the Teatro, the Teatro had approached me, or we both approached each other. I realized that there is such a thing as being approached in order to force one's hand into making what only appears to be an approach, which is actually a non-approach that negates the whole concept of approaching. It was all a fix from the start, because I belonged to an artistic underworld, because I was an artist whose work would be brought to an end by an encounter with the Teatro Grottesco. And so I was outraged by the eyes of Dr. Groddeck, which were the eyes of the Teatro, and I was resentful of all insane realities and the excruciating functions of the Teatro. Although I knew that the persecutions of the Teatro were not exclusively focused on the artists and highly artistic persons of the world, I was nevertheless outraged and resentful to be singled out for *special treatment*. I wanted to punish those persons in this world who are not the object of such special treatment. Thus, at the top of my voice, I called out in the dim corridor, I cried out the summons for others to join me before the stage of the Teatro. Strange that I should think it necessary to compound the nightmare of all those damaged bodies in that backstreet hospital, as well as its staff of sleepwalkers who moved within a world of outdated fixtures. But by the time anyone arrived Dr. Groddeck was gone, and his office became nothing more than a room full of dirty laundry.

My escapade that night notwithstanding, I was soon released from the hospital pending the results of several tests I had been administered. I was feeling as well as ever, and the hospital, like any hospital, always needed the bedspace for more damaged bodies. They said I would be contacted in the next few days.

It was in fact the following day that I was informed of the outcome of my stay in the hospital. "Hello again," began the letter, which was typed on a plain, though waterstained sheet of paper. "I was so pleased to finally meet you in person. I thought your performance in our interview at the hospital was really first rate, and I am authorized to offer you a position with us. There is an opening in our organization for someone with your resourcefulness and imagination. I'm afraid things didn't work out with Mr. Spence. But he certainly did have a camera's eye, and we have gotten some wonderful pictures from him. I would especially like to share with you his last shots of the soft black stars, or S.B.S., as we sometimes refer to them. Veritable super-art, if there ever was such a thing!

"By the way, the results of your tests — some of which you have yet to be subjected to — are going to come back positive. If you think an intestinal virus is misery, just wait a few more months. So think fast, sir. We will arrange another meeting with you in any case. And remember – *you* approached *us*. Or was it the other way around?

"As you might have noticed by now, all this artistic business can only keep you going so long before you're left speechlessly gaping at the realities and functions of . . . well, I think you know what I'm trying to say. I was forced into this realization myself, and I'm quite mindful of what a blow this can be. Indeed, it was I who invented the appellative for our organization as it is currently known. Not that I put any stock in names, nor should you. Our company is so much older than its own name, or any other name for that matter. (And how many it's had over the years – The Ten Thousand Things, Anima Mundi, Nethescurial.) You should be proud that we have a special part for you to play, such a talented artist. In time you will forget yourself entirely in your work, as we all do eventually. Myself, I go around with a trunkful of aliases, but do you think I can say who I once was *really*? A man of the theater, that seems plausible. Possibly I was the father of Faust or Hamlet . . . or merely Peter Pan.

"In closing, I do hope you will seriously consider our offer to join us. We can do something about your medical predicament. We can do just about anything. Otherwise, I'm afraid that all I can do is welcome you to your own private hell, which will be as unspeakable as any on earth."

The letter was signed Dr. Theodore Groddeck, and its prognostication of my physical health was accurate: I have taken more tests at the backstreet hospital and the results are somewhat grim. For several days and sleepless nights I have considered the alternatives the doctor proposed to me, as well as others of my own devising, and have yet to reach a decision on what course to follow. The one conclusion that keeps forcing itself upon me is that it makes no difference what choice I make, or do not make. You can never anticipate the Teatro . . . or anything else. You can never know what you are approaching, or what is approaching you. Soon enough my thoughts will lose all clarity, and I will no longer be aware that there was ever a decision to be made. The soft black stars have already begun to fill the sky.

SEVERINI

I was the only one among a local body of acquaintances and associates who had never met Severini. Unlike the rest of them I was not in the least moved to visit him along with the others at that isolated residence which had become known as "Severini's Shack." There was a question of my *deliberately* avoiding an encounter with this extraordinary individual, but even I myself had no idea whether or not this was true. My curiosity was just as developed as that of anyone else, more so in fact. Yet some kind of scruple or special anxiety kept me away from what the others celebrated as the "spectacle of Severini."

Of course I could not escape a second-hand knowledge of their Severini visits. Each of these trips to that lonesome hovel some distance outside the city where I used to live was a great adventure, they reported, an excursion into the most obscure and idiosyncratic nightmares. The figure that presided over these salon-like gatherings was extremely unstable and inspired in his visitors a sense of lurid anticipation, an unfocused expectation that sometimes reached the pitch of lunacy. Afterward I would hear detailed accounts from one person or another of what occurred during a particular evening within the confines of the notorious shack, which was situated at the edge of a wildly overgrown and swampy tract of land known as St. Alban's Marsh, a place that some claimed had a sinister pertinence to Severini himself. Occasionally I would make notes of these accounts when later I returned to my apartment, indulging myself in a type of imaginative and also highly analytical record-keeping. For the most part, however, I simply absorbed all of these Severini anecdotes in a wholly natural and organic fashion, much as I assimilated so many things in the world around me, without any awareness – or even a possibility of awareness – that these things might be nourishing or noxious or purely neutral. From the beginning, I admit, it was my tendency to be highly receptive to whatever someone might have to say regarding Severini, his shack-like home, and the marshy landscape in which he had ensconced himself. Then, during private moments, I would recreate in my imagination the phenomena that had been related to me in conversations held at diverse places and times. It was rare that I actively urged the others to elaborate on any specific aspect of their adventures with Severini, but several times I did betray myself when the subject arose of his past life before he set himself up in a marshland shack.

According to first-hand witnesses (that is, persons who had actually made the pilgrimage to that isolated and crumbling shack), Severini could be quite talkative about his personal history, particularly the motives and events that most directly culminated in his present life. Nevertheless, these persons also admitted that the "marvelous hermit" (Severini) displayed a conspicuous disregard for common facts and for truths of a literal sort. Thus he was often given to speaking about himself by way of ambiguous parables and metaphors, not to mention outrageous anecdotes the facts of which always seemed to cancel out one another, as well as outright lies which afterward he himself would sometimes expose as such. But much of the time – and in the opinion of some, *all* of the time – Severini's speech took the form of total nonsense, as though he were talking in his sleep. Despite these difficulties in communication, all of the individuals who spoke to me on the subject somehow conveyed to my mind a remarkably focused portrait of the hermit Severini, an amalgam of hearsay that attained the status of a potent legend.

This impression of a legendary Severini was no doubt bolstered by what certain persons were describing as "Exhibits from the Imaginary Museum." The entourage of visitors to the hermit's dilapidated shack was a crowd of more or less artistic persons, or at least individuals with artistic *leanings*, and their exposure to Severini proved a powerful inspiration that resulted in numerous artworks in a variety of media and genres. There were sculptures, paintings and drawings, poems and short prose pieces, musical compositions sometimes accompanied by lyrics, conceptual works that existed only in schematic or anecdotal form, and even an architectural plan for a "ruined temple on a jungle island some-where in the region of the Philippines." While on the surface these productions appeared to have their basis in a multitude of dubious sources, each of them claimed the most literalistic origins in Severini's own words, his *sleeptalking*, as they called it. Indeed, I myself could perceive the underlying coherence of these artworks and their integral relationship to the same unique figure of inspiration that was Severini himself, although I had never met this fantastical person and had no desire to do so. Nevertheless, these so-called "exhibits" helped me to recreate in my imagination not only those much discussed visits to that shack in the marsh country but also the personal history of its lone inhabitant.

As I now think about them – that is, recreate them in my imagination – these Severini-based artworks, however varied in their genres and techniques, brought to the surface a few features that were always the same and were always treated in the same way. I was startled when I first began to recognize these common features, because somehow they closely replicated a number of peculiar images and concepts that I myself had already experienced in moments of imaginative daydreaming and especially during episodes of delirium brought on by physical disease or excessive psychic turmoil.

A central element of such episodes was the sense of a place possessing qualities that were redolent, on the one hand, of a tropical landscape, and, on the other hand, of a common sewer. The aspect of a common sewer emerged in the feeling of an enclosed but also vastly extensive space, a network of coiling passages that spanned incredible distances in an underworld of misty darkness. As for the quality of a tropical landscape, this shared much of the same kind of darkly oozing ferment as the sewer-aspect, with the added impression of the most exotic forms of life spawning on every side, things multiplying and also incessantly *mutating* like a time-lapse film of spreading fungus or multi-colored slime molds totally unrestricted in their form and expansion. While I experienced the most intense visions of this tropical sewer, as it recreated itself in my delirious imagination year after year, I was always outside it at some great remove, not caught within as if I were having a nightmare. But still I maintained an awareness (as in a nightmare) that something had happened in this place, some unknown event had transpired that left these images behind it like a trail of slime. And then a certain *feeling* came over me and a certain *concept* came to my mind.

It was this feeling and its companion concept that so vividly occurred to me when the others began telling me about their strange visits to the Severini place and showing me the various artworks that this strange individual had inspired them to create. One by one I viewed paintings or sculptures in some artist's studio, or heard music being performed in a club that was frequented by the Severini crowd, or read literary works that were being passed around – and each time the sense of that tropical sewer was revived in me, although not with the same intensity as the delirious episodes I experienced while suffering from a physical disease or during periods of excessive psychic turmoil. The titles of these works alone might have been enough to provoke the particular feeling and the concept that were produced by my delirious episodes. The concept to which I have been referring may be stated in various ways, but it usually occurred to my mind as a simple phrase (or fragment), almost a chant that overwhelmed me with vile and haunting suggestions far beyond its mere words, which are as follows: *the nightmare of the organism*. The vile and haunting suggestions underlying (or inspired by) this conceptual phrase were, as I have said, called up by the titles of those Severini-based artworks, those Exhibits from the Imaginary Museum. While I have difficulty recalling the type of work to which each title was attached – whether a painting or a sculpture, a poem or a performance piece – I am still able to cite a number of the titles themselves. One of them that easily emerges in recollection was *No Face among Us*. Another such title was *Defiled and Delivered*. And now many more of them are coming to my mind: *The Way of the Lost*, *On Viscous and Sacred Ground* (a. k. a. *The Tantric Doctors*), *In Earth and Excreta*, *The Black Spume of Existence*, *Integuments in Eruption*, and *The Descent into the Fungal*. All of these titles, as my artistic acquaintances and associates informed me, were taken from selected phrases (or fragments) spoken by Severini during his numerous episodes of *sleeptalking*.

Every time I heard one of these titles and saw the particular artwork that it named, I was always reminded of that tropical sewer of my delirious episodes. I would also feel myself on the verge of realizing what it was that happened in this place, what wonderful or disastrous event that was so intimately related to the conceptual phrase which I have given as *the nightmare of the organism*. But I never attained more than a remote sense of some vile and haunting revelation. And it was simply not possible for the others to illuminate this matter fully, given that their knowledge of Severini's past history was exclusively derived from his own nonsensical or questionable assertions. As nearly as they were willing to speculate, it appeared that this incoherent and all-but-incognito person known as Severini was the willing subject of what was variously referred to as an "esoteric procedure" or an "illicit practice." At this point in my discoveries about the strange Severini I found it difficult to inquire about the exact nature of this procedure, or practice, while at the same time pretending a lack of interest in actually meeting the resident of that ruined shack stuck out in the marshland backroads some distance outside the city where I used to live. It did seem, however, that this practice or procedure, as nearly as anyone could speculate, was not a medical treatment of any known variety. Rather, they thought that the procedure (or practice) in question involved some type of mysticism, possibly even occultist or quasi-magical traditions that, in their most potent form, are able to exist – inconspicuously – in only a few remaining parts of the world. Of course, all of this speculation could have been a cover-up orchestrated by Severini or by his disciples – for that is what they had become – or by all of them together. In fact, for some time I had suspected that Severini's disciples, despite their parade of artworks and outlandish accounts of their visits to the marshland shack, were nevertheless concealing from me some vital element of their new experiences. There seemed to be some truth of which they had knowledge and I had not. Yet they also seemed to desire that I might, in due course, share with them this truth.

My suspicions of the others' deception – perhaps it might be called a *tentative* deception – derived from a source that was admittedly subjective. This was my imaginative recreation, as I sat in my apartment, of the spectacle of Severini as it was related to me by those who had participated in the visits to his residence in the marsh. In my mind I pictured them seated upon the floor of that small, unfurnished shack, the only illumination being the hectic light of candles that they brought with them and placed in a circle, at the center of which was the figure of Severini. This figure always spoke to them in his uniquely cryptic way, his sleeptalking voice fluctuating in its qualities and even seeming to emanate from places other than his own body, as though he were practicing a hyper-ventriloquism. Similarly, his body itself, as I was told and as I later imagined to myself in my apartment, appeared to react in concert with the fluctuations in his voice. These bodily changes, the others said, were sometimes subtle and sometimes dramatic, but they were consistently ill-defined – not a matter of clear transformation as much as a *breakdown* of anatomical features and structures, the result being something twisted and tumorous like a living mound of diseased clay or mud, a heap of cancerous matter that slowly thrashed about in the candlelight which illuminated the old shack. These fluctuations in both Severini's voice and his body, the others explained to me, were not in any way under his own guidance but were a totally spontaneous phenomenon to which he submitted as the result of the esoteric procedure or illicit practice worked upon him in some unknown place (possibly "in the region of the Philippines"). It was now his destiny, the others elaborated, to comply with whatever was demanded of his flesh by what could only be seen as utterly mindless and chaotic forces, and even his consciousness itself – they asserted – was as deranged and mutable as his bodily form. Yet as they spoke to me about these particulars of Severini's condition, none of them conveyed any real sense of the nightmarish quality of the images and processes they were describing. Awestruck, yes; passionate, yes; somewhat demented, yes. But nightmarish – no. Even as I listened to their account of a given Severini meeting, I too failed to grasp fully their nightmarish qualities and aspects. They would say to me, referring to one of Severini's metamorphoses, "The naked contours of his form twisted about like a pool of snakes, or twitched like a mass of newly hatched spiderlings." Nevertheless, upon hearing statement after statement of this kind I sat relatively undisturbed, accepting without revulsion or outrage these revolting and outrageous remarks. Perhaps, I thought at the time, I was simply under the powerful spell of social decorum, which so often may explain otherwise incomprehensible feelings (or lack of feelings) and behaviors (or lack of behaviors). But once I was alone in my apartment, and began to imaginatively recreate what I had heard about the spectacle of Severini, I was overwhelmed by its nightmarish essence and several times lapsed into one of my delirious episodes with all of its terrible sensations of a tropical sewer, and all the nightmares of exotic lifeforms breaking out everywhere like rampant pustules and suppurations. And then I suspected that there was a deception involved in this whole Severini business, although even then I thought the deception might be tentative, a period of surreptitious initiation until that perfect moment when I could be accepted into their ranks.

Finally, on a rainy afternoon, as I was working alone in my apartment (making Severini notes), the buzzer signaled that someone was downstairs. The voice over the intercom belonged to a woman named Carla, who was a sculptress and whom I barely knew. When I let her in my apartment she was wet from walking in the rain without a coat or umbrella, although her straight black hair and all-black clothes looked very much the same whether wet or dry. I offered her a towel but she refused, saying she "kind of liked feeling soggy and sickish," and we went on from there. The reason for her visit to my apartment, she revealed, was to invite me to the first "collective showing" of the Exhibits from the Imaginary Museum. When I asked why I should be receiving this personal invitation in my apartment on a rainy afternoon, she said: "Because the showing is going to be at *his place*, and you've never wanted to go there." I said that I would think seriously about attending the showing and asked her if that was all she had to say. "No," she said as she dug into one of the pockets of her tight damp slacks. "*He* was really the one who wanted me to invite you to the exhibit. *We* never told him about you, but he said that he always felt someone was missing, and for some reason we assumed it was you." After extracting a piece of paper that had been folded several times, she opened it up and held it before her eyes. "I wrote down what he said," she said while holding the limp and wrinkled note close to her face with both hands. Her eyes glanced up at me for a moment over the top edge of the unfolded page (her heavy mascara was running down her cheeks in black rivulets), and then she looked down to read the words Severini had told her to write. "He says, 'You and Severini' – he always calls himself Severini, as if that were someone else – 'you and Severini are sympathetic . . .' something – I can hardly read this; it was dark when I wrote it down. Here we go: 'You and Severini are *sympathetic organisms*'." She paused to push away a few strands of black, rain-soaked hair that had fallen across her face. She was smiling somewhat idiotically.

"Is that it?" I asked.

"Hold on, he wanted me to get it right. Just one more thing. He said, 'Tell him that the way into the nightmare is the way out'." She folded the paper once again and crammed it back into the pocket of her black slacks. "Does any of that mean anything to you?" she asked.

I said that it meant nothing at all to me. After promising that I would most seriously consider attending the exhibit at Severini's place, I let Carla out of my apartment and back into that rainy afternoon.

I should say that I had never spoken to either Carla or the others about my delirious episodes, with their sensations of a tropical sewer and the emergent concept of the "nightmare of the organism." I had never told anyone. I had thought that these episodes and the deranged concept of the nightmare of the organism were strictly a private hell, even one that was unique. Until that rainy afternoon, I had considered it only a coincidence that the artworks inspired by Severini, as well as the titles of these works, served to call up the sensations and suggestions of my delirious episodes. Then I was sent a message by Severini, through Carla, that he and I were "sympathetic organisms" and that "the way into the nightmare is the way out." For some time I had dreamed of being delivered from the suffering of my delirious episodes, and from all the suggestions and sensations that went along with them –

the terrible vision that exposed all living things, including myself, as no more than a fungus or a collection of bacteria, a kind of monumental slime-mold quivering across the landscape of this planet (and very likely others). Any deliverance from such a nightmare, I thought, would involve the most drastic (and esoteric) procedures, the most alien (and illicit) practices. And, ultimately, I never believed that this deliverance, or any other, was really possible. It was simply too good, or too evil, to be true – at least this is how it seemed to my mind. Yet all it took was a few words from Severini, as they reached me through Carla, and I began to dream of all kinds of possibilities. In a moment everything had changed. I now became ready to take those steps towards deliverance; in fact, *not* to do so seemed intolerable to me. I absolutely had to find a way out of the nightmare, it seemed, whatever procedures or practices were involved. Severini had taken those steps – I was convinced of that – and I needed to know where they had led him.

As might be imagined, I had worked myself into quite a state even before the night of the showing (of the Exhibits of the Imaginary Museum). But it was more than my frenzy of dreams and anticipation that affected my experiences that night and now affects my ability to relate what occurred at the tumble-down shack on the edge of St. Alban's Marsh. My delirious episodes previous to that night were nothing (that is, they were the perfection of lucidity) when compared to the delirium that over-takes me every time I attempt to sort out what happened at the marshland shack, my thoughts disintegrating little by little until I pass into a kind of sleeptalking of my own. I saw things with my own eyes and other things with other eyes. And everywhere there were voices . . .

It was all weedy shadows and frogs croaking in the blackness as I walked along the narrow path that, according to the directions given to me, led to Severini's place. I left my car parked alongside the road where I saw the vehicles of the others. They had all arrived before me, although I was not in the least bit late for this scheduled artistic event. But they had always been anxious, I had long before noticed, whenever a Severini visit was planned, all that day fidgeting with some restless impulse until nightfall would come and they could leave the city and go out to St. Alban's Marsh.

I expected to see a light ahead as I walked along that narrow path, but all I heard were frogs croaking in the blackness. The full moon in a cloudless sky revealed to me where I should next step along the path leading to the shack at the edge of the marsh. But even before I reached the clearing where the old shack supposedly stood, my sense of everything around me began to change. A warm mist drifted in from either side of the path like a curtain closing in front of my eyes, and I felt something touch my mind with images and concepts that were from elsewhere. "We are sympathetic organisms," I heard from the mist. "Draw closer." But that narrow path seemed to have no end to it, like those passages in my delirious episodes which extended such great distances in the misty darkness of a tropical landscape, where on every side of me there were exotic forms of life spawning and seething without restraint. *I must go to that place*, I thought as if these were my own words and not the words of another voice altogether, a voice full of desperate intensity and confused aspirations. "Calm yourself, Mr. Severini, if you insist I still address you by that name. As your therapist I cannot advise you to pursue this route . . . chasing miracles, if that is what you *imagine* . . . this 'temple,' as you call it, is an escape from any authentic confrontation with . . ."

But he did find his way to freedom, although without properly being discharged from the institution, and he went to that place. "*Documentes. Passportas!*" Looking around at those yellow-brown faces, you were finally there. You went to that jungle island, that tropical sewer, a great temple looming out of the misty darkness in your dreams. It rained in every town, the streets streaming like sewers. "*Disentaría*," pronounced the attending physician. But he was not like any of the doctors whom you sought in that place. Amoebic dysentery – there it was, the nightmare continued, so many forms it could take. *The way into the nightmare is the way out.* And you were willing to follow that nightmare as far as you needed in order to find your way out, just as I was following that narrow path toward your shack on the edge of St. Alban's Marsh to enter that same nightmare you had brought back with you. The Exhibits of the Imaginary Museum. Your shack was now a gallery of the nightmares you had inspired in the others with your sleeptalking and the *fluctuations* of your form, those outrageous miracles which had not outraged anyone. Only when I was alone in my apartment, imaginatively recreating what the others had told me, could I see those miracles as the nightmares they were. I knew this because of my delirious episodes, which none of the others had known. *They* were the sympathetic organisms, not I. I was antagonistic to you, not sympathetic. Because I would not go into the nightmare, as you had gone. The Temple of Tantric Medicine, this is what you dreamed you would find in that tropical sewer – a place where miracles took place, where that sect of "doctors" could minister with the most esoteric procedures and could carry out their illicit practices. But what did you find instead? "*Disentaría*" pronounced the attending physician. Then a small group of those yellow-brown faces told you, told *us*, about that other temple which had no name. "For the belly sickness," they said. Amoebic dysentery, simply another version of the nightmare of the organism from which none of the doctors you had seen in the past could deliver you. "How can the disease be cured of itself?" you asked them. "My body – a tumor that was once delivered from the body of another tumor, a lump of disease that is always boiling with its own disease. And my mind – another disease, the disease of a disease. Everywhere my mind sees the disease of other minds and other bodies, these other organisms that are only other diseases, an absolute nightmare of the organism. Where are you taking me!" you screamed (we screamed) at the yellow-brown faces. "Fix the belly sickness. We know, we know." They chanted these words along the way, it seemed, as the town disappeared behind the trees and the vines, behind the giant flowers that smelled like rotting meat, and the fungus and muck of that tropical sewer. They knew the disease and the nightmare because they lived in that place where the organism flourished without restraint, its forms so varied and exotic, its fate inescapable. "*Disentaría*" pronounced the attending physician. They knew the way through the stonework passages, the walls seeping with slime and soft with mold as they coiled toward the central chamber of the temple without a name. Inside the ruined heart of the temple there were candles burning everywhere; their flickering light revealed an array of temple art and ornamentation. Intricate murals appeared along the walls, mingling with the slime and the mold of that tropical sewer. Sculptures of every size and all shapes projected out of the damp, viscous shadows. At the center of the chamber was a large circular altar, an enormous mandala composed of countless jewels, precious stones, or simply bits of glass that gleamed in the candlelight like a pool of multi-colored slime molds.

They laid your body upon the altar; they knew what to do with you (us) – the words to say, the songs to sing, and the esoteric procedures to follow. It was almost as if I could understand the things that they chanted in voices of tortured solemnity. *Deliver the self that knows the sickness from the self that does not know. There are two faces which must never confront each other. There is only one body which must struggle to contain them both.* And the phantom clutch of that sickness, that amoebic dysentery, seemed to reach me as I walked along that narrow path leading to Severini's shack at the edge of St. Alban's

Marsh. Inside the shack were all the Exhibits of the Imaginary Museum, the paintings lining the damp wood of the walls and the sculptures projecting out of the shadows cast by the candles which always lighted the single room of that ruined hovel. I had imaginatively recreated the interior of Severini's shack many times according to the accounts related to me by the others about this place and its incredible inhabitant. I imagined how you could forget yourself in such a place, how you could be delivered from the nightmares and delirious episodes that tortured you in other places, even becoming someone else (or something else) as you gave yourself up entirely to the fluctuations of the organism at the edge of St. Alban's Marsh. You needed that marsh because it helped you to imaginatively recreate that tropical sewer (where you were taken *into* the nightmare), and you needed those artworks in order to make your shack into that temple (where you were supposed to find your way *out* of the nightmare). But most of all you needed them, the others, because they were sympathetic organisms. I, on the other hand, was now an antagonistic organism who wanted nothing more to do with your esoteric procedures and illicit practices. *Deliver the self that knows the sickness from the self that does not know. The two faces . . . the one body.* You wanted them to enter the nightmare, who did not even know the nightmare as *we* knew it. You needed them and their artworks to go into the nightmare of the organism to its *very end* so that you could find your way out of the nightmare. But you could not go to the very end of the nightmare unless I was with you, I who was now an antagonistic organism without any hope that there was a way out of the nightmare. We were forever divided, one face from the other, struggling within the body – the organism – which we shared.

I never arrived at the shack that night; I never entered it. As I walked along that narrow path in the mist I became feverish. ("Amoebic dysentery," pronounced the doctor whom I visited the following day.) The face of Severini appeared at the shack that night, not mine. It was always his face that the others saw on such nights when they came to visit. But I was not there with them; that is, my face was not there. His face was the one they saw as they sat among all the Exhibits from the Imaginary Museum. But it was my face which returned to the city; it was my body which I now fully possessed as an organism that belonged to my face alone. But the others never returned from the shack on the edge of St. Alban's Marsh. I never saw them again after that night, because on that night he took them with him into the nightmare, with the candle flames flickering upon those artworks and the fluctuations of form which to the others appeared as a pool of twisting snakes or a mass of spiderlings newly hatched. He showed them the way into the nightmare, but he could not show them the way out. There is no way out of the nightmare once you have gone so far into its depths. That is where he is lost forever, he and the others he has taken with him.

But he did not take me into the marsh with him to exist as a fungus exists or as a foam of multi-colored slime mold exists. That is how I see it in my *new delirious episodes*. Only at these times when I suffer from a physical disease or excessive psychic turmoil do I see how he exists now, he and the others. Because I never looked directly into the pools of oozing life when I stopped at the shack on the edge of St. Alban's Marsh. I was on my way out of the city the night I stopped, and I was only there long enough to douse the place in gasoline and set it ablaze. It burned with all the brilliance of the nightmares that were still exhibited inside, casting its illumination upon the marsh and leaving the most obscure image of what was back there – a vast and vague impression of that great black life from which we have all emerged and of which we all are made.

GAS STATION
CARNIVALS

Outside the walls of the Crimson Cabaret was a world of rain
and darkness. At intervals, whenever someone entered or
exited through the front door of the club, one could actually see the
steady rain and was allowed a brief glimpse of the darkness. Inside
it was all amber light, tobacco smoke, and the sound of the
raindrops hitting the windows, which were all painted black.
On such nights, as I sat at one of the tables in that drab little
place, I was always filled with an infernal merriment, as if I were
waiting out the apocalypse and could not care less about it. I also
liked to imagine that I was in the cabin of an old ship during a
really vicious storm at sea or in the club car of a luxury passenger
train that was being rocked on its rails by ferocious winds and
hammered by a demonic rain. Sometimes, when I was sitting in
the Crimson Cabaret on a rainy night, I thought of myself as
occupying a waiting room for the abyss (which of course was
exactly what I was doing) and between sips from my glass of wine
or cup of coffee I smiled sadly and touched the front pocket of my
coat where I kept my imaginary ticket to oblivion.

However, on that particular rainy November night I was not
feeling very well. My stomach was slightly queasy, as if signalling
the onset of a virus or even food poisoning. Another source for my
malaise, I thought to myself, might well have been my long-
standing nervous condition, which fluctuated from day to day
but was always with me in some form and manifested itself in a
variety of symptoms both physical and psychic. I was in fact
experiencing a faint sensation of panic, although this in no way
ruled out the possibility that the queasiness of my stomach was due
to a strictly physical cause, either viral or toxic. Neither did it rule
out a *third* possibility which I was trying to ignore at that point in
the evening. Whatever the etiology of my stomach disorder, I felt
the need to be in a public place that night, so that if I should
collapse – an eventuality I often feared – there would be people

around who might attend to me, or at least shuttle my body off to the hospital. At the same time I was not seeking close contact with any of these people, and I would have been bad company in any case, sitting there in the corner of the club drinking mint tea and smoking mild cigarettes out of respect for my ailing stomach. For all these reasons I brought my notebook with me that night and had it lying open on the table before me, as if to say that I wanted to be left alone to mull over some literary matters. But when Stuart Quisser entered the club at approximately ten o'clock, the sight of me sitting at a corner table with my open notebook, drinking mint tea and smoking mild cigarettes so that I might stay on top of the situation with my queasy stomach, did not in the least discourage him from walking directly to my table and taking the seat across from me. A waitress came over to us. Quisser ordered some kind of white wine, while I asked for another cup of mint tea.

"So now it's mint tea," Quisser said as the girl left us.

"I'm surprised you're showing your face around here," I said by way of reply.

"I thought I might try to make up with the old crimson woman."

"Make up? That doesn't sound like you."

"Nevertheless, have you seen her tonight?"

"No, I haven't. You humiliated her at that party. I haven't seen her since, not even in her own club. I don't know if you're aware of this, but she's not someone you want to have as an enemy."

"Meaning what?" he asked.

"Meaning that she has connections you know absolutely nothing about."

"And of course *you* know all about it. I've read your stories. You're a confessed paranoid, so what's your point?"

"My point," I said, "is that there's hell in every handshake, never mind an outright and humiliating insult."

"I had too much to drink, that's all."

"You called her a *deluded no-talent*."

Quisser looked up at the waitress as she approached with our drinks, and he made a hasty hand-signal for silence. When she was gone he said, "I happen to know that our waitress is very loyal to the crimson woman. She will very probably inform her about my visiting the club tonight. I wonder if she would be willing to act as a go-between with her boss and deliver a second-hand apology from me."

"Look around at the walls," I said.

Quisser set down his glass of wine and scanned the room.

"Hmm," he said when he finished looking. "This is more serious than I thought. She's taken down all her old paintings. And the new ones don't look like her work at all."

"They're not. You *humiliated* her."

"And yet she seems to have done up the stage since I last saw it. New paint job or something."

The so-called stage to which Quisser referred was a small platform in the opposite corner of the club. This area was entirely framed by four long panels, each of them painted with black and gold sigils against a glossy red background. Various events occurred on this stage: poetry readings, tableaux vivants, playlets of sundry types, puppet shows, artistic slideshows, musical performances, and so on. That night, which was a Tuesday, the stage was dark. I observed nothing different about it and asked Quisser what he imagined he thought was new.

"I can't say exactly, but something seems to have been done. Maybe it's those black and gold ideographs or whatever they're supposed to be. The whole thing looks like the cover of a menu in a Chinese restaurant."

"You're quoting yourself," I said.

"What do you mean?"

"The Chinese menu remark. You used that in your review of the Marsha Corker exhibit last month."

"Did I? I don't remember."

"Are you just saying you don't remember, or do you really *not* remember?" I asked this question in the spirit of trivial curiosity, my queasy stomach discouraging the strain of any real antagonism on my part.

"I *remember*, all right? Which reminds me, there's something I wanted to talk to you about. It came to me the other day, and I immediately thought of you and your . . . stuff," he said, gesturing toward my notebook of writings open on the table between us. "I can't believe it's never come up before. You of all people should know about them. No one else seems to. It was years ago, but you're old enough to remember them. You've *got* to remember them."

"Remember what?" I asked, and after the briefest pause he replied:

"The gas station carnivals."

And he said these words as if he were someone delivering a punchline to a joke, the proud bringer of a surprising and profound hilarity. I was supposed to express an astonished recognition, that much I knew. It was not a phenomenon of which I was *entirely ignorant*, and memory is such a tricky thing. This, at least, is what I told Quisser. But as Quisser told me *his* memories, trying to arouse mine, I gradually realized the true nature and purpose of the so-called gas station carnivals. During this time it was all I could do to conceal how badly my stomach was acting up on me, queasy and burning. I kept telling myself, as Quisser was talking about his memories of the gas station carnivals, that I was certainly experiencing the onset of a virus, if in fact I had not been the victim of food poisoning. Quisser, nevertheless, was so caught up in his story that he seemed not to notice my agony.

Quisser said that his recollections of the gas station carnivals derived from his early childhood. His family, meaning his parents and himself, would go on long vacations by car, often driving great distances to a variety of destinations. Along the way, naturally, they would need to stop at any number of gas stations that were located in towns and cities, as well as those that they came upon in more isolated, rural locales. These were the places, Quisser said, where one was most likely to discover those hybrid enterprises which he called gas station carnivals.

Quisser did not claim to know when or how these specialized *carnivals*, or perhaps specialized *gas stations*, came into existence, nor how widespread they might have been. His father, whom Quisser believed would be able to answer such questions, had died some years ago, while his mother was no longer mentally competent, having suffered a series of psychic catastrophes not long after the death of Quisser's father. Thus, all that remained to Quisser was the memory of these childhood excursions with his parents, during which they would find themselves in some rural area, perhaps at the crossroads of two highways (and often, he seemed to recall, around sunset), and discover in this isolated location one of those curiosities which he described to me as gas station carnivals.

They were invariably *filling stations*, Quisser emphasized, and not *service stations*, which might have facilities for doing extensive repairs on cars and other vehicles. There would be, in those days, four gas pumps at most, often only two, and some kind of modest building which usually had so many signs and advertisements applied to its exterior that no one could say if anything actually stood beneath them. Quisser said that as a child he always took special notice of the signs that advertised chewing tobacco, and that as an adult, in his capacity as an art critic, he still found the sight of chewing tobacco packages very appealing, and he could not understand why some artist had not successfully exploited their visual and imaginative qualities. It seemed to me, as we sat that night in the Crimson Cabaret, that this chewing tobacco material was intended to lend greater credence to Quisser's story. This detail was so vivid to him. But when I asked Quisser if he recalled any particular brands of chewing tobacco being advertised at these filling stations which had carnivals attached to them, he became slightly defensive, as if my question was intended to challenge the accuracy of his childhood recollection. He then shifted the focus of the issue I had raised by asserting that the carnival aspect of these places was not exactly *attached* to the gas station aspect, but that they were never very far away from each other and there was definitely a commercial liaison between them. His impression, which had been instilled in him like some founding principle of a dream, was that a substantial purchase of gasoline allowed the driver and passengers of a given vehicle free access to the nearby carnival.

At this point in his story Quisser became anxious to explain that these gas station carnivals were by no means elaborate – quite the opposite, in fact. Situated on some empty stretch of land that stood alongside, or sometimes behind, a rural filling station, they consisted of only the remnants of fully fledged carnivals, the *bare bones* of much larger and grander entertainments. There was usually a tall, arched entranceway with colored lightbulbs that provided an eerie contrast to the vast and barren landscape surrounding it. Especially around sunset, which was usually, or possibly always, when Quisser and his parents found themselves in one of these remote locales, the colorful illumination of a carnival entranceway created an effect that was both festive and sinister. But once a visitor had gained admittance to the actual grounds of the carnival, there came a moment of letdown at the thing itself – that spare assemblage of equipment that appeared to have been left behind by a travelling amusement park in the distant past.

There were always only a few carnival rides, Quisser said, and these were very seldom in actual operation. He supposed that at some time they were in functioning order, probably when they were first installed as an annex to the gas stations. But this period, he speculated, could not have lasted long. And no doubt at the earliest sign of malfunction each of the rides was shut down. Quisser said that he himself had never been on a single ride at a gas station carnival, though he insisted that his father once allowed him to sit atop one of the wooden horses on a defunct merry-go-round. "It was a *miniature* merry-go-round," Quisser told me, as if that gave his recollected experience an aura of meaning or substance. All the rides, it seemed, were miniature, he asserted –

small-scale versions of carnival rides he had elsewhere known and had actually ridden upon. Beside the miniature merry-go-round, which never moved an inch and always stood dark and silent in a remote rural landscape, there would be a miniature ferris wheel (no taller than a bungalow-style house, Quisser said), and sometimes a miniature tilt-a-whirl or a miniature roller coaster. And they were always closed down because once they had malfunctioned, if in fact any of them was ever in operation, they were never subsequently repaired. Possibly they never could be repaired, Quisser thought, given the antiquated parts and mechanisms of these miniature carnival rides.

Yet there was a single, quite crucial amusement that one could almost always expect to see open to the public, or at least to those whose car had been filled with the requisite amount of gasoline and who were therefore free to pass through the brightly lit entranceway upon which the word CARNIVAL was emblazoned in colored lights against a vast and haunting sky at sundown somewhere out in a rural wasteland. Quisser posed to me a question: how could a place advertise itself as a carnival, even a gas station carnival, if it did not include that most vital element – a sideshow? Perhaps there was some special law or ordinance regulating such matters, Quisser imagined out loud, an old statute of some kind that would have particular force in remote areas where certain traditions have an endurance unknown to urban centers. This would account for the fact that, except under extraordinary circumstances (such as dangerously bad weather), there was always some type of sideshow performance at these gas station carnivals, even though everything else on the grounds stood dark and damaged.

Of course these sideshows, as Quisser described them, were not terribly sophisticated, even by the standards of the average carnival, let alone those that served as commercial enticements for some out-of-the-way gas station. There would be only a single sideshow attraction at a given site, and outwardly they each presented the same image to the carnival patrons: a small tent of torn and filthy canvass. At some point along the perimeter of the tent would be a loose flap of material through which Quisser and his parents, though sometimes only Quisser himself, would gain entrance to the sideshow. Inside the tent were a few wooden benches that had sunken a little bit into the hard dirt beneath them and, some distance away, a small stage area that was raised perhaps just a foot or so above ground level. Illumination was provided by two ordinary floor lamps – one on either side of the stage – that were without lampshades or any other kind of covering, so that their bare lightbulbs burned harshly and cast dramatic shadows throughout the interior of the tent. Quisser said that he always noticed the frayed electrical cords that trailed off from the base of each lamp and, by means of several extension cords, ultimately found a source of power at the gas station, that is, from within the small brick building which was obscured by so many signs advertising chewing tobacco and other products.

When visitors to a gas station carnival entered the sideshow tent and took their places on one of the benches in front of the stage, they were not usually alerted to the particular nature of the performance or spectacle that they would witness. Quisser remarked that there was no marquee or billboard of any type that might offer such a notice to the carnival-goers either before they entered the sideshow tent or after they were inside and seated on one of the old wooden benches. However, with one important exception, each of the performances, or spectacles, was much the same rigmarole. The audience would settle itself on the wooden benches, most of which were about to collapse or (as Quisser observed) were so unevenly sunken into the ground that it was impossible to sit on them, and the show would begin.

The attractions varied from sideshow to sideshow, and Quisser said he was unable to remember all of the ones he had seen. He did recall what he described as the Human Spider. This was a very brief spectacle during which someone in a clumsy costume scuttled from one side of the stage to the other and back again, exiting through a slit at the back of the tent. The person wearing the costume, Quisser added, was presumably the attendant who pumped gas, washed windows, and performed various services around the filling station. In many sideshow performances, such as that of the Hypnotist, Quisser remembered that a gas station attendant's uniform (greasy gray or blue coveralls) was quite visible beneath the performer's stage clothes. Quisser did admit that he was unsure why he designated this particular sideshow act as the "Hypnotist," since there was no hypnotism involved in the performance, and of course no marquee or billboard existed either outside the tent or within it that might lead the public to expect any kind of mesmeric routines. The performer was simply clothed in a long, loose overcoat and wore a plastic mask which was a plain, very pale replica of a human face, with the exception that instead of eyes (or eyeholes) there were two large discs with spiral designs painted upon them. The Hypnotist would gesticulate chaotically in front of the audience for some moments, no doubt because his vision was obscured by the spiral-patterned discs over the eyes of his mask, and then stumble off stage.

There were numerous other sideshow acts that Quisser claimed to have seen, including the Dancing Puppet, the Worm, the Hunchback, and Dr. Fingers. With one important exception, the routine was always the same: Quisser and his parents would enter the sideshow tent and sit upon one of the rotted benches, soon after which some performer would appear briefly on the small stage that was lit up by two ordinary floor lamps. The single deviation from this routine was an attraction that Quisser called the Showman.

Whereas every other sideshow act began and ended *after* Quisser and his parents had entered the special tent and seated themselves, the one called the Showman always seemed to be *in progress*. As soon as Quisser stepped inside the tent – invariably preceding his parents, he claimed – he saw the figure standing perfectly still upon the small stage *with his back to the audience*. Of course there were never any other persons in the audience when Quisser and his parents stopped at twilight and visited one of these gas station carnivals – with their second-hand, defective amusements – there was only the figure of the Showman standing with his back to a few rows of empty benches that might break up altogether even as you were attempting to sit on them. And whenever Quisser entered the sideshow tent and saw that it was the Showman onstage, he wanted to immediately turn around and leave that place. But then his parents would come pushing into the tent behind him, he said, and before he knew it they would all be sitting on one of the benches in the very first row looking at the Showman. His parents never knew how terrified he was of this peculiar sideshow figure, Quisser repeated several times. Furthermore, visiting these gas station carnivals, and especially taking in the sideshows, was all done for Quisser's benefit, since his father and mother would have preferred simply filling up the family car with gasoline and moving on toward whatever vacation spot was next on their itinerary.

Quisser contended that his parents actually enjoyed watching him sit in terror before the Showman, until he could not stand it any longer and asked to go back to the car. At the same time he was quite transfixed by the sight of this sideshow character, who was unlike any other that he could remember. There he was, Quisser said, standing with his back to the audience and wearing an old top hat and a long cape that touched the dirty floor of the small stage on which he stood. Sticking out from beneath the top hat were the dense and lengthy shocks of the Showman's stiff red hair, Quisser said, which looked like some kind of sickening vermin's nest. When I asked Quisser if this hair might actually have been a wig, deliberately testing his memory and imagination, he only gave me a contemptuous look that seemed to reply that *I* was not the one who had seen the stiff red hair; *he* was the one who had seen it sticking out from beneath the Showman's old top hat. The only other feature that was visible to the audience, Quisser continued, were the fingers of the Showman, which grasped the edges of his long cape. These fingers appeared to Quisser to be somehow deformed, curling together in little claws, and were a pale greenish color, Quisser said. Apparently, as Quisser viewed it, the entire stance of the figure was calculated to suggest that at any moment he might twirl about and confront the audience full-face, his moldy fingers lifting up the edges of his cape, reaching to the height of his stiff red hair. Yet the figure never budged. Sometimes it did seem to Quisser that the Showman was moving his head a little to the left or a little to the right, threatening to reveal one side of his face or the other, playing a horrible game of peek-a-boo. But ultimately Quisser concluded that these perceived movements were illusory and that the Showman was always posed in perfect stillness, a nightmarish mannikin that invited all kinds of imaginings by its very forbearance of any gesture.

"It was all a nasty pretence," Quisser said to me and then paused to finish off his glass of wine.

"But what if he had turned around to face the audience?" I asked. While awaiting his response I sipped some of my mint tea, which did not seem to be doing much good for my queasy stomach, yet at the same time was causing no harm either. I lit one of the mild cigarettes that I was smoking on that occasion. "Did you hear what I said?" I said to Quisser, who had been looking toward the stage located in the opposite corner of the Crimson Cabaret. "The stage is the same," I said to Quisser quite sternly, attracting some glances from persons sitting at the other tables in the club. "The panels are the same and the designs on them are also the same."

Quisser played nervously with his empty wine glass. "When I was very young," he said, "there were certain occasions on which I would see the Showman, but he wasn't in his natural habitat, so to speak, of the sideshow tent."

"I think I've heard enough tonight," I interjected, my hand pressing against my queasy stomach.

"What are you saying?" asked Quisser. "You remember them,

don't you? The gas station carnivals. Maybe just a *faint* memory. I was sure you would be the one to know about them."

"I think I can say," I said to Quisser, "I've heard enough of your gas station carnival story to know what it's all about."

"What do you mean, 'what it's all about'?" asked Quisser, who was still looking over at the small stage across the room.

"Well, for one thing, your later memories, your *purported* memories, of that Showman character. You were about to tell me that throughout your childhood you repeatedly saw this figure at various times and in various places. Perhaps you saw him in the distance of a schoolyard, standing with his back to you. Or you saw him on the other side of a busy street, but when you crossed the street he wasn't there any longer."

"Something like that, yes."

"And you were then going to tell me that lately you've been seeing this figure, or faint suggestions of this figure – sketchy reflections in store windows along the sidewalk, flashing glimpses in the rear-view mirror of your car."

"It's very much like one of your stories."

"In some ways it is," I said, "and in some ways it isn't. You feel that if you ever see the Showman figure turn his head around to look at you . . . that something terrible will happen, most likely that you'll perish on the spot from some kind of monumental shock."

"Yes," agreed Quisser. "An unsustainable horror. But I haven't told you the strangest part. You're right that lately I have had glimpses of . . . that figure, and I did see him during my childhood, outside of the sideshow tent, I mean. But the strangest part is that I remember seeing him in other places even *before* I first saw him at the gas station carnivals."

"This is just my point," I said.

"What is?"

"That there *are no gas station carnivals*. There never were any gas station carnivals. Nobody remembers them because they never existed. The whole idea is preposterous."

"But my parents were there with me."

"Exactly – your dead father and your mentally incompetent mother. Do you remember ever discussing with them your vacation experiences at these special gas stations with the carnivals supposedly annexed to them?"

"No, I don't."

"That's because you never went to any such places with them.

Think about how ludicrous it all sounds. That there should be filling stations out in the sticks that entice customers with free admission to broken-down carnivals – it's all so ridiculous. *Miniature* carnival rides? Gas station attendants doubling as sideshow performers?"

"Not the Showman," interrupted Quisser. "He was never a gas station attendant."

"No, of course he wasn't a gas station attendant, because he was a delusion. The whole thing is an outrageous delusion, but it's also a very particular type of delusion."

"And what type would that be?" asked Quisser, who was still sneaking glances at the stage area across the room of the Crimson Cabaret.

"It's not some type of common psychological delusion, if that's what you were thinking I was about to say. I have no interest at all in such things. But I am very interested when somone is suffering from a *magical* delusion. Even more precisely, I am interested in delusions that are a result of *art-magic*. And do you know how long you've been under the influence of this art-magic delusion?"

"You've lost me," said Quisser.

"It's simple," I said. "How long have you imagined all this nonsense about the gas station carnivals, and specifically about this character you describe as the Showman?"

"I guess it would be more or less absurd at this point to insist to you that I've seen this figure since childhood, even if that's exactly how it seems and that's exactly what I remember."

"Of course it would be absurd, because you're definitely delusional."

"So I'm delusional about the Showman, but you're *not* delusional about . . . what do you call it?"

"Art-magic. For as long as you've been a victim of this particular art-magic, this is how long you've been delusional about the gas station carnivals and all related phenomena."

"And how long is that?" asked Quisser, not quite sincerely.

"Since you humiliated the crimson woman by calling her a *deluded no-talent*. I told you that she had connections you knew absolutely nothing about."

"I'm talking about something from my childhood, something I've remembered my entire life. You're talking about a matter of days."

"That's because a matter of days is exactly the term that you've been delusional. Don't you see that through her art-magic she has caused you to suffer from the worst kind of delusion, which might be called a *retroactive* delusion. And it's not only you who've been afflicted in the past days and weeks and even months. Everyone around here has sensed the threat of this art-magic for some time now. I'm beginning to think that I've found out about it too late myself, much too late. You know what it is to suffer from a delusion of the retroactive type, but do you know what it's like to be the victim of a severe stomach disorder. I've been sitting here in the crimson woman's club drinking mint tea served by a waitress who is the crimson woman's friend, thinking that mint tea is just the thing for my stomach when it very well may be aggravating my condition or even causing it to transform, in accordance with the principles of art-magic, into something more serious and more strange. But the crimson woman is not the only one practicing this art-magic. It's happening everywhere around here. It drifted in unexpectedly like a fog at sea, and so many of us are becoming lost in it. Look at the faces in this room and then tell me that you alone are the victim of a horrible art-magic. The crimson woman has quite a few adversaries, just as she is connected with powerful allies. How can I say exactly who they are – some group specializing in art-magic, no doubt, but I can't just say, with a fatuous certainty, 'Yes, it must be some particular gang of illuminati,' or *esoteric scientists*, as so many have begun styling themselves these days."

"But it all sounds like one of you stories," Quisser protested.

"Of course it does, don't you think *she* knows that. But I'm not the one with that grotesque yarn about the gas station carnivals and the sideshow tent with a small stage not unlike the stage on the opposite side of this room. You can't keep your eyes off it, I can see that and so can the other people around the room. And I know what you think you're seeing over there."

"Assuming *you* know what you're talking about," said Quisser, who was now forcing himself to look *away* from the stage area across the room, "what am I supposed to do about it?"

"You can start by keeping your eyes off that stage across the room. There's nothing you can see over there except an art-magic delusion. There is nothing necessarily fatal or permanent about the affliction. But you must *believe* that you will recover, just as you would if you were suffering from some non-fatal physical disease. Otherwise these diseases may turn into something far more deadly, because ultimately all diseases are magical diseases, especially your art-magic delusion."

I could now see that the intense conviction carried by my words had finally had its effect on Quisser. His gaze was no longer drawn toward the small stage on the opposite side of the room but was directed full upon me. He did remain somewhat distraught in the face of the truth about his delusion, yet he seemed to have settled down considerably.

I lit another of my mild cigarettes and glanced around the room, not looking for anything or anyone in particular but merely gauging the atmosphere. The tobacco smoke drifting through the club was so much thicker, the amber light was several shades darker, and the sound of raindrops still played against the black painted windows of the Crimson Cabaret. I was now back in the cabin of that old ship as it was being cast about in a vicious storm at sea, utterly insecure in its bearings and profoundly threatened by uncontrollable forces. Quisser excused himself to go to the rest room, and his form passed across my field of vision like a shadow through dense fog.

I have no idea how long Quisser was gone from the table. My attention became fully absorbed by the other faces in the club and the deep anxiety they betrayed to me, an anxiety that was not of the natural, existential sort but one that was caused by peculiar concerns of an uncanny nature. What a season is upon us, these faces seemed to say. And no doubt their voices would have spoken directly of certain peculiar concerns had they not been intimidated into weird equivocations and double entendres by the fear of falling victim to the same kind of unnatural affliction that had made so much trouble in the mind of the art critic Stuart Quisser. Who would be next? What could a person say these days, or even think, without feeling the dread of repercussion from powerfully connected groups and individuals? I could almost hear their voices asking, "Why here, why now?" But of course they could have just as easily been asking, "Why not here, why not now?" It would not occur to this crowd that there were no special rules involved; it would not occur to them, even though they were a crowd of imaginative artists, that the whole thing was simply a matter of random, purposeless terror that converged upon a particular place at a particular time for no particular reason. On the other hand, it would also not have occurred to them that they might have wished it all upon themselves, that they might have had a hand in bringing certain powerful forces and connections into our district simply by wishing them to come. They might have wished and wished for an unnatural evil to fall upon them but, for a while at least, nothing happened. Then the wishing stopped, the old wishes were forgotten yet at the same time gathered in strength, distilling themselves into a potent formula (who can say!), until one day the terrible season began. Because had they really told the truth, this artistic crowd might also have expressed what a sense of meaning (although of a negative sort), not to mention the vigorous thrill (although of an excruciating type), this season of unnatural evil had brought to their lives.

It was during the moments that I was looking at all the faces in the Crimson Cabaret, and thinking my own thoughts about those faces, that a shadow again passed across my foggy field of vision. While I expected to find that this shadow was Quisser, my table-companion for that evening, on his way back from his trip to the rest room, I instead found myself confronted by the waitress who Quisser had claimed was so loyal to the crimson woman. She asked if I wanted to order yet another cup of mint tea, saying it in exactly these words, *yet another cup of mint tea*. Trying not to become irritated by her queerly sarcastic tone of voice, which would only have further aggravated my already queasy stomach, I answered that I was just about to leave for the night. Then I added that perhaps my friend wanted to drink *yet another* glass of wine, pointing across the table to indicate the empty glass Quisser had left behind when he excused himself to use the rest room. But there was no empty wine glass across the table; there was only my empty cup of mint tea. I immediately accused the waitress of taking away the empty wine glass while I was distracted by my reverie upon the faces in the Crimson Cabaret. But she denied ever serving any glass of wine to anyone at my table, insisting that I had been alone from the moment I arrived at the club and sat down at the table across the room from the small stage area. After a thorough search of the rest room, I returned and tried to find someone else in the club who had seen the art critic Quisser talking to me at great length about his gas station carnivals. But all of them said they had seen no one of the kind.

Even Quisser himself, when I tracked him down the next day to a hole-in-the-wall art gallery, maintained that he had not seen me the night before. He said that he had spent the entire evening at home by himself, claiming that he had suffered some indisposition – some *bug*, he said – from which he had since fully recovered. When I called him a liar, he stepped right up to me as we stood in the middle of that hole-in-the-wall art gallery, and in a tense whisper he said that I should "watch my words." I was always shooting off my mouth, he said, and that in the future I should use more discretion in what I said and to whom I said it. He then asked me if I really thought it was wise to open my mouth at a party and call someone a *deluded no-talent*. There were certain persons, he said, that had powerful connections, and I, of all people, he said, should know better, considering my awareness of such things and the way I displayed this awareness in the stories I wrote. "Not that I disagreed with what you said about you-know-who," he said. "But I would not have made such an open declaration. You *humiliated* her. And these days such a thing can be very perilous, if you know what I mean."

Of course I did know what he meant, though I did not yet understand why he was now saying these words to me, rather than I to him. Was it not enough, I later thought, that I was still suffering a terrible stomach disorder? Did I also have to bear the burden of another's delusion? But even this explanation eventually fell to pieces upon further inquiry. The stories multiplied about the night of that party, accounts proliferated among my acquaintances and peers concerning exactly *who* had committed the humiliating offence and even who had been the *offended party*. "Why are you telling me these things?" the crimson woman said to me when I proffered my deepest apologies. "I barely know who you are. And besides, I've got enough problems of my own. That bitch of a waitress here at the club has taken down all my paintings and replaced them with her own."

All of us had problems, it seemed, whose sources were untraceable, crossing over one another like the trajectories of countless raindrops in a storm, blending to create a fog of delusion and counter-delusion. Powerful forces and connections were undoubtedly at play, yet they seemed to have no faces and no names, and it was anybody's guess what we – a crowd of deluded no-talents – could have possibly done to offend them. We had been caught up in a season of hideous magic from which nothing could offer us deliverance. More and more I found myself returning to those memories of gas station carnivals, seeking an answer in the twilight of remote rural areas where miniature merry-go-rounds and ferris wheels lay broken in a desolate landscape.

But there is no one here who will listen even to my most abject apologies, least of all the Showman, who may be waiting behind any door (even the rest room of the Crimson Cabaret). And any room that I enter may become a sideshow tent where I must take my place upon a rickety old bench on the verge of collapse. Even now the Showman stands before my eyes. His stiff red hair moves a little toward one shoulder, as if he is going to turn his gaze upon me, and moves back again; then his head moves a little toward the other shoulder in this neverending game of horrible peek-a-boo. I can only sit and wait, knowing that one day he will turn full around, step down from his stage, and claim me for the abyss I have always feared. Perhaps then I will discover what it was I did – what any of us did – to deserve this fate.

THE BUNGALOW HOUSE

Early last September I discovered among the exhibits in a local art gallery a sort of performance piece in the form of an audio tape. This, I later learned, was the first of a series of tape-recorded dream monologues by an unknown artist. The following is a brief and highly typical excerpt from the opening section of this work. I recall that after a few seconds of hissing tape noise, the voice began speaking: "There was far more to deal with in the bungalow house than simply an infestation of vermin," it said, "although that too had its questionable aspects." Then the voice went on: "I could see only a few of the bodies where the moonlight shone through the open blinds of the living room windows and fell upon the carpet. Only one of the bodies seemed to be moving, and that very slowly, but there may have been more that were not yet dead. Aside from the chair in which I sat in the darkness there was very little furniture in the room, or elsewhere in the bungalow house for that matter. But a number of lamps were positioned around me, floor lamps and table lamps and even two tiny lamps on the mantle above the fireplace."

A brief pause occurred here in the opening section of the tape recorded dream monologue, as I remember it, after which the voice continued: "'The bungalow house was built with a fireplace,' I said to myself in the darkness, thinking how long it had been since anyone had made use of this fireplace, or anything else in the bungalow. Then my attention returned to the lamps, and I began trying each of them one by one, twisting their little grooved switches in the darkness. The moonlight fell upon the lampshades without shining through them, so I could not see that none of the lamps was equipped with a lightbulb, and each time I turned the switch of a floor lamp or a table lamp or one of the tiny lamps on the mantle, nothing changed in the dark living room of the bungalow house: the moonlight shone through the dusty blinds and revealed the bodies of insects and other vermin on the pale carpet.

"The challenges and obstacles facing me in that bungalow house were becoming more and more oppressive," whispered the voice on the tape. "There was something so desolate about being in that place in the dead of night, even if I did not know precisely what time it was. And to see upon the pale, threadbare carpet those verminous bodies, some of which were still barely alive; then to try each of the lamps and find that none of them was in working order – everything appeared in opposition to my efforts, everything aligned against my taking care of the problems I faced in the bungalow house. For the first time I noticed that the bodies lying for the most part in total stillness on the moonlit carpet were not like any species of vermin I had ever seen," the voice on the tape recording said. "Some of them seemed to be deformed, their naturally revolting forms altered in ways I could not discern. I knew that I would require specialized implements for dealing with these creatures, an arsenal of advanced tools of extermination. It was the idea of poisons – the toxic solutions and vapors I would need to use in my assault upon the bungalow hordes – that caused me to become overwhelmed by the complexities of the task before me and the paucity of my resources for dealing with them."

At this point, and many others on the tape (as I recall), the voice became nearly inaudible. "The bungalow house," it said, "was such a bleak environment in which to make a stand: the moonlight through the dusty blinds, the bodies on the carpet, the lamps without any lightbulbs. And the incredible silence. It was not the absence of sounds that I sensed, but the stifling of innumerable sounds and even voices, the muffling of all the noises one might expect to hear in an old bungalow house in the dead of night, as well as countless other sounds and voices. The forces required to accomplish this silence filled me with awe. *The infinite terror and dreariness of an infested bungalow house,* I whispered to myself. *A bungalow universe,* I then thought without speaking aloud. Suddenly I was overcome by a feeling of euphoric hopelessness which passed through my body like a powerful drug and held all my thoughts and all my movements in a dreamy, floating suspension. In the moonlight that shone through the blinds of that bungalow house I was now as still and as silent as everything else."

The title of the tape-recorded artwork from which I have just quoted an excerpt was *The Bungalow House (Plus Silence)*. I discovered this and other dream monologues by the same artist at Dalha D. Fine Arts, which was located in the near vicinity of the public library (main branch) where I was employed in the Language and Literature department. Sometimes I spent my lunch breaks at the gallery, even consuming my brown-bag meals on the premises. There were a few chairs and benches on the floor of the gallery, and I knew that the woman who owned the place did not discourage any kind of traffic, however lingering. Her actual livelihood was in fact not derived from the gallery itself. How could it have been? Dalha D. Fine Arts was a hole in the wall. One would think it no trouble at all to keep up the premises where there was so little floor space, just a single room that was by no means overcrowded with artworks or art-related merchandise. But no attempt at such upkeeping seemed ever to have been made. The display window was so filmy that someone passing by could barely make out the paintings and sculptures behind it (the same ones year after year). From the street outside, this tiny front window presented the most desolate hallucination of bland colors and shapeless forms, especially on late November afternoons. Further inside the gallery, things were in a similar state – from the cruddy linoleum floor, where some cracked tiles revealed the concrete foundation, to the rather high ceiling, which occasionally sent down small chips of plaster. If every artwork and item of art-related merchandise had been cleared out of that building, no one would think that an art gallery had once occupied this space and not some enterprise of a lesser order.

But as many persons were aware, if only through second-hand sources, the woman who operated Dalha D. Fine Arts did not make her living by dealing in those artworks and related items which only the most desperate or scandalously naive artist would allow to be put on display in that gallery. By all accounts, including my own brief lunchtime conversations with the woman, she had pursued a variety of careers in her time. She herself had worked as an artist at one point, and some of her works – messy assemblages inside old cigar boxes – were exhibited in a corner of her gallery. But evidently her art gallery business was not self-sustaining, despite minimal overhead, and she made no secret of her true means of income.

"Who wants to buy such junk?" she once explained to me, gesturing with long fingernails painted emerald green. This same color also seemed to dominate her wardrobe of long, loose garments, often featuring incredible scarves or shawls that dragged along the floor as she moved about the art gallery. She paused and with the pointed toe of one of her emerald green shoes gave a little kick at a wire wastebasket that was filled with the miniature limbs of dolls, all of them individually painted in a variety of colors. "What are people thinking when they make these things? What was I thinking with those stupid cigar boxes? But no more of that, definitely no more of that sort of thing."

And she made no secret, beyond a certain reasonable caution, of what sort of thing now engaged her energies as a businesswoman. The telephone was always ringing at her art gallery, always upsetting the otherwise dead calm of the place with its cracked, warbling voice that called out from the back room. She would then quickly disappear behind a curtain that hung in the doorway separating the front and back sections of the art gallery. I might be eating my sandwich or a piece of fruit, and then suddenly, for the fourth or fifth time in a half-hour, the telephone would scream from the back room, eventually summoning this woman behind the curtain. But she never answered the telephone with the name of the art gallery or employed any of the stock phrases of business protocol. Not so much as a "good afternoon, may I help you?" did I ever hear from the back room as I sat eating my midday meal in the front section of the art gallery. She always answered the telephone in the same way with the same quietly expectant tone in her voice. *This is Dalha,* she always said.

Before I had known her very long she even had me using her name in the most familiar way. The mere saying of this name instilled in me a sense of *access* to what she offered all those telephone-callers, not to mention those individuals who personally visited the art gallery to make or confirm an appointment. Whatever someone was eager to try, whatever step someone was willing to take – Dalha could arrange it. This was the true stock in trade of the art gallery, these *arrangements*. When I returned to the library after my lunch break, I continued to imagine Dalha back at the art gallery, racing between the front and back sections of the building, making all kinds of arrangements over the telephone, and sometimes in person.

On the day that I first noticed the new artwork entitled *The Bungalow House,* Dalha's telephone was extremely vocal. While she was talking to her clients in the back section of the art gallery, I was practically left alone in the front section. Just for a thrill I went over to the wire wastebasket full of dismembered doll parts and lifted one of the painted arms (emerald green!), hiding it in the inner pocket of my sportcoat. It was then that I spotted the old audio tape recorder on a small plastic table in the corner. Beside the machine was a business card on which the title of the artwork had been hand-printed, along with the following instructions: PRESS PLAY. PLEASE REWIND AFTER LISTENING. DO NOT REMOVE TAPE. I placed the headphones over my ears and pressed the PLAY button. The voice that spoke through the headphones, which were enormous, sounded distant and was somewhat distorted by the hissing of the tape. Nevertheless, I was so intrigued by the opening passages of this dream monologue, which I have already transcribed, that I sat down on the floor next to the small plastic table on which the tape recorder was positioned and listened to the entire tape, exceeding my allotted lunchtime by over half an hour. By the time the tape had ended I was in another world – that is, the world of the infested bungalow house, with all its dreamlike crumminess and foul charms.

"Don't forget to rewind the tape," said Dalha, who was now standing over me, her long gray hair, like steel wool, almost brushing against my face.

I pressed the REWIND button on the tape recorder and got up from the floor. "Dalha, may I use your lavatory?" I asked. She pointed to the curtain leading to the back section of the art gallery. "Thank you," I said.

The effect of listening to the first dream monologue was very intense for reasons I will soon explain. I wanted to be alone for a few moments in order to preserve the state of mind which the voice on the tape had induced in me, much as one might attempt to hold on to the images of a dream just after waking. However, I felt that the lavatory at the library, despite its peculiar virtues which I have appreciated over the years, would somehow undermine the sensations and mental state created by the dream monologue, rather than preserving this experience and even enhancing it, as I hoped the lavatory in the back section of Dalha's art gallery would do.

The very reason why I spent my lunchtimes in the surroundings of Dalha's art gallery, which were so different from those of the library, was exactly why I now wanted to use the lavatory in the back section of that art gallery and definitely not the lavatory at the library, even if I was already overdue from my lunch break. And, indeed, this lavatory had the same qualities as the rest of the art gallery, as I hoped it would. The fact that it was located in the back section of the art gallery, a region of mysteries to my mind, was significant. Just outside the door of the lavatory stood a small, cluttered desk upon which was the telephone that Dalha used in her true business of making arrangements. The telephone was centered in the weak light of a desk lamp, and I noticed, as I passed into the lavatory, that it was an unwieldy object with a straight – that is, *uncoiled* – cord connecting the receiver to the telephone housing, with its enormous dial. But although Dalha answered several calls during the time I was in her lavatory, these seemed to be entirely legitimate conversations having to do either with her personal life or with practical matters relating to the art gallery.

"How long are you going to be in there?" Dalha asked through the door of the lavatory. "I hope you're not sick, because if you're sick you'll have to go somewhere else."

I called out that there was nothing wrong (quite the opposite) and a moment later emerged from the lavatory. I was about to ask for details of the art performance tape I had just heard, anxious to know about the artist and what it would cost me to own the work entitled *The Bungalow House*, as well as any similar works that might exist. But the phone began ringing again. Dalha answered it with her customary greeting as I stood by in the back section of the art gallery, which was a dark, though relatively uncluttered, space that now put me in mind of the living room of the bungalow house that I had heard described on the tape recorded dream monologue. The conversation in which Dalha was engaged (another non-arrangement call) seemed interminable, and I was becoming nervously aware how long past my lunch break I had stayed at the storefront art gallery.

"I'll see you tomorrow," I said to Dalha, who responded with a look from her emerald eyes while continuing to speak to the other party on the telephone. And she was smiling at me, *like muted laughter*, I remember thinking as I passed through the curtained doorway into the front section of the art gallery. I glanced at the tape recorder standing on the plastic table but decided against taking the audio cassette back to the library (and afterward home with me). It would be there when I visited on my lunch break the following day. Hardly anyone ever bought anything out of the front section of Dalha's art gallery.

For the rest of the day – both at the library and at my home – I thought about the bungalow house tape. Especially while riding the bus home from the library, I thought of the images and concepts described on the tape, as well as the voice that described them and the phrases it used throughout the dream monologue on the bungalow house. Much of my commute from my home to the library, and back home again, took me past numerous streets lined from end to end with desolate-looking houses, any of which might have been the inspiration for the bungalow house audio tape. I say that these streets were lined from "end to end" with such houses, even though the bus never turned down any of these streets, and I therefore never actually viewed even a single one of them from "end to end." In fact, as I looked through the window next to my seat on the bus – on either side of the bus I always sat in the window seat, never in the aisle seat – the streets I saw appeared endless, vanishing from my sight toward an infinity of old houses, many of them derelict houses and a great many of them being dwarfish and desolate-looking houses of the bungalow type.

The tape-recorded dream monologue, as I recalled it that day while riding home on the bus and staring out the window, described several features of the infested bungalow house – the dusty window blinds through which the moonlight shone, the lamps with all their lightbulb sockets empty, the threadbare carpet, and the dead or barely living vermin that littered the carpet. The voice on the tape only presented an interior view of the bungalow house, never a view from the exterior. Conversely, the houses I gazed upon with such intensity as I rode the bus to and from the library were only seen by me from an exterior perspective, their interiors being visible solely in my imagination as I projected it into these houses. And my memory of these interiors, once I had emerged from one of my imaginative projections, was always spotty and vague, lacking the precise physical layout provided by the bungalow house audio tape. Even my recollection of the dreams I often had of these houses was spotty and vague, highly imperfect. Yet the sensations and the mental state created by my imaginative projections *into* and my dreams *of* these houses perfectly corresponded to those I experienced at Dalha's art gallery when I listened to the tape entitled *The Bungalow House*. That feeling of being in a trance among the most vile and pathetic surroundings was communicated to me in the most powerful way by the voice on the tape, which described a silent and secluded world where one existed in a state of abject hypnosis. While sitting on the floor of the art gallery listening to the voice as it spoke through those enormous headphones, I had the sense not that I was simply *hearing* the words of that dream monologue but also that I was *reading* them. What I mean is that whenever I have the occasion to read words on a page, any words on any page, the voice that I hear saying these words in my head is always recognizable in some way as my own, even though the words are those of another. Perhaps it is even more accurate to say that whenever I read words on a page, the voice in my head is my own voice *as it becomes merged* (or lost) within the words that I am reading. Conversely, when I have the occasion to write words on a page, even a simple note or memo at the library, the voice that I hear dictating these words does *not* sound like my own – until, of course, I read the words back to myself, at which time everything is all right again. The bungalow house tape was the most dramatic example of this phenomenon I had ever known. Despite the poor overall quality of the recording, the distorted voice reading this dream monologue became merged (or lost) within my own perfectly clear voice in my head, even though I was listening to its words over a pair of enormous headphones and not reading the words on a page. As I rode the bus home from the library, observing street after street of houses so reminiscent of the one described on the tape-recorded dream monologue, I regretted not having acquired this artwork on the spot or at least discovered more about it from Dalha, who had been occupied with what seemed an unusual number of telephone calls that afternoon.

The following day at the library I was anxious for lunchtime to arrive so that I could get over to the art gallery and find out everything I possibly could about the bungalow house tape, as well as discuss terms for its acquisition. Entering the art gallery, I immediately looked toward the corner where the tape recorder had been set on the small plastic table the day before. For some reason I was relieved to find the exhibit still in place, as if any artwork in that gallery could possibly have come and gone in a single day.

I walked over to the exhibit with the purpose of verifying that everything I had seen (and heard) the previous day was exactly as I remembered it. I checked that the audio cassette was still inside the recording machine and picked up the little business card on which the title of the exhibit was given, along with instructions for properly operating the tape-recorded artwork. It was then that I realized that this was a different card from the first one. Printed on this card was the title of a new artwork, which was called *The Derelict Factory with a Dirt Floor and Voices*.

While I was very excited to find a new work by this artist, I also felt intense apprehension at the absence of the bungalow house dream monologue, which I had planned to purchase with some extra money I brought with me to the art gallery that day. Just at that moment in which I experienced the dual sensations of excitement and apprehension, Dalha emerged from behind the curtain separating the back and front sections of the art gallery. I had intended to be thoroughly blasé in negotiating the purchase of the bungalow house artwork, but Dalha caught me off-guard in a state of disorienting conflict.

"What happened to the bungalow house tape that was here yesterday?" I asked, the tension in my voice betraying desires that were all to her advantage.

"That's gone now," she replied in a frigid tone as she walked slowly and pointlessly about the gallery, her emerald skirt and scarves dragging along the floor.

"I don't understand. It was an artwork exhibited on that small plastic table."

"Yes," she agreed.

"Now, after only a single day on exhibit, it's gone?"

"Yes, it's gone."

"Somebody bought it," I said, assuming the worst.

"No," she said, "that one was not for sale. It was a performance piece. There was a charge, but *you* didn't pay."

A sickly confusion now became added to the excitement and disappointment already mingling inside me. "There was no notice of a charge for listening to the dream monologue," I insisted. "As far as I knew, as far as anyone could know, it was an item for sale like everything else in this place."

"The dream monologue, as you call it, was an exclusive piece. The charge was on the back of the card on which the title was written, just as the charge is on the back of that card you are holding in your hand."

I turned the card to the reverse side, where the words "twenty-five dollars" were written in the same hand that appeared on all the price tags around the gallery. Speaking in the tones of an outraged customer, I said to Dalha, "You wrote the price only on this card. There was nothing written on the bungalow house card." But even as I said these words I lacked the conviction that they were true. In any case, I knew that if I wanted to hear the tape recording about the derelict factory I would have to pay what I owed, or what Dalha claimed I owed, for listening to the bungalow house tape.

"Here," I said, removing my wallet from my back pocket, "ten, twenty, twenty-five dollars for the bungalow house, and another twenty-five for listening to the tape now in the machine."

Dalha stepped forward, took the fifty dollars I held out to her, and in her coldest voice said, "This only covers yesterday's tape about the bungalow house, which was clearly priced at fifty dollars. You must still pay twenty-five dollars if you wish to listen to the tape today."

"But why should the bungalow house tape cost twenty-five dollars more than the tape about the derelict factory?"

"That is simply because this is a less ambitious work than the bungalow house."

In fact the tape recording entitled *The Derelict Factory with a Dirt Floor and Voices* was of shorter duration than *The Bungalow House*

(Plus Silence), but I found it no less wonderful in picturing the same "infinite terror and dreariness." For approximately fifteen minutes (on my lunch break) I embraced the degraded beauty of the derelict factory – a narrow ruin that stood isolated upon a vast plain, its broken windows accepting only the most meager haze of moonlight to shine across its floor of hard-packed dirt where dead machinery lay buried in a grave of shadows and languished in the echoes of hollow, senseless voices. Yet how lucid was the voice that communicated its message to me through the medium of a tape recording. To think that another person shared my love for the *icy bleakness of things*. The comfort I felt at hearing that monotonal and somewhat distorted voice singing words that I knew so well – this was an experience that even then, as I sat on the floor of Dalha's art gallery listening to the tape through enormous headphones, might have been heartbreaking. But I wanted to believe that the artist who created these dream monologues about the bungalow house and the derelict factory had not set out to break my heart or anyone's heart. I wanted to believe that this artist had escaped the dreams and demons of all *sentiment* in order to explore the foul and crummy delights of a universe where everything had been reduced to three stark principles: first, that there was nowhere for you to go; second, that there was nothing for you to do; and third, that there was no one for you to know. Of course I knew that this view was an illusion like any other, but it was also one that had sustained me so long and so well – as long and as well as any other illusion and perhaps longer, perhaps better.

"Dalha," I said when I had finished listening to the tape recording, "I want you to tell me what you know about the artist of these dream monologues. He doesn't even sign his works."

From across the front section of the art gallery Dalha spoke to me in a strange, somewhat flustered voice. "Well, why should you be surprised that he doesn't sign his name to his works – that's how artists are these days. All over the place they are signing their works only with some idiotic symbol or a piece of chewing gum or just leaving them unsigned altogether. Why should you care what his name is? Why should I?"

"Because," I answered, "perhaps I can persuade him to allow me to buy his works instead of sitting on the floor of your art gallery and renting these performances on my lunch break."

"So you want to cut me out entirely," Dalha shouted back in her old voice. "I am his dealer, I tell you, and anything he has to sell you will buy *through me*."

"I don't know why you're getting so upset," I said, standing up from the floor. "I'm willing to give you a percentage. All I ask is that you arrange something between myself and the artist."

Dalha sat down in a chair next to the curtained doorway separating the front and back sections of the art gallery. She pulled her emerald shawl around herself and said, "Even if I wished to arrange something I could not do it. I have no idea what his name is myself. A few nights ago he walked up to me on the street while I was waiting for a cab to take me home."

"What does he look like?" I had to ask at that moment.

"It was late at night and I was drunk," Dalha replied, somehow evasively it seemed to me.

"Was he a younger man, an older man?"

"An older man, yes. Not very tall, with bushy white hair like a professor of some kind. And he said that he wanted to have an artwork of his delivered to my gallery. I explained to him my usual terms as best I could, since I was so drunk. He agreed and then walked off down the street. And that's not the best part of town to be walking around all by yourself. Well, the next day a package arrived with the tape-recording machine and so forth. There were also some instructions which explained that I should destroy each of the audio tapes before I leave the art gallery at the end of the day, and that a new tape would arrive the following day and each day thereafter. There was no return address on the packages."

"And did you destroy the bungalow house tape?" I asked.

"Of course," said Dalha with some exasperation, but also with insistence. "What do I care about some crazy artist's work or how he conducts his career. Besides, he guaranteed I would make some money on the deal, and here I am already with seventy-five dollars."

"So why not sell me this dream monologue about the derelict factory? I won't say anything."

Dalha was quiet for a moment, and then said, "He told me that if I didn't destroy the tapes each day he would know about it and that he would do something. I've forgotten exactly what he said, I was so drunk that night."

"But *how* could he know?" I asked, and in reply Dalha just stared at me in silence. "All right, all right," I said. "But I still want you to make an arrangement. You have his money for the bungalow house tape and the tape about the derelict factory. If he's any kind of artist, he'll want to be paid. When he gets in touch with you, that's when you make the arrangement for me. I won't cheat you out of your percentage. I give you my *word* on that."

"Whatever that's worth," Dalha said bitterly.

But she did agree that she would try to arrange something between myself and the tape-recording artist. I left the art gallery immediately after these negotiations, before Dalha could have any second thoughts. That afternoon, while I was working in the Language and Literature department of the library, I could think about nothing but the derelict factory that was so enticingly pictured on the new audio tape. The bus that takes me to and from the library each day of the working week always passes such a structure, which stands isolated in the distance just as the artist described it in his dream monologue.

That night I slept badly, thrashing about in my bed, not quite asleep and not quite awake. At times I had the feeling there was someone else in my bedroom who was talking to me, but of course I could not deal with this perception in any realistic way, since I was half-asleep and half-awake, and thus, for all practical purposes, I was out of my mind.

Around three o'clock in the morning the telephone rang. In the darkness I reached for my eyeglasses, which were on the nightstand next to the telephone, and noted the luminous face of my alarm clock. I cleared my throat and said hello. The voice on the other end said hello back to me. It was Dalha.

"I talked to him," she said.

"Where did you talk to him?" I asked. "On the street?"

"No, no, not on the street," she said, giggling a little. I think she must have been drunk. "He called me on the telephone."

"He called you on the telephone?" I repeated, imagining for a moment what it would be like to have the voice of that artist speak to me over the telephone and not merely on a recorded audio tape.

"Yes, he called me on the telephone."

"What did he say?"

"Well, I could tell you if you would stop asking so many questions."

"Tell me."

"It was only a few minutes ago that he called. He said that he would meet you tomorrow at the library where you work."

"You told him about me?" I asked, and then there was a long silence. "Dalha?" I prompted.

"Yes, I told him about you. But I never knew what you did for a living. How long have you worked at the library?"

"Fifteen years. Did he say anything else to you?" I asked Dalha.

"No, nothing."

"Maybe it was only a coincidence that he said he would *meet* me at the library and that I also *work* at the library," I said. "People meet all the time at the library. I see them meeting there every day."

"Of course they do," said Dalha, a little patronizing it seemed for someone who was so drunk at three o'clock in the morning. Then she said good-bye and hung up before I could say good-bye back to her.

After talking to Dalha I found it impossible to sleep anymore that night, even if it was only a state of half-sleeping and half-waking. All I could think about was meeting the artist of the dream monologues. So I got myself ready to go to work, rushing as if I were late, and walked up to the corner of my street to wait for the bus.

It was very cold as I sat waiting in the bus shelter. There was a sliver of moon high in the blackness above, with several hours remaining before sunrise. Somehow I felt that I was waiting for the bus on the first day of a new schoolyear, since after all the month was September, and I was so filled with both fear and excitement. When the bus finally arrived I saw that there were only a few other early risers headed for downtown. I took one of the back seats and stared out the window, my own face staring back at me in black reflection.

At the next shelter we approached I noticed that another lone bus rider was seated on the bench waiting to be picked up. His clothes were dark colored (including a long loose overcoat and hat), and he sat up very straight, his arms held close to the body and his hands resting on his lap. His head was slightly bowed, and I could not see the face beneath his hat. His physical attitude, I thought to myself as we approached the lighted bus shelter, was one of disciplined repose. I was surprised that he did not stand up as the bus came nearer to the shelter, and ultimately we passed him by. I wanted to say something to the driver of the bus but a strong feeling of both fear and excitement made me keep my silence.

The bus finally dropped me off in front of the library, and I ran up the tiered stairway that led to the main entrance. Through the thick glass doors I could see that only a few lights illuminated the spacious interior of the library. After rapping on the glass for a few moments I saw a figure dressed in a maintenance man's uniform appear in the shadowy distance inside the building. I rapped some more and the man slowly proceeded down the library's vaulted central hallway.

"Good morning, Henry," I said as the door opened.

"Hello, sir," he replied without standing aside to allow my entrance to the library. "You know I'm not supposed to open these doors before it's time for them to be open."

"I'm a little early, I realize, but I'm sure it will be all right to let me inside. I work here, after all."

"I know you do, sir. But a few days ago I got talked to about these doors being open when they shouldn't be. It's because of the stolen property."

"What property is that, Henry? Books?"

"No, sir. I think it was something from the media department. Maybe a video camera or a tape recorder, I don't know exactly."

"Well, you have my word – just let me through the door and I'll go right upstairs to my desk. I've got a lot of work to do today."

Henry eventually obliged my request, and I did as I told him I would do.

The library was a great building as a whole, but the Language and Literature department (second floor) was located in a relatively small area – narrow and long with a high ceiling and a row of tall, paned windows along one wall. The other walls were lined with books, and most of the floor space was devoted to long study tables. For the most part, though, the room in which I worked was fairly open from end to end. Two large archways led to other parts of the library, and a normal-sized doorway led to the stacks where most of the bibliographic holdings were stored, millions of volumes standing silent and out of sight along endless rows of shelves. In the pre-dawn darkness the true dimensions of the Language and Literature department were now obscure. Only the moon shining high in the blackness through those tall windows revealed to me the location of my desk, which was in the middle of the long narrow room.

I found my way over to my desk and switched on the small lamp that years ago I had brought from home. (Not that I required the added illumination as I worked at my desk at the library, but I did enjoy the bleakly old-fashioned appearance of this object.) For a moment I thought of the bungalow house where none of the lamps were equipped with lightbulbs and moonlight shone through the windows upon a carpet littered with vermin. Somehow I was unable to call up the special sensations and mental state that I associated with this dream monologue, even though my present situation of being alone in the Language and Literature department some hours before dawn was intensely dreamlike.

Not knowing what else to do, I sat down at my desk as if I were beginning my normal workday. It was then that I noticed a large envelope lying on top of my desk, although I could not recall its being there when I left the library the day before. The envelope looked old and faded under the dim light of the desk lamp. There was no writing on either side of the envelope, which was bulging slightly and had been sealed.

"Who's there?" a voice called out that barely sounded like my own. I had seen something out of the corner of my eye while examining the envelope at my desk. I cleared my throat. "Henry?" I asked the darkness without looking up from my desk or turning to either side. No answer was offered in reply, but I could feel that someone else had joined me in the Language and Literature department of the library.

I slowly turned my head to the right and focused on the archway some distance across the room. At the center of this aperture, which led to another room where moonlight shone through high, paned windows, stood a figure in silhouette. I could not see his face but immediately recognized the long, loose overcoat and hat. It was indeed the one whom I saw in the bus shelter as I rode to the library in the pre-dawn darkness. Now he was there to meet me that day in the library, as he had told Dalha he would do. At that moment it seemed beside the point to ask how he had gotten into the library or even to bother about introductions. I simply launched into a monologue that I had been constantly rehearsing since Dalha telephoned me earlier that morning.

"I've been wanting to meet you," I started. "Your dream monologues, which is what I call them, have impressed me very much. That is to say, your *artworks* are like nothing else I have ever experienced, either artistically or extra-artistically. It seems incredible to me how well you have expressed subject matter with which I myself am intimately familiar. Of course, I am not referring to the subject matter as such – the bungalow houses and so on – except as it calls forth your underlying vision of things. When – in your tape-recorded monologues – your voice speaks such phrases as 'infinite terror and dreariness' or 'ceaseless negation of color and life,' I believe that my response is exactly that which you intend for those who experience your artworks, perhaps even that which you yourself have experienced that gives you the inspiration for your artworks."

I continued in this vein for a while longer, speaking to the silhouette of someone who betrayed no sign that he heard anything I said. At some point, however, my monologue veered off in a direction I had not intended it to take. Suddenly I began to say things that had nothing to do with what I had said before and that even contradicted my former statements.

"For as long as I can remember," I said, continuing to speak to the figure standing in the archway, "I have had an intense and highly aesthetic perception of what I call the *icy bleakness of things*. At the same time I have felt a great loneliness in this perception. This conjunction of feelings seems paradoxical, since such a perception, such a view of things, would seem to preclude the emotion of loneliness, or any sense of a *killing sadness*, as I think of it. All such heartbreaking sentiment, as usually considered, would seem to be on its knees before artworks such as yours, which so powerfully express what I have called the icy bleakness of things, submerging or devastating all sentiment in an atmosphere potent with desolate truths, permeated throughout with a visionary stagnation and lifelessness. Yet I must observe that the effect, as I now consider it, has been just the opposite. If it was your intent to evoke the icy bleakness of things with your dream monologues, then you have totally failed on both an artistic and an extra-artistic level. You have failed your art, you have failed yourself, and you have also failed me. If your artworks had really evoked the bleakness of things, then I would not have felt this need to know who you are, this killing sadness that there was actually someone who experienced the same sensations and mental states that I did and who could share them with me in the form of tape-recorded dream monologues. Who are *you* that I should feel this need to go to work hours before the sun comes up, that I should feel this was something I had to do and that you were someone that I had to know? This behavior violates every principle by which I have lived for as long as I can remember. Who are you to cause me to violate these long-lived principles? I think it's all becoming clear to me now. Dalha put you up to this. You and Dalha are in a conspiracy against me and against my principles. Every day Dalha is on the telephone making all kinds of arrangements for profit, and she cannot stand the idea that all I do is sit there in peace, eating my lunch in her hideous art gallery. She feels that I'm cheating her somehow because she's not making a profit from me, because I never paid her to make an arrangement for me. Don't try to deny what I now know is true. But you could say something, in any case. Just a few words spoken with that voice of yours. Or at least let me see your face. And you could take off that ridiculous hat. It's like something Dalha would wear."

By this time I was on my feet and walking (staggering, in fact) toward the figure that stood in the archway. All the while I was walking, or staggering, toward the figure I was also demanding that he answer my accusations. But as I walked forward between the long study tables toward the archway, the figure standing there receded backward into the darkness of the next room, where moonlight shone through high, paned windows. The closer I came to him the farther he receded into the darkness. And he did not recede into the darkness by taking steps backward, as I was taking steps forward, but moved in some other way that even now I cannot specify, as though he were floating.

Just before the figure disappeared completely into the darkness he finally spoke to me. His voice was the same one that I had heard over those enormous headphones in Dalha's art gallery, except now there was no interference, no distortion in the words that it spoke. These words, which resounded in my brain as they resounded in the high-ceilinged rooms of the library, were such that I should have welcomed them, for they echoed my very own, deeply private, principles. Yet I took no comfort in hearing another voice tell me that there was nowhere for me to go, nothing for me to do, and no one for me to know.

The next voice I heard was that of Henry, who shouted up the wide stone staircase from the ground floor of the library. "Is everything all right, sir?" he asked. I composed myself and was able to answer that everything was all right. I asked him to turn the lights on for the second floor of the library. In a minute the lights were on, but by then the man in the hat and long, loose overcoat was gone.

When I confronted Dalha at her art gallery later that day, she was not in the least forthcoming with respect to my questions and accusations. "You are crazy," she screamed at me. "I want nothing more to do with you."

When I asked Dalha what she was talking about, she said, "You really *don't* know, do you? You really are a crazy man. You don't remember that night you came up to me on the street while I was waiting for a cab to show up."

When I told her I recalled doing nothing of the kind, she continued her anecdote of that night, and also subsequent events. "I'm so drunk I can hardly understand what you are saying to me about some little game you are playing. Then you send me the tapes. Then you come in and pay to listen to the tapes, exactly as you said you would. Just in time I remember that I am supposed to lie to you that the tapes are the work of a white-haired old man, when in fact you are the one who is making the tapes. I knew you were crazy, but this was the only money I ever made off you, even though day after day you come and eat your pathetic lunch in my gallery. When I saw you that night, I couldn't tell at first who it was walking up to me on the street. You did look different, and you were wearing that stupid hat. Soon enough, though, I can see that it's you. And you're pretending to be someone else, but not really pretending, I don't know. And then you tell me that I must destroy the tapes, and if I don't destroy them something will happen. Well, let me tell you, crazy man," Dalha said, "I did not destroy those tape recordings. I let all my friends hear them. We sat around getting drunk and laughing our heads off at your stupid *dream monologues*. Here, another one of your artworks arrived in the mail today," she said while walking across the floor of the art gallery to the tape machine that was positioned on the small plastic table. "Why don't you listen to it and pay me the money you promised? This looks like a good one," she said, picking up the little card that bore the title of the work. "*The Bus Shelter*, it says. That should be very exciting for you – a bus shelter. Pay up!"

"Dalha," I said in a laboriously calm voice, "please listen to me. You have to make another arrangement. I need to have another meeting with the tape-recording artist. You are the only one who can arrange for this to happen. Dalha, I'm afraid for both of us if you don't agree to make this arrangement. I need to speak with him again."

"Then why don't you just go talk into a mirror. There," she said, pointing to the curtain that separated the front section from the back section of the art gallery. "Go into the bathroom like you did the other day and talk to yourself in the mirror."

"I didn't talk to myself in the bathroom, Dalha."

"No? What were you doing then?"

"Dalha, you have to make the arrangement. You are the go-between. He will contact you if you agree to let him."

"*Who* will contact me?"

This was a fair question for Dalha to ask, but it was also one that I could not answer. I told her that I would return to talk to her the next day, hoping she would have calmed down by then.

Unfortunately, I never saw Dalha again. That night she was found dead on the street. Presumably she had been waiting for a cab to take her home from a bar or a party or some other human gathering place where she had gotten very drunk. But it was not her drinking or her exhausting bohemian social life that killed Dalha. She had, in fact, choked to death while waiting for a cab very late at night. Her body was taken to a hospital for examination. There it was discovered that an object had been lodged inside her. Someone, it appeared, had violently thrust something down her throat. The object, as described in a newspaper article, was the "small plastic arm of a toy doll." Whether this doll's arm had been painted emerald green, or any other color, was not mentioned by the article. Surely the police searched through Dalha D. Fine Arts and found many more such objects arranged in a wire wastebasket, each of them painted different colors. No doubt they also found the exhibit of the dream monologues with its unsigned artworks and tape recorder stolen from the library. But they could never have made the connection between these tape-recorded artworks and the grotesque death of the gallery owner.

After that night I no longer felt the desperate need to possess the monologues, not even the final bus shelter tape, which I have never heard. I was now in possession of the original handwritten manuscripts from which the tape-recording artist had created his dream monologues and which he had left for me in a large envelope on my desk at the library. Even then he knew, as I did not know, that after our first meeting we would never meet again. The handwriting on the manuscript pages is somewhat like my own, although the slant of the letters betrays a left-handed writer, whereas I am right-handed. Over and over I read the dream monologues about the bus shelter and the derelict factory and especially about the bungalow house, where the moonlight shines upon a carpet littered with the bodies of vermin. I try to experience the infinite terror and dreariness of a bungalow universe in the way I once did, but it is not the same as it once was. There is no comfort in it, even though the vision and the underlying principles are still the same. I know in a way I never knew before that there is nowhere for me to go, nothing for me to do, and no one for me to know. The voice in my head keeps reciting these old principles of mine. The voice is his voice, and the voice is also my voice. And there are other voices, voices I have never heard before, voices that seem to be either dead or dying in a great moonlit darkness. More than ever, some sort of new arrangement seems in order, some dramatic and unknown arrangement – anything to find release from this heartbreaking sadness I suffer every minute of the day (and night), this killing sadness that feels as if it will never leave me no matter where I go or what I do or whom I may ever know.

THE CLOWN PUPPET

It has always seemed to me that my existence consisted purely and exclusively of nothing but the most outrageous nonsense. As long as I can remember, every incident and every impulse of my existence has served only to perpetrate one episode after another of conspicuous nonsense, each completely outrageous in its nonsensicality. Considered from whatever point of view – intimately close, infinitely remote, or any position in between – the whole thing has always seemed to be nothing more than some freak accident occurring at a painfully slow rate of speed. At times I have been rendered breathless by the impeccable chaoticism, the absolutely perfect nonsense of some spectacle taking place outside myself, or, on the other hand, some spectacle of equally senseless outrageousness taking place within me. Images of densely twisted shapes and lines arose in my brain. *Scribbles of a mentally deranged epileptic*, I often said to myself. If I may allow any exception to the outrageously nonsensical condition I have described – and I *will* allow *none* – this single exception would involve those *visits* which I experienced at scattered intervals throughout my existence, and especially one particular visit that took place in Mr. Vizniak's medicine shop.

I was stationed behind the counter at Mr. Vizniak's modest establishment very late one night. At that hour there was practically no business at all, none really, given the backstreet location of the shop and its closet-like dimensions, as well as the fact that I kept the place in almost complete darkness both outside and inside. Mr. Vizniak lived in a small apartment above the medicine shop, and he gave me permission to keep the place open or close it up as I liked after a certain hour. It seemed that he knew that being stationed behind the counter of his medicine shop at all hours of the night, and in almost complete darkness except for a few lighting fixtures on the walls, provided my mind with some distraction from the outrageous nonsense which might otherwise occupy it. Later events more or less proved that Mr. Vizniak indeed possessed a special knowledge and that there existed, in fact, a peculiar sympathy between the old man and myself. Since

Mr. Vizniak's shop was located on an obscure backstreet, the neighborhood outside was profoundly inactive during the later hours of the night. And since most of the streetlamps in the neighborhood were either broken or defective in some way, the only thing I could see through the small front window of the shop was the neon lettering in the window of the meat store directly across the street. These pale neon letters remained lit throughout the night in the window of the meat store, spelling out three words: BEEF, PORK, GOAT. Sometimes I would stare at these words and contemplate them until my head became so full of meat nonsense, of beef and pork and goat nonsense, that I had to turn away and find something to occupy myself in the back room of the medicine shop, where there were no windows and thus no possibility of meat-store visions. But once I was in the back room I would become preoccupied with all the medicines which were stored there, all the bottles and jars and boxes upon boxes stacked from floor to ceiling in an extremely cramped area. I had learned quite a bit about these medicines from Mr. Vizniak, although I did not have a license to prepare and dispense them to customers without his supervision. I knew which medicines could be used to most easily cause death in someone who had ingested them in the proper amount and proper manner. Thus, whenever I went into the back room to relieve my mind from the meat nonsense brought on by excessive contemplation of the beef-pork-and-goat store, I almost immediately became preoccupied with fatal medicines; in other words, I then would become obsessed with death nonsense, which is one of the worst and most outrageous forms of all nonsense. Usually I would end up retreating to the small lavatory in the back room, where I could collect myself and clear my head before returning to my station behind the counter of Mr. Vizniak's medicine shop.

It was there – behind the medicine-shop counter, that is – that I experienced one of those *visits*, which I might have allowed as the sole exception in an existence of intensely outrageous nonsense, but which in fact, I must say, were the nadir of the nonsensical. This was my *medicine-shop visit*, so called because I have always experienced only a single visitation in any given place – after which I begin looking for a new situation, however similar it may actually be to my old one. Each of my situations prior to Mr. Vizniak's medicine shop was essentially a medicine-shop situation, whether it was a situation working as a night watchman who patrolled some desolate property, or a situation as a groundskeeper for a cemetery in some remote town, or a situation in which I spent endless gray afternoons sitting in a useless library or shuffling up and down the cloisters of a useless monastery. All of them were essentially medicine-shop situations, and each of them sooner or later involved a *visit* – either a monastery visit or a library visit, a cemetery visit or a visit while I was delivering packages from one part of town to another in the dead of the night. At the same time there were certain aspects to the medicine-shop visit that were unlike any of the other visits, certain new and unprecedented elements which made this visit unique among the ones which came before it.

It began with an already familiar routine of nonsense. Gradually, as I stood behind the counter late one night at the medicine shop, the light radiated by the fixtures along the walls changed from a dim yellow to a rich reddish-gold. I have never developed an intuition that would allow me to anticipate when this is going to happen, so that I might say to myself: "This will be the night when the light changes to reddish-gold. This will be the night of another visit." In the new light (the rich reddish-gold illumination) the interior of the medicine shop took on the strange opulence of an old oil painting; everything became transformed beneath a thick veneer of gleaming obscurity. And I have always wondered how my own face appears in this new light, but at the time I can never think about such things because I know what is about to happen, and all I can do is hope that it will soon be over.

After the business with the tinted illumination, only a few moments pass before there is an appearance, which means that the visit itself has begun. First the light changes to reddish-gold, then the visit begins. I have never been able to figure out the reason for this sequence, as if there might be a reason for such nonsense as these visits or any particular phase of these visits. Certainly when the light changes to a reddish-gold tint I am being forewarned that an appearance is about to occur, but this has never enabled me to witness the *actual manifestation*, and I had given up trying by the time of the medicine-shop visit. I knew that if I looked to my left, the appearance would take place in the field of vision to my right; conversely, if I focused on the field of vision to my right, the appearance would take place, in no time at all, on my left. And of course if I simply gazed straight ahead, the appearance would take place just beyond the edges of my left or right fields of vision, silently and instantaneously. Only after it had appeared would it begin to make any sound, clattering as it moved directly in front of my eyes, and then, as always happened, I would be looking at a creature that I might say had all the appearances of an antiquated marionette, a puppet figure of some archaic type.

It was almost life-sized and hovered just far enough above the floor of the medicine shop that its face was at the same level as my own. I am describing the puppet creature as it appeared during the medicine-shop visit, but it always took the form of the same antiquated marionette hovering before me in a reddish-gold haze. Its design was that of a clown puppet in pale pantaloons over-draped by a kind of pale smock, thin and pale hands emerging from the ruffled cuffs of its sleeves, and a powder-pale head rising above a ruffled collar. I always found it difficult at first to look directly at the face of the puppet creature whenever it appeared, because the expression which had been created for that face was so simple and bland, yet at the same time so intensely evil and perverse. In the observation of at least one commentator on puppet theater, the expressiveness of a puppet or marionette resides in its arms, hands, and legs, never in its face or head, as is the case with a human actor. But in the case of the puppet thing hovering before me in the medicine shop, this was not true. Its expressiveness was all in that face with its pale and pitted complexion, its slightly pointed nose and delicate lips, and its dead puppet eyes – eyes that did not seem able to fix or focus themselves upon anything but only gazed with an unchanging expression of dreamy malignance, an utterly nonsensical expression of stupefied viciousness, dumbfounded cruelty. So whenever this puppet creature first appeared I avoided looking at its face and instead I looked at its tiny feet which were covered by a pair of pale slippers and dangled just above the floor. Then I always looked at the wires which were attached to the body of the puppet thing, and I tried to follow those wires to see where they led. But at some point my vision failed me; I could visually trace the wires only so far along their neat vertical path . . . and then they became lost in a thick blur, a ceiling of distorted light and shadow that always formed some distance above the puppet creature's head – and my own – beyond which my eyes could perceive no clear image, nothing at all except a vague sluggish movement, like a layer of dense clouds seen from far away through a gloomy reddish-gold twilight. This phe-nomenon of the wires disappearing into a blur supported my observation over the years that the puppet thing did not have a life of its own. It was solely by means of these wires, in my view, that the creature was able to proceed through its familiar motions. (The term "motions," as I bothered myself to discover in the course of my useless research into the subject, was commonly employed at one time, long ago, to refer to various types of puppets, as in the statement: "The motions recently viewed at St. Bartholomew's Fair were engaged in antics of a questionable probity before an audience which might have better profited by deep contemplation of the fragile and uncertain destiny of their immortal souls.") The puppet swung forward toward the counter of the medicine shop behind which I stood. Its body parts rattled loosely and noisily in the late-night quiet before coming to rest. One of its hands was held out to me, its fingers barely grasping a crumpled slip of paper.

Of course I took the tiny page, which appeared to have been torn from an old pad used for writing pharmaceutical prescriptions. I had learned through the years to follow the puppet creature's cues obediently. At one time, years before the visit at the medicine shop, I was crazy or foolish enough to call the puppet and its visits exactly what they were – outrageous nonsense. Right to the face of that clown puppet I would say, "Take your nonsense somewhere else," or possibly, "I'm sick of this contemptible and disgusting nonsense." But none of these outbursts counted for anything. The puppet simply waited until my foolhardy craziness had passed and then continued through the motions which had been prepared for that particular visit. So I examined the prescription form the creature had passed across the counter to me, and I noticed immediately that what was written upon it was nothing but a chaos of scrawls and scribbles, which was precisely the sort of nonsense I should have expected during the medicine-shop visit. I knew that it was my part to play along with the clown puppet, although I was never precisely certain what was expected of me. From previous experience I learned that it was futile to determine what would eventually transpire during a particular visit, because the puppet creature was capable of almost anything. For example, once it visited me when I was working through the night at a skid-row pawn shop. I told the thing that it was wasting my time unless it could produce an exquisitely cut diamond the size of a yo-yo. Then it reached under its pale smock-like garment and rummaged about, its hand seeking deep within its pantaloons. "Well, let's see it," I shouted at the clown puppet. "As big as a yo-yo," I repeated. Not only did it come up with an exquisitely cut diamond that was, generally speaking, as large as a yo-yo, but the object that the puppet thing flashed before my eyes – brilliant in the pawn-shop dimness – was also made in the *form* of a yo-yo . . . and the creature began to lazily play with the yo-yo diamond right in front of me, spinning it slowly on the string that was looped about one of those pale puppet-fingers, throwing it down and pulling it up over and over while the facets of that exquisitely cut diamond cast a pyrotechnic brilliance into every corner of the pawn shop.

Now, as I stood behind the counter of the medicine shop staring at the scrawls and scribbles on that page torn from an old prescription pad, I knew that it was pointless to test the clown puppet in any way or to attempt to determine what would occur during this particular visit, which would be unlike previous visits in several significant ways. Thus I tried only to play my part, my medicine-shop part, as close as possible to the script that I imagined had already been written, though by whom or what I could have no idea.

"Could you please show me some proper identification?" I asked the creature, while at the same time looking away from its pale and pasty clown face and its dead puppet eyes, gazing instead through the medicine-shop window and focusing on the sign in the window of the meat store across the street. Over and over I read the words BEEF-PORK-GOAT, BEEF-PORK-GOAT, filling my head with meat nonsense, which was infinitely less outrageous than the puppet nonsense with which I was now confronted. "I cannot dispense this prescription," I said while staring out the medicine-shop window. "Not unless you can produce proper identification." And all the time I had no idea what to do once the puppet thing reached into its pantaloons and came up with what I requested.

I continued to stare out the medicine-shop window and think about the meat nonsense, but I could still see the clown puppet gyrating in the reddish-gold light, and I could hear its wooden parts clacking against one another as it struggled to pull up something that was cached away inside its pantaloons. With stiff but unerring fingers the creature was now holding what looked like a slim booklet of some kind, waving it before me until I turned and accepted the object. When I opened the booklet and looked inside I saw that it was an old passport, a foreign passport with no words that I recognized save those of its rightful owner: Ivan Vizniak. The address below Mr. Vizniak's name was a very old address, because I knew that many years had passed since Mr. Vizniak emigrated from his homeland, opened the medicine shop, and moved into the rooms directly above it. I also noticed that the photograph had been torn away from its designated place in the document belonging to Mr. Vizniak.

Nothing like this had ever occurred during one of these puppet visits: no one else had ever been involved in any of the encounters I had had over the years with the clown puppet, and I was now at a loss for my next move. The only thing that occupied my mind was the fact that Mr. Vizniak lived in the rooms above the medicine shop, and here in my hands was his passport, which the puppet creature had given me when I asked it to provide some identification so that I could fill the prescription it had given me, or rather, go through the motions of filling such a prescription, since I had no hope of deciphering the scrawls and scribbles on that old prescription form. And all of this was nothing but the most outrageous nonsense, as I well knew from past experience. I was actually on the verge of committing some explosive action, some display of violent hysterics by which I might bring about an end, however unpleasant, to this intolerable situation. The eyes of the puppet creature were so dark and so dead in the reddish-gold light that suffused the medicine shop; its head was bobbing slightly and also quivering in a way that caused my thought processes to race out of control, becoming all tangled in a black confusion. But exactly at the moment when I approached my breaking point, the head of the puppet thing turned away from me and its eyes seemed to be looking toward the curtained doorway that led to the back room of the medicine shop. Then it began to move in the direction of the curtained doorway, its limbs swinging freely with the sort of spastic and utterly mindless gestures of playfulness that only puppets can make. Nothing like this had ever happened before in the course of the creature's previous visits: it had never left my presence in this manner. And as soon as it disappeared entirely behind the curtain of the doorway leading to the back room, I heard a voice calling to me from the street outside the medicine shop. It was Mr. Vizniak. "Open the door," he said. "Something has happened."

I could see him through the paned windows of the front door, the eyes of his thin face squinting into the dimness of the medicine shop. With his right hand he kept beckoning, as if this incessant gesturing alone could bring me to open the door for him. *Another person is about to enter the place where one of these visits is occurring*, I thought to myself. But there seemed to be nothing I could do, nothing I could say, not with the clown puppet only a few feet away in the back room. I stepped around the counter of the medicine shop, unlocked the front door, and let Mr. Vizniak inside. As the old man shuffled in I could see that he was wearing an old robe with torn pockets and a pair of old slippers.

"Everything is all right," I whispered to him. And then I pleaded: "Go back to bed. We can talk about it in the morning."

But Mr. Vizniak seemed to have heard nothing that I said to him. From the moment he entered the medicine shop he appeared to be in some unusual state of mind. His whole manner had lost the vital urgency he displayed when he was rapping at the door and beckoning to me. He pointed one of his pale, crooked fingers upward and slowly gazed around the shop. "The light . . . the light," he said as the reddish-gold illumination shone on his thin, wrinkled face, making it look as if he were wearing a mask that had been hammered out of some strange metal, some ancient mask behind which his old eyes were wide and bright with fear.

"Tell me what happened," I said, trying to distract him. I had to repeat myself several times before he finally responded. "I thought I heard someone in my room upstairs," he said in a completely toneless voice. "They were going through my things. I thought I might have been dreaming, but I was awake when I heard something going down the stairs. Not footsteps," he said. "Just something quietly brushing against the stairs. I wasn't sure. I didn't come down right away."

"I didn't hear anyone come down the stairs," I said to Mr. Vizniak, who now seemed lost in a long pause of contemplation. "I didn't see anyone on the street outside. You were probably just dreaming. Why don't you go back to bed and forget about everything," I said. But Mr. Vizniak no longer seemed to be listening to me. He was staring at the curtained doorway leading to the back room of the medicine shop.

"I have to use the toilet," he said while continuing to stare at the curtained doorway.

"You can go back to your room upstairs," I suggested.

"No," he said. "Back there. I have to use the toilet."

Then he began shuffling toward the back room, his old slippers lightly brushing against the floor of the medicine shop. I called to him, very quietly, a number of times, but he continued to move steadily toward the back room, as if he were in a trance. In a few moments he had disappeared behind the curtain.

I thought that Mr. Vizniak might not find anything in the back room of the medicine shop. I thought that he might see only the bottles and jars and boxes upon boxes of medicines. *Perhaps the visit has already ended*, I thought. It occurred to me that the visit could have ended the moment the puppet creature went behind the curtain of the doorway leading to the back room. I thought that Mr. Vizniak might return from the back room, after having used the toilet, and go upstairs again to his rooms above the medicine shop. I thought all kinds of nonsense in the last few moments of that particular visit from the clown puppet.

But in a number of its significant aspects this was unlike any of the previous puppet visits I had experienced. I might even claim

THE RED TOWER

The ruined factory stood three stories high in an otherwise featureless landscape. Although somewhat imposing on its own terms, it occupied only the most unobtrusive place within the gray emptiness of its surroundings, its presence amounting to no more than a faint smudge of color upon a desolate horizon. No road led to the factory, nor were there any traces of one that might have led to it at some time in the distant past. If there had ever been such a road it would have been rendered useless as soon as it arrived at one of the four, red-bricked sides of the factory, even in the days when the facility was in full operation. The reason for this was simple: no doors had been built into the factory, no loading docks or entranceways allowed penetration of the outer walls of the structure, which was solid brick on all four sides without even a single window below the level of the second floor. The phenomenon of a large factory so closed off from the outside world was a point of extreme fascination to me. It was almost with regret that I ultimately learned about the factory's subterranean access. But of course that revelation in its turn also became a source for my truly degenerate sense of amazement, my decayed fascination.

The factory had long been in ruins, its innumerable bricks worn and crumbling, its many windows shattered. Each of the three enormous stories that stood above the ground level was vacant of all but dust and silence. The machinery, which densely occupied the three floors of the factory as well as considerable space beneath it, is said to have evaporated, I repeat, *evaporated*, soon after the factory ceased operation, leaving behind it only a few spectral outlines of deep vats and tanks, twisting tubes and funnels, harshly grinding gears and levers, giant belts and wheels that could be most clearly seen at twilight – and later, not at all. According to these strictly hallucinatory accounts, the whole of the Red Tower, as the factory was known, had always been subject to *fadings* at certain times. This phenomenon, in the delirious or dying words of several witnesses, was due to a profound hostility between the noisy and malodorous operations that I was not the one whom the puppet creature was visiting on this occasion, or at least not exclusively so. Even though I had always felt that my encounters with the clown puppet were nothing but the most outrageous nonsense, the very nadir of the nonsensical, as I have said, I nonetheless always had the haunting sense of being singled out in some way from all others of my kind, of being *cultivated* for some special fate. But after Mr. Vizniak disappeared behind the curtained doorway I discovered how wrong I had been. Who knows how many others there were who might say that their existence consisted of nothing but the most outrageous nonsense, a nonsense that had nothing unique about it at all and that had nothing behind it or beyond it except more and more nonsense – a new order of nonsense, perhaps an utterly unknown nonsense, but all of it nonsense and nothing but nonsense.

Every place I had been was only a place for puppet nonsense. The medicine shop was only a puppet place like all the others. I came there to work behind the counter and wait for my visit, but I had no idea until that night that Mr. Vizniak was also waiting for his. Upon reflection, it seemed that he knew what was behind the curtained doorway leading to the back room of the medicine shop, and that he also knew there was no longer any place to go except behind that curtain, since any place he could ever go would only be another puppet place. Yet it still seemed he was surprised by what he found back there. And this is the most outrageously nonsensical thing of all – that he should have stepped behind the curtain and cried out with such profound surprise as he did. *You*, he said, or rather, cried out. *Get away from me.* These were the last words that I heard clearly before Mr. Vizniak's voice faded quickly out of earshot, as though he were being carried away at incredible velocity toward some great height.

When morning finally came, and I looked behind the curtain, there was no one there. I told myself at that moment that I would not be so surprised when my time came. No doubt, Mr. Vizniak, at some time, had told himself the same, utterly nonsensical, thing.

of the factory and the desolate purity of the landscape surrounding it, the conflict occasionally resulting in temporary erasures, or fadings, of the former by the latter.

Despite their ostensibly mad or credulous origins, these testimonies, it seemed to me, deserved more than a cursory hearing. The legendary conflict between the factory and the grayish territory surrounding it may very well have been a fabrication of individuals who were lost in the advanced stages of either physical or psychic deterioration. Nonetheless, it was my theory, and remains so, that the Red Tower was not always that peculiar color for which it ultimately earned its fame. Thus the *encrimsoning* of the factory was a betrayal, a breaking-off, for it is my postulation that this ancient structure was in long-forgotten days the same pale hue as the world which encompassed it. Furthermore, with an insight born of dispassion to the point of total despair, I envisioned that the Red Tower was never solely devoted to the lowly functions of an ordinary factory.

Beneath the three soaring stories of the Red Tower were two, possibly three, other levels. The one immediately below the ground floor of the factory was the nexus of a unique distribution system for the goods which were manufactured on all three of the floors above. This first subterranean level in many ways resembled, and functioned in the manner of, an old-fashioned underground mine. Elevator compartments enclosed by a heavy wire mesh, twisted and corroded, descended far below the surface into an expansive chamber which had been crudely dug out of the rocky earth and was haphazardly perpetuated by a dense structure of supports, a criss-crossing network of posts and pillars, beams and rafters, that included a variety of materials – wood, metal, concrete, bone, and a fine sinewy webbing that was fibrous and quite firm. From this central chamber radiated a system of tunnels that honeycombed the land beneath the gray and desolate country surrounding the Red Tower. Through these tunnels the goods manufactured by the factory could be carried, sometimes literally by hand, but more often by means of small wagons and carts, reaching near and far into the most obscure and unlikely delivery points.

The trade that was originally produced by the Red Tower was in some sense remarkable, but not, at first, of an extraordinary or especially ambitious nature. These were a gruesome array of goods that could perhaps best be described as novelty items. In the beginning there was a chaotic quality to the objects and constructions produced by the machinery at the Red Tower, a randomness that yielded formless things of no consistent shape or size or apparent design. Occasionally there might appear a particular ashen lump that betrayed some semblance of a face or clawing fingers, or perhaps an assemblage that looked like a casket with tiny irregular wheels, but for the most part the early productions seemed relatively innocuous. After a time, however, things began to fall into place, as they always do, rejecting a harmless and uninteresting disorder – never an enduring state of affairs – and taking on the more usual plans and purposes of a viciously intent creation.

So it was that the Red Tower put into production its terrible and perplexing line of unique novelty items. Among the objects and constructions now manufactured were several of an almost innocent nature. These included tiny, delicate cameos that were heavier than their size would suggest, far heavier, and lockets whose shiny outer surface flipped open to reveal a black reverberant abyss inside, a deep blackness roaring with echoes. Along the same lines was a series of lifelike replicas of internal organs and physiological structures, many of them evidencing an advanced stage of disease and all of them displeasingly warm and soft to the touch. There was a fake disembodied hand on which fingernails would grow several inches overnight, every night like clockwork. Numerous natural objects, mostly bulbous gourds, were designed to produce a long deafening scream whenever they were picked up or otherwise disturbed in their vegetable stillness. Less scrutable were such things as hardened globs of lava into whose rough igneous forms were set a pair of rheumy eyes that perpetually shifted their gaze from side to side like a relentless pendulum. And there was also a humble piece of cement, a fragment broken away from any street or sidewalk, that left a most intractable stain, greasy and green, on whatever surface it was placed. But such fairly simple items were eventually followed, and ultimately replaced, by more articulated objects and constructions. One example of this complex type of novelty item was an ornate music box that, when opened, emitted a brief gurgling or sucking sound in emulation of a dying individual's death rattle. Another product manufactured in great quantity at the Red Tower was a pocket watch in a gold casing which opened to reveal a curious timepiece whose numerals were represented by tiny quivering insects while the circling "hands" were reptilian tongues, slender and pink. But these examples hardly begin to hint at the range of goods that came from the factory during its novelty phase of production. I should at least mention the exotic carpets woven with intricate abstract patterns that, when focused upon for a certain length of time, composed themselves into fleeting phantasmagoric scenes of the kind which might pass through a fever-stricken or even permanently damaged brain.

As it was revealed to me, and as I have already revealed to you, the means of distributing the novelty goods fabricated at the Red Tower was a system of tunnels located on the first level, not the second (or, possibly, third), that had been excavated below the three-story factory building itself. It seems that these subterranean levels were not necessarily part of the original foundation of the factory but were in fact a perverse and unlikely development that might have occurred only as the structure known as the Red Tower underwent, over time, its own mutation from some prior state until it finally became a lowly site for manufacturing. This mutation would then have demanded the excavating – whether from above or below I cannot say – of a system of tunnels as a means for distributing the novelty goods which, for a time, the factory produced.

As the unique inventions of the Red Tower achieved their final forms, they seemed to have some peculiar location to which they were destined to be delivered, either by hand or by small wagons or carts pulled over sometimes great distances through the system of underground tunnels. Where they might ultimately pop up was anybody's guess. It might be in the back of a dark closet, buried under a pile of undistinguished junk, where some item of the highest and most extreme novelty would lie for quite some time before it was encountered by sheer accident or misfortune. Conversely, the same invention, or an entirely different one, might be placed on the night-table beside someone's bed for near-immediate discovery. Any delivery point was possible, none was out of the reach of the Red Tower. There has even been testimony, either intensely hysterical or semi-conscious, of items from the factory being uncovered within the shelter of a living body, or one not long deceased. I know that such an achievement was within the factory's powers, given its later production history. But my own degenerate imagination is most fully captured by the thought of how many of those monstrous novelty goods produced at the Red Tower had been scrupulously and devoutly delivered – solely by way of those endless underground tunnels – to daringly remote places where they would never be found, nor ever could be.

Just as a system of distribution tunnels had been created by the factory when it developed into a manufacturer of novelty goods, an expansion of this system was required as an entirely new phase of production gradually evolved. Inside the wire-mesh elevator compartment that provided access between the upper region of the factory and the underground tunnels, there was now a special lever installed which, when pulled back, or possibly pushed forward (I do not know such details), enabled one to descend to a second subterranean level. This latterly excavated area was much smaller, far more intimate, than the one directly above it, as could be observed the instant the elevator compartment came to a stop and a full view of things was attained. The scene which now confronted the uncertain minds of witnesses was, in many ways, like that of a secluded graveyard, one surrounded by a rather crooked fence of widely spaced pickets held together by rusty wire. The headstones inside the fence all closely pressed against one another and were quite common, though somewhat antiquated, in their design. However, there were no names or dates inscribed on these monuments, nothing at all, in fact, with the exception of some rudimentary and abstract ornamentation. This could be verified only when the subterranean graveyard was closely approached, for the lighting at this level was dim and unorthodox, provided exclusively by the glowing stone walls enclosing the area. These walls seemed to have been covered with phosphorescent paint which bathed the grave-yard in a cloudy, grayish haze. For the longest time – how long I cannot say – my morbid reveries were focused on this murky vision of a graveyard beneath the factory, a subterranean graveyard sur-rounded by a crooked picket fence and suffused by the highly defective illumination given off by phosphorescent paint applied to stone walls. For the moment I must emphasize the vision itself, without any consideration paid to the utilitarian purposes of this place, that is, the function it served in relation to the factory above it.

The truth is that at some point all of the factory functions were driven underground to this graveyard level. Long before the complete *evaporation* of machinery in the Red Tower, something happened to require the shut-down of all operations in the three floors of the factory which were above ground level. The reasons for this action are deeply obscure, a matter of contemplation only when a state of hopeless and devouring curiosity has reached its height, when the burning light of speculation becomes so intense that it threatens to incinerate everything on which it shines. To my own mind it seems entirely valid to reiterate at this juncture the longstanding tensions that existed between the Red Tower, which I believe was not always stigmatized by such a hue and such a title, and the grayish landscape of utter desolation that surrounded this structure on all sides, looming around and above it for quite incalculable distances. But below the ground level of the factory was another matter: it was here that its operations at some point retreated; it was here, specifically at this graveyard level, that they continued.

Clearly the Red Tower had committed some violation or offense, its clamoring activities and unorthodox products – perhaps its very existence – constituting an affront to the changeless quietude of the world around it. In my personal judgement there had been a betrayal involved, a treacherous breaking of a bond. I can certainly picture a time before the existence of the factory, before any of its features blemished the featureless country that extended so gray and so desolate on every side. Dreaming upon the grayish desolation of that landscape, I also find it quite easy to imagine that there might have occurred a lapse in the monumental tedium, a spontaneous and inexplicable impulse to deviate from a dreary perfection, perhaps even an unconquerable desire to risk a move toward a tempting defectiveness. As a concession to this impulse or desire *out of nowhere*, as a minimal surrender, a creation took place and a structure took form where there had been nothing of its kind before. I picture it, at its inception, as a barely discernible irruption in the landscape, a mere sketch of an edifice, possibly translucent when making its first appearance, a gray density rising in the grayness, embossed upon it in a most tasteful and harmonious design. But such structures or creations have their own desires, their own destinies to fulfil, their own mysteries and mechanisms which they must follow at whatever risk.

From a gray and desolate and utterly featureless landscape a dull edifice had been produced, a pale, possibly translucent tower which, over time, began to develop into a factory and to produce, as if in the spirit of the most grotesque belligerence, a line of quite morbid and disgusting novelty goods. In an expression of defiance, at some point, it reddened with an enigmatic passion for betrayal and perversity. On the surface the Red Tower might have seemed a splendid complement to the grayish desolation of its surroundings, a unique, picturesque composition that served to define the glorious essence of each of them. But in fact there existed between them a profound and ineffable hostility. An attempt was made to reclaim the Red Tower, or at least to draw it back toward the formless origins of its being. I am referring, of course, to that show of force which resulted in the *evaporation* of the factory's dense arsenal of machinery. Each of the three stories of the Red Tower had been cleaned out, purged of its offending means of manufacturing novelty items, and the part of the factory that rose above the ground was left to fall into ruins.

Had the machinery in the Red Tower *not* been evaporated, I believe that the subterranean graveyard, or something very much like it, would nonetheless have come into existence at some point or another. This was the direction in which the factory had been moving, as was suggested by some of its later models of novelty items. Machines were becoming obsolete as the diseased mania of the Red Tower intensified and evolved into more experimental, even visionary projects. I have previously reported that the headstones in the factory's subterranean graveyard were absent of any names of the interred, or dates of birth and death. This fact is also confirmed by numerous accounts rendered in borderline-hysterical gibberish. The reason for these blank headstones is entirely evident as one gazes upon them standing crooked and closely packed together in the phosphorescent haze given off by the stone walls covered with luminous paint. None of these graves, in point of fact, could be said to have anyone buried in them whose names and dates of birth and death would require inscription on the headstones. These were not what might be called *burying graves*. This is to say that these were in no sense graves for burying the dead, quite the contrary: these were graves of a highly experimental design from which the newest productions of the Red Tower were to be born.

From its beginnings as a manufacturer of novelty items of an extravagant nature, the factory had now gone into the business of creating what came to be known as "hyper-organisms." These new productions were also of a fundamentally extreme nature, representing an even greater divergence on the part of the Red Tower from the bland and gray desolation in the midst of which it stood. As implied by their designation as *hyper-organisms*, this line of goods displayed the most essential qualities of their organic nature, which meant, of course, that they were wildly conflicted in their two basic features. On the one hand, they manifested an intense *vitality* in all aspects of their form and function; on the other hand, and simultaneously, they manifested an ineluctable element of *decay* in these same areas. That is to say that each of these hyper-organisms, even as they scintillated with an obscene degree of vital impulses, also, and at the same time, had degeneracy and death written deeply upon them. In accord with a tradition of dumb-struck insanity, it seems the less said about these offspring of the *birthing graves*, or any similar creations, the better. I myself have been almost entirely restricted to a state of seething speculation concerning the luscious particularities of all hyper-organic phenomena produced in the subterranean graveyard of the Red

Tower. Although we may reasonably assume that such creations were not to be called beautiful, we cannot know for ourselves the mysteries and mechanisms of, for instance, how these creations moved throughout the hazy luminescence of that underground world; what creaky or spasmic gestures they might have been capable of executing, if any; what sounds they might have made or the specific organs used for making them; how they might have appeared when awkwardly emerging from deep shadows or squatting against those nameless headstones; what trembling stages of mutation they almost certainly would have undergone following the generation of their larvae upon the barren earth of the graveyard; what their bodies might have produced or emitted in the way of fluids and secretions; how they might have responded to the mutilation of their forms for reasons of an experimental or entirely savage nature. Often I picture to myself what frantically clawing efforts these creations probably made to deliver themselves from that confining environment which their malformed or non-existent brains could not begin to understand. They could not have comprehended, any more than can I, for what purpose they were bred from those graves, those incubators of hyper-organisms, minute factories of flesh that existed wholly within and far below the greater factory of the Red Tower.

It was no surprise, of course, that the production of hyper-organisms was not allowed to continue for very long before a second wave of destruction was visited upon the factory. This time it was not merely the *fading*, and ultimate evaporation of machinery, that took place; this time it was something far more brutal. Once again, forces of ruination were directed at the factory, specifically the subterranean graveyard located at its second underground level, its three-story structure that stood above ground having already been rendered an echoing ruin. Information on what remained of the graveyard, and of its cleverly blasphemous works, is available to my own awareness only in the form of shuddering and badly garbled whispers of mayhem and devastation and wholesale sundering of most unspeakable sort. These same sources also seem to regard this incident as the culmination, if not the conclusion, of the longstanding hostilities between the Red Tower and that grayish halo of desolation that hovered around it on all sides. Such a shattering episode would appear to have terminated the career of the Red Tower.

Nevertheless, there are indications that, appearances to the contrary, the factory continues to be active despite its status as a silent ruin. After all, the evaporation of the machinery which turned out countless novelty items in the three-story red-brick factory proper, and the ensuing obsolescence of its sophisticated system of tunnels at the first underground level, did not prevent the factory from pursuing its business by other and more devious means. The work at the second underground level (the graveyard level) went very well for a time. Following the vicious decimation of those ingenious and fertile graves, along with the merchandise they produced, it may have seemed that the manufacturing history of the Red Tower had been brought to a close. Yet there are indications that below the three-story above-ground factory, below the first and the second underground levels, there exists a *third* level of subterranean activity. Perhaps it is only a desire for symmetry, a hunger for compositional balance in things, that has led to a series of the most vaporous rumors of this third under-ground level, in order to provide a kind of complementary proportion to the three stories of the factory that rise into the gray and featureless landscape above ground. At this third level, these misty rumors maintain, the factory's schedule of production is being carried out in some new and strange manner, representing its most ambitious venture in the output of putrid creations, ultimately consummating its tradition of degeneracy, reaching toward a perfection of defect and disorder, according to every polluted and foggy rumor concerned with this issue.

Perhaps it seems that I have said too much about the Red Tower, and perhaps it has sounded far too strange. Do not think that I am unaware of such things. But as I have noted throughout this document, I am only repeating what I have heard. I myself have never seen the Red Tower – no one ever has, and possibly no one ever will. And yet wherever I go people are talking about it. In one way or another they are talking about the nightmarish novelty items or about the mysterious and revolting hyper-organisms, as well as babbling endlessly about the subterranean system of tunnels and the secluded graveyard whose headstones display no names and no dates designating either birth or death. Everything they are saying is about the Red Tower, in one way or another, and about nothing else but the Red Tower. We are all talking and thinking about the Red Tower in our own degenerate way. I have only recorded what everyone is saying (though they may not know they are saying it), and sometimes what they have seen (though they may not know they have seen it). But still they are always talking, in one deranged way or another, about the Red Tower. I hear them talk of it every day of my life. Unless of course they begin to speak about the gray and desolate landscape, that hazy void in which the Red Tower – the great and industrious Red Tower – is so precariously nestled. Then the voices grow quiet until I can barely hear them as they attempt to communicate with me in choking scraps of post-nightmare trauma. Now is just such a time when I must strain to hear the voices. I wait for them to reveal to me the new ventures of the Red Tower as it proceeds into ever more corrupt phases of production, including the shadowy workshop of its third subterranean level. I must keep still and listen for them; I must keep quiet for a terrifying moment. Then I will hear the sounds of the factory starting up its operations once more. Then I will be able to speak again of the Red Tower.